PENGUIN BOOKS

THE COLLECTED STORIES

Paul Theroux was born in Medford, Massachusetts in 1941 and published his first novel, *Waldo*, in 1967. His subsequent novels include *The Family Arsenal*, *Picture Palace*, *The Mosquito Coast*, *O-Zone*, *Millroy the Magician*, *My Secret History*, *My Other Life* and, most recently, *A Dead Hand*. His highly acclaimed travel books include *Riding the Iron Rooster*, *The Great Railway Bazaar*, *The Old Patagonian Express*, *Fresh-Air Fiend*, and *Ghost Train to the Eastern Star*. He divides his time between Cape Cod and the Hawaiian Islands.

Books by Paul Theroux

FICTION

Waldo
Fong and the Indians
Girls at Play
Murder in Mount Holly
Jungle Lovers
Sinning with Annie
Saint Jack
The Black House
The Family Arsenal
The Consul's File
A Christmas Card
Picture Palace
London Snow
World's End
The Mosquito Coast
The London Embassy
Half Moon Street
Doctor Slaughter
O-Zone
The White Man's Burden
My Secret History
Chicago Loop
Millroy the Magician
The Greenest Island
My Other Life

Kowloon Tong
Hotel Honolulu
The Stranger at the Palazzo d'Oro
Blinding Light
The Elephanta Suite
A Dead Hand

CRITICISM

V. S. Naipaul

NON-FICTION

The Great Railway Bazaar
The Old Patagonian Express
The Kingdom by the Sea
Sailing Through China
Sunrise with Seamonsters
The Imperial Way
Riding the Iron Rooster
To the Ends of the Earth
The Happy Isles of Oceania
The Pillars of Hercules
Sir Vidia's Shadow
Fresh-Air Fiend
Nurse Wolf and Dr Sacks
Dark Star Safari
Ghost Train to the Eastern Star

The Collected Stories

PAUL THEROUX

PENGUIN BOOKS

PENGUIN BOOKS

Published by the Penguin Group
Penguin Books Ltd, 80 Strand, London WC2R ORL, England
Penguin Group (USA) Inc., 375 Hudson Street, New York, New York 10014, USA
Penguin Group (Canada), 90 Eglinton Avenue East, Suite 700, Toronto, Ontario, Canada M4P 2Y3
(a division of Pearson Penguin Canada Inc.)
Penguin Ireland, 25 St Stephen's Green, Dublin 2, Ireland (a division of Penguin Books Ltd)
Penguin Group (Australia), 250 Camberwell Road, Camberwell, Victoria 3124, Australia
(a division of Pearson Australia Group Pty Ltd)
Penguin Books India Pvt Ltd, 11 Community Centre, Panchsheel Park, New Delhi – 110 017, India
Penguin Group (NZ), 67 Apollo Drive, Rosedale, Auckland 0632, New Zealand
(a division of Pearson New Zealand Ltd)
Penguin Books (South Africa) (Pty) Ltd, 24 Sturdee Avenue, Rosebank, Johannesburg 2196, South Africa

Penguin Books Ltd, Registered Offices: 80 Strand, London WC2R ORL, England

www.penguin.com

This collection first published by Hamish Hamilton 1997
First published in Penguin Books 2011

1

Some of these stories first appeared in *Atlantic, Commentary, Confrontation, Encounter, Harper's,
Harper's Bazaar, London Magazine, Mademoiselle, Malahat Review, New Review, New Statesman, New
Yorker, North American Review, O. Henry Prize Stories 1977, Penthouse, Playboy, Punch, Shenandoah,
Tatler, The Times, The Times Anthology of Ghost Stories* and *Transatlantic Review*.
Except for 'Polvo', 'Low Tide', 'Jungle Bells' and 'War Dogs', these stories have previously been published
by Hamish Hamilton and Penguin Books in *World's End, Sinning with Annie, The Consul's File* and *The
London Embassy*.

Sinning with Annie and *The Consul's File* copyright © Paul Theroux,
1969, 1970, 1971, 1972, 1975 and 1977
World's End and *The London Embassy* copyright © Cape Cod Scriveners Co., 1980 and 1982
'Polvo' copyright © Cape Cod Scriveners Co., 1982
'Low Tide' copyright © Cape Cod Scriveners Co., 1983
'Jungle Bells' copyright © Cape Cod Scriveners Co., 1993
'Warm Dogs' copyright © Cape Cod Scriveners Co., 1996
Introduction copyright © Cape Cod Scriveners Co., 1997
All rights reserved

The moral right of the author has been asserted

Printed in England by Clays Ltd, St Ives plc

ISBN: 978-0-241-95052-4

www.greenpenguin.co.uk

Contents

CONTENTS

Part III Jungle Bells

Part IV Diplomatic Relations (i): The Consul's File

Part V Diplomatic Relations (ii): The London Embassy

CONTENTS

Introduction

When I was small my family thought I was deaf. No, I was dreaming. Later on I heard of people harmed in accidents, scarred or crippled; and the same trauma produced in these victims mathematical genius, or an original line in art, or a quirk. *She hit her head on the dashboard and after that she couldn't stop eating.* I know that hunger.

Certain episodes in infancy or early childhood are a version of such accidents. In my case, I was left with a sense of separation. *He's not all there*, people said. The joke was true. I had been made lonely, and given a happy capacity to dream, and a need to invent. I did not understand the question, until I realized that writing my stories was the answer. They were my earliest literary effort, and I have gone on believing that such stories are almost the whole of my imaginative task as a writer. In a novel I try to make each chapter as complete and harmonious as a story. My travel books are a sequence of traveler's tales.

People who have no idea who they are talking to have told me that they love Paul Theroux's stories; yet I can see they aren't impressed with me. Of course! Other people have told me to my face that they dislike my stories, but that I am a good sort. Why is this? As a person I am hurt and incomplete. My stories are the rest of me. I inhabit every sentence I write! I tear them out of my heart!

After a long, fruitful and friendly time in London (1971–1990), I came to realize that I hated literary society for the very reasons I had once liked it: the shabby glamour, the talk, the drink, the companionship, the ambition, the business, and the belief: You are your stories. I protested, *No, no – my stories are better than me*, and went away.

Conspicuousness is not for me. My pleasure is that of a specter. I am calmest in remote places, haunting people who have no need of books and no idea what I do. I understand magicianship, murder, guilt, and motherhood; I also understand the demented people who late at night telephone strangers and whisper provocative words to them. Sometimes I feel like someone who has committed the perfect crime, an offender on the loose, who will never be caught. Please don't follow me, or ask me what went wrong. Please don't watch me eat.

My secret is safe. No one ever sees me write. One of the triumphs of fiction is that it is created in the dark. It leaves my house in a plain wrapper, with no bloodstains. Unlike me, my stories are whole and indestructible. In a reversal of the natural order, I am the shadow, my fiction is the substance. If my books are buried by time they can be dug up. The most powerful of the Chinese emperors, Qin Shi huangdi – who tried – could not make printed books vanish.

I planned to be a medical doctor (who also wrote books) and on the days I cannot write, and especially when I am in a place like New Guinea or Malawi, I regret that I do not have a doctor's skill to heal. I am too old to learn now. But I would like to speak Spanish fluently, and tap-dance, and study celestial navigation. I intend to paddle for months down a long river, the Nile or one of the long Chinese rivers, or hike for a year or more across an interesting landscape. I dream of flying, using only my arms. I am well aware that some of these activities are metaphors for writing, but not the writing of stories.

Pretty soon I will be gone, and afterwards when people say, *He is his stories*, the statement will be true.

Part I

World's End

World's End

Robarge was a happy man who had taken a great risk. He had transplanted his family – his wife and small boy – from their home in America to a bizarrely named but buried-alive district called World's End in London, where they were strangers. It had worked, and it made his happiness greater. His wife, Kathy, had changed. Having overcome this wrench from home and mastered the new routine, she became confident. It showed in her physically – she had unstiffened; she adopted a new hairstyle; she slimmed; she had been set free by proving to her husband that he depended on her. Richard, only six, was already in what Robarge regarded as the second grade: the little boy could read and write! Even Robarge's company, a supplier of drilling equipment for offshore oil rigs, was pleased by the way he had managed; they associated their success with Robarge's hard work.

So Robarge was vindicated in the move he had made. He had considered marriage the quietest enactment of sharing, connubial exclusiveness the most private way to live – a sheltered life in the best sense. And he saw England as upholding the domestic reverences that had been tossed aside in America. He had not merely moved his family but rescued them. His sense of security made him feel younger, an added pleasure. He did not worry about growing old; he had put on weight in these four years at World's End and began to affect that curious sideways gait, almost a limp, of a heavy boy. It was a game – he was nearly forty – but games were still possible in this country where he could go unrecognized and so unmocked.

Most of all, he liked returning home in the rain. The house at World's End was a refuge; he could shut his door on the darkness and smell the straightness of his own rooms. The yellow lights from the street showed the rain droplets patterned on the window, and he could hear it falling outside, the drip from the sky, as irregular as a weeping tree, which meant in London that it would go on all night. Tonight he was returning from Holland – a Dutch subsidiary machined the drilling bits he dispatched to Aberdeen. Without waking Kathy, he took the slender parcel he had carried from Amsterdam and crept upstairs to his son's room. On the plane he had kept it on his lap – there was nowhere to stow it. A man in the adjoining seat had stared and prompted Robarge to say, 'It's a kite. For my son. The Dutch import them from the Far East. Supposed to be foolproof.' The man had answered him by taking out a pair of binoculars he had bought for his own boy at the duty-free shop.

'Richard's only six,' said Robarge.

The man said that the older children got the more expensive they were. He said it affectionately and with pride, and Robarge thought how glad he would be when Richard was old enough to appreciate a really expensive present – skis, a camera, a pocket calculator, a radio. Then he would know how his father loved him and how there was nothing in the world he would not give him. And he felt a casual envy for the man in the next seat, having a son old enough to want the things his father could afford. His own uncomprehending son asked for nothing; it made fiercer Robarge's desire to show his love.

The lights in the house were out; it was, at midnight, as gloomy as a tunnel and seemed narrow and empty in all that darkness. Richard's door was ajar. Robarge went in and found his son sleeping peacefully under wall posters of dinosaurs and fighter planes. Robarge knelt and kissed the boy, then sat on the bed and delighted in hearing the boy's measured breaths. The breaths stopped. In the harsh knife of light falling through the curtains from the street Robarge saw his son stir.

'Hello.' The word came whole: Richard's voice was wide-awake.

'It's me.' He kissed the boy. 'Look what I brought you.'

Robarge brandished the parcel. There was a film of rain on the plastic wrapper.

'What is it?' Richard asked.

Robarge told him: A kite. 'Now go back to sleep like a good boy.'

'Can we fly it?'

'You bet. If it's windy we'll fly it at the park.'

'It's not windy enough at the park. You have to go in the car.'

'Where shall we go?'

'Box Hill's a good place for kites.'

'Is it windy there?'

'Not half!' whispered the child.

Robarge was delighted by this odd English expression in his son's speech, and he muttered it to himself in amazement. He was gladdened by Richard's response; he had pondered so long at the gift shop at Schiphol wondering which toy to buy – like an eager indecisive child himself – he had nearly missed his flight.

'Box Hill it is then.' It meant a long drive, but the next day was Saturday – he could devote his weekend to the boy. He crossed the hall and undressed in the dark. When he got into the double bed, Kathy touched his arm and murmured, 'You're back,' and she swung over and sighed and pulled the blankets closer.

'I think I made a hit last night,' said Robarge over breakfast. He told Kathy about the kite.

'You mean you woke him up to give him that thing?'

Kathy's tone discouraged him: he had hoped she would be glad. He said, 'He was already awake – I heard him calling out. Must have had a bad dream. I went straight up.' All these lies to conceal his impulsive wish to kiss his sleeping child at midnight. 'We'll fly the thing today if there's any wind.'

'That's nice,' said Kathy. Her voice was flat and unfocused, almost belittling.

'Anything wrong?'

She said no and got up from the table, which was her abrupt way of showing boredom or changing the subject. And yet Robarge was struck by how attractive she was; how, without noticeable effort, she had discovered the kind of glamour a younger woman might envy. She was thin and had soft heavy breasts and wore light expensive blouses with her jeans.

Robarge said, 'Are you angry because I travel so much?'

'You take your job seriously,' she said. 'Don't apologize. I haven't nagged you about that.'

'I'm lucky I'm based in London – think of the rest of them in Aberdeen. How would you like to be there?'

'Don't say it in that threatening way. I wouldn't go to Aberdeen.'

'I might have been posted there.' He said it loudly, with the confidence of one who has been reprieved.

'You would have gone alone.' He guessed she was poking fun;

he was grateful for that, grateful that things had worked out so well in London.

'You didn't want to come here,' he said. 'But you're glad now, aren't you?'

Kathy did not reply. She was clearing the table and at the same time setting out Richard's breakfast.

'Aren't you?' he repeated in a taunting way.

'Yes!' she said, with unreasonable force, reddening as she spoke. Then she burst into tears. 'There,' she stuttered, 'are you satisfied?'

Robarge, made guilty by her outburst (what had he said?), approached his wife to calm her. But she turned away. He heard Richard on the stairs, and the rattle of the kite dragging. He saw with relief that Kathy had fled into the kitchen, where Richard could not hear her sobbing.

He had dropped Kathy on the Kings Road and proceeded – Richard in the back seat – out of London toward Box Hill. It was only then that he remembered that he had failed to tell Kathy where they were going. She hadn't asked: her tears had made her stubbornly silent. It was late May and once they were past Epsom he could see bluebells growing thickly in the shade of pine woods, and the pale green of the new leaves of beeches, and – already high and drooping from the weight of their blossoms – the cow parsley at the margins of plowed fields.

Richard said, 'There are seagulls here.'

Robarge smiled. There were no seagulls – only newly plowed fields set off by windbreaks of pines, and some crows fussing from tree to tree, to squawk.

'The black ones are crows.'

'But seagulls are white,' said Richard. 'They follow the tractor and eat the worms when the farmer digs them up.'

'You're a smart boy. But seagulls –'

'There they are,' said Richard.

The child was right; at the edge of a field a tractor turned and just behind it, hovering and swooping – seagulls.

They parked near the Burford Bridge Hotel, and above them Robarge saw the long scar of exposed chalk, a whole eroded chute of it, and the steep green hill rising beside it to the brow of a grassy slope where the woods began.

'Mind the cars,' said Richard, warning his father. They paused at the road near the parking lot. A motorcyclist sped past, then the child led his father across. He was being tugged by the child to the far left of a clump of boulders at the base of the hill, and then he saw the nearly hidden path. He realized he was being led by the boy to this entrance, then up the path beside the chalk slide to the gentler rise of the hill. Here Richard broke away and ran the rest of the way up the slope.

'Shall we fly it here?'

'No – over there,' said Richard, out of breath and pointing at nothing Robarge could see. 'Where it's windy.'

They resumed, Robarge trudging, the child leading, until they were on the ridge of the hill. It was as the child had said, for no sooner had he walked to the highest point on that part of the hill than Robarge felt the wind. The path was sheltered, but here the wind was so strong it almost tore the kite from his hands. Robarge was proud of his son for leading him here.

'This is fun!' said Richard excitedly, as Robarge fixed the cross-piece and looped the twine, tightening and flattening the paper butterfly. He took the ball of string from his pocket and fastened it to the kite.

Richard said, 'What about the tail?'

'This kite doesn't need a tail. It's foolproof.'

'All kites have tails,' Richard said. 'Or they fall down.'

The certainty in the child's voice irritated Robarge. He said, 'Don't be silly,' and raised the kite and let the wind pull it from his hand. The kite rose, spun, and then plummeted to the ground. Robarge tried this two more times and then, fearing that he would destroy the frail thing, he squatted and saw that a bit of it was torn.

'It's broken!' Richard shrieked.

'That won't make any difference.'

'It needs a tail!' the child cried.

Robarge was annoyed by the child's insistence. It was the monotonous pedantry he had used in speaking about the seagulls. Robarge said, 'We haven't got a tail.'

Richard planted his feet apart and peered at the kite with his large serious face and said, 'Your necktie can be a tail.'

'I don't know whether you've noticed, Rich, but I'm not wearing a necktie.'

'It won't work then,' said the child. Robarge thought for a

moment that the child was going to stamp on the kite in rage. He kicked the ground and said tearfully, 'I told you it needs a tail.'

'Maybe we can use something else. How about a handkerchief?'

'No – just a tie. Or it won't work.'

Robarge pulled out his handkerchief and tore it into three strips. These he knotted together to make a streamer for the tail. He tied it to the bottom corner of the kite, and while Richard sulked on the grass, Robarge, by running in circles, got the kite aloft. He tugged it and paid out string and made it bob; soon the kite was steadied on the curvature of white line. Richard was beside him, happy again, hopping on his small bow legs.

Robarge said, 'You were right about the tail.'

'Can I have a go?'

A go! Robarge had begun to smile again. 'You want a go, huh? Think you can do it?'

'I know how,' said Richard.

Robarge handed his son the string and watched him lean back and draw the kite higher. Robarge encouraged him. Instead of smiling, the child was made serious by the praise. He worked the string back and forth and said nothing.

'That's it,' said Robarge. 'You're an expert.'

Richard held the string over his head. He made the kite climb and dance. The wind beat against the paper. The child said, 'I told you it needed a tail.'

'You're doing very well. Walk backward and you'll tighten the line.'

But Richard, to Robarge's approval, wound the string on the ball. The kite began to rise. Robarge was impatient to fly the kite himself. He said he could get it much higher and then demanded his turn. He got the kite very high and while it swung he said, 'You're a smart boy. I wouldn't have thought of coming here. And you're good at this. Next time I'll get you a bigger kite – not a paper one, but plastic. They can go hundreds of feet up.'

'That's against the law.'

'Don't be silly.'

'Yes. You can get arrested. It makes the planes crash,' said the child. 'In England.'

Robarge was still making sweeping motions with the string, lifting the kite, making it dive. 'Who says?'

'A man told me.'

Robarge snorted. 'What man?'

'Mummy's friend.'

The child screamed. The kite was falling on its broken string. It crashed against the hill and came apart, blowing until it was misshapen. Robarge thought: I am blind.

Later, when the child was calm and the broken kite stuffed beneath a bush (Robarge promised to buy a new one), he confirmed what Robarge had feared: he had been there before, seen the gulls, climbed the hill, and the man – he had no name, he was 'Mummy's friend' – had taken off his necktie to make a tail for the kite.

The man had worn a tie. Robarge created a lover from this detail and saw someone middle aged, middle class, perhaps prosperous, a serious rival, out to impress – British, of course. He saw the man's hand slipped beneath one of Kathy's brilliant silk blouses. He wondered whether he knew the man; but who did they know? They had been happy and solitary in this foreign country, at World's End. He wanted to cry. He felt his face breaking to expose all his sadness.

'Want to see my hide-out?'

The child showed Robarge the fallen tree, the pine grove, the stumps.

'Did Mummy's friend play with you?'

'The first time –'

Kathy had gone there twice with her lover and Richard! Robarge wanted to leave the place, but the child ran from tree to tree, remembering the games they had played.

Robarge said, 'Were they nice picnics?'

'Not half!'

It was the man's expression, he was sure; and now he hated it.

'What are you looking at, Daddy?'

He was staring at the trampled pine needles, the seclusion of the trees, the narrow path.

'Nothing.'

Richard did not want to go home, but Robarge insisted, and walking back to the car Robarge could not prevent himself from asking questions to which he did not want to hear answers.

The man's name?

'I don't know.'

Did he have a nice car?

9

'Blue.' The child looked away.

'What did Mummy's friend say to you?'

'I don't remember.' Now Richard ran ahead, down the hill.

He saw that the child was disturbed. If he pressed too hard he would frighten him. And so they drove back to World's End in silence.

Robarge did not tell Kathy where they had gone, and instead of confronting her with what he knew he watched her. He did not want to lose her in an argument; it was easy to imagine the terrible scene – her protests, her lies. She might not deny it, he thought; she might make it worse.

He directed his anger against the man. He wanted to kill him, to save himself. That night he made love to Kathy in a fierce testing way, as if challenging her to refuse. But she submitted to his bullying and at last, as he lay panting beside her, she said, 'Are you finished?'

A few days later, desperate to know whether his wife's love had been stolen from him, Robarge told Kathy that he had to go to Aberdeen on business.

'When will you be back?'

'I'm not sure.' He thought: Why should I make it easier on her? 'I'll call you.'

But she accepted this as she had accepted his wordless assault on her, and it seemed to him as though nothing had happened, she had no lover, she had been loyal. He had only the child's word. But the child was innocent and had never lied.

On the morning of his departure for Aberdeen he went to Richard's room. He shut the door and said, 'Do you love me?'

The child moved his head and stared.

'If you really love me, you won't tell Mummy what I'm going to ask you to do.'

'I won't tell.'

'When I'm gone, I want you to be the daddy.'

Richard's face grew solemn.

'That means you have to be very careful. You have to make sure that Mummy's all right.'

'Why won't Mummy be all right?'

Robarge said, 'I think her friend is a thief.'

'No – he's not!'

'Don't be upset,' said Robarge. 'That's what we're going to find out. I want you to watch him if he comes over again.'

'But why? Don't you like him?'

'I don't know him very well – not as well as Mummy does. Will you watch him for me, like a daddy?'

'Yes.'

'If you do, I'll bring you a nice present.'

'Mummy's friend gave me a present.'

Robarge was so startled he could not speak; and he wanted to shout. The child peered at him, and Robarge saw curiosity and pity mingled in the child's squint.

'It was a little car.'

'I'll give you a big car,' Robarge managed.

'What's he stealing from you, Daddy?'

Robarge thought a moment, then said, 'Something very precious –' and his voice broke. If he forced it he would sob. He left the child's room. He had never felt sadder.

Downstairs, Kathy kissed him on his ear. The smack of it caused a ringing in a horn in his head.

He had invented the trip to Aberdeen; he invented work to justify it, and for three days he knew what madness was – a sickening and a sorrow. He was deaf, his feet and hands were stupid, and his tongue at times seemed to swell and choke him when he tried to speak. He wanted to tell his area supervisor that he was suffering, that he knew how odd he must appear. But he did not know how to begin. And strangely, though his behavior was clumsily childlike, he felt elderly, as if he were dying inside, all his organs working feebly. He returned to London feeling that a burned hole was blackened on his heart.

The house at World's End was so still that in the doorway he considered that she was gone, that she had taken Richard and deserted him with her lover. This was Sunday evening, part of his plan – a surprise: he usually returned on Monday. He was not reassured to see the kitchen light on – there was a telephone in the kitchen. But Kathy's face, when she answered the door, was blank.

She said, 'I thought you might call from the station.'

He tried to kiss her – she pulled away.

'My hands are wet.'

'Glad to see me?'

'I'm doing the dishes.' She lost her look of boredom and said, 'You're so pale.'

'I haven't slept.' He could not gather the phrases of the question in his mind because he dreaded the simple answer he saw whole: yes. He felt afraid of her, and more deaf and clumsy than ever, like a helpless orphan snatched into the dark. He wanted her to say that he had imagined the lover, but he knew he would not believe words he craved so much to hear. He no longer trusted her and would not trust her until he had the child's word. He longed to see his son. He started up the stairs.

Kathy said, 'He's watching television.'

On entering the television room, Robarge saw his son stand up and take a step backward. Richard's face in the darkened room was the yellow-green hue of the television screen; his hands sprang to his ears; the blue fibers of his pajamas glowed as if sprinkled with salt. When Robarge switched on the light the child ran to him and held him – so tightly that Robarge could not hug him.

'Here it is.' Robarge disengaged himself from the child and crossed the room, turning off the television as he went. The toy was gift wrapped in bright paper and tied with a ribbon. He handed it to Richard. Richard put his face against his father's neck. 'Aren't you going to open it?'

Robarge felt the child nodding against his shoulder.

'Time for bed,' said Robarge.

The child said, 'I put myself to bed now.'

'All by yourself?' said Robarge. 'Okay, off you go then.'

Richard went to the door.

'Don't forget your present!'

Richard hesitated. Robarge brought it to him and tucked it under the child's arm. Then, pretending it was an afterthought, he said softly, 'Tell me what happened while I was away – did you see anything?'

Richard shook his head and let his mouth gape.

'What about Mummy's friend?' Robarge was standing; the question dropped to the child like a spider lowering on its own filament of spittle.

'I didn't see him.'

The child looked so small; Robarge towered over him. He knelt and asked, 'Are you telling the truth?'

And it occurred to Robarge that he had never asked the child that question before – had never used that intimidating tone or looked so hard into the child's eyes. Richard backed away, the gift-wrapped parcel under his arm.

At this little distance, the child seemed calmer. He shook his head as he had before, but this time his confidence was pronounced, as if in the minute that had elapsed he had learned the trick of it. With the faintest trace of a stutter – when had he ever stuttered? – he said, 'It's the truth, Daddy. I didn't.'

Robarge said, 'It's a tank. The batteries are already inside. It shoots sparks.' Then he shuffled forward on his knees and took the child's arm. 'You'll tell me if you see that man again, won't you?'

Richard stared.

'I mean, if he steals anything?'

Robarge saw corruption in the unblinking eyes.

'You'll tell me, won't you?'

When Robarge repeated the question, Richard said, 'Mummy doesn't have a friend,' and Robarge knew he had lost the child.

He said, 'Show me how you put yourself to bed.'

Robarge was unconsoled. He found Kathy had already gone to bed, and though the light was on she lay on her side, facing the dark wall, as if sleeping.

Robarge said, 'We never make love.'

'We did – on Wednesday.'

She was right; he had forgotten.

She said, 'I've locked the doors. Will you make sure the lights are out?'

So he went from room to room turning out the lights, and in the television room Robarge sat down in the darkness. There, in the house which now seemed to be made of iron, he remembered again that he was in London, in World's End; that he had taken his family there. He was saddened by the thought that he was so far from home. The darkness hid him and hid the country; he knew that if he appeared calm it was only because the darkness concealed his loss. He wished he had never come here, and worrying this way he craved his child and had a hideous reverie, of wishing to eat the child and eat his wife and keep them in that cannibal way. Burdened by this guilty thought, he went upstairs to make sure his son was safe.

Richard was in darkness, too. Robarge kissed the child's hot cheek. There was a bright cube on the floor, the present from Aberdeen. He picked it up and saw that it had not been opened.

He put it beside Richard on the bed and leaning for balance he pressed something in the bedclothes. It was long and flat and the hardness stung his hand. It was the breadknife with the serrated blade from the kitchen, tucked beneath these sheets, close to the child's body. Breathless from the shock of it Robarge took it away.

And then he went to bed. He was shaking so badly he did not think he would ever sleep. He wanted to smash his face against the wall and hit it until it was bloody and he had torn his nose away. He dropped violently to sleep. When he woke in the dark he recalled the sound that had wakened him – it was still vibrant in the air, the click of the front gate: a thief was entering his house. Robarge waited for more, and perspired. His fear left him and he was penetrated by the fake vitality of insomnia. After an hour he decided that what he had heard, if anything, was a thief leaving the house, not breaking in. Too late, too far, too dark, he thought; and he knew now they were all lost.

Zombies

Miss Bristow was certain she had dreamed of a skull because on waking – gasping to the parlor and throwing open the curtains – the first face she had seen was skull-like, a man or woman looking directly in at her from the 49 bus. It verified her dream but was simpler and so more horrible, with staring eyes and bony cheeks and sharp teeth and the long strings of dirty hair they called dreadlocks. She went to the small cabinet and plucked at the doors with clumsy fingers before she remembered that Alison had the key. And then she felt abandoned in dismal terror, between the bedroom where she had dreamed the skull and the window where she had seen the face moving down Sloane Street.

She was still in her slippers and robe when Alison arrived at ten. Alison was an efficient girl with powerful shoulders, a nurse's sliding tread and humor in her whole body; the distress was confined to her eyes. She said, 'Have we had a good night?'

Miss Bristow did not reply to the question. She was tremulous with thought. Her arthritis gave her the look of someone cowering.

'You took the key.'

Alison appeared not to hear her. 'I hope you haven't forgotten that you have a lunch date today.'

She had forgotten. She saw the skull, the teeth, the cowl of hair grinning from the far side of a table in a restaurant where she was trapped. She said, 'Who is it?'

'Philippa – that nice girl from Howletts. She left a message last week.'

Miss Bristow was relieved. She said, 'The Italian.'

'Philippa is not Italian,' said Alison in the singsong she used when she repeated herself. 'Now you must put some clothes on. You haven't had your bath.' She opened the blue diary and said, 'She's coming here at twelve. She'll have news of your book.'

'In a moment you're going to say you've lost the key.'

Alison said, 'We promised we weren't going to be naughty, didn't we?'

*

The Italian, she thought in her bath. At the party, months ago, the girl Philippa had sat at her feet and a sentence was fully framed in Miss Bristow's mind. 'I can remember,' she said, rapping the words on the arm of her chair, struggling to say them, 'I can remember when we were Romans.'

'And now we're Italians,' the girl had said quickly.

Miss Bristow peered at the girl's blank face. The girl scarcely knew how witty she had been, and so Miss Bristow felt better about appropriating the remark and making it her own: *We are Romans turning into Italians*.

The girl had been attentive, with a hearty dedication, saying, 'Your glass is empty again!' But the criticism in the words was not in her tone. Miss Bristow felt the need to sip; she panicked and became breathless when there was nothing to sip. But the girl had made sure there was something in the glass all evening. Miss Bristow sensed the girl's watchfulness as she sipped. How could she explain the paradox she herself did not understand? The contents of this glass worsened her fears, but made her better able to bear them.

'I take no pleasure in this,' said Miss Bristow. 'It is a necessity, like a splint on a fracture.'

Or, she thought, *embalming fluid*. At eighty-two, Miss Bristow felt like a corpse. A celebrated writer in the thirties, she had, after a period of obscurity, lived on to see her work rediscovered and treated – those angry and unhappy books – with a serene reverence. The critical essays about her had the slightly fraudulent forgiving tone of obituaries, publication days the solemnity of exhumations. She knew the talk, that people believed she had been dead for years. When it was learned (and this was news in London) that she was not dead, but had only fallen silent, living on gin in solitude in a tiny Welsh village, she was invited to parties. The books that were republished sold well. She was regarded as a survivor, a voice from the past. And part of her past, the earliest, was a small island in the Caribbean. For the first time in her life, she could afford to live in London. She could not remember when people had listened to her so keenly. She began to write again.

Philippa had asked all the predictable questions, and then they had started to discuss the country. Strangers meeting in London these days spoke of the condition of England as they had once spoken of the weather – cherishing the subject, as people did a harmless illness or a plucky defeat. England was in a pickle: they made it comedy, without consequences, as the girl had done: 'And now we're Italians.'

All evening Miss Bristow had been in the chair. Philippa had carried drinks to her, and a heaped plate of food from the buffet downstairs. Miss Bristow had eaten a pinch of watercress and some of the swollen raisins from the risotto. The ease made her reflective, and the girl relaxed, too.

'I love it here,' said Philippa. 'So many literary people!'

'Do you think so?' Miss Bristow liked the girl's dullness. Lively people required listeners and close attention.

'Sarah's fantastic.'

'That woman,' said Miss Bristow, indicating Sarah, the hostess, who was a poet's widow. 'She is to her late husband's work what Anne Hathaway's cottage is to *Hamlet*.'

Philippa moved her lips and laughed.

Miss Bristow said, 'And I am a zombie.'

Miss Bristow was aware that her fame made bright people shy. But the girl was dull and bold. She was attentive without fawning. She was carelessly pretty, like a beauty in an old snapshot. Miss Bristow wanted to know the girl better, not so much to make a friend as to reacquaint herself with the person she had once been. Already she had seen the re-enactment of some of her own traits – going downstairs for the food the girl had flirted with a black man; she had a slyness in her stare; she knelt on the floor unselfconsciously; she had a frank laugh and a nervous cough – the sounds were harshly similar and seemed to give no relief.

Miss Bristow had been like this – hard and pretty and reckless in ways that had later, as memories, lessened her loneliness. She had emerged from her twenty years' solitude whole, impatient, her imagination undiminished and with an added strength, a directness. She hated discussion, talk of terms, Howletts' ritual respect whenever she turned in a new book. And memory: years of her life which she had thought irretrievable, when she had been as young as that girl, she recovered and wrote about. It startled her to remember these years – other lives in another world. She was glad that she had that girl to talk to. She was, she felt, speaking to her younger self.

'I hope it's not too strong,' said Philippa returning again, the glass between two fingers. Miss Bristow noticed the physical difference in their hands. Her own, twisted with arthritis, was so shaped by habit that it snugly fitted the glass.

'You are so right,' said Miss Bristow. 'Romans turning into Italians.'

Philippa looked baffled. Miss Bristow remembered: the girl had not said precisely that.

'Oh, yes,' Philippa finally said. 'But no one has described it better than you.'

Had she? Perhaps – in a book or story long ago which had not enjoyed the revival. There had been so many books, too great a number for any disinterment to be complete. And now, like everyone else, she knew only the work that had been revived, that was spoken about. The rest was lost to her.

The girl said, 'I admire your work enormously.'

It was not exactly what Miss Bristow wished to hear. She felt sisterly, but her affection was being returned to her more formally, as to a grandmother or great-aunt, and it obliged her with the impulse to do something for this girl – to help her in some way, if only to prevent her from squandering her attention on worthless people like Sarah.

'Do you write?' said Miss Bristow, dreading the girl's reply.

'I tried,' said Philippa. 'I spent a summer in the Caribbean. I wrote poems, part of a play. I started a novel. Then I came home and burned the lot.'

'Ah,' sighed Miss Bristow, seeing the flames – swift and yellow, they consumed the luxury of error and wasted time. It matched a memory of hers and was too much for her. She said, 'And did you visit Isabella?'

Isabella had been Miss Bristow's island.

'Only for a holiday.'

'A holiday?' It dignified the place absurdly. A holiday *there*!

The girl coughed her nervous cough. She said, 'More of a pilgrimage, actually. But I had been there so often already in your books it was as if I were simply returning. It is such a lovely island.'

'It was lovely once.' Miss Bristow thought a moment, and sipped, and said, 'In Roman times.'

'Changeless, like so many of those islands.'

Miss Bristow said, 'The Romans became Italians. It has altered beyond recognition.'

'You reckon?' said Philippa.

Miss Bristow smiled at the expression.

'You really ought to go back.'

'I did. I couldn't bear it. Everything has changed. I was lost – I went to the beach, for a stroll, for my sanity. It was ghastly.'

'The hotels,' said Philippa.

'I like hotels,' said Miss Bristow. 'We built our share of hotels. No, it was the tidewrack, the detritus on the sand. Once, it was all driftwood and torn nets, barrel staves, rope – beautiful things. You expected to find pirate treasure, messages in bottles. Now it is all plastic beakers, tins and tubs, broken glass, bits of rubber. Junk. And oil. And worse.'

'Pollution,' said Philippa.

Miss Bristow glanced at the girl, wondering if with this idiot word she was satirizing her.

'I must write about it.'

'You will.'

'Yes, encourage me,' said Miss Bristow. She looked at her crooked fingers and she whispered, 'I write so slowly now.'

'No one writes about the really important things.'

'Exactly,' said Miss Bristow. 'And what are you writing, my dear?'

Philippa said, 'I think it is ever so important to realize that if one has no talent one ought not to waste one's time in self-deception. I would rather help others, who really have a gift.'

'You are so right.'

Philippa winced. 'I am on the dole.'

Miss Bristow could not hide her shock. This pretty girl, this drawing-room, the talk of her holiday. For a moment, Miss Bristow thought this girl was speaking figuratively: rich parents, idleness.

'I've as much right to it as anyone else,' said the girl, and as she spoke of having lost her job selling antiques, of the Employment Exchange, Miss Bristow looked at the girl's hands – the ring, the silver bracelet: the girl collected her money with these perfect hands.

'Terrible,' said Miss Bristow. 'An American asked me just the other day, "How can you live here?" I said, "I can live here because I once lived on an island that was overrun by savages."'

'Actually,' said Philippa, 'I'd like to be in publishing. But there aren't any jobs going just at the moment.'

'They are the enemy,' said Miss Bristow. 'But if you are

absolutely determined I might be able to help you. My publisher is looking for someone. Do you know Howletts?'

'They're awfully grand.'

Miss Bristow laughed. 'I used to think that!'

'But their list is –'

'It is all trade,' said Miss Bristow. 'They are in business to make money, like everyone else. In Isabella, before the Great War, there were icehouses in the capital. Yes, water was a commodity! They sold it by the cake to planters who carried it upcountry, so they could have cool drinks. The ice merchants were on to a good thing – isn't that the phrase? They might have been selling anything – cloth by the yard, soap, matches, motor cars.' Miss Bristow pursed her lips and added, 'Or books.'

'You're being a bit unfair.'

'Am I? I mean it as praise. What a very great pity it would be if they were not interested in profit,' said Miss Bristow. 'But they are, which is why I have no friends there.'

'Drink,' said Philippa briskly. And before Miss Bristow could react, her empty glass was lifted from her hand.

'You are very kind,' said Miss Bristow.

The girl was immediately hired at Howletts on Miss Bristow's recommendation. And Miss Bristow knew she had assigned the girl to the firm to approve her new book, to eliminate the ritual. Miss Bristow wanted an ally. Dull people mattered more than the spirited ones who mystified her with praise that sounded like mockery.

And now, rising carefully from the bath so she would not break her bones, and hating the feeble image that made the full-length glass seem a ridiculous distorting mirror, she thought how, in the months Philippa had been at Howletts, she had been able to work. She had her ally; and she wasn't fooled: the girl knew very little of her, but how could she? The girl was as she had once been – bold and untruthful, undemanding, generous, and a little foolish. But the girl believed, and the girl did not judge her – that was worth anything. Miss Bristow remembered that she had liked the girl for a phrase, a single observation – Romans, Italians. She had put this into a story and afterward had felt grateful and a bit guilty using words that were not wholly hers. The indebtedness was nothing compared to the fears she remembered and the faces she saw, sleeping, waking, so often now as she tunneled in the past, living in it more intensely now and blinking the zombies away to write about it.

The door chimes rang. Miss Bristow became eager.

'Won't you have something to drink?' said Miss Bristow, entering the parlor, taking the girl's hand. She kept her back to the window so as not to see any skulls. This fear made her seem prim, and even somewhat stately.

Alison said, 'I have already asked her. She doesn't want anything.'

'Go on, my dear. A gin and tonic perhaps?'

'Oh, all right,' said Philippa.

'You see?' said Miss Bristow.

Alison reached through the neck of her jumper and brought out a blunt key on a thong. She went to the cabinet, removed the gin bottle, and made Philippa's drink.

'I will join you,' said Miss Bristow. She smiled at Alison. 'The usual.'

Alison mixed the gin and vermouth for Miss Bristow with a kind of defeated disregard.

'I am feeling a bit shaky today,' said Miss Bristow, slowly fitting herself into the chair and reaching for her drink. She sipped, gulped, sipped again, and said, 'It was that film on the television about the mummy. They unwrapped it and I thought, "Oh, my, I must turn this off." But I couldn't. I just sat there while they unwrapped it. I thought, "I know I'm going to have a bad night if I watch this" but I kept watching and they kept unwrapping. Finally, I couldn't stand it any more. I switched it off and went to bed. And I had a bad night.'

'I didn't see it,' said Philippa. 'I was at a party. A publisher's thrash.'

'It reminded me of something.'

'The mummy?'

'Something else. A face I knew, a face from the catacombs – a long time ago.'

'I didn't know you'd been in Rome.'

'I have never been to Rome,' said Miss Bristow.

Philippa looked at her watch. 'I booked the table for one o'clock and the traffic's pretty bad. We ought to make a move.'

'I'll just fetch my hat,' said Miss Bristow. From the bedroom she heard Alison speaking to Philippa in a harsh accusing whisper.

'We've got lots to talk about,' said Philippa in the restaurant. 'And I have two ideas for you.'

'Before you say another word,' said Miss Bristow, pushing down her hat, 'I want you to get that young man's attention and ask him for two drinks. There's a dear.'

Philippa ordered the drinks and even began talking, but it was not until the gin and French was set before her that Miss Bristow's eyes lost their vacancy and took on a glaze of attention.

'I've been thinking,' Philippa was saying, 'that it's about time you wrote your autobiography. I don't know why you haven't done it before! What an absolutely marvelous book it would be. Of course, I haven't mentioned it to Roger' – 'Roger' to Philippa had been Mister Howlett to Miss Bristow for ten years – 'but I know he'll be fantastically sweet about it.'

'My autobiography?'

'Yes! It just occurred to me the other day,' said Philippa. 'I don't know how I thought of it! What do you say?'

Not one day of my life has gone by, Miss Bristow thought, without that book appearing to me. The book was constant, not as a mass of papers, but finished, a hefty lettered spine, occupying a thick space in a shelf in her mind.

She said, 'It is a nice idea. But who would want to read it?'

'I certainly would!' said Philippa.

The girl was being unhelpful. Miss Bristow wanted more than this.

Philippa said, 'London in the First World War, Paris in the twenties, London again –'

'My island,' said Miss Bristow.

'Of course,' said Philippa, but seemed disappointed.

'I haven't been back to Paris since 1938. It's such a long time ago. I wouldn't go back, not now. People say it's changed so much. I'd go back if I could do it – somehow – like being a fly on the wall, just watching and listening. But that's impossible. How can one be a fly on the wall? And my island. It wasn't what you might think. Some people think it was paradise – "That beautiful life you must have had there," they say. I say, "What beautiful life?"'

'You could explain,' said Philippa. 'In the book.'

22

'Montparnasse was small, too. It was a village. One knew every-one who lived there. I saw James Joyce. This was at a party. We spoke for a while, and I thought, "What a kind man!" He had dark spectacles; he must have been nearly blind. I loved him – I don't think I even knew he was a writer – and I felt that this was a man that one could depend on. *Dependable*, that's what I thought. Gertrude Stein was very noble – a very noble face. And there was Alice B.'

'What did she do?' said Philippa.

'Knitting – something of the sort. Just sitting there and knitting, while Gertrude looked great and noble. I saw Hemingway – I didn't know him. But Djuna Barnes – how grand she looked! She had a huge cape on her shoulders, a huge black cape.'

'So I was right!' said Philippa in triumph. 'It will be a lovely book. I'm sure Roger will be thrilled. I don't know what gave me the idea, but I just knew it was a good one.'

Miss Bristow smiled and put her glass down and pushed it until it hit the ashtray. Hearing the clink, Philippa looked down and then searched for the waiter. Fresh drinks were brought.

Miss Bristow said, 'Once, at a party, I met the lunatic Crosby. He wanted to talk and he noticed I was wearing a pretty ring. This ring. "I've been admiring your ring," he said. "The boy who gave me this ring just got out of prison," I said.'

Philippa lowered her head and frowned.

Miss Bristow said, 'Crosby was very shocked. He looked at me and said, "And you mean you kept it?" That's all he said. "And you mean you kept it?" And he went away.'

Philippa said, 'That's just what I had in mind. Funnily enough, I never thought of James Joyce as dependable.'

'I am telling you what I felt.'

'It would be a marvelous book.'

'What was the other thing?'

'What other thing?'

'You said you had two ideas,' said Miss Bristow. 'You have told me only one.'

'Oh, yes,' said Philippa. 'Would you like another drink?'

'The same,' said Miss Bristow.

Philippa's glass was full: one drink was brought. Miss Bristow sipped and watched Philippa trying to begin. The girl was having difficulty. Miss Bristow said, 'Is it my new collection?'

'Partly. But first of all I want to tell you what a brilliant collection it is –'

With this preface, Miss Bristow thought, the news can only be bad. She was aware that it was an old woman's book, rather a monochrome, all memory, without adornment or invention. But Miss Bristow had discovered this as her strength.

Philippa was still praising her: the news was very bad.

Instead of speaking, Miss Bristow drank, and the drink was like speech, calming her, relieving the apprehension she felt, so that by the time the drink was gone and Philippa had finished, Miss Bristow was smiling and had forgotten her initial uneasiness about the girl's reservations. She heard herself saying, 'Why, that's all right then, isn't it?'

'Gosh, you're quick.' Philippa turned. Now the waiter was nearby and ready, anticipating the order. He brought Miss Bristow another drink.

'Lastly,' said Philippa suddenly, surprising Miss Bristow.

Miss Bristow peered over the rim of her glass.

'The icehouse story.'

'Rather short, I'm afraid,' said Miss Bristow.

'I have no objection to its length,' said Philippa, looking very frightened.

'Does it seem overobvious to you?'

'Not that.' The girl was lost. She looked around as if searching for a landmark and the right way through this confusion.

Miss Bristow said, 'These waiters must be wondering what's keeping us.'

Philippa took a deep breath and said, 'Miss Bristow' – the name alone was warning of worse to come – 'Miss Bristow, some of us at Howletts think it will hurt your reputation.'

Saying so, Philippa sighed and squinted as if expecting the ceiling to crack and drop in pieces on her head.

Miss Bristow laughed hard at the girl in disbelief. And as she laughed she saw the people in the restaurant alter: they were skulls and bones and rags, and even Philippa was skeletal and sunken-eyed, with a zombie's stare.

'Who thinks that?' said Miss Bristow, spacing out her words.

'Roger – some others.' Philippa used her teeth to clamp her lip and chafe it. 'And I do, sort of. I mean, I can see their point.'

'My reputation is no concern of mine. It is a figment in other

24

people's imaginations. It does not belong to me. You should know that.'

'I'm not sure I understand,' said Philippa. 'But I think I understand the icehouse story. It's easily one of the best-written things you've done, and maybe that's why I think it's going to hurt you.'

'How can it possibly hurt me?'

Philippa said, 'Well, it's anti-Negro for one thing.'

'Yes?' Miss Bristow was incredulous; her eyes asked for more.

'And for another thing –' Philippa tried to go on, started twice, and finally said, 'Isn't that enough?'

'If what you said were true it would, I suppose, be more than enough. But it is not true.'

'It's what some readers will think.'

'I don't care about "some readers." It's the others that I care about – and I do care, passionately.'

'Roger thinks –'

'Tell me what you think,' Miss Bristow said sharply.

'I think it presents the black people – oh, God, I hate people who say things like this, but anyway – I think it presents the black people in a bad light.'

'It happened a long time ago,' said Miss Bristow.

'Still –'

'Nineteen seventeen. The light could not have been worse.'

'It worries me.'

'Splendid. The story is a success.'

'I'm sure it is,' said Philippa. 'Miss Bristow, would you like another drink?' Miss Bristow said she would appreciate a small one. Philippa said, 'It seems racial.'

'It is not about race. It is about condition.'

Philippa said, 'I hate to say this, but I think you should take it out.'

Miss Bristow said, 'It is true from start to finish. It is a memory. "But they did not know that they were dying, like Romans becoming Italians" – the last line says it all. You are not interested, you do not want to know. Why won't you see?'

'You were so young then,' said Philippa. 'You might have been wrong.'

Miss Bristow said, 'I was about your age.'

Philippa had not heard the sarcasm.

'But things are different now. You said so yourself.'

'Did I say that?' Miss Bristow saw the faces – the dream skull, the one on the moving bus. And from a bus, on the street, six of them carrying placards, as savage seeming as long ago. She was not imagining those ghastly faces, the teeth, the red eyes, the dreadlocks. She said, 'I have seen them.'

And saw them now. The drink had come. She did not sip. She gulped from the glass, and spilled some.

Philippa said, 'I feel terrible about this. Roger was fantastically sweet. Roger –'

In the restaurant, as in the dream and through the window, bony cheeks, dirty hair, and dusty bitten fingers. They were there, left and right, at the watery offside of her field of vision surrounding the men she saw; in shadow. They had swarmed like rats from the island and now they were here, lurking; they had gained entrance to this restaurant.

Miss Bristow said, 'Perhaps you are right.' She turned and no longer saw the ones in the corner. But there were others. 'Perhaps.' They returned in their rags, but still she said, 'You are right' and 'Yes, yes,' hoping the words would drive them away. Her agreement was merely ritual, like the effect of this glass: it made the fright worse but enabled her to bear it.

The young waiter hurried to Miss Bristow's side, as if instructed, and said, 'The same again, madam?'

The Imperial Icehouse

Of all the grand buildings on my island, the grandest by far was The Imperial Icehouse – white pillars and a shapely roof topped by ornate lettering on a gilded sign. Unlike the warehouses and the shops on the same street, it had no smell. It was whiter than the church, and though you would not mistake it for a church, the fresh paint and elongated windows – and the gold piping on the scrollwork of the sign – gave it at once a look of holiness and purpose. I cannot think of human endeavor without that building coming to mind, shimmering in my memory as it did on the island, the heat distorting it like its reflection in water.

The icehouse did more than cater to the comforts of the islanders. It provided ice for the fisherman's catch and the farmer's delicate produce. A famous Victorian novelist visited us in 1859 and remarked on it, describing it as 'a drinking shop.' It was certainly that, but it was more. It was 'well attended' he said. He was merely passing through, a traveler interested in recording our eccentricities. He could not have known that The Imperial Icehouse was our chief claim to civilization. Ice in that climate! It was shipped to the island whole, and preserved. It was our achievement and our boast.

Then one day, decades later, four men came to town for a wagonload of ice. Three were black and had pretty names; the fourth was a white planter called Mr Hand. He had made the trip with his Negroes because it was high summer and he wanted cold drinks. His plan was to carry away a ton of ice and store it in his estate upcountry. He was a new man on the island and had the strengths and weaknesses peculiar to all new arrivals. He was hard-working and generous; he talked a good deal about progress; he wore his eagerness on his face. He looked stunned and happy and energetic. He did not listen or conceal. On this the most British of the islands it was a satisfaction to newcomers to see the Victoria Statue on Victoria Street, and the horses in Hyde Park, and Nelson in Trafalgar Square. Mr Hand saw no reason why he should not drink here as he had done in England.

He had taken over Martlet's estate, which had been up for sale ever since Martlet's death. That again revealed Mr Hand as a newcomer, considering what had happened to old Martlet. And the estate was as far from town as it was possible to be on this island: Mr Hand, a bachelor, must have needed consolation and encouragement.

He had, against all good advice, taken over the Martlet Negroes, and three of these accompanied him on that trip to town for the ice. Mr Hand closed the deal at the icehouse by having a drink, and he sent a bucket of beer out to his men. They were called John Paul, Macacque, and Jacket. He had another drink, and another, and sent out more beer for those men who kept in the shade. It was not unlawful for Negro estate workers to drink in the daytime, but it was not the custom either. Even if he had known, Mr Hand probably would not have cared.

The Negroes drank, conversing in whispers, shadows in shadow, accepting what they were offered, and waiting to be summoned to load the ice.

They had arrived in the coolness of early morning, but the drinking meant delay: by noon the wagon was still empty, the four horses still tethered to a tree, the Negroes sitting with their backs to the icehouse and their long legs stretched out. Perhaps the racket from inside told them there would be no hurry. In any case, they expected to leave at dusk, for not even the rankest newcomer would risk hauling ice across the island in the midafternoon heat.

Just as they had begun to doze, they were called. Mr Hand stood and swayed on the verandah. He was ready, he yelled. He had to repeat it before his words were understood. Some other men came out of the icehouse and argued with him. Mr Hand took them over to the wagon and showed them the sheets of canvas he had brought. He urged the men to watch as the Negroes swung the big wagon to the back door; and he supervised the loading, distributing sawdust between the great blocks of ice as if cementing for good the foundations of an imperial building.

For an hour or more the Negroes labored, two men to a cake, and Mr Hand joked to them about it: Had they known water to be so heavy? An enormous block was winched from the door. John Paul, who was the leader of the three, withdrew an ice pick from his shirt and began to work its stiletto point on that block. There was a shout from Mr Hand – again, the unexpected voice – and

John Paul stood and patiently wiped the ice pick on his arm. When the block was loaded, the wheels were at a slant and the floor of the wagon had squashed the springs to such an extent that the planks rested on the axle trees. Mr Hand continued to trowel the sawdust and separate the cakes with canvas until at last all the ice was loaded and the four horses hitched.

The news of the loading had reached the men drinking in the icehouse. A noisy crowd gathered on the verandah to watch the tipping wagon creak down Regent Street, Mr Hand holding the reins, Macacque and Jacket tugging the bridles of the forward horses, John Paul sauntering at the rear. Their progress was slow, and even before they disappeared past the tile kiln at the far end of the street many of the icehouse men had left the verandah to seek the cool bar.

Past the Wallace estate, and Villeneuve's dairy, the milestone at the flour mill; children had followed, but they too dropped back because of the heat. Others had watched from doorways, attracted by the size of the load and the rumble and wobble of the wheels in the rutted lanes. Now, no one followed.

There were no more houses. They had begun to climb the first range of hills. In this heat, on the exposed road, the birds were tiny and silent, and the flowers had no aroma. There was only a sawing of locusts and a smell of dust. From time to time, Jacket glimpsed the straining horse he held and looked over at Macacque, who frowned at the higher hills beyond.

The hills loomed; no one saw the hole in the road, only the toppling horses, the one behind Jacket rearing from a broken trace and free of one strap swinging himself and snapping another. Empty, the wagon had seemed secure; but this weight, and the shock of the sudden hole, made it shudder feebly and look as if it might burst. Jacket calmed the horse and quickly roped him. The others steadied the wagon.

Mr Hand, asleep on his seat, had tumbled to his knees. He woke and swore at the men, then at the horses, and he cursed the broken straps. But he had more straps in the chest he had brought, and he was so absorbed in the repair he did not leave the road. He mended the traces – spurning the men's help – in the middle of the North Road, squinting in the sunshine.

They were soon on their way. There was a rime of froth on the necks and fetlocks of the horses, and great syrupy strings of yellow saliva dripped from their jaws. The road narrowed as it grew steep; then it opened again. The horses fought for footing and the wheels chimed as they banged against the wagon. The Negroes did not sing as they had on the early-morning ride, nor did they speak. Mr Hand nodded, sat upright, slumped again, and was asleep.

Sensing the wagon slowing, John Paul put his shoulder under the back flap and gave a push. His shoulder was soaked; the wagon had begun to drip, dark pennies in the dust that dried almost as soon as they formed. He placed his forearms on the flap and put his head down and let the wagon carry him.

Passing the spring where they had stopped that morning for a drink, John Paul called out to Mr Hand and asked if they could rest. No, said Mr Hand, waking again and spreading his fingers to push at the sunlight. They would go on, he said; they were in a hurry. Now Jacket sang out – a brief squawking ditty, interrupting the silence of the hot road. He was answered by John Paul, another birdlike cry, and then Macacque's affirming gabble. John Paul took his ice pick and reached beneath the canvas. He chopped a wedge, and sucked it, then shared it with the two other Negroes. Mr Hand gasped in sleep.

There was a cracking, a splintering of wood like a limb twisting from a tree. John Paul tossed his chunk of ice into the grass by the roadside, and he saw the rear wheel in pieces, a bunch of spokes settling under the wagon.

Glassy eyed from his nap, Mr Hand announced to them that he had a spare wheel. He unbolted it from the bottom of the wagon and fitted it to the axle, but from where the others stood idle they could see that the ice had shifted and cracked the side boards. And yet, when the trip was resumed, the wagon rolled more smoothly, as if the load were lighter than before – the springs had bounce, the wheels were straighter.

More ice was chopped away by John Paul, and this he shared, and while Mr Hand slept the three Negroes quarreled silently, sniffing and sighing, because John Paul had the ice pick and he would not let any of the others use it.

The road became bumpy again; the ice moved in the wagon. It had been securely roped, but now it was loose; it was a smaller load; its jarring woke Mr Hand. He worked himself into a temper when he saw the diminished load. He stopped to tighten the canvas around it and screamed at the puddle that collected under the wagon. He would not let the Negroes drink. There will be cold drinks in plenty, he said, when we arrive home. Later, he got down from the seat on a steep grade and got behind and pushed with his shoulder like John Paul, and he said: That's how we do it.

They passed a fragrant valley. Negroes in that valley whispered and laughed and jeered at the Negroes in this procession. Now the ice was melting so quickly there was a stream of water pouring from the wagon and its cracks. The mockery was loud and several Negroes followed for some distance, yelling about the melting ice and the trail of mud they left through the pretty valley. The wagon wood was dark with moisture, as dark as the Negroes' faces, which were streaming with sweat.

Mr Hand began to talk – crazy talk about England – and his men laughed at the pitch of his voice, which was a child's complaint. They did not understand his words; he ignored their laughter.

The left trace snapped as the right had done, a spoke worked loose and dropped from a wheel, although the wheel itself remained in position. One horse's shoe clanged as he kicked it into the belly of the wagon. These incidents were commented upon, and now the Negroes talked loudly of the stupidity of the trip, the waste of effort, the wrong time of day, the color of Mr Hand's cheeks. Mr Hand sat holding the reins loosely, his head tipped onto his shoulder. His straw hat fell off and the Negroes left it on the road where it fell. John Paul looked back and saw his footprint crushed into the crown.

They had gained the second range of hills, and descending – slowly, so that the wagon would not be shot forward – the late-afternoon sun, unshielded by any living tree, struck their faces like metal. The road was strewn with boulders on which the horses did a tired dance, stepping back. There was a curve, another upward grade, and at that corner the horses paused to crop the grass.

There was no sound from Mr Hand. He was a crouching infant in his seat, in the sun's glare, his mouth open. The horses tore at the grass with their lips. The Negroes crept under the wagon, and there they stayed in the coolness, for an hour or more, the cold water dripping on them.

Mr Hand woke, stamping his feet on the planks. They scrambled to their places.

His anger was exhausted in three shouts. He promised them ice, cold drinks, a share for everyone, and as he spoke the Negroes could see how the ice beneath the sagging canvas was a quarter the size of what it had been. Divided, it would be nothing. They did not respond to Mr Hand's offer: it was a promise of water, which they had already as their right, from their own spring.

Mr Hand tugged the reins and the men helped the horses, dragged the wagon, dragged the ice, dragged this man through the tide of heat. Mr Hand chattered, repeating his promises, but when he saw the impassive faces of the Negroes he menaced them with whining words. He spoke sharply, like an insect stirred by the sun.

If you don't pull hard, he said to the men, I'll free the horses and hitch you to the wagon – and you'll take us home. He thwacked the canvas with his whip. There was no thud, nothing solid, only a thin echoless smack, and he clawed open the canvas. Shrunken ice blocks rattled on the planks.

He stopped the wagon and leaped out and faced each man in turn and accused him. The men did nothing; they waited for him to move. And he did. He hit Macacque and called him a thief. Jacket was lazy, he said, and he hit him. John Paul prepared himself for worse. Mr Hand came close to him and screamed and, as he did, the wagon lurched. The horses had found grass: they pulled the wagon to the roadside.

The sounds of the horses chewing, the dripping of the wagon in the heat; it was regular, like time leaking away. Mr Hand raised his whip and rushed at John Paul. And then, in that low sun, Mr Hand cast three shadows; two helped him aside, and he struggled until a sound came, the sound John Paul had made in town with his ice pick, like ice being chipped, or bone struck, and the hatless man cried out – plea, promise, threat, all at once – and staggered to the wagon and shouted at the water dripping into the dust. The ice was no larger than a man, and bleeding in the same way.

At last it was cool and dark and they were passing the first fences of the farm and turning into the drive. There were lighted huts and lights moving toward them, swinging tamely on nothing in the darkness. Voices near those lanterns cried out – timid questions. The three men answered in triumph from the top of the heavy wagon, which rumbled in the road like a broken catafalque, streaming, still streaming, though all the ice was gone.

Yard Sale

As things turned out, Floyd had no choice but to spend the summer with me in East Sandwich. To return home to find his parents divorced was awkward; but to learn that they had already held their yard sale was distinctly shaming. I had been there and seen my sister's ghastly jollity as she disposed of her old Hoover and shower curtains and the chair she had abandoned caning; Floyd senior, with a kind of hostile generosity, turned the whole affair into a potlatch ceremony by bestowing his power tools on his next-door neighbor and clowning among his junk with the word 'freebie.' 'Aunt Freddy can have my life jacket,' he crowed. 'I'm not your aunt,' I said, but I thanked him for it and sent it via the local church to Bangladesh, where I hoped it would arrive before the monsoon hit Chittagong. After the yard sale, they made themselves scarce – Floyd senior to his Boston apartment and his flight attendant, my sister to the verge of a nervous breakdown in Cuttyhunk. I was glad to be deputized to look after little Floyd, and I knew how relieved he would be, after two years in the Peace Corps in Western Samoa, to have some home cooking and the sympathetic ear of his favorite aunt. He, too, would be burdened and looking for buyers.

At Hyannis Airport, I expected a waif, an orphan of sorts, with a battered suitcase and a heavy heart. But Floyd was all smiles as he peered out of the fuselage, and when the steps were lowered and he was on them, the little plane actually rocked to and fro: Floyd had gained seventy-five pounds. A Henry Moore muppet of raw certainty, he was dark, with hair like varnished kapok and teeth gleaming like Chiclets. He wore an enormous shirt printed with bloated poppies, and the skirtlike sarong that Margaret Mead tells us is called a *lava-lava*. On his feet were single-thong flip-flops, which, when he kicked them off – as he did in the car, to sit cross-legged on the bucket seat – showed his toes to be growing in separate directions.

'Wuppertal,' he said, or words to that effect. There was about him a powerful aroma of coconut oil and a rankness of dead leaves and old blossoms.

'Greetings,' I said.

'That's what I just said.'

'And welcome home.'

'It doesn't seem like home anymore.'

We passed the colonial-style (rough-hewn logs, split-rail fence, mullion windows) Puritan Funeral Home, Kopper Krafts, the pizza joints, and it occurred to me that this part of Route 132 had changed out of all recognition. I thought: Poor kid.

The foreknowledge that I would be led disloyally into loose talk about his father's flight attendant kept me silent about his parents' divorce. I asked him about Samoa; I was sure he was aching to be quizzed. This brought from him a snore of approval and a native word. I mentioned his sandals.

He said, 'My mother never wears sandals. She's always barefoot!'

I determined upon delicacy. 'It's been a hard year.'

'She says the craziest things sometimes.'

'Nerves.'

Here was the Hyannis Drive-In Movie. I was going to point out to him that while he had been away, they had started holding drive-in church services on Sunday mornings – an odd contrast to Burt Reynolds in the evenings, the sacred and the profane in the same amphitheatre. But Floyd was talking about his father.

'He's amazing, and what a sailor! I've known him to go out in a force-nine gale. He's completely reckless.'

Aren't the young downright? I thought. I did not say anything about the life jacket his old man had given me; I was sure he had done it out of malice, knowing full well that what I had really coveted was the dry pinewood sink lost in the potlatch.

'Floyd,' I said, with a shrill note of urgency in my voice – I was frantic to drag him off the topic I knew would lead him to his parents' fractured marriage – 'what about Samoa?'

'Sah-moa,' he said, moving his mouth like a chorister as he corrected my pronunciation. So we have an emphatic stammer on the first syllable, do we? I can take any amount of well-intentioned pedantry, but I draw the line at condescension from someone I have laboriously diapered. It was so difficult for me to mimic this unsayable word that I countered with 'And yet, I wonder how many of them would get Haverhill right?'

Floyd did not move from his Buddha posture. 'Actually, he's wicked right-wing, and very moralistic about things. I mean, deep down. He hates change of any kind.'

'You're speaking of –?'

'My father.'

Your psychiatrists say grief is a great occasion for rationalizing. Still, the Floyd senior I knew was indiscernible through this coat of whitewash. He was the very engine of change. Though my sentence was fully framed, I didn't say to his distracted son, That is a side of your father I have not been privileged to observe.

'Mother's different.'

'How so?'

'Confident. Full of beans. Lots of savvy.'

And beside herself in Cuttyhunk. Perhaps we do invent the friends and even the parents we require, and yet I was not quite prepared for what Floyd said next.

'My sister's pretty incredible, too. I've always thought of myself as kind of athletic, but she can climb trees twice as fast as me.'

This was desperate: he had no sister. Floyd was an only child. I had an overwhelming desire to slap his face, as the hero does in B movies to bring the flannel-mouthed fool to his senses.

But he had become effusive. 'My sister . . . my brother . . . my grandmother' – inventing a fictitious family to make up for the one that had collapsed in his absence.

I said, 'Floyd dear, you're going to think your old auntie is horribly literal-minded, but I don't recognize your family from anything you've said. Oh, sure, I suppose your father *is* conservative – the roué is so often a puritan underneath it all. And vice versa. Joseph Smith? The Mormon prophet? What was it, fifty wives? 'When I see a pretty girl, I have to pray,' he said. *His* prayers were answered! But listen, your mother's had a dreadful time. And, um, you don't actually have any brothers or sisters. Relax. I know we're under a little strain, and absolutely bursting with Samoa, but –'

'In Samoa,' he said, mocking me with the half sneeze of its correct pronunciation, 'it's the custom to join a local family. You live with them. You're one of them.'

'Much as one would join the Elks around here?'

'It's wicked complicated.'

'More Masonic – is that it?'

'More Samoan. You get absorbed kind of. They prefer it that way. And they're very easygoing. I mean, there's no word for bastard in Samoan.'

'With so little traffic on the roads, there's probably no need for it. Sorry. I see your point. But isn't that taking the extended family a bit far? What about your parents?'

'He thatches roofs and she keeps chickens.'

'Edith and Floyd senior?'

'Oh, them' was all he said.

'But you've come home!'

'I don't know. Maybe I just want to find my feet.'

Was it his turn of phrase? I dropped my eyes and saw a spider clinging to his ankle. I said, 'Floyd, don't move – there's a creature on your foot.'

He pinched it lovingly. 'It's only a tattoo.'

That seemed worse than a live spider, which had the merit of being able to dance away. I told him this, adding, 'Am I being fastidious?'

'No, ethnocentric,' he said. 'My mother has a mango on her knee.'

'Not a banjo?' When I saw him wince, I said, 'Forgive me, Floyd. Do go on – I want to hear everything.'

'There's too much to tell.'

'I know the feeling.'

'I wouldn't mind a hamburger,' he said suddenly. 'I'm starving.'

Instead of telling him I had cassoulet waiting for him in East Sandwich, I slowed down. It is the fat, not the thin, who are always famished; and he had not had a hamburger in two years. But the sight of fast food woke a memory in him. As he watched the disc of meat slide down a chute to be bunned, gift wrapped, and clamped into a small styrofoam valise, he treated me to a meticulous description of the method of cooking in Samoa. First, stones were heated, he said, then the hot stones buried in a hole. The uncooked food was wrapped in leaves and placed on the stones. More hot stones were piled on top. Before he got to the part where the food, stones, and leaves were disinterred, I said, 'I understand that's called labor intensive, but it doesn't sound terribly effective.'

He gave me an odd look and excused himself, taking his little valise of salad to the drinking fountain to wash it.

'We always wash our food before we eat.'

I said, 'Raccoons do that!'

It was meant as encouragement, but I could see I was not doing at all well.

Back at the house, Floyd dug a present out of his bag. You sat on it, this fiber mat. 'One of your miracle fibers?' I said. 'Tell me more!' But he fell silent. He demurred when I mentioned tennis, and at my suggestion of an afternoon of recreational shopping he grunted. He said, 'We normally sleep in the afternoon.' Again I was a bit startled by the plural pronoun and glanced around, half expecting to see another dusky islander. But no – Floyd's was the brotherly folk 'we' of the native, affirming the cultural freemasonry of all Polynesia. And it had clearly got into his bones. He had acquired an almost catlike capacity for slumber. He lay for hours in the lawn hammock, swinging like a side of beef, and at sundown entered the house yawning and complaining of the cold. It was my turn to laugh: the thermometer on the deck showed eighty-one degrees.

'I'll bet you wish you were at Trader Vic's,' I said over the cassoulet, trying to avert my ethnocentric gaze as Floyd nibbled the beans he seized with his fingers. He turned my Provençal cuisine into a sort of astronaut's pellet meal.

He belched hugely, and guessing that this was a ritual rumble of Samoan gratitude, I thanked him.

'Ironic, isn't it?' I said. 'You seem to have managed marvelously out there in the Pacific, taking life pretty much as you found it. And I can't help thinking of Robert Louis Stevenson, who went to Samoa with his sofas, his tartans, his ottoman, and every bagpipe and ormolu clock from Edinburgh in his luggage.'

'How do you know that?' he asked.

'Vassar,' I said. 'There wasn't any need for Stevenson to join a Samoan family. Besides his wife and his stepson, there were his stepdaughter and her husband. His wife was a divorcée, but she was from California, which explains everything. Oh, he brought his aged mother out, too. She never stopped starching her bonnets, so they say.'

'Tusitala,' said Floyd.

'Come again?'

'That was his title. "Teller of tales." He read his stories to the Samoans.'

'I'd love to know what they made of "Weir of Hermiston."' It was clear from Floyd's expression that he had never heard of the novel.

He said gamely, 'I didn't finish it.'

'That's not surprising – neither did Stevenson. Do much reading, Floyd?'

'Not a lot. We don't have electricity, and reading by candlelight is really tough.'

'"Hermiston" was written by candlelight. In Samoa. It would be an act of the greatest homage to the author to read it that way.'

'I figured it was pointless to read about Samoa if you live there.'

'All the more reason to read it, since it's set in eighteenth-century Scotland.'

'And he was a *palagi*.'

'Don't be obscure, Floyd.'

'A white man.'

Only in the sense that Pushkin was an octoroon and Othello a soul brother, I thought, but I resisted challenging Floyd. Indeed, his saturation in the culture had made him indifferent to the bizarre. I discovered this when I drew him out. What was the food like after it was shoveled from beneath the hot stones? On Floyd's report it was uninspired: roots, leaves, and meat, sweated together in this subterranean sauna. What kind of meat? Oh, all kinds; and with the greatest casualness he let it drop that just a week before, he had eaten a flying fox.

'On the wing?' I asked.

'They're actually bats,' he said. 'But they call them –'

'Do you mean to tell me that you have eaten a bat?'

'You act as if it's an endangered species,' he said.

'I should think Samoans are if that's part of their diet.'

'They're not bad. But they cook them whole, so they always have a strange expression on their faces when they're served.'

'Doesn't surprise me a bit. Turn up their noses, do they?'

'Sort of. You can see all their teeth. I mean, the bats'.'

'What a stitch!'

He smiled. 'You think that's interesting?'

'Floyd, it's matchless.'

Encouraged, he said, 'Get this – we use fish as fertilizer. Fish!'

'That's predictable enough,' I said, unimpressed. 'Not far from where you are now, simple folk put fresh fish on their vegetable gardens as fertilizer. Misguided? Maybe. Wasteful? Who knows?

Such was the nature of subsistence farming on the Cape three hundred years ago. One thing, though – they knew how to preach a sermon. Your agriculturalist is so often a God-fearing man.'

This cued Floyd into an excursion on Samoan Christianity, which sounded to me thoroughly homespun and basic, full of a good-natured hypocrisy that took the place of tolerance.

I said, 'That would make them – what? Unitarians?'

Floyd belched again. I thanked him. He wiped his fingers on his shirtfront and said it was time for bed. He was not used to electric light: the glare was making him belch. 'Besides, we always go to bed at nine.'

The hammering some minutes later was Floyd rigging up the hammock in the spare room, where there was a perfectly serviceable double bed.

'We never do,' I called.

Floyd looked so dejected at breakfast, toying with his scrambled egg and sausage, that I asked him if it had gone cold. He shrugged. Everything was hunky-dory, he said in Samoan, and then translated it.

'What do you normally have for breakfast?'

'Taro.'

'Is it frightfully good for you?'

'It's a root,' he said.

'Imagine finding your roots in Samoa!' Seeing him darken, I added, 'Carry on, Floyd. I find it all fascinating. You're my window on the world.'

But Floyd shut his mouth and lapsed into silence. Later in the morning, seeing him sitting cross-legged in the parlor, I was put in mind of one of those big lugubrious animals that look so home-sick behind the bars of American zoos. I knew I had to get him out of the house.

It was a mistake to take him to the supermarket, but this is hindsight; I had no way of anticipating his new fear of traffic, his horror of crowds, or the chilblains he claimed he got from air conditioning. The acres of packaged foods depressed him, and his reaction to the fresh-fruit department was extraordinary.

'One fifty-nine!' he jeered. 'In Samoa, you can get a dozen bananas for a penny. And look at that,' he said, handling a whiskery coconut. 'They want a buck for it!'

'They're not exactly in season here on the Cape, Floyd.'

'I wouldn't pay a dollar for one of those.'

'I had no intention of doing so.'

'They're dangerous, coconuts,' he mused. 'They drop on your head. People have been known to be killed by them.'

'Not in Barnstable County,' I said, which was a pity, because I felt like aiming one at his head and calling it an act of God.

He hunched over a pyramid of oranges, examining them with distaste and saying that you could buy the whole lot for a quarter in a village market he knew somewhere in remote Savai'i. A tray of mangoes, each fruit the rich color of old meerschaum, had Floyd gasping with contempt: the label stuck to their skins said they were two dollars apiece, and he had never paid more than a nickel for one.

'These cost two cents,' he said, bruising a grapefruit with his thumb, 'and they literally give these away,' he went on, flinging a pineapple back onto its pile. But his disbelief was nothing compared to the disbelief of shoppers, who gawped at his *lava-lava*. Yet his indignation at the prices won these people over, and amid the crashing of carts I heard the odd shout of 'Right on!'

Eventually I hauled him away, and past the canned lychees ('They grow on trees in China, Floyd!') I became competitive. 'What about split peas?' I said, leading him down the aisles. 'Scallops? Indian pudding? Dreft? Clorox? What do you pay for dog biscuits? Look, be reasonable. What you gain on mangoes, you lose on maple syrup!'

We left empty-handed. Driving back, I noticed that Floyd had become even gloomier. Perhaps he realized that it was going to be a long summer. I certainly did.

'Anything wrong, Floyd?'

He groaned. He put his head in his hands. 'Aunt Freddy, I think I've got culture shock.'

'Isn't that something you get at the other end? I mean, when the phones don't work in Nigeria or you find ants in the marmalade or the grass hut leaks?'

'Our huts never leak.'

'Of course not,' I said. 'And look, this is only a *palagi* talking, but I have the unmistakable feeling that you would be much happier among your own family, Floyd.'

We both knew which family. Mercifully, he was gone the next

day, leaving nothing behind but the faint aroma of coconut oil in the hammock. He never asked where I got the price of the Hyannis–Apia airfare. He accepted it with a sort of extortionate Third Worlder's wink, saying, 'That's very Samoan of you, Aunt Freddy.' But I'll get it back. Fortunately, there are ways of raising money at short notice around here.

Algebra

Ronald had threatened to move out before, but I always begged him not to. He knew he had power over me. He was one of those people who treats flattery as if it is mockery, and regards insult as a form of endearment. You couldn't talk to him. He refused to be praised, and if I called him 'Fanny' he only laughed. I suppose he knew that basically he was worthless, which led him to a kind of desperate boasting about his faults – he even boasted about his impotence. What Ronnie liked best was to get drunk on the cheap wine he called 'Parafino' and sprawl on the chaise and dig little hornets out of his nose and say what scum most people were. I knew he was bad for me and that I would have another breakdown if things went on like this much longer.

'God's been awful good to me,' he said once in the American accent he affected when he was drunk.

'That's blasphemy,' I said. 'You don't mean that. You'll go to Hell.'

'Wrong!' he shrieked. 'If you *do* mean it you'll go to Hell.'

When I met him he had just joined Howletts, the publisher. Quite early on, he began to sneer at the parties he sometimes took me to by boasting that he could go to one every day of the week. I thought he had a responsible position but afterwards, when I got to know the others, particularly Philippa and Roger, I came to realize that he was a rather insignificant person in the firm. I think this is why he seemed so embarrassed to have me along and took me so seldom. He implied that I wasn't attractive or intelligent enough for his publishing friends, and he would not let me near the real writers.

'This is Michael Insole, a friend,' he'd say, never letting on that we were living together in my flat. That sort of thing left me feeling incredibly depressed.

Then everything changed. I have not really analyzed it until now. It certainly wasn't an idea – nothing as solemn or calculated as that. It was more an impulse, a frenzy you might say, or a leap in the dark. At one of the parties I was talking to Sir Charles Moon-man, the novelist and critic. 'And what do you do?' he asked me. At another time I might have said, 'I live with Ronald Brill,' but I was feeling so fed up with Ronnie I said, 'Basically, I'm a writer.'

'Do I know your work?' asked Sir Charles.

'No,' I said. It was the truth. I worked then, as I do now, at the Arcade Off-License near the Clapham South tube station, but living with Ronnie had made me want to go into writing.

Sir Charles found my prompt reply very funny, and then an odd thing happened. He relaxed and began to talk and talk. He was hugely old and had the downright manner and good health of a country doctor. He was reading Kingsley, he said, and squeezed air with his hands. He described the book, but it was nothing like any Kingsley I had ever read. He said, 'It has, don't you agree, just the right tone, an elasticity one associates with fiction –' I nodded and tried to add something of my own, but could not get a word in.

At this point, Virginia Byward, the novelist and traveler, ambled over and said hello.

'This is Mister Insole. He's a writer,' said Sir Charles. 'We've just been talking about Kinglake.'

Kinglake, not Kingsley. I was glad I had not said anything.

'*Eothen*? That Kinglake?' said Miss Byward.

'*The Invasion of the Crimea*. That Kinglake,' said Sir Charles.

'Well, I'll let you two get on with it,' said Miss Byward, laughing at her mistake. 'Very nice to have met you, Mister Insole.'

'She's so sweet,' said Sir Charles. 'And her reportage is devastating.' He clawed at his cuff. 'Bother. It's gone eight. I must rush – dinner engagement.'

'I'll be late for mine, as well,' I said. 'My hostess will tear a strip off me.' But I was not going anywhere.

'Such a bore, isn't it?' he said. 'We are both being called away. So unfortunate. I would much rather stand and chat about the Crimean War.'

'So would I!' I said. Then, I could think of nothing else to say, so I said, 'I am one of your most passionate fans.'

This was my leap in the dark. I had never read a word he had written. I suppose I looked terrified, but you would not have known it from the look on Sir Charles's face – pure joy. He removed his pipe from his mouth and stuffed his finger in the bowl.

'I'm so glad.'

'I'm not joking,' I said. 'I find your work a real consolation. It genuinely engages me.'

'It is awfully good of you to say so.'

He sounded as if he meant it. More than that, he reacted as if no one had ever said these words to him before.

'We must meet for lunch one day.' He clenched the pipe stem in his teeth and beamed.

I said, 'How about dinner at my place? When you're free.'

And Sir Charles Moonman, the eminent novelist and critic, said to me, 'I am free most evenings.'

'Next week?'

'I can do Monday, or Tuesday, or –'

'Monday,' I said. I gave him my address and that was that. He clapped me on the shoulder in his bluff country doctor way, and I was still somewhat dazed when Ronald came over.

'What are you grinning about?'

'I've just invited Sir Charles Moonman for dinner.'

Ronald was horrified. 'You can't,' he said. 'I'll phone him in the morning and tell him it's off.'

'You'll do no such thing,' I said, raising my voice to a pitch that had Ronald shushing me and steering me to a corner.

'What are you going to give him?'

He had me there. I do a nice shepherd's pie, and Ronald had often praised my flan, but truly I had not given the menu much thought, and told him so.

'Shepherd's pie!' Ronald was saying as Virginia Byward sidled up to me.

'Hello, Mister Insole,' she said. She had remembered my name! 'Has Charles gone?'

Ronald was speechless.

'Charles had to be off,' I said. 'A dinner party – he was rather dreading it.'

Miss Byward was staring at Ronald.

'I know Mister Insole is a writer,' she said. 'But what do you do?'

Ronald turned purple. He said, 'I sell worthless books,' and marched away.

'I hope I didn't say anything to offend him,' said Miss Byward. 'Too bad about Charles. I was hoping he'd still be here. I meant to lock horns with him.'

'If you're free on Monday, come along for dinner. Charles will be there.'

'I couldn't crash your dinner party.'

'Be my guest,' I said. 'It won't be fancy, but I think of myself as a good plain cook.'

'If you're sure it's no trouble –'

'I'd be honored,' I said, and then I could think of nothing to say except, 'I am one of your most passionate fans,' the statement that had gone down so well with Sir Charles. I was a bit embarrassed about saying it, because repeating it made it sound formulated and insincere. But it was my embarrassment that brought it off.

'Are you?' she said. She was clearly delighted.

'Your reportage is devastating.'

It was as easy as twisting a tap. I said nothing more. I simply listened to her talk, and finally she said, 'I've so enjoyed our little chat. See you Monday.'

Ronald was silent on the way home until we got to Kennington or The Oval. Then he said, 'Are you a writer?'

At Stockwell, I said, 'Are you a publisher?'

As the train drew into Clapham Common, he stood up and said, 'You're shameless.' He pushed past me and ran up the escalator.

That night Ronald slept on the chaise and the next day he moved out of the flat and out of my life.

I had not known how easy it would be to make the acquaintance of Sir Charles Moonman and Miss Byward. It had only been necessary to learn a new language, and it was one that Ronald either despised or did not know. When I went broody about Ronald's absence over the weekend I remembered the guests I'd invited for Monday and I cheered up.

But on Sunday I began to worry about the numbers. Three people did not seem much of a dinner party and I kept hearing myself saying, 'I like the intimate sort of party.' So I invited Mr Momma, too. Mr Momma, a Cypriot, was a house painter who lived in the top-floor flat. He never washed his milk bottles, so Ronald had named him 'Inky,' which was short for 'inconsiderate.' Mr Momma said he would do a salad.

On Monday I went to the library and got copies of Sir Charles's and Miss Byward's books. I was setting them out, arranging them on tables, when the phone rang. I must have been feeling a bit insecure still because I thought at once that it was either Sir Charles or Miss Byward who had rung to say they couldn't make it after all.

'Michael?'

It was Tanya Moult, one of Ronald's authors. I should say one of Ronald's victims, because he had strung her along for years. She was working on a book about pirates, women pirates, and Ronald had said it was just the ticket, a kind of robust woman's thing. That was very Ronald. He had other people doing books on cowboys – black cowboys; hair-dressers and cooks – all men; gay heroes, and cats in history. Tanya sent him chapters and at the same time she scraped a living writing stories for women's magazines under a pseudonym. Ronald was very possessive about Tanya, but perversely so: he kept me away from her while at the same time being nasty to her.

I told her that Ronald had moved out. It was the first she had heard of it and I could tell that she was really down. Ronald had not been in touch with her about her newest chapter.

'Look, Tanya,' I said – it was the first time I had used her Christian name. 'Why don't you come round tonight? I'm having a few friends over for dinner.'

She hesitated. I knew what she was thinking – I couldn't blame her.

'Sir Charles Moonman,' I said. 'And Virginia Byward.'

'Gosh, Michael, really?'

'And Mister Momma from upstairs.'

'I've met him,' she said. 'I don't know whether I have anything to wear.'

'Strictly informal. If I know Sir Charles he'll be wearing an old cardigan, and Virginia will be in a rather shapeless tunic.'

She said she would be there. At seven, Mr Momma appeared in a bulging blue jumpsuit, carrying plastic bags of lettuce and onions and some tubs of dressing. He said, 'How do you know I like parties?' and pulled one bulge out of his pocket – an avocado. His teeth were big, one was cracked, he wore a gold crucifix on a chain around his neck, and he smelled of sweat and soap. He sniffed. 'Cooking food!' He swung his bags onto the table. 'Salad,' he said. 'I make fresh. Like my madder.'

I had never seen Mr Momma happier. He shooed me out of the kitchen and then busied himself chopping and grating, and whistling through the crack in his tooth.

Tanya arrived on the dot of eight with a bottle of Hungarian Riesling. 'I'm so excited,' she said, and I realized just how calm I was. The bell rang again.

'Oh, my God,' cried Mr Momma.

Tanya went to the kitchen door and smiled.

'Like my madder,' Mr Momma said.

Sir Charles was breathless when I met him on the landing.

'I should have warned you about those stairs,' I said.

But his breathlessness helped. He was panting, as if he had been cornered after a long chase and he could do nothing but smile and gasp his thanks as he was introduced to Tanya. He found a chair and propelled himself backward into it and sighed.

'Wine?' I said.

'That would be lovely.'

I poured him a glass of Montrachet, gave him its pedigree (but omitted the fact that I had got it at a staff discount from Arcade Off-License) and left him to Tanya.

' – it's not generally known, but there were a fantastic number,' Tanya was saying, and she was off: women pirates. Sir Charles was captivated.

'Do you know,' said Virginia Byward when she arrived, glancing around the flat and relaxing at the sight of two copies of her books, 'this is only the second time in my life I've been to Clapham? I'd rather not talk about the first time. I came a cropper that night!' She spoke to Sir Charles: 'It was during the war.'

'Something for your biographer,' said Sir Charles.

We all laughed at this. But I thought then, and I continued to think throughout the evening, that I was now a part of their lives and that the time they were spending with me mattered. Each great writer seems to me to contain a posthumous book, the necessary and certain biography. Writers carry this assurance of posterity around with them. This was a page of that book.

This: my chaise, on which Miss Byward was sitting; my brass Benares ashtray with a smoldering thimble shape of Sir Charles's pipe tobacco in it; my tumbling tradescancia; my gate-legged dining table on which one of Ronald's dents was still visible; my footstool with its brocade cushion; my crystal sugar bowl; the wine glass Miss Byward was holding; the pillow Tanya was hugging; my basketwork fruit holder; me.

I excused myself and went into the kitchen. Mr Momma was

putting the finishing touches to his salad. He had made a little hill of chopped lettuce leaves and sprinkled it with olives and pimentoes and drips of dressing.

'You love it?'

I said it was perfect.

'It is a woman's tee-tee,' he said, and made a knob-turning gesture with his hand.

In the parlor, my other guests were engrossed in conversation. I thought they were talking about an author they all respected; a name seemed to repeat (*Murray?* Gilbert Murray?). I pretended to straighten the leg of the table so I could get the drift of their conversation, but I quickly grasped that they were talking about money. (And I heard myself saying on a future occasion, *I thought they were talking about an author they all respected . . .*)

'I don't know how some people manage,' said Sir Charles. 'I really don't. By the way, Michael, this wine is superb. You didn't tell me you had a cellar.'

'I have an attic too,' I said.

'Isn't he a poppet!' said Virginia.

Mr Momma brought out his salad.

'Bravo,' said Virginia, and hearing Mr Momma's accent, she asked him where he was from. His mention of Cyprus had Virginia asking him which particular village was his and brought a long very practiced-sounding story from Sir Charles about a hotel in Limassol. Throughout the meal we talked intimately about Lawrence Durrell and I even found myself chipping in every now and then. I could see that it was considered quite a coup to have Mr Momma on hand.

'And what is our friend from Cyprus doing in London?' asked Virginia.

'I am a painter.'

Mr Momma did not have the English to amplify this. He was quickly taken to be a tormented artist in exile rather than the hard-working house painter he was. We talked about the Mediterranean sense of color, and afterward Mr Momma ran upstairs for his Cypriot records. He played them, he danced with Virginia, and he told her he loved her. Then he sat down and sobbed into his handkerchief.

'I've been admiring this wine glass,' said Virginia over Mr Momma's muted hoots. 'Is it part of a set?'

I said, 'Just the one,' and filled it with the claret I had brought out for the shepherd's pie.

I was relieved when Sir Charles said he had to go, because that was my signal to open the Krug, which went down a treat. Then Sir Charles and Virginia shared a taxi back to Hampstead and Tanya (making a crack about Ronald) said she had never enjoyed herself more. Hearing what Tanya had said, Mr Momma put his arm around me. He smelled strenuously of his dancing.

'No,' I said, and led him to the door. 'Let's not spoil it.'

I slept alone, but I was not alone. The evening had been a great success. Both Sir Charles and Virginia sent me notes, thanking me for having them. They were brief notes, but I replied saying that the pleasure had been all mine.

Afterward, I wondered why they had agreed to come. I decided that their very position had something to do with it. They were so grand that most people thought that they must be very busy, so no one dared to invite them. And people believed that they were beyond praise. But my flattery, my offer of a meal, my discount wines had done the trick.

I had worked hard to make the evening festive, and Mr Momma had been an unexpected success. And what had I asked of them? Nothing – nothing but for them to be there.

I had told them I was a writer. Because I had said this no one talked about it: I was one of them. Anyway, a good host is preoccupied with managing his party. His graciousness is silence when it is not encouragement. He isn't supposed to say much, only to keep the dishes coming and the glasses filled. So, in the end, they did not know much about me. They talked to each other.

The proof that Miss Byward meant what she said about enjoying herself was her invitation to me several weeks later for drinks at her very tiny flat in Hampstead. It was not until I saw her flat that I fully understood how she could have seen something to admire in mine. She was clearly an untidy person, but I was grateful when she introduced me as 'Michael Insole, the writer.' There were six others there, all writers whose names I instantly recognized, but because of the seating arrangements, I had no choice but to talk to Wibbert the poet. He told me a very entertaining story about giving a poetry reading in Birmingham, and he finished by saying, 'The pay's appalling. They always apologize when they hand it over.'

Henry Wibbert was a tall balding youth with the trace of a regional accent, and bitten fingernails, something I had always hated until I met him. His socks had slipped into his shoes and I could see his white ankles. His poet's love of failure was written all over him, and when I told him I did not write poetry he seemed to take this as a criticism – as if I were acting superior – and I wanted to tell him that, in fact, I had never written anything at all.

'I do the odd spot of reviewing,' he said, somewhat defensively. And then, 'I can always go back to teaching yobboes if I find myself really hard up.' He twisted his finger into his mouth and chewed. 'I'm sure your earnings have you in the supertax bracket.'

'Far from it,' I said. 'I find it very hard to manage.'

At once, he was friendlier. We had found common ground as struggling writers.

'It's hand to mouth with me,' he said.

I said, 'I was having this very conversation with Sir Charles Moonman just the other night.'

'He hasn't got my worries,' said Wibbert, though when I had said Sir Charles's name Wibbert looked closely at me, the way a person peers from a high window to an interesting spectacle below.

'You'd be surprised.'

'If it was a struggle for that pompous overpraised old bastard?' he said. 'Yes, I'd be very surprised.'

'Have you ever met him?'

Wibbert shook his head.

'Why don't you come over some evening? You might change your mind.'

Wibbert said, 'He'd probably hate me.'

'Absolutely not,' I said.

'How can you be so sure?'

'Because I'm sure he's read your poetry, and if he has how could he fail to be an admirer of yours?'

This did the trick. Wibbert wrote his telephone number on the back of my hand in ballpoint, and as he had to hold my hand in his in order to do this it was noticed by the others at Miss Byward's as a rather eloquent gesture.

'You're not leaving,' said Miss Byward, when I asked for my cape.

'A dinner engagement. Unfortunately. I would so much rather stay here and chat. It's been lovely.'

She released me and afterward I wondered whether she had not said those very words to me. On the bus home I thought how much more satisfying it was to be a host than a guest.

I went home and after four tries typed a letter to Sir Charles, which I copied out in longhand – I liked the look of spontaneous intimacy in a handwritten letter. I was sure he would appreciate it. I told him about Wibbert and said that Wibbert was dead keen to meet him, if we could fix a day.

The reply from Sir Charles came in the form of an invitation from the Royal Society of Literature in which I was named as his guest at a lecture by Cyril Crowder on 'Our Debt to Hugh Walpole.' Although a reply was not requested I dashed off a note to the Society's secretary and said I'd be delighted to attend. And another to Sir Charles. On the day, I was so impatient I arrived early and chatted to the only person I could find, a little old lady fussing at a table. I had very nearly invited her to meet Sir Charles when she revealed herself as one of the tea ladies and said, 'I should have a cream bun now if I was you. They're always the first to go.'

Just before the lecture the room filled with people, Sir Charles among them. I blushed when a man, on being introduced to me by Sir Charles, said yes, indeed, he knew my work well. Sir Charles was pleased, and so was I, but I quickly took myself to a corner of the room. Here, a group of people were talking to a man who was obviously the center of attention. I made a beeline for this man, but instead of speaking, simply listened to what the others were saying. The man smiled at me a number of times.

'His friendship with James amounted to influence,' someone said. 'I believe it was very great.'

'Deep,' said the man, and smiled at me.

I swallowed my fear and said, 'Profound.'

'That's it,' said the man and thanked me with his eyes.

'They're calling you, Cyril,' said a woman. 'You're on.'

This was Cyril Crowder! But he took his time. He said, 'You'll have to excuse me. I must do my stuff. Perhaps I'll see you afterward. There are drinks downstairs in the Lodge.'

Cyprus sherry, Hungarian Bull's Blood that was red ink, a semi-sweet Spanish white, and a mongrel Corsican rosé.

*

The dinner I gave for Cyril Crowder, Sir Charles and Lady Barbara, Virginia Byward, and Wibbert was one of my most memorable. It was further enhanced by the appearance after dinner (I had only six chairs) of Tanya and Mr Momma – and Mr Momma brought his records. Naturally I left them to themselves, kept their glasses filled with some vintage Muscadet (1971), and let them become quite tipsy. Very late in the evening, Cyril took me aside. I told him again how much I had enjoyed his lecture, but he interrupted, saying, 'Have you ever thought of addressing the Society?'

'I wouldn't dare.'

'Oh, do.'

'I'm not even a member,' I said.

'We can put that right,' he said, and he hollered across the room, 'Charles – how about making Michael a Fellow at the next committee meeting? All in favor say, "Aye!"'

'Aye!' came the shout from the sofa.

And Mr Momma said, 'High!'

'Motion carried,' said Cyril. 'Now what will you speak on?'

'First things first,' I said, and uncorked a bottle of port (1972), decanted it through my hanky, and poured three inches into a schooner.

'That wine's a gentleman,' said Cyril.

'So you can understand why I was so keen to lay it down.'

After Sir Charles and Lady Barbara left, Mr Momma put his records on the gramophone and did his drunken Cypriot shuffle. Wibbert waltzed with Tanya. I was tapped on the shoulder. Cyril had taken off his spectacles. He said, 'May I have the pleasure?' and slipped his arm around my waist.

Friendship is algebra, but there are operations most people are too impatient or selfish to perform. Any number is possible! There is a cynical side to this. Ronald used to say that you can sleep with anyone you like – you only have to ask. That is almost entirely selfish. But one can be unselfish, even in sleeping around – in giving everything and expecting nothing but agreeable company. 'Giving everything,' I say; but so little is actually required – a good-natured remark, a little flattery, a drink.

But I have been bold. Not long after my election to the Royal Society I saw a production of *Streetcar Named Desire*, with Annette Frame playing Blanche Dubois. I wrote her a fan letter. She replied.

I replied. We exchanged letters on a weekly basis – mine were letters, hers postcards. Then I popped the question. Would she join me for a drink? We agreed on a date and though she was leery at first she stayed until the wee hours. Now I count her as one of my dearest friends. Algebra.

I sometimes think that in my modest way I have discovered something that no one else knows. When Virginia Byward got her OBE it was I who helped her choose her dress and I who drove her to the Palace. A year before I would not have believed it to be possible, and yet as we rounded Hyde Park Corner I realized we were hurrying to meet the Queen. 'Alice,' Virginia calls me when she is a little tipsy and tearful. But the life I have is the life I have always wanted. I am surprised that no one has realized how simple it is.

Once, I thought that in agreeing to attend my parties these people were doing me an enormous favor, taking time off from busy schedules to flatter my vanity. Later I saw how empty their lives were. 'I'd have lunch with anyone remotely human,' Wibbert once said. It was the saddest thing I had ever heard. Now it is clear that if it were not for me they would drearily write their books and live drearily alone and be too proud and unimaginative to invite each other round.

They take me as I am. I pose no threat; but more, I believe I have brought some joy into their lives – as much into Mr Momma's as Sir Charles's. It is only awkward when, very late in the evening, their gratitude gets the better of them and they insist on hearing something about my latest book. I say it's dreadful, everything's up the wall, I haven't written a word for ages. And they accept this. They even seem a bit relieved when I change the subject and uncork another bottle.

The English Adventure

'You have read already *The Times*?'

'I just did so.'

'For my lateness I am deeply sorry, but there was the parking. So much of traffic in this town now. I think it is the Germans and their campings. It is fantastic.'

'I hate the campings. And the Germans are a shame. You see? There are some at that table. Listen to them. Such a language.'

'I much prefer the English.'

'Indeed. Quite so.'

'Why are you drinking *genever* at this hour?'

'For *The Times*. I had the tea and finished it. But there was still more of *The Times*. I could not have more tea, so I took some *genever*. And so I finished *The Times*, but I still have the *genever*.'

'Henriet! You will be drunk for Janwillem!'

'It is easier to speak English if one is drunk, and tonight is Janwillem's church.'

'A lousy night for Janwillem.'

'He likes the church, Marianne. Last week he has missed the church and he has been so ashamed.'

'I mean that. Happy as a louse on a dirty head. We say "a lousy time" for a happy time.'

'We say a jolly time.'

'A jolly time, thank you. Did you learn this in *The Times*?'

'I learned this in England.'

'Have you had a jolly time in England?'

'A lousy time.'

'Henriet! You are drunk already. So I will have the tea. Last week, I had the tea, but no English. I said to the boy, "One pot of tea and two cakes, if you please." But he did not reply in English. It was so insulting to me. I think he did it to be wicked. When he brought the tea I said, "Please," but he only smiled at me. I was so deeply sorry you were not here. You would have said more.'

'The young boy?'

'The old boy.'

'I would have said more.'

'I have been thinking last week of you in England. Proper tea, proper English. I know you already for ten years, but since we are starting this English I know you better. "Lucky Henriet," I have been thinking last week, "in London with the plays and the shows, and speaking English to all the people. And I have nothing but this news and this wicked boy." You buy that shoot in London?'

'I have bought this suit in London.'

'Please. And the weather, it was nice?'

'London weather. London rain.'

'It is fantastic. And the hotel, it was good?'

'We will not speak of the hotel.'

'Janwillem, he enjoyed?'

'Janwillem is Janwillem. Here he is Janwillem, and in another place we go – how much money, tickets, taxis, rain, different people – he is still Janwillem. In London, at the hotel, we are in the room and I am sitting in the chair. I look out the window – a small square, with grass, very nice, and some flowers, very nice, and the wet street, so different. I turn again and I am happy until I see Janwillem is still Janwillem.'

'You are not going to speak of the hotel you say!'

'I was mentioning my husband.'

'He is a good man.'

'Quite so, a good man. I love him. But even if he had a few faults I would love him. I would love him more and wish him to understand. The faults make the love stronger. I want him to be a bit faulty, so I can show him my love. But he is a good man. It is so hard to love a good man.'

'Your English is fantastic. It is London. Last week I am here with this tea and this old boy. I am learning nothing. You are learning more English. It is London.'

'It is this *genever*. And my sadness.'

'We will then speak of the news. You have read already?'

'And the hotel and Janwillem. So many times I ask of him to understand this thing. "No," he says. "Do not speak of it." And he goes to his church. Even in London – the church, he is missing the church. And the children and the house. He is a good father, such a good one. But at the church, I have seen him three weeks ago, a festival, he is dancing with the other ladies, hugging them.

He is so happy. Kissing them and holding hands. What is wrong with that? A man can do such things and it means nothing, but a woman cannot. No hugging – this is the fault. For a man it means nothing. He is going home in the car laughing, so happy while I am so very sad.'

'I have read the front page, Henriet. And some letters. Have you seen "appalling lack of taste"? We can discuss.'

'I have seen "appalling lack of taste" and I have seen the program on television to which it is referring.'

'Fantastic.'

'But I cannot discuss. I will have another *genever*. See? He knows I want it and I have not even asked. Such a pleasant boy.'

'He is the boy who insulted me.'

'It is only natural, Marianne. You speak in English. He is wishing to be friendly.'

'I do not wish to be friendly.'

'He is not the old boy. He is the young.'

'I am drinking tea. He is the old.'

'Perhaps he would enjoy an adventure. It means nothing to them.'

'We shall speak of the news instead.'

'It is the thing Janwillem does not understand at all and he will never understand. "Do not speak of it!" But if he has an adventure I can understand. I can love him more. But he has no adventure. I have told you about Martin?'

'The librarian. He gives you books.'

'He gives me pinches.'

'We shall talk of the books.'

'And he tells me how easy it is. It means nothing to him. He wants me to spend the night with him. I tell him impossible. An afternoon, he says. After the lunch period he puts the library in the hands of his assistant and we leave. To my house. Four hours or five. Before Janwillem comes home, before Theo breaks from school. How does he know it is so easy? But he knows too much about this. How does he know? I ask him. He has three girl friends, or two – anyway, more than one. He boasts about them, and of course I cannot have an adventure with Martin. He would boast of me.'

'Maybe he would boast of you.'

'Or talk about me. Men talk.'

'Janwillem would be so sad.'

'Janwillem would kill me. He could not stand it. I wonder if I can stand it? One day I am home with my throat – one afternoon. I am walking around the house. Strolling around the house. Not in our bedroom. Janwillem's clothes are there. He is so neat. In Theo's room. Yes, I think, that is where we would have our adventure. I go into Theo's room. Stamp collection, maps, Action-Man.'

'Fantastic.'

'I cannot have an adventure in my son's room with Martin. Action-Man. It would make me sad.'

'I am glad I am older than you, even if my English is not good. But we will go to Croydon in April.'

'In London it is wonderful even in the rain. The people are different, and so polite. If you speak to them they speak. If you don't speak they are still polite.'

'*The Times* – it is very cheap in Croydon. It is cheap in London?'

'I never read the newspaper, not once. Janwillem read it. I saw him reading it and I did not want to. I can read it here, but not there. There, I can read novels, only novels. In the hotel room, having some gin, with the rain outside, and Janwillem in his offices. No Theo, no Action-Man. There I am different, too. No headaches. I was so worried about Martin I began the migraines. Always on my day off – the migraines. And we did nothing! He only boasted and pinched, and I said, "Yes, it is a good idea, an adventure, but not here."'

'This talk is a bit silly and it is shaming me. Shall we discuss the news? I still have some tea left. Or books? I have seen that there is a new novel by Mister Dursday.'

'Tom Thursday. Extremely violent. He shows an appalling lack of taste. I wish to speak of thumsing else.'

'I have read all his books. Tom's.'

'Do you remember that young American fellow – Jewish fellow – he spoke of the American novel to the Society?'

'He was fantastic.'

'He asked me to meet him. That young fellow. How could I meet him? I have my family to think of, I have Janwillem. I cannot simply go off because this young Jewish fellow wishes to have an adventure. He writes me letters: "Come! Come!" I think he is like Martin.'

'Martin is not Jewish. You never said so.'

'Martin and his boasting and his girl friends.'

'Do not think of him, Henriet. He will give you migraines.'

'Martin is gone, but I still have the migraines. I have to scream sometimes because of the migraines. Do you ever scream, Marianne?'

'I like this. This is better. Yes, one day I was making some soup. Some carrot, some potato, and chicken broth. I am looking for the, yes, the barley. The soup was in an enormous pot. The soup was boiling furiously. It was a very hot day. And then I reached for the barley. The barley was on a high shelf. I reached for it. I hit with my elbow the pot of soup and it splashed upon my arm. And then I screamed.'

'I scream at Janwillem because he is so good. He mentions the church and I scream. I scream when I think of Martin, and Martin is bad.'

'As you say, Martin is wicked.'

'Martin is not wicked, but I cannot trust him. Always his girl friends. I would prefer to have an adventure with another man.'

'I am too old for adventures, Henriet. And this is not the place.'

'Those Germans – they drive twenty kilometers and have their adventures here. Look at them. You're not looking.'

'I have seen Germans.'

'The English people hate them as much as we do. But some do not even remember.'

'How can they not remember the Germans? If once you see them you remember!'

'The young ones. They do not remember.'

'Even the young ones remember!'

'In England.'

'The young ones in England? I do not know the young ones in England. This tea is cold. How do you know?'

'I have asked.'

'What do they say?'

'They do not know. They do not care now. It is old history.'

'Where do you meet these young ones?'

'I meet them in England. In London.'

'In the hotel.'

'Yes, in there.'

'I have not met them in Croydon.'

'Do you know young ones in Croydon?'

'Henriet, everyone I meet is younger than me. So I do not notice.'

'I notice. The young ones remind me.'

'That they are young?'

'That I am old.'

'But you are not old. What? Forty-five? Very slim and smart. Nice shoot.'

'Forty-three.'

'It's not old.'

'If you are twenty, forty-three is old.'

'This is good English conversation. Question-answer. Those Germans must think we are two English ladies, having our tea.'

'I am not having tea.'

'You know what I am saying.'

'I did not have tea in London. In London, Janwillem has tea, he reads *The Times*, he takes his umbrella. People think he is a schoolmaster. In London, I sit by the window and read my novel and watch the rain fall. And I wait – what for? For the young to knock on my door and say, "Madam, your adventure."'

'You are being silly.'

'In a uniform. A dark jacket and a small black tie and a tray. My adventure is on the tray. "Just one moment," I say. And I get up from my chair and pull the curtains so that he won't notice my age. I am very nervous, but he is more nervous, so it does not matter. I go very close to him. If you go close and he does not draw away, you know he is saying yes.'

'Henriet, you have had too much to drink. Please, the news.'

'I am telling you the news.'

'This is not a discussion. We must discuss.'

'There is nothing to discuss. I need my adventure. I have gone to London with Janwillem for my English, but what is English if you cannot use it except to say, "Please close the door" and "Where is the post office?" and "How much?" Or if you only speak it once a week at a hotel restaurant in a terrible town as this one is.'

'I enjoy it. It is good enough for me. I am happy.'

'I am not happy. English is not enough, Marianne. Books are very enjoyable, and lectures. But always there is Martin in the library, and that American fellow at the lectures. I ask myself: "Am I here because of English, or do I want an adventure?"'

'What is the answer?'

'There is no answer. But English is not enough, I know that. If that could be so I could sit in the chair in the hotel and talk with the boy and be happy.'

'There was a boy?'

'I have told you of the boy. With the tray and the tie. Twenty. English. Thin face. Very nervous.'

'You talked with him in English?'

'Very little.'

'You are smiling. No more English!'

'I can only tell you in English.'

'You have said you talked very little.'

'He took his clothes off, I took my clothes off. We were naked. After that, there is very little to say. "We were naked." It is so easy to say, "We were naked," if you say it in another language. It would be harder to tell Janwillem – I could say it to him in English. But he would not understand, would he? No, he would shout at me. "Do not speak of it!" and then he would go to his church and hug and kiss those women. And formerly, I had the migraine and I have thought all those years of shooicide. Instead, I have the lessons – we have them here. But in London I know why I have the lessons. It is clear to me there. The boy. We say very little because we both can speak. So we don't need to speak. It is a small thing. As for Janwillem, it means nothing. Now we are here and it is gone, but it is not gone. There is only the English.'

'A good lesson today, Henriet.'

'Yes, Marianne.'

'Some new words. A jolly time.'

'We will say no more about my adventure.'

'Next week we will read *The Times*.'

'I will drink tea.'

'You are fantastic.'

'Yost so. That is the most faluable ting.'

After the War

Delia lay in bed and listened and studied the French in the racket. Downstairs, Mr Rameau shouted, 'Hurry up! I'm ready!' Mrs Rameau pleaded that she had lost her handbag. The small bratty boy they called Tony kicked savagely at the wall, and Ann Marie who five times had said she could not find her good shoes had begun to cry. Mr Rameau announced his movements: he said he was going to the door and then outside to start the car; if they weren't ready, he said, he would leave without them. He slammed the door and started the car. Mrs Rameau shrieked. Ann Marie sobbed, 'Tony called me a pig!' Someone was slapped; bureau drawers were jiggled open and then pushed. There were urgent feet on the stairs. 'Wait!' The engine roared, the crying stopped. The stones in the walls of Delia's small room shook, transmitting accusations. Mrs Rameau screamed – louder and shriller than anyone Delia had ever heard before, like a beast in a cage, a horrible and hopeless anger. Mr Rameau, in the car, shouted a reply, but it came as if from a man raging in a stoppered bottle. There were more door slams – the sound of dropped lumber – and the ratchetings of gears, and with a loosening, liquefying whine the car's noise trickled away. They had set out for church.

In the silence that followed, a brimming whiteness of cool vapor that soothed her ears, Delia pushed down the sheet and breathed the sunlight that blazed on her bedroom curtains. She had arrived just the night before and was to be with the Rameaus for a month, doing what her mother had called 'an exchange.' Later in the summer Ann Marie would join her own family in London. Arriving late at the country cottage, which was near Vence, Delia had dreaded what Ann Marie would think about a stay in London – the semi in Streatham, the outings to the Baths on the Common, the plain meals. She had brought this embarrassment to bed, but she woke up alarmed at their noise and looking forward to Ann Marie's visit, since that meant the end of her own.

The cottage, Mr Rameau had told her proudly, had no electricity.

They carried their water from a well. Their water closet (he had used this English word) was in the garden. He was, incredibly, boasting. In Paris, everything they had was modern. But this was their vacation. 'We live like gypsies,' he had said, 'for one month of the year.' And with a candle he had shown Delia to her room. He had taken the candle away, and leaving her in the darkness paused only to say that as he did not allow his daughter to use fire he could hardly be expected to let Delia do so.

The Rameaus at church, her thoughts were sweetened by sleep. She dreamed of an unfenced yellow-green field, and grass that hid her. She slept soundly in the empty house. It was not buoyancy, but the deepest submersion in sleep. She was as motionless as if she lay among the pale shells on the ocean floor.

She woke to the boom of the door downstairs swinging against the wall. Then she was summoned. She had no choice but to face them. She reached for her glasses.

'Some people,' said Mr Rameau at lunch – he was seated at the far end of the table, but she could feel the pressure of his gaze even here – 'some people go out to a restaurant on Sunday. A silly superstition – they believe one should not cook food on the Lord's Day. I am modern in this way, but of course I expect you to eat what you are given, to show your appreciation. Notice how my children eat. I have told them about the war.'

His lips were damp and responsive to the meat he was knifing apart, and for a moment his attention was fixed on this act. He speared a finger of meat and raised it to his mouth and spoke.

'Madame Rameau asked me whether English people ever go to church. I said I believed they did and that I was surprised when you said you would not go –'

He had a dry white face and a stiff lion-tamer's mustache. When he put his knife and fork down, and clasped his hands, his wife stopped eating and filled his plate. Madame Rameau's obedience made Delia fear this man. And Ann Marie, the friend whom she did not yet know, remained silent; her face said that she had no opinion about her father – perhaps she chose not to notice the way he held his knife in his fist. Both mother and daughter were mysteries; Delia had that morning heard them scream, but the screams did not match these silent faces. And Tony: a brat, encouraged because he was a boy, pawing his father's arm to ask a question.

Now something jarred Delia. The faces searched hers. What was it? She had been asked a question. She listened carefully to remember it.

'Yes, my parents go to church,' she said. 'But I don't.'

'My children do as I do.'

'It is my choice.'

'Fifteen is rather young for choices.' He said *choices* solemnly, as if speaking of a mature vice.

'Ann Marie is fifteen,' said Tony, tugging the man's sleeve. 'But she is bigger.'

The breasts, thought Delia: Ann Marie had the beginnings of a bust – that was what the boy had meant. Delia had known she was plain, and though her eyes were green and cat-like behind her glasses – she knew this – she had not realized how plain until she had seen Ann Marie. Delia had grown eight inches in one year and her clothes, depending on when they had been bought, were either too tight or too loose. Her mother had sent her here with shorts and sandals and cotton blouses. These she was wearing now, but they seemed inappropriate to the strange meal of soup and cutlets and oily salad. The Rameaus were in the clothes they had worn to church, and Mr Rameau, drinking wine, seemed to use the gesture of raising his glass as a way of scrutinizing her. Delia tried hard to avoid showing her shock at the food, or staring at them, but she knew what they were thinking: a dull girl, a plain girl, an English girl. She had no religion to interest them, and no small talk – she did not even like to chat in English. In French, she found it impossible to do anything but reply.

'We want you to enjoy yourself,' said Mr Rameau. 'This is a primitive house, or should I say "simple"? Paradise is simple – there is sunshine, swimming, and the food is excellent.'

'Yes,' said Delia, 'the food is excellent.' She wanted to say more – to add something to this. But she was baffled by a pleasantry she knew in advance to be insincere.

'The lettuce is fresh, from our own garden.'

Why didn't Ann Marie say anything?

'Yes. It is very fresh.'

Delia had ceased to be frightened by the memory of those accusatory morning noises. Now she was bored, but thoroughly bored, and it was not a neutral feeling but something like despair.

'Enough.' Mr Rameau emptied his glass of wine and waved away his wife's efforts to pour more. He said that he was going to sleep.

'I have no vacation,' he said to Delia – he had been speaking to her, she realized, for the entire meal: this was her initiation. 'Tomorrow I will be in town and while you are playing I will be working. This is your holiday, not mine.'

In the days that followed, Delia saw that when Ann Marie was away from her father she was happier – she practiced her English and played her Rolling Stones records and they took turns giving each other new hair styles. Every morning a boy called Maurice came to the cottage and delivered to the Rameaus a loaf from his basket. Delia and Ann Marie followed him along the paths through the village and giggled when he glanced back. This was a different Ann Marie from the one at meal times and as with the mother it was Ann Marie's submissiveness that made Delia afraid of Mr Rameau. But her pity for the girl was mingled with disbelief for the reverence the girl showed her father. Ann Marie never spoke of him.

At night, Mr Rameau led the girls upstairs and waited in the hall with his candle until they were in bed. Then he said sharply, 'Prayers!' – commanding Ann Marie, reproaching Delia – and carried his light haltingly downstairs. He held the candle in his knife grip, as if cowering from the dark.

One week, two weeks. From the first, Delia had counted the days and it was only for the briefest moments – swimming, following Maurice the breadboy, playing the records – that time passed without her sensing the weight of each second.

After breakfast Mr Rameau always said, 'I must go. No vacation for me!' And yet Delia knew, without knowing how she knew, that the man was enjoying himself – perhaps the only person in the cottage who was. One Sunday he swam. He was rough in the water, thrashing his arms, gasping, spouting water from his mouth. Pelts of hair grew on his back and, more sparsely but no less oddly, on his shoulders. He wrestled in the waves with Tony and when he had finished Madame Rameau met him at the water's edge with a dry towel. Delia had never known anyone she disliked more than this man. Her thoughts were kind toward her own father who had written twice to say how much he missed her. She could not imagine Mr Rameau saying that to Ann Marie.

At lunch one day Tony shoved some food in his mouth and gagged. He turned aside and slowly puked on the carpet. Delia put her fork down and shut her eyes and tasted nausea in her own throat, and when she looked up again she saw that Mr Rameau had not moved. Damp lips, dry face: he was smiling.

'You are shocked by this little accident,' he said. 'But I can tell you the war was much worse than this. This is nothing. You have no idea.'

Only Tony had left the room. He moaned in the parlor. And they finished their meal while Madame Rameau slopped at the vomit with a yellow rag.

'If you behave today,' said Mr Rameau on the Friday of her third week – when had they not behaved? – 'I may have a surprise for you tomorrow.' He raised a long crooked finger in warning and added, 'But it is not a certainty.'

Delia cared so little for the man that she immediately forgot what he had said. Nor did Ann Marie mention it. Delia only remembered his promise when, after lunch on Saturday, he took an envelope from his wallet and showed four red tickets.

'For the circus,' he said.

Delia looked at Ann Marie, who swallowed in appreciation. Little Tony shouted. Madame Rameau regarded Tony closely and with noticeable effort brought her floating hands together.

Delia felt a nervous thrill, the foretaste of panic from the words she had already begun to practice in her mind. She was aware she would not be asked to say them. She would have to find an opportunity.

She drew a breath and said, 'Excuse me.'

'A German circus,' Mr Rameau was saying. 'I am told they have performed for the President, and they are at this moment in Nice. They have just come from Arabia where the entire circus was flown to perform for a sheik. They will only be in Nice for four days. We will go tomorrow. Of course, if there is any bad behavior between now and tomorrow you'll stay home.'

'Excuse me,' said Delia again. To steady her hand she clutched her empty glass.

Pouring Delia a glass of water, Mr Rameau continued, 'I am told there is no circus like it anywhere in the world. It is lavish in all ways. Elephants, tigers, lions –'

'I won't go to the circus,' said Delia. She was at once terrified and ashamed by what she had said. She had intended to be graceful.

She had been rude. For the first time this vacation her French had failed her.

Mr Rameau was staring at her.

'I cannot go to the circus,' she said.

He pushed at his mustache and said, 'Well!'

Delia saw that Madame Rameau was rubbing at her mouth with her napkin, as if she wished to remove that part of her face.

Mr Rameau had also seized his napkin. Stiff with fury he snapped the cloth at the crumbs of bread on his shirtfront. 'So,' he said, 'you intend to misbehave?'

'I don't understand.' She knew each word, but they made no pattern of logic. By not going – was that misbehaving?

He faced her. 'I said that if there was any bad behavior between now and tomorrow you'd stay home.'

'Oh, no!' said Delia, and choked. Something pinched her throat, like a spider drawing a web through her windpipe. She gasped and drank some water. She spoke a strangled word, an old woman's croak, and tears came to her eyes from the effort of it.

At his clean portion of table, Mr Rameau watched her struggle to begin.

'I don't go –' The words came slowly; her throat was clearing, but still the spider clung.

'Perhaps you would rather discuss this some other time?'

'I don't want to discuss it at all,' she managed. 'I don't go to circuses.'

'There are no circuses in England?'

'Yes,' she said. The word was perfect: her throat was open. 'There are circuses in England. But I haven't gone since I was very young.'

Mr Rameau said to his wife, 'She has not gone since she was very young.' And to Delia, 'Have you a reason?'

'I don't enjoy circuses.'

'Ah, but you said that you once went! When you were young.' He smiled, believing he had trapped her. 'You enjoyed them then?'

'But I was very young,' she said, insisting on the importance of the word he had mocked. 'I did not know anything about them.'

'The English,' said Mr Rameau, and again he turned to his wife. 'Such seriousness of purpose, such dedication. What is there to know about a circus? It exists purely for enjoyment – there is nothing to understand. It is laughter and animals, a little exotic and out of the ordinary. You see how she makes it a problem?'

Mrs Rameau, who had mistaken Delia's gasping for terror, said, 'She does not want to go. Why don't we leave it at that?'

'Why? Because she has not given a reason.'

The words she had practiced formed in her mind, her whole coherent reason. But it was phrased too pompously for something so simple, and as the man would have no reply for it she knew it would give offense. But she was glad for this chance to challenge him and only wished that her French was better, for each time he replied he seemed to correct by repeating it the pronunciation of what she said.

'I don't believe she has a reason, unless being English is the reason. Being English is the reason for so much.'

'Being French' – she was safe merely repeating what he had said: his manner had shown her the rules – 'being French is the reason for so much.'

'We enjoy circuses. This is a great circus. They have performed for kings and presidents. You might say we are childish, but' – he passed a finger across his mustache – 'what of those kings?' He spoke to his wife. 'What of those kings, eh?'

Ann Marie took a deep breath, but she said nothing. Tony made pellets of bread. Madame Rameau, Delia could see, wanted her husband to stop this.

Delia said, 'The animals do tricks. People think they are clever tricks. A tiger jumps through a hoop. An elephant dances. The dogs walk on their back legs –'

'We are familiar with the tricks,' said Mr Rameau testily. 'We have been to circuses.'

'The circus people are cruel to the animals.'

'This is totally untrue!' His hands flew up and Delia thought for a moment that he was about to slap her face.

The violence in his motioning hands spurred her on. 'They are cruel to them in the way they teach the animals to do tricks.'

'She knows so much for someone who never goes to circuses,' said Mr Rameau, and brought his hands down to the table.

'They use electric shocks. They starve them. They beat them.' She looked up. Mr Rameau showed no emotion, and now his hands were beneath the table. 'They bind their legs with wire. They inflict pain on the animals. The animals are so hurt and afraid they do these tricks. They seem clever, but it is fear. They obey because they are afraid.'

Delia thought this would move him, but he had begun again to smile.

'You are fifteen. You were born in nineteen sixty-two, the same year as Ann Marie.'

'Yes.'

'So you don't know.'

'I have been told this about the circus by people who do know.'

'Now I am not speaking about the circus. I am speaking about the war. You are very concerned about the animals –'

She hated this man's face.

'– but have you any idea what the Germans did to us in the war? Perhaps you are right – the animals are mistreated from time to time. But they are not killed. Surely it is worse to be killed or tortured?'

'Some animals are tortured. It is what I said.'

But he was still speaking. 'Of course, one hears how bad it was for the Jews, but listen – I was your age in nineteen forty-two. I remember the Germans. The Jews tell one story – everyone knows this story. Yes, perhaps it was as bad for them as they say. I don't speak for other people – I speak for myself. And I can tell you that we starved. We were beaten. Our legs were tied. And sometimes for days we were left in the dark of our houses, never knowing whether we would live to see the light. It made some people do things they would not normally do, but I learned to respect my parents. I understood how terrible it must have been for them. I obeyed them. They knew more than I did and later I realized how dreadful it was. It was not a circus. It was war.'

He made it an oration, using his hands to help his phrases through the air, and yet Delia felt that for all the anonymity of his blustering he was expressing private thoughts and a particular pain.

Madame Rameau said, 'Please be calm, Jean. You are being very hard on the girl.'

'I am giving this young girl the benefit of my experience.'

Still the woman seemed ashamed, and she winced when he began again.

'I have seen people grovel to German army officers, simply to get a crust of bread. It did not horrify me. It taught me respect, and respect is something you do not know a great deal about, from

what you have said. The Jews tell another story, but remember –
it was very bad for us. After the war, many people forgot, but I
suffered, so I do not forget.'

'It might be better if we did not go to the circus,' said Madame
Rameau.

'I don't want to go to the circus,' said Ann Marie.

Tony had already begun to protest. 'I do! I am going!'

'Yes,' said Mr Rameau and struck his son affectionately on the
shoulder. 'We will all go to the circus. The tickets are paid for.'

Delia had resolved to say nothing more.

Madame Rameau said, 'The girl does not have to go, if she
would rather stay home with me.'

'If she wishes to stay at home she may stay. So we have an extra
ticket. You will come to the circus with us, my dear.'

'I am not sure I want to go.'

'You will go,' he said promptly. 'We will all go. It is what our
English guest insists upon.'

Madame Rameau reached for Delia but stopped short of touching her. She said, 'I will leave some soup for you. And a cutlet.'

'No need for the cutlet,' said Mr Rameau. 'She never eats much
of what we give her. She will only leave it on her plate.'

'You won't be afraid to be here alone?' Madame Rameau was
close to tears.

Mr Rameau answered for Delia. 'It is the animals who are afraid!
You heard what she said. She will not be afraid while we are away.
She might be very happy.'

His white face was a hard dull slab when in the flower-scented
twilight, and just before taking his family away to the circus, he
stood in the doorway and said, 'No matches. No candles. My
advice to you is to eat now while there is some light, and then go
to bed. We will not be late. Eight o'clock, nine o'clock. And
tomorrow we will tell you what you missed.'

He sounded almost kindly, his warning a gentle consolation. He
ended softly, but just as she thought he was going to lean forward
to touch her or kiss her he abruptly turned away, making Delia
flinch. He drove the car fast to the road.

Delia ate in the mottled half-dark of the back kitchen. She had
no appetite in the dim room, and the dimness which rapidly soaked
into night made her alert. The church bell in the village signaled

eight; the Rameaus did not come back. At nine she grew restive. It was less dark outside with stars and the moon in ragged clouds like a watch crystal. The windows were open, the sound of distant cars moved through the hedges, the trees in the garden – it was a trick of the dark – rattled dry leaves in her room.

She wondered if she were afraid. She started to sing and frightened herself with her clear off-key cry. She toyed with the thought of running away, leaving a vague note behind for Mr Rameau – and she laughed at the thought of his panic: the phone calls, the police, his helplessness. But she was not young enough or old enough to run. She was satisfied with the stand she had taken against him, but what sustained her was her hatred for him. It was not the circus anymore, not those poor animals, but the man himself who was in his wickedness more important than the animals' suffering. She had not given in. He was the enemy and he was punishing her for challenging him. Those last coy words of his were meant to punish her. She went to the doorway to hear the church bell better.

At midnight she anxiously counted and she was afraid – that their car had been wrecked and the whole family killed; afraid of her hatred for him that had made her forget the circus. It was too late to remain in the doorway, and when Delia withdrew into the house she knew by the darkness and the time how he had calculated his punishment. She saw that his punishment was his own fear. The coward he was would be afraid of the thickened dark of this room. It took her fear away.

So she did not hear the car. She heard their feet on the path, some whispers, the scrape of the heavy door. He was in front; Madame Rameau hurried past him, struck a match to a candle and held the flame up. He was carrying his son.

'Still awake?' he said. His exaggerated kindness was mockery. 'Look, she is waiting for us.'

The candle flame trembled in the woman's trembling hand.

'You'll go next time, won't you?'

Delia was smiling. She wanted him to come close enough in that poor light to see her smile.

He repeated his question, demanding a reply, but he was so loud the child woke and cried out of pure terror, and without warning arched his back in instinctive struggle and tried to get free of the hard arms which held him.

Words are Deeds

On entering the restaurant in Corte, Professor Sheldrick saw the woman standing near the bar. He decided then that he would take her away with him, perhaps marry her. When she offered him a menu and he realized she was a waitress he was more certain she would accompany him that very day to the hotel, where he had a reservation, on the coast at Ile-Rousse. Not even the suspicion that it was her husband behind the counter – he had a drooping black mustache and was older than she – deterred him as he planned his moves. The man looked like a brute, in any case; and Sheldrick was prepared to offer that woman everything he had.

His wife had left him in Marseilles. She said she wanted to live her own life. She was almost forty and she explained that if she waited any longer no man would look twice at her. She refused to argue or be drawn; her mind was made up. It was Sheldrick who did all the imploring, but it did no good.

He said, 'What did I do?'

'It's what you said.'

Words are deeds: he knew that was what she meant. And not one but an accumulation of them over a dozen years. The marriage, he knew, had been ruined long before. He was content to live in those ruins and he had believed she needed him. But there in Marseilles she declared she was leaving him. The words she said with such simple directness weakened him; he ached as if in speaking to him that way she had trampled him. He agreed to let her have the house and a certain amount of money every month.

He said, 'I'll suffer.'

'You deserve to suffer.'

Her manner was girlish and hopeful, his almost elderly. She went home; but when it was time for him to return home he could see no point to it, nor any reason to work. He was a professor of French literature at a college in Connecticut: the semester was starting. But from the day his wife left him, Sheldrick answered no letters and made no plans and did not think about the future. What was the point? He did nothing, because nothing mattered. He had set out on this trip feeling lucky, if a bit burdened by his wife. Now the summer was over, his wife had left him, and he began to believe that she had taken the world with her.

He no longer recognized the importance of anything he had ever done before, but his feeling of failure was so complete he felt he did not exist except as a polite and harmless creature who, all his defenses removed, faced extinction. His wife had pushed their boulder aside and left him exposed, like a soft blind worm.

In this mood, one of uselessness, he felt entirely without obligation. The world was illusion – he had invented a marriage and an existence, and it had all vanished. He was a victim twitching in air, with a small voice. What he had mistaken for concreteness was vapor. Only lovers had faith. But he didn't want his wife back; he wanted nothing.

His surprise was that he could enter a strange restaurant in a remote Corsican town and see a woman and want to marry her. He wondered if defeat had made him bold. This island, the first landscape he had seen as a newly single man, had a wild ship-wrecked look to it that suited his recklessness. He would ask that woman to leave with him.

He was bewitched by her peculiar beauty, which was the beauty of certain trees he had been admiring all afternoon in the drive from the stinks of Cateraggio. She was slim, like those trees, and unlike any woman he had seen on this island. He knew then that he would not leave Corte without her. She was the embodiment of everything he loved in Corsica. The idea that he would take her with him was definite. There was no doubt in his mind; it was rash and necessary. And while he found a seat and ordered a drink and then chose at random from the menu, he had already decided on his course of action. It only remained for him to begin.

His French was fluent. Indeed, he affected a slight French accent, a stutter in his throat and the trace of a lisp, when he spoke English. But language was the least of it. She had small shoulders and almost no breasts, and slender legs, and her hair was cut short. He spoke to her about the food, but only to detain her, so he could be near her. She smelled of lilies. She brought the wine; his meal; the dessert – fruit; coffee, which her husband – almost certainly her husband – made on the machine. And each time, he said something more, trying to grow intimate, to make her see him. He had no clear plan. He would not leave the town without her. He was due in Ile-Rousse that night. She wore a finely spun sweater. She was not dressed for a restaurant: she was no waitress. Her husband owned the place – he forced her to help him run it. Sheldrick guessed at these things and by degrees he began to understand that though he had only happened upon her, she was waiting for him.

She approached him with the bill folded on a saucer. He invited her to look at it, and when she bent close to him, peering at the bill, he said, 'Please – come with me.'

He feared she might be startled: for seconds he knew he had said something dangerous. But she was looking at the bill. Was this pretense? Was she stalling?

He said, 'I have a car.'

She was expressionless. She touched the bill with a sharp red claw.

Trying to control his voice, Sheldrick said, 'I love you and I want you to come with me.'

She faced him, turning her green eyes on him, and he knew she was scrutinizing him, wondering if he were crazy. He smiled helplessly, and her gaze seemed to soften, a pale glitter pricking the green.

His hands trembled as he placed his money on the saucer.

She said, 'I will bring you your change.'

Then she was gone. Sheldrick forced himself to stare at the tablecloth, so as not to betray his passion to the man he supposed was her husband.

She did not return immediately. Was she telling her husband what he had said? He could hardly blame her. What he had asked her in a pleading whisper was so insane an impulse that he knew he must have frightened her. And yet he did not regret it. He knew he had had to say it or he would not have forgiven himself and would have suffered for the rest of his life. After five minutes he assumed she had gone to the police; he imagined that now many people knew the mad request he had made to this woman.

In the same stately way that she had approached before, she crossed the restaurant with the saucer, and with some formality, bowing slightly as she did so, placed it before him. She went away, back to the bar where he had first seen her.

There was nothing more. She had not replied; she had not said a word. So, without a word, there was no blame; and it had all passed, like a spell of fever. Now it could remain a secret. She had been kind enough to let him go without making a jackass of himself.

He plucked at his change, keenly aware of the charade he was performing in leaving her a tip. But gathering the coins, he saw the folded bill at the bottom of the saucer, and the sentence written on it. The scribbled words made him breathless and stupid, the fresh ink made him flush like an illiterate. He labored to read it, but it was simple. It said: *I will be at the statue of Paoli after we close.*

He put the bill into his pocket and left her ten francs, and not looking at her again he hurried out of the restaurant. He walked, turning corners, on rising streets that became steps, and climbed a stone staircase on the ramparts that towered over Corte. Alone here, he read the sentence again and was joyful on these ruined battlements and thrilled by the wind in the flag above him. Beneath him in the rocky valleys and on hillsides were the trees he had come to love.

He gave her an hour. At five, in brilliant twilight, he found his car, which was parked near the restaurant. The steel shutters of the restaurant were across the windows and padlocked. It was Sunday; the cobblestone streets of this hilltop town were deserted, and he could imagine that he was the only person alive in Corte. Not wishing to be conspicuous, he decided that it was better to drive slowly through the Place Paoli than to walk.

He found it easily, an irregular plaza of sloping cobbles, and rounding the statue he saw her, wearing a short jacket, carrying a handbag, her white face fixed on him. He stopped. Before he could speak she was beside him in the car.

'Quickly,' she said. 'Don't stop.'

Her decisiveness stunned him, his feet and hands were numb, he was slow.

'Do you hear me?' she said. 'Drive – drive!'

He remembered how to drive, and skidded out of the town, making it topple in his rearview mirror. She looked back; she was afraid, then excited, her face shining. She looked at him with curiosity and said, 'Where are we going?'

'Ile-Rousse,' he said. 'I have a room at the Hotel Bonaparte.'

'And after that?'

'I don't know. Maybe Porto.'

'Porto is disgusting.'

This disconcerted him: his wife had often spoken of Porto. One of her regrets when she left him, perhaps her only regret – though she had not put it this way – was that they would not be able to visit Porto, as they had planned.

The woman said, 'It is all Germans and Americans.'

'I am an American.'

'But the other kind.'

'We're all the same.'

She said, 'I would like to visit America.'

'I hope I never see the place again as long as I live,' he said.

She stared at Sheldrick but said nothing.

'You are very beautiful.'

'Thank you. You are kind.'

'Beautiful,' he said, 'like Corsica.'

She said, 'I hate Corsica. These people are savages.'

'You're not a savage.'

'I am not a Corsican,' she said. 'My husband is one.' She glanced through the rear window. 'But that is finished now.'

It had all happened quickly, the courtship back in the restaurant, and she had greeted him at the statue like an old busy friend ('Do you hear me?'). This was something else, another phase; so he dared the question. 'Why did you come with me?'

She said, 'I wanted to. I have been planning to leave for a year. But something always goes wrong. You worried me a little. I thought you were a policeman – why do you drive so slow?'

'I'm not used to these roads.'

'André – my husband – he drives like a maniac.'

Sheldrick said, 'I'm a university professor,' and at once hated himself for saying it.

The road was tortuous. He could not imagine anyone going fast on these curves, but the woman (what was her name? when could he ask her?) repeated that her husband raced his car here. Sheldrick was aware of how the car was toiling in second gear, of his damp palms slipping on the steering wheel. He said, 'If you're not Corsican, what are you?'

'I am French,' she said. Then, 'When André sees that I have left him, he will try to kill me. All Corsicans are like that – bloodthirsty. And jealous. He will want to kill you, too.'

Sheldrick said, 'Funny. I hadn't thought of that.'

She said, 'They all have guns. André hunts wild boar in the

mountains. Those mountains. He's a wonderful shot. Those were our only happy times – hunting, in the first years.'

'I hate guns,' said Sheldrick.

'All Americans like guns.'

'Not this American,' he said. She sighed in a deliberate, almost actressy way. He was trying, but already he could see she disliked him a little – and with no reason. He had rescued her! On a straight road he would have leaned back and sped to the hotel in silence. But these hills, and the slowness of the car, made him impatient. He could think of nothing to say; and she was no help. She sat silently in her velvet jacket.

Finally, he said, 'Do you have any children?'

'What do you take me for?' she said. Her shriek jarred him. 'Do you think if I had children I would just abandon them like a slut in the afternoon and go off with a complete stranger? Do you?'

'I'm sorry.'

'You're not sorry,' she said. 'You did take me for a slut.'

He began again to apologize.

'Drive,' she said, interrupting him. She was staring at him again. 'Your suit,' she said. 'Surely, it is rather shabby even for a university professor?'

'I hadn't noticed,' he said coldly.

She said, 'I hate your tie.'

White Lies

Normally, in describing the life cycle of ectoparasites for my notebook, I went into great detail, since I hoped to publish an article about the strangest ones when I returned home from Africa. The one exception was *Dermatobia bendiense*. I could not give it my name; I was not its victim. And the description? One word: *Jerry*. I needed nothing more to remind me of the discovery, and though I fully intend to test my findings in the pages of an entomological journal, the memory is still too horrifying for me to reduce it to science.

Jerry Benda and I shared a house on the compound of a bush school. Every Friday and Saturday night he met an African girl named Ameena at the Rainbow Bar and brought her home in a taxi. There was no scandal: no one knew. In the morning, after breakfast, Ameena did Jerry's ironing (I did my own) and the black cook carried her back to town on the crossbar of his old bike. That was a hilarious sight. Returning from my own particular passion, which was collecting insects in the fields near our house, I often met them on the road: Jika in his cook's khakis and skullcap pedaling the long-legged Ameena – I must say, she reminded me of a highly desirable insect. They yelped as they clattered down the road, the deep ruts making the bicycle bell hiccup like an alarm clock. A stranger would have assumed these Africans were man and wife, making an early-morning foray to the market. The local people paid no attention.

Only I knew that these were the cook and mistress of a young American who was regarded at the school as very charming in his manner and serious in his work. The cook's laughter was a nervous giggle – he was afraid of Ameena. But he was devoted to Jerry and far too loyal to refuse to do what Jerry asked of him.

Jerry was deceitful, but at the time I did not think he was imaginative enough to do any damage. And yet his was not the conventional double life that most white people led in Africa. Jerry had certain ambitions: ambition makes more liars than egotism does.

But Jerry was so careful, his lies such modest calculations, he was always believed. He said he was from Boston. 'Belmont actually,' he told me, when I said I was from Medford. His passport – *Bearer's address* – said Watertown. He felt he had to conceal it. That explained a lot: the insecurity of living on the lower slopes of the long hill, between the smoldering steeples of Boston and the clean, high-priced air of Belmont. We are probably no more class conscious than the British, but when we make class an issue it seems more than snobbery. It becomes a bizarre spectacle, a kind of attention seeking, and I cannot hear an American speaking of his social position without thinking of a human fly, one of those tiny men in grubby capes whom one sometimes sees clinging to the brickwork of a tall building.

What had begun as fantasy had, after six months of his repeating it in our insignificant place, made it seem like fact. Jerry didn't know Africa: his one girl friend stood for the whole continent. And of course he lied to her. I had the impression that it was one of the reasons Jerry wanted to stay in Africa. If you tell enough lies about yourself, they take hold. It becomes impossible ever to go back, since that means facing the truth. In Africa, no one could dispute what Jerry said he was: a wealthy Bostonian, from a family of some distinction, adventuring in Third World philanthropy before inheriting his father's business.

Rereading the above, I think I may be misrepresenting him. Although he was undeniably a fraud in some ways, his fraudulence was the last thing you noticed about him. What you saw first was a tall good-natured person in his early twenties, confidently casual, with easy charm and a gift for ingenious flattery. When I told him I had majored in entomology he called me 'Doctor.' This later became 'Doc.' He showed exaggerated respect to the gardeners and washerwomen at the school, using the politest phrases when he spoke to them. He always said 'sir' to the students ('You, sir, are a lazy little creep'), which baffled them and won them over. The cook adored him, and even the cook's cook – who was lame and fourteen and ragged – liked Jerry to the point where the poor boy would go through the compound stealing flowers from the Inkpens' garden to decorate our table. While I was merely tolerated as an unattractive and near-sighted bug collector, Jerry was courted by the British wives in the compound. The wife of the new headmaster, Lady Alice (Sir Godfrey Inkpen had been knighted for his work in the Civil Service) usually stopped in to see Jerry when her husband was away. Jerry was gracious with her and anxious to make a good impression. Privately, he said, 'She's all tits and teeth.'

'Why is it,' he said to me one day, 'that the white women have all the money and the black ones have all the looks?'

'I didn't realize you were interested in money.'

'Not for itself, Doc,' he said. 'I'm interested in what it can buy.'

No matter how hard I tried, I could not get used to hearing Ameena's squawks of pleasure from the next room, or Jerry's elbows banging against the wall. At any moment, I expected their humpings and slappings to bring down the boxes of mounted butterflies I had hung there. At breakfast, Jerry was his urbane self, sitting at the head of the table while Ameena cackled.

He held a teapot in each hand. 'What will it be, my dear? Chinese or Indian tea? Marmalade or jam? Poached or scrambled? And may I suggest a kipper?'

'*Wopusa!*' Ameena would say. 'Idiot!'

She was lean, angular, and wore a scarf in a handsome turban on her head. 'I'd marry that girl tomorrow,' Jerry said, 'if she had fifty grand.' Her breasts were full and her skin was like velvet; she looked majestic, even doing the ironing. And when I saw her ironing, it struck me how Jerry inspired devotion in people.

But not any from me. I think I resented him most because he was new. I had been in Africa for two years and had replaced any ideas of sexual conquest with the possibility of a great entomological discovery. But he was not interested in my experience. There was a great deal I could have told him. In the meantime, I watched Jika taking Ameena into town on his bicycle, and I added specimens to my collection.

Then, one day, the Inkpens' daughter arrived from Rhodesia to spend her school holidays with her parents.

We had seen her the day after she arrived, admiring the roses in her mother's garden, which adjoined ours. She was about seventeen, and breathless and damp; and so small I at once imagined this pink butterfly struggling in my net. Her name was Petra (her parents called her 'Pet'), and her pretty bloom was recklessness and innocence. Jerry said, 'I'm going to marry her.'

'I've been thinking about it,' he said the next day. 'If I just invite her I'll look like a wolf. If I invite the three of them it'll seem as if I'm stage-managing it. So I'll invite the parents – for some inconvenient time – and they'll have no choice but to ask me if they can bring the daughter along, too. *They'll* ask *me* if they can bring her. Good thinking? It'll have to be after dark – they'll be afraid of someone raping her. Sunday's always family day, so how about Sunday at seven? High tea. They will deliver her into my hands.'

The invitation was accepted. And Sir Godfrey said, 'I hope you don't mind if we bring our daughter –'

More than anything, I wished to see whether Jerry would bring Ameena home that Saturday night. He did – I suppose he did not want to arouse Ameena's suspicions – and on Sunday morning it was breakfast as usual and 'What will it be, my dear?'

But everything was not as usual. In the kitchen, Jika was making a cake and scones. The powerful fragrance of baking, so early on a Sunday morning, made Ameena curious. She sniffed and smiled and picked up her cup. Then she asked: What was the cook making?

'Cakes,' said Jerry. He smiled back at her.

Jika entered timidly with some toast.

'You're a better cook than I am,' Ameena said in Chinyanja. 'I don't know how to make cakes.'

Jika looked terribly worried. He glanced at Jerry.

'Have a cake,' said Jerry to Ameena.

Ameena tipped the cup to her lips and said slyly, 'Africans don't eat cakes for breakfast.'

'*We* do,' said Jerry, with guilty rapidity. 'It's an old American custom.'

Ameena was staring at Jika. When she stood up he winced. Ameena said, 'I have to make water.' It was one of the few English sentences she knew.

Jerry said, 'I think she suspects something.'

As I started to leave with my net and my chloroform bottle I heard a great fuss in the kitchen, Jerry telling Ameena not to do the ironing, Ameena protesting, Jika groaning. But Jerry was angry, and soon the bicycle was bumping away from the house: Jika pedaling, Ameena on the crossbar.

'She just wanted to hang around,' said Jerry. 'Guess what the bitch was doing? She was ironing a drip-dry shirt!'

*

It was early evening when the Inkpens arrived, but night fell before tea was poured. Petra sat between her proud parents, saying what a super house we had, what a super school it was, how super it was to have a holiday here. Her monotonous ignorance made her even more desirable.

Perhaps for our benefit – to show her off – Sir Godfrey asked her leading questions. 'Mother tells me you've taken up knitting' and 'Mother says you've become quite a whiz at math.' Now he said, 'I hear you've been doing some riding.'

'Heaps, actually,' said Petra. Her face was shining. 'There are some stables near the school.'

Dances, exams, picnics, house parties: Petra gushed about her Rhodesian school. And in doing so she made it seem a distant place – not an African country at all, but a special preserve of superior English recreations.

'That's funny,' I said. 'Aren't there Africans there?'

Jerry looked sharply at me.

'Not at the school,' said Petra. 'There are some in town. The girls call them nig-nogs.' She smiled. 'But they're quite sweet actually.'

'The Africans, dear?' asked Lady Alice.

'The girls,' said Petra.

Her father frowned.

Jerry said, 'What do you think of this place?'

'Honestly, I think it's super.'

'Too bad it's so dark at the moment,' said Jerry. 'I'd like to show you my frangipani.'

'Jerry's famous for that frangipani,' said Lady Alice.

Jerry had gone to the French windows to indicate the general direction of the bush. He gestured toward the darkness and said, 'It's somewhere over there.'

'I see it,' said Petra.

The white flowers and the twisted limbs of the frangipani were clearly visible in the headlights of an approaching car.

Sir Godfrey said, 'I think you have a visitor.'

The Inkpens were staring at the taxi. I watched Jerry. He had turned pale, but kept his composure. 'Ah, yes,' he said, 'it's the sister of one of our pupils.' He stepped outside to intercept her, but Ameena was too quick for him. She hurried past him, into the parlor where the Inkpens sat dumbfounded. Then Sir Godfrey, who had been surprised into silence, stood up and offered Ameena his chair.

Ameena gave a nervous grunt and faced Jerry. She wore the black satin cloak and sandals of a village Muslim. I had never seen her in anything but a tight dress and high heels; in that long cloak she looked like a very dangerous fly which had buzzed into the room on stiff wings.

'How nice to see you,' said Jerry. Every word was right, but his voice had become shrill. 'I'd like you to meet –'

Ameena flapped the wings of her cloak in embarrassment and said, 'I cannot stay. And I am sorry for this visit.' She spoke in her own language. Her voice was calm and even apologetic.

'Perhaps she'd like to sit down,' said Sir Godfrey, who was still standing.

'I think she's fine,' said Jerry, backing away slightly.

Now I saw the look of horror on Petra's face. She glanced up and down, from the dark shawled head to the cracked feet, then gaped in bewilderment and fear.

At the kitchen door, Jika stood with his hands over his ears.

'Let's go outside,' said Jerry in Chinyanja.

'It is not necessary,' said Ameena. 'I have something for you. I can give it to you here.'

Jika ducked into the kitchen and shut the door.

'Here,' said Ameena. She fumbled with her cloak.

Jerry said quickly, 'No,' and turned as if to avert the thrust of a dagger.

But Ameena had taken a soft gift-wrapped parcel from the folds of her cloak. She handed it to Jerry and, without turning to us, flapped out of the room. She became invisible as soon as she stepped into the darkness. Before anyone could speak, the taxi was speeding away from the house.

Lady Alice said, 'How very odd.'

'Just a courtesy call,' said Jerry, and amazed me with a succession of plausible lies. 'Her brother's in Form Four – a very bright boy, as a matter of fact. She was rather pleased by how well he'd done in his exams. She stopped in to say thanks.'

'That's *very* African,' said Sir Godfrey.

'It's lovely when people drop in,' said Petra. 'It's really quite a compliment.'

Jerry was smiling weakly and eyeing the window, as if he

expected Ameena to thunder in once again and split his head open. Or perhaps not. Perhaps he was congratulating himself that it had all gone so smoothly.

Lady Alice said, 'Well, aren't you going to open it?'

'Open what?' said Jerry, and then he realized that he was holding the parcel. 'You mean this?'

'I wonder what it could be,' said Petra.

I prayed that it was nothing frightening. I had heard stories of jilted lovers sending aborted fetuses to the men who had wronged them.

'I adore opening parcels,' said Petra.

Jerry tore off the wrapping paper, but satisfied himself that it was nothing incriminating before he showed it to the Inkpens.

'Is it a shirt?' said Lady Alice.

'It's a beauty,' said Sir Godfrey.

It was red and yellow and green, with embroidery at the collar and cuffs; an African design. Jerry said, 'I should give it back. It's a sort of bribe, isn't it?'

'Absolutely not,' said Sir Godfrey. 'I insist you keep it.'

'Put it on!' said Petra.

Jerry shook his head. Lady Alice said, 'Oh, do!'

'Some other time,' said Jerry. He tossed the shirt aside and told a long humorous story of his sister's wedding reception on the family yacht. And before the Inkpens left he asked Sir Godfrey with old-fashioned formality if he might be allowed to take Petra on a day trip to the local tea estate.

'You're welcome to use my car if you like,' said Sir Godfrey.

It was only after the Inkpens had gone that Jerry began to tremble. He tottered to a chair, lit a cigarette, and said, 'That was the worst hour of my life. Did you see her? Jesus! I thought that was the end. But what did I tell you? She suspected something!'

'Not necessarily,' I said.

He kicked the shirt – I noticed he was hesitant to touch it – and said, 'What's this all about then?'

'As you told Inky – it's a present.'

'She's a witch,' said Jerry. 'She's up to something.'

'You're crazy,' I said. 'What's more, you're unfair. You kicked her out of the house. She came back to ingratiate herself by giving you a present – a new shirt for all the ones she didn't have a chance to iron. But she saw our neighbors. I don't think she'll be back.'

'What amazes me,' said Jerry, 'is your presumption. I've been sleeping with Ameena for six months, while you've been playing with yourself. And here you are trying to tell me about her! You're incredible.'

Jerry had the worst weakness of the liar: he never believed anything you told him.

I said, 'What are you going to do with the shirt?'

Clearly this had been worrying him. But he said nothing.

Late that night, working with my specimens, I smelled acrid smoke. I went to the window. The incinerator was alight; Jika was coughing and stirring the flames with a stick.

The next Saturday, Jerry took Petra to the tea estate in Sir Godfrey's gray Humber. I spent the day with my net, rather resenting the thought that Jerry had all the luck. First Ameena, now Petra. And he had ditched Ameena. There seemed no end to his arrogance or – what was more annoying – his luck. He came back to the house alone. I vowed that I would not give him a chance to do any sexual boasting. I stayed in my room, but less than ten minutes after he arrived home he was knocking on my door.

'I'm busy,' I yelled.

'Doc, this is serious.'

He entered rather breathless, fever-white and apologetic. This was not someone who had just made a sexual conquest – I knew as soon as I saw him that it had all gone wrong. So I said, 'How does she bump?'

He shook his head. He looked very pale. He said, 'I couldn't.'

'So she turned you down.' I could not hide my satisfaction.

'She was screaming for it,' he said, rather primly. 'She's seventeen, Doc. She's locked in a girls' school half the year. She even found a convenient haystack. But I had to say no. In fact, I couldn't get away from her fast enough.'

'Something *is* wrong,' I said. 'Do you feel all right?'

He ignored the question. 'Doc,' he said, 'remember when Ameena barged in. Just think hard. Did she touch me? Listen, this is important.'

I told him I could not honestly remember whether she had touched him. The incident was so pathetic and embarrassing I had tried to blot it out.

'I knew something like this was going to happen. But I don't understand it.' He was talking quickly and unbuttoning his shirt. Then he took it off. 'Look at this. Have you ever seen anything like it?'

At first I thought his body was covered by welts. But what I had taken to be welts were a mass of tiny reddened patches, like fly bites, some already swollen into bumps. Most of them – and by far the worst – were on his back and shoulders. They were as ugly as acne and had given his skin that same shine of infection.

'It's interesting,' I said.

'Interesting!' he screamed. 'It looks like syphilis and all you can say is it's interesting. Thanks a lot.'

'Does it hurt?'

'Not too much,' he said. 'I noticed it this morning before I went out. But I think they've gotten worse. That's why nothing happened with Petra. I was too scared to take my shirt off.'

'I'm sure she wouldn't have minded if you'd kept it on.'

'I couldn't risk it,' he said. 'What if it's contagious?'

He put calamine lotion on it and covered it carefully with gauze, and the next day it was worse. Each small bite had swelled to a pimple, and some of them seemed on the point of erupting: a mass of small warty boils. That was on Sunday. On Monday I told Sir Godfrey that Jerry had a bad cold and could not teach. When I got back to the house that afternoon, Jerry said that it was so painful he couldn't lie down. He had spent the afternoon sitting bolt upright in a chair.

'It was that shirt,' he said. 'Ameena's shirt. She did something to it.'

I said, 'You're lying. Jika burned that shirt – remember?'

'She touched me,' he said. 'Doc, maybe it's not a curse – I'm not superstitious anyway. Maybe she gave me syph.'

'Let's hope so.'

'What do you mean by that!'

'I mean, there's a cure for syphilis.'

'Suppose it's not that?'

'We're in Africa,' I said.

This terrified him, as I knew it would.

He said, 'Look at my back and tell me if it looks as bad as it feels.'

He crouched under the lamp. His back was grotesquely inflamed.

The eruptions had become like nipples, much bigger and with a bruised discoloration. I pressed one. He cried out. Watery liquid leaked from a pustule.

'That hurt!' he said.

'Wait.' I saw more infection inside the burst boil – a white clotted mass. I told him to grit his teeth. 'I'm going to squeeze this one.'

I pressed it between my thumbs and as I did a small white knob protruded. It was not pus – not liquid. I kept on pressing and Jerry yelled with shrill ferocity until I was done. Then I showed him what I had squeezed from his back; it was on the tip of my tweezers – a live maggot.

'It's a worm!'

'A larva.'

'You know about these things. You've seen this before, haven't you?'

I told him the truth. I had never seen one like it before in my life. It was not in any textbook I had ever seen. And I told him more: there were, I said, perhaps two hundred of them, just like the one wriggling on my tweezers, in those boils on his body.

Jerry began to cry.

That night I heard him writhing in his bed, and groaning, and if I had not known better I would have thought Ameena was with him. He turned and jerked and thumped like a lover maddened by desire; and he whimpered, too, seeming to savor the kind of pain that is indistinguishable from sexual pleasure. But it was no more passion than the movement of those maggots in his flesh. In the morning, gray with sleeplessness, he said he felt like a corpse. Truly, he looked as if he was being eaten alive.

An illness you read about is never as bad as the real thing. Boy Scouts are told to suck the poison out of snakebites. But a snakebite – swollen and black and running like a leper's sore – is so horrible I can't imagine anyone capable of staring at it, much less putting his mouth on it. It was that way with Jerry's boils. All the textbooks on earth could not have prepared me for their ugliness, and what made them even more repellent was the fact that his face and hands were free of them. He was infected from his neck to his waist, and down his arms; his face was haggard, and in marked contrast to his sores.

I said, 'We'll have to get you to a doctor.'

'A witch doctor.'

'You're serious!'

He gasped and said, 'I'm dying, Doc. You have to help me.'

'We can borrow Sir Godfrey's car. We could be in Blantyre by midnight.'

Jerry said, 'I can't last until midnight.'

'Take it easy,' I said. 'I have to go over to the school. I'll say you're still sick. I don't have any classes this afternoon, so when I get back I'll see if I can do anything for you.'

'There are witch doctors around here,' he said. 'You can find one – they know what to do. It's a curse.'

I watched his expression change as I said, 'Maybe it's the curse of the white worm.' He deserved to suffer, after what he had done, but his face was so twisted in fear, I added, 'There's only one thing to do. Get those maggots out. It might work.'

'Why did I come to this fucking place!'

But he shut his eyes and was silent: he knew why he had left home.

When I returned from the school ('And how is our ailing friend?' Sir Godfrey had asked at morning assembly), the house seemed empty. I had a moment of panic, thinking that Jerry – unable to stand the pain – had taken an overdose. I ran into the bedroom. He lay asleep on his side, but woke when I shook him.

'Where's Jika?' I said.

'I gave him the week off,' said Jerry. 'I didn't want him to see me. What are you doing?'

I had set out a spirit lamp and my surgical tools: tweezers, a scalpel, cotton, alcohol, bandages. He grew afraid when I shut the door and shone the lamp on him.

'I don't want you to do it,' he said. 'You don't know anything about this. You said you'd never seen this thing before.'

I said, 'Do you want to die?'

He sobbed and lay flat on the bed. I bent over him to begin. The maggots had grown larger, some had broken the skin, and their ugly heads stuck out like beads. I lanced the worst boil, between his shoulder blades. Jerry cried out and arched his back, but I kept digging and prodding, and I found that heat made it simpler. If I held my cigarette lighter near the wound the maggot wriggled, and by degrees, I eased it out. The danger lay in their breaking: if I pulled too hard some would be left in the boil to decay, and that I said would kill him.

By the end of the afternoon I had removed only twenty or so, and Jerry had fainted from the pain. He woke at nightfall. He looked at the saucer beside the bed and saw the maggots jerking in it – they had worked themselves into a white knot – and he screamed. I had to hold him until he calmed down. And then I continued.

I kept at it until very late. And I must admit that it gave me a certain pleasure. It was not only that Jerry deserved to suffer for his deceit – and his suffering was that of a condemned man; but also what I told him had been true: this was a startling discovery for me, as an entomologist. I had never seen such creatures before.

It was after midnight when I stopped. My hand ached, my eyes hurt from the glare, and I was sick to my stomach. Jerry had gone to sleep. I switched off the light and left him to his nightmares.

He was slightly better by morning. He was still pale, and the opened boils were crusted with blood, but he had more life in him than I had seen for days. And yet he was brutally scarred. I think he knew this: he looked as if he had been whipped.

'You saved my life,' he said.

'Give it a few days,' I said.

He smiled. I knew what he was thinking. Like all liars – those people who behave like human flies on our towering credulity – he was preparing his explanation. But this would be a final reply: he was preparing his escape.

'I'm leaving,' he said. 'I've got some money – and there's a night bus –' He stopped speaking and looked at my desk. 'What's that?'

It was the dish of maggots, now as full as a rice pudding.

'Get rid of them!'

'I want to study them,' I said. 'I think I've earned the right to do that. But I'm off to morning assembly – what shall I tell Inky?'

'Tell him I might have this cold for a long time.'

He was gone when I got back to the house; his room had been emptied, and he'd left me his books and his tennis racket with a note. I made what explanations I could. I told the truth: I had no idea where he had gone. A week later, Petra went back to Rhodesia, but she told me she would be back. As we chatted over the fence

I heard Jerry's voice: *She's screaming for it.* I said, 'We'll go horse-back riding.'

'Super!'

The curse of the white worm: Jerry had believed me. But it was the curse of impatience – he had been impatient to get rid of Ameena, impatient for Petra, impatient to put on a shirt that had not been ironed. What a pity it was that he was not around when the maggots hatched, to see them become flies I had never seen. He might have admired the way I expertly pickled some and sealed others in plastic and mounted twenty of them on a tray.

And what flies they were! It was a species that was not in any book, and yet the surprising thing was that in spite of their differently shaped wings (like a Muslim woman's cloak) and the shape of their bodies (a slight pinch above the thorax, giving them rather attractive waists), their life cycle was the same as many others of their kind: they laid their eggs on laundry and these larvae hatched at body heat and burrowed into the skin to mature. Of course, laundry was always ironed – even drip-dry shirts – to kill them. Everyone who knew Africa knew that.

Clapham Junction

'The satisfaction of working snails out of shells,' said Cox, 'is the satisfaction of successfully picking one's nose.' He had been hunched over his plate, screwing the gray meat out of the glistening yellow-black shell. Now he looked up and said, 'Don't you think so?'

Mrs Etterick looked at him sideways. She said, 'I'm glad Gina is upstairs.'

But her expression told him that he had scored. Encouraged, he said, 'A horrible, private sort of relief. Like finding exactly what you need at Woolworth's. A soap dish. Those plastic discs you put under chair legs so they won't dent the carpet.'

'Now you've gone too far,' said Mrs Etterick.

Rudge said, 'And how is dear Gina? Is she any better?'

'She seems happy. In that sense she is better,' said Mrs Etterick. 'But hers is not the sort of affliction that can be cured in a place like Sunbury. She is so very backward in some ways. I say "affliction" – but that doesn't describe it. She is like a different racial type altogether, like someone from a primitive tribe. Terribly sweet, but terribly uncivilized. I sometimes think what a pity it was, when she was born that –'

Mrs Etterick faced her snails and reproached herself with a shudder.

'There is a kind of light in her face,' Rudge said. 'I noticed it when she let me in tonight. She was standing there like a very serious head prefect.'

'She is nearly thirty,' said Mrs Etterick. 'I still have to wash her face and comb her hair. Head prefects, in my experience, can manage those things.'

Cox had finished his snails. He was smiling at Rudge.

Rudge said, 'I meant there was a gentleness about her, something distinctly proper.'

'She broke a vase this afternoon. She kept asking me where she should put it. I could hardly hear her. She gets very exasperated, awfully flustered. I came down the stairs. When she saw me she started to juggle it. They don't have the same joints in their fingers that we do. Then it went crash.' Mrs Etterick dropped a snail shell with her tongs, as if intending to give drama to what Gina had done. She said, 'I think she did it on purpose.'

'Perhaps a plea for love,' Rudge said.

'Rubbish,' said Mrs Etterick. 'That vase cost less than a pound.'

Cox began to laugh. He was not a man given to expression, but the laugh accomplished his purpose; it complimented Mrs Etterick and it mocked Rudge. But it also slewed in his throat, and it was loud with greed.

Rudge said, 'I've always wanted a daughter. Particularly at a time of year like this. Christmas. It seems part of the season.'

'You sound like her,' said Mrs Etterick, rising, collecting the plates. Rudge rose to help her, but she waved him aside, saying that she could manage.

Cox rocked his chair back and yawned. Then he said, 'Those snails were marvelous.'

'It's a sort of kit,' said Mrs Etterick. 'You get snail mince and empty shells in a box. You stuff the shells and heat them through. It's really very simple.'

She returned with a casserole dish on which spills of juice had been baked black on the rim. 'Cassoulet,' she said. 'I put it in the oven this morning. I had to spend the day shopping.'

'When I didn't see you in your office,' said Cox, 'I thought you were home, cooking. Now I don't feel so guilty.'

'I couldn't face the party.'

'It was all secretaries,' Rudge said.

'So you noticed,' Cox replied.

'I noticed you,' said Rudge.

Cox turned to Mrs Etterick. 'Are you going away for Christmas?'

'My plans are still pretty fluid,' she said. 'Gina's been on at me to make a week of it. That's a fairly grim prospect.'

Cox said, 'So you might be alone?'

'I'm not sure.'

The two men ate in silence. Upstairs, the radio was loud.

Mrs Etterick said, 'Gina's transistor. I decided to give her her present early. She *will* leave the door open.'

Cox said, 'I hate Christmas.'

Mrs Etterick filled Rudge's glass with claret and said, 'You'll be spending Christmas here in London, then?'

'I have an open invitation in Scotland,' Rudge said.

'Snow in the Highlands!' said Cox.

'Rain, more likely. The Lowlands – Peebles,' said Rudge. 'It's my mother.'

'Will you go?' asked Mrs Etterick.

Rudge stared, holding his knife and fork, and with hunger on his face he seemed on the point of cutting a slice from Mrs Etterick's white forearm and stuffing it into his mouth. He lowered the implements and in a subdued voice said, 'That depends.'

'Such a lovely house you have, Diana. I hadn't realized you'd such a passion for oriental art. It's all frightfully dazzling.' Cox had finished eating and had lit a cigarette. 'Is this an ashtray, or a funerary urn?'

'Both,' said Mrs Etterick. 'Yes, we were in Thailand. That's where I lost my husband. He was at the university.'

'An academic in the family,' said Cox. 'Forgive me – I wasn't mocking.'

'He was the bursar.'

'Was it one of these tropical diseases?' asked Rudge.

'Yes,' said Mrs Etterick. 'She was about twenty, one of these heartless Chinese girls that are determined to leave Thailand. I can't tell you how beautiful she was. She set about him like an infection. They're in Australia now. I imagine she's quite bored with Richard these days. I got the Buddhas, the bronzes, the porcelain. You could pick it up for next to nothing then. The looters, you know. It was all looters.'

Rudge said, 'I was thinking of staying in town over Christmas. Perhaps taking in a show or a concert. Last year, I saw Verdi's *Otello*. Placido Domingo. Overwhelming. I've always wanted to attend the carol service at Saint Paul's. Something traditional.'

'Last year,' Cox said, 'Boxing Day, I went up to the Odeon in Holloway and saw a double bill. *The Godfather* – both parts. Best afternoon I'd spent in ages. Place was full of yobs.'

Mrs Etterick said, 'I'd like to close my eyes and open them and discover it's January.'

'I'd like to spend the next eight days in bed, watching rubbish on television and eating buttered toast. I mean, really pig it until London's back to normal,' Cox said.

'In Bangkok, you never knew it was Christmas. The heat was dreadful – I loved it. And Gina had an amah then. Amazing, isn't it? They were both seventeen, only the amah was about a foot shorter. But she kept Gina well in check. There were parties, but none of this bogus nostalgia. All the Christmas decorations were in the massage parlors and the brothels – well, that's what Richard told me. The Americans carried on, of course. But they would.'

'I had no idea there was another Far East hand at Alliance,' Cox said.

'Another?' said Mrs Etterick.

'I was in Malaya during the war,' Cox said. 'It was long before your time. But I stayed on. I rather enjoyed the Japanese surrender. It was a terrible shambles. They handed Kota Bahru over to me – can you imagine?'

Rudge said, 'There is so much that we have yet to understand about the East. Yes, I suppose one can treat it all as a great joke. Those funny little people. But our destiny lies in the hands of those funny little people.'

'They go out of their way to insult us,' Cox said. 'They make no serious attempt to understand us. Never did. I have always taken the view that we should offer them all the friendly attention they offer us. I mean, if they turf out our people we should immediately turf out one of theirs. Only language they understand.'

'Who are we talking about?' asked Rudge.

'Orientals,' Cox said.

'You lump them all together.'

'My dear boy, they lump *us* all together. We are westerners, they are orientals.'

Rudge said, 'Did Shiner ever tell you that terrible story about his visit to the Canton Trade Fair? It was when Alliance sent that industrial software delegation over, about three years ago.'

Cox said, 'I never speak to Shiner. I don't like his eyes, or his software, for that matter.'

'His secretary had that nervous breakdown,' said Mrs Etterick. 'That spoke volumes.'

'It makes no difference whether we like Shiner or not,' Rudge said. 'The story still stands.'

Cox said, 'Get on with it, then. I can see there is no way of stopping you.'

'Apparently they went all out to impress our delegation,' Rudge said. 'Took them to spindle factories, steel mills, hydroelectric plants. Well, you know. Then they took them to a model commune. The interpreter got hold of the headman and translated what he said. "In five years our cotton acreage has risen fiftyfold," says the headman. "We have increased production of vegetable fiber by two hundred percent." Shiner was terribly impressed. They inspected the schools, the electricity plant, the kitchens. All this time, the headman is raving about the progress they've made and saying how happy everyone is. "Under the wise leadership of Chairman Mao, we have gone from strength to strength." Shiner signed the visitor's book and said he'd have to leave. "No," said the headman, "there is one more thing I must show you." Out of politeness, Shiner agreed. Then there was a bit of by-play between the interpreter and the headman. The headman said that he wanted to take Shiner upstairs, but that the staircase was very narrow and the room was small and so forth. The interpreter relented, and off they went, Shiner and the headman, to inspect this attic.'

'Now comes the interesting part,' Cox said.

'There was a cradle in this attic. The headman leaned over to Shiner and said, "That is my daughter." He spoke in English! Shiner was astonished, but before he could recover himself, the headman had picked up the child. He was frantic. He put the child in Shiner's arms and said, "Take her with you! Please, take her away from here! You must do this! She has no future here in China!"'

'Is this an ashtray, too?' said Cox to Mrs Etterick. But she was squinting at Rudge.

'Shiner never said a word,' said Rudge. 'He simply put the child back into the cradle and took himself away. But he told me he was really quite shaken by it.'

'I'd divide anything Shiner says by ten,' said Cox.

'The story is true,' Rudge said. 'There were others present. He had witnesses.'

'But there were only two of them in the attic. You said so.'

'I think it is a heart-rending story,' Rudge said. He appealed to Mrs Etterick. 'I sometimes wonder what I would have done if I'd been in Shiner's position.'

'If you'd had any sense you'd have taken the next rickshaw out of the place,' Cox said.

'I'd like to think I was the sort of man who could get that infant out of the country.'

'And where would you bring this ashen-faced tot? To England? What future would she have here?'

Mrs Etterick said, 'Gina was very happy in Bangkok. She hasn't been nearly so happy since.'

'I have nothing so dramatic to offer as Shiner's story,' Cox said. 'I wasn't on a company swan to the Canton Trade Fair. I was in the army, and Kota Bahru was about the grimmest place I'd ever seen. I couldn't imagine why the Japanese had wanted to capture it, or why we were so bloody keen to get it back. But I was an officer and I was put in charge of the reoccupation. What made me think of this? I suppose it was your mention of looters, Diana. After the surrender, Malaya was swarming with looters and Kota Bahru seemed to have more than its fair share. They made me livid. They spent the war hiding behind trees while British soldiers were dying in battle or rotting in prison camps. One day, I was driving along in my jeep. This was just outside of town. I saw a looter running across the road with an enormous great sack. I slammed on the brakes and hopped out of the jeep. And I suppose I yelled at him to stop – I really can't remember. It all happened so fast. I then took out my pistol – the chap was still beetling away with his sack – and fired. One shot. The man fell dead.'

'That's horrible,' Rudge said.

'I was afraid,' Cox said, 'that he might still be alive. He was lying there. I couldn't see any blood. I wasn't even a good shot! I thought he was faking – the way animals pretend they're dead. He had flopped over so quickly, just like a rabbit. I kept my pistol aimed at him as I walked over to him, and then I saw that I had got him right through the heart. The blood had started to clot on his blouse. It was a woman's blouse. I imagine he had stolen that, too.'

'What a thing to have on your conscience,' Rudge said.

'Precisely,' Cox said. 'I thought I'd have a terrible night. But not a bit! I went back to my bungalow and ate a huge meal and then slept like a baby.'

Mrs Etterick said, 'And I'll bet everyone blamed you afterward and said you hadn't any right.'

'Some fools did, but I don't suppose anyone really cared.'

'There's no dessert,' Mrs Etterick said. 'I have some fresh fruit and some cheese, if anyone's interested.'

'I'll help you clear away these things,' said Cox.

'Leave them, please, Austin,' Mrs Etterick said. 'I rather like sitting in the rubble.'

Rudge said, 'Some years, there's lots of snow in Peebles.' He stood up. 'I ought to be off,' he said. 'Are you going? We're both crossing the river. We could share a taxi.'

'I'm going to linger a bit in the rubble,' Cox said. 'But don't let me hold you up.' Now he looked at Mrs Etterick, 'Or would it be simpler if we both left?'

Though it was almost eight-thirty, it was still dark the following morning as the mother and daughter walked down St John's Hill to Clapham Junction. Mrs Etterick was brisk and silent, keeping four steps ahead of Gina, who was unusually talkative for this early hour. Passing the sweet shops on the hill, Gina remarked that they might buy their chocolate oranges on the way back; at the Granada, Gina said they'd have to see the Disney film – perhaps tomorrow; and there were Christmas trees stacked at the flower shop: Gina fell behind, choosing one. Mrs Etterick had not paused, or replied, and Gina had toiled on clumsy feet to catch up with her. The daughter was big, but had the stumbling round-shouldered gait of a small child. Her eyes were hooded slits in her fat solemn face and her arms swung uselessly in her sleeves.

Gina said, 'After Daddy died and went to Heaven –'

Mrs Etterick quickened her pace.

A crowd of people stood at the ticket window. Mrs Etterick joined them. Now Gina entered the lobby.

'Mum,' she said in a pleading voice. 'After Daddy died –'

'You're talking much too loud,' Mrs Etterick said sharply. 'You'll have to stand in the corner. Over there.'

Gina lugged herself to the corner and waited, murmuring.

It was Mrs Etterick's turn. She put her money down and leaned toward the plastic grille. 'One single and one return to Sunbury, please.'

The Odd-Job Man

Every spring, on the first free day after exams, Lowell Bloodworth
and his wife, Shelley, drove to Boston from Amherst and then flew
to London. He told people he was seeing his publisher. But he had
no publisher. The London visits had begun when, as an associate
professor, Bloodworth was working on his edition of *The Family
Letters of Wilbur Parsons*. He had brought a box of the letters,
rented a room near Sloane Square, and stuck them into a thick
album, working by the window with a brush and a bottle of glue;
he added footnotes in ink and gave each personal observation a
crimson exclamation mark. English academics mocked his enterprise. He would not be drawn, but Shelley said, 'It's not easy editing
the letters of a living poet.' English academics said they had never
heard of Parsons. Bloodworth had a reply: 'The only difference
between Wallace Stevens and Wilbur Parsons is that Stevens was
vice president of an insurance company and Parsons was president
– still is.'

'Why is it,' an Englishman once said to him, 'American academics
are forever putting their fingers down their throats and bringing
up books like these?' Bloodworth had thought of asking that man
to help him find an English publisher. It struck Bloodworth as odd
that the mere mention of his book caused shouts of laughter in
London. Especially odd since this book, brought out in America
after several delays by a university press, got Lowell Bloodworth
the tenure he wanted, and now he was earning thirty thousand
dollars a year. But it was the salary that embarrassed him, not
the book. There was an additional bonus: *The Times Literary
Supplement* gave him one of Parson's collections to review, and
years afterward Bloodworth said, 'I do a little writing for the *TLS*,'
often claiming credit for anonymous reviews he admired.

He liked London, but his links with the life of the city tended
to be imaginary. There was that huge party at William Empson's.
Bloodworth had gone with one of Mr Empson's former students
(who, as it turned out, had not been invited either). Bloodworth

talked the whole evening to an elderly man who told malicious stories against Edith Sitwell. The stories became Bloodworth's own, and later, describing that summer to his Amherst colleagues, he said, 'We spent quite a bit of time with the Empsons . . .' He appropriated gossip and gave it the length of anecdote. One summer he saw Frank Kermode across a room. In the autumn, for a colleague, he turned this glimpse into a meeting.

Nine summers, nine autumns had been spent this way; and always Bloodworth regretted that he had so little to show after such long flights. He craved something substantial: a literary find, an eminent friend, a famous enemy. Inevitably his rivalries were departmental; the department had grown, and for the past few years Bloodworth's younger colleagues, all of whom flew to England in June, had come back with similar stories. In the warm, early-autumn afternoons they would meet at Bloodworth's 'Little Britain' on the Shutesbury Road; the wives in Liberty prints swapping play titles, the children jerking at Hamleys' toys, and the men discussing London as if it were no larger or more complicated than Amherst itself: 'Leavis is looking a lot older . . . ,' 'We saw Iris Murdoch in Selfridge's . . . ,' 'Cal's divorce is coming through . . .' This last remark from Siggins, whose preposterous anecdotes Bloodworth suspected were nimble parodies of his own: lately, Bloodworth had felt (the word was Parsons's) outgunned.

This was the first year the Bloodworths had spent their English vacation outside London. They were flushed from Sloane Square by the department. On their second day in London they met Cliff Margoulies on Pont Street. He had a story about Angus Wilson. That afternoon, they bumped into Siggins at the Byron exhibition. Bloodworth said he was just leaving. The next day he had gone back to the Byron exhibition and seen Arvin Prizeman: there was just no escaping them. He ran into Milburn at the Stoppard play, and Shelley had seen the Hoffenbergs at Biba's. Each encounter was alarming, producing a keen embarrassment Bloodworth disguised unwillingly in heartiness. The prospect of a summer of these chance meetings made Bloodworth cringe, and so, at the end of their first week, the Bloodworths took a train to the village of Hooke, in Kent, where they rented a small cottage ('Batcombe') for the remainder of their vacation.

It was not a coincidence that a mile from this village was the house of the American poet Walter Van Bellamy, who had been living in England since the war. Bellamy was an irascible man of about seventy who had known both Pound and Eliot – and been praised by them – and who (though the airfare to New York was less than his well-publicized phone bill) described himself as an exile. Bloodworth was not the first American to get the idea of going to Hooke with the intention of making Walter Van Bellamy's acquaintance; there had been others – poets, Ph.D. candidates, anthologists – but invariably they were turned away. Out of spite they reported how they had found Bellamy drunk. The more Bellamy protected his privacy, the more scandalous the stories became.

Bloodworth, who gave a Bellamy seminar, was anxious to verify the stories. He had often talked to Wilbur Parsons about Bellamy's influence: Parsons acknowledged the fact that Bellamy was the greater poet, but they had, Parsons said, been good friends and had once dated the same Radcliffe girl. Now, Bloodworth's ambition went beyond verifying the scandalous stories or even meeting the man. He had in mind an edition of poems that would be different from anything scholarship had so far produced. This book, 'Presented by Lowell Bloodworth,' would consist of poems in Bellamy's hand, photographs of work sheets and fair copies, discovered drafts, inky lyrics, all of them nobly scrawled instead of diminished by the regularity of typefaces. It would be a collector's item: Introduction by Bloodworth, Notes by Bloodworth – the sort of book got up to honor a dead poet's memory, an exhibit showing crossed-out lines, second thoughts, hasty errors in the poet's own handwriting. Bloodworth's sections, of course, would be printed in Times Roman. In his mind the book became such a finished thing that when he remembered he had not yet met the man he grew restless to see samples of his handwriting.

'I've seen him,' Shelley said, several days after their arrival in Hooke. It was at the off-license. Bellamy (confirming scandal) was buying an enormous bottle of gin. The man behind the counter had said, 'Will that be all, Mr Bellamy?' and Bellamy had grunted and gone away in a car. Shelley described Bellamy closely: the hair, the walking stick, the green sweater, the car, even the brand of gin.

Bloodworth was excited. The next morning he saw the car parked near the village's cricket ground, and on the grass Bellamy was throwing a mangled ball for his dog to fetch.

'There are people,' said Bloodworth, 'who'd risk losing tenure to be right here at this moment.'

The poet shambled after his dog.

'Say something,' said Shelley.

'This is an historic moment,' said Bloodworth. He added, 'I mean, in my life.'

'No, say something to *him*.'

But Bellamy was headed in the opposite direction, flinging the ball.

'Rain,' said Shelley, looking up. She spread her palms to the sky. There was a sound, far off, of thunder, and a spark of lightning from the underside of a black cloud.

Bloodworth shook out the umbrella he habitually carried in England. He said, 'Bellamy doesn't have one.'

The poet seemed not to notice the rain. He tramped slowly, circled by the excited dog. For a moment Bloodworth imagined Walter Van Bellamy, the American poet, struck by lightning and killed instantly while he watched from the boundary of the field. He drew grim cheer from the reflection, and saw the thunderbolt's jagged arrow enter Bellamy's head, saw the poet stagger, and himself sprinting across the cricket pitch, then kneeling: critic administering the kiss of life to poet. Bellamy's death would make an attractive article, but if Bloodworth managed to bring him back to life the poet would be grateful, and it was a short distance from lifesaver to literary executor; indeed, they were much the same.

The sun broke through the sacking of clouds, and it was then, in the barely perceptible rain, that Bloodworth ran across the grass and offered his umbrella to the poet.

'What do you want?' said Walter Van Bellamy, wheeling around, startled by Bloodworth's panting.

His ferocity did not stop Bloodworth, who said, 'I thought you might need this. I happened to be passing –'

'Who's that?' said Bellamy. Shelley – her plastic raincoat flying like a cape – was making her way to where the men stood.

'That's my wife,' said Bloodworth. 'Shelley, I'd like you to meet Walter Van Bellamy.'

'Who the hell are *you*?' demanded Bellamy.

Bloodworth introduced himself.

'I'm just going home,' said Bellamy.

'We'll walk you back to your car.'

Bellamy said something, but Bloodworth realized he was talking to his dog.

Bloodworth said, 'Wilbur's a great friend of ours.'

'Richard Wilbur?' Bellamy seemed to relax.

'Wilbur Parsons.'

'Never heard of him,' said Bellamy.

Bloodworth started to describe Parsons's contribution to American poetry and Bellamy's profound influence on the man ('Going back to what you said about mankind's terrible . . .').

'Say,' said Bellamy, interrupting him, 'do you happen to know anything about light plugs?'

'Light plugs?'

'These English plugs have three colored wires, and they just changed the goddamned colors, if you please. I've been trying to figure out which wire goes where. Ralph's never around when I want him, and I spent the whole morning trying to connect my new shaver.'

'Leave it to me,' said Bloodworth with energy.

'I really appreciate that,' said Bellamy. 'Come over this afternoon around drink time. Bring your wife if you want. This plug's driving me nuts.' Bellamy helped his dog into the car and without another word sped down the road.

'Talk about luck,' said Bloodworth.

Shelley said, 'He seems kind of rude.'

'You'd be rude, too, if you'd had his life. Shelley, he's got *wounds*!'

In the pub, The King's Arms, at lunchtime Bloodworth inquired about the way to Bellamy's house. The landlord started to tell him, but halfway through the explanation the door flew open and a tall muscular man came in. The man was young, but balding like a man of sixty. He wore a leather jacket, and under it a T-shirt. He grinned and ordered a beer.

'Here's the man who'll tell you the quickest way to Bellamy's,' said the landlord. 'Ralph, come here.'

'What's the problem?' asked Ralph.

'Ralph here works for your friend Bellamy. He's the odd-job man.'

'It's a husband and wife thing,' said Ralph. 'My wife does the housework and cooking. I do the odd jobs – gardening, that lark.'

'When he feels like it,' said the landlord.

'When I feels like it,' said Ralph.

'I know a lot of people who'd give their right arm to work for Walter Van Bellamy,' said Bloodworth.

'Not in Hooke you don't,' said Ralph. He winked at the landlord. 'Right, Sid?'

Bloodworth suppressed a lecture. 'You were saying, the quickest way . . .'

'Oh, yeah. Here, I'll draw you a map.' He made the map carefully, sketching the streets and labeling them, marking the way with arrows, noting landmarks. Bloodworth was surprised by the stubborn, conscientious way the odd-job man worked with his pencil, and when Ralph said, 'I think that's worth a beer, don't you?' Bloodworth dumped change on the counter for three pints.

At half past four, the Bloodworths walked the pleasant mile along winding country roads to Bellamy's house. The house was not signposted, nor did it have a name. It was a converted farmhouse at the end of a close lane, set amid crumbling farm buildings, a roofless barn, broken sheds, and fences with no gates. They were met at the front door by a woman of about thirty with a white, suspicious face.

'Mrs Bellamy?'

'She's in Italy.'

Bloodworth explained his errand. The woman said, 'Wait here.' She closed the door in their faces and bounded through the house; they heard her on the stairs. Then she returned and led them to an upstairs room, where Bellamy sat at a cluttered table. On the table were papers, unopened letters, a stack of books, a wine bottle, a glass, and the electric shaver with its flex exposed.

'I'll have that fixed in a jiffy,' said Bloodworth. He lifted the shaver and, pretending to examine it, looked past it to the swatches of paper with their blocks of blue stanzas. He was glad, but it was not the simple thrill he had once invented for himself ('Walter was showing me some of his rough drafts . . .'): in this script he saw his finished book, that album of scribbles.

'Doris,' said Bellamy to the woman, 'bring a couple of glasses, will you?'

Bloodworth took the plug apart, stripped the wires, and said, 'Looks like you're hard at work.'

But Bellamy was staring at the plug. 'I don't understand why they don't sell the shaver with the plug on. I suppose that's too simple.'

Bloodworth repeated, 'Looks like you're hard at work. New book?'

'What's that?' Bellamy said. 'Oh, fiddling around. My wife's out of town. That usually gets me writing.'

'Lowell's a writer,' said Shelley.

'Robert Lowell?' said Bellamy.

'No – me,' said Bloodworth. 'I do a little teaching on the side to pay the grocery bill, that sort of thing. Well, I mentioned my Parsons edition this morning. I like to *present* a poet, get him an audience. Some people call it criticism, but I think of it as presentation. And' – Bloodworth bit a length of plastic from one of the wires – 'I do quite a bit of reviewing.'

'You don't say,' said Bellamy.

Bloodworth saw he had not roused him. He took a breath. 'I've even done some reviews of your work.'

'That's funny,' said Bellamy, turning from the plug to Bloodworth, 'I don't recall your name.'

'It wasn't signed. Actually it was for the *TLS*, so you could hardly be expected –'

'The *TLS*? Was it about a year ago, that review of *Hooked*?'

Bloodworth did not hesitate. He stuck the last wire into the plug and said, 'Yup.'

Bellamy struggled to his feet and snatched the plug out of Bloodworth's hands. He weighed it like a grenade – Bloodworth thought he might throw it – and said fiercely, 'Get out of here this minute and take your wife with you. Doris!' (She stood in the doorway, a wineglass in each hand.) 'See these people out. You, sir,' he said to Bloodworth, 'are over-certain to the point of libel, and if there's one thing I will not stand –'

Bloodworth did not wait to hear what it was. Bellamy was a big man, and enraged he looked even bigger. There was a story that Ezra Pound had taught Bellamy to box. The fact was pertinent, for it is well known that Pound had sparred with Hemingway. The Bloodworths bolted.

At the road they paused for a last look at the house. The house was lighted; the lingering storm had darkened the late afternoon. But as they watched, the lights went out, all at once, just like that. And they heard within the house the poet howl.

'The plug,' said Bloodworth. 'I think I've made a mess of that too.'

Bloodworth thought of writing Bellamy a letter, explaining everything. But it had gone too far for that, and Shelley said, 'Let's forget it, Lowey. It was a horrible mistake. There's no sense crying about it. We can go back to London and see some plays.'

'And Siggins, and Margoulies, and Prizeman . . .' Bloodworth flinched: a return to London was a return to the department.

'But we can't stay here. Not after that.'

Bloodworth said, 'I hate to leave empty-handed. Let's give it a few more days.'

They saw no more of Bellamy. Bloodworth watched for his car, his dog, for any sign of him; but the poet had withdrawn to his farmhouse. Bloodworth hiked through the damp fields, hoping to meet him, and he imagined a situation in which he could undo all his bungling. He might happen upon the poet drowning, or lamed by a fall, or cursing a blowout Bloodworth could fix. It might rain again: a crippling thunderbolt. No opportunity presented itself. And Bloodworth walked alone, for Shelley had come down with a cold. She sat in 'Batcombe' with the electric fire on, reading a Dick Francis she'd found on the bookshelf.

One evening, leaving Shelley at the cottage, Bloodworth went to The King's Arms and saw Ralph. Ralph said, 'If you know what's good for you, you won't come over to the farm!'

'I guess he's pretty mad.'

'He's been screaming his head off for the past three days,' said Ralph. 'I don't know why, but he takes it out on Doris and me. I mean, I don't care myself. I tell him to his face to leave me alone. But not my wife. She's the quiet type. Just sits there and takes it. He's a bastard, he is. You Yanks are all alike.'

Bloodworth didn't know what to say. Finally he said, 'Bellamy is a very gifted poet. But his reputation has suffered. I wanted to help him.'

Ralph said, 'You're a great help. He had to get an electrician in. For the lights. You fused 'em.'

'An American poet,' said Bloodworth, still thinking of Bellamy, 'needs an American critic, an American audience.'

Ralph said, 'Hey, is it true that one third of all the dog food in America is eaten by human beings?'

'No,' said Bloodworth.

'I heard that somewhere,' said Ralph. 'The thing is, I suppose, my wife has no sense of smell. She burns things. What I'm trying to say is, it's hard to be a cook if you can't smell.'

'Funny. I'd never thought of that.'

'Some people are born that way. Old Bellamy shouts about his food – says it's too salty, or overdone, or underdone. My wife's disabled and he shouts. Sympathy? Not him – just poems.'

'Why do you put up with it, then?'

'I take a pride in my work,' said Ralph. 'And you can't beat the money; Bellamy's rolling in it. You buggers make a fortune. But Christ, *I* could write the stuff he does! Ever seen it?'

'I teach it,' said Bloodworth.

'It's rubbish,' said Ralph. He recited in a lilting voice, '"I was walking down the road. I seen two cows. The sky turned green. My uncle don't like me. Oh-oh-oh. I remember them cows. Hum-hum-hum. My heart she's shaking like a big fat drum."'

'He never wrote that.'

'Oh no? I *seen* it. The most awful crap. I could do it myself. I *do* do it – tried it once or twice, pretty good stuff. Pomes.' Ralph grinned. 'You know what I think? I think he gets people to write it. He's got so much money, and these sickly looking buggers are always sloping around the place – "Don't touch this, don't touch that."'

'You haven't read any of his books,' said Bloodworth.

'The hell I haven't,' said Ralph. 'And I've done a tidy sight more than that. I've read the stuff on his desk, all the scribbly papers. "My heart was walking down the road and seen two fat cows," that stuff. "Chickenzola, how's your father." I've read the lot. It stinks.'

'I don't believe you.'

'I don't care if you believe me or not,' said Ralph. 'If I wasn't making money off him I'd go and give some lectures. Rent a church hall somewhere and say, "Well, here's the truth about your so-called great poet, Mr Bellamy –" That'd shake him!'

Bloodworth said, 'Suppose I was to say to you, man to man, "Prove it"? What would you say to that?'

'I'd say, "Why?"'

'Let's say I'm interested, I want to give you a chance,' said Bloodworth. 'I know what you've been through.'

'It would cost you something.'

'How much?'

'More than ten quid, I can tell you that.'

'Let's say fifteen,' said Bloodworth.

'Let's say thirty,' said Ralph.

'You drive a hard bargain.'

'Like I say, I'm me own man. My wife, she just takes it from him. Bellamy thinks an odd-job man is someone you shout at, but I do my work and I shout back. I take a pride in my work – whatever I do, I take a pride in it.'

Ralph, Bloodworth could see, was three-parts drunk. He wanted to cut the business short. He said, 'Now let's get this straight. What you're going to do is bring me two or three examples of his bad poetry . . .'

'Listen,' said Ralph, 'make it fifty quid and I'll bring you the whole bloody lot in a bushel basket!'

That evening Bloodworth told his wife Ralph's extraordinary story. Shelley was fearful, but Bloodworth said, 'After what he's done to us? Thrown us out of his house – and we went over there with the best of intentions. I tell you, he deserves what's coming to him.'

'I didn't like the look of that Ralph. He's probably wrong.'

'Probably,' said Bloodworth. 'But think of the manuscripts, work sheets! Shelley, they're gold! And what if he's right?'

Ralph was not in The King's Arms the next day. Bloodworth stopped in at lunchtime, then returned at six-thirty and stayed until closing. He watched an interminable darts game, he made himself ill on cider, and briefly he wondered if the whole affair might not be the blunder Shelley feared it was. But the critic's rules were not the poet's, and what the poet called ruthlessness the critic might give another name. Bloodworth sympathized with Ralph, the odd-job man; he saw the similarity in his tasks and the critic's: they received orders from the man whose poetry had earned him privileges, and stood at the margins of the poet's world, listening for a shout, waiting for a poem. But what critic had marched forward and snatched a poem from under the poet's nose? None had dared – until now. Bloodworth saw himself on the frontier of criticism, where there was danger, and not the usual tact required, but elaborate deceits and stratagems, odd ways of doing odd jobs. He went to bed with these thoughts, though Shelley woke him throughout the night with her coughing.

'It's not like Ralph to miss a day,' said Sid, the landlord, the next day.

Bloodworth said, 'It's not important.' He wondered if Ralph had betrayed him to Bellamy, and he knew a full minute of panic.

He met Ralph after closing time on the road. Ralph said, 'Running away, are you?'

'I thought you weren't coming.'

'It's all in here,' said Ralph. He slapped his shirtfront. Bloodworth heard the sound of paper wrinkling at the stomach of the shirt. He was excited. His Introduction would be definitive. The book would be boxed. It might cost twenty dollars. Ralph said, 'Let's go somewhere private.'

They chose the churchyard, a shield of gravestones. Ralph said, 'My wife was off yesterday. She gets these depressions. I might as well be frank. It's her tits, see. I don't understand women. I keep telling her they're not supposed to stick out. Look around, I says, lots of women have the same thing. But she –'

'What about the poems?' Bloodworth said.

'Don't rush me,' said Ralph. 'You don't care about anybody's problems but your own, do you? Just like old Bellamy.'

'We're taking the evening train.'

'First the money.'

Bloodworth peeled off five five-pound notes and counted five more ones into Ralph's dirty hand.

Ralph said, 'Why not make it forty? You're rolling in it.'

'We agreed on thirty.' Bloodworth hated the odd-job man for putting him through this.

'Have it your way.' Ralph undid the buttons on his shirt and took out a creased brown envelope. 'I hope you appreciate all the work I put into this. It seemed a lot of trouble to go to, but I said to Doris, "Thirty quid is thirty quid."' He handed the envelope to Bloodworth.

'I'm glad you're a man of your word,' said Bloodworth.

'Well, you seemed to want them awful bad.'

Bloodworth shook the hand of the odd-job man and hurried to 'Batcombe' to tell Shelley. But partly from fear, and partly from superstition, he did not open the envelope until he was on the train and rolling through the Kent hopfields. At first he thought he had been swindled; the folded sheets, about ten of them, looked blank. But they were only blank on one side. On the other side were the collapsing rectangles of typed stanzas, lines which broke and sloped, words so badly typed they had humps and troughs. And there was a letter: *I hope you apreciate all the work I put into this but a deals a deal altho it take me a whole day to type up this stuff and any time you want some more lets see the colour of your money! Yours faithfully, R. Tunnel. PS I enclosed herewith one I wrote meself so you can compare.*

But the drunken typing and misspelling that made them valueless to Bloodworth did not disguise the beauty of the lines. Reading them made his eyes hurt. He turned quickly to Ralph's own poem, which began,

> *The odd-job man thats me*
> *Messing around in my bear feat*
> *Can make a stie from some tree*
> *Raise up pigs for the meat.*

The polecat, he thought, and his anger stayed with him for four English days. But back in Amherst he recovered himself, and when the department met for drinks and showed their trophies – Waterford crystal, a Daniell engraving of Wick, a first edition of *Howards End* – Bloodworth brought out his folder and said, 'I've got some unpublished Bellamy variants in here, and the work of a new poet; he's terribly regional but quite exciting.' Prizeman squinted; Margoulies smirked; the others stared. He shuffled the summer's result, but as he passed the poems around to convince the men, it struck him that he had the oddest job of all.

Portrait of a Lady

A hundred times, Harper had said to himself: *I am in Paris*. At first he had whispered it with excitement, but as the days passed he began mouthing it in a discouraged way, almost in disbelief, in the humiliated tones of a woman who realizes that her lover is not ever going to turn up. His doubt of the city made him doubt himself.

He was in Paris waiting for a sum of money in cash to be handed to him. He was expected to carry this bundle back to the States. That was the whole of his job: he was a courier. The age of technology demanded this simple human service, a return to romance: he tucked his business under his arm – the money, the message – as men had a century ago. It was a delicate matter; also, it was illegal.

Harper had been hired for his loyalty and resourcefulness. His employer demanded honesty, but implied that cunning would be required of him. He had impressed his employer because he wasn't hungry and wasn't looking for work. And, a recent graduate of Harvard Business School, Harper was passionate about real estate investment. Afterward he discovered that real estate investment was carrying a flat briefcase with eighty-five thousand dollars in used hundreds from an Iranian in Paris to an office in Boston, to invest in an Arizona supermarket or a chain of hamburger joints. They probably didn't even eat hamburgers, the Iranians – probably against their religion; so much was. Money (he, from Harvard Business School, had to be told this) shows up in a luggage x-ray at an airport security check as innocently as laundry, like so many folded hankies.

I am in Paris. But his first sight of the place gave him the only impression that stayed with him: there were parts of Paris that resembled Harvard Square.

He had told his wife that he would be back by the following weekend, and had flown to Paris on Sunday believing that he could pick up the cash on Monday. A day to loaf, then home on

Wednesday, and his surprised wife seeing him grinning in the doorway would say, 'So soon?'

He had not known that Monday was a holiday; this he spent furiously walking, wishing the day away. On Tuesday, he found Undershaw's office closed – Undershaw was the Iranian's agent, British: everyone got a slice. Harper's briefcase felt ridiculously light. That afternoon he tried the telephone. The line was busy; that made him hopeful. He took a taxi to the office but found it as he had that morning, locked, with no message on the dusty glass. On Wednesday he canceled his flight and tried again. This time there was a secretary in the outer office. She did not know Undershaw's name; she was temporary, she explained. Harper left a message, marked it *Urgent* and returned to his hotel near Les Invalides and waited for the phone to ring. Then he regretted that he had left his number, because it obliged him to stay in his room for the call. There was no call. He tried to ring his wife, but failed; he wondered if the phone was broken. Thursday he wasted on three trips to the office. Each time, the secretary smiled at him and he thought he saw pity in her eyes. He became awkward under her gaze, aware that a certain frenzy showed in his rumpled clothes.

'I will take your briefcase,' she said. She was French, a bit bucktoothed and angular, not what he had expected.

Harper handed it over. Not realizing its lightness until it was too late, she juggled it and almost dropped it. Harper wondered whether he had betrayed his errand by disclosing the secret of its emptiness. A man with an empty briefcase must have a shady scheme.

The street door opened and a man entered. Harper guessed this might be Undershaw; but no, the fellow was young and a moment later Harper knew he was American – something about the tortoiseshell frames, the new raincoat, the wide-open face, the way he sat with his feet apart, his shoes and the way he tapped them. Brisk apology and innocent arrogance inhabited the same body. Still sitting, he spoke to the secretary in French. She replied in English. He gave her his name – it sounded to Harper like 'Bumgarner.' He turned to Harper and said, 'Great city.'

Harper guessed that he himself had been appraised. He said, 'Very nice.'

Bumgarner looked at his watch, did a calculation on his fingers, and said, 'I was hoping to get to the Louvre this afternoon.'

He is going to say, You can spend a week there and still not see everything.

But Bumgarner said, 'What part of the States are you from?'

Harper told him: Boston. It required less explanation than Melrose.

'I'm from Denver,' Bumgarner said, and before Harper could praise it, Bumgarner went on, 'I'm over here on a poetry grant. National Endowment for the Arts.'

'You write poems?' But Harper thought of his taxes, paying for this boy's poems, the glasses, the new raincoat.

Bumgarner smiled. 'I've published quite a number. I'll have enough for a collection soon.'

The secretary stared at them, seeing them rattling away in their own language. Bumgarner seemed to be addressing her as well as Harper.

'I've been working on a long poem ever since I got here. It was going to be simple, but it's become the history of Europe, and in a way kind of autobiographical.'

'How long have you been in Paris?'

'Two semesters.'

Harper thought: *Doesn't that just sum it up.*

'Are you interested in poetry?' Bumgarner asked.

'I read the usual things at college. Yeats, Pound, Eliot. "April is the cruellest month."' Bumgarner appeared to be waiting for him to say something more. Harper said, 'There's a lot of naive economic theory in Pound.'

'I mean modern poetry.'

'Isn't that modern? Pound? Eliot?'

Bumgarner said, 'Eliot's kind of a back number.'

And Harper was offended. He had liked Eliot and found it a relief from marketing and accountancy courses; even a solace.

'What do you think of Europe?' Bumgarner asked.

'That's a tough one, like, "Is science good?"' But seeing that Bumgarner looked mocked and wary, Harper added, 'I haven't seen much more than my hotel and this office. I can't say.'

'Old Europe,' said Bumgarner. 'James thought it corrupted you – Daisy Miller, Lambert Strether. I've been trying to figure it out. But it does do something to you. The freedom. All the history. The outlook.'

Harper said, 'I can't imagine any place that has more freedom than the States.'

'Ever been to Colorado?'

'No,' said Harper. 'But I'll bet Europeans go. And for the same reason that characters in Henry James used to come here. To escape, find freedom, live a different life. Listen, this is a pretty stuffy place.'

'Depends,' Bumgarner said. 'I met a French girl. We're living together. That's why I'm here. I mean, I have to see this lawyer. My wife and I have decided to go our separate ways.'

'Sorry to hear it.' *He will go home*, thought Harper, *and he will regret his folly here.*

'It's not like that. We're going to make a clean break. We'll still be friends. We'll sell the house in Boulder. We don't have any kids.'

Harper said, 'Is this a lawyer's office?'

'Sure. Are you in the wrong place?'

'Anywhere away from home is the wrong place,' said Harper. 'I'm in brokerage. I haven't fallen in love yet. As a matter of fact, I'm dying to leave. Is Undershaw your lawyer?'

'I don't know Undershaw. Mine's Haebler – Swiss. Friend of a friend.' Then Bumgarner said, 'Give Paris a chance.'

'Paris is an idea, but not a new one,' said Harper. 'I tried to call my wife. The phones don't work. Where do these people park? The restaurants cost an arm and a leg. Call this a city?'

Bumgarner laughed in a patronizing way; he didn't argue. It interested Harper to discover that there were still Americans – poets – finding Paris magical. But this poet was getting a free ride: who was paying? Only businessmen and subsidized students could afford the place. Harper had had a meal at a small restaurant the previous day. The portions were tiny, the waiter was rude, the tables were jammed together, his knees ached from the forced confinement. The meal had cost him forty-seven dollars, with wine. No wonder poets had credit cards. It was a world he understood, but not one that he had expected.

Soon after, a tall man entered: Bumgarner's lawyer. Recognizing him, Bumgarner galloped after him. Harper was annoyed that the poet had shown so little interest in him, and *Eliot's kind of a back number* had stung him. The divorce: he would make it into a poem, deal with it like a specimen in a box and ask to be excused. But the other things – the dead phones, the restaurants, the bathtubs that couldn't take your big end, the pillow bolster that was hard as a log, the expense account, the credit card – they couldn't be poems. Too messy; they didn't rhyme. *Go home*! Harper wanted to scream at Bumgarner. *Europe's more boring than Canada*!

The secretary made a sorrowful click of her tongue when Harper rose to go. She had to remind him that he had left his briefcase; empty, it hardly seemed to matter. He was thinking about his wife.

On Friday, Undershaw rang him at ten-thirty, moments before Harper, who had started sleeping late – it was boredom – was preparing to leave his hotel room. Undershaw said he had been out of town, but this was not an apology.

'I've come for the merchandise,' said Harper. He wanted to say, *I've wasted a week hanging around for you to appear*. He said, 'I'd like to pick up the bundle today.'

'Out of the question.'

Harper tried to press him, but gently: the matter was illegal.

Undershaw said, 'These things take time. I won't be able to do much before next week.'

'Monday?'

'I can't be that definite,' said Undershaw. 'I'll leave a message at your hotel.'

No, thought Harper. But he could not protest. He was a courier, no more than that. Undershaw did not owe him any explanation.

Harper had come to the city with one task to perform, and as he had yet to perform it his imagination wouldn't work. He had concentrated his mind on this one thing; thwarted, he could think of nothing else. He was on the hook. His boss had sent him here to hang. Paris seemed very small.

Waiting in Paris reminded Harper of his childhood, which was a jumpy feeling of interminable helplessness. And childhood was another country, too, one governed like this by secretive people who would not explain their schemes to him. He had suspected as a child that there were rules he did not know. In adulthood he learned that there were no particular rules, only arbitrary courtesies. Children were not important, because they had no power and no menace: it took a man twenty-eight years to realize that. You wait; but perhaps it is better, less humiliating, if people don't know you're waiting. Children were ignorant. The strength of adulthood lay in being dignified enough not to expose this impatience. It was worse for women. Now Harper could say to his wife: *I know how you feel*.

The weekend was dreary. Sunday in a Catholic country punished atheists by pushing them into the empty streets. Harper felt unwelcome. He did not know a soul except Bumgarner, who was smug and lucky and probably in bed with his 'mistress' – the poet from Colorado would have used that silly word. Harper lay on his bed alone, studying the repetitions in the patterned wallpaper, and it struck him that it is the loneliest traveler who remembers his hotel wallpaper. He was exhausted by inaction; he wanted to go home.

He had been willing to offer the city everything. There were no takers. He thought: All travelers are like aging women, now homely beauties; the strange land flirts, then jilts and makes a fool of the stranger. There is less risk, at home, in making a jackass of yourself: you know the rules there. The answer is to be ladylike about it and maintain your dignity. But he knew as he thought this that he was denying himself the calculated risks that might bring him romance and a memory to carry away. There was no hell like a stranger's Sunday.

I'll leave a message at your hotel, Undershaw had said. That was a command. So Harper loitered in the hotel on Monday, and when he was assailed by the sense that he was lurking he went out and bought a *Herald-Tribune*; then he felt truant. At five there was no message. He decided to go for a walk, and soon he discovered himself to be walking fast toward Undershaw's office.

'He is not here,' the secretary said. She knew before he opened his mouth what Harper wanted.

To cover his embarrassment, Harper said, 'I knew he wasn't here. I just came to say hello.'

The girl smiled. She began to cram papers and envelopes and keys into her handbag.

'I thought you might want a drink,' said Harper, surprising himself at his invention.

The girl tilted her head and shrugged: it was neither yes nor no. She picked up her coat and switched off the lights as she walked to the door. Still, Harper was not sure what all this meant, until with resignation she said, 'We go.'

At the bar – she chose it; he would never have found it in that alley – she told him her name was Claire.

Harper began describing the emptiness he had felt on Sunday, how the only thing it was possible to do was go to church.

Claire said, 'I do not go to church.'

'At least we've got that in common.'

A man in the bar was reading a newspaper; the headline spoke of an election. Harper mentioned this.

Claire thrust forward her lower lip and said, 'I am an anarchist.' She pronounced the word *anarsheest*.

'Does that mean you don't take sugar?' Harper playfully moved the sugar bowl to one side as she stirred her coffee.

She said, 'You have a ring.' She tapped it with a pretty finger. 'Are you married?'

Harper nodded and made a private vow that he would not deceive his wife.

She said, 'How is it possible to be married?'

'I know,' Harper said. 'You don't know anyone who's happily married. Right? But how many single people are happy?'

'Americans think happiness is so important.'

'What do the French think is important?'

'Money. Clothes. Sex. That is why we are always so sad.'

'Always?'

'We have no humor,' she said, proving it in her solemn tone of voice. 'We are – how do you say – *melancholique*?'

And Harper, who knew almost no French, translated the word. Then he complimented her on her English. Claire said that she had lived for two years in London, with an English family.

He wanted her to drink. She said she only drank wine, and that with meals. He took her to a restaurant – again she chose: a narrow noisy room. Why did they all look like ticket offices? Harper stared at the young men and women in the restaurant. The men had close-cropped hair and earrings, the women were white-faced and smoked cigarettes over their food. Harper said, 'There's something about this place.'

Claire smiled briefly.

'That guy in the corner,' Harper said. 'He's gay.' Claire squinted at Harper. 'A pederast.'

Claire glanced at the man and made a noise of agreement.

Harper smiled. 'A sodomite.'

'No,' she said. 'I am a sodomite. But he is a pederast. *Un pédé*.'

'I knew there was something about this place.' Harper's scalp prickled.

'You seem a bit shocked.'

'Me?' Harper tried to laugh.

'Didn't you do it at school? Playing with the other boys?'

'They would have killed me. I mean, the teachers. Anyway, I didn't want to. What about you?'

She thrust out her lower lip and said, 'Of course.'

'And now?'

'Of course.'

The food came. They ate in silence. Harper could think of nothing to say. She was an anarchist who had just disclosed that she was also a lesbian. And he? A courier with an empty briefcase, killing time. He thought of the poet Bumgarner: Paris belonged to him. Harper could not imagine the feeling, but Bumgarner would know what to say now.

'It is easier for a woman,' said Claire. He guessed that she had perceived his confusion. 'I don't care whether I make love to a man or a woman. Though I have a fiancé – he is a nice boy. It is the personality that matters. I like clever men and stupid women.'

'That guy who was in the office the other day,' Harper said. 'He's a poet. He writes poems.'

Claire said, 'I hate poems.'

It was the most passionate thing she had said so far, but it killed his ardor.

In the twilight, under a pale watery-blue sky, they walked past biscuity buildings to the river. Although this was his eighth day in Paris, Harper's yearning for home had deserted him, and he could ignore his errand, which seemed trivial to him now. He no longer felt humiliated by suspense; and another thing released him: the girl Claire, who was neither pretty nor ugly, seemed indifferent to him. It did not matter whether he slept with her or not – he felt no desire, so there could be no such thing as failure. He enjoyed this perverse freedom, walking along the left bank of the Seine, on a mild spring evening, feeling no thrill, only a complacent lack of urgency. But that was how it was, in spite of Paris; and urgency had been no help the previous week. He did not speak French. The churches and stonecrusts were familiar; he recognized them from free calendars and jigsaw puzzles and the lids of fancy cookie tins.

He had never been overseas before. It was the stage set he had imagined, but he felt unrehearsed.

'I'm tired,' he said, to give Claire an excuse to go home.

She shrugged as she had before, but now the gesture irritated him because she did it so well, using her shoulders and hands and sticking out her lower lip.

'I'm staying at a hotel near Les Invalides,' he said. 'Would you like a drink there?'

She shrugged again. This one meant yes – it was pliable and positive.

By the time they found a taxi rank it was ten-thirty. There was traffic – worse than Boston – and they did not arrive at the hotel until after eleven. The concierge stepped from behind a palm to tell Claire the bar was closed.

Harper said, 'We can drink in my room,' although he had nothing there to drink.

In the room, Harper filled a tumbler with water from the sink. This he brought to Claire and presented it with a waiter's flourish. She drank it without a word.

He said, 'Do you like it?'

'Yes. Very much. It is a pleasant drink.'

'Would you like some more?'

'Not now,' she said.

He sat beside her on the bed, and kissed her with a clownish sweetness, holding her elbows, and she responded innocently, putting her cool nose against his neck. Then she said, 'Wait.'

She untied the drawstring at her waist and shook herself out of her dress. She did this quickly, like someone impatient to swim. When she was naked they kissed again, and he was almost alarmed by the way her tongue insisted in his mouth and her foraging hands pulled clumsily at his clothes. Soon after, they made love, and in the darkness, when it had ended, Harper thought he heard her whimper with dissatisfaction.

He woke. She was across the room, speaking French.

'What is it?'

'I am calling a taxi, to go home.'

'Don't go,' he said. 'Besides, I don't think the phone works.'

'I have to take my pill.'

The phone worked. *I am in Paris:* he said it in a groggy foolish voice.

Claire, who was dressing, said, 'Pardon?'

The next day was a repetition of the previous day. He waited at the hotel for Undershaw to ring. At four, he went to the office. This time there were no preliminaries; only romance required them, and this was no romance. Harper was glad of that, and glad too that he was not particularly attracted to Claire. Since his marriage – and he was happy with his wife – he had not been attracted to any other woman. It did not make him calm; indeed, it worried him, because he knew that if he did fall for another woman it would matter and he would have to leave home. They skipped the bar, ate quickly, then hurried to the hotel and went to bed, hardly speaking.

In the pitch dark of early morning, he waited for her to make her telephone call. But she was asleep. He woke her. She was startled, then seemed to remember where she was. He said, 'Don't you have to go?'

She muttered rapidly in French, then came fully awake and said, 'I brought my pill.'

Harper slept badly; Claire emitted gentle satisfied snores. In the morning she opened her eyes wide and said, 'I had a *cauchemar*.'

'Really?' The word, which he knew, bewitched him.

She said, 'You have a beautiful word in English for *cauchemar*.'

'*Cauchemar* is a beautiful word,' he said, and quoted,

> How much it means that I say this to you –
> Without these friendships – life, what *cauchemar*!

'I don't understand,' she said.

'A poem,' said Harper.

She pretended to shudder. She said, 'What is *cauchemar* in English?'

'Nightmare.'

'So beautiful,' she said.

'What was your *cauchemar* about?'

'My – nightmare' – she smiled, savoring the word – 'it was about us. You and me. We were in a house together, with a cat. It was quite an ordinary cat, but it was very hungry. I wanted to make love with you. That is my trouble, you see. I am too direct. The cat was in our bedroom.'

'Where was this bedroom – Europe?'

'Paris,' she said. 'The cat was so hungry it was sitting on the floor and crying. We couldn't make love until we had fed it. We gave it some food. But when the cat ate the food it caught fire and burned – oh, it was horrible! Each time it swallowed it burned some more. It did not burn like a cat, but like a human, like Jan Palach. You know Jan Palach?'

Harper did not know the name. He said, 'A saint?' – because her tone seemed to describe a martyr.

'No, no, no,' said Claire. She was troubled.

Harper said, 'It's about being a lesbian – your dream. Killing the cat, us making love.'

'Of course,' she said. 'I have thought of that.'

Her troubled look had left her; now she was abstracted, her features stilled by thought.

A fear rose in Harper that he was not in Europe at all, but trapped in a strange place with a sad crazy woman. He had made a great mistake in becoming involved with her. It was worse when they were dressing, for the telephone rang and Harper panicked and screamed, 'Don't touch it!' He imagined that it was his wife, and he felt guilty and ashamed to be in this room with this incomprehensible woman. He had never loved his wife more. He seized the phone: Undershaw.

'It's ready. You can come over.'

'Thank you,' said Harper, tongue-tied with gratitude. He turned to Claire. 'I've got to go to the office.'

But she was buckling her small watch to her wrist. 'Look at the time,' she cried. 'I'm late!'

They arrived separately – it was his idea – so that no one would suspect what they had done. Harper, who had spent days wishing to punch Undershaw in the face, introduced himself to the gray, rather tall Englishman feeling no malice at all. He took the parcel of money and locked himself in a small room to count it. He repeated the procedure, and when he was satisfied the amount was correct he packed the money in neat bundles in the briefcase. And, as if he knew how long it took to count eighty-five thousand dollars, Undershaw knocked at the door just as Harper finished.

'If everything's in order I'll be off then,' said Undershaw.

'Take care,' said Harper, and watched him go.

In the outer office, Claire was filling her handbag. Harper paused, because he believed it was expected of him to ask her out to dinner – he would not be able to leave until the next day.

Claire said, 'I can't see you tonight. I am meeting a woman. I may have an adventure. You can stay – shut the door and it will lock.'

'I hope she's nice,' said Harper. 'Your woman.'

'Yes,' said Claire, ladylike in concentration. She went to the door and stuck out her lower lip. 'She is my fiancé's girl friend.'

When she had left, Harper wanted to sit down. But the chairs disgusted him. There were four of them in this dreadful yellow room, this rallying place for the crooked – they were not evil, but idle. The room had held Bumgarner, and Claire, and Undershaw; and now they had gone on their tired errands. But their snailtracks were still here. There are rooms – his hotel room was one – in which the weak leave their sour hope behind; from which they set out to succeed at small deceptions and fail in the hugest way. Harper wanted to be home. He felt insulted and had never hated himself more. The briefcase, weighted with money, reminded him that he was still in Paris, and that he would have to complete his own shameful errand before he could look for a new job in the United States of America.

Part II

Sinning with Annie

The Prison Diary of Jack Faust

Shortly after I discovered America (the word *defect* suggests error rather than flight to me) it became known that I had in my possession a valuable smuggled manuscript, and I was whisked to New York and interviewed on a number of early-morning and late-night television shows. At some point during every interview I found myself mumbling through my mustache, 'Being a member of the Party was for me like being in prison.' This awkward simile, intended as a slur on a bungling but well-intentioned organization, was misleading; in fact, I spent all my card-carrying years in real prisons of one sort or another. My convictions, moreover, have always been political. More of this later.

Speaking in a glare of arc lights with the snouts of television cameras sniffing my face, and of course exhausted by what the newspapers correctly described as my ordeal, I tend – I think most people do when speaking off the cuff – to simplify. To simplify is to falsify; I am grateful for this opportunity to set the record straight.

I am frankly tired of being badgered by sneering interviewers about the mistress whom I am suspected of having abandoned, the dozen or so children I am supposed to have fathered, and my so-called 'Nazi connections' (I will certainly get to the bottom of this last fabrication and make the inventor pay). Oh, all sorts of lies about my part in the Writers' Union ado over a writer of clearly libelous novels; my mother – rest her soul – has been mentioned as having unkindly informed on my dad; I have been made out to be a perfectly horrible old menace. One interviewer asserted that I received a phone call late one night from our Party Chairman who asked, 'What shall we do about Osip?' My alleged reply to this was a silence resulting in Osip's banishment and death. Rubbish! This fantastic concoction is made all the more crazy when one knows, as I do, that our Party Chairman, a superstitious soul, would never touch a telephone: he thought the mouthpiece of the receiver was a source of deadly germs. Another interviewer had the impertinence to ask, 'Why was it that you were known as the Mephisto of the Twentieth Plenum?' Spurning the assistance of the translator, I shot back quickly, 'Could I help it if I was all things to all men?' smartly putting a stop to *his* nonsense. I am especially sick of these interviewers looking over their clipboards into the camera lens and solemnly prefacing their questions with my full name – something that would only be done in my country in a courtroom or a grade school. Is this intentional ridicule (perhaps my name sounds a bit silly to the American tin ear?) or is it done for the benefit of viewers who have tuned in late and wonder, in their ample distraction, who is the hairy chap on the stool being abused? I know I lost my temper in front of (or so I was told) ten million viewers. There was a simple explanation for that. I had, at that point in the program, reached the conclusion that I was not being interviewed but having my head examined. I have more than compensated the studio for all breakage and all injuries sustained.

On my arrival I graciously consented to the interviews, and now I am terminating them. I have four lawyers working day and night on what I believe are serious breaches of contract; it would be unfair of me to make more work for them by engaging in yet more of these abusive television shows. Editorial innuendo has not escaped my notice either. You are not easy with strangers, you are not above the petty suspicions of your peasant ancestors who left their plows and groped toward these shores as stowaways.

It is not as if I came to this country cap in hand pleading for asylum. Far from it. A narrow-shouldered Italian publisher of Iron Curtain horror stories dogged my heels throughout Europe. He tossed lire my way and, alternately whining and shrugging in the Italianate style, pestered me for a peek at the manuscript I kept photographed on a roll of film in my pocket. Others, French, German and English, each clamored for a hearing. I lunched with each but said no and fled west, leaving in my wake many a crestfallen editor. I am nagged by the thought that my negatives – the ones on my lips, not in my pocket – were a mistake. Both *Stern* and the London Sunday *Observer* offered particularly good terms, and *Paris-Match* dumped lashings of francs beside my plate. My accountant is understandably furious and keeps reminding me that on Jersey, in the Channel Islands, I could be living like a king, whereas here in America I am subjected to your spiteful taxes. But let this pass. The early brouhaha here has, after the expensive legal tangle, neither soothed nor enriched me. The bungalow that was so grandly presented to me after my arrival has a leaky roof and a perpetually flooded cellar; and my television is, as you say, on the fritz. Still, I can't complain.

My concern is the diary. It is to this I now turn.

The manuscript that caused so many powerful Europeans to cluster about me is indeed a rare document and deserves patient study. I am happy to report that my present editor has consented to print it in full and has paid a substantial sum for the American rights. This is especially gratifying for, after getting to know you better, I find that you have really no taste for literature at all. Not like my country, where any garbage collector can sing grand opera or quote you whole cantos of the classics. You make a whole literature out of the sordid and silly nuances of Jewish behavior and, ironically, the writing style you most admire sounds like a direct translation from Perplexed Old Teutonic. You love obvious symbols and popular science. Long sentences annoy you, sentiment embarrasses you; you feel safe with alliteration – you think that is a sign of genius. Your heroes are as unlettered as their creators, your gods are all dogs, you have no appreciation of the simple human story.

The following diary if published in my country would be unacceptable and might land the author in jail. But this is not to say that we are an artless people. Other books have readerships in the millions, they go through forty editions in a matter of weeks and have workers banging through the doors of bookshops at all hours. They are read on factory and farm; the authors are mobbed on the pavement, their names are household words, they get proposals of marriage in the morning mail.

Mind you, the present manuscript is an exception. The author is not heroic; he never did a stroke of work in his life. That he is a simple soul is apparent in every craven line he writes. He is not to be emulated, only studied. His story shows just the sort of quaint dilemma expressed in grumbles that is common to a certain sort of person – though no more common, I repeat, no more common in my country than in yours. Frankly speaking, when I left I was under the impression that this was someone only our system chucked up; but since being warmly welcomed in your very lovely country I have noticed that you get these deluded cranks too. And so take this as a cautionary tale: read it to those unkempt sons of yours who stuporously slope along wearing garish beads around their filthy necks; read it to your daughters who lick at drugs and keep condoms in their handbags, and to those uncles of yours who when their god failed began striking out, cursing us with the sorry wrath of the recently reconverted. And those of you who chaffed me about my 'convenient departure' and 'untrustworthy explanations,' remember that although I am hesitant to use this manuscript as a *visa de voyage*, I am aware that it gained me access to your country, and with it in my pocket I know I am welcome anywhere. You need me much more than I need you.

The pseudonymous author of this diary was known to me from youth. As the poet Drunina puts it so skillfully, 'We were as twinned lambs that did frisk in the sun, / and bleat one at the other: what we changed / Was innocence for innocence . . .' The difference, a large one, was that he made at least one big mistake and possibly more. This is clear in the text. The diary requires very little explanation except the following two points.

Number one, his name was not Jack Faust. Another Slav scurrying westward dropped half the letters from the dozen of his name and in doing so earned a permanent place in English literature (would anyone seriously believe a man called Korzeniowski capable of writing a story called 'Because of the Dollars'?). I have taken that hint and expunged his real name and, on the advice of my present editor, adopted this crisp two-syllable alias. It is intentionally symbolic: a *jack* is used to hoist a heavy object; he is *Jack*, the object a weighty truth he was too simple to grasp wholly. For consistency I will neither name the country nor the prison in which this diary was written. This will not confuse anyone. Western readers are not unfamiliar with this prison, despite its edited anonymity. Our dungeons are as familiar to students of Eastern European political fortunes as our boarded-up synagogues are to anxiously vocal Western Jews who have never set foot in our country (name-calling is easy at that distance!). One has the impression that any regular reader of the current crop of frenzied memoirs by ex-Bolsheviks ('The man of steel took me on his lap and cooed, "My little sparrowchik"') would have no difficulty at all finding his way about in a penal colony in Pskov, though he would probably become irretrievably lost in the rather grand Moscow metro or the modern Warsaw sink works. Even a dispirited and disaffected Party hack like myself is appalled by the general ignorance in the West of my country's achievements: sharp new flats have replaced cheesy peasant cottages, to name but one. Progress is progress; one should not hate the jackboot so much that one fails to notice whether it is down at the heel or making great strides. And simply because I was never given a chance to mention these things on television does not make them untrue.

Number two, what follows is a translation of the photographed manuscript I carried to America at great personal risk and sacrifice. I won't rub it in. No more explanation is in order. I can vouch for the truth of every word that 'Jack Faust' wrote and for the gaumlessness with which he set each down. I can see him licking his pencil lead and scribbling, scribbling.

12 Nov. I have committed no crime, but today I was arrested. My arm is still stiff from being twisted. I cannot write any more now except <u>I am innocent</u>. And this, though my hand pains me, I underline.

13 Nov. My arm still hurts.

14 Nov. Better. It happened in this way. Two burly secret policemen in shiny boots and well-cared-for truncheons beat at my door at five A.M. and told me to get dressed. I offered them buns. They refused saying, 'This is not a social call, Comrade Faust. We are here on Party business.' I asked one to pass me my new felt boots. 'You won't be doing much walking where you're going,' he said, and with that he kicked them out of my reach. As it turns out they would have come in quite handy. It is true I am in a small cell and do not walk much; but my feet are cold and I miss those boots. I hope Madam Zloty found them when she came to tidy up and had the good sense to pass them on to the chauffeur. The dopes will probably sell them, in which case I have the feeling the boots will eventually end up here: there seems to be quite a bit of black marketeering in this prison. Last night a voice whispered through the high window, 'Cigarettes, chewing gum, razor blades.' A small boy's voice, but I thought of Marushka with her little tray and her pathetic bunny costume and how she was so grateful when I befriended her. I mocked her crucifix and taught her to love the Party. If only she could see what the Party has done to me! And yet . . . and yet I find it hard to believe that the committee knows of this. Surely this is a trick. They are testing me. I make no observation except the following: it is said that the Marquis de Sade wrote *Justine* in prison on a roll of toilet paper. This strikes me as incredible. Mine is already coming to bits under the flint of my stubby pencil, and I am hardly past square one.

15 Nov. The warder's name has a familiar ring. 'Comrade Goldpork doesn't allow reading in this prison,' the guard said when he saw me looking over some scraps of newspaper I found in the ticking of my mattress. 'Goldpork, Goldpork,' I murmured, shredding the newspaper, 'I know that name.' I believe we were in the Youth Wing together. He used to slouch horribly, a poor specimen of a Youth Winger. How I remember him being shouted at by the Platoon Commander! 'Pig! Dog! Twist of dogshit!' the PC called at him. Goldpork stiffened under this abuse. Of course he could make no reply. A Youth Winger simply does not slouch. He stands straight as a ramrod; he snaps his salutes; he keeps his knickers in good order; he assiduously oils his truncheon. He coldly reports the activities of his grasping parents and notes how many pounds of lard have been hoarded by his mother. The Youth Wing is the backbone of the Party. Goldpork slouched and so was given the job of looking after this shabby penitentiary while I was composing rather hush-hush memoranda for B. And Goldpork doesn't allow reading! I wonder if he himself can read? The guard gave the order so stupidly (Can he know who I am?) I am not surprised Goldpork never got further than this prison. If I had my way he would be scrubbing the toilets – that is, all the toilets except the one in which I scribble this!

17 Nov. Just to while away the time I have spent the past day and a half itemizing a clean-up and renovation memorandum. I haven't lost my touch.

Memo to Goldpork

(a) As this is not a fish tank surely moss and fungus are not needed to keep the inmates well and happy. Scrape those tiles and make them shine.

(b) In my day, guards clicked their heels and polished their boots; the fact that guards are seen by no one but detainees should not excuse sloppy habits. Look smart.

(c) Note that chamberpots are designed for easy emptying. It is axiomatic that the full chamberpot overflows.

(d) There is an accumulation of rust on every iron bar in this prison. Prisoners should be made to feel that this is *their* prison as much as it is every citizen's. A sense of pride and purpose is wanted; a rust-scrubbing session with wire brushes would do wonders for morale. Let's buckle down.

(e) We have noted a preponderance of nightly comings and goings of small boys in frocks. This seems a questionable way of passing an evening. Must moral fiber necessarily break down because a man is behind bars? Work, cold showers, an honest fatigue: such things build the Party.

(f) We would like to see more prunes on the menu.

(g) If reading is not allowed, surely the ticking of all prison mattresses should be winnowed for bits of newspaper. This is a sensible measure: any of these newspapers may have reports of past events which have since proved to be malicious fabrications. We know many news items have been planted by foreign spies. Here, it is possible they will fall into the wrong hands. Sift, winnow, purge; get straw in those mattresses.

(h) Laughter. Why in the world are prisoners allowed to laugh and shriek? A more somber note could be struck if each laugh were awarded five of the best. Experience has shown a yard of bamboo to be most useful for this.

(i) The bindery is a shambles, a positive disgrace. We would like to see those glue pots kept in better order.

(j) The inspections are a joke.

The above are noted in a spirit of cooperation, with the following in mind: a good prison is a clean one; no one will accuse the warder of being soft because he wants to run 'a tight ship.' Skimping will not do. The habits of youth are carried into middle age; there is a definite slouch about this place.

(signed) *J. Faust*

23 *Nov.* Have decided not to send the above to Goldpork as he may take it amiss and think I am trying to tell him how to do his job. I could send him memos until I was blue in the face and he would not pay any attention to me. When I am out of here he will have a lot of questions to answer. I shall keep my memo safe. I have submitted my request to see the minister of internal affairs when he makes his tour of this prison. I'll give him an earful!

24 Nov. Why didn't I think of this before? The guard's words were, 'No books, no papers, no pencils, no writing tablets.' In my haste a few days ago I wrote something about Goldpork 'not allowing reading' – probably for brevity's sake. I should have remembered the order. It was almost certainly Minute 345/67ZB in the Prisons Ordinance, Appendix D. I wrote that myself after we caught that Jew with his volume of reminiscences stuffed in his phylactery. And here I am giving Goldpork all the credit for it.

(*later*) The reason it all comes back to me is the typist. We worked late at the ministry that evening finishing up odds and ends of Party business. I was a stickler for detail, I wanted those minutes letter-perfect. I saw her slowing down, mumbling and erasing.

'Dinner?' I said, looking up from a foolscap file.

She turned away from her heavy black Yalor Office Console and flexed her fingers.

I snapped open my briefcase and handed her a sausage, a bit of bread, a cold potato. Gratefully she took them and, munching them, told me something about herself. I don't remember a word she said, but I recall thinking, 'Yes, with a girl like that we have succeeded. Strong as a mule. Her tits are like turnips. She types a good rate and works like a dog. In the West she would be a frump at twenty.'

Nor was typing her only talent.

I begin to understand these handsome little striplings mincing through the night corridors of this dungeon.

27 Nov. Cement did very well, ten editions in a year. And *Logs* was to do even better. Those two secret policemen interrupted me halfway through *Spindles*. I wonder if they destroyed the fragment of manuscript I kept on my writing table? No, I don't wonder at all. They did, of course they did. To do otherwise would have been a flagrant disregard of their orders. They had a duty to perform. Is it bourgeois of me to hope that before those pages were incinerated some soul read them and had doubts about my guilt?

30 Nov. Find this notebook, Goldpork! Here is one manuscript you won't unearth. I write nearly every day, squatting on this bucket in your unclean stall. You would never think to look here! You have not discovered me, and until you reform this prison you never shall! I am noting this under your very nose! Pig! Dog!

2 Dec. The minister's visit was brusquely announced for the first of December. I handed in my chit and said that I would like a word with him in private. 'I know my rights,' I said. I walked on eggshells all day, with the crumpled squares of the Memo to Goldpork tucked into the elastic of my underpants. No minister. I waited all day today. No minister.

3 Dec. No minister.

4 Dec. No minister.

5 Dec. No minister.

6 Dec. What this country needs is a good solid overhaul by some merciless but farsighted Party man. When a minister announces a visit he has made a promise; this promise must be kept. The Memo to Goldpork of 17 Nov. is all but deteriorated in my underpants. I shall recopy it while waiting for the minister. I am not surprised Goldpork kept his job for so long. He would not last a minute in my charge.

7 Dec. No minister. I shall put the memo squares with the rest of this little diary. That minister is asking for a sacking.

8 Dec. 'It was like battling with a pillow. Squeezed at one end it bulged at the other . . .' (*Cement*, Ch. 10). I was writing of the landlords and moneylenders and the bullies in the ballroom. I could have been writing of my present difficulties.

Item: Enemies

(1) Goldpork
(2) The minister of internal affairs
(3) Fatso, G's toad
(4) The little chap who visited me several nights ago and played hard to get

9 Dec. The film version of *Logs* was praised and won a coveted medal. It opened with a panorama of a great banqueting hall. Fat men slobbering over pigs' trotters, ladies yelling, young men reaching into the bosoms of dowagers, dogs lapping up scraps. The camera moved to the cellar of the house: bearded old men reclining in coal piles, little boys whimpering. Back to the banqueting hall: fat men begin to dance with one another. Jigs and reels. 'Spin the floor!' cries one man (close shot of hairy face, hog jowls, food-flecked fangs). He stamps on the floor with his big boots. Cut below to cellar: old men and young boys putting on harnesses; they begin to tug and yank, little cattle on a threshing floor. Above, the people dance, the floor revolves gently; music plays. Fat men clutch their partners' bums. 'Faster! Faster!' they call; they stamp. Below, the proletariat get the message. They summon all their strength; they run on their harnesses: they are literally dancing. The old men become young, the young men strong. Above, the floor is spinning, revolving crazily, much too fast. The first fat man falls, then another. A dowager sprawls and spills her pearls. Skirts fly. The dancers are spun from the revolving floor by centrifugal force; some are knocked cold. Below, the workers strip off their harnesses and sing. A small boy makes a fist and raises his arm. Last shot: this dirty little fist.

I used to know what all this represented. I am not so sure now.

10 Dec. Clearly, the inner Party has gone soft. My analogy is the potato raked out of the coals too soon. Break open that crusty jacket, dig your fork into the soft mealy white . . . but *wait*! Grasp the potato with two hands and pinch it open: a cold hard center will be revealed. Burned on the outside, but cold and uncooked at the center . . . and that indigestible lump is enough to ruin the whole meal.

In our discussions, particularly at the Twentieth Plenum, we decided on and minuted the reverse of this. It was, so to say, the center of the potato we were certain was nourishing; we were not so sure of the rest.

Problem: Identify the potato's components, the fire, the tongs.

Who eats this potato?

There are rumors flying about. They say the minister has come and gone. But how could he? He hasn't seen me. He is fiddling his mileage claim, there is no doubt of that.

Ask yourself, Comrade Minister, which Party member penned the second Five-Year Plan? Yes, I wear manacles, but none of my chains weighs as heavily as this ingratitude.

11 Dec. Are there compensations here? Yes, I confess there are. Today, during our ten-minute fresh-air stroll we clanked as usual in a circle, reminding me of the painting by that insane Dutchman of a prison scene – blue convicts in a blue exercise yard – a painting, let me record, hanging in the Pushkin Museum in Moscow (who said the Russians are an insensitive people?). And one, then another and another of my fellow prisoners whispered hoarsely, 'That's him! There he is!' This continued ('That's *him!*') until the guard knocked one of the whisperers to the ground and told him to pipe down. But they continued to look at me with their gray faces. Several lifted their chains at me and shook them. It's nice to be recognized in a crowd.

14 Dec. At night now they scream my name.

15 Dec. They're still doing it. It gives me quite a lift.

16 Dec. Today I was set upon by six inmates and beaten. It was just after breakfast while we were emptying our chamberpots into the swill vat. The guards stand as far away as possible (the stink is overpowering) and these six, seeing their chance, gagged me with a mitten and knocked me insensible. I was not found until half-past ten. I was given broth and told to report to Goldpork. He recognized me immediately.

'Comrade Faust, we meet again.'

'Under less happy circumstances than before, Goldpork, I don't have to remind you.'

'Sit down, I want to have a word with you. What's this I hear about the stir you're causing in your cell-block?'

'They scream my name. I liked it at first, but today they beat me. They dug their fingers into my eyes and plucked at my neck and cheeks. I hated it.'

'And what do you conclude from this little affair?'

'Simple. They belong here. I don't. You know, Goldpork, we built this prison for them, not for ourselves. It is they who should be munching on scraps and wiping the rims of their soiled chamberpots . . . not me. If only I had known!'

'You didn't deserve to be beaten, then? Don't you see that these men are relatives of all the people you liquidated?'

'I have one regret. I should have searched the houses more carefully. I might have turned up one or two of these oafs in cupboards and liquidated them as well.'

'And so you're trying to tell me you are a faithful Party member still?'

'I have committed no crime. I am not one of these comrades who runs shrieking into the arms of a Western publisher as soon as I am wronged, though I know I could live quite a nice little life if I did that. But I am not one of your backsliders. I was put in here, and here I will stay until the Party feels I have been punished enough. When I am set free I will work as always, with fervor.'

'It's pleasant to hear that, Comrade Faust. You bear us no ill will?'

'None at all.'

But I had. Though I only realized it after I went back to my cell and reread all the entries in this diary. I was dreadfully afraid. I held these scraps of paper up to the light and, as my name boomed through the corridors, I read with a sinking heart. I begin by saying I am innocent. I go on to complain about Goldpork and itemize ten objections to this prison. I slander the minister and the guard. I indulge in bourgeois nostalgia about my tenth-rate film. And as if this is not enough six days ago I describe the Inner Party as a lump of underdone potato.

Furthermore, and much worse, I withheld all of this from Goldpork. I tried to pass myself off as a good Party member. But what is a good Party member doing in prison? I had said when I pocketed my Party card that I would serve. I am doing nothing of the sort. I am a complainer, like the chap on the commune who won't dig sugar beets because his mattock is bent. I should have told Goldpork exactly where I stood. If I were honest I would hand over this diary. What earthly good is it? It represents nothing. Who would bother to read it except one of our magistrates or those Western publishers? It is an indulgence. I will write no more today.

17 Dec. Spent the whole day poking through my mattress looking for reactionary newspaper clippings to read. Found nothing. Knock on door. Fatso. Asked what pile of straw and oakum on floor might be. Told him to his face.

Note: Delete (g), (h) and (j) from Memo to Goldpork. These have apparently been remedied while I was busy with this diary. They know what they are doing. This is further evidence that I am a scab. It was no trick. My guilt shows in every square I fill. After this knowledge, what forgiveness?

24 Dec. There is some satisfaction, when in prison, in knowing that one is guilty. The time passes quickly, one stops talking to oneself, one bears no grudges. I look forward to seeing Goldpork again and telling him everything, perhaps producing this diary from my shirtfront and letting it spill over his desk. They were right all along. My imagined innocence weighed on me and made me lax; but, guilty, I have a place – I belong. I see the logic of their decision to thump on my door with truncheons and drag me bootless from my flat. Today I sat and mused, humming a tune I once heard with Marushka when we secretly listened – as we did countless times! – to the broadcast of a foreign power. I am not Party material, and it is clear that Goldpork is. I shall see him tomorrow and cheerfully convey my guilt by wishing him a Merry Christmas.

Those were the last words Jack Faust was to write. He handed over his diary and freely confessed to all his crimes. They were mostly imaginary ones, but they contained such a wild note of threat that he was hanged before the new year. He was not mourned. I know this is true. My reward for extracting his confession from him – I did little more than listen to him and nod to the steno – was a very agreeable posting in Rome, attached to our Embassy; my job was to round up people who had fled the country and were seeking asylum in Italy. I got to know the ins and outs of fleeing, and I was helped in my searches by Marushka, whose full name and address I had found scratched on the wall of Jack's cell. In our six months in Rome we drugged many an escapee and posted each back to the capital in a mailbag. Only Marushka could have been expected to mourn Jack Faust, yet when I asked her she denied all knowledge of him. I could only smile.

And smiling one night I said I was stepping out for a breath of fresh air. I did so and never returned. The morning I left Italy (this was in Milan) I thought I saw Marushka whiz past me, straddling the back of a Vespa and clutching the Italian driver with one hand and what I believe was the manuscript of Jack's unfinished novel (*Spindles*) with the other. But I may be wrong; many Italian girls had Marushka's knees, and all girls jounce the same on a scooter: I love to see their rolling bottoms and hear the seat springs oink! In any case, Marushka is doing all right for herself. I am pretty sure she pinched *Spindles* from Jack's flat; I know I never discovered what happened to it. The police were no help. I have a feeling that one of these days I'm going to see it in translation on the revolving paperback bookstand at my corner drugstore.

During our last conversation Jack had a moment of panic. He saw the toilet roll of his whole incriminating diary spread out on my desk and said, 'Wait, Goldpork, I'll make a deal with you!' I flapped my hand and brushed aside the terms he was stammering at me. I said, 'But don't you see you've already made one?' Then the guards appeared and led him away. I had not finished speaking. I wanted to say that we all make deals. It is a pity he did not live long enough to see that mine at least had a reasonably happy ending.

A Real Russian Ikon

Fred Hagberg, forewarned by his travel agent in Cleveland of the Russian hunger for hard cash, had been in Moscow for two days and there had not been even a glimmer of interest in his dollars. The plastic cover of his American Express wallet stayed buttoned; Intourist paid all the bills. He expected to be guided to seedy black-market shops off the beaten track or, at the very least, pestered for cigarettes and Chiclets. There wasn't a peep from the Muscovites, and Fred thought maybe his travel agent meant somewhere else.

On the evening of the third day he was ambling along Karl Marx Prospekt, where it runs into Manège Square, returning from the Palace of Congresses where he had seen Verdi hysterically acted and shrieked to an audience of cows. The Mob of Shuffling Humanity, he called them, as they slushed along the sidewalk in felt boots, oblivious of everything, ignoring everything, tramping nowhere into the night. Fred hated their guts. He had just turned away from the revolting sight of two Russians eating (eating! on the sidewalk! at night!) when it happened.

There was a voice, the thickened tongue lap of the impossible language, audible but disembodied. Fred looked down. A small boy in a blue Bolshevik beanie, hands crammed into the pockets of a capelike coat, lurched alongside him. The boy was looking away, looking around in the direction of a slapping banner which, secured by cables, was being driven against the trolley wires by the wind and making sparks.

'Cherman?'

The boy turned from the slapping banner to the Obelisk to Revolutionary Thinkers, peered at the spikes and spoke again.

'Enklis?'

'American,' said Fred.

'Unidestates?'

Fred nodded and blew on his hands. He saw that the boy was still avoiding his gaze, looking distractedly elsewhere, slouching along the salt-gritty sidewalk, the perfection of KGB aplomb, furt-ive but at the same time very cool.

The next exchange took Fred a while to understand, for each time the boy spoke he looked away. The boy apparently wanted chewing gum: Fred had none. The boy wanted a ballpoint pen (he called it a 'pallboint'): Fred said yes. He fingered his Parker Jotter. The boy turned sharply right and headed toward a newspaper kiosk, closed up for the night. Fred followed.

In the glare of the sputtering arc lamp high above, Fred saw in the boy's palm a small enamel pin stamped with the gold head of Lenin and the dates *1917–1967*. 'Nice medal, good, best,' said the little boy. 'For the pen.'

'Deal,' said Fred, offering it.

The boy took a deep breath, rolled his eyes up, prodded the Parker up his sleeve and, turning away, deftly passed the little pin to Fred. The blue beanie disappeared into the darkness at the steps that led to 25th Oktober Street, behind the Ploshchad Revolutsii Metro entrance.

Back at the Metropole Hotel, in a room heated to a skin-crinkling eighty, Fred flicked on the fake chandelier and examined the pin. He knew, with that certainty that comes quickly to travelers, that he had been swindled. He ground it into the squares of shrunken parquet with his heel, and then spat.

Over a breakfast of syrupy coffee and flaking pastry Fred collected his thoughts. He had not, he decided, lost completely: a deal had been made. Only shrewdness had been missing, and that on his part. He had been too eager. Furthermore he had been dealing with a kid. But several things stood out in the incident, and these were important: the Russians made deals, they talked to foreigners, and they were cagey. Pondering these Russian qualities Fred missed the English Speakers' tour of the city. There was only one thing left, something Fred had counted on seeing: the graveyard of the Novod-evichy Convent, where Svetlana's mother was buried. She was the lady, mentioned in the *Twenty Letters*, to whom Stalin had called, 'Hey you!' and who, miffed, had gone upstairs and shot herself.

The taxi stand was at Sverdlovsky Square, near the Bolshoi Theater. A long line of people, laden with fishnet shopping bags (some showing withered fruit), stood morosely in mangy fur hats

and ankle-length overcoats. Their noses glowed red, redder than
the flags on the light poles or the banners on the Bolshoi which
praised the Komsomol for fifty years of tireless devotion.

Fred fumbled for a cigarette with cold hands. He picked open
the crushed pack of Luckies and withdrew a bent one. Smoothing
it slowly, he felt subtle pressure on his sides, two warm bears, then
a voice, a steamy word.

'Enklis?'

'United States,' said Fred, squirming, feeling for his wallet of
traveler's checks. He smelled pickpockets.

'Amerikansk?'

'Yeah,' said Fred, looking up into a raw knobby face.

'Toureest?'

'Mm.'

Without moving a muscle Fred felt himself turning in the taxi
line, revolving on an axis like a slow-motion soldier. Again, without
any effort on his part, he was borne by the pressure of the two bears
to the near sidewalk where the giant seated figure of Ostrovsky in
bronze brooded over a bird-limed manuscript.

Shortly, they were in a tearoom, the Uyut (Cozy) on Leninsky
Prospekt, exchanging names. The bears were Igor and Nikolai and,
by way of introduction, said they liked Willis Conover, someone
Fred had never heard of, though Igor insisted he was a great American. Other names were dropped – Jim Reeves, the Beatles, Dave
Brubeck, Jack London, President Kennedy – and then they got
down to business.

'Dollars?'

'You mean, do I have dollars?'

'To have dollars,' said Nikolai.

'Sure, I've got everything. I'm going around the world on the
Pan Am flight. Pan American. You know what I mean?'

'American dollars. Very nice,' said Igor. 'You want rubles?'

'I want an ikon,' said Fred. And added, 'For my mother.'

Neither Russian understood.

'Ikon, ikon, ikon.'

Nikolai mumbled to Igor, whose face brightened. 'You want
eekone?'

Fred nodded. It seemed useless to speak.

'Eekone,' said Nikolai. He giggled.

'We find eekone, you pay dollars us,' said Igor. 'To want rubles.'

'It's got to be a good one. A *good one*.'

'Don't whorry.'

They were in a battered taxi, Fred in the back seat with Nikolai, the silent one. Igor, taller, more garrulous, sat in front with the driver, giving instructions. Down the wide avenues they sped, jockeying through the traffic, the little taxi slipping between a Zyl and a Zym, two tanklike cars resembling old Packards, complete with chrome jaws. They drew up to a shop that looked like a pawnbroker's, where Igor fought to the front of a mob of people around a counter and shouted the familiar word. A shopgirl folded her arms across her smock and shook her head.

At another similar place a shopgirl pointed to an inferior painting on the wall depicting a muscular bleeding Christ. Igor looked questioningly at Fred. Fred said, '*Nyet*.'

The taxi driver seemed to take an interest in the search. He muttered to Igor; Igor muttered back; Nikolai emitted a cluck, sucking at his front teeth, the sound that in most of Europe means yes. They were off again, and from the way the Russians settled back in their seats it looked as if it was going to be a long ride. They passed under the red banners which Fred drew their attention to. When they saw that Fred was interested they read each one – quite a feat, since there were three to a block and the taxi was going fast.

'Great Russian People,' said Igor, pointing. 'Good Komsomol Fifty Year . . . Hail Russian Worker.' He interspersed the banners with sales talk as well: 'Work Hard . . . Dollars very nice . . . Build State . . . Cash or check? . . . Remember Comrade Lenin . . . We find real Russian eekone . . . Crush Imperialism . . .'

They rode for several miles more, into a dingy suburb squeezed with old one-story houses. The eaves of these houses were carved, but all were in disrepair. The taxi parked on the sidewalk. The driver got out, shouted something to Igor, and then disappeared through a gray wooden door. Fred made a move to get up, but Igor waved him back.

'Nice scarf,' Igor finally said.

'This one?' Fred fingered his scarf.

'Sell?'

'I need it. It's cold here.'

'Ten rubles, fifty kopeks.'

'I want an ikon, an ikon! I *need* this scarf. It's cold –'

Igor stirred. The driver was giving a signal from the doorway of the ramshackle house. 'We go,' said Igor.

Fred was allowed to go in first. On entering, he did not notice the old lady, but when his eyes grew accustomed to the darkness he saw her – small, pale, standing fretfully among draped furniture, her white hair appearing in several tendrils from under her shawl. Her facial skin was loose and wrinkled, as if she had once been fat, the skin stretched and retaining its former size. Her eyebrows were heavy, her hands were large, she wore three sweaters and appeared much afraid.

Igor addressed the old lady. In the conversation that went on Fred heard the word *Amerikansk* again. The second time he heard it he smiled at the old lady, who looked incredulous for a moment, then stepped closer to Fred and smiled. It was an open, trusting smile which revealed her small fine teeth and creased her whole face like an old apple. She spoke to Fred in Russian.

'She asking you to want tea. She have her brother in America.'

'Look, I didn't come here for tea,' said Fred. The old lady implored him with an odd grace. 'Okay, I'll have a cup of tea.'

A smoking, steaming samovar was brought. It was brass and, even in that dingy room stuffed with junk, gleamed like a church fixture. A small valve at the top popped open, shooting jets of steam into the chill air. The old lady placed a teapot under the spigot and twisted the key: hot water bubbled out. There were no wires anywhere.

Fred smacked his lips. 'That's some contraption!'

'You like?' It was Igor, smiling like a cat and rubbing his hands. 'How much?'

The smile left Igor's face. He turned to the old lady who, when Igor spoke, shut the hot water off and looked quickly at Fred. She showed her large gnarled hands, shrugged and said several words.

'No sell, she say.'

'I'll give her fifty dollars.' Fred began flashing fingers at the old lady, two hands at a time, ten, twenty, thirty . . .

'*Karasho*,' said Igor impatiently, 'Okay, okay.' He spoke again, his voice rising, his eyeballs rolling. The old lady muttered another reply and drew her shawl tighter.

'She want. For tea. No sell.'

'Oh, for God's sake,' said Fred. 'Listen, for fifty bucks she can buy *two* of them, electric ones, any kind she wants. Doesn't she want a nice electric one?'

Nikolai said nothing. He simply snatched up a candle and wagged it in Fred's face, giving Fred a crazy grin that said, 'No electricity – isn't it awful?'

'Okay, forget it.'

But he wanted his trophy. The faint stamp in his passport CCCP, MOCKBA and a date was not enough. Something substantial was needed, like the *bierstein*, the rosary, the blue Wedgwood pot. And even if he could not be the traveler who brought home a demure full-breasted peasant girl, he would have his modest souvenir. If not, what was the sense in coming so far? And to Russia, no less.

In silence, the tea was drunk. Fred finished his first. He placed his chipped cup on the floor and said, 'What about the ikon? I haven't got all day.'

'Eekone, yes.'

The three Russian men gathered around the old lady. Igor did all the talking, pointing to Fred and, once, asking the taxi driver's opinion. While he spoke Fred saw a vivid moment in his mind, a very familiar one: he was back in Cleveland with his pals and they were making a deal. The faces were eager, joshing American ones, reddish, large nosed, rough. The Russians even had crew cuts, the same thick ears and deep wrinkles. They were grinning and pushy-looking in a Midwestern way. They even seemed to be yakking in English!

The sight of the worn carpet, the sheets over the furniture, the coldness of the room, brought Fred back to reality. He was halfway around the world from Cleveland, in enemy territory. He reminded himself to be careful.

The discussion was still going on, the old lady appearing not to understand. She asked many questions and got many shrugs, many gestures, many little sharp cries of admonishment as replies. Then the old lady rose very reluctantly, with sighs, and beckoned Fred into a little room at the side. The room was damp and even darker than the outer parlor. It was hung with heavy tapestries which, when the old lady lit a candle, appeared to be delicately embroidered. The room had the eerie glow of a chapel; in fact, the candle was in a red glass chimney on a gold-wrought stand. It was a vigil light and could have come from a very large church.

Warming the wax, the candle flared up. Above it gleamed the

ikon, a painting the size of an airline calendar, Mary and child with tiny carefully made faces and thin hands. Each head wore a coronet of little sparkling gems; in places there were pocks where gems had been. And Fred noticed that the paint had cracked, the boards had warped, the cloth around the frame had frayed. Still, it was beautiful. The candle flame grew higher, picking out tiny cherubs with trumpets, lilies, roses and fishes, scrolls and, at the top of the ikon, a wordy motto in elongated characters like gold washing hung on a line.

'Boy,' said Fred.

'You like?' asked Igor. To Nikolai he said, 'He like.'

Nikolai grunted.

'Is good,' said Igor, turning to Fred. 'Is nice Russian eekone.'

'How much?' asked Fred.

'Is good eekone,' Igor replied. 'Not much. Three hundred.'

'Rubles?'

'Dollars.'

'Two fifty,' said Fred.

'Okay. Two fifty.'

Fred cursed himself for not saying two hundred. 'Traveler's checks?'

'Is better dollars cash.'

'I don't carry that kind of money around in cash,' said Fred obstinately. 'So it's traveler's checks or nothing. You understand? *Traveler's checks!*'

Ignor winced. Fred realized he had shouted in the little chapel; he apologized. The apology seemed to bewilder them more than the offense.

'Ask her if it's okay.'

Igor sidled up to the old lady and spoke, flicking his finger at the ikon. At Igor's words the old lady drew away, her back to the little altar, as if protecting it. She clapped her hands to her mouth, stifling a shriek; then, petrified, she wagged her head rigidly from side to side.

'No sell,' said Igor, inexplicably grinning.

'No sell,' mumbled Fred. 'Did you tell her the price?'

'Now I tell.' Igor shot fingers into the old lady's face and, at the same time, brayed numbers.

The old lady lowered her eyes and shook her head in a gentle negative.

Fred understood. 'Not enough, eh? Fine, how much does she want for it?'

The old lady glanced up at Fred and spoke quickly. Her head dropped once more.

Grinning in the manner of Igor, Nikolai blessed himself with the sign of the cross, finishing by kissing his bitten finger tips.

'She wants. For pray,' said Igor.

'What?'

Igor blessed himself as Nikolai had done, but Igor did it with his left hand and cast his eyes up to the ikon. Fred looked at the taxi driver. He smiled sheepishly and did the same.

'What! Are you *kidding* me? Listen, you people don't pray – it's against the law, for God's sake. Listen . . .' Fred knew he was talking too fast for the Russians. He tried in broken English: 'Communist no like church. Huh? Church very bad. Praying bad. Priests bad. No pray in Soviet Union. Huh?' His patience was exhausted. He went on angrily, 'So what the hell is this old lady talking about, will you just tell me that?'

Igor got the point. He leered. 'Komsomol no like this.' He clapped his hands prayerfully under his chin and attempted an appearance of devotion.

'Right. Tell *her* that,' Fred said coldly.

Igor began to speak, but was interrupted by Fred again. 'And tell her,' Fred went on, 'that she'll get into trouble if she keeps on praying, because it's against the law. And you know what *that* means! Siberia, right? Right. Go ahead, tell her.'

'Is good idea,' said Igor. He tapped the side of his head and puckered his mouth appreciatively, as if to say, 'Good thinking.' And then he spoke to the old lady. He had not said ten words when the old lady looked fearfully at Fred and sucked in her breath. She seemed trapped, as if the floor of the fragile chapel was about to give way and drop her onto a rock pile. She started to protest, but broke off in the middle of a word and wept. She averted her eyes from the four men in the room; she stared at the frayed carpet and, taking the knotted end of her shawl into her mouth, bit it, the way a person being tortured tries to endure pain. She moaned.

'Tell her to cut that out!' said Fred. She seemed to be doing it on account of him, pretending it was all his fault. He began to hate the old lady for making him feel that way. 'All right,' Fred finally said, 'no deal. The deal's off. I don't want it! Will you tell her to cut it out!'

Fred was now shouting louder than the old lady was crying. It had a chastening effect on her; her sobbing died to a sniffle.

Igor spoke and, as he did, the old lady continued to sniff. 'She wants sell eekone very much.' He winked. 'Two hundred fifty dollars, American.'

'But I thought you said –'

'Wants sell to you,' Igor said. He stood near Nikolai and the taxi driver. Their faces were triumphantly rosy.

'Doesn't she want it for praying?'

Igor translated with evident malice.

The old lady looked at Fred with red eyes full of pleading fear, more fear than she had shown toward the three Russians. Her voice was small, her face puffy with grief, her unusually large arthritic-knuckled hands clenched tightly over her knees.

'She no pray. She say to me, *No pray, comrade*!'

In the men's toilet of the Uyut tearoom Fred coated his hands with slimy Soviet soap and scalded them in the sink while a customer kecked into the commode. At last the customer left. Fred and Igor made the final transaction. Fred passed the traveler's checks wadded in brutally heavy toilet paper to Igor who reached under the gap in the wall of an adjoining water closet.

Outside, at their table, the deal complete, they touched teacups.

'Chin-chin,' said Igor.

'Wait a minute, wait a minute, wait a minute,' said Fred, feeling oddly abandoned and fearful. 'What am I going to tell them at the customs desk at the airport? They're going to ask me where I got this thing.' The bundle lay beside Fred's chair, innocuous-looking in *Pravda* and old twine. Fred pointed cautiously, then cupped his hands to his mouth and whispered, 'I'll get into trouble. They'll know I changed my money illegally.' Fred looked to Igor for reassurance. 'I don't want any trouble.'

'No trouble,' said Igor.

'*What do you mean* –'

Igor hushed him; people at other tables had turned to watch the man shouting in English.

'What,' said Fred with pained hoarseness, 'do you mean, no trouble? They're looking for people who've changed their money on the black market. I'm an American, for God's sake, *an American*! They'll lock me up. I know they will.' Fred was inconsolable. He sighed. 'I *knew* this whole thing was a mistake.'

Igor chuckled. 'No trouble. Tell police this eekone present.'

'Sure, a present. You're a great help.'

'Present, yes,' Igor said calmly. 'Find young policeman. Young man. Tell him, heh, you fack Russian gorl. She say, heh, yes, very good, thank you. Gorl give you eekone as present for fack. Easy.'

'Oh, my God.'

'Don't whorry.' Igor winked. 'We go.' He took Nikolai by the arm and departed, leaving Fred to pay the bill.

Fred was upset. Walking back to the Metropole he decided to throw the ikon away and forget the whole business. The decision calmed him, but he grew tense when he realized there was nowhere to throw the ikon. The alleys were bare; there was not a scrap of rubbish or even a trash can on any of the streets. The gutters were being scrubbed by old women in shawls with big brushes. The bundle would be noticed as a novelty (no one threw anything away in Moscow) and would attract attention.

It was all the more worrying for Fred when the elevator operator, a sullen, wet-lipped man in a faded braided uniform, gave the bundle cradled in Fred's arm a very queer look. Fred shoved it under his bed, downed three neat vodkas and went to the Bolshoi to see *The Tsar's Bride*. He had been cheated on the tickets: he sat behind a post in the sixty-kopek heights, in the darkness, shredding his program with anxious hands.

That night he could not sleep. The haggard face of the old lady appeared in his room. She accused him of stealing her valuable ikon. A Russian policeman with a face like raw mutton tore Fred's passport in half and twisted his arm. Igor, in a chair under a bright light, confessed everything. Nikolai wept piteously and pointed an accusing finger at Fred. Toward dawn Fred lapsed into feverish sleep. He awoke with a vow on his lips.

It was not easy for him to find the old lady's house. The banners were some help in figuring the general direction, but it was not until a day and a half after the visit with Igor and Nikolai – one day before he was due to leave for Tokyo – that he found the right street.

He rapped hard at the gray door, so hard he skinned some leather from his glove knuckles. He soon saw why there was no answer: a heavy padlock clinked in a hasp at the bottom of the door. Turning, Fred was brought up short by a figure on the sidewalk, standing with his hands in his pockets, eyeing him closely.

'Do you speak English?'

'If you zpeak zlowly.'

'Where is the old lady?'

'Not here,' said the man. At that moment a chauffered Zyl drew up to the curb. 'You are friend?'

'In a way. See, a couple of days ago –'

'Come,' said the man darkly.

They drove through narrow streets, then out to the wide Sadov-aya that rings Moscow, and across the canal to more narrow gray streets, in the bare district of black stumps and boarded-up houses near the Church of the Assumption in Gonchary. They passed the church and continued for about half a mile over frost heaves in the empty street.

'Where are we?'

'Gvozdev,' said the man, and he gave the driver a direction.

The car pulled in through a low gate cut in a thick stone wall. At the far end of a scrubby courtyard was a sooty brick building, the shape of Monticello on the back of the nickel, a domed roof but with one difference: this one had a chimney at the rear belching greasy smoke. It was too squat, too plain, too gloomy for a church. Fred pulled the ikon out of the car and followed the man into the building.

The front entrance – there were no doors – opened onto a vast, high-ceilinged room, empty of furniture. The walls were covered with small brown photographs of men and women, framed in silver and set into the cement, not hung. The cold wind whistling through the front entrance blew soot and grit into the faces of people milling about in the center of the room. It was a silent group, apparently workers; Fred saw that their eyes were fixed on three men who sat on a raised platform at the far end.

The three men were dressed in long coats and boots. They all wore gloves. This would not have seemed so strange except that two of the men were holding violins; the third was seated at an organ. They began to play, still gloved, a mournful and aching song.

From a side door two men entered, carrying a coffin which they set in front of the musicians' platform. One of the pallbearers placed a small sprig of flowers on the coffin and touched the wood with his fingers.

'Old lady,' said the man next to Fred. 'She die I am not zurprised. It is formidable how she live zo long in this cold.'

The scraping of the violins and the heavy breathing of the organ continued as the coffin descended into the floor, accompanied by the steely clanking of a hidden chain. The coffin bumped down and out of sight. Two trap doors shot up, met and shut with a bang which echoed in the stone room. When the echo died out the musicians stopped playing and at once began tuning their instruments.

'Say.' Fred turned to the man. He cleared his throat. 'Can you direct me to the Novodevichy Convent?' He said nothing about Svetlana. There might have been trouble. On the other hand he felt sure he would get the ikon past customs now.

A Political Romance

To calm his wife after a quarrel, Morris Rosetree always recalled to her how they had met in the National Library in Prague, how he had said, 'Excuse me, miss, could you tell me where the reading room is?' and how she had replied, 'You are excused. It is in this vichinity.'

He had been doing research for his doctoral dissertation on the history of the Czechoslovak Communist Party. But he had lost interest in it. He asked about the reading room because he heard it was well heated: he wanted to sit comfortably and write a letter to his folks. Several days after asking the dark-eyed girl the question he saw her on the library steps and he offered her a lift home. She refused at first, but Morris was insistent and finally he persuaded her. She remained silent, seemed to hold her breath throughout the journey. Morris invited her for coffee the next day, and later to have lunch. He told her he was an American. On Valentine's Day he bought her some fur-lined gloves. She was glad to get them, she said. She was an orphan. When they were married it was noticed by several American newspapers; one paper printed a picture of the bride and groom and titled it *A Political Romance*, explaining in the text that love was bigger than politics. At that time very little was happening in Czechoslovakia: Morris Rosetree's marriage there to Lepska Kanek was news.

With the help of Lepska, Morris finished his research. A year later, in the States, Morris got his Ph.D., and he told Lepska that if it hadn't been for her he would never have managed it. Some chapters of the dissertation were published in political journals, but no publisher seemed interested in the whole book. What depressed Morris some time after his book had been turned down was a review he saw of a similar book. The review was enthusiastic ('. . . valuable, timely . . .'), but judging from quotations used in the review the book was no better than his own. He knew his own was dull, so he was irritated reading praise of a book equally dull on the same subject. He became so discouraged that he moved away from Eastern European affairs and began a fitful study of the ruling parties of certain African countries.

It was at about this time that his quarrels started with Lepska who, once she had arrived at the Massachusetts college, nicknamed herself Lil. Morris had found her accent attractive in the early years of their marriage: 'You could cut that accent with a knife.' She had learned Morris' swearwords ('Kleist!' 'Sanvabeach!'). Morris had been charmed by her way of asking dinner guests innocently, 'There was big – how do you say *rayseestonce* in English?' (this provoked 'Resistance!' from the guests). But now the accent annoyed Morris. When she said, 'You Americans hev zoch dirty manners,' he corrected her English. If there were friends present he said, 'Sure, Americans have bad manners. Look at this. This is the way your Czechs eat their grub.' He reached across the table, speared a potato on his fork and made noises of chewing and growling as he cut the potato savagely on his plate. The friends laughed. Lil went silent; her face shut. Afterward she cried and said she was going back to Prague with the children. They had two girls: one had been born while Morris was finishing his disser-tation; one a year later. Both had Czech names. Lil cried in their room.

'Remember the library?' Morris would say whenever Lil cried. He could do both voices well, his bewildered American question, her stiff mispronounced reply.

One night she rejected the memory and said bitterly, 'I vish I had not met you.'

'Aw, Lil.'

'You make me zo unhappy,' she sniffed. Then she shrieked, 'I do not vant to leave!'

'Christ, I don't want you to either.'

'No, not *leave* . . . leave!' she insisted, and burst into tears again. She was, Morris guessed, talking of suicide.

He went easy on her for a while and was careful not to criticize her accent. But something had happened to the marriage: it had become impersonal; he felt they did not know each other very well, and he didn't care to know her any better. Her accent made him impatient and set his teeth on edge: he interrupted her as you do a stutterer. She moped like a hostage. Her hips were huge, her face and hands went florid in the January cold, though her face was still pretty. But she was like so many Czech women he had seen in Prague, like his landlady, like the librarians and the shrews in the ministries who would not allow him to interview officials. Those women who tried to kill his research: they wore brown, belted dresses and heavy shoes; not old in years, they were made elderly by work. Somehow, they were fat.

His daughters were fat, too, and once Morris had said to his office mate O'Hara (the Middle East), 'I think if we gave them American names they'd get skinny again.' O'Hara laughed. Morris was, afterward, ashamed of having revealed his exasperation. Exasperation was the name he gave it, despair was what he felt: because nothing would change for him. He would have no more kids; he would not marry again. He had tenure: this was his job for life. He could hope for promotion, but in thirty years he would be – this hurt him – the same man, if not a paler version. The manuscript of his book, the letters from publishers containing phrases of terse praise and regret and solemn rejection clipped to the flyleaf, would stay in the bottom drawer of his desk. Once he had had momentum and had breathed an atmosphere of expectancy; he had flown across Europe and been afraid. But he had been younger then, and a student, and he had been in love.

The study he planned of ruling parties was getting nowhere. He could not keep up with the revolutions or the new names (the presidents and generals in these countries were so young!). He taught Political Theory and used a textbook that a colleague had written. Morris knew it was not a good one.

Then the Russians invaded Czechoslovakia. Morris looked at his newspaper and saw photographs of chaos. He was tempted to throw the paper away and pay no further attention, for he could not separate in his mind the country from that woman in his house (Lil!) urging food into the two fat little girls whose Slavic names, instead of being dimmed by three and four years of utterance, had acquired queer, unfamiliar highlights and were the roots of even sillier diminutives, encouraging ridicule.

Morris fought that impulse, and he did not want the oblique revenge which his indifference to the invasion would have been. So he read the story and looked at the pictures, and he felt exhilaration, anger stoked by a continuous flow of indignant shame, as if he had returned to a deserted neighborhood and realized, standing amid abandoned buildings, that he too had been a deserter. The pictures were of Prague: tanks in formation on a thoroughfare's cobbles, their slender cannon snouts sniffing at rumpled citizens; some boys near the tanks with their hands cupped at their mouths, obviously shouting; others, reaching, in the act of pitching stones; people being chased into doorways by soldiers wearing complicated boots and carrying rifles; people laying wreaths; pathetically small crowds wagging signs; two old ladies, with white flowers, weeping. Morris read the news reports and the editorial, and he fumbled with a cigarette, discovering as he puffed that he had put the wrong end in his mouth and lighted the filter tip.

'What's that awful stink?' It was O'Hara. He saw the paper spread out, the headline. He said, 'Incredible, isn't it?'

'I could have predicted it,' said Morris. He was shaking his head from side to side, but he was smiling.

O'Hara invited Morris over for a meal the next night. He said, 'And don't forget to bring the wife! *She's* the one I want to chew the fat with.'

Remembering Lil, Morris folded the paper and started down the corridor. He was stopped by Charlie Shankland (Latin America). Shankland said, 'I'm sorry about this,' meaning the invasion, and invited the Rosetrees for Saturday.

Lil cried that afternoon. She saw the paper and said, 'Brave, brave people,' and 'My poor country, always trouble.' At the O'Haras' and the Shanklands' Lil was asked about the Russians: how did she feel about them? what would she do if she were in Prague today? who would she support?

'You do not know how . . . messianic . . . are the Russians,' she said. Morris had never heard her use that word before. He was pleased. 'My husband,' she went on, looking at Charlie and lowering her eyes, 'my husband thinks they are okay, like you all do. But we know they are terrible –' She could not finish.

She had said 'sinks' instead of 'thinks.' Morris was angry with himself for having noticed that. He wanted her to say more; he was proud and felt warm toward her. He was asked questions. Twice he replied, 'Well, my wife says she thinks,' ending each time 'Isn't that right, Lil?' And each time Lil looked at him and bowed her head sadly in agreement.

Morris dug out his dissertation and read it, and threw half of it away. He made notes for new chapters and began consulting Lil, asking detailed questions and not interrupting her answers. He gave a lecture for the Political Science Club, and he was invited to

Chicago to present a paper at a forum on the worsening situation in Czechoslovakia. He started buying an evening paper; he read of more students defying soldiers and scrawling Dubček's name on the street with chalk. He followed the funeral of the boy who was shot, and he saw the Czechs, whom he often felt were *his* Czechs, beaten into silence by the Russians. But the silence did not mean assent; even less, approval. It was resistance. He knew them, better than most people knew them. Time had passed, but it was not very long after the first Russian tank appeared in Prague that Morris Rosetree came home from a lecture and whispered to his wife, 'Lepska, I love you.'

Sinning with Annie

Make no mistake about it, I, Arthur Viswalingam, was married in every sense of the word, and seldom during those first years did I have the slightest compunction. Acceptance is an Asiatic disease; you may consider me one of the afflicted many. I was precisely thirteen, still mottled with pimply blotches, pausing as I was on that unhealthy threshold between puberty and adolescence. Annie (Ananda) was a smooth eleven, as cool and unripe as the mango old Mrs Pushpam brings me each morning on a plate when I sit down to my writing. (Is it this green fruit before me now that makes me pause in my jolly memoir to take up this distressing subject, one that for so long has troubled my dreams and made my prayers pitiful with moans of penitential shame?) It was a long time before the eruptions of adolescence showed with any ludicrous certainty (I almost said absurtainty!) on Annie's face. I imagine it was around our third anniversary, the one we celebrated at the home of that oaf Ratnam, my cousin (his mother, another yahoo, unmercifully repeated a jape about our childlessness: 'Perhaps they are not *doing* it right!'). I cannot be sure exactly when Annie became a woman: she always seemed to be a small girl playing at being grown-up, worrying the cook and sweeper with her pouts, dressing in outlandish styles of sari, crying often and miserably – all of this, while we were married, an irritating interruption of my algebra homework.

At my present age I am certain of very little; I only know that I can no longer expect God to listen to my incessant wailing, and so I turn to my fellow man, not for indulgence but simply to give God a rest. This is the wet season in Delhi; the temple monkeys are drenched: they sit mournfully under the crassly painted arches, their fur sticking out in wet prickles, their pale blue flesh chilled with the monsoon, giving them the deathly look of the gibbons that turn up now and again, bloated and drowned in the open drains of this city. My pen spatters ink; I write slowly on unbleached foolscap with many half-starts and crossings-out. I can hear the wheezing of wind through the little midden of Asiatic rubbish that has accumulated in my lungs; I can feel my heart stretching and straining with each pump, like an old toad squatting in the basket of my ribs. To misquote the celebrated poet from Missouri, I am an old man in a wet month.

But imagine me, if you can, seventy years ago, standing on spindly legs (I thought all the world stood on spindly legs until I saw English shopgirls) – as I was saying, standing on spindly legs at the temple entrance, in my pint-sized turban, my hands clasped against my thirteen-year-old breast. All manner of hooting and shrieking from the street echoed in the temple: bargains being struck, coins and brown rupees exchanged for flesh and fruit. That was long ago; it has taken all this time for me to see the irony of those beastly hawkers.

Little imbecile that I was, I had no idea I was being swapped. I did not know that Annie's father had promised five thousand rupees to my father if the marriage transpired as arranged. Chits and promises had been exchanged; my parents had haggled while I played dawdling puddle games and kicked my football. And little did I know of my father's bankruptcy, my mother's idle, spendthrift ways; no, it pleased me that my father always seemed to be on holiday, my mother dressed richly in excellent shawls. How was I to know my father was lazy, my mother foolish; or, indeed, that I would have to pay for their sins with my chaste flesh?

We lived in princely fashion, with leisure and comfort that for all I know even a prince would envy: the lower class's idea of the voluptuous is always grander than the prince's, because it is unattainable. Their demons and gods, about which I shall speak presently, show them to be a very imaginative lot; coupled with their idleness this breeds a grotesquery all its own. My father's credit remained solid; had my father declared himself bankrupt very early on, or had my mother gone about in the market in tattered sari and worn sandals, a splintery wooden comb stuck in her hair instead of the ivory one she habitually wore, the final reckoning would have, I am convinced, come sooner. The people in our village were quite ignorant and easily gulled. Foolishness was a plague which descended on us early and stayed, not killing, but maiming: cripples abounded. In evidence of this, which I am sure my parents took careful note of, the villagers worshiped a whole zoo of beasts, a pseudospiritual menagerie: snakes, monkeys, elephants, goddesses with six arms and dreadful snouts, gods with elephantine ears, tusks and even wrinkled trunks. To be human was a crime against everyone; it was grotesque. Have I mentioned the cows? It pains me to recall the bovine benedictions I performed: I have stroked the hindquarters of a plaster cow until the paint flaked off and the stone itself was worn smooth – nay, made indentations in the plaster flanks with my praying fingers! I donged bells and keened, lit tapers, strewed petals. We Hindus have a curious faith that, in a manner of speaking, transforms a farmyard into a place of worship – a backward, rat- and snake-infested farmyard at that. The more dumb and stupid the idol, the more devoutly we pray. Mrs Pushpam, for example, is at this moment with a hundred other yelping women, beating her tambourine before a smudged mezzotint of Shiva in a squalid bazaar. It should surprise no one to learn that two of the dozen or so words which English takes from my language are *goon* and *thug*; I would not be amazed, further, if *fanatic* and *dunderhead* had Sanskrit roots.

Where was I? Yes, at the temple. I was there because my father's credit had run out at last. No one else knew this of course: the bluff was still working. I think of a card game, symbol of bluff. I have never seen a child's face on a pack of cards, though I have in my mind a special pack, my father's, the cards marked Foolishness, Pomp, Ego, Greed, Idleness, Boastfulness; there is a face card as well: the painted image of a sallow prince, dressed ludicrously in finery, the little demented face staring with big eyes. It was this card my father played in the spring of 1898 (it was a 'marrying year,' as they say in my language) in the Laxshminarayan Temple, when he was released from his years of bluff, and I was bound up irrevocably with sin.

The Savior of the faith I embraced only this year similarly stood in a temple; he spoke wise words to his elders about Work, Duty and His Father's Business. The comparison with me is crude and unworthy, but it serves to throw my sin into bold relief. I too stood in an Eastern temple, but less confidently than the Nazarene; I stood with sweating elders and uttered inanities (God help me, I have already said something of my father's 'business'!), stroked for the umpteenth time the cow's behind, the monkey's flank, mooed and crowed, in a tongue I would very willingly now like to disremember, the shrill syllables of my pagan faith, trumpeted like Ganpati, the elephant god, chattered like Hanuman, and let myself be anointed (under the circumstances, a sacrilegious verb) with unguents, perfumes, juices, nectars, spots of dust, rare oils and essences and – it shames me to mention this, though I promised to be ingenuous – devoured a reeking pudding made up of the excrement, dung I should say, of all the above-mentioned animals. Meanwhile a medium went into a trance and, eyeballs rolled up, scraped his tongue with a rusty sword after which he wrote asinine charms on yellow slips of paper with the blood. Talk about barbarism! You have no idea.

My bride, the child Annie, was heavily veiled, clotted with blossoms, orchids, a paraphernalia of frangipani and jacaranda, anything the idlers who arranged the wedding could lay their hands on. She was so small she could have been a corsage; and she was as mobile as Birnam wood. None of it meant much to me, neither the incantations nor the odors, the clanging temple nor the avaricious side glances of my 'elders.' My attention was fixed elsewhere: in the corner of the temple a beggarly snake charmer on his haunches blew a swollen flute, coaxing a sleek, swaying cobra out of a basket.

Picture our wedding night: two children entering an empty house, a small boy with dripping sweets clasped in one hand and, in the other hand, a sequined turban crammed with stale flower petals and old rupees; a small girl, head down, follows closely behind, clutching flowers, shuffling in gilt slippers that clack on the stone floor. The children are moving cautiously: both are afraid of the dark.

Our house was an extension to my father's. Annie and I had six rooms, though for that first year we lived in one; as children, even though the house was ours, we felt we were not entitled to more than that. In every way except one did we behave as children: we needed our parents' permission to buy sweets; we were not allowed to go to plays or to music shows alone; all our clothes and all my schoolbooks were bought by my father (we had not one piece to call our own); Annie, though my wife, never cooked, sewed or scrubbed; there were times when we were not allowed to dress ourselves. I can remember several occasions when we were tucked into bed (consider the implications of that phrase!). Thrice I was birched by my father in the presence of my wife.

Bear all this in mind as you read on. But before I begin, let me say that I have noticed in Western countries a certain evidence of urges before there is action on the part of the very young. Theirs, those gay souls, is a constant rehearsal of marital obligation long before the deed is done, a relatively harmless form of physical foolery, touching at private parts, playing Mommy and Daddy, dressing up like the oldsters do. This goes on manifesting itself in various forms up to the age of eighteen or twenty when, quite understandably, they are allowed the privacy and license to, as it were, get on with it.

In my savage country things are different, to say the least. While in the West you have, during this exploratory period, adults always within earshot, in our case (I should say village), for all practical purposes, we had none. Unlike the little chappies frolicking and dabbing at each other in English country gardens, our experience was painfully real and immediate, unrelieved by sport or jest. Sex, in marriage, loses much of its heartiness. I suppose our parents thought that one of the many semibeasts we went about worshiping would swoop down and rescue us at the crucial moment. To be frank, I haven't the slightest idea of what goes on in the Asian mind.

That first night was fairly typical of the ones that followed. There were so many. I led the way into the room; inside, Annie crept into a corner. Suspecting that I had lost her, I lighted a taper and slammed the door. She jumped, startled; I spied her crouching near a little altar. I wanted very much to talk to her, but could think of nothing to say except 'Where do you live?' and I refrained from asking that; her reply would have been a polite, 'Here, my husband.' I offered her a sweet, one of our large vulgar *gulabjam*, made of paste and broken milk and covered with sugary syrup. She took it and ate it noisily, licking her fingers with her cat's tongue.

There was a screen in the room, a wicker frame with silk stretched across it and decorated with clumsy flowers: more of our degraded culture. When my sweets were gone I stuffed my money-filled turban under my pillow and went behind the screen to change into my pajamas. This done, I blew out the candle and crept into bed, ignoring my wife. It was not until I rolled over and shut my eyes that I heard the rustle of Annie's clothes. I could tell what she was taking off from the sounds each garment made when it was fumbled with: there was first the flutter of the withered flower strands as they were lifted over her head, the lisp of silk unwinding, and the hush of her stepping out of her petticoat; the thump and tinkle as she pulled her slippers off, the heel click as they were placed side by side at the foot of the bed; a tiny noise, the slow zip of fingernails scraping on flesh, her thumbs in the waistband of her bloomers, pulling them down her legs. Then the *fee, fee, fee* of a comb being drawn through young and silky hair.

I find this description unbearably arousing! Was that really *me* in that bed? Alas, yes. I must go on. There were no more noises, not even the padding of her little feet as she crossed to her side of the bed. She slipped under the sheet (I felt the cool breath of the sheet ballooning air past me). At my age I could not be expected to have any idea of female nakedness: even as I listened to Annie removing her clothes I could not imagine what she looked like and, believe me, lying next to her in bed hadn't the foggiest idea what would happen next. I thought we might go quietly to sleep: I had eaten a sufficiency of sweets, slurped yogurt, gorged myself on rice and *dhal*; my head rang from the powerful incense of the ceremony. I shut my eyes tightly and tried to sleep, but this seemed to give me a bad case of insomnia. I was trying too hard. And then it came, against my will: a little animal, a nasty little beast like the sort we worshiped, awoke in me and made me very warm. Annie seemed to have something to do with it. The image came to me then (it persists even now) of the small girl's circus act: she waves her hand over the slumbering puppy and, with only this gesture, makes him rise on his haunches, his forepaws up, his jaws apart, begging, his tongue sagging juicily through his teeth. This is the only perception I keep from my youth, that sinful score of years. I keep it like a little shell plucked from the shores of my childhood, never thrown away: the little girl dancing innocently in naked grace around the puppy, the puppy rising from haunches to hind legs and leaping up, nipping at the little girl with sharp teeth, snarling – not a puppy, but that more bestial word, *dog* – and knocking the girl over roughly. The dog is on all fours, standing on her frail little newly budded breasts and barking insistently in quivering jerks. They are not playing, they are beyond that, and no one is watching; there is something fierce about the whole thing. Fierce, fumbling and unsatisfying. It was thus with Annie and me.

The next morning, when I awoke, I found a string tied to the underpart of the bedstead. I followed it out of the room and down to my parents' parlor where there were chairs. The string ended in a small silver bell. Annie must have been making the bed or something as I stared at the bell, for it tinkled (was she patting the covers?), reminding me of my lack of success, *ting-a-ling*.

There was no shame, only a temporary sense of defeat. You would say I was not man enough. We have no equivalent phrase in our language. How could we? With small folk leaping into bed, fully married, at the age of eleven and thirteen, could we possibly have any sane concept of maturity? I am not a sociologist; I am a tired old man, an ashamed and angry tired old man, but I know that this is a different kettle of fish from what you are used to. You never saw anyone so young bunged into marriage as I was.

In a phrase you have it: a nation of children. It is cruel, but exceedingly accurate. If I was not a child, why should I leap on my bride of one day and bark like a dog, sniff her, butt her with my head, squeeze her until she cried out? Mind you, I squeezed her ankles, I squeezed her wrists: I did not know any better. Half my body had swollen in an unfamiliar manner and I was looking for a place to put it, to fit it in, a socket which I imagined was hidden somewhere on her pathetic little body. She lay; when I touched her roughly she squealed, but I must say that she did all she could. She tried her level best. I nuzzled, bit, screwed up my face and whined piteously into her cheek, all to no avail. If I may say so, it made matters somewhat worse, for nothing is so inflammatory to lust as delay. I burned. I married *and* burned. This went on for many months.

At the same time I was at school, preoccupied with the trivia that besets the schoolboy. My education, in light of the bizarre circumstances of my private life, pained me as often as it gave me release. How I envied the simple lives of those characters we read about, Oliver Twist whose only problem was to find a way of coping with those rogues and ruffians, all the others oiling their cricket bats, having tea and buttered scones in well-appointed parlors, throwing their hats in the air at rugger matches. All so jolly next to what I had to face! Naturally I could explain none of this to my wife. Our marriage was now a year old (I was in Form Two), and we spent our time sitting dumbly in our house or picking flowers for festivals, always avoiding the subject that seemed to turn the sharp Indian sunlight into deep gloom. I cannot say I dreaded going to bed; I will say that I viewed the whole affair with some little apprehension. My desire to succeed befogged my mind and made me less capable of success.

Inevitably of course we did succeed; I will not trouble you with details which, in their entirety, do not make a very pretty parcel; my gift for expression begins to lurch some distance this side of stark nakedness. It would be an error to venture nearer than I have already. What intrigued me during this time was that once I had succeeded I could not understand why I had ever failed. This success marked the onset of school latenesses that very nearly ended in my expulsion, my failure to complete the most rudimentary homework or, in brief, any task that was performed outside the confines of our wretched little bedroom. I puffed and panted (we are not a hardy race, in spite of what the rabble of nationalists may assert when speaking with a rank foreigner: never trust an Asiatic); my lust knew no bounds, yet there was a limit to my competence, of that I am shamefully aware, doubly so as I write this.

I should now very much like to say a thing or two about my sin, namely lust. This sin is commonly, and not altogether mistakenly, classed with gluttony, envy and the other four deadly sins. Alcoholism, a manifestation of gluttony, may serve as a preliminary comparison: one sees drunken louts shambling about the streets searching for a drink shop. Their behavior is unseemly. But lust is worse; it is in a class all its own, for it afflicts man in a more acute way than does the craving for spirits. Besides being a most private degradation, gluttony for drink lacks a certain urgency which is essential to any definition of lust. Thirst, sometimes associated with lust, should not be at all; thirst is a sense of wasting, together with the slimy accumulation on the mouth, tongue and throat of a layer of bubbly but not juicy saliva that wants slaking. It comes in stages, the swelling tongue, the parching throat beginning to build up that slimy coat, and then the urge. Lust, on the other hand, *is* urge, a fullness that is in actual fact closer to anger than to gluttony: a fit of full feverish temper which puts the blood immediately on the boil, causes muscles to tense and harden with something approaching criminal determination and starts a warm diabolical rosiness to effervesce throughout one's limbs, drenching the body in one's own sweat like a sputtering joint of basted beef. You readers who are not lustful but who may have quick tempers may usefully compare your tantrums with reechy passion; even the descriptive vocabulary remains somewhat constant: one is aroused quickly to both anger and lust; one grows excessively hot with both, loses one's reason and turns beefy red. The emotions of lust and anger proceed with equal speed, which is to say they are frantically brief when given the most liberty, and longest in duration (and more intense) when an attempt is made to curb or conceal them. The difference is this: one may take out one's wrath on the leg of a table, but lust is only satisfied by the leg of a strumpet. It is possible to allay one's angry feelings in private; lust involves other people and I believe because it does so, is the greater corruption. It takes two, as the saying has it, to do the tango. Having said that, I shall say no more about it.

Annie changed. No longer the hard coil of dark wires I had married, but indolent and alluring, and yet remarkably compact, like those bready sweets we in Asia addict ourselves to and canker our teeth with. Her cheeks grew plump, her budding breasts swelled into two tingling and pipped morsels of fruit, and indeed all her flesh took on a sleepy thickness which I took the devil's own delight in pinching in this wise: extending my claw, I would grasp a bit of her flesh between my thumb and forefinger and give a sharp tweak, pretending all the while that I had scooped a collop of meat from, say, her cheek or belly; and then I would pretend to eat it. I realize now that had she grown ugly I might have ceased sinning and taken my solemn vow of celibacy much sooner. But she grew ever more attractive, which goes to show that the devil may take many forms, even that of grace and beauty, provided that it is dark enough to conceal his cloven hoof: where lust is concerned, darkness is just around the corner. Far from being horrible, the object of our lust may appear virginal; the sin itself, to the wanton child with the corrupt parents, seems incredibly delicious on first taste.

Prying old Pushpam has returned from her fatuous orgy of monkey worship. I must be quick; the hag is snorting and fretting in the hallway, wondering which vegetables to stew. And just as well; I should say no more about sinning with Annie and its attendant sorrows. There were times when I wanted to be done with the whole business: my penitent trembling transformed me from hermit to nut case, and brutality welling within me sloshed up past my gizzard to splash at the back of my eyes. With my prayers wobbling every which way like bats in my closed room, and pleas squeaking past my numb lips, I felt the urge to punish: I was at the Delhi Gate when the British returned; I led them to the flea pots and flesh pits, the drink shops and temples and, in a bloody crusade, we crushed the life out of the verminous population. This accomplished, we peopled the country anew, cleanly, without mess, with colder holy folk from frozen places. Those times, had Annie walked through the door, as Mrs P. has just done, I would have put my pen down, risen and wrapped my still-nimble fingers around her neck to throttle the life out of her. Taking into account the extent of my sin and general misery, that action must seem to you totally justifiable. I cannot say. Latterly, I get fewer and fewer of these brutal urges. No, I doubt that I would do that now, I very much doubt it. You will call me silly, but most likely I would fumble out of my chair and screech across the carpet, sleeves and cuffs billowing, sandals aflap; and, pity me deeply, I would fall before her and touch my lips to her instep as if she were the Queen of Heaven.

A Love Knot

On rainy nights in that part of Boston, the Charles Street area, antique gas lamps lighted the narrow side streets which were swollen with a paving of cobblestones. Like the lamps, the stones had been left intact, and they were so carefully preserved in a way that caused such inconvenience that the nostalgia they represented was vulgar, an obnoxious pride. There was no love in it. It is that way with keeping old things: they are flaunted and handled and gaped at. Collectors and conservers are arrogant; many Bostonians are that way, and several I knew flinched when I told them how I had once seen my cousin tear the brass guts out of an expensive Victorian oil lamp and solder in a light socket. He thought it looked better with a plastic flex trailing from a hole he punched in its base. My cousin should have seen those gas lamps in Boston. Their clean windows framed small bags of white light and made the cobblestones gleam like glazed loaf tops.

With the love knot in my pocket Walnut Street was my destination, but all those streets had the same effect on me: turning into one from the traffic and honkings of busy Charles, I began to walk more slowly, as if I had been hurried back a hundred years and cooled on the way. I didn't see the nostalgia as arrogance: the discovery of this oldness was private and all my own, not urged on me by an anxious host. Because I was young and a stranger and because my first experience of that city had been vicarious in the most distancing way – through reading about it in novels – I wished to prolong these sensations of the age I understood, the city of quaintness and crime. By slowing down and remembering, I exhumed in my memory of grateful reverence for the solidness and the apparent calm, and hoped that the feeling would remain at least until I reached that crusted hydrant or that angular leaning house with the mullioned windows at the corner. I strained to hear the hoofbeats and creaking leather of a gasping horse, the wobbling clatter of carriage wheels approaching, or the man in the black opera cape tapping his cane toward a doorway draped in fog boas.

I saw no one's face and I sensed that behind the brick walls of houses lay intrigue's moist dread and expectancy: a shadowy drawing room, chairs arrayed facing each other like old aunts who refuse to die, a cold fire, untouched sandwiches curling on the edges of a plate, a mantelpiece clock set in porcelain, an odor of foreign tobacco, a male corpse lying in a posture of frozen hilarity, some blood running into the pile of an expensive carpet – all the props in the literary stage set of a finished murder.

I was a student then, and on an errand, and if I made a great deal of the atmosphere it was because I had recently arrived from the worst city in the world, my birthplace, Calcutta – not, as I was often forced to explain to Americans, a fancifully named town in a Midwestern state, but the real place, in Bengal. Having left Calcutta I knew I would never go back, though I was bonded to the Government of West Bengal and I had promised that on my return I would work at a low salary for five years in the civil service to repay the loan that had been given to me. I am not a liar by nature; it hurt me to make the promise of returning after I earned my degree. But my family no longer exists for me: most are dead, and those who are not dead I never knew well. It was my plan to flee. The university in the Boston suburb was also part of my plan – I would not have gone anywhere else.

The idea of crime in those parts was not wholly literary remembrance of Bostonians with swords sheathed in walking sticks or genteel poisonings (strychnine has the sound and feel of a long, sharp knife – the sword-cane and the poisoning are linked in my imagination). All this was ten years ago, a time when so many women, most of them elderly, were sexually outraged and then strangled – I may have reversed the order here – by a lunatic handyman. On my first visit to Walnut Street a daily newspaper displayed in a steel rack in front of a drugstore had the alarming headline FEAR STALKS THE HILL. Idling foreigners were reported to the police, and I expected to be stopped and subjected to a frisking and made to explain my errand. I was a total stranger in that place. Although my mother was a white American and my father a German, my passport was Indian and so is my accent still: I speak with my lips pursed and subtly transpose the first letters of the words *very well*. I had always been taught to think of myself as an Indian, more particularly Bengali, for in addition to being born near Calcutta, I lived there until the age of twenty-one, at which time I received my bursary. In Boston at the time of these stranglings, I felt that I, an Indian, was conspicuous. I was surprised that no one took the slightest notice of me. In coffee shops and, occasionally, buying subway tokens, I was asked to repeat myself; the requests were extremely polite. But in large cities speech is seldom necessary, and when it is used it is functional phrase-book language; except for the few times when I was asked to repeat what I said, a number or the name of a subway station, my accent went unnoticed. My color, of course, blended perfectly. At that time the word *colored* was still used to describe black people. I was not taken for, though I felt, colored.

My background was of interest to the girls I dated, and the information that I had resolved to suppress I found myself elaborating upon, as soon as I saw that it caused no discomfort to the listener. I am not a gregarious person and these petty details of my life were a relief from small talk. It soon reached the point where if I was not asked, I offered, saying, 'Did you know that I'm an Indian?' which never failed to produce the question, 'You mean an *Indian* Indian or the other kind?' I was envied for my origins but I selected, leaving many details unspoken, for I had once dwelt on some squalid aspects of my upbringing with a girl I especially liked, thinking of ways to interest her and casting about in my memory for impressive sorrows and hardships, and I was so absorbed in this that it was some time before I looked up and saw that I was making her cry.

The love knot, in gold, I found among my mother's possessions after she died, of an illness diagnosed as cerebral malaria, in our house in Calcutta in 1957. It was in an envelope sealed on the flap with red wax, a buff-paper envelope, much thumbed and furry with use, bearing on the front an address in my mother's handwriting, *To: George Chowdree, 22 Walnut Street, Boston, Massachusetts.* It was with three bangles, an out-of-date passport, my birth certificate and some things of my father's (his spectacles, some old coins, green-brown paper money, his copy of the *Ramayana* in a German translation), items of no value. He had died years before, alone my mother said, in another city in India. The sealed envelope had been addressed a very long time ago, and it looked as if it had been carried around, for the corners were tearing and the wrinkles and bulges in the envelope were a shadowy pattern the shape of the small object inside. It could not be mailed. I opened it, for these reasons and also because I was curious. There was no note inside, only the love knot, worked in the most delicate filigree perhaps by one of our Bengali goldsmiths. That the name was George Chowdree amused me. He was obviously a Christian Indian, one of a group my mother detested: she spat at the sight of a black priest and she said that if I ever entered a Catholic church she would kill me. This anger in her was rare. She was a peaceful soul, and she was a very devout Hindu.

I am, I suppose, a Hindu myself. My interest in the name George Chowdree lay in the fact that its pattern was nearly my own name in reverse: my first name is Hindu and my surname European. Danny, as I'm called, is given as Daneeda on my passport; my surname, Schum, which is German, rhymed with zoom in India and now, in America, it rhymes with thumb. Persons of mixed identity like me find it simpler to agree with the stranger's assessment. I am what other people take me for; I never challenge their assumptions. When they say, 'I guess your father went to India during the war,' I say he did. They are probably right. I never knew my father, and the little I know of my background is enough to prevent me from wondering further. It was my mother who raised me, her only child; she took me to the temple, she enrolled me in school and stitched and mended my uniforms, she encouraged me to get a job in the civil service, she tried to keep me innocent. While she was certainly puritanical, she had developed the Indian habit of going to the movies on Saturday afternoons; it was her one recreation, and I shared it purely to please her. The films were extremely boring, their plots predictable and melodramatic (defiant lovers, feuding families, women dying in childbirth), but the songs – a dozen or so in each movie – were pleasant. My mother hummed them as she cooked, crouching next to a smoky fire and stirring and slapping dough cakes and turning from the smoke to sigh and push her hair – which was light brown – out of her eyes. I know now that my mother was a very beautiful woman; it is something that one discovers late – it may even be the mark of manhood to see one's mother as a woman who was once beautiful. As an orthodox Hindu, my mother never wore jewelry; her only ornament was a vermilion caste mark, the shape of a narrow candle flame, on her very white forehead. It surprised me that she had owned a love knot.

But there it was, after her cremation, in my hand. I slipped it into a clean envelope and wrote out the address of George Chowdree, and for weeks afterward I repeated the address to myself. I took the same comfortable refuge in it that one does in an incantation. Studying for my Higher School Certificate, I copied this address on the flyleaf of my volume of *The Secret Agent*, which was one of the set books in English that year and which, now that I think of it, may have provided some of the London atmosphere that I later associated with that area of Boston: Verloc could have managed his seedy shop on Charles Street, and Winnie's carriage bumped over cobblestones just like those I saw on Walnut. I made one alteration in the address. Instead of Chowdree's name, I wrote, with the yearning one feels in the solitude of early youth, my own name, and under it *Walnut Street* and the city. For as long as I could remember I had wanted to escape from India, and now I had a place to escape to. It might have been the reason I did so well in my examinations.

In my mind I saw a street in America lined with walnut trees; there was only one house on the street that I could see clearly, the others were smaller and much blurred. Number twenty-two was a cheerful house, freshly painted, and it resembled a colonnaded house in Calcutta I was fond of walking past, an elegant but deserted one, where an Englishman had once lived. My scholarship went through after some delays; I was given a folder of directions and authorizations, printed on villainous paper; and I sailed from Madras.

I did not go to Walnut Street immediately. I wanted to discover the place slowly, as one does a painting in a museum, approaching it from a great distance and picking out details as one draws nearer for the close, final dazzle. I bought a map; I studied that. I walked in other parts of the city, where the docks are, where the insurance companies are, the bookstores, the Irish bars with old photographs of bare-fisted boxers in the windows, along the river near the hospitals, the Chinese district of four streets bordered by strip clubs and a large school of dentistry. And when I had explored the peripheries of the Charles Street area, noticing on the way a gloomy building housing the Theosophical Society, many antique shops and boarding houses (the doors ajar, pay phones on the wall), I walked to the corner of Beacon and Charles and then down Charles, pausing often, to Walnut, where I first saw that newspaper headline. I examined my map one last time. It was late on a rainy afternoon in August and I shielded the map in my hand as I looked from it to the street sign and then down the sidewalk. People walked quickly past me in the warm drizzle with their heads down, holding bright umbrellas or, if they had no umbrella, making visors over their eyes with their hands. I was splashed by a car just before I turned into Walnut; but this was not the street I expected. The antique gas lamps were lighted, and so were most of the cobbles beneath them, glazed individually in pools of illumination. But the rest was dark, and there were few trees, all with wet, heavy green leaves, planted in holes in the sidewalk and protected by cylindrical wooden fences. The houses were all three-storied, most of them joined, with narrow plots of grass at the fronts. The even numbers were on the opposite side of the street. I went cautiously and found number twenty-two, watched for a moment, then walked around the block to a coffee shop where I had a sandwich and tea. The darkness outside was false, caused by the storm; I wanted night, and I walked until it enclosed the city. I went back to Walnut Street again, and passing the house, I saw through the lighted front window a girl's face, laughing at someone I could not see, and the face of the girl was as dark as all those I had left in Calcutta.

That was strange. I had prepared myself for a man's face, and, even more, for a particular man, one I had seen in a Bengali film, a plump-necked actor who always played the role of a businessman, a frequent traveler, a man of some importance; I had superimposed this important actor's face on George Chowdree. He was my stereotype – healthy Indians traveled, skinny ones stayed at home. Here I betray the theatrical side of my plan. It was melodrama, worthy of the Indian film which is filled with such paraphernalia: my dead mother's piece of ornate jewelry always in my pocket, my cleverly obtained scholarship, my search, my wanderings about the city – striking poses as if I was being watched. And soon I fitted that dark girl's face into this melodrama, as more appropriate than the man's I expected.

It was not my purpose to knock on the door and introduce myself. The busy strangler made everyone suspicious, doors were closed to strangers; it was not even a time for casual visiting, for people were no less anxious on an unfamiliar sidewalk than they were in their own houses, and footsteps behind one took on the jarring insistence of summoning nighttime knocks on a door.

169

I saw the girl's face; I was satisfied; I went away. For many days I called the laughing face to mind, the street, the lighted window, until all the anticipated details of my previous fantasy had been replaced by the actual details – unanticipated but now appropriate – of what I saw that evening. It was still fantasy, but substantiated by enough reality to make me patient in my errand. Something of my patience, deliberately exercised to sustain my little drama, may be seen when I say that I did not look up Chowdree's name in the telephone directory until after I visited the house. I could have done this as soon as I landed in America. I did not. And finally, when I did, it was as I expected, the only one in the book, at the right address. But to my surprise his initials were followed by the abbreviation for medical doctor.

For minutes I searched for credible symptoms, envisaging an allusive chat with Chowdree the physician as he tapped my back and crushed the wooden tongue depresser into his wastebasket. I could become his patient. I rejected this as too convenient and, as I had by now become acquainted with American medical charges, too expensive. I think I might have tried it, but after I saw that girl's face I knew my approach would be through her. She was about my own age; she was pretty, probably a student like me and, quite black, was me in negative. It was a symmetry I enjoyed. While I thought about this I fancied that the shadow I cast in that late summer reverie was like this girl, dark and altering in rippling angles as I walked on uneven ground, a foreshortened reflection of my own personality, changeable and intriguing, joined at my foot sole.

I did what the solitary person or the lonely lover often does. He knows that it is morbid to sit in his room and chew on his misery; he goes out and, at the slightest suggestion, he follows women, marking them in buses or in stores and then trailing after them, keeping at a safe undetectable distance and relentlessly keeping them in sight, so that their resolution – those quick woman's steps – becomes this, promising fulfillment. Women march more hectically than men and as they approach their destination they become positively frantic because women do not watch their feet or swing their arms, and when they speed up they acquire a mechanical bustle, and nearly always their calves stand out in smooth oblongs and the backs of their ankles become hard and pinched. A foreigner in a city watches other people; he tries to imitate their rhythm so he studies their movements. The reason I assigned for the women's speeding up was that unlike men they never glanced around as they walked and I decided that this provoked uneasiness and, consequently, a nervous speed.

So it was with this dark girl. She attended a school of fine arts that was housed in an old building on Marlborough Street; I had followed her to the place and later wrote a letter asking whether I might do a part-time course with them. The fees were out of the question. I continued to follow the girl to other likely spots. She used the Boston Public Library twice a week, the section devoted to Oriental art. I applied for a borrower's card and began studying there myself twice a week at the little tables adjacent to the ones she used. When she entered a stack, I entered a parallel one and, pretending to read, peered at her back. One day I saw her take a book; the subject was Indian miniatures of the Mogul period. She used it for the afternoon. I stayed at my desk, watching. After she was gone I looked on the shelf and saw that it was not there. She had checked it out.

A month later, on a day when normally she did not use the library, I looked for the book. It was not on the shelf. I looked it up in the card catalogue and noted down the author's name, and then I requested it at the main desk. The white-haired lady there wore spectacles hung on a chain around her neck. I showed her the card and asked when the book was due to be returned. Spectacles were put on, drawers pulled out, index cards flipped and thumbed. The book had not been borrowed, said the lady, and was I absolutely sure it was not on the shelf? She repeated the call number. I said no. She said, rising, that it may have been put on another shelf.

We searched; she for a long time, I for only a few minutes. I knew then the book had been stolen.

And I knew the thief! A discovery! I had found her laughing and recorded her way of walking; I knew her subject and her school and many of her habits. These were obvious things. Now I had discovered a weakness, a deep secret. Many husbands would have trouble discovering this in their wives, but I was more patient than any husband, and more persistent than most lovers. I fantasized the kind of device necessary for such a theft: a sling, a pocket hung between her thighs on straps attached to a belt, the whole business hidden by her long skirt. (I knew her complete wardrobe and the ways she varied it, though once she surprised me with a new silk scarf.)

Her long skirts were out of fashion, but her face was so pretty that in clothes cut the wrong length, and so plain and featureless, she seemed to be anticipating a bold fashion. Her face was the same shade as her arms, deeply colored, with a high dark polish, the gloss of the race, a prominent nose balanced above by a strong forehead and brow, and below by full brown lips. She was Bengali, there was no doubt of that; the face, the thick black hair told it, the warm melancholy of her large eyes, the thin arms and sharp elbows, the long fingers, busy with mischief and pencils, nacreous fingernails, her air of independence, walking so swiftly, her responsible innocence concealing her crime.

I had followed her for months, through Boston streets, in department stores, stood with my back to her and watched her reflection in the window of a travel agency as she walked like a ghost through the sign *Puerto Rico $49*, as she browsed among the sidewalk bins of a secondhand bookshop. Her movements were unchanging: I could meet her bus, join her discreetly at the Hayes-Bickford for a coffee or follow her blindly, streets away, walking parallel on Boylston as she walked on Commonwealth Avenue, and I knew precisely when I could turn and allow our paths to cross. I was daring in the Main Reading Room of the library, sitting across the varnished table from her, memorizing her hands, for the lamps at eye level prevented her from seeing me. I kept maps of her movements; I could meet her head-on; I passed by her school and rehearsed conversations with her, and during her school's winter break, when her movements became slightly irregular (no school, more stores and library) I was half in love with her.

Her name was Dorothy Chowdree. I learned that early in December in the ridiculously painstaking way I had found out that she stole the book on Indian miniatures (and two others, also about Indian art). Now borrowing is done with numbers, but at that time the borrower wrote his name on two cards that were kept in a brown pocket glued to the inside back cover of the book; these cards were handed over when the book was taken out. I noted one book she had taken; it was returned on the date due; it bore her name. Simple. I noticed one other thing from my watching slot in

Middle Eastern Art: there was a book she always used but never took out. It wasn't possible for her to steal this one; it was very large, with color plates, bound in full calf. Its subject was Indian ornaments and jewelry.

For several weeks in March I neither followed her nor used the library, and toward the beginning of April I picked up again and found her exactly where I knew she would be, at 4:30 on a Friday, walking away from her school to a cup of coffee at the Hayes-Bickford and then a two-hour session in the Oriental collection. I saw her disappear around the corner; I lingered at the school and then went in. Some students, long-haired girls with green book bags and bulging portfolios were clomping down a wooden, spiral staircase. They paused at a bulletin board, read, and passed by me. I had a look at the bulletin board myself: a tea was announced ('Pourer, B. Yardley'), a lecture at a museum, a summer school in Vermont. Dorothy's name was given twice, as organizer of a dance at the Biltmore for the Spring Weekend ('Single, $3.50') and as chairman of a lecture on Mondrian. The lecture was in a week's time, the dance in mid-May. Savoring the pure pleasure of expectation, I decided on the dance.

The weather grew mild; it still rained often, but the rain did not dry so quickly on the streets as it had done in the winter freeze. Streets, grass and sidewalks stayed wet, and in the early evenings and at night there were reflections on Walnut Street, reminding me of my first day, when I discovered that house and Dorothy's face in the lighted window. I was less patient now, for I had decided that Dorothy's industry at the library must mean that she was in her last year at the school. It would not be easy to trace her after her graduation. All my energies went into planning for the dance. I ferreted out a student from my college who knew where tickets could be bought for the Spring Weekend dance at the Biltmore. I borrowed money, bought a dark suit and a new tie and had my shoes resoled. Dorothy was also preparing for the dance: she bought shoes and yards and yards of silk from an importer just off Washington Street.

A week before the dance I entered the library early and went to the Oriental section. Dorothy had not arrived. I found the large leather volume on Indian ornaments and slipped an envelope inside. It was a new envelope, addressed to Dorothy; inside was my mother's love knot. I replaced the book on the shelf and took my usual place at Middle Eastern Art. I could see a tweed coat moving slowly through Dorothy's stack, fingering the spines. A man's ringed hand took a book from the shelf, opened it to the flyleaf, put it back. He then sidled toward the Indian ornaments book and, just as quickly, stepped away. Dorothy was beside him, her shoes clicking, heaving the book down.

American bars are the darkest places imaginable. In the Biltmore bar I had a whiskey and watched the students, dressed for the dance, walking past the window of the bar into the hotel lobby. I counted them so as to be sure that the ballroom would be full when I arrived, and when I had thirty-two couples I followed. Dorothy had not passed the bar, but I knew that as organizer she must have arrived early. I saw her as soon as I entered the ballroom; she was not hard to miss.

She was wearing a sari, blue with a gold border and not the shoes I had seen her buy but small embroidered slippers with curling toes. Her dress was correct, the sort that might be worn for an Indian festival or a wedding. She wore bangles on both wrists and one on her left ankle and when I saw her she was deep in conversation with an elderly gentleman whom I took to be the president of her school; he was bearded and wore a silk handkerchief in his breast pocket. I remained in a corner, near a palm, an intruder, and I saw, as I expected, that Dorothy was wearing the love knot on a chain around her neck. I squinted and made out a neatly painted caste mark on her forehead, vermilion.

I do not know how to dance, and although I had prepared for the dance by deviously getting the ticket and borrowing money for my clothes, I should have included a few dancing lessons, for I knew that I was going to talk to Dorothy this evening. The conversation I had practiced I imagined taking place as we were twirling around the room. But the band was playing loudly and I could see from the couples already on the floor that this dance step was beyond me. Half a dozen songs and an hour later I decided that unless the lights were lowered and the band was playing more slowly my plans would be ruined. A bad dancer can fake it if the music is slow and no one is watching. I went out of the ballroom and found a man in overalls and genially bribed him to dim the lights.

The first slow number was 'Blue Moon.' Dorothy danced with the elderly bearded gentleman. So she was a bad dancer, too! As she moved around the floor I edged over to where she had been standing; the music ended. There was clapping. She walked toward me. I smiled at her, an over-rehearsed grin that was nearly wild, but she returned it. I had to speak to her now.

I did so, but to this day I have no idea what happened to my tongue. I often think of this – I think of it as much as I do her face – and I still cannot understand it; there seems no explanation. I opened my mouth; my sentence was 'I've been admiring your sari all evening,' but I spoke it not in English but in Bengali.

Her eyes widened. I blushed and stared at the love knot, and I saw it as I had once done, in my hands in my mother's room in Calcutta.

'You speak Hindi,' said Dorothy. An American accent in that beautiful Bengali mouth.

'No,' I said in Bengali, and then, 'No, not Hindi,' I said in English, with my Indian accent. I was not doing well.

She wrinkled her nose.

'I have been admiring your sari all evening,' I said, almost in panic. 'But when I saw your jewel – it is a Bengali jewel, is it not? – I felt I had to speak in Bengali.'

'Where did you learn it?' she asked, eager.

'A few lessons . . . private teacher . . .'

'Can you give me his name? I'm trying to learn –'

'He died,' I said, and she made me regret my lie.

'Oh, I'm awfully sorry,' she said, her face going sad.

'A long time ago,' I added, and hearing 'These Foolish Things' asked her to dance. My head was swimming.

She placed her hand on my shoulder; I embraced her and we were off, intimate as lovers. She said, 'Some idiot put practically all the lights off. You can't see your hand in front of your face.'

It was true. Perhaps I had given the man in overalls too much money. I said, 'Oh, but I can see you wery vell.'

She was humming the song in my ear.

'You must have lived in the States for a long time to pick up such a strong American accent. Not so?'

'I was born here,' said Dorothy. 'But my father was born in India, in Calcutta.'

'Imagine that,' I said. 'And your mother?'

'Indian, too. But born in England. Kinda complicated, huh?'

'They met here?'

'In England,' she said, 'where my father was studying.'

'Forgive my questions.'

'That's okay. I have to explain this about once a week. As a matter of fact I was just saying the same thing to the dean. That's him over there with the beard, if you can see him in this spooky room.'

'Odd,' I said, 'your father coming all this way. To America.'

'Not so odd when you consider that his first wife was an American. But like they say, that was in another country.'

I had no more questions. The dance ended. People were clapping.

But she was saying, 'I can't understand why he came here. I'm leaving for India the day after tomorrow. I can hardly wait.'

'Who knows,' I said. 'You might meet an Indian boy and marry him and never leave India.'

'Not if my father has anything to do with it!' she said, and she raised her eyebrows and laughed loudly and I watched the love knot rising and falling at her throat, a jewel pulsing warmly on that dark velvet skin. She excused herself and disappeared, but I still saw the love knot, the gold threads of the filigree, meeting and crossing and meeting again. And I had a vision of a child I once saw in Calcutta, tracing figure eights in the dust with a wobbling stick. I watched and he drew a dozen or more, and the more he traced the more the figure changed, so that just before he left off, the final lines in each figure which had touched with such symmetry at the beginning ceased to meet at all and left a line curving at an angle in the dust, the open hourglass of an imperfect eight.

What Have You Done to Our Leo?

At the end of the meal, the Sunday curry lunch which many of the expatriates in Dar es Salaam ate in the upstairs dining room of the Rex Hotel, Ernie Grigson leaned over and whispered seriously and slowly to Leo Mockler's ear: 'I'm going to ask you for a big favor some time when I'm sober.' Ernie found his glass and swallowed some beer. He added, 'Mention it to me tomorrow, okay?'

Leo said yes, expelling it quickly with a vaporous belch, and as he did he saw Margo at the end of the table watching the two of them. Although Margo did not speak, she had the staring look of the practiced wife who knows without hearing him what her husband is saying.

But Ernie and Margo weren't married. They had planned to be months before, and then, out of the blue, Amy – Ernie's wife – went to India with the two children. Amy was living in an *ashram* outside Bombay. She wrote letters which were vague and dreamy and which always ended with demands for money. She never mentioned divorce. Ernie wondered if perhaps she was ill (the food? the heat? – Amy had never been strong). He wrote to the elderly Canadian lady who ran the *ashram*; he asked about Amy. The lady wrote back in shaky script on handmade paper, stamped at the top with a Hindu symbol in blue: Amy was fine and the children were happy; 'Amy's thoughts are serene and with us. She has many friends here. It will confuse her to preoccupy her mind with the separation. Amy needs time.'

Ernie was angry: Amy in India had all the time in the world! And it had been understood that the divorce was a mutual wish. In those last months before Amy left for Bombay they had even stopped discussing the divorce: the arguments ended and the indifference that followed was more final than silence, worse than their quarreling had ever been.

Margo had moved in with Ernie the day Amy left. Leo visited them. He could sense their tension, which was lovers' tension, haphazardly pitching them into moods. Marriage, they agreed, was a trivial, nearly silly ceremony – but Ernie was still married to Amy and that mattered. Three times Leo heard the elderly Canadian lady's letter being read out; the last time it was read by Margo, who was pregnant now.

It was April in Dar es Salaam, and the rains were on them. The road to Ernie's house was sodden, and the raised sections at the edges broke off in chunks. There were a number of simple brown puddles which proved bottomless and swallowed the wheels of cars. And insects, seemingly given life by the floods of rainwater, crawled over the furniture and clung to windows. Even when it was not raining the air was heavy with wetness and insect racket. Ernie said that screens killed the breeze.

Leo, who lived at a boarding house, The Palms, a mile up the Oyster Bay Road, stopped driving all the way out to Ernie's. He saw the couple only on Sundays at the curry lunch. He was glad he did not see them often, because Margo's mood now did not concern the divorce anymore but was rather a tight shrewish incomprehension over why Ernie had married Amy in the first place. And Leo, once used as a witness, was expected to take sides. So it was 'What do *you* think, Leo?' and also the rain that kept him away.

On Monday at five Leo pushed through the swinging saloon doors of the Rex and saw Ernie at the end of the bar, standing with one foot on the brass rail, studying the deeply scarred dart board.

'Large Tusker,' said Leo to the barman, drawing beside Ernie and startling him.

'Rough day?' asked Ernie. He held his glass to his lips.

'The usual,' said Leo. He worked at the National and Grindlays on Shirazi Street. He seldom spoke about his job to Ernie, who had something to do with traffic control at the airport, and thought naively (but like most other people) that Leo was rich because he worked in a bank. 'I get long leave in September,' said Leo. 'I need it, too. I'm thinking of going back via Beirut and Athens.'

'I might be able to do something for you – get you a concession, reduced rates, that sort of thing,' said Ernie.

'Really?' Ernie had never made an offer like that before; and the most Leo had allowed Ernie at the bank was jumping the queue on Saturday mornings at the end of the month. 'As a matter of fact I was also thinking of going to Prague, but it costs a bit extra.'

'I could fix it for you,' said Ernie. 'There's a connecting flight to Prague from Athens. Have you booked?'

'No,' said Leo.

'Write down the places you want to go on a piece of paper. Leave it to me. I'll take care of it.'

Then Leo remembered what Ernie had said on Sunday. He was going to mention it. But it seemed so obvious: the favor in return.

'What are you drinking?' asked Leo.

'I'm all right,' said Ernie. He looked into his glass and said, 'You remember what I asked you yesterday?'

'The favor?'

'That's right,' said Ernie, and tried to chuckle. 'Well, the other day I was trying to think who was my best friend. I thought of Charlie and Agnes, Alan, the boys at the airport. And you know what? I couldn't think of one that I could rely on.'

'Money?' asked Leo. He felt sure it was not, but said it to help Ernie along.

'No. I don't have much, but that's the thing, see? This is the one thing money won't buy.'

'You've got me in suspense,' said Leo.

'It's my divorce,' said Ernie. He put his glass down, and with his hands empty he seemed to become conscious of their trembling. He picked them up and made fists and began to rub his eyes, speaking tiredly as he did so: 'I've been seeing lawyers about it, and they all say it's hopeless. There are only two legal grounds for divorce here in Tanganyika.' A long-time resident, Ernie always used the country's colonial name. 'Nonconsummation and adultery, just like UK. And since I've got two kids I can't very well say I never poked my wife, can I?' He laughed briefly and took his fists from his eyes, which were now very red. 'So that leaves me with adultery.'

'It happens in the best of families,' said Leo.

'Sure,' said Ernie, 'but did you ever think how hard it is to prove? The lawyers tell me that I have to supply the name of the chap and of course his address. Then I have to give the number of times and the places where I think it happened. If I can't give the details my divorce is up the spout.' Ernie shook his head. 'God, I haven't had a good night's sleep in ages.'

'Amy's no help, I suppose.'

'Useless,' said Ernie. 'Absolutely useless. I send a check every bloody month and she never thanks me. She's only written a couple of times. She wants a tape recorder, she wants a camera. I don't know what she *does* with the money – a hundred quid goes a long way in India.' In a resigned tone Ernie said, 'But she always took me for granted, you know.'

'Well, who do you think it was that –' Leo stopped deliberately, but Ernie simply watched Leo's eyes and showed no inclination to speak. 'That, um, committed adultery with her?'

'That's just it!' Ernie said. 'She *didn't*. That's only the grounds.'

'Oh, the grounds,' said Leo. 'But in order to get your divorce here you've got to prove she went off with someone, isn't that right?'

'I could go to Mexico. Divorces are easy there – mental cruelty, incompatibility, lots of vague stuff,' said Ernie. 'But I can't spare the time.'

'It really is hopeless,' said Leo. 'Funny, I thought Amy was playing around.'

'She wasn't,' said Ernie, seemingly offended by what Leo had said. 'I'm no fool. We weren't suited to each other – I knew that before we got married. But she went on about how she'd kill herself if I wouldn't have her. That sort of thing. We got married and that was a mistake, but no one made a monkey out of me, not even when my marriage was breaking up.'

The image suggested a great ship foundering in a boiling sea; but marriage was a flimsy agreement, its only drama was its legality, the image was arrogant. It was the male pride, thought Leo: Ernie denying his cast-off wife's adultery. Her sin was his humiliation. He wanted it all ways.

'Maybe,' said Leo, '*she'll* divorce *you*. After all, you were playing around, weren't you?'

'I found a woman I loved,' said Ernie. His sincerity reproached Leo.

'It's still adultery,' said Leo quickly, trying to cover his embarrassment. 'Amy can divorce you for it, can't she?'

'She's up in the clouds,' said Ernie. 'She's in that *ashram*. You know what they *do* there? They pray, sort of, and meditate, silly things like that. Besides, she's got her money coming every month. They all have in these *ashrams* – they're all rich or divorced there. They don't care; they go around barefoot and write poems. No, she'll never divorce me. I'll have to divorce her, and if I don't do it soon Margo's going to have a bastard in five months' time. A bastard with no passport,' Ernie said bitterly.

'But how do you expect to –' Again Ernie did not speak. He waited for Leo to finish. 'You can't divorce her. You haven't got any grounds. It's impossible, you said so yourself.'

'No, I didn't,' said Ernie.

Leo laughed. 'Yes, you did!'

'It's possible,' said Ernie slowly, 'but it's illegal. Did you ever hear of connivance?'

'I suppose conniving is what we're doing now,' said Leo.

'Not yet,' said Ernie. 'Have another drink?' Leo said yes, and Ernie went on. 'Amy never committed adultery with anyone and you know it. She wouldn't know where to begin. But if I say she did and can prove it, I can get the divorce – providing she agrees to the whole business.'

'You mean, concoct a story about a boy friend she had?'

'They call them corespondents.'

'So you have to find a corespondent.'

'That's the favor I was going to ask you,' said Ernie, and he said it with the same sincerity that had picked at Leo's shame earlier – that reproachful sentence, 'I found a woman I loved.'

'Me?' said Leo, but couldn't laugh. In a very thin voice he said, 'I only met her once.'

'Twice,' said Ernie. He took out a worn pocket diary and fingered the pages.

Leo remembered the first time. He was new in the country, and, having met Ernie casually in the Rex, Ernie had invited him home for a last drink. Amy had made a show of surprise, so wooden and deliberate that the word *theatrical* occurred to Leo; and then she used halting sarcasm: 'At least you could have given me a ring and let me know you were bringing someone.'

Ernie, much to Leo's discomfort, turned his back on his wife.

Leo said, 'I'm terribly sorry if I'm intruding.'

'It's not you,' Amy had said, 'it's him.'

It was clear they were not getting on well, and Leo thought: if a man was kind to her she would take him as a lover. Amy left the room. She came back without the ribbon in her hair; her hair was long and alive with the electricity the comb had left in it. She was charming to Leo, got him a drink, lit his cigarette, sat beside him and said, 'Have you got pots and pots of money?' when Leo told her he worked at the National and Grindlays.

'No, I'm just a clerk on the foreign exchange side, though I started out on fixed deposits. As a matter of fact, I'm trying to save enough money so that I can resign in a few years and go back to university.'

'I was at Exeter,' Amy said. Her reply was pleasing: she was one of the few people who had not said, 'At your age?' when he mentioned going back to university. 'I did art history, but I read fiction most of the time.'

'I read a lot of novels,' said Leo. 'I'm very fond of –'

'I haven't read a book since –' Here Amy looked at Ernie. 'Since I met you.'

'Well, children must take up a great deal of your time,' said Leo.

'Not here,' she said. 'We've got slaves – *ayahs*. They do everything, washing, cooking . . . the children are devoted to them. I've plenty of time. But no . . . interest. Are you married?'

Leo shook his head.

'God, how I envy you.' Amy closed her eyes and seemed to relax, and Leo took a good look at her. She was pale, small boned, blonde as a Swede, with a sharp lean nose and breasts which were probably small – it was hard to tell: she was wearing a loose shirt, one of Ernie's perhaps, and the breasts were only suggestions at the pockets. But she had a lovely fragile face, and with her eyes closed Leo could imagine her head on a pillow.

'You could do a little art history here,' Leo said.

'Bongo drums,' said Amy contemptuously. 'India – that's where the art is. Have you ever been to India, Leo?'

'No.' When had he told her his name? 'But I've always wanted to go.'

'Indians are fabulous creatures – very catlike, I always think, very gentle and smooth,' she said, stroking her forearm as she spoke. 'Erotic sculpture on temples. Yes! On holy temples! Fantastic things. They worship the *lingam*, you see. You wouldn't believe what they get up to,' she said, her eyes flashing. 'Look at poor Ernest – he's *blushing*!'

'I am not blushing,' said Ernie. 'I've heard all this rubbish before. Here, Leo, you want to have a look at those temples? There they are.' He pointed to a shelf of large books, boxed editions; art books, Leo knew, even from across the room.

Leo stayed late, talking mostly to Amy ('My aunt was a character,' Amy said at one point, 'I once saw her lose her temper and down a whiskey, then smash her glass into the fireplace . . .'). After twelve Ernie drove Leo back to The Palms. In the car Leo said, 'I like your wife. She's very intelligent.'

'We're getting a divorce,' said Ernie.

It was a statement to which the only tactful response was silence. And Leo knew as Ernie said it that he would have nothing to do with Amy. A married lover, it was said, was a convenient if temporary pleasure; but a woman on the verge of divorce was a terrible risk, a man-eater.

Apparently there *was* a second meeting – Ernie swore it was so, it was marked in his pocket diary – but Leo could not recall it. His interest in Amy died with the news of the divorce. He could remember being a bit sorry, because he had never made love to a married woman, and now his courage failed him. The next time Leo saw Ernie in the Rex, Ernie was with Margo. Leo knew that he could not be friends with both wife and lover. His friendships had to be Ernie's or there would be misunderstandings. And Leo felt mild relief, as if something cloudy and uncertain in his life had disappeared, when Amy went to India. It was a surprising feeling: he barely knew the woman.

'. . . happens all the time,' Ernie was saying. Used to giving orders at the airport and unfamiliar with persuading people to do things, Ernie got excited and distracted telling Leo his idea. He began by saying that he considered it a big favor, but later in the evening he said in a wheedling tone that there was no risk; it was a small thing really, if Leo could see it in its proper perspective. 'Look at the paper. Every Thursday they give the court proceedings, and, Christ, they're practically all divorces – even in a little dump like Tanganyika.'

Ernie took out his handkerchief and wiped his face. The bar had filled up with seamen who stood, like Ernie, with one foot on the brass rail, glancing around. The regulars were at tables, drinking slowly or not at all, and looking up and commenting when people left or entered through the swinging doors of the bar.

'It's a strange request,' Leo said finally. 'I don't know what to do.'

'There's no one else I can turn to,' said Ernie.

'So it really isn't such a small matter, is it?'

'For me, no. It's a life-or-death business for me. But you – God, it's nothing.'

'It's a lie, though.'

'Oh, yes, I know that,' said Ernie. 'There's no getting around that.'

'And a lie is serious, especially in a legal matter. It's perjury. The whole thing could backfire. I could lose my job at the bank.'

'It won't backfire, I swear.'

'Everyone knows we're friends. They'll know we made it up.'

'That's just it. These divorces, look at them. Who is it that's always named as the third party – it's friends every single time! How else would the wife meet the bloke? The women here don't get out much. The only men they meet are the friends of their husbands. That's how it happens –'

'You mentioned the court proceedings in the paper,' said Leo. 'I read the paper every day and I've never noticed them, but what bothers me is that other people here probably read them all the time. It would be just like my manager, Farnsworth, to see something like that. If he did I'd be finished.'

'Nothing to worry about,' said Ernie, becoming eager again. 'Don't give that a thought. The editor of the *Standard* is an old pal of mine. I could ask him not to print our names. He'd do it, I know he would. He's a very old friend. I've known him for years.'

'Then why don't you name him as corespondent?' said Leo. But he was sorry as soon as he said it.

'Leo, for God's sake!' Ernie said helplessly. 'Don't you see I can't? You're my last hope. If you refuse me, I'm stuck – Margo says she'll go away. She'll leave me.' Ernie began to sigh softly. 'Everyone lets me down, Amy, Margo, my kids – those kids mean a lot to me. You don't have any kids. You don't know what it's like to be away from them. It kills me. Leo, I cry when I think of them – I'm not ashamed, I *do*.' Ernie looked mournfully at Leo and said, 'If you did this for me, you can't imagine what I'd do for you. I'd do anything –' Ernie put his hand on Leo's wrist: the fingers were wet and Leo felt disgust, felt his arm turn clammy as Ernie said, 'Just name it – anything –'

'Stop,' said Leo, and drew away. 'I don't want to make a deal with you,' he said. But he said it to convince himself, because at the source of Leo's disgust was the thought that he could have had anything he named; and what was most sinister to him was that he was tempted to ask. But he said: 'First put it to Amy. See if she'll agree to it. I take it Margo already agrees. Then – this is crucial – make sure that nothing appears in the *Standard*. Get a definite promise from the editor. If Amy agrees and nothing gets into print, I'll be satisfied.'

Ernie beamed. 'We're halfway there! Amy's already said yes.'

'What? But how did you know I'd agree?'

'I didn't.' Ernie grinned. 'I just said that I was going to ask you. Here's her letter. I think she means business.' Ernie took out a wrinkled aerogram with a pink stamp printed on it. He showed it to Leo, smoothing it on the bar. The handwriting was large, willful, done with a felt marking pen: *I suppose it will happen eventually, so it might as well be your way. Better with Leo than others I could name – he's a nice boy.* There was no signature. Leo folded the aerogram and before he handed it back to Ernie he looked at the unusual return address: *Amy/Ashram/Kolhapur.*

The following Sunday at lunch Ernie was exuberant; he sat a few feet away from the table and held his beer mug on his knee; he laughed loudly and often. He said that he had seen the editor of the *Standard* and got the promise from him; and the lawyer, who was an Indian, knew of the connivance and was drawing up the papers. It was all set.

'Have a beer,' said Ernie. 'You're not drinking, Leo. Cheer up!'

'I've stopped drinking,' said Leo. He hadn't, but the lie was necessary: he wanted nothing from Ernie. On his way to the toilet Leo paid for his own meal. He said he had a headache and went back to The Palms. He did not want Ernie to think that the favor, which already he regretted, could be repaid so easily, or at all. He withdrew into spiteful lassitude and stopped seeing Ernie altogether.

Some weeks after that lunch he was visited by the Indian lawyer, whose name was Chandra and who drove out to The Palms and said softly, 'Are you alone?' and then 'I've come to deliver a subpoena.'

That was ominous; it gave Leo a fright, but Chandra said, 'Not to worry – it's just a formality,' and stayed for tea. They talked, and as they did, Leo thought: Here is a good man; he would never ask of me what Ernie did. And Leo wished that he had met Chandra instead of Ernie.

Walking to Chandra's car, Leo asked, 'Did you know Amy?'

Eagerly Chandra said, 'Yes – oh, she was a fine person. She knew a great deal about Indian art – very interested in Indian culture. A graduate, did you know? I was hoping Ernie would try to patch things up – but –'

'He wasn't interested,' said Leo.

'I should not say this,' said Chandra. 'But he did not deserve her.'

'You're right,' said Leo. And he startled the Indian by saying, 'He's a selfish bastard.'

Chandra looked warily at Leo and then said good-bye.

He's wondering how I can say that, thought Leo. But the betrayal was not Leo's – it was Ernie's. Ernie's lie had changed Leo and made him restless. He slept badly and had disturbing dreams. In a dream he watched his mother snarling at Ernie and saying, 'What have you done to our Leo?' Ernie had replied by sticking his tongue out at the old lady.

A month after he agreed to act as corespondent he admitted his hatred of Ernie to himself. Leo found himself falling into conversations with bank customers who knew Ernie; Leo made a point of calling Ernie a shit, and he encouraged the customers to agree with him. He saw each of Ernie's enemies – there were quite a number, Leo realized – as his own friends.

Amy as well. He thought of her in ramshackle India with her two children, living from day to day, in a silent *ashram*, in retreat from the world. It seemed a kind of destitution that he had connived with Ernie in forcing upon her. How she must hate me, he thought. But Amy did not know that his part in the conspiracy had ruined his friendship with Ernie and Margo. Amy didn't know that in his agreeing to the favor he had accepted the blame and had had to construct the adultery in his mind in order to convince himself of his blame. That preoccupation had begun to obsess and arouse him, almost as if it had all been true and he was looking back at a recent half-completed passion which had confused rather than exhausted his feelings.

On an impulse he wrote to her. It was late in the morning, just after coffee, and there were no customers in the bank because it was raining very hard. He felt lonely, but writing the letter lifted his spirits. An impediment, the cramp of language he had some-times experienced in letter writing, did not arise this time. The hollowness of letters with all their inadequate phrases had caused him to stop writing letters entirely, but the letter to Amy gave him pleasure. He said, *I rather like the idea of being your lover.* He said, *I agreed to it because Ernie seemed so upset, but I don't like him anymore.* He said, in his last long paragraph, *I'm sitting in the bank and looking out into the empty foyer and the rainy street* – and that was especially strange because as he wrote it he did look around the bank and he tried to explain all the things he saw to this lonely woman.

She replied. It came quickly and it made Leo realize that India was just across the water, closer than England. Amy talked about the children, how brown they had become; about the *ashram*'s activities, the poetry magazine, the outings, the play school that was being organized. She said, *I've seen those sexy temples, by the way. Fantastic!* She said she was learning a bit of Hindi. And she finished her letter with a long paragraph similar to Leo's: *It's late now and our chickens are silent. The room seems quite empty and I'm smoking a cigarette I rolled from the air edition of the* Guardian Weekly . . .

That was an aerogram. Her next was many sheets of notepaper in a thick envelope. She unburdened herself and responded to Leo's remark about Ernie (*I don't like him anymore*). She analyzed her marriage more candidly and more fairly than Ernie had ever done; it was a little history, their first meeting and their first disappoint-ments. She said how excited she had been when Leo had come home unexpectedly with Ernie. Leo read, fascinated: she was a victim and here she was alone; Leo had had a part in victimizing her. The deception was like a fishbone in his throat.

Leo wrote Amy a long apology; he asked her to forgive him for agreeing to the lie. He said he was sorry and that if he had it to do over again he would refuse. Amy's reply was: *Don't say that. Don't regret what you've said. You did something fine because you believed Ernie was your friend. I think about you often, Leo, and I sometimes wish we really had gone off together. But it's too late for that now. You're a very sweet person. If you regret what you did, then I'll have to as well. And I don't want that. I'm happy here.*

*

The bank manager, Farnsworth, frowned at Leo when the coffee boy knocked on the glass partition and said Leo had a telephone call.

'Take your call,' said Farnsworth. 'I'll check these figures in the meantime.'

'Sorry,' said Leo. 'I'll be right back.'

'*Shauri kwisha*!' It was Ernie. 'It's all settled! I've just come out of court this minute. It'll be final in three weeks. God, the judge gave me the third degree, asked me how well I knew you and did I know what you were up to ... Leo, are you there?'

'Yes. Look, I'm busy –'

'I thought you'd laugh when I told you. Say, Leo, is there anything wrong?'

'I'm with the manager. Piles of work –'

'I understand. But what a weight off my shoulders! It's like – just like a big weight lifted off my shoulders. I can breathe again! I feel like celebrating. How about a drink at the Rex?'

'It's not even *noon*, Ernie.'

'I can drive right over. Say yes.'

'No, I've got work to do.'

'Leo, are you feeling all right?'

'I'm fine; I have to go. The manager's waiting. I'll ring you back.'

But he didn't ring Ernie back that day; he busied himself with the July figures. And the next day he could have rung, but he had no excuse for neglecting to ring the previous day, none that Ernie would believe. Ernie would still say he was ill or out of sorts. Leo was waiting – for courage, he told himself. He did not want to hear about the divorce and he did not want to see Ernie until he could say what he felt: that Ernie had betrayed him and made him victimize poor Amy.

The third day Ernie rang three times in the morning. Leo told the switchboard operator that if Ernie Grigson rang again – she was to ask for the name – she should tell him that Leo was not available. Leo tried to stay out of sight; he worked in the vault, then in a back office hidden from the street. But late in the afternoon, when he was standing at the front counter and going over his transactions on the electric adding machine, he sensed someone pause at the window, and he felt it must be Ernie, peering in at him.

It wasn't. Two European ladies had stopped. Leo looked up and they began walking. He didn't recognize them – they were deeply tanned; one wore a headscarf, the other a straw hat – but their gestures were distinct. As they moved along the sidewalk, one looked through the bank's window, directly at him with her broad brown face and bright red lips, and then she quickly looked away and seemed to mumble; the second turned and stared at Leo, shielding her eyes from the glare in a kind of salute. And they walked on. The women did not face each other, but Leo could tell they were speaking. He realized it was Thursday.

Farnsworth came over as Leo was searching the columns of the *Standard* for the Court Record. He couldn't find it at first, and when he did find the right column (it resembled the account of a cricket match) it was with difficulty that he located his name among the many there.

'I see we've got our name in the papers, Mockler,' said Farnsworth curtly. 'Feel like talking about it?'

'No,' said Leo.

The Palms was run by a small, neat widow of sixty or more whose husband had been a District Officer in Morogoro. She had a son Leo's age who was an accountant with a public relations firm in Capetown, and usually, before dinner, when Leo was having his drink on the verandah, she joined him and spoke about her son. The other guests tried to avoid her chatter, but Leo was grateful for her company and even listened with patient interest to her reading her son's letters.

But that Thursday, the day Leo's name appeared in the *Standard*'s Court Record, the widow avoided him. She sat at another table with an older resident, a man Leo knew by his nickname, and only once looked at Leo: wickedly, he thought, as if at a traitor. The widow and her elderly companion spoke in rapid whispers, then very loudly and irrelevantly ('Are the Browns in nine?' 'I believe they are, yes') to disguise their whispering.

Leo ate alone and felt eyes on him and voices behind him. But he was determined not to be intimidated; after dinner he had his coffee on the verandah instead of the lounge. He turned his back to the people in the bar, which adjoined the verandah, and he faced the sea. The waves lapped, making a breathless splashing, and the palm fronds rattled out of sight, high above him. In the darkness, across that ocean, were India and Amy. He felt like going up to his room and writing her a note. He fought the impulse. If he walked through the bar they would say, 'Expect he's going up to write to the other party.' They would laugh, because now they believed they knew his closest secret.

A silence consumed the bar sounds; it was as if the sea had mysteriously risen inside and drowned every person there. It happened like that, unnaturally, and the only sounds were the palms and the regular waves and, far-off, one or two barking voices, perhaps of fishermen, the shouts skipping in from the water.

Leo turned to see Ernie walking through the bar. The widow said, 'He's outside.'

Ernie was at the doorway. He paused and smiled weakly, then came toward Leo with both hands out.

'Leo, I'm sorry,' he said, too loud. The people in the bar must have heard because they went silent in a hush once again and Leo could hear the ice rattling in their glasses.

'Go away,' the whisper was barely audible. 'Don't talk to me here.'

'It was the African –'

'Lower your voice,' Leo hissed.

'The African,' said Ernie. But it was a poor whisper. 'At the printery. The stupid bugger forgot what the editor told him about leaving out your name. It's all his fault –'

'Get out,' said Leo. He tossed his head. 'They're listening.'

'I just wanted to tell you that I promised I'd make your bookings – for your long leave. But you never gave me a list of places. You mentioned Vienna, wasn't it? And I forgot the others. So write them down on a piece of paper –'

'All right,' said Leo. 'Tomorrow. Now do me a favor.'

'Yes, of course,' said Ernie.

'Get out of here this minute.'

'You hate me, don't you? I don't blame you –'

'Ernie!' In his exasperation he raised his voice, and again he heard the ice in the glasses.

'Margo's in the car. She said to thank you,' said Ernie.

'Leave by the beach, so they don't see you.'

Leo went up to bed by entering the building from the back door, avoiding crossing through the bar. Going up the stairs he thought he heard the widow's voice, '– Indian lawyer came to see him – Knew it then, of course –' her voice was a high, satisfied whine.

Chandra, the widow, the people in the bar, Margo, Amy, Ernie

– everyone had got what he wanted out of the divorce, except Leo. All the blame was his and he was suffering for no good reason, as if he alone had been made to sit in a zone of dead air.

'Coffee?' inquired Farnsworth; Leo said yes, Farnsworth suggested the Gymkhana Club, and Leo knew it was serious: it was in the Billiard Room of the Gymkhana Club that Leo's predecessor, a man who traded currency on the side, was sacked.

Farnsworth was relaxed. He talked about the club, how long he had been a member, all the changes he had seen, how women weren't allowed in the upstairs lounge, how he and others in the old days used to wait every second Friday for the mailboat and the English papers. He leaned forward and said, 'Let's take the bull by the horns –'

A man entered the club and, greeting Farnsworth, smiled at Leo.

'You're due for leave in September, am I right?'

'The fifteenth,' said Leo.

'Well, I've been thinking,' said Farnsworth. 'We're not all that busy. I think you can take it a bit earlier than that.'

'How soon would that be?' asked Leo.

'Say – within the next fortnight,' said Farnsworth. 'That'll give you time to make your bookings. If you have any difficulty I'll see what I can do.'

'I won't have any trouble with that,' said Leo.

'Better settle up with the tax people before you go.'

'Aren't I coming back here?' asked Leo.

'Do you *want* to?' Farnsworth looked surprised. 'I would have thought not.'

'I don't know,' said Leo.

'This club has seen its share of scandal,' said Farnsworth, and then he smiled. He stood up and put his arm on Leo's shoulder. 'I know how it is,' he said. 'Don't do anything foolish. Things look pretty black to you now. But when you're back in the UK, everything will seem different. You'll see.'

'Can you drop me at the post office? I have a cable to send.'

Later in the morning Leo rang Ernie.

'About those plane bookings,' Leo said. 'I've changed my mind about Beirut –'

'Very sensible,' said Ernie. 'How do you want me to route you?'

'I'm going to London,' said Leo.

'Any stops?'

'Yes,' said Leo, 'Bombay.'

'That's in India,' said Ernie. He laughed. 'It'll cost a lot extra.'

'You can afford it,' said Leo.

She had said she would be at the airport, but it was a man who stepped out of the crowd of people with bundles and took Leo by the arm and spoke his name. The man was English; he was dressed like a holy man, in a dusty white robe. His hair was to his shoulders and he had a full beard, the tip of which he clutched as he spoke to Leo: 'Amy's told me all about you,' he said, but not unkindly. His eyes were extremely gentle, and he held Leo's arm the way one holds an invalid's.

His name was Bob, he said. He was agreeable and helpful, and even recognizing the vast differences in their appearances, Leo felt close to him, saw him as one who had perhaps lived on the periphery of Amy's marriage – probably helped her through the divorce – as Leo had lived alongside Ernie.

'Amy couldn't get away,' said Bob. 'I'm supposed to take you to the *ashram*.' He guided Leo through the crowd and hailed a taxi, and they bumped along through more crowds to a railway station which had the appearance of a busy refugee encampment.

They traveled second class; it was a compromise. Leo wanted first class, which was air-conditioned, and Bob said he always went third. In the train Bob said, 'You look petrified!'

'What's that?' asked Leo, glancing out the window.

'A rice field,' said Bob.

'No, those naked people.'

'Oh, beggars. India's full of them.'

They arrived at the *ashram* at night. It was an enormous compound, as plain as an army barracks, surrounded by a freshly painted wall which was floodlit. Amy's house was big, two storied, and she was at the upper window, a white face with darkness behind it.

Leo bounded up the stairs ahead of Bob, but when he saw her his nerve failed and he could not kiss her. Then Bob was in the room, putting Leo's suitcase against the wall and saying awkwardly, 'Well here you are. I'll be going now.'

'You're a dear,' said Amy. Bob had opened the door. She said, 'Narendra?'

'*Baroda*,' said Bob, and was away.

'I see you speak the language,' said Leo.

'Pardon?' said Amy, and then, 'Oh that,' and smiled.

She was wearing a sari and gold bangles, and her hair was loosely braided in one thick strand with a tassel at the tip in the Indian style. She was not the person Leo had written to, not the person he had seen at Ernie's house. She was thinner, more angular, awkward, plain even, and her speech was shallow. She was not pretty; she was any English housewife in an Indian costume, and Leo noticed she was smoking and wore a watch.

Leo fumbled with his hands and finally said, 'It's a nice house you've got.'

'Very old,' said Amy. 'It belonged to one of the first residents of the *ashram*. A wonderful old man. It's got a fantastic view of the place. You'll see in the morning.'

'The kids,' said Leo. 'Are they asleep?'

'Hours ago,' said Amy.

'They didn't wait up,' said Leo.

'They didn't know you were coming.'

Leo was going to ask why, but didn't. He found it hard to speak to Amy, and it was odd, because he could have written to her very easily; but now he could hardly think of anything to say. She seemed a vague acquaintance, met after a long time, someone he barely knew.

'That's a very handsome oil lamp,' said Leo, pointing to the lantern on a carved table; it was the only light in the room.

'Only five rupees at the bazaar,' said Amy. 'It's solid brass.'

'Do you mind if I blow it out?' said Leo. He did not wait for Amy's reply. He walked over, raised the chimney and puffed on it. The room was dark. Leo said, 'Where am I going to sleep?'

'Silly,' said Amy, and Leo heard the gold bangles clink and saw the sparks from the cigarette being stubbed out. He heard her walking toward him and saw her arm move outward as if flinging her sari off.

They made love ineptly, in silence, with unsatisfying speed on a rocking *charpoy*. Leo apologized, saying that it had been a long plane journey and that he was tired. And Amy confessed that she was upset, too. It had been dutiful; there was no passion, and Leo felt that he had lived through the act a hundred times already, even to the apology.

He was too excited to sleep, as if he had been rushed through a tunnel, and he told himself that it was the plane. He lay beside Amy and now the room did not seem so dark: he could make out large squares on the ceiling. He still heard the plane, the roar of the landing, and felt the deafening pressure in his ears. He said to himself, 'I'm in India,' but he felt nothing. All the utterance brought to him was India's flat map shape, the vast red patch, the sharp triangle drooping into green ocean, the black borders and dots of cities. But he would get to know it, and 'Yes,' he thought, 'this could be home for me.'

'I want to marry you,' said Leo at last.

'No,' said Amy, 'don't say that.'

'Yes,' he held her, but felt her struggle slightly.

'I can't,' she said; and then pulling away, 'What was that?'

Amy rose up on her elbow and looked at the ceiling.

'Did you hear a bicycle?'

'A bicycle?'

'Go look – go to the window,' said Amy.

Leo walked to the window. Down in the yard a bicycle leaned on its kickstand. An Indian, hard to make out except for the gleaming whiteness of his *dhoti*, was walking away from it.

'What?' asked Amy.

But Leo did not answer until he had lain down again. 'Nothing,' he said, 'just an Indian.'

Amy put her hand to her throat and started to laugh. 'It might be Narendra,' she said. 'My husband.' Her laugh was coarse, that stranger's laugh that fitted the new image Leo had of her.

Leo leaped up and looked for his pants, but just as he caught sight of them – they were knotted in a pile ten feet from the bed – he heard feet quickly mounting the stairs.

Memories of a Curfew

It was not odd that the first few days of our curfew were enjoyed by most people. It was a welcome change for us, like the noisy downpour that comes suddenly in January and makes a watery crackle on the street and ends the dry season. The parties, though these were now held in the afternoon, had a new topic of conversation. There were many rumors, and repeating these rumors made a kind of tennis match, a serve and return, each hit slightly more savage than the last. And the landscape of the city outside the fence of our compound was fascinating to watch. During these first days we stood in our brightly flowered shirts on our hill; we could see the palace burning, the soldiers assembling and making people scatter, and we could hear the bursts of gunfire and some shouts just outside our fence. We were teachers, all of us young, and we were in Africa. There were well-educated ones among us. One of them told me that during the Roman Empire under the reign of Claudius rich people and scholars could be carried in litters by *lecticarii*, usually slaves, to camp with servants at a safe distance from battles; these were curious Romans, men of high station who, if they so wished, could be present and, between feasts, witness the slaughter.

But the curfew continued, and what were diversions for the first days and weeks became habits. Although people usually showed up for work in the mornings, work in the afternoons almost ceased. There were too many things to be done before the curfew began at nightfall: buses had to be caught, provisions found, and some people had to collect children. We visited the bars so that we could get drunk in the company of other people; we played the slot machines and talked about the curfew, but after two weeks it was a very boring subject.

The people who never went out at night before the curfew was imposed – some Indians with large families used to matinees at the local movie houses, the Africans who did manual labor and some settlers – felt none of the curfew's effects. And there were steady ones who refused to let the curfew get to them; they were impatient with our daily hangovers, our inefficiency, our nervous comments. Our classes were not well-attended. One day I asked casually where our Congolese student was – a dashing figure, he wore a silk scarf and rode a large old motorcycle. I was told that he had been pulled off his motorcycle by a soldier and had been beaten to death with a rifle butt.

We left work early. In the afternoons it was as if everyone was on leave but couldn't afford to go to Nairobi or Mombasa, as if everyone had decided to while away his time at the local bars. At the end of the month no one was paid because the ministry was short-staffed. Some of us ran out of money. The bar owners said they were earning less and less: it was no longer possible for people to drink in bars after dark. They would only have been making the same amount as before, they said, if all the people started drinking in the middle of the morning and kept it up all day. The drinking crowd was a relatively small one, and there were no casual drinkers. Most people in the city stayed at home. They were afraid to stay out after five or so. I tried to get drunk by five-thirty. My memory is of going home drunk, with the dazzling horizontal rays of the sun in my eyes.

The dwindling of time was a strange thing. During the first weeks of the curfew we took chances; we arrived home just as the soldiers were drifting into the streets. Then we began to give ourselves more time, leaving an hour or more for going home. It might have been because we were drunker and needed more time, but we were also more worried: more people were found dead in the streets each morning when the curfew lifted. For many of us the curfew began in the middle of the afternoon when we hurried to a bar; and it was the drinkers who, soaked into a state of slow motion, took the most chances.

Different prostitutes appeared in the bars. Before the curfew there were ten or fifteen in each bar, most of them young and from the outskirts of Kampala. But the curfew was imposed after two tribes fought; most of the prostitutes had been from these tribes and so went into hiding. Others took their places. Now there were ones from the Coast, there were half-castes, Rwandans, Somalis. I remember the Somalis. There was said to be an Ethiopian at the Crested Crane, but I never saw her; in any case, she would have been very popular. All these women were old and hard, and there were fewer than before. They sat in the bars, futile and left alone, slumped on the broken chairs, waiting, as they had been waiting ever since the curfew started. Whatever other talents a prostitute may have she is still unmatched by any other person in her genius for killing time and staying on the alert for customers. The girls held their glasses in two hands and followed the stumbling drinkers with their eyes. Most of us were not interested in complicating the curfew further by taking one of these girls home. I am sure they never had to wait so long with such dull men.

One afternoon a girl put her hand on mine. Her palm was very rough; she rubbed it on my wrist and when I did not turn away she put it on my leg and asked me if I wanted to go in the back. I said I didn't mind, and so she led me out past the toilets to the back of the bar where there was a little shed. She scuffed across the shed's dirt floor, then stood in a corner and lifted her skirt. Here, she said, come here. I asked her if we had to remain standing up. She said yes. I started to embrace her; she let her head fall back until it touched the wood wall. She still held the hem of her skirt in her hand. Then I said no, I couldn't nail her against the wall. I saw that the door was still open. She argued for a while and said in Swahili, 'Talk, talk, we could have finished by now!' I stepped away, but gave her ten shillings just the same. She spat on it and looked at me fiercely.

Anyone who did not crave a drink went straight home. He took no chances. There were too many rumors of people being beaten up at five or six o'clock by drunken soldiers impatient for the curfew to start. As I say, the drinkers took the risks, and with very little time to spare dashed for their cars and sped home. For many the curfew meant an extra supply of newspapers and magazines; for others it meant an extra case of beer. A neighbor of mine had prostitutes on his hands for days at a time, and once one of the girls' babies in a makeshift cot. Many people talked about rape.

The car accidents were very strange, freak accidents, ones that could only happen during a curfew. One man skidded on a perfectly dry road and drove his car through a billboard six feet wide; dozens of people, as if they had been struck blind, plowed straight across the grass of rotaries. And there were accidents at intersections: not hitting oncoming cars, but smashing into the rears of the cars ahead of them. These rear-end collisions were quite numerous and there were no street sweepers to cope with all the broken glass. It was hard to go a hundred yards without seeing shards, red plastic and white glass, sprinkled on the road. Overturned cars on the verge of the road are rare in Africa, but they became very common around Kampala. Accidents in Africa are usually serious; few end with only a smashed headlight or simple bruises. Either the car is completely ruined or the car and driver disappear. We had some of these fatal accidents during the curfew, but there was also, for the first time, a rash of trivial accidents: broken lights, smashed fenders, bent bumpers, bruised foreheads. I think these were caused by the driver glancing around as he drove, half expecting to see angry people about to stone him, or troops aiming rifles at him. I know I tried to pick out soldiers as I drove along, and I always watched carefully for roadblocks which were so simple (two soldiers and an oil drum) as to be invisible. But it was death to drive through one.

There were so many petty arguments those days. In the bars there were fights over nothing at all; with this, a feeling of tribe rather than color. It was not racism. It was a black revolt, northern Ugandans were killing Bugandans, and neither side was helped to any great extent by anyone who was not black. The lingua franca in Kampala was bad Swahili instead of the usual vernacular which was Luganda. At any other time Swahili would have been a despised language, because only the fringe people used it – refugees, Indians, white men, foreigners. But after the curfew began it was mainly the fringe people who took over the bars.

The curfew reminded many of other curfews they had sat through in their time. During the day, in the bars, if the curfew was mentioned, old-timers piped up contemptuously, 'You think *this* is bad? Why, when I was in Leopoldville it was a lot worse than this . . .' Sometimes it was London, Palermo, Alexandria or Tunis, or for the Indians Calcutta, Dacca or Bombay during the Indian emergency. It brought back memories which, though originally violent, had become somewhat glamorous in the long stretch of intervening time: days spent in haggard platoons in the Western Desert, in the dim light of paraffin lamps in Congolese mansions, in London basements with the planes buzzing overhead, in Calcutta with the sound of blood running in the monsoon drains. These men enjoyed talking about the other more effective curfews, and they said that we really didn't know what a curfew was. They had seen men frightened, they said, but this curfew only bored people. Still, I knew then that some time in the future I would recall the curfew – perhaps recall it with the same fanciful distortions that these men added to their own memories. It is so strange. I was in Africa for five years; I remember nothing so clearly as the curfew.

The cripples who sold newspapers at the hotels and down by the Three Stars Bar no longer had to shout and point at their stacks of papers. As soon as the new papers arrived they were sold. The ones from Kenya and Tanzania were in demand since they were printing all the facts and even some of the rumors. The local papers which showed some courage during the first weeks were banned or their reporters beaten up. They now began all their curfew stories, 'Things are almost back to normal . . .'

More and more people began tuning to the External Service of Radio South Africa, and after a time they didn't even apologize. People traded rumors of atrocities (the gorier the story the more knowledgeable the storyteller was considered). No one except the anthropologists chose sides. The political scientists were silent (it was said that as soon as the tribal dispute started a half a dozen doctoral dissertations were rendered invalid). We waited for the curfew to end. But the weeks passed and the curfew stayed the same. At night there was stillness where there had been the rush of traffic in town, the odd shout, or the babbling of idle boys in the streets. Barking dogs and the honk and cackle of herons in our trees replaced the human noises. The jungle had started to move in. Every hour on the hour the air was thunderous with the sound of news broadcasts, but after that, at our compound, you could stand on the hill and hear nothing. Lights flashed soundlessly and to no purpose. Nothing outside the fence moved. Viewed from that hill the curfew seemed a success.

'This is your friend?' asked the Somali girl in Swahili.

The Watusi next to her ignored the question. He turned to me, '*C'est ma fille, Habiba.*' When I looked at the girl he said in Swahili, 'Yes, my friend Paul – *rafiki wangu.*'

'*Très jolie,*' I said, and in English, 'Where'd you find her?'

'*Sur la rue!*' He laughed.

For the rest of the evening we spoke in three languages, and when Habiba's friend, Fatma the Arab, joined us the girls spoke their own mixture of Swahili and Arabic. Gestures also became necessary.

I did not know the Watusi boy well. We had spoken together, our French was equally bad, but it was interlarded with enough Swahili and English for us to understand each other. And that was a strange enough *patois* to create a bewildered silence around us in the bar. I knew he was from Burundi; he claimed a vague royal connection – that was one of the first things he had told me. I had bought him a drink. His name was Jean. His surname had seven syllables.

He leaned over. 'She has a sister,' he said.

At six o'clock we drove to the Somali section of town, a slum like all the sections inhabited by refugees. Even the moneyed refugees – the fugitive *bhang* peddlers, the smugglers – seemed to prefer the anonymity of slums. Habiba's sister came out. She was tall, wearing a veil and silk trousers, but with that sable grace – long-necked, eyes darting over the veil, thin, finely made hands, a jewel in her nostril – that makes Somali women the most desired in Africa. Jean talked to her in Swahili. I smoked and looked around.

There were about a dozen Somali families in this compound of cement sheds; they leaned against the walls, talked in groups, sat in the deep mud ruts that coursed through the yard, eroded in the last rain. Some men at the windows of the sheds sent little boys over to beg from us. We refused to give them any money, but one begged a cigarette from me which he quickly passed to a tough-looking man who squatted in a doorway.

Habiba came back to the car and said it was impossible for her sister to come with us. The men would be angry. The Somali men, forced by the curfew to meander about the yard of their compound, the ones sending little boys to beg from us and chewing the stems of a green narcotic weed (the style was the hillbilly's, but the result was delirium) – these refugees with nothing to do and nowhere to go might lose their tempers and kill us if they saw two of their girls leaving with strangers. They could easily block the drive that led out of the compound; they would have had no trouble stopping our car and beating us. They had nothing to lose. Besides, they were within their rights to stop us. Habiba had a husband, now on a trip (she said) upcountry; technically these other Somali men were her guardians until her husband returned. Two dead men found in a drain. It would not have been a very strange sight. Corpses turned up regularly as the curfew was lifted each morning.

Habiba got into the car and we drove away. I expected a brick to be tossed through the back window, but nothing happened. Several men glared at us; some little boys shouted what could only have been obscenities.

Take a left, take a right, down this street, left again, chattered Habiba in Swahili. I drove slowly; she pointed to a ramshackle cement house with a wooden verandah pocked by woodworm and almost entirely rotted at the base. Some half-caste children were playing nearby, chasing each other. The racial mixtures were apparent: Arab-African, Indian-Somali, white-Arab. The texture of the hair told, the blotched skin; the half-African children had heavy, colorless lips. We entered the house and sat in a cluttered front room. There were pictures on the walls, film stars, a calendar in Arabic, and other calendar pictures of huntsmen in riding gear and stiff squarish dogs. And there was a picture of the ruler whose palace had been attacked. No one knew whether he had been shot or managed to escape.

Some half-castes and Arabs drifted in and out of a back room to look at us, the visitors, and finally Fatma came. She was unlike Habiba, not ugly, but small, tired-looking and – the word occurred to me as I looked at her in that cluttered front room – dry. Habiba was very black, with a sharp nose, large, soft eyes and long, shapely legs; Fatma was small, ageless in a shriveled way, with frizzed hair and one foreshortened leg which made her limp slightly. Her eyes were weary with lines; she could have been young and yet she seemed to have no age. She was cautious – now seated and carefully smoothing her silk wrappings, not out of coyness but out of the damaged reflex of pride that comes with generations of poverty. Even the small children in that room looked as concerned as little old men. I felt like a refugee myself who, moving from slum to slum, took care in an aimless, pointless way. Fatma offered us tea.

At that moment I changed my seat. I moved into a chair with my back to the wall. I know why I did it: I was sitting in front of a window and I had the feeling that I was going to be shot in the back of the head by a stray bullet. During the curfew there was always gunfire in Kampala. That was four years ago, and in Africa, but I am still uneasy sitting near windows.

'No time for tea,' Jean said in Swahili. He pointed to his watch and said, 'Curfew starts right now.'

Fatma left the room and Jean nudged me. 'That girl,' he said in English, 'I support her.'

'*Comment?*'

'*La fille est supportable, non?*'

We had only fifteen minutes to get back. We drove immediately to a shop and bought some food and a case of beer, then hurried back to my apartment and locked ourselves in. It was precisely seven when we started drinking. The girls, although Muslims, also drank. They said they could drink alcohol 'except during prayers.'

As time passed the conversation lapsed and there was only an occasional gulp to break the silence. We had run through their life stories very quickly. Habiba was eighteen, born in Somalia. She came to Uganda because of the border war with Kenya which prevented her from living in her own district or migrating to Kenya where she was an enemy. She married in Kampala. Her husband was away most of the time; in the Congo, she thought, but she was not sure. Fatma's parents were dead, she was twenty-two, not married. She was from Mombasa but liked Kampala because, as she said, it was green. The rest of the conversation was a whispered mixture of Arabic and Swahili which the girls spoke, and the French-English-Swahili which Jean and I spoke. Once we turned on the radio and got Radio Rwanda. Jean insisted on switching it off because the commentator was speaking the language of the Bahutu, who were formerly the slaves of Jean's tribe. That tribal war, that massacre, that curfew had been in 1963.

Jean told me what ugly swine the Bahutu were and how he could not stand any Bantu tribe. He squashed his nose with his palm and imitated what I presumed to be a Hutu speaking. He said, 'But these girls – very *Hamite*.' He traced the profile of a sharp nose on his face.

The girls asked him what he was talking about. He explained, and they both laughed and offered some stories. They talked about the Africans who lived near them; Fatma described the fatal beating of a man who had broken the curfew. Habiba had seen an African man stripped naked and made to run home. She mimicked the man's worried face and flailed her long arms. 'Curfew, curfew,' she said.

Jean suddenly stood and took Habiba by the arm. He led her to a back room. It was eight o'clock. I asked Fatma if she was ready. She said yes. She could have been a trained bird, brittle and obedient. She limped beside me into the bedroom.

At eleven I wandered into the living room for another drink.

Jean was there with his feet up. He asked me how things were going. We drank for a while, then I asked him if he was interested in going for a walk. If we went to sleep now, I said, we'd have to get up at four or five. We switched off all the lights, made sure the girls were asleep, and went out.

The silence outside was absolute. Our shoes clacking on the stones in the road made the only sound and, at intervals, the city opened up to us through gaps in the bushes along the road. Lights can appear to beckon, to call in almost a human fashion, like the strings of flashing lights at deserted country fairs in the United States. The lights cried out. But we were safe inside the large compound; no one could touch us.

When we were coming back to my apartment an idea occurred to me. I pointed to the dark windows and said, choosing my words carefully, 'Supposing we just went in there without turning on any lights . . . Do you think the girls would notice if we changed rooms?'

'*Changez de chambres?*'

'*Je veux dire, changez de filles.*'

He laughed, a drunken sort of sputtering, then explained the plan back to me, adding, '*Est-ce que c'est cela que vous voulez faire?*'

'*Cela me serait égal, et vous?*'

Habiba was amused when she discovered, awaking as the act of love began, that someone else was on top of her. She laughed deep in her throat; this seemed to relax her, and she hugged me and sighed.

Jean was waiting in the hallway when I walked out an hour later. He was helpless with suppressed giggling. We stood there in the darkness, our clothes slung over our shoulders, not speaking but communicating somehow in a wordless giddiness which might have been shame. At the time I thought it was a monstrous game, like a child's, but hardly even erotic, played to kill time and defeat fear and loneliness – something the curfew demanded.

But after the curfew ended, I changed my mind. I had not been playing; all my gestures had been scared and serious. I stopped trusting. I became rather jumpy and found I could not teach anymore. And so I left Africa, deciding I needed a rest, and checked into a hotel in the south of France. One day while I was sunning myself at the swimming pool, a large black man appeared between two flowering bushes at the far end. He was wearing a light suit and he carried a briefcase. He walked heavily along the poolside, toward me, and I imagined for a moment – a moment in which the memory of the curfew rubbed and mumbled – that he had come to kill me. He passed by me and entered the bar. He was, I found out later, a famous Nigerian economist. He stayed at the hotel for three days, and committed no outrage.

Biographical Notes for Four American Poets

'Robert Frost was sitting right where I am now,' said Denton Fuller, the American poet, in Amherst. 'In this very rocking chair –'

In *The Hub*, A Magazine of Verse, Fuller's biographical note read: *Born Conway, N. H., 1922; attended Green Mountain School and Bowdoin College; after graduation, 'army and Byronesque ramblings.' Worked for PORTLAND (Me.) HERALD, wrote verse late at night and far into the morning on rolls of newsprint. First book* No News *(1946) followed by* Barefoot Boy *(1949);* Good Fences *(1956) won Mr Fuller a John Wheeler Fellowship. He is presently teaching part-time and writing. Married, two daughters. Hobbies: mushrooms, dogs, farming.*

'– just staring off this porch, looking meaningfully at the Common there. He could have been Tiresias, with his shock of white hair and that wise old clapboard face. And he said to me, "Denton, I once ran away from this college – there were so many things I wanted to do."'

'And miles to go before he slept,' murmured Wilbur Parsons, the American poet.

In *The Hub*, Parsons' biographical note read: *Born Worcester, Mass., 1918; educated Worcester Academy and Harvard Business School; Rhodes Scholar (Oxford University, England) 1940–41; published first book shortly after joining Homemakers Mutual Insurance Co. (Boston and New York, with branches around the world); now Executive Vice-President of this company. In 1949 Mr Parsons founded* The Hub, A Magazine of Verse, *which he edits today when the world of finance is too much with him. Author of* The Muse and Mammon *(1943),* Predilections *(1950) and* Bull and Bear *(1957).* Curtain Raisers *(1965) is a collection of Mr Parsons' translations from the Russian of Iosip Brodsky. Married, no children. Hobbies: wines, travel, yachting, golf.*

'I can't say that I knew Frost,' Parsons went on. 'Of course we chatted dozens of times at Breadloaf. And I was responsible for putting lots of his stuff in *The Hub*. He was a marvelous old man. My wife used to say he was salty.'

'Oh, he was an old salt,' said Denton Fuller. 'He could have been the skipper of some great sailing ship.'

'I always thought of him as the yeast at Breadloaf,' said Sumner Bean, the American poet. 'I mean no disrespect.'

In *The Hub*, Bean's biographical note read: *Born Kennebunk-port, Me., 1921; educated at The Friends School, Cambridge, and Antioch College. A conscientious objector, Mr Bean served as an ambulance driver, 1942–45; published his war poems,* Back to Front *(1946), and taught for two years in Kyoto, Japan, 1949–51; published* Enemies No More *(1953). For some years he has been working on a verse play set at the time of Hiroshima and tentatively titled* Seeing the Light. *Presently teaching at Webster Friends College (Webster, Mass.). Married, four sons and a daughter. Hobbies: cycling, swimming, baking bread. Describes himself as 'The oldest "younger poet" in the USA.'*

'It was his sense of humor,' said Wilbur Parsons.

'He said he wrote his poems in couplets' – Sumner Bean grinned brightly – 'because that's how the world goes on – by coupling!'

'I remember him chaffing Ciardi for telling him what "The Road Not Taken" meant,' said Fuller. 'I mean, symbolically, you see. He would say –'

Here Stanley Gold, the American poet, said, 'For God's sake, how long is this going on! You talk about Frost as if he was some old local druggist that made great banana splits.'

Gold's biographical note was long and breezy, and usually magazines only printed part of it. *The Hub* had never done that much, for Gold had never published there. But the *New Republic, Harper's, Commentary* and (once) *The New Yorker* had published his poems. His fullest biographical note appeared in the *Beloit Poetry Journal: Born NYC, 1931. Educated PS 119 (Flatbush) and Brooklyn College. Awarded MA Columbia, 1955. Worked as bus boy, steamfitter, garage mechanic, welfare inspector, high school teacher. Nervous breakdown (1958)* [once, a magazine in Iowa printed this as if it was the title of a book of poems] *followed by a period of intensive 'lenitive, purgative, cathartic' writing. Mr Gold is the author of* The Jew's Ruse *(1960),* Hitler Riddles *(1962). A Guggenheim Fellow in 1965, Mr Gold traveled to Israel, which resulted in* Ruthless in Gaza *(1967), a travel diary. Divorced, no hobbies.*

'What do you mean by that?' demanded Fuller.

'That's how the world goes on, by coupling. Doesn't that sound a little *cute* to you? There was a lot of schmaltz in Frost. You must be kidding about Tiresias. Let's face it, Frost was a Yankee Harry Golden. You know, *Enjoy, Enjoy!* Except that Frost was writing for English department phonies, not fat Jews at Grossingers', so he wrote *Provide, Provide!* But it's the same cruddy ethos.' Stanley Gold started to recite 'Birches' in a Yiddish accent ('Ven I zee boiches . . .') but was cut off sharply by Fuller.

'You never met Frost, did you?' snapped Fuller.

'Me?' Stanley Gold shrugged under the severe gazes of the others. 'I don't know what you mean by met. I heard him recite his poems at the YMHA in Manhattan. Then I saw him on television, at Kennedy's inauguration. His papers blew off the podium, remember? I saw him at Trilling's house, too, I forget when. He read his poems in a crackly voice, a kind of Spencer Tracy croak –'

Wilbur Parsons' finger had been pointed directly at Gold's chin for some minutes. Gold frowned at the finger and cocked his head to the side comically. But no one laughed.

'I'll tell you something,' said Parsons. 'You don't know the first thing about Frost and I'll tell you how I know and you can correct me if I'm wrong, Denton.' Parsons paused, sipped his drink, then said simply, 'Frost never recited his poems to anyone, anywhere.'

'I heard him,' said Gold. 'At the YMHA. Then at Trilling's. I *heard* him recite his poems, I'm telling you. "Boiches," for example.'

'Frost never recited his poems,' Parsons continued, as if Gold had not said anything. 'Frost used to . . . *say* . . . his poems. Am I right, Denton?'

'Absolutely, Wilbur. That's what he called it.' Denton Fuller jutted his jaw out and said in a rasping voice, 'I am now going to say a poem called "Desert Places."'

'He never *recited*, he always *said* his poems,' Parsons recited.

'Said, read,' Gold muttered. 'It's pretty cute, pretty stagy.'

'Would you put your *Hitler Riddles* next to *A Boy's Will*?' Parsons challenged.

'What *is* this, some kind of stock market?' Gold snarled. Then he fell silent.

Sumner Bean steered the conversation to Robert Lowell's world view. He ordered drinks for everyone, a grapefruit juice for himself.

*

The day had not started badly. In the car, driving to Bradley Field to meet Parsons' plane, Fuller had said to Bean, 'I've been excited about this seminar for weeks. I was writing night and day, night and day. I was on to something very big and very important to me personally. I knew I had to finish it in time for the seminar, so I could show you. And by God I *did* finish it. It's back at the hotel. Frankly speaking I think it's the best thing I've done, but I'll let you be the judge of that.'

'I want to see it, Denton. You know I do.' Sumner Bean's gentle Quaker voice soothed Fuller.

'You look at this poem,' said Fuller. 'But be brutal, tear it to pieces if you want to.'

Sumner Bean smiled.

Fuller relaxed and drove the car with confidence, reducing his speed on the thinly iced road. 'Working like a mule,' he said. 'I shut myself off completely when I work. Don't talk to a soul. Just pick at my food. I go for long walks. Refuse to answer the telephone.'

'We don't have a telephone,' said Sumner Bean. As he said it he sensed a stiffening in Fuller and was jogged by a thumped throttle. He realized he had hurt Fuller in making the nonownership of a telephone somehow virtuous. 'We're planning to get one installed, though,' he lied. 'Say, Denton, how's the farm?'

'Big Bertha's calved,' said Fuller proudly, recovering.

'What a lovely verb,' said Bean. '*Calved.*'

'Well, it's mine,' said Fuller, and he lifted his head and recited, '"All around the green farm the acres are waking, / And hard by her stanchion old Bertha's calved –"'

'I thought that sounded familiar,' said Bean.

'"Good Fences,"' said Fuller, and he cheered up.

Parsons arrived tanned, an odd figure crossing the snow-swept runway, with jaunty, befeathered alpine hat and a trim topcoat, overnight bag and briefcase. He shook hands: 'Denton, Sumner, good to see you again,' and said that he had just returned from Nassau, where he had 'dickered with some offshore properties, did a little fishing, and worked on a poem.'

'You're brown as a berry,' said Fuller.

'But not as dark as Berryman,' said Bean.

'Ha-ha,' said Parsons. 'But odd you should mention him. I was talking with John just this morning in New York. I'm anthologizing him.'

'How's business?' asked Fuller when they were in the car and driving toward Amherst.

Parsons, in the back seat, said, 'I'm working on a sonnet.'

'I meant your company.'

'Oh, *that*,' laughed Parsons. 'Going great guns. I'm negotiating a bauxite contract.'

'How do you do it,' said Bean with admiration. 'It's all I can do to keep up with marking the freshman themes. And you, with your bauxite and ballads!'

'There's a title for you, Wilbur,' said Fuller.

But Parsons had leaned forward, resting his forearms on the top of the front seat, near Sumner Bean. He was looking meditatively at the dashboard. 'How do I do it? Let me ask you something: how did Wallace Stevens do it?'

'I've always wondered,' said Sumner Bean.

'I'll tell you,' said Parsons. 'My secretary, Martha, takes my first draft down in shorthand, and then types it up with wide margins, triple spaced. I work like blazes on that, penciling in words, crossing things out, adding new stuff. It's a beautiful mess when I'm through with it, like one of Balzac's galley proofs.'

'The Buffalo Library's buying work sheets,' said Fuller. 'They're paying well for them, too.'

'They've got some of mine,' said Parsons, 'some early drafts of *The Muse and Mammon*. They've got some graduate students doing their Ph.D.'s on my work. But as I was saying. Martha's the only one who can read my hand-writing. I give her my fussed-up page and she hands me back a clean copy. I mess that one up; she does another. And that's the way it goes. I keep working the thing into shape until it's letter-perfect. And, you know, the poem I start with is never the poem I finish up with – it's a completely different poem. Take that sonnet I started in Nassau. That will keep changing and changing. I'll give it to Martha on Monday. She says I'm a perfectionist. I don't know what I'd do if she ever left the firm.'

'How did Wallace Stevens do it?' asked Sumner Bean.

'Well, that's my point. Exactly the same way,' said Parsons. 'But he did it in Key West.'

'Eliot had his typist, too,' said Bean. He chuckled.

Parsons dozed, his jaunty hat over his eyes, his hands folded across his briefcase.

'I carry all sorts of scraps of paper around with me,' said Fuller eagerly. 'Some I carry around for years, with little bits and pieces of writing on them, phrases, words, you see. They don't mean a thing to anyone else: it's a kind of code. Then, when I get a free month, I go up to the farm and sit down and put it all together, scratching away like mad on yellow legal-size paper with a four-B pencil.'

'I use a typewriter, an old Remington,' said Bean.

'It's so mysterious, writing poems,' said Fuller. 'I don't know how it happens. It's a kind of magic, I guess.'

'I haven't written a poem in three years,' said Bean sadly. 'Really, I haven't. It's terrible, isn't it?'

Fuller could not think of any words of consolation for Bean at first. But driving across a dry stretch of road near the greenhouses on the Amherst outskirts, Fuller was inspired. He spoke to the snowy corrugations of a distant field: 'We all have our dry patches. Be patient. It'll come bubbling up when the mood takes you.'

After lunch (roast chicken, new potatoes, fresh corn, Indian pudding) they adjourned to the hotel piazza, where in the chill afternoon air they sat and waited for Stanley Gold, who had said he would be driving up from New York in his own car.

'They must think we're a bunch of crazy bohemian poets,' said Parsons, rubbing his hands and tossing his head in the direction of nearby windows. Lunching couples sat at festive tables, watched the poets, and chewed. 'They're staring at us because we're doing what we damn please.'

'I was looking at that tree,' said Fuller reflectively. 'It's a willow tree. When I was a boy I used to pretend I was a bell ringer and pull the branches of willow trees down, *dong-dong-dong*.'

'A weeping willow,' said Bean.

'It's supposed to be a sad tree,' said Parsons. 'But I don't think of it as a sad tree. For me it's a happy tree. Look at it.'

Rooted in the Common, the tree was a cold fountain of black leafless wires, the trunk battered and icy.

'Yes, it is a happy tree,' said Fuller. 'Not a weeping tree at all.'

'It droops, of course,' said Parsons. 'But that's part of its charm. No, it's not a sad tree.'

'Like' – Bean struggled with a phrase – 'like ... so many ... graceful ...' He could not go on. He had not written a poem for three years. He drank his juice.

When Stanley Gold arrived they were still watching the tree and discussing the happy aspect it presented. Gold seated himself with them (he wore a thick woolen scarf and an army jacket; his hair was wild and bushy, his ears bright red, his glasses iced with frozen crystal needles of scattered breath). He listened for a while, blowing on his fingers, then asked, 'Say, in the winter, how can you tell which trees are dead and which aren't?' and here the conversation turned to Robert Frost.

At six-fifteen that same evening on the steps of the Amherst town hall, Parsons, Fuller and Bean waited for Stanley Gold. They had arranged to meet at six; Fuller said that he had 'a little surprise' for them before their early meal, a pizza and a pitcher of beer at one of the local hangouts. Parsons said he had not had a pizza for years; Bean said he was game; Gold had nodded and said (rather too quickly, Fuller thought), 'Okay, okay.' Parsons said that it was customary for the English department sponsoring such seminars to give a cocktail party before the talks and a little cold buffet afterward ('They had quite a spread for me when I read at Swarthmore'), but added that he was frankly quite anxious to see what Fuller's surprise was. There would be drinks at Professor Bloodworth's after the evening session. At six-twenty Fuller said he didn't think Gold would show.

'Nothing gold can stay,' said Bean. He was dressed for the weather: a fur hat and thick duffel coat, corduroy trousers stuck in high, freshly oiled lumberjack boots, heavy woolen mittens. The others paid no attention to Bean's compulsive pun. Bean himself had been ten minutes late: Parsons, watching Bean approach, had said, 'Look, Denton, he even *dresses* like a Quaker!' Fuller had replied, 'Sumner's got a heart of gold,' and Parsons quipped, 'Let's hope not.' They were laughing softly even as Bean joined them.

Now Parsons was saying, 'I'd never take that young man on my firm. Oh, I know he's supposed to be a good poet – very popular with campus audiences, they say – but in business punctuality is essential. If he were coming for an interview right now I would simply say to him, "Sorry, the post has been filled by a prompt applicant," and that, my friends, would be that. I say we push off.'

'Let's give him another five minutes,' said Fuller, flashing his watch crystal toward the streetlamp and trying to read it. 'Starting now.'

'What's the hurry?' Bean asked inoffensively. 'Maybe he's doing something important, a call from home or something.'

'Very charitable of you, Sumner,' said Parsons, 'but don't waste your charity. Five'll get you ten he's inside the hotel sitting on his butt. I'm telling you, I know an unreliable man when I see one. Besides, he's divorced – so we know he's not calling his wife, don't we?'

Bean did not reply.

'Dylan Thomas was always late,' said Fuller. He detected that Bean disapproved of Parsons' remark about Gold's divorce. Bean made a point of counseling unhappy couples and, discouraging gossip, trying to patch things up.

'Stanley Gold is not Dylan Thomas,' said Parsons. 'I met Dylan at Williams College back in – was it fifty-two? You could excuse that man for anything, anything at all.' Parsons blew a jet of steamy breath into the night air and said, 'I've had it. Gentlemen, shall we lead on?'

'I don't see,' said Bean, 'how you can be so hard on Stanley. He strikes me as a very sincere person. And I've read his poems. They're darned good.'

'Well, I haven't read as many of his poems as you have, I'm sure. He's never sent any to *The Hub*,' said Parsons, aggrieved. 'But I'll tell you something. I stand here waiting for him and I say to myself: This isn't how poems get written. With poetry it's fish or cut bait. It takes discipline, application, plain old work. Gold would probably call me an old fogy for saying this: it takes a lot of things that young man doesn't have.'

'I don't think Stanley would call you an old fogy,' said Bean.

Parsons continued. 'That's why Stevens will always be a greater poet for me than, say, Hart Crane. One basic reason is that Stevens knew about discipline, and there was no nonsense about it. He ordered his life. He invested wisely. He ordered his poems. There's something very, very American about that. Hart Crane was a sot. Granted, his death was tragic. I'm not saying it wasn't. But Wallace Stevens knew how a poem is made, the way real poets do.'

'I haven't written a poem for three years,' said Bean. He said it with a certain pride.

'Marilyn Monroe was always late,' said Fuller. 'I'm thinking of writing a poem about her. She was America.'

'She had a lot of talent,' said Parsons. 'But hasn't someone already done a poem about her? Was it Thom Gunn?'

'He did Elvis Presley,' said Fuller, piqued.

'They say Marilyn Monroe had a very unhappy childhood,' said Bean.

'The worst,' said Fuller. 'Boy, could I tell you some stories. They'd stand your hair on end.'

Bean had been watching the distant sidewalk. He saw a figure loping along. He said, 'I think that's Gold, isn't it? He's headed in this direction.'

Parsons squinted. 'Could be.' He turned to Bean. 'I tell you what. I'm going to ask him where he's been. Watch him squirm. A fellow like that never gets asked why he's late. It'll be a good experience for him.'

'You might call this a threat,' said Bean in a steady voice, facing the much taller Parsons, 'but if you ask him that I will go straight back to the hotel in protest. You have no right to ask that man for an explanation. None whatsoever.'

Parsons turned away. When Gold came near and Fuller led the way down the icy sidewalk, Parsons paired up with Fuller and Gold fell in with Bean. The four poets shuffled, so as not to fall.

'You see a lot of stars around here,' said Gold.

Bean obligingly indicated several constellations.

Up front Parsons talked about Nassau. They walked two hundred yards, then Fuller said to stop right where they were and to look across the street. There was a high wall of shrubbery – evergreens – some bare trees, and just visible the large-windowed top floor of a very old house. Gold and Bean caught up. They all stared at the house.

'What I want you to look at,' said Fuller, 'is that upper right-hand window over there.' He pointed to the window with a gloved hand. The window gleamed black. 'A great poet lived there her whole life. Barely stirred from her room. Great poems were written right up there behind that window.' Fuller paused, saying with some emotion, 'The poems of Emily Dickinson.'

'When I was reading my poems in England,' said Parsons, 'an Englishman came up to me and said, "I know you have Edna Ferber, but we have Emily Brontë." I looked him straight in the eye and said, "We have Emily Dickinson, and they don't come any better than that." He shut up, of course.'

But Bean had started reciting 'Much Madness is divinest Sense' and Parsons' story went unnoticed. Fuller followed with 'After great pain, a formal feeling comes,' and Parsons, with a glance at Gold, recited 'A narrow fellow in the grass.' And then they went for their pizza.

The seminar ('Poetry: Meaning and Being') was held in the overheated chapel. The poets spoke in turn. With a rustic twinkle in his eye, Fuller talked about his own poems ('Who knows where a poem comes from?') and his ardent cultivation of cabbages ('And that's a kind of creating, too!'). Parsons was candid about the rat race and said there was no money in poetry, but writing poems was 'a lot cheaper than paying five grand to a headshrinker'; he told about his secretary and how he often composed poems right in Wall Street itself ('Who needs a vernal wood?'); and he read some of his Russian translations. Bean spoke movingly of Vietnam: 'At this moment a young poet in Bienhoa is trying to unstick fiery napalm from his fingers,' and he finished with a sequence of verses written not by himself (he confessed his three-year barrenness) but by Ho Chi Minh, Dag Hammarskjöld, Mao Tse-tung, the wife of Harold Wilson, Léopold Senghor and John Kennedy. The Kennedy was prose, but he read it as verse. Gold shouted love lyrics scattered with references to elimination; he refused to comment on or explain any of them. At the end of the seminar the questions, mumbled by admiring students, hairy and in greasy jackets, were all directed at Gold. The chairman, closing the seminar, said confidently, 'I think we've all learned something this evening,' and he led the four poets to a party at Professor Bloodworth's.

The party continued for nearly three hours, climaxing in a magical but unfortunate sudden hush in the din during which the young wife of a graduate student was heard in an insistent voice to say, 'I wouldn't mind if Mailer buggered me!' Guests winced. One associate professor said, 'Well, I guess that about wraps it up.' There was laughter; the room emptied.

At the front door, Mrs Dorothy Margoulies, M.A. candidate ('Ferlinghetti and the Coney Island Ethos') and wife of the witty associate professor, said good night to Parsons and Fuller. She was moved to a violent nervous shuddering. She caught her breath and said, 'I haven't felt this way since William Golding read here. I don't know what to say –'

She prattled. In the living room someone clinked ashtrays, empty-ing them; in the kitchen, someone else was stacking dishes in the plastic-basket innards of an automatic dishwasher; in the study, Sumner Bean thumbed a book he had been wait-listed for at the Webster Library for months; Stanley Gold, slumped in a wing chair, tried to tune in on the conversation at the door.

'– So enjoyed your talks and readings, and I can't *tell* you how much –' There was a false pause as her voice fell, the low pitch making a purring silence. Gold heard his name, and laughter.

Then Parsons. '– Must get back to New York tomorrow –' A pause. '– No, ha-ha, not exactly. You see, Stevens worked in Connecticut. I guess that's your only major difference.'

'My farm's at Ripton,' said Fuller. 'I'm going to shoot right up there as fast as I can.'

In a cheerful frame of mind, Parsons and Fuller entered the living room. Stanley Gold stared at Parsons, then asked, '*Kak viy pozhivaete?*'

'I beg your pardon,' said Parsons, still wearing the warm grin with which he had sent off the grateful Mrs Margoulies.

'It's Russian,' said Gold.

'If you say so,' said Parsons. He looked at his watch.

'It's a question.'

'I thought I detected an interrogatory note there somewhere,' said Parsons. He checked his watch again.

'So what's your reply?'

'My reply' – and here Parsons glanced at Professor Bloodworth and Fuller – 'is I don't know what the hell you're up to, but I'm going back to the hotel and get some sleep or I won't be able to do a lick of work tomorrow.'

'Why?' Gold's eyes were big behind thick lenses. 'Are you think-ing of doing a few translations tomorrow?'

'See here,' Parsons began.

But Gold had already started speaking: 'I'd like to know where the hell you get the right to pretend you do translations from a language you don't know! Just tell me that and I'll be satisfied.'

'Auden translated *Markings* and he doesn't know a word of Swedish. He said so.' Bean called from the study.

'Shakespeare didn't speak Latin or Greek,' said Fuller. 'And he –'

'A little Latin and less Greek,' said Bloodworth in humorous reproof. He gave the quotation its source.

'Settle down, young fellow,' said Parsons. 'Oh, I know you're thinking I'm a faker. But, hell, Kunitz doesn't speak Russian.'

'I'm not talking about Kunitz. I'm talking about you, Daddy Warbucks.'

'If you can't talk in a civil manner I'm not going on with this. You have no right to ask me for an explanation for anything. I stand by my poems and my magazine. If you think you can do a better translation of Brodsky you're welcome to try.' Parsons calmed himself and added, 'And while you're at it, you can send your poems to *The Hub*. We'd be mighty pleased to get them. You've never sent us any, you know.'

'And I don't intend to,' said Gold.

'Come on, son,' said Fuller, as if to a juvenile delinquent. 'Parsons is trying to help you.'

'Your magazine is financed by you, isn't it?' said Gold to Parsons; he did not wait for a reply. 'And your money comes from your insurance company, right? A company that for the past five years has owned controlling interest in a chemical plant that produces defoliant for the Defense Department! Who are you trying to kid!'

'Hold on a minute,' said Parsons.

Bean appeared at the study door. 'Say, Wilbur, that's a very serious charge. You never told me anything about that.'

'Let me say this,' said Parsons. 'We're Americans. Each of us, in his own way, directly or indirectly, whether we want to or not, has something to do with war. I'll give you a small example. Do you know where your tax money goes?'

'I don't pay taxes,' said Gold. 'I don't earn enough.'

'I haven't paid taxes for ten years,' said Bean. 'It's downright immoral, contributing to a corrupt government. I'm prepared to go to jail if necessary.'

'You're off your head,' said Parsons to Bean. 'It's your business, I know that. But if you ask me –'

'It's been a long day,' said Fuller sheepishly to Bloodworth.

'– I've endowed a lot of magazines,' Parsons was saying, 'a hell of a lot of them. That doesn't mean I agree with their editorial policies, no indeed! I have nothing but respect for Dr Spock's views, don't think I haven't –'

'What about your chemical plant?' asked Bean.

'I didn't come here to talk shop,' said Parsons. 'I came here as a poet. We're all poets. I don't know why we're behaving like this if we're poets.' He stopped momentarily and looked at Bean's face, Gold's face, Fuller's face; he saw something witless and fatigued on each one. He guessed that the same thing showed on his own face. He spoke again, his tongue feeling very large in his mouth. 'Come to my office. I can explain everything.' He turned to Gold. 'And as for you, I can tell you that I've been getting together a little anthology, and I was sort of counting on using your poem "Moshe Dayan's Other Eye" – '

'I wouldn't let you print that poem if you gave me ten grand,' Gold said fiercely.

'The fee was fifty dollars,' said Parsons. He strode to the kitchen; before Mrs Bloodworth could dry her hands on her apron Parsons took them both and shook them, thanking her for a delightful evening. He bade good night to Professor Bloodworth, and, still urging Bean to come and see him, left with a shaken Fuller.

Sumner Bean and Stanley Gold left the house together. It was four in the morning; they walked in the middle of the street. They did not speak; at one point, and without warning, Bean crooked his arm through Gold's the way a stiff old-time lover might. This was the way they walked to the hotel, silently, arm in arm, feeling frail, as poetry was. And when they went to their separate rooms they did not say good night, but bowed slightly, trying to smile. In his bed, Gold continued the poem he had put aside the previous evening at 6:30. At his undersized hotel desk, Bean fiddled with headed note-paper; he did not begin writing immediately, but a poem was arranging itself in his head. Bean's and Gold's were only two of the poems Bloodworth later claimed as the seminar's own. There were two more: 'A Night Call on Miss Dickinson' and 'Pizza – A Sonnet.'

Hayseed

Ira Hubbel was talking to his two attentive boys at the single pump of his Jenney station on the main street of Stockton Springs. They heard a car slowing down, but seeing it was Warren Root's new Chevy convertible, the two boys walked over to a stack of tires which, for a time, they kicked, glancing back at their father and Root. And then they sauntered closer to the car and stood gaping in their beaked baseball caps and greasy overalls like two birds, trying to hear.

'Just up from Bangor this minute,' Root was saying.

Ira looked into Root's reckless face from under the long visor of a faded green fisherman's cap on which a license was pinned. Ira's face was tanned, creased rather than wrinkled, and gave the impression of having been smoked and cured like a tobacco leaf. His alert eyes were a luminous blue and watched Root with the close curiosity of pity.

'Better check the water,' said Ira. He motioned to one of the boys, who heard. The boy got a large watering can and carried it to the front of the car. He hoisted the hood.

'Same old damn town,' said Root, looking across the main street. He shifted away from the steering wheel and made a right angle of his arms, one extended across the top of the front seat, the other along the door. He hooked his thumbs and began drumming emphatically with his fingers.

'Ain't Bangor.' Ira was squirting water in droplets from a Windex bottle onto the mud-speckled windshield.

'Leave that be, Ira. I'm going to wash the car soon's I get home.'

'Never mind, Chub.' Ira rubbed the windshield with a handful of squeaking chamois.

'Ain't Bangor is right,' said Root, shaking his head. 'Why they got a ritzy new hotel opened up there, with two or three bars and a big ballroom and what all. People come all the way down from Portland to have a gander at it.'

Ira was silent, busy with the windshield. Then he said, 'That so.'

'Picked me up some chicken wire at the feed store,' said Root.

'Trunk wired down good?'

'Not too good. But it didn't flap open.'

'That's a blessing,' said Ira. He looked at the pump. 'You wanted it full up?'

'I guess.'

'It's full up now,' said Ira. 'That's five sixty.'

Root gave Ira a ten-dollar bill.

'Expected you yesterday,' said Ira, taking the bill.

'Gave myself an extra day,' said Root. In reflection, he pulled on his nose.

'Myron says you wasn't at the boarding house,' Ira said politely.

'Now how does Myron know that?'

'Tried to call you up last night. They said you wasn't there.'

'Moved to the new one on Thursday,' said Root. 'The hotel I was telling you about. The boys that carry your bags got these funny little suits and say yes sir. I got sick of that Jesus boarding house.'

'Myron didn't know.'

'No, Myron didn't know,' said Root. 'And I'll tell you something else. Lavinia didn't know neither.' Root grinned.

Ira looked at the ground, then said softly, 'I'll get your change.'

'Stoved-in front,' said Hubbel's boy, slamming down the hood.

'Skunk,' said Root. He measured with his hands. ''Bout yay big. I stove *him*!'

Root was outside the car, stretching, examining the dent on the grill, when Ira came back with the change. Ira counted it into Root's hand, pressing the coins, flattening the bills, saying, 'Five sixty. And forty is six, and one is seven, and two is nine –'

'But I'll tell you something,' said Root, closing his hand on the money, 'they still haven't learned to shoot pool in Bangor, and that's the God's truth. How about a quick game?' Root rubbed his palms and nodded at the drugstore, where there was a pool table.

'Maybe later,' said Ira.

'I'm all stiff with the driving,' said Root. 'Come on, Ira.'

'Got to watch the station,' said Ira.

'You got your two boys to watch your Christly gas station, Ira. Now get over and shoot a game with me.'

Ira hitched up his pants and followed Root across the street.

A game was in progress, but the two players looked up and backed away from the table when Root and Ira entered the store. A man in an apron behind the soda fountain greeted Root solemnly.

'Hi, Wayne,' said Root to the man in the apron. To the players he said, 'You boys should be in school.'

The boys put down their cues.

'That's okay,' said Root. 'I don't care if you play hooky. Used to do quite a bit of that myself, didn't I, Ira?'

'They're giving us the table,' said Ira.

'Finish your Jesus game,' said Root.

'You go ahead, Mr Root,' said one of the boys.

'I don't like to horn in,' said Root.

Ira took a cue and began chalking it. Root did the same.

The boys obligingly racked the balls and dusted chalk marks off the rails.

'Didn't know you two worked here,' said Root, and laughed. He spotted the cue ball and lined up his shot, then gently sent the cue ball into the triangular formation. It nicked a corner and came to rest an inch from the barely troubled formation.

'Don't leave me with much,' said Ira. But instead of nudging the cue ball, he blasted, breaking the formation and spreading the balls all over the table.

'You want me to win,' said Root.

Ira coughed.

'I'd like a drink,' said Root, sinking a ball.

'It ain't three yet,' said Ira.

'I'd like a drink. Here,' Root said to one of the boys, 'go get us half a pint of vodka next door. Tell them who it's for.'

The game proceeded quickly, Ira fumbling his shots, Root scoring often. The boy returned with the vodka.

'Oil up with Orloff's!' said Root. He knocked back two swallows, then gasped and wiped his mouth with the back of his hand. He passed the bottle to Ira.

Ira looked around the store before he drank; then he took a sip.

'Take a real slug,' said Root. 'Oil up, Ira!'

Ira tipped the bottle and took a mouthful. His eyes were watering when he handed it back to Root. He said, 'Don't that stuff burn.'

'First time I heard you complain about a free drink,' said Root.

'I'm not complaining, Chub,' Ira said quickly. 'I appreciate it.'

'Then have another one,' said Root. He lined up a new shot.

'I'm seeing spots,' said Ira. He screwed the cap onto the bottle. Root said, 'Son of a whore. That was an easy one.'

One of the boys came forward and held the pool chalk out to Root. 'Thank *you*,' said Root, and smiled at the boy. The boy crept back to the raised bench and sat down.

As Ira was taking his next shot the door flew open with a bang and a man came in. He was heavy, rawboned, wearing a torn felt hat and overalls dusted with yellow chicken meal. He saw Root and closed the door carefully, turning the knob and making no sound. He said, 'Sorry,' and squinted, then bought some cough drops, nodded respectfully toward Root and, easing the door open, slipped out.

'What's he tiptoeing around for?' said Root. He rested the pool cue on his thumb and whacked a ball into a corner pocket. 'I don't say this is the grandest town, but people treat you right.'

'Yep,' said Ira.

'Bangor's a waste from that point of view. Mighty unfriendly – reminds me of the navy, Bangor does. Those crazy Indians come up from Stillwater. Oh, they're a tough bunch when they get a little Orloff's in them. Look at you with them big square faces. I saw a hell of a fight a few nights back.'

'Don't get down Bangor way very often,' said Ira.

'It's a good experience,' said Root, watching the table. 'Like the navy. We'll go down there together next time, what do you say?'

'I'd like that, Chub.'

Root grinned. 'Might even get laid, eh? What would your old woman say to that?'

Ira cleared his throat and looked around. He grasped his pool cue with two hands. One of the high school boys was smiling.

'You mind your own business, sonny,' said Root.

'Sorry, sir,' said the boy.

The next time Root looked over both boys had gone.

'Have another swig, Ira. It won't kill you.'

'Chub, I don't think –'

'Ira.'

'I think I'll just have a bottle of tonic,' said Ira.

'Put some of this into it,' said Root. He showed the vodka.

'All right,' said Ira. He smiled while Root splashed some vodka into his glass of orangeade. But he did not drink. He set the glass down on the raised bench.

'I can finish this game in three shots,' said Root. He walked around the table, then began knocking the balls into the pockets. The balls dropped in three gulps. Root said, 'How about another? You gave me that one, didn't you?'

'No, no,' said Ira. 'I'd better scoot back to the station.'

'Another game wouldn't hurt.' Root looked at his watch. 'Half-past three,' he said. 'Bet Lavinia's tearing her hair.'

Ira didn't move.

Root giggled. 'She'll bust a gut when I get back, so I'm in no hurry. Women,' he said, facing Ira, 'they're so damn con-trary, ain't they?'

Ira flicked his head up and down. 'Sure are,' he said. He glanced at Wayne, the man behind the soda fountain. At the glance, Wayne picked up a coffee cup and started to wipe it.

'You know what I always say, Ira?' Root held up the vodka bottle, saw there was still an inch left, and took a long pull. 'I always say: You can't live *with* 'em, and you can't live with*out* 'em. And frankly, Ira, I know what the hell I'm talking about.'

'You do, Chub. A good woman –'

'Ain't no such animal!' said Root. He laughed and drank again. 'Now my name's Warren, as you know, and that's the name I use in Bangor.'

'Warren,' said Ira.

'Know what they call me? Take a guess.'

'Can't guess,' said Ira.

'I'll tell you. It's Don Warren – like Don Juan. Get it?'

'Oh, I see,' said Ira.

Root shook his head and said, 'Jesus.'

'I'd better scoot back to the station,' said Ira.

'You do that.' But as Ira was leaving, Root called, 'Ira, wait!' startling the old man. Root pointed to the glass of orangeade on the bench. 'You forgot your drink, Ira. Set down and finish it.'

Ira picked up the glass and drank it down with his eyes closed. He left, coughing.

'He's a funny old hayseed,' said Root. 'Ain't that right, Wayne?'

'Yes, sir,' said Wayne, and began to blink and sniff in a rabbity way.

*

222

One of Ira Hubbel's boys was standing near the convertible. 'I washed your car, Mr Root.'

'Much obliged,' said Root. He tried to give the boy a tip. The boy refused it. 'Groceries,' said Root.

At Mason's, the grocery store, Root took a wire carriage and wheeled it around, filling it with cans. Harold Mason was at the cash register. Root said, 'No cartons of Luckies.'

'Aren't there any on the shelf, Mr Root?'

'Not a one.'

'Must be in the stockroom. I'll get you a carton.'

'That's all right. I'll be back later.'

'I won't be a minute,' said Mason, hurrying to the back of the store.

'Didn't mean to cause him any bother,' said Root to a woman holding a child. The woman, gawking by the door, seemed surprised that Root should address her. Root smiled. The woman turned away and left the store.

'Here you are,' said Mason. 'One carton of Luckies.'

'Didn't mean to cause any bother,' said Root.

'No bother at all.'

'What's the bad news?'

'Pardon?' Mason looked shocked.

'The bill. How much do I owe you?'

'You don't have to pay now,' said Mason. 'You must have your hands full.'

Root smiled. 'I don't have an account here, do I?'

'No, you don't. But –'

'So how can I put it on account if I don't *have* an account? You tell me.' Root looked around for a witness. He saw no one except Mason's wife, watching from the frozen-food section at the rear of the store.

'Suit yourself,' said Mason. He added the column of figures on the paper bag, then rang up the amount on the clanking cash register. 'That will be nine dollars and forty-eight cents.'

Root paid and started to leave.

'Mr Root?'

Root turned.

'I'm very sorry,' said Mason, and he did not take his eyes from Root's.

Root shrugged and went out to his car.

The Root farm was just outside town, on a slope, at the end of a stony, rain-eroded driveway. Root put the car into second and drove casually, holding a knob attached to the steering wheel, spinning it slightly as the car slid sideways on the gravel and shuddered and jounced to the front of the house. He was out of the car and reaching into the back seat for the bag of groceries; drunk, he spoke his thoughts: 'Hell with it. I bought them, she can lug them in.'

Inside the house he called, 'Lavinia! I'm back!' And again, 'Lavinia!' sharply.

There was no reply and not even much of an echo. The doors were open all the way out to the sunlight on a saw-horse at the back. A plump, reddish chicken bustled mechanically, as if it ran on a spring, and pecked at the floor just inside the kitchen. Root turned and looked back at the car, then at the driveway. At his split-rail fence, which bordered the road, some children stood and were staring up at him. He went to shoo the chicken, but he did not go all the way to the kitchen, for halfway down the hall the sound of his own feet stopped him. He called his wife's name again, now softly, nearly a question; and then he took a sip of air and held it in his mouth.

Later, upstairs, he found the severed length of rope, the note, the overturned stool.

A Deed without a Name

We have known the Crowleys ever since we arrived in Singapore, and to be honest neither Harry nor I found it the least bit strange that they should ring us up in the middle of the night to tell us about that horrid ship disaster in the harbor. It was only later that Harry said he had had a few inklings all along, that it was 'just like the Crowleys,' but that from practically every point of view it was (as he put it) 'very strange indeed,' which I take to mean he agrees with me.

Both Les and Beth – or as I now think of them, Lester and Elizabeth – fancied themselves amateur detectives, better than the fictional ones. At first there was not a bit of this. He puffed his pipe and talked about meerschaum and dottle and Turkish mixtures; and she was frightfully women's pagey, with black stockings and eye make-up and funny beads. He wore a medallion around his neck which embarrassed Harry, though he said he had been wearing it a lot longer than the youngsters these days, and she said the same about her get-up. I shall never know how they got away with it in London just after the war, a trying time for us all; they could have got away with it in Hampstead or Chelsea, I suppose, but certainly not in Sutton where they claimed they had a maisonette. The boring thing about people who dress in this odd way is that they do so to invite comment and challenge approval, like children in company saying to their parents 'I hope you die.' They made Harry's life a misery simply because he always wore a cricketing tie, and Harry worked jolly hard as treasurer of the club. He earned that tie, but I'll never know where they earned the right to dress like an up-dated incubus and succubus, who might be known to their friends as Inky and Sucky. And they always said my frocks were *infra*.

I was saying about the Crowleys and their detective stories. This subject came up one evening when I told her how thrilled I had been by *The Mousetrap* and had they seen it? She held a sip of sherry in her mouth and tasted it with a tight little smile. She swallowed; the smile was gone. 'Did you hear that?' she called to

225

Lester. 'Yes,' he said, and getting terribly excited he turned to me and said, 'I thought it was such a lot of –'

Do people *have* to talk that way?

Ellery Queen was going off, they said. And Poirot ('with his mon doos and sacra bloos') was already beyond the pale. 'The only writer worth mentioning is Simenon in the original,' she said, though 'mon doo' I shouldn't think recommended her as much of a French scholar. As I look back on Elizabeth and her nastiness and her French novels I always suspect that her great pleasure must have been in cutting the pages with some ever-so-interesting Oriental dagger. 'And Doyle at his best,' said Lester, 'and B— and Gr—.' (These last two names, which he mumbled, were unfamiliar to me: I am positive that is why he said them.)

'You see, to have a proper murder story there has to be a real sense of sin,' she said.

A sense of sin! Well, that's the Crowleys all over. *The Mousetrap*, a diverting little gem by the mistress of the genre, didn't have a sense of sin, was that it? I remember the evening Harry and I saw it; I can imagine how it would have been spoiled for us if the Crowleys had been in the next stall and got all shirty about this gripping play not having a sense of sin. And neither will I repeat the uncharitable, not to say the beastly things the Crowleys said about Dame Margaret Rutherford.

I hold no brief for detective stories. Usually I find them very gloomy and always I find them badly written. I suppose Harry and I defended Agatha Christie and Arthur Conan Doyle because the Crowleys were being such awful bores. I get no joy from murder, though I admit some do, but in the normal way I would not have lifted a finger to defend a writer of crime fiction, except from an onslaught of prigs. I would cheerfully defend anyone in the same way – it is my nature – unless it was another prig. Elizabeth, I hope you and Lester can hear me.

Their infatuation was with murder stories of quite a different stripe. I have already admitted that I did not catch the names of the writers Lester mentioned, but when people say, 'Oh, you know who I mean – I'm sure you must have heard of him,' you can be fairly certain they know you haven't any idea who they mean. But I can well imagine what sort of stories the Crowleys liked. I had some indication of their tastes when they confessed that they too had thought of being murder-story writers. This is the chief characteristic of people who read rubbishy books; they take a shameless comfort in the fact that in a pinch they could quite easily duplicate them. Readers of murder stories are the biggest offenders here. I doubt that there is one of them who has not thought of setting pen to paper and dashing off a shilling shocker of his own. These aficionados of gore never actually write their stories, though they insist that with a typewriter and a bank holiday they would 'type it up' (writing, for them, being something like crocheting a doily) and it would be a best seller. Sheer bloody-mindedness prevents them from ever attempting it; they much prefer telling it, with pauses, putting finger to lips and saying um-um, holding a roomful of people captive with boredom. Lester and Elizabeth did this all the time, they were forever going on about their 'own story,' interrupting each other to add bloody minutiae and getting terribly excited about what were (to me, at any rate, and Harry) rather dreary little mysteries with obvious clues, intended only to shock. I have no doubt that there was a sense of sin in *theirs*!

But their infatuation was with murder stories of quite a different stripe. For Lester and Elizabeth, the crime was everything and solving it did not worry them for a moment; in fact, the crimes they concocted were seldom solved at all. Their theory, I suppose, was that not all crimes are solved – that is, the best ones aren't. Their shockers took ages to tell and always had the servant in a terrible state (Ah Ho doesn't live in this compound and has to be driven home when the guests leave; Harry used to be furious and it always rained). A typical Crowley shocker was about a murder trial in which all the jury, the magistrate, the entire prosecution – everyone in the courtroom except the accused – was guilty of the crime. Of course the poor chap was found guilty and later gassed. (Was it that old gray-haired judge with a nose so big 'it seemed,' Lester put in, 'as if he was perpetually eating a banana' who dreamed up that mess? I forget.) Here the point was that the honest man has no business in society: society is evil and will kill him. For the Crowleys there was no such thing as a good sleuth and no one was innocent except the accused, no one guilty except the law; I think that was how it went, and there was an awful lot of torturing. Positively diabolical.

I do not mean to suggest that the Crowleys were cruel to us or hurt us in any way, or for that matter that they were not, underneath it all, decent people in many ways. Her soufflés and his imitation of a West Country rustic (I can still hear him saying, 'Ur, it bain't very furr . . .') did more than make up for their rather childish insistence on ticking off the writers of detective stories and their championing of the two I suppose infinitely more tiresome and bloodthirsty writers whose names were lost in the nimbus of Turkish tobacco smoke which hung between Lester's lips and my ear; I mean, B — and Gr—. Perhaps it was the amusing working-class accent which Lester adopted when speaking about very serious subjects. (The middle class often use such devices as a cover for their embarrassment.) And the Crowleys, for all their admitted kinks and quirks, had excellent taste in antiques, little ikons and altars, maps and occult charts which fascinated Harry, who has been looking into old atlases ever since he heard of their annual appreciation of 10 per cent – a good deal sounder than most British investments, which are a scandal. They had cute little black drapes fitted across Lester's 'meditation room' and inside very interesting snapshots of a bald and bug-eyed gentleman Lester said was his father. 'A beastly man, a beastly man,' Lester would say, and this for a reason I cannot guess at sent both Lester and Elizabeth into gales of laughter. They had such things as tiger skins and opium pipes, fascinating Oriental pots, and bric-à-brac imprinted with abracadabra. It was all, Lester said, his father's.

'Your father must have been quite a character,' I said to Lester on one occasion. Harry and Elizabeth were in another room sampling a sort of rice dumpling very popular here with the Chinese.

'Oh, he was,' said Lester, and with that he brushed his hand neatly across the curve of my bottom, so neatly that I could not accuse him of getting fresh, barely comprehending what he had done to me. I thought at the time that it was a skirt pleat freeing itself and touching me softly. I know better now. He never spoke again about his father, nor did I ask.

Our relationship, because it was not a relationship at all but rather an awareness of each other, had a forced heartiness about it and a bonhomie (how Elizabeth made a shambles of the pronunciation of this simple French word!) that was impossible to suppress. We were not good friends of the Crowleys' and never had been; this resulted in an uncertain distance which compelled us to do more for them than their best friends would have done, though God only knows who or where their best friends were. It is easier to say no to a friend than to one of these fumbling strangers; I much prefer the honesty of friendship, so does Harry. One is always doing something one finds unpleasantly intimate with someone one barely knows. It is always the way and it is the reason Harry and I make a point of 'screwing our courage to the sticking place,' so to speak, and getting to know people really well. As we have no children (Harry has a low 'count') this is usually quite simple. We tried with the Crowleys but it never worked: we were always the new visitors, obliging them with kindnesses and remembering not to interrupt or offend either of them, and often going out of our way for them, always an inconvenience. Harry is such a dreadful sleeper; I remember how they used to urge us to stay on and dope Harry with coffee. We could not say no. We only said no once to the Crowleys, and that was the last time we saw them, when our so-called friendship ended; and this happened shortly after the incident I intend to tell you about right now.

It was near midnight when they rang. I know that because Harry was soaking his teeth, and he never does that before midnight. It is a small but useful courtesy he has practiced throughout our marriage and I am grateful to him for it. It is my luck that I have been blessed with very strong teeth, and let me note here that Lester, although of Irish stock, had an unexpectedly fine set of teeth which he said were all his own. 'That,' I ribbed him, 'comes of a long residence in England. In Ireland they'd be rotted to stumps!' Lester did not, happily for me, take offense at my harpish dig.

They spoke of two separate items when they rang and they did this in a rather clever way. Lester spoke to Harry first and told him of the ship disaster in the harbor. Apparently a tanker approaching the harbor spied another tanker just leaving. They were in the deep channel, near the islands called the Sisters, that leads to Collyer Quay. The approaching tanker signaled the other (two short blasts) to turn off. But it was early morning and the captain who had signaled had the impression he had not been heard, and so shortly after gave two more strong blasts on his whistle, or whatever it is they signal with on tankers. Here destiny dealt another card. Two short blasts means 'turn to port' (left) but four short blasts means 'turn to starboard' (right). The second tanker turned to starboard, was rammed amidships and sank in seventeen minutes, just long enough for four wild Chinese to find life jackets and leap to safety. The rest perished, the Scots captain and thirty of the crew. As for the other tanker, the one that had done all the signaling and ramming; well, that tanker steamed out to sea and was last heard of in Japan where it discharged its entire crew, including its (Liberian) captain. It suffered a bit of damage in the bow (front). A tragic tale, and one worthy of a Humphrey Bogart film if not a Joseph Conrad novel.

Then Elizabeth spoke to me. Were we interested in getting up a swimming party? I said an emphatic yes. One is able to see a great deal of one another on a swimming trip; there is candid revelation in seminakedness. We fixed it for the following Sunday and I said I'd bring sandwiches and my own liver pâté if they could be responsible for fruit and drink (I hinted at a jug of simple orange squash so that they would not feel obligated to hump a crate of beer). I was beside myself when I rang off.

Harry was pale. He told me what Lester had said about the ship disaster and added, 'I fancy the poor blokes didn't have a chance.' Poor *blokes*, you see; it sounds frightfully low, and Harry's father was a bishop. But I have said somewhere above that the middle class often uses working-class language when the thought expressed is unbearably serious. Harry, you are forgiven for this. I understand.

Then I told Harry what Elizabeth had said to me about swimming. Harry said fine, 'as long as it isn't near the Sisters,' and he tried a charmless laugh.

The scene at the Jardine Steps where we booked our motor launch was so picturesque: sampans and fisherfolk here, smugglers in undervests there, mothers giving suck to their round-cheeked kids on the quayside, and over there a foursome of RAF hearties with goggles and flippers setting out for a day of snorkeling in the Straits! Much as I would like to linger here on the steps and allow a thorough consideration of the colorful comings and goings, I feel I must press on. Landscape is all very well, and there is much to say of the quaint splendor of these 'pampered jades of Asia,' but for my present purpose I am afraid it would only delay the telling of what is a far more important (to me, at any rate) if less pretty story.

Leaning against the gunwales (sides) of the launch as we putt-putted out into the harbor, I realized that we were not headed in the direction of Pulau Blakang Mati – where the bathing facilities are excellent and 'the water is like ginger beer' in the unambitious simile of one of the local poets – but for the Sisters. These two heaps of stones, topped with stunted cacti and patient pitcher plants, loomed up in the channel of swirling water. And behind them, the low blue *blancmange* of Indonesia.

The two druids sat inside, leafing through the Sunday papers and smiling to themselves. Harry, poor Harry, tried to strike up a conversation with the Chinese pilot. The unmuffled engine roared, Harry shouted, the pilot replied in clacking Cantonese. The pilot's small daughter had come along, though for no more sinister reason than the daughter of the *Hesperus'* captain: 'To bear him company.' She stared in an intensely embarrassing way at Harry, who does not know a word of Cantonese but talks a great deal when he is upset.

I put on a brave face. I was not going to let the Crowleys know they had succeeded in spoiling what could have been quite a pleasant swimming party. But though my expression did not betray my alarm, I searched the water anxiously for the wreck of the tanker and thought at one point that just beneath the surface I saw the funnel (chimney) of the sunken ship. It turned out to be a rotten basket astir with seaweed.

The pilot communicated to us by means of clever wrist play and a series of little grunts that the tide was down and that he would have to drop anchor there while we swam ashore to the Sisters. This was agreed upon. There was no need for an elaborate change of clothes as we were wearing our bathing costumes under our street things. We folded our slacks and jumpers and dived into the channel and made for the shore, the Crowleys with morbid slowness, Harry and I thrashing desperately.

I felt the tug of the ripping tide on my arms, the slimy uprooted loofahs brushing my knees, and I thought with horror of the ghostly hulk which lay – who knew how close? The Crowleys probably did – beneath me, manned by the corpses of thirty Chinese and one valiant Scot. I have no idea how I made it to shore, but I did, and so did Harry. How ironic that the sun should beat down on us, that the sky should be so impossibly blue! A blasted heath would have been more appropriate, especially as in trendy bathing costumes the Crowleys crawled up the beach.

It was clear that both of them wished to raise the subject of the tanker, for they remarked on the rainbows of oil slick that slapped in the shallows. 'Must be from our launch,' said Harry, who is nobody's fool and certainly knew better than that. They also spoke about the curious shadows in the water, and Lester said in that pompously knowledgeable way of his: 'Modern science really hasn't a clue what goes on under the sea.'

'Another one of your detective stories?' I remarked, and I could tell it wounded him because he visibly winced at me.

Seeing that they were getting nowhere, the Crowleys then began telling Harry and I of something that had happened to them in I think Panama. The story does not bear repeating; it is too horrible for that. But simply let me say that it was about a stray dog they picked up, thinking it was a worthy little animal. They fed it and cared for it; it loved them and appeared perfectly docile. After a month or two of care its coat was glossy and it showed tenderness, fetching sticks and wagging its tail. The family next door, imitating the Crowleys' example, bought a small puppy at a pet shop in the city. On seeing the puppy, the Crowleys' hound leaped the hedge that divided the gardens and set upon the poor animal and tore it to pieces. It turned out that the dog the Crowleys had befriended was a 'fighting dog' which is trained from birth to kill other dogs, but is in all other respects quite normal. Apparently your Panamanian enjoys such sport and makes bets on these dogfights in the same way as other savages gamble on fighting cocks. I have told more of this story than I had planned to. I don't have to say it chilled me to the bone. And Lester had the impertinence to add, 'You see, there's a lesson in that.'

The only lesson I could see was that one should be careful in choosing one's friends, and I as much as told him so.

We lunched on the launch. Another frantic swim. They remarked politely on my cucumber sandwiches ('frail but cooling') and ate all the pâté. Harry, who *will* let himself be bullied, had their leavings. I made up for their gluttony by having more than my share of wine (they did after all bring a few bottles of a very acid Australian red). Harry, sampling the wine, remarked, 'It's a sincere little chappie' – very much to the point, I thought. And then we dozed, eyed by the Chinese father and daughter from the stern (back).

Around three I suggested returning home, saying that the sun had given me a rather splitting headache and didn't they think enough was enough? They insisted on another swim; Harry refused to stand by me, he let himself be chivvied by them once again. We remained on board while the Crowleys floated on their backs and spat infantile little waterspouts into the air. 'Thar she blows!' said Harry, but he ceased this when he detected an expression of severe reprimand on my face. It was at this point that, gazing off the side of the launch, I noticed a long and bejewelled snake slithering through the water, making its way amongst the rocks and coral. I did not call attention to it; even Harry was unaware of its existence (yes, dear). They are said to be quite poisonous and I thought then as I think now, that death can end an unsatisfying relationship as soon as rudeness, and I don't mind saying that I was hoping with all my heart that one or both of the Crowleys would sustain the fatal bite of that snake. It was not to be. Laughing absurdly they clambered into the launch and gave the pilot instructions for the voyage home.

Instead of taking the direct route back, we made what I thought was a pointless detour around St John's Island, where the mental hospital is. It is also, at the south shore, the place where the channel meets the open sea, and consequently there is a terrific choppiness in the water. I was absolutely disgusted and decided to sun myself on the roof of the launch; but the pounding of the waves across the rocking bow of the launch was too much for me, and I realized that it was the express intention of the Crowleys to drown Harry and me, as they had signally failed to cow or frighten us. The sea hit and broke, hit and broke, setting the launch into an indescribable pitching, and tossing up bundles of lathered flotsam onto the foredeck.

And here, just south of that island madhouse, in the frothy sea, I looked up and saw that very strange thing. I peered at it for a long moment.

'Look at that,' said Harry, who had also seen it. 'Is it a lobster trap?'

Neither of the Crowleys spoke, though they watched it intently. On the cabin bench the small Chinese girl was peacefully, mercifully asleep.

It bobbed toward us, bloated to a grotesque buoyancy, very high in the water, rigid in the attitude of a resting swimmer.

'A sack of meal,' said Harry.

We all watched it pass twenty yards off. It had limbs, but the hands were out of the water, and black, and clawing the air. It was much worse than seeing a corpse far off and deliberately averting your eyes. We did not take our eyes off it for a second! We pretended it wasn't human! Then it was too late: we knew we had been staring at a dead man for ten minutes or more.

The Chinese boatman threw his head back and laughed, for a corpse is considered unlucky, and it is by laughing hysterically that your Chinese reacts to mortal terror.

'You can't fool me,' I said. 'I know it's dead.'

'No one is trying to fool you,' said Lester. 'But look – it's spinning so grandly.'

The corpse wheeled around and around, like an inflated beach toy in a breeze.

'It *is* floating rather well,' said Elizabeth, and she smiled: the lewd satisfaction of the torturer.

I closed my eyes and instantly wanted to kill them both. With my eyes shut I heard Harry say, 'Quite possibly a fugitive bale of jute.'

Poor Harry. That was no bale of jute. You knew what it was. But why didn't you say so then? Why did you wait until after we had paid the boatman and were home to agree with me? Don't you see that we could have confronted those two hellhounds with their beastliness? And why, whenever I bring this matter up, do you simply say that 'we learned our lesson'?

As for me, I was brusque with the Crowleys. I remembered not to say cheerio but snapped a sharp good-bye into their faces. Harry will go on denying this, but I know pretty well what those arch bitches were up to, though I have not yet discovered the name for their deed, and without this word I cannot make a coherent accusation. Harry keeps muttering that some people are intentionally devilish while others are plain crazy, and these days you don't know who to trust. This, as Harry knows perfectly well, explains nothing whatsoever. Now he refuses to discuss the matter and has talked repeatedly of leaving Singapore and taking me 'for a long rest somewhere cool.' If I do not know the name of what they did to us it is not because there is none. It is only a matter of time, and I have assured Harry that when I find out what it is I shall report all the findings which I have carefully noted here to the proper authorities.

You Make Me Mad

'I think you're going colorblind,' said Ambrose McCloud.

Doris McCloud hitched herself forward to turn and stare at her husband. They had just pulled into their driveway and Doris was twisting the emergency brake when he took his pipe out of his mouth and spoke.

'I didn't want to mention it back there. Thought you might get rattled,' said Mr McCloud. He chuckled, a pitying kind of mirth, and said, 'You went sailing right through two red lights. Scared the pants off me.'

'You're imagining things, Ambrose,' said Mrs McCloud. But she did not sound convinced; her tone of voice contradicted what she said.

'Here,' said Mr McCloud, 'feel my hand.'

Mrs McCloud took her husband's hand. 'Why, it's gone all clammy!'

'You gave me a fright,' said Mr McCloud. 'Back there.'

'God,' said Mrs McCloud to herself, 'I thought they were green.'

'Better watch your step, Doris, or you'll rack yourself up,' said Mr McCloud. 'Say, what's on television?'

Mrs McCloud didn't reply, not even when they were in the house and sitting in front of the television set. Mr McCloud filled his pipe; he did it methodically, packing it with his thumb and then brushing the little stringy droppings of tobacco on his shirtfront back into his cracked plastic pouch. He was a man of sixty-three, two years younger than his wife. It was a difference in age she particularly resented, since he was very spry and chirpy and she was not. He was short, his gestures were precise; and he had a beautiful head of white hair which gave emphasis to his tanned face.

In the three months they had been in Singapore, Mr McCloud had got the tan, and his healthy color was matched by a new vigor, the kind of rejuvenation that is promised to old people on the labels of patent medicine. During the same period his wife's face had grown waxen and she had begun to seem especially aged. It was as if, since coming to Singapore, she had learned feebleness, the way a younger woman might learn to put on airs. She shook, she forgot things and mislaid her shopping lists; she repeated herself and she had started that habit of the very old, of announcing what she was about to do: 'Think I'll have a bite to eat ... Time for my bath ... Gosh, it's time I was in bed.' She often accused her husband of making her that way, but still her doubt lingered to produce fear in her; the uncertainty was like being elderly and she had begun to be afraid.

'I want to go home,' she said finally.

'We've been through this one before.'

'I mean it. Two old duffers like us shouldn't be living in a nasty place like this.'

'*I'm* not an old duffer,' said Mr McCloud irritably. 'Anyway, the company won't allow it. They'll probably keep me here until retirement, is what they'll probably do.' Mr McCloud thought a moment. 'Not many younger fellers are interested in marketing plastics like I am.'

'We should have rented an apartment in town,' said Mrs McCloud.

'They cost the earth,' said Mr McCloud. 'What we save now we can spend later.'

'Money,' said Mrs McCloud. 'Your penny-pinching makes me mad. Take the car. I think we're the only people in the world with an old Japanese car. You'd think we'd have a new one, as it's Japanese. But no. It's cheap, and what's cheap is dangerous.'

'Some folks call it cheap,' said Mr McCloud. 'And some –'

'I know what you're going to say,' said Mrs McCloud.

Mr McCloud puffed his pipe. He said, 'Lots of people would give their right arm to live in the country, instead of that noisy city. We're air-conditioned, no neighbors, lots of nice flowers, and it's quiet as –'

'Quiet as a grave,' said Mrs McCloud.

'Well, that's what I was going to say.'

Mrs McCloud went reflective. 'I was thinking about those lights,' she said. 'The ones I went through. What color were they, anyway?'

'Red,' said Mr McCloud. 'I guess they looked like green to you. Take care when you pick me up tomorrow.'

*

'Why, Doris,' said Mr McCloud the following afternoon. 'You're all pale. You look like you've seen a ghost.'

Mrs McCloud was not sitting in the driver's seat. She shook her head and said, 'You drive. I'm afraid.'

'What the devil happened?'

'I almost crashed the car. The other man slammed on his brakes. He swore at me. I could hear him.'

'What color was the light?'

'I don't know!' said Mrs McCloud, and she looked as if she might cry.

'You're a bundle of nerves, Doris. I suggest we get a drink at that new hotel over on Orchard Road. What do you say?'

'That would be nice,' said Mrs McCloud.

Only the lower portion of the hotel was finished, the lobby, the cocktail lounge, and two floors for guests. The rest of the hotel, in various stages of completion, rose from this solid lighted foundation and seemed to disintegrate, from lighted windows, to a floor of glassless windows, to a floor of wall-less rooms, to brick piles and finally to a rickety structure of bamboo scaffolding at the top.

After two drinks, Mr McCloud said, 'I'll bet you could get a terrific view from the roof.'

'Except,' said Mrs McCloud, 'there's no roof. It's not up that far.'

'I mean the top floor,' said Mr McCloud. 'Bet we could sneak up there and get a really nice breeze and see the whole harbor.'

Mr McCloud seemed very eager, 'like a college boy,' said his wife, which made them both smile.

'You go,' said Mrs McCloud. 'I'll just park myself right here.'

'Doris, you're no damned fun, you know that?' said Mr McCloud. 'To hear you talk anyone would think you're sixty-six years old.'

'I *will* be,' said Mrs McCloud, 'next March,' and she started to cry.

'Aw, come on,' said Mr McCloud. 'People are looking at you.'

'I can't help it,' said Mrs McCloud. 'Ambrose, you're so good and I'm such an old bag.'

'You're as young as you feel,' said Mr McCloud, winking.

'I feel eighty-seven,' said Mrs McCloud.

'Let's skitter up to that top floor and have us a look, eh?'

'You know how I am about heights,' said Mrs McCloud. 'I can't even climb a ladder to change a bulb. I go dizzy and feel limp as a rag.' Her last phrase seemed to depress her and she cried again; many people in the cocktail lounge turned to watch her.

Mr McCloud dropped the subject and put his arm around his wife.

On the way home Mrs McCloud said, 'Ambrose, you just went through a red light!'

'Wrong again,' said Mr McCloud, driving fast. 'It was green.'

Mrs McCloud stayed home for a week. She said it was a kind of convalescence, but instead of getting better she seemed to worsen, and each time Mr McCloud came home his wife was paler and more feeble than she had been in the morning.

'I wish you'd come home for lunch,' said Mrs McCloud one day.

'I can get me a nice cheap lunch in town,' said Mr McCloud. 'Little bowl of noodles, little bit of boiled fish, tasty little omelette.' He lighted his pipe. 'Sixty cents,' he said, puffing.

'If you came home for lunch you could give me a hand when things go wrong.'

'Don't tell me things have been going wrong, Doris.'

'So many things,' said Mrs McCloud. 'The other day it must have been something I ate. I think it was that sandwich you made for me, or it might have been a rotten egg, gave me tummy pains. I threw up. Today I blew a fuse. I just plugged in my hair dryer and it made a fizz and the TV shut off.'

'Who fixed the fuse?'

'The gardener,' said Mrs McCloud.

'You didn't mention it when I called up.'

'I was ashamed to,' said Mrs McCloud. 'Thought I'd make you mad.'

Mr McCloud was looking at the hair dryer; it was pistol shaped and blackened. 'She's all burned out inside. Wires must have shorted,' he said. 'Good thing you didn't get a shock,' and he looked closely at his wife.

'I did,' said Mrs McCloud. 'But it wasn't a bad one.'

'That hair dryer cost a pretty penny,' said Mr McCloud.

'You can get a Japanese one to replace it.'

'Not this month,' said Mr McCloud. 'Oh, no! That'll have to wait, my dear. I can't be throwing my money away on hair dryers. I've got the insurance coming up and God knows what else.'

'How will I dry my hair?' asked Mrs McCloud.

'Sit in front of the air conditioner and shake your head,' said Mr McCloud gruffly. He stamped the floor with one foot, as he often did when he was very angry.

Several minutes of tuning, twisting the knobs with two hands, had produced only squawks, the underwater babble of Tamil, a high-pitched Chinese opera and some Malay gongs; though they came in clearly, the Chinese salesman said these foreign noises were not showing the radio to best advantage, and he became anxious. He apologized to Mr McCloud and rearranged the antenna, whipping it around and just missing Mr McCloud's left eye. Mr McCloud touched at the lucky eye, making a light tear-wiping motion with his finger; but he was smiling.

The salesman offered to demonstrate a powerful shortwave radio.

Mr McCloud said not to bother. 'This one's going to do me just fine.'

'Let me search some English,' said the salesman breathlessly, still hunting. He flicked the antenna again.

Mr McCloud leaned over and switched the radio off. He took out his wallet and grinned at the perspiring salesman. He asked, 'How much?' He removed the pipe when he counted the money, licking his thumb and peeling the bills into the salesman's palm.

'That's a mighty fine little radio,' said Mr McCloud. 'Get me some nice programs on that radio.'

'Don't mention,' said the salesman, smiling and opening the door. 'See you next time.'

That evening Mr McCloud turned on all the air conditioners in the house. His wife complained, 'I'm going to catch a death of cold,' but Mr McCloud calmed her by saying, 'Don't worry – I put them on low. Freshen up the room a bit,' he said over the roaring of the air conditioners.

Mrs McCloud said, 'Time for my bath,' and Mr McCloud said, 'you do that. I'll just sit here and fill my pipe.'

Mrs McCloud was singing softly to herself when Mr McCloud entered the bathroom. She stopped singing and covered her breasts, holding one in each hand, as her husband, chuckling, turning the radio he carried in his hand onto full volume, said 'Alley-oop' and pitched the yelling thing into the water at his wife's feet. He stepped quickly out and shut the door.

'*Ambrose!*' Mr McCloud heard his wife scream. He nibbled on his pipe stem and smiled.

But she was out of the bathroom a minute later, wrapped in a towel and still wearing her plastic cap. 'You silly old fool,' she said, and slapped him with a force that sent his pipe flying out of his mouth.

Mr McCloud did not retrieve the pipe. He watched his wife with the extreme attention of disbelief. She looked very angry, but not ill. At once, her face lighted with a thought, became concerned, grew rather small; she murmured, 'Oh, God,' and sat down, as if exhausted.

'Oh, shoot,' said Mr McCloud, and went to pack.

Dog Days

The Indian said: 'I take hand of woman and I squeeze and look in eyes, and if she return look and do not take hand away I know I can make intercourse. If also she squeeze my hand back it is most certain I can do it that very day. Only thing is, husband must be elsewhere.'

He smiled and lifted his long brown hands, displaying their emptiness like a conjurer. He went on in his lilting voice: 'In Asia, namely India, Pakistan, Indochina, Siam, here in Singapore, wherever, it is enough to touch body of woman, even arm or whatnot. If they do not object to that, path is quite open. And what,' he inquired, 'is done in States?'

'In the States?' Len Rowley thought a moment. 'I don't know. I suppose we just come out and ask the girl if she wants to.'

'Just looking and saying, "Cheerio, let us make intercourse"?'

'No, probably something like, "Would you care to come up for a drink?"'

'A *drink*?' The Indian threw his head back and gave a dry croaking laugh. His teeth were bony and stained dark red with betel juice.

'Or to see your pictures. Any excuse, really. The idea is to get her up to your room. If she says yes you know you can do it.'

The Indian nodded and spoke to the empty chair beside him, solemnly rehearsing: 'You would like to come up to take drink, yes?' Then he said to Len, 'I think it is same as touching body. Woman enjoys, but she do not like to name.'

That conversation had taken place in a bar on Serangoon Road, the heart of the Indian district of Singapore. Len had been out walking and had stopped at the bar. He hadn't intended to drink. But the Indian sitting by the door had given him a welcoming wobble of the head, and had smiled and tapped a chair seat and said, 'Try some toddy?' They had talked, first about toddy, then about hot food, then about women. Len did not ask the Indian's name, nor did he ever see the Indian again.

But Len had replayed the Indian's voice many times. He found the explanation satisfying and revealing, such a close glimpse into the mind of Asia that he had never divulged it to anyone. It was like a treasure map, described by a casually met pirate and committed to memory. *I take hand of woman and I squeeze . . . It is enough to touch body*. The Indian had a way of saying *body* – he had pronounced it *bho-dhee*, speaking it with wet lips and heavy tongue-working – that made it sound the leering name for something vicious.

Len Rowley was a private soul, and marriage had increased his loneliness by violating his reveries. His attachment to Marian was not deep: he had lingered beside her for nearly seven years. She had put him through college, and now as an expatriate lecturer in English literature he was paying the bills. Marian was learning to play the guitar which hung on a hook in their living room. Friends found them an odd couple. Len and Marian talked of divorce, in company; this frightened listeners, but it always seemed to bring them together. Len was sometimes startled to recall that he had been unfaithful only once – with a prostitute in Newark, a year after the marriage. That was like making love to a chair tipped on its back and it cost Len twelve dollars.

The Forbeses and the Novaks were over for drinks. In a room full of people, Len became a recluse: he was still mentally speaking to the Indian.

But Ella Novak was saying, 'In *Midnight Cowboy*, yes, that party. Remember? When Ratso faints? It was actually filmed at Andy Warhol's! That was a *real party*!'

'It's the new thing,' Tom Forbes said. 'Of course, your French have been doing it for years – at least Truffaut has.'

Marian said, 'Interesting, isn't it? Like Eldridge Cleaver's wife being in *Zabriskie Point*.'

'Which one was she?' asked Ella in annoyance.

'At the beginning, when those students – I think they were students – were talking. With the hair. Holding the pencil and sort of . . . leading the discussion.'

'Has anyone here seen *Easy Rider*?' Joan Forbes put in.

'That hasn't come to Singapore yet,' said Ella.

'And probably won't,' said Tony Novak. 'Unless the Film Society gets it.'

'Len still refuses to join,' said Marian, looking at Len in the corner, slumped in the Malacca chair with a dreamy look in his eyes.

Roused, returned to the living room by Marian's words and the ensuing silence, Len said, 'Film Society. Foreigners out of focus. Too much work reading all those subtitles!'

'I knew he was going to say that,' said Marian to Tony. 'He's really very puritanical.'

Len smiled. He heard: *It is enough to touch body. Bho-dhee.*

'Tom and I saw it when we were on leave,' said Joan, adding, '*Easy Rider.*'

'I didn't know you got home leave every year,' said Marian.

'Ford Foundation,' said Joan, and put her hands primly into her lap.

'We don't go home until seventy-two,' said Marian. 'Seventeen months more.'

Tom Forbes asked Marian about Len's contract, and he commiserated while Joan Forbes explained to Ella and Tony what happened in *Easy Rider*.

Len was silent. He heard the Indian's piratical voice and he watched the kitchen. Ah Meng was at the sideboard flexing a plastic freezer tray and popping the ice cubes into a pewter bucket. She stood in the bright rectangle of the half-open door, a shelf of corn flakes and Quaker Oats behind her head making her unremarkable profile more interesting. Her forehead was long and sloping, her pug nose set just below the rise of her high cheeks; her chin was small but definite, her mouth narrow and almost grim. Len could see her stiff black hair which was wound in a pile on her head, and he knew what her eyes were like: hooded, the sly changeless shape of the skeptic's; they were amused eyes, but some would say contemptuous. She was all but breastless and only her hands could be called beautiful, but it was the total effect that excited Len, the flower and stalk of face and body, the straightness of her length, her carriage. In a slim woman posture was beauty. She was tall for a Chinese and she moved in nervous strides like a deer.

Len had compared her with others' servants: the Forbeses' Ah Eng had muscular legs, bowed as a pair of nutcrackers. The Novaks' Susan was a pale, pudgy, worried-looking little thing who always wore the same dress and once went bald. Tony was on the verge of firing her but, fortuitously, her hair grew back, porcupiny at first, then to her old bush.

When there was company, as on this evening, Ah Meng wore a loose blouse (raising to show a flat stomach when she reached for clean glasses on the top shelf), and tight, red skier's slacks. She went about the house swiftly, treading on the ankle loops of her slacks, in bare feet: Len found the feet attractive for the wildness they suggested. She had been with the Rowleys for nearly three months – replacing the bossy old Hakka woman – and for much of that time Len Rowley had been trying to get into bed with her.

Trying was perhaps the wrong word. He had been thinking constantly about it, the way he thought of the Indian's advice. But something a man at the university had said made him hesitate. It was in the Staff Club. A man from Physics left, and Davies from Economics said, 'See that bloke?' Davies told a story which cautioned by horrifying: the man from Physics had pinched his house girl's bottom. That very evening the girl disappeared, and the following day at a stoplight three youths jumped into the man's car, beat him with bearing scrapers, slashed him, and fled. The man still wore bandages. The house girl's boy friend was in a secret society, and the boy friend's final piece of revenge was upon the next girl the man employed. She was threatened; she resigned. This became known, and no one would work for the man. Davies said the man was going to break his contract and go home. That for a bottom-pinching.

This story had to be balanced against the easy explanation of the Indian; it made Len hesitate but he did not put the thought of sleeping with Ah Meng out of his mind. Sometimes he wondered why and decided it was lust's boldness, lechery's curiosity for the new. Unlike the man who feels challenged by the unwilling, Len was aroused by those who were passive, who would say yes instantly. He didn't like the devious ploys of love, and it was Ah Meng's obedience ('Shut the door' 'Yes, mister') that made an affair seem possible.

For his lust he blamed his dog days. In some of the books he lectured on they were mentioned as days of excessive heat, unwholesome influences, practically malignant. The dog days were the hottest time of the year; the days Len passed, replaying the Indian's words and staring into the kitchen at Ah Meng were the hottest in his life. And it was literally true: it was always ninety in Singapore.

But hotter on Thursdays, Marian's Film Society night. These nights Len sat, soaking his shirt with sweat and wondering if he should make a move. Ah Meng would be in the downstairs shower, the one that adjoined her room, sluicing herself noisily with buckets of water and hawking and spitting. Later she would sit on the backstairs, holding her small transistor to her ear.

The story of the man in Physics restrained him; but there was something more. It was shame. It seemed like exploitation to sleep with your house girl. She might be frightened; she might submit out of panic. The shame created fear, and fear was an unusual thing: it made you a simpleton, it unmanned you, it turned you into a zombie. It was as a zombie that he had passed nearly three months.

'. . . early class tomorrow,' Tom Forbes was saying. He was in the center of Len's living room, stretching and yawning, thanking Marian for a lovely evening.

Len looked up and saw that everyone was standing, the Forbeses, the Novaks, Marian, waiting for him to rise and say good night. He leaped to his feet, and then bent slightly to conceal his tumescence.

'What's on?' asked Len, who was marking essays on the dining-room table. Marian clawed at objects inside her handbag.

'*Knife in the Water*,' she said, still snatching at things inside the bag. She muttered, 'Where are those car keys?'

'They usually show that one,' said Len. 'Or a Bergman.'

'And some cartoons,' said Marian, who hadn't heard what Len had said. 'Czech ones,' she said, looking up, dangling the car key.

'Enjoy yourself,' said Len.

'I've told Ah Meng to heat the casserole. Tell her whether you want rice or potatoes.' Patting her hair, snapping her handbag shut, Marian left the house.

As soon as Marian had gone Len pushed the essays aside and lit a cigarette. He thought about Ah Meng, the man in Physics, what the Indian had said. It occurred to him again – this was not a new perception – that the big mistake the man had made was in pinching the girl's bottom. That was rash. The Indian would have advised against it. There were subtler ways.

Ah Meng was beside him.

'Yes?' He swallowed. She was close enough to touch.

'Want set table.'

'Okay, I'll take these papers upstairs. Make some rice.' Distracted, he sounded gruff.

And upstairs at his desk, he continued to pursue his reverie. A squeezed hand was ambiguous and had to be blameless, but a pinched bottom signaled only one thing – and was probably offensive to a Chinese. Also: if Ah Meng had a boy friend, where was he? She took a bus home on her day off. A boy friend would have picked her up on his motorbike, a secret society member in his car. The Indian's way seemed unanswerable: his method was Asian, bottom-pinching was not.

'Mister?' Ah Meng was at the study door. 'Dinner.'

Len got up quickly. Ah Meng was in the kitchen, scraping rice from the pot, by the time he had reached the second landing. He was breathless for a moment, and he realized as he gasped for air that he had hurried in order to catch her on the stairs.

He ate, forking the food in with one hand and with the other retuning the radio each time the overseas station drifted off into static. He stared at the sauce bottles, and forked and fiddled with the radio knobs.

He put down his fork. It made a clank on the plate. Ah Meng was in the room, and now leaning over the table, gathering up silverware, piling plates, rolling up placemats. She said, 'Coffee, mister?'

Len reached over and put his hand on hers. It was as sudden and unexpected as if his hand belonged to someone else. His hand froze hers. She looked at the wall. *I take hand of woman and I squeeze* . . . but the damned girl wouldn't look him in the eyes! It was getting awkward, so still squeezing he said, with casualness that was pure funk, 'No, I don't think I'll have a coffee tonight. I think I will have –' He relaxed his grip. Her hand didn't move. He tapped her wrist lightly with his forefinger and said, 'A whiskey. I think I'll have a whiskey upstairs.'

Ah Meng turned and was gone. Len went upstairs to think; but it took no deep reflection for him to know that he had blundered. It had happened too fast: the speed queered it. She hadn't looked at him. He thought, I shouldn't have done it then. I shouldn't have done it at all.

Ah Meng did not bring the whiskey. She was in the shower below Len's study, hawking loudly. Spitting on me. He took his red ballpoint and, sighing, poised it over an essay. '"The Canonization" is a poem written in indignation and impatience against those who censored Donne because of what is generally considered to have been his –'

Len pushed the essay (Sonny Poon's) away, threw down the ball-point and put his head in his hands.

The front door slammed. The house was in silence.

This is the end, he told himself, and immediately he began thinking of where he might find another job. He saw a gang of Chinese boys carrying weapons, mobbing a street. He winced. An interviewer was saying, 'Why exactly did you leave Singapore, Mr Rowley?' He was on a plane. He was in a dirty city. He was in an airless subway, catching his cock on a turnstile's steel picket.

There was a chance (was it too much to hope for?) that she was just outside, on the back steps, holding her little transistor against her ear. He prayed it was so, and in those moments, leaving his study, he felt that strange fear-induced fever that killed all his desire.

He took the banister and prepared to descend the stairs. Ah Meng was halfway up, climbing purposefully, silently, on bare feet. There was a glass in her hand. She wore pajamas.

'I heard the door. I –'

'I lock,' she said. She touched his hand and then bounded past him, into the spare bedroom. Len heard the bamboo window blind being released and heard it unroll with a flapping rattle and thump.

His first thought the next morning was that she had left during the night. Shame might have come to her, regret, an aftertaste of loathing. There was also the chance that she had gone to the police.

Len dressed hurriedly and went downstairs. Ah Meng was in the kitchen, dropping slices of toast into the toast rack as she had done every morning since the Hakka woman left. Marian took her place at the table across from Len and Ah Meng brought their eggs. Ah Meng did not look at him. But that meant nothing: she never did.

Marian chewed toast, spooned egg and stared fixedly at the corn-flakes box. That was habitual. She wasn't ignoring him deliberately. Everything seemed all right.

'How was the film?'

Marian shrugged. She said, 'Russian film festival next month.'

'*Ivan the Terrible, Part One*,' said Len. He grinned. But he could not relax. That girl in the kitchen. He had made love to her only hours before. Her climax was a forlorn cry of 'Mister!' Afterward he had told her his name and helped her pronounce it.

'I thought you'd say something like that.' Marian turned the corn-flakes box and read the side panel.

'Just kidding,' said Len. 'I might even go to that festival. I liked the Russian *Hamlet*.'

'Members only,' said Marian. She looked bored for a moment, then her gaze shifted to the tablecloth. 'Where's your lunch?'

Every morning it was beside Len's plate, in a paper bag, two sandwiches with the crusts trimmed off, a banana, a hard-boiled egg, a tiny saltcellar, rambutans or mangosteens if they were available at the stalls. Ah Meng, neat and attentive, made sharp creases in the bag, squaring it. The Staff Club food – maybe it was the monosodium glutamate? – gave him a headache and made him dizzy.

Today there was no lunch bag.

'Must be in the kitchen,' said Len. 'Ah Meng!'

There was no cry of 'Mister?' There was no cry.

'I don't think she heard me,' said Len. He gulped his coffee and went into the kitchen.

Ah Meng sat at the sideboard, sipping tea from a heavy mug. Her back was to him, her feet hooked on the rung of her stool.

'Ah Meng?'

She didn't turn. She swallowed. Len thought she was going to speak. She sipped again at her mug.

'My lunch. Where is it?'

She swallowed again, gargling loudly. That was her reply. It was as if she had said, 'Get stuffed.'

'Is it in the –' Len opened the refrigerator. The lunch was not inside. He was going to speak again, but thought better of it. Marian was around the corner, at the table – out of sight but probably listening. Len found a paper bag in a drawer. He put three bananas in it and looked for something more. He saw a slice of bread on the sideboard and reached for it. Ah Meng snatched it up. She bit into it, and sipped at her mug. Her back seemed to wear an expression of triumph. Len left the kitchen creasing the bag.

'Got it,' he said. He went behind Marian and kissed her on her ear. She was raising a spoonful of egg to her mouth, which was open. She stopped the spoon in midair, held it, let Len kiss, and then completed the interrupted movement of the spoon to her mouth.

That evening, when Len returned from the department, Marian said, 'Ah Meng wants a raise.'

'Really?' said Len. 'I thought we just gave her one.'

'We did. At least you were supposed to. I wouldn't put it past you to hold back the five dollars and buy something for yourself.'

'No,' said Len. He ignored the sarcasm. He *had* given Ah Meng the raise. He remembered that well: it was one of the times he had been about to seize and press her hand; but he had handed over the money and panicked and run. 'I did give it to her. When was that? About a month ago?'

'I told her she gets more than the Novaks' Susan, and doesn't have children to mind. She gets her food and we pay her Central Provident Fund. I don't know what more she wants.'

'What did she say?'

'She insisted. "Want five dollar, *mem*,"' said Marian, imitating absurdly. Her mimicry was all the more unpleasant for the exaggerated malice of its ineptness. 'It's not the five dollars, it's the principle of the thing. We gave her a raise a month ago. If we give in this time she'll ask again next month, I know. I told her to wait until you came home. You're better with her.'

'Maybe we should give it to her,' Len said. 'Five bucks Singapore is only one sixty US.'

'No, I expect you to be firm with her. No raise this month!'

In the kitchen, Ah Meng faced him – was that a sneer or a smile? Len said, '*Mem* says you want a raise. Is that right?'

She didn't blink. She continued to sneer, or perhaps smile. There was a red mark, just at the base of her neck, near the bump of her shoulder bone, a slight love scratch. From his own hand.

'Says you want five dollars more.'

Her expression was that of a person looking at the sun or facing a high wind. It was a look only the Chinese could bring off. It revealed nothing by registering the implausible, severe pain. And this pain had to be discounted, for the face, on closer inspection, bore no expression at all: the eyes were simply a shape, they were not lighted, they gave Len no access.

Marian, out of sight, called from the dining room: 'Tell her if she does her work properly we'll give her something around Christmas!'

'If you do your work properly,' said Len loudly, taking out his wallet, fishing around and discovering that he had three tens and two ones, and then giving her a ten which she folded small and put in her handkerchief and tucked into the sleeve of her blouse,

'– if you do your work properly we *might* give you something around Christmas. But we can't give you anything now.'

The *might* came to him on the spur of the moment, and Marian, who overheard, thanked him for it.

Len felt cold and started to shake. He went upstairs and clicked his red ballpoint at the unmarked essays. His dog days were over. But something new was beginning: intimidation. He didn't like it.

For the next few days he stayed up until Marian went to bed. Then he made his lunch in the kitchen, remembering to crease the paper bag, and this he placed on the dining-room table, which was set for breakfast.

On Tuesday he had an idea. Marian was having her Pernod on the verandah, a touch she learned from a foreign film; she played with the small glass and watched its cloudy color.

'Is Ah Meng around?' Len whispered.

'At the market. We ran out of salt.'

'Then I don't have to whisper.' But this was a whisper. Len had downed five stengahs on the way home. 'Marian, seriously, I think we should fire her.'

'Why?' Marian frowned.

Len expected to be challenged, but not so quickly or (Marian was squinting at him) aggressively.

'Lots of reasons,' said Len, starting.

'I thought you were so pally with her.'

'Me? Pally? That's a laugh.' Len forced a laugh. He heard its cackling falsity as a truly horrible sound, and stopped. 'Here, look what she did to my pants.'

Len stood and showed Marian his leg. On the thigh was a brown mark of an iron, the shape of a rowboat. Between the Conrad lecture and the Donne tutorial Len had borrowed an iron from a Malay woman at the Junior Staff Quarters, and he had scorched his pants in his locked and darkened office. 'Burned the hell out of them.'

'That's a shame,' said Marian.

'Burned the hell out of them,' Len repeated.

Marian said, 'You know, I've never said anything, but she's done that lots of times to my dresses. She scorches the collars.'

'That's it then! Out she goes!'

'Okay, Len, if you say so. But there's going to be trouble with the Labor Exchange. It'll be just like the Novaks.'

'What about the Novaks?'

'Investigated,' said Marian. 'By the Labor Exchange. After Susan's hair fell out, Tony said he didn't want to see her around, couldn't stand that bald head, or so he said. The Labor Exchange came to investigate – Susan told them of course – and there was a great to-do.'

'I didn't know they did things like that.'

'Went on for weeks,' said Marian. The Pernod was to her lips. Ah Meng entered the house and went into the kitchen.

'I'll speak to her,' said Marian.

'That's okay. I will – they're my pants,' said Len.

He went into the kitchen and closed the door. Ah Meng's back was to him; she was removing small parcels wrapped in newspaper, bound with rubber bands from her market basket. Len made himself a gin and tonic.

'I guess we ran out of salt, eh?'

Ah Meng walked past him and closed the refrigerator door hard. Len went out to the verandah.

'She says she's sorry.'

Thursday came. Len asked, barely disguising the desperation in his voice, 'Say Marian, how about letting me come with you to the Film Society. We can go out to eat afterward. What do you say?'

'Are you putting me on?'

'No, honest to God,' said Len, his voice cracking. 'Take me. I won't make any comments. I'd love to come.'

'Mister is coming with me,' said Marian to Ah Meng later.

Momentarily, Ah Meng faced a high wind; then she turned away.

The film was *L'Avventura*. Len watched with interest. He murmured that he was enjoying it, and he meant it. At the end, when Sandro sits abjectly on the bench and wrings his hands and starts to cry, blubbering with a pained look, Len understood, and he snuggled close to Marian in the darkness of the Cultural Center. Marian patted him on the knee. Afterward, as Len promised, they went to the Pavilion and he had cold, silky oysters with chili sauce, and tankards of stout.

Marian said, 'We should do this more often,' and at home, confidentially, 'Keep me awake, Len,' which was the whispered euphemism she used when she wanted to make love. Len was tired, but put the fan on full and made love to Marian with resolve, allowing his vigor to announce his new fidelity. Then he turned the fan down.

He lay on his back, his hands folded across his chest, proceeding feetfirst into sleep; but even much later, in the stillness of deep night, sleep was only to his knees. His eyes were open, his mouth clamped shut, and he was apprehensive, at that stage of fatigue where one's mind is vulnerable enough to suggestion to be prodded and alarmed and finally reawakened by a sequence of worrying images, broken promises, papers not marked, unpaid bills. He shooed his thoughts as they appeared tumbling and circling like moths attracted to the glowing bulb of his half-awake brain. He made an effort to switch off his mind – as one would a lamp in an upper room on a summer night, so as to quiet what had collected and not to attract more. But something in that darkness stung him: it was the thought of his lunch.

He went down to the kitchen. The sleepiness made him look like a granny in rumpled pajamas and electrified hair – like the elderly Hakka woman with the simian face and loose *sam foo*, her silk trousers with cuffs a yard wide, her narrow shoulders and square, swollen knuckles. He muttered like her and nodded at what he was doing, and just like her, in the curious conserving motion of the very old, fussed nimbly with his hands and at the same time shuffled slowly in broken shoes. He opened and closed cupboards, found a lunch bag, cut tomatoes, and he dealt out bread slices onto the sideboard as if starting a game of solitaire. With his impatient fingernail he pecked the boiling egg into its suds of froth.

A hand brushed the back of his neck. It was a caress, but he reacted as if dodging a dagger swipe.

'You scared the life –'

Ah Meng took his hand and did not let go. 'Ren,' she said, giving his name the rising intonation of a Chinese word.

Len shook his head. He said, 'No.'

Ah Meng pressed his hand. She was unhurried, looking at him without blinking. She tugged. Len tried to pull away. But she was the stronger; with his free hand Len turned the gas off under the cooking egg. She led him to her room. He would have time before dawn to finish making his lunch.

A Burial at Surabaya

After Abe Sassoon died in Tretes, his cook got a *jaga* to guard the house and then took a taxi to Surabaya to tell me. He chose me because my cook was related to him, and what he said was that Abe, normally an early riser – always in his vegetable gardens by six o'clock – was not up for breakfast that morning. The cook had forced the door and found Abe in bed clutching the mosquito netting he had yanked right off its pulley. It was draped in tangles over his face, giving the cook the impression he had smothered. I knew this couldn't be true. Abe had a bad heart.

I was having lunch at the time. The cook stood in the kitchen doorway, shouting the information, awkwardly trying to convey sorrow in his shrill parrot's voice. He said he came quickly because he knew we had to bury the old man before nightfall according to *Yehudi* custom. I thanked him for remembering that, gave him his taxi fare and told him to go back to the house and wait for us.

Hesitantly he asked for some 'coffee money' for the *jaga*.

We have known better times, and I can recall when that cook would not have had to take a taxi to tell me. We even had a synagogue in Malang – the rabbi there was a very learned fellow who always had his nose in a book. The telephones were better then, and you could pick it up and tell the operator the town you wanted and in minutes you would be gabbing away, clear as a bell. Now, the telephone squawks, then goes dead in your hand, and no one risks sending a cable. People will say it was when the Dutch left that things went to pot, but it wasn't: it was when the sugar prices fell. It doesn't matter now; there aren't enough Jews in Surabaya to support one synagogue, and business hasn't been good since the early fifties. Our age is an advantage. It means fewer interruptions – no marriages, no births. We don't observe the holi-days, and it seems that every death over the past ten or fifteen years has happened after the person went to a hospital in Singapore. I can't say I looked forward to these deaths, but they gave me a chance to pick up a little stock for my business, which is mainly ship's hardware. I was thinking to myself, as I was driving over to Mr Aaron's, that it would have been simpler for all of us if Abe had died in Singapore.

'I'm not surprised,' Mr Aaron said. But he had closed his eyes on hearing the news, and his wife had groaned. 'We haven't seen Abe down here for months.' He shook his head. 'We should have visited him, you know. And the funny thing is, I passed through Tretes a week ago. It was so late I thought I'd better hurry back. My driver is hopeless after dark. I bought a basket of apples and didn't see anyone.'

Mrs Aaron was sitting next to her husband. Her plump shoulders shook with sobs, and when Mr Aaron mentioned buying the apples and coming straight back she groaned again in what struck me as the deepest grief, disappointment.

'What time did it happen?' Mr Aaron asked.

I had forgotten to ask the cook, but he had discovered him in the morning, so I guessed it was after midnight.

'Let's call it four A.M.,' said Mr Aaron. Mrs Aaron looked at him and seemed slightly horrified; but she didn't say anything.

Mr Aaron shrugged, not carelessly but hopelessly. 'I was just going to have my nap,' he said, pulling off his corduroy slippers and showing them to me.

'I thought we could use your van,' I said.

'Oh, yes,' he said, lacing his shoes. 'Gunawan will be back about three. We can go up together. We'll have to leave the burial till tomorrow.'

'Disgraceful!' Mrs Aaron said.

'We can't bury him any quicker than that,' said her husband. 'It's lucky he hasn't got a wife who'll see us doing it this way. That would be awful for her.'

'It *is* awful,' Mrs Aaron said in a whisper more terrifying than a shout.

'It can't be helped,' said Mr Aaron. 'Benjamin can conduct the ceremony. Is that cousin of Abe's still in Hong Kong, do you think?'

'Benjamin will know,' I said.

'Try to calm yourself, Lool,' said Mr Aaron to his wife. 'Get Benjamin on the phone and tell him about Abe. He can cable – what's the fellow's name? Greenman? Greenberg? We'll go around town and tell the people here. Everyone's going to be napping: it's after two.' He sighed. 'I haven't finished my papaya.'

Mrs Aaron said, 'What if it was you? That's what I keep thinking! I don't want it to be like this, to make a chore out of your funeral.'

Mr Aaron, like me, was born in Baghdad; but he looks like a man of the desert, and I have always looked like an iron-monger. His lean face has the furrows of dry soil, aging like erosion; he has a skinny hawk nose, his teeth are bad, black from cheroots and the poor food at Tjimahi Camp during the war. He often jokes, though he never smiles. He said to his wife, 'At least, when I die no one will have to drive all the way to Tretes to pick up my body.'

Glassman was the cousin's name. I remembered it as we were driving back in the van. None of us had ever seen him, but Abe had told us that if we were ever in Hong Kong we should look him up – he'd be glad to see us. Abe made a point of saying that this Glassman was something important in one of the banks there.

In the old days we might have seen him at a wedding, like the Meyer girl's in Djakarta. Old Meyer invited people from all over. They looked out of place – they kept saying how hot it was – and asked us how was business and why not try Manila or Singapore or wherever, if it's so bad? No one admitted it was bad, but these strangers knew the sugar price was down; and none of us said that Surabaya was hotter than Djakarta. You could look at people's shoes and know exactly how business was, and more than that, you could tell from their shoe styles where their business was. The Philippine friends had these huge pebbly-orange or purplish American shoes, the ones from Singapore and Hong Kong had English-style, rather smaller, without laces, and other people had low, narrow Italian ones with thin soles, bankers' shoes. Ours were old-fashioned, square-toed and stitched, and some were scuffed from the train. We were staying with friends, not in hotels where the room boys polish them every night. It was quite a wedding, and after the champagne some of us sat up all night, liking the company, drinking cold little glasses of Bols *genevaer* and eating beady caviar on small squares of toast. 'I wish we could meet like this every year,' said Meyer. 'We've got enough money – we owe it to ourselves.' *He* had enough money, but he went to Zurich a few years later, and they say his daughter's in Israel. The rest of us took our hangovers to Surabaya.

'Glassman wasn't at the Meyer wedding,' I said to Benjamin the next day.

'Who says?' Benjamin is a sharp one, pretending to be a bit older than he actually is, because he knows he can have the last word that way. He uses an old man's preoccupied gestures, and looking thoughtful says as little as possible.

'I didn't see any Glassman there,' I said. 'And I'm sure I met everyone.'

'He was there,' said Benjamin.

'I didn't see him either,' said Mr Aaron. 'I think you're making this up, Ben.'

Benjamin sniffed in annoyance. 'He was ten years old then.'

Mr Aaron looked at me. 'I hadn't thought of that.' After a moment he said, 'Why didn't we meet his parents?'

'How do I know?' said Benjamin, acting more irritated than he was. 'Maybe he didn't come with his parents. Maybe he's an orphan. Anyway, you can ask him this afternoon.'

This was news. 'He's coming?'

'From Singapore,' said Benjamin. He had withheld the information, the old person's privilege and pleasure. 'I just got a cable. His people in Hong Kong must have rung him up there – his bank has a Singapore branch. I don't know the details. He's due in at two-twenty.'

'I hope the plane's on time,' said Mr Aaron. 'The burial's at three. We can hold it up for a little while. But if he's late?'

'Who's picking him up?' I asked.

'Morris,' said Benjamin. Morris is the Honorary Austrian Consul in Surabaya, and with the CC plates on his car he can be counted on to get through the airport confusion with the least delay.

'I hope the plane's on time,' said Mr Aaron again. He looked out the window. 'I would go over to my house if it weren't for those women. Their weeping upsets me worse than Abe's coffin. Would it be disrespectful to have a drink? It's a hot day.'

Benjamin got a bottle of whiskey, three glasses and a bucket of ice. We drank without speaking, in the still, dusty air of the narrow parlor, sitting in hard chairs. I propped myself up on a cushion and tried to think of something to say. One disadvantage about drinking in silence is that you become self-conscious if you drink quickly. I sipped mine. Benjamin held his drink under his nose and inhaled it.

We had walked to Benjamin's, followed by *betjak* drivers, a half a dozen of them cycling along urging us to ride. Mr Aaron told them we weren't going far. It didn't do any good. Now the *betjak* drivers – I could see them through the barred windows of Benjamin's parlor – were curled in the seats of their green vehicles, their feet resting on the handlebars, parked in front of the house. Their number had attracted a few hawkers, some women selling fruit and one man with a noodle stall on wheels. 'Have some respect for the dead,' I was going to say to them. I thought: In a few hours Sassoon will be in the ground and I can go home and sleep. I was sorry it was Saturday; that meant a whole day tomorrow with nothing to do except think about him. I'd rather go to work after a funeral, to remind myself that I can still work.

Someone out front sat up in his *betjak* and began shouting. His hat was still pulled down over his eyes. They're always camped against your fence. Mr Aaron said, 'Lool's right. It is awful.'

Lool's crazy, I was going to say: Why should death make someone your brother? But that truth was an inappropriate argument.

Ponderously, Benjamin addressed his glass: 'Sassoon was a good man. He had some money, but he was a very simple man –' He went on, and Mr Aaron agreed. I knew what was starting and I dredged around for a complimentary reminiscence of old Sassoon.

The word that came to me was: *ruins*. We had seen them at Sassoon's house in Tretes. I said, 'Look at that,' but Mr Aaron had gone straight into the house. I was standing under a mango tree – fruit had ripened and dropped and turned black on the ground – and I was looking toward the back of the house. Once it had belonged to a Dutchman, a happy one to judge from the back garden. There was a swimming pool, children's swings, a miniature golf course with toy bridges and stone chutes and plump low posts. The swimming pool was sooty, filled with tall weeds; the bolts of the diving board remained, but they were large with rust. The swings were rusty, too, the chains had snapped, and the odd stone shapes of the golf course, sticking up from the overgrown yard, looked like the baffling gravestones you see in a Chinese burying ground.

It was dusk, soon dark as a cellar, and I wasn't sure I had seen all those decaying, neglected things: I couldn't verify in the blackness what might have been my imagination. I went into the house. Later, Mr Aaron said the house held the smell of death, but what I noticed was an odor of vinegar and cabbage, boiled meat – probably what Abe had eaten the previous evening. That, and the mangoes which, newly rotting on the ground, gave off a high ripe smell and filled the house with sweetness.

'We should be starting,' Mr Aaron was saying in Benjamin's parlor.

I had been daydreaming. On the way I told them a story the cook had told me about Abe's giving the Javanese kids English lessons at night.

'And look what he gets for it,' said Benjamin.

The signboard, lettered *Graveyard for Foreigners* in yellow and blue – but in Indonesian – was nailed to a high archway at the entrance. There was a little argument at the parking lot over our taking the van in. A Javanese came out carrying a long, rusty *parang*; he laughed when he saw us glancing at his knife, and he explained that he was head gardener. We'd have to leave the van outside, he said, and carry the coffin ourselves. Benjamin told him to lower his voice. We had attracted ten or fifteen onlookers, young boys mostly, in faded shirts. They watched us, smiling, as we heaved the coffin onto our shoulders and shuffled up the dusty road.

Benjamin walked in front, with his head down. Mr Aaron and I were at the head of the coffin, Solomon and Lang had the other end; and behind us walked Mrs Aaron, Benjamin's daughter and her husband – the Manassehs – Mrs Lang, Mrs Solomon and Joel Solomon. Joel is a fleshy fifteen-year-old with a big backside and mustache fur on his upper lip. We must have looked very strange, walking so solemnly in our black clothes, past the torn and carved-up trunks of the casuarina trees which lined the road, their needles glistering in the bright sun and making a mewing moan, a sinuslike sound over our heads – an especially odd sound, for the breeze causing it didn't drift near the hot road, and we could hear the coolness we couldn't feel. Squatting around these trees and next to scarred sisal clumps were groups of boys, most of them about Joel Solomon's age, captivated by the sight of eleven black crows marching with a box through the heat.

At the top of the road we turned right, past a monument in white marble with black graffiti painted on the wide plinth. There had been names and dates carved into the peeling casuarinas, and more names – nicknames, names of gangs – were painted on the gravestones. But it didn't strike me as blasphemous to scrawl your name on a broken monument or carve it into a dying tree. Down the cinder path, on an embankment, two goats were ripping grass with their lips, brushing the ground with their beards, their hoofs planted on *Rudy van Houten Feb. 1936–Dec. 1936*, a tombstone not much bigger than a water-swollen bread loaf: *Rust zacht kleine lieveling en tot wederziens*. A little farther along there was a broken, lamed angel, face down in the grass. There were no trees anywhere – we had left the moaning casuarinas behind – and the ground was so dry it opened in jagged cracks the width of your heel, big enough to trip you. The cloudless sky was enormous without the trees, and the flat plain of graves, the markers leaning this way and that, pushed over by the eruption of a rough grassy tussock – not even green – and scarred and scratched with charcoal – this baking plain was the kind you sometimes see in remoter places in east Java, a few acres of stony rubble signifying a dead story of habitation, which people visit to photograph. But this was not very far gone – more like Sassoon's own swimming pool, blackened and filled with tall grass, a recent ruin, in an early, unremarkable stage of decay, obviously crumbling but not far enough for alarm or interest. I wanted this history to be dust, and the dust to blow away.

We passed the children's graves. The next were families – stone shelters, flat white roofs on posts. Three boys sat under one for the shade, playing cards and listening to loud music on a portable radio. They looked up as we passed, and I heard Solomon curse them. I was fascinated by the heated ruins, the grasshopper whine, the awful litter inspiring not funereal sadness but the simple familiarity of this as a dumping ground in an old country with so many junkyards of cracked tombs and smashed statuary anyone can cart away. Here was a cluster of Chinese graves, photographs of old men and old black-haired women, wincing in egg-sized lockets and posed like the faces in newspapers of men wanted by the police, but much more blurred: *Anton Tjiung Koeng Li*, and beside those stacked slabs, another set of slabs with deep, once gold letters: *Hier Rust onze Dierbare echtgenoot em vader Hubertus Tshaw Khoer Tan*. I had never been a pallbearer here, and today the slow march down the cemetery path, the fact that I was carrying a heavy coffin on my shoulder, made me curious about the details of the graves I was passing: *Geboren Solo 1877, Batavia 1912, Pontianak 1883, Soerabaja 1871*. The Dutchman born in Solo died in Surabaya. I saw a husband and wife; both were born in Malang, both died there: what journey? The next stone made me pause, and the coffin lurched as I read it: *In Memoriam Augusta Baronesse van Lawick-Hercules*. I made a point of remembering it for Mr Aaron.

The Jewish corner of the cemetery adjoins the Chinese Buddhist section on one side, with a dingy crematorium the size and shape of a warehouse on the other side. I was hoping our section would be either in good repair or completely fallen to bits and covered by ashes and gnawed at and pissed on by goats. It was neither; in that intermediate stage of decay that characterized the whole place, a crack through a name, a date effaced, a dry turd cake against a column, weeds uncut, it was resisting pathetically, in the squeezed posture of indignity – but you knew it would disappear. Small boys with grass clippers and sickles had been following us, hoping for a chance to earn a few rupiahs trimming the weeds on our plot. As soon as we arrived at our corner, Mrs Solomon and Mrs Aaron turned and hissed to shoo them away. The boys stepped back, but this wasn't good enough: the women didn't want these urchins to watch. Mrs Solomon pretended to chase them. The boys ran, stopping once to see if she was still after them.

We had put the coffin over the narrow, newly dug trench, and I was wiping my face. Benjamin compared his watch with Mr Aaron's. 'I thought he might catch up with us. I don't see any sign of him.' Benjamin shaded his eyes and looked down the path.

'Let's give him ten minutes or so,' said Mr Solomon.

'The sun,' I said, wrinkling my nose and squinting. 'We should move over there.' I felt a whiskey headache creeping across the back of my eyes. Our black clothes weren't doing us any good. 'Mrs Aaron,' I said. 'Wouldn't you like to stand over there, in the shade?'

'I won't leave him,' she said, nodding at the coffin.

'Irma?'

'No.'

Mrs Aaron shook out her umbrella and pushed it open.

'Very nice,' I mumbled to Mr Aaron, 'we all get sunstroke.' Just behind him I read: *Mȳn geliefde broer Hayeem Mordecai Mizrahie*.

I closed my eyes and imagined myself keeling over; I was on my feet when I opened them, and the sun's dazzle blinded me. I held the lapels of my jacket and worked them back and forth trying to fan myself. Sweat crawled down my chest like harmless ants, tickling the hairs there, and my eyes were stinging with salt. I read the gravemarkers to pass the time; it might have looked like veneration. *Our beloved Hilda Wife of Adolf Lisser Died 19th Elool 5701 –*

11th Sept. 1941, and a little lozenge-shaped stone, *Joseph Haim Bar 4¹/₂ Years*. I counted the ones born in Baghdad: two, three, five – six altogether, one with the inscription *Born in Baghdad (Aged 49) Died on Wed. 28th Nov. 1945*. That was Isaac Abraham, but something was missing on his stone: where had he died, a Wednesday in what place? It was Tjimahi, the concentration camp in west Java – I knew him there. It would be forgotten. Here was a misspelled one: *These memory of loving uncle Solomon Judah Katar – Decierd* (what was that?) *10 Feb. 1945 Saterday Tjimahi Kamp His Soul Rest in Peace*. Not quite rubble, not yet incomprehensible: I wanted them dust, or else impossible to decipher, nameless as the stone with the top half missing and only *Died on Sat. Night 13 June 1926*.

'We should start,' said Mr Lang. Thank God, I thought.

'Do you hear a car?' asked Benjamin. He nibbled air, listening.

'It's those trees down there,' said Mr Aaron.

I read: *Selma Liebman-Herzberger*.

'Maybe Morris got a puncture,' said Mr Solomon.

'I'm thinking of the women,' Mr Lang said. 'If it was just me I'd wait until five, or even later. But these women can't take the heat. Look. Covered with sweat, your wife's back. I'd hate to see one of them faint. Something like that would hold things up.'

'Lool was awake most of the night,' said Mr Aaron.

'That's what I mean,' said Mr Lang.

'So was my Irma,' said Mr Solomon. 'Her feet are killing her.' He looked in her direction. 'She never complains.'

'Look at this,' I said, holding my jacket open. My shirt was darkly plastered, bubbled in places, on my chest. 'Sopping wet!'

'I didn't think it would take so long for Morris to get here from the airport,' said Benjamin.

'It shouldn't,' said Mr Lang. 'That's why I suggested we start.'

'If David thinks so –' I started to say.

Benjamin was looking uneasy. He didn't want to make the decision alone. He said, 'Who thinks we should go ahead?'

'I do,' said Mr Lang promptly.

'Who's this cousin?' Mr Solomon was asking Mr Aaron.

'I'll go along with David,' I said.

Mr Solomon and Mr Aaron nodded, and 'All right, then,' said Benjamin. The women were still standing around the coffin, holding their shiny black handbags tightly against their stomachs. Mrs

Aaron was sharing her umbrella with the Manasseh girl. Benjamin said, 'We've decided to start.'

'What about Glassman?' asked Mrs Aaron.

'He's not coming.'

The coffin rested on two beams which had been placed across the trench of the grave. Benjamin stood on the red mound of dirt lumps that had been shoveled out. We made a little circle around the coffin and listened to Benjamin read the prayers. The cover of his leather-bound siddur had sweatstains on it from being carried in the heat, black finger marks on the cover, a black patch on the spine.

He started reading slowly, but after a few verses his voice quickened to a reciting pace, a hurrying drone that emphasized only the last word before he sucked in a breath. The death chant for Abe Sassoon was being muttered to himself; this speeded rendition made it private. *Jakob Sassoon*, I was reading on the stone next to Benjamin, *Born in Baghdad*, and then Joel Solomon's whining voice, 'Dad, I hear a car.'

It was the screech of a car braking in gravel, and one after another, two doors slamming. We all heard.

Benjamin slowed down and read in a louder voice. Each of us sneaked a look down the dusty path to the entrance, but only the little boys were on the path. Two figures in black appeared, both running – one on long legs was far ahead of the other. This was Glassman, for just as I had turned to concentrate on what Benjamin was saying, he was on us. He came panting, a yarmulke in his hand, his face red, preparing to frown. We made room for him, and he fell on his knees beside the coffin, at the same time clapping the yarmulke on his head. He let out a great affronted wail. The women stopped crying and stared at him. Benjamin faltered in the verses, then continued, as Glassman hugged the coffin, knocking our black-bowed wreath askew. Now Glassman was crying piteously.

Benjamin stopped reading.

'Why stop now?' said Glassman angrily to Benjamin, a youthful quaver in his voice. 'You started without me – *why stop now*! Go ahead, if you're in such a hurry!'

Benjamin lifted the book and read slowly.

Mrs Aaron touched Glassman's shoulder. He raised himself, slapping the dust off his knees, to stand next to her. He had an expression on his face that showed horror and pain, his lips pressed shut, his cheeks blown out, his eyes narrowed to slits, his crumpled yarmulke slightly to one side.

I listened for Benjamin but I heard Glassman, who was breathing heavily, making a thin whistling in his nose and heaving his chest up and down and nodding his head with each long breath. He was wearing a beautiful suit. With the distraction of Glassman's panting, and with his screams still ringing in my ears, I felt a sharp embarrassment that was becoming terror.

It was time to put the coffin into the grave. We lifted the ropes under each end while the beams were slid away. Glassman watched us. We lowered the coffin on the ropes and Benjamin scooped up some dirt with a spade and threw it in, and said a prayer after it. Each person took a turn with the spade, the first ones making very loud thuds with their dry dirt clods on the coffin lid, the later ones making no sound at all. Glassman, the last to throw in some dirt, burst into fresh tears as he did so. He peered down. I have heard of close relations leaping into the grave, and I was afraid that Glassman might try this, perhaps breaking his leg. He shook his head – but he was indignant rather than sorrowful. What did he expect? Javanese *babus* in shiny silk pajamas holding umbrellas over our heads, a gilded coffin, the hot air split by mourners' shrieks, a wise old rabbi chanting into his nest of beard, a resolute throng of relatives at the graveside, shaking their fists at death? I knew this Glassman: 'Why not try Manila or Hong Kong?' He walked back to where he had been standing, under Mrs Aaron's umbrella.

'Brothers and sisters,' said Benjamin. He spoke in Dutch, tasting each syllable separately, relishing the long words and closing his eyes as he finished a phrase. 'These are very sad days for us –'

'What's that?' Glassman's shout made me jump. 'What are you saying?'

We looked at him, then at Benjamin.

Benjamin proceeded, 'But we must remember that our brother Abraham is now in a happy –'

'Stop that!' screamed Glassman, his voice cracking.

Benjamin glanced into the partially filled grave. He looked up and bit on a word which, displaying his teeth, he showed Glassman on the tip of his tongue. 'Home,' he said in Dutch, 'he is home now. And someday –'

'What the *hell* is going on here?' Glassman asked Mrs Aaron. 'This is a bloody mockery. I won't have him talking in that language.'

'Ben,' said Morris. 'Maybe you should –'

'And someday,' Benjamin continued, more rapidly, 'we will join our brother. Joyfully, yes, our hearts full –'

'No!' Glassman broke away from Mrs Aaron, who reached for him. He vaulted the grave and his hands were on Benjamin's throat. Mr Lang snatched at Glassman's arms, I yanked on his collar; it took five of us to pull him away. He kicked out, catching me on the shin with the sharp heel of his fancy buckled boot. 'You!' he shouted at Benjamin. 'What are you saying?'

Benjamin clasped his hands and tried to finish: 'We should not mourn our brother – we should be glad he is at peace –'

'Let me *go*!' yelled Glassman, struggling.

'– enjoying the rewards of a virtuous life and hard work and let us all say a silent prayer for him.'

We released Glassman and bowed our heads, praying silently. Glassman was surprised at his sudden freedom and then enraged by our silence. A yellow and gray bird with a head like the top of a claw hammer flew past.

'Shame on you,' said Glassman while we prayed. 'You should be ashamed of yourselves. What kind of people are you?' He went on in this vein, in his British accent, accusing us of savagery, looking quite comical with his jacket twisted around and his yarmulke slipping off and the knot of his tie pulled down and made small.

Benjamin signaled to some workmen to fill the hole. These three men in faded clothes had been standing under the eaves of the crematorium and had seen the whole business. They smiled as they ambled out of the shade, squinting and ducking as they entered the bright sunlight, and holding their spades ready.

Glassman, leaning, held each woman's shoulders and kissed her cheek. He left with Morris.

'What does it matter?' Benjamin said, when we were in the car and driving back to town. 'It's his own fault for being late. *Bleddy mockery*.' He snorted. 'I wonder what they do in Hong Kong.'

'The next problem,' Mr Aaron said – he hadn't been listening to Benjamin – 'is where does he stay?'

It wasn't a problem. Glassman was on the evening flight to Djakarta. The rest of us stayed just where we were, and no one said that young man's name again.

Part III

Jungle Bells

Polvo

Even farther S., the Pan-American Highway, unpaved at this point, passes a mule track (km 1,024, not signposted), at the very end of which is the town of **Polvo** (pop. 87, Census of 1935). Mutton, lanolin, wool, and cactus fiber are the main products. Many travelers regard Polvo as the true Gateway to Patagonia. It was perhaps here, in 1832, that General Juan Manuel de Rosas began his mission of subduing the Indians. The conjecture is reasonable, as the Indians in the area are subdued to the point of invisibility. It is likely that the young Charles Darwin, who met Rosas during his (Rosas's) onslaught, might also have trod Polvo's narrow gravelled street and, on the precipitous rockslides nearby, collected the specimens of black toads he painstakingly describes in his 'Journal of Researches' (often wrongly titled 'The Voyage of the Beagle').

Unprepossessing in appearance, little more than two acres of habitation, and hardly discernible above the tops of its own low thornbushes, Polvo, although part of the former Kingdom of Araucanía and Patagonia, has been called 'the hamlet without a prince.' And yet it is not devoid of the charm that characterizes many another sheep-raising town. The annual sheep-clip (May 10–17) draws a score of visitors. Polvanos refuse to be drawn, but their silence implies that it may be worth the tourist's while to endure the overcrowded conditions and generally stretched amenities to which the town is subject during such local fiestas. (Jan. 4, Druids' Day, and July 22, Feast of Martyrs, are others.) At sheep-clip, the Market Square (*Plaza*) is said to take on something of the atmosphere of Act IV, Scene 4, of 'The Winter's Tale,' with a Wool Queen in her ancient cardigan and a good-humored Shearer's Dance, which has proved fatal to many an unwary onlooker! Once every ten years there is an *eisteddfod* – Welsh poems being sung and shouted. The simultaneous translation in Tehuelche is perhaps a hangover from the days of colonization.

Visitors to Polvo cannot fail to notice the scarcity of water in the town, and the sensible wayfarer will carry enough to last him his stay. A visit of any length will necessitate the boring of a well, and the budget-minded traveler will want to allow for this additional expense. Years of privation have left their mark on the settlers, who tend to give the impression of truculence – an impression that is only confirmed by long acquaintance. Unaccustomed to strangers, and somewhat outside the mainstream of the tourist boom that has brought modernity to his distant neighbors, the Polvano is inclined to be brusque, except toward visitors who are thoroughly fluent in colloquial Welsh. More than usual care should be exercised in entering a farmhouse unannounced, and no one ought to expect a clear set of directions to the downtown area and hotel (*Residencial Penrhyndeudraeth*). Well stocked with some of the better Fuegian vintages, the restaurant, sumptuous by Polvo's standards, is nearly always shut. There is limitless scope in the hills for the spelunker.

Once the haunt of Patagonian giants, who are said to have been numerous in the region and to account for early maps bearing the reference 'Regio Gigantum,' Polvo has seen these natives dwindle in number as well as in size over the years, until by mid-century there was but one. That he was hunted for sport is part of Polvo's rich folklore. What remains of his small earthen hut may still be seen, though not every traveler will wish to make the two-day journey, as it can only be accomplished on foot. (Stout shoes a must.) Those who do (and the jaunt is a welcome relief from the odor of sheep-dip and uncured hides, which casts a blight on the otherwise attractive town) will glimpse herds of roving guanacos and, smeared on rocks, odd fingerprint markings reputed to be 10,000 years old. The trip to the gravesites of the early settlers takes slightly longer, at just under a week, and is to be recommended for the hardy. Those who manage it are rewarded by the simple grandeur of three solitary markers, shaped not unlike hubcaps, carved from local stone and bearing indistinct inscriptions in the Welsh language. Round about this tiny necropolis an impressive desolation soothes the eye of the footsore traveler.

Municipal buildings in Polvo include the Central Jail, the Founders' Orphanage, the Carding House, and the Methodist Chapel. The chapel is, in the words of the French traveler Gaston, 'typical of its kind . . . notwithstanding its window, which is open to criticism.' A Christian Science Reading Room is in the planning stages, and this will be housed in a chamber now known as the *Zona*

Rosa (open most weekdays), where in former times gauchos are supposed to have gathered during the sheep-clip. (Note hook and scarred doorjamb, where, according to legend, spurs were hung.)

The *Mercado* (market) is close by, and although Polvo's barter system is almost certain to divest the enthusiastic traveller of his wristwatch, a visit is well worth the risk. Apart from the root vegetables and the carcasses of sheep arranged sandbag-style around the dour venders, there are traditional Indian ornaments on sale, some thought to be of ancient manufacture, including penwipers, calendar holders, napkin rings, buckles, tie clasps, book-marks, and plinths for digital clocks, all fashioned from dried cactus fiber, to which magical properties have been ascribed. Some distance from the market, but now derelict, are the shacks of quarrymen who worked the iron-ore deposit. There are few organized tours of this part of town.

Steeped in Patagonian history, Polvo nonetheless wears its antiquity lightly, and it has steadily diminished in population. The youths of the town are understandably siphoned off by the oil pipeline and the bright lights of Río Gallegos. Consequently, the average age in Polvo is seventy-three. The petrochemical plant, promised for the next decade, ought to go some way toward altering the scope of tourism. Bird life abounds, and the sky above Polvo is frequently black with the soaring Turkey Buzzard (*Cathartes aura*). Polecats and skunks (*Zorrillos*) must also be mentioned here. The flora is tenacious but thin, and limited to scrub thorn and the cactus from which the local artifacts are made. Oblivious of the stranger's taunt about the monotony of their unremarkable surroundings, Polvanos delight in their landscape's occasional fits of natural crankishness and will walk any distance to hear the rumble of a glacier 'calving.'

In another epoch, dinosaurs must have ranged this dusty plateau and laid eggs where sheep now graze, though all have vanished without a trace. The *Museo de Polvo* (Polvo Museum, open Mondays) contains a plaster model of a settler's homestead, a sketch map of the Spanish advance, an authentic Welsh dresser, a collection of skins and hides, a stuffed albatross, a fusilier's epaulets, and a canoe. Murals depict Rosas's massacres (north wall) and the flood damage of 1899 (west wall). The attendant on duty wakes from time to time to remind the browser not to lean on the display cases.

Low Tide

The woman with the have-a-nice-day face in the post office they call 'Buttons'? The one that's always saying 'Can I share something with you?' and then complains about her feet, ruined by Uncle Sam, how she has to spend so much time at the counter selling stamps that she has to put cookies into her shoes for arch support? That lost her husband to a brain tumor and always asks me about Alice in an irritating way, as if I lost *her* to a brain tumor? With the apron?

She stuck a leaflet in my box, not to me personally, but to one of those all-purpose addresses – 'Box-Holder,' it said, and it advertised a 'Parenting Clinic,' and I said to myself: *'Parenting?'* So I said to her, 'Now can I share something with *you*, Buttons?' and handed it back – didn't want it, didn't need it, because there is no such word and now am I going to get huge bills addressed to me as 'Box-Holder' that I have to pay – Minimum Payment and New Balance – regular as the tide, whether I like it or not? She took the leaflet back. She saw my point.

The tide was still going down as I searched my stack of mail for a word from Skip or Larry – nothing today; and still ebbing as I read the young fellow's T-shirt motto 'You Are Dealing With An Animal,' and I hurried towards his car to set him straight, but he drove off before I could say anything.

'The hell are you doing, Stanley?' I heard and turned and saw Ned Clark leaving the box lobby of the post office. 'Chasing cars?'

'One of these T-shirts,' I said, pointing in the direction where the car had gone.

He just shook his head – could not have cared less about the way people advertise their aggression with T-shirts and bumper stickers – but who would notice in a town where the local garbage truck is lettered IRANIAN LUNCH CART?

'Anything I can do for you?' he said, as though to an invalid, and then took my arm to steer me through the parking lot.

I snatched my arm back and said, 'As a matter of fact, yes. Can you explain what "parenting" means?'

'All I know is that no one truly understands the dynamics of family life, and I suppose the best counsel is from the Bible, "Judge not less ye be judged."' And he tried to put his arm round me again. 'As for Alice and the boys – sometimes people need space.'

All this gabble from my simple question; and I kept thinking, *The tide is falling*.

'Ned,' I said. 'The word "parenting." What's it all about?'

'It's a gerund,' he said, with his hands out.

'It is no such thing. It is not even a word.'

He insisted it was, I swore it wasn't, and finally to clinch his argument he said, 'Any noun can be verbed, Stanley.'

'Now I've heard everything,' I said and just walked off as he called out *Don't go away mad* – but who wouldn't? It was low tide by the time I got to the landing.

I was still thinking about Skip and Larry, why they hadn't written in so long, and trying to heave my boat across the mud-flats when I looked up and saw my children, both of them, standing there on the shore watching me; Skip and Larry, exactly the way they were when they were eight and ten, in their bare feet and bathing suits, with their skinny arms and bony shoulders, except they were black.

I said, 'Don't just stand there.'

They didn't move.

'Give me a hand,' I said. 'Look alive.'

Anyone could see that I was about to lose forty feet of line that had slid off the stern cleat as I plowed the skiff forward through the mud. And I was angry: low tide, because of all that business at the post office.

'Pick it up,' I said.

'The rope?'

'It's not a rope, son. It's a line. If you're going to mess around in boats – grab it!'

He scooped up the line and at the same time moved across the mud to me on stepping-stones, finding one after another, his brother behind him, following him just as Larry used to follow Skip.

I took an end of the rope and tied a bowline through a hole in the breasthook and said, 'Give me some slack.'

He just stood there.

'Pay me out some slack,' I said.

I thought: 'I've been giving English lessons all morning.' It was as though I had found myself on another planet, and at low tide it seemed that way.

'Let go of the line, sonny.'

He threw it at me.

'Doesn't anyone speak English anymore?' I said.

This made him very solemn and attentive, just like Skip waiting for me to set him straight. His face was smooth, his head shaved, the whites of his eyes were slightly flecked, and his skin black beneath little scaly ashes. His brother was a smaller version of him. They looked to me as children do – waterproof and unsinkable and unfinished – unfinished most of all. So many things they didn't know, so much they couldn't do. How would they ever learn? The world was all tall strangers to them. And their being black only made it all worse. Who had ever shown them compassion?

'Hop aboard,' I said.

They didn't move. Onshore, a big bearded man in shorts yelled 'Wallace and Ferdy! Get over here!'

They tensed, looking very compact, as they prepared to leap back on the stepping-stones.

'No problem,' I said. 'They want to come with me.'

Only then did this bearded man look at me. 'You sure?'

'I've got two of my own,' I said. I settled my oars into the oarlocks and eased the stern towards the boys. 'Get in. One at a time. Hold tight.'

They glanced back at the bearded man as they did so, and I could tell they were relieved to get away from him. There was something tyrannical-looking about his beard, and the way he walked, those shoes. He watched us row away through the weedy water.

'Ever been in a boat before?'

'Nope,' the big boy said.

'Scared?' I said.

He looked up sharply and denied it.

The little one said, 'Hey, mister – that a Chinese boat?'

A gaff-rigged 40-footer was passing us. Red sails – and so the boy had drawn a simple conclusion. I told him what it was and made him repeat it, and then I held up a line and said, 'What's this?'

'Rope,' the little boy said.

'Line,' I said and got them chanting. After they had stopped I said 'Don't worry. You'll learn. It took my kids years to learn these things. We'll have to cram it all into a few hours today. But I'll make you into two sailors, you'll see.'

'Where are your kids, mister?'

Something bothered me about being called 'mister' like that.

'Call me captain,' I said. They nodded and went quiet. 'Which one of you is Wallace and which is Ferdy?'

The big one was Wallace, and the little one said that Ferdy was not short for anything. It was his whole name.

I said, 'Got any brothers and sisters?'

'Four,' the little one piped up.

'Six,' Wallace said, and when the little boy challenged him with a look, Wallace said, 'LaToya and LaRetta.'

I asked them to spell these names, and they did so.

'They's the twins,' Wallace said. 'They's living with my father.'

'Was that your father on the beach?'

'Nope.'

'"No, Captain."'

'No, Captain. That's the Reverend. Of our church. Heavengate Baptist.'

'Boston?'

'Roxbury.'

Hot streets, black gangs, crazed Irishmen in cars racing by and screaming abuse at them, boarded up storefronts and brick tenements, junked vans and jalopies rusting by the roadside, radios playing too loud and planes descending overhead – never mind the rape, the murder, the mayhem – just the simple visible facts were bad enough; and they knew they were in heaven here, being rowed across the harbor.

They were sitting together, big and little on the thwart.

'How old are your kids?' Wallace said, and when I did not reply he added 'Captain.'

'That's it, son. You're learning,' I said. 'Twenty-one and twenty-four. They're big now. But they were once your age, sitting there, just like you. They went to California. Why is it that people who go to California never seem to come back? And they don't write letters. That's not a California thing, is it? But they're different.

273

Know why? Because I raised them to be different. I taught them how to be clean-cut. Yes, sir. No, sir. I taught them the fundamentals. I kept them off the streets and on the water. You never learn any harm on the water. You give me a week or two – I could set you straight. I could teach you to row. Skip and Larry could row like demons. I had them sprinting across here, from the beach to the tip of the jetty. They didn't learn that at school. Of course not. There was a smoking room at school. Imagine. For 15–16-year-olds. They had driver education. Naturally. So they could use their parents' car. That was very hard on Alice. But, you know? I went up to the school and saw the principal. Henry T. Wing. I explained everything very carefully to him, the pressure we were under, the strain that driver ed was putting on our vehicle. I told him about Alice's condition. Her hair had started to fall out in bunches, and nothing is more troubling to a woman than losing her hair. I'm dead sure that contributed to it. Notice how I am just dipping the oars into the water. Not trying to overdo it – just sinking the blades and gliding and lifting, and feathering slightly because of the wind.' I took three more long pulls. 'Does that answer your question?'

They had gone silent – we were in the channel and I was fighting a short breaking chop that had been whipped up by the westerly wind smacking the last of the ebbing tide.

'What are the other ones called?' I said.

They just stared.

'Your brothers and sisters,' I said.

'Shonelle, Shanice, Valia, and Troy,' Wallace said.

'Interesting,' I said, but privately I found the names heartbreaking, like brands of floor polish or shampoo.

'Shonelle got married,' Ferdy said.

'Would you like to get married?' I asked Wallace.

'Maybe,' he said.

'You're going to have to be more definite than that, son. If you meet the right woman there'll be no question,' I said. 'A marriage isn't just a romantic thing. Oh, sure. You're all fired up at first, but you have to look at that woman's face at breakfast the next morning. You're going to have to plan and save. You want to keep your life shipshape. Like this boat. Notice how I coil the line? We had a knot in that line. Remember how I undid it before I coiled it? Marriage is like that. Think about it.'

This made a definite impression on Wallace, but then Ferdy

smirked and said, 'If you get married you can see her panties.'

I cut him off with, 'We don't need that kind of talk on this boat.'

'Shut up, Ferdy,' Wallace said, and looked towards shore.

'Your wife belongs on a pedestal, and you don't put her on a pedestal just so that you can look up her dress. Respect, that's what I'm talking about. You don't have to take your clothes off just to have a good time, sonny. What are you looking at, Wallace?'

'Thought I saw the Reverend,' he said. 'I was going to axe him a question.'

'No, you weren't.'

He seemed hurt – baffled, anyway.

'You were going to *ask* him a question.'

'Mister, I have to go to the bathroom,' Ferdy said.

'You should have thought of that before we left,' I said. 'You'll just have to hold on to it. I know it's hard but it's for your own good. See, next time you won't make that mistake, will you?'

He winced at me and put his knees together, and I knew that no one had ever put it like that to him. He needed to be told that in just that way. I felt that I had nipped a bad habit right in the bud and I saw again Skip and Larry on that same thwart, and all the lessons they had learned in this boat.

'What were you going to ask the Reverend? Something about the church service?'

'Yup.'

'"Yes, Captain."'

'"Yes, Captain."'

'How did I know that you were going to ask him about the church service?' I said. 'I guess I read your mind, didn't I? See, when you get to be my age and been around like I have you don't have to be told things. You know what a person is going to say before he or she opens his or her mouth. Used to amaze Skip and Larry. "Don't tell me," I'd say. "You're hungry. You've got to see somebody. You're going out of town." Whatever. I'll bet you're in the choir.'

'Yes, Captain,' Wallace said.

'I'll bet you've got a lovely voice,' I said.

'Yes, Captain.'

'Want to sing something for me? I love gospel music.'

He seemed to be thinking this over, and then he said, 'Captain, Ferdy's crying.'

'That's because he's learning a lesson. Sometimes tears are a good teacher. And the more he cries the less he'll pee.'

The child was shuddering. No jokes from him now. None of this *If you get married you can see her panties* nonsense.

'What's wrong, Wallace? Why don't you want to sing? Would you rather do it tomorrow?'

'Yes, sir, Captain,' he said eagerly.

'Suit yourself,' I said.

We were now parallel to the end of the jetty, at the mouth of the harbour. 'This is a steep and confused sea,' I said, as the boat pitched. 'What if we went over?'

And a wave slapped the stern and wet the boys as I spoke.

'What if we just got swamped? What's the first thing you'd do? Would you swim for shore?'

'I sure would,' Wallace said and became gray at the thought of it.

'You'd be making the biggest mistake of your life,' I said. 'You never leave your craft. You never swim for shore. You stay with your craft until help comes.'

'We gonna drown, mister?' Ferdy wailed, and he began to sob.

Wallace said, 'Captain, we got church.'

'And I suppose you want to turn back?'

'Yes, Captain.'

'But you want to come out tomorrow, don't you?'

'Yes, Captain.'

'You want to learn a thing or two about seamanship?'

'Yes, Captain.'

'What about you, Ferdy?'

'Yes, Captain,' the little boy said.

I was still rowing, and I thought how precisely like Skip and Larry they were at this moment, sitting in the stern nodding and agreeing. They were showing manners. And how long had we been out? No more than forty-five minutes. Give me a week with them – just a week, Reverend – and I will give you back two adults.

With that, I turned the boat and rowed back towards shore, still fighting the tide. But I made use of the time. *We ain't got but one*, Wallace said, speaking of his parents. I explained the grammatical mistake and I thought; 'No – you can count on me, and that makes two.' I told them what had happened that morning at the post office, of the business with the leaflet, and 'parenting,' and *Any noun can be verbed*. We had a good laugh over that.

'Be here tomorrow at nine sharp, so we can catch the tide,' I said.

They said '*Yes, sir*' – all politeness now – and scampered off the boat and up the beach. I didn't see the Reverend but I suppose he was putting on his dog-collar. I wasn't happy, but I was satisfied. I felt I had rescued the day and kept it from being a waste, and maybe saved a few young lives in the process.

That was yesterday. Today I went back, launched the boat and waited. Nine – ten – eleven. No sign of them. So I went out alone. It's not funny when the water recedes and shows bottles and old rope and clam shells and crab claws and dead weeds on a long shore of mud.

Jungle Bells

On Christmas eve, 1964, I was just about to leave a run-down bar in Lusaka, Zambia, when I offered two bottles of Lion Lager to an African couple I had just met. The Christmas decorations on the walls were tattered – strings of frayed tinsel, dusty cotton snow, a cardboard sleigh covered with fly-specks. Posters from the brewery showed African women posing in Santa hats. They mocked the season and were the opposite of festive. But so what? I had come to Africa, partly as an act of rebellion. I was receptive to the sort of unintentional satire I saw in this bar. It strengthened me; it was an undiscovered world, something else to write about.

'Merry Christmas,' I said. 'And that one's for your wife.'

'Happy Christmas. She is not my wife,' the man said.

The young woman looked frankly at me. A red turban was wound tightly around her head, and its color matched her tight red dress.

'She is my sister,' the man said. 'And she likes you.'

'I like you too much,' the young woman said, meaning very much. 'Happy Christmas.'

She touched her turban and smiled, and toasted me, drinking from the bottle I had just bought her.

None of this was ambiguous to me. I had been living in Africa for a year and I was used to the way, at any moment, anything could happen. It suited my curiosity and my impatient temperament. I was twenty-three, and game for almost anything. I was very skinny and looked harmless – even a bit foolish. My traveling method then was: Arrive and hope for the best; make the fewest possible plans; take the plunge; rely on the kindness of strangers; just say yes. So far it had worked.

A week before this, I had flown from southern Malawi (formerly Nyasaland), where I was a Peace Corps schoolteacher, to Salisbury (now Harare) in Rhodesia (now Zimbabwe), intending to travel to Zambia (formerly Northern Rhodesia). From black country to white country to black country and back. These were times of transition and racial uneasiness.

White Rhodesians confided in me: 'Don't stay at the Jameson. They're taking Africans there now.' In Bulawayo I fell in with an English plumber who was living in South Africa. He gorged on french fries, got roaring drunk, then collapsed, and when he woke up he vomited hugely. He said he usually spent Christmas doing that. 'So, how about it, mate. Let's go back to that poxy chip shop.'

I did not think I would. Christmas was still a few days off. I took a train to Victoria Falls and onward to Lusaka. On the Rhodesian section the whites were drunk, singing their hearts out, and the Africans (all in Second Class) very silent. When the train crossed from white Rhodesia into black Zambia, at Livingstone, the Africans from Second Class entered the bar coach and they quickly became drunk and abusive. 'Happy Christmas! You!' they would say to the whites. 'Buy me a Christmas present!' Bottles of beer went back and forth.

We arrived in Lusaka at about noon on Christmas Eve, and that was how I happened to be speaking to the African couple, the brother and sister.

In this African bar, with a dirt floor that stank of dampness and cat piss, some of the people held old rinsed-out oil cans on their knees, which they raised from time to time, to drink African beer. Sour and thick, the consistency of porridge, it was plopped from a plastic bucket into the cans. The rest of us drank warm bottled beer. There was nagging music and smoke and shouting, and occasionally the squalling of babies, because the women wore their children on their backs, slung like papooses. Every so often a fight would start, but before they became dangerous the men went outside, and fought there. Even then, Zambia was well known for its beer-party stabbings.

Around midnight, the brother said, 'Happy Christmas. My sister wants you to come with us.'

'Happy Christmas,' I said, drunkenly, and shortly afterwards we were in the back seat of an old car bumping on a back road. It seemed a long ride and when we arrived, and I was swaying, blinded by the headlights, the brother said, 'Happy Christmas. You give him money.'

I gave some money to the taxi driver and when he was gone we were in darkness. They led me to their hut. The sister took my hand. And then I was lying on a damp mattress, by candlelight, and thinking: There are other people in this room. I heard them but I could not see them.

The following morning I saw who they were, small children – three or four of them – tangled in blankets on the floor, and snoring in a heap like kittens in a basket.

'Happy Christmas,' the sister said. She was squirming into her red dress. She was slim, she had a brown scowling face, she never went out without a turban that matched her dress.

It was then that she told me her name – Nina; and her brother was George. I slowly put together the chronology of events that had led me here to this African hut on Christmas morning. I felt ill, I was hung over, unshaven, and my tongue felt like a dead mouse. I had been wearing a tan suit that was now rumpled, and a shirt that had wilted. I dressed, yawned, and said, 'I have to get back to town.'

George put his head into the room. He looked fairly dapper, in a suit. He had brown flecks on the whites of his eyes. 'Happy Christmas. We have breakfast.'

They took me down the dusty village road to a ramshackle building. It was about nine in the morning, a day that was already hot; radios playing plonking Christmas music, children shouting. I had no idea where this village was, except that it was some distance from Lusaka.

'Happy Christmas,' George said in the bar, signaling and muttering to the bartender. The bar, much seedier than the one of the night before, stank of kerosene. In Africa kerosene always meant no electricity and breathing the fumes gave me a headache.

'What do they have to eat here?'

But the ragged barman had already begun to open three bottles of warm Lion Lager.

'I don't want beer,' I said. 'I'd like something to eat.'

'Christmas!' George said fiercely and thumped a bottle against my chest until I grasped it. Nina was swigging hers, as though to show me how.

The bartender asked for money. When I hesitated, George said, 'Christmas!' and I paid.

I sipped the beer, I bought a pickled egg from a cloudy bottle of them that looked like a museum exhibit, and ate it. Long before

I had finished my beer, George was ready for another, and so was Nina. I bought them, I sipped, I felt very ill.

'Where's the *chimbudzi*?'

'Come with me,' George said.

It was a roofless shed behind the tin-roofed building, upright planks and poles enclosing a shallow hole that was furious with struggling maggots. George was waiting when I left it, retching.

Back in the bar, he introduced me to various Africans. 'My brother ... Also my brother ... My sister – same mother, same father,' and he called to the barman to serve us. Now, when he opened his mouth to say, 'Christmas,' I hated his grin and the spittle on his teeth. And his brown-flecked eyes seemed sinister. But I paid.

Nina sat beside me, as though we had overnight become a couple and had an understanding. Several hours passed in this way. George demanded that the radio be turned louder. He recognized the melody, and he sang,

> *Jungle bells,*
> *Jungle bells,*
> *Jungle all the way ...*

'Sing,' he said to me. He made a tyrannous insisting face.

I was too weak to do anything but listen. And I began to feel ill again. When I got up, Nina said, as though to a small child, 'Where are you going?'

'Outside,' I said.

'George,' she said, nodding at her brother.

And then George was by my side.

'To the *chimbudzi*.'

'I go with you.'

'I don't need you,' I said, and walked outside.

He scowled at me and poked my chest with his finger the way he had with the beer bottle. 'If I no come with you, you run away.'

I said, 'I have to go back to Lusaka.'

'No. You stay.'

Sometimes in Africa, faced by Africans, I felt very pale, very skinny, very weak, and almost incoherent. This was one of those times.

George was drunk. I had made him drunk. I tried to calm him, but he was already suspicious and irritable and hovered around me like a jailer. When we got back inside the bar, the others demanded more beer, and I paid, and I again tried to think how I might get away from them. I especially wanted to leave when a group of Africans near us began making remarks about the *mzungu* – I was the only white man in the bar – and Nina infuriated them by answering back.

By late afternoon, I had begun to drink again and became less alarmed; then I was as drunk as everyone else and we went back to the hut, where I fell asleep on the mattress that lay on the dirt floor.

I woke in darkness, and I wondered whether it was still Christmas. I remembered: *Jungle bells.* I contemplated sneaking away, but I had no idea of the way to Lusaka, and I was further worried by the barking dogs I heard. In African villages, dogs are mainly dangerous to white people. I imagined my hotel room in Lusaka, my bag where I had left it two days ago, the bed I had not slept in.

In the morning, I looked at the children on the floor of the hut, damp and sighing in a little heap, and was silently grateful to them for being there. As long as they slept there Nina would keep her distance. My financial entanglement was bad enough; so far, thanks to the sleeping children, I had avoided a sexual entanglement.

Two of them were Nina's children. So she was married?

'Yes. To you,' she said, with a horrible greedy face, patting her turban.

That made my heart sink. I said, 'I'm leaving.'

'No,' Nina said. 'It's Boxing Day.'

It was the first time in my life I had ever heard that unusual pairing of words. I did not have the slightest idea of what they meant. I put on my clothes again – the same clothes: grubby suit pants, stained jacket, clammy shirt.

George was waiting for us outside the hut.

'We go,' he said. His smile meant: You do what I tell you to do.' He poked my lapel with his yellow fingernail. 'Boxing Day.'

At the bar down the road I bought two pickled eggs and beer for the three of us, and I smiled, and we clinked bottles, and we toasted Happy Boxing Day, and I thought: *Get out of here.*

The others showed up, the four from yesterday, a few more. I bought them all beer, and I reflected that there was no conversation.

They drank, they mumbled the words of the songs from the transistor radio playing loud on the bar, they did not speak to each other. They drank, they scowled, they grunted; their faces seemed to thicken with incomprehension and obscure anger.

They clamored for more beer, provoked by George, and no one noticed that I had not drunk any of my beer. Yesterday a couple of them had bought a round of beer. Today, it was all mine. They drank, I paid; they drank again, I paid again. The cranky men came back. They made remarks, Nina scoffed at them, they replied; she shouted back, defending me, abusing them. A man stood up and yelled directly at her. That made me very nervous.

Soon, there was more shouting, some of it mirthful, and the group of Africans I sat with had ceased to notice me, except when they wanted more beer. It was about two in the afternoon of a very hot day and I felt a rising sense of panic.

'I'll be right back,' I said.

'George,' Nina said.

I did not protest. I laughed. I said, 'I don't need George to show me the *chimbudzi*.'

'He will not come back,' Nina said, and I realized how shrewd she was in her witchlike way.

'Of course I will,' I said. I took off my suit jacket and folded it on the bar. 'Here's my jacket, here's some money. Buy me a beer, get some for yourselves, and hand over that jacket when I get back.'

Before they could reply, I walked away, left the bar. I did not hurry. The sun was overhead, the trees so thin there was no shade, the soil was pale dust. I glanced back; no one had followed me.

It was then that I ran, in a desperate flight, realizing that I had very little time. I made it to the edge of the village. Some children playing on the road looked up, startled.

The village road intersected with another road. I was gasping, still jogging along. A car approached. I waved to it.

'Taxi?'

'As you like,' the driver said.

'Lusaka,' I said, and got in. I rode, continually turning back, to see whether we were being followed.

At the hotel I asked the driver to wait. I retrieved my bag and paid my bill and got back into the car.

'Let's go,' I said.

'Where?'

'Just drive – there,' I said, and pointed to a road.

'That's south, to Kafue.'

'How many miles?'

'Maybe twenty.'

'Take me to Kafue.'

There was a motel at Kafue, by the side of the road. I stayed there and though there was little nighttime traffic, each time my room was raked by the yellow glare of headlights I grew worried, and trembled with a fugitive's fear, feeling that they had come for me.

The next day, after I hitch-hiked out of the country, back to Rhodesia, my fear eased, and later all I remembered were the children, and wondered what became of them – the sleepers who had protected me, and the surprised ones who had seen me running. It was an uncommon, even remarkable, sight in Central Africa, in 1964, a white man running in the bush.

Warm Dogs

When the broker's message came that a child was available the Raths went home and put their suits on and made love in a solemn methodical way, as though mimicking conception. Afterwards they peeled their clothes off and lay exhausted, in the bubble of the balcony Arvin and Hella themselves had designed, eagerly speculating about the broker's child. He called himself a broker. But he was probably just an opportunist who knew someone as desperate to sell a child as they were desperate to buy one.

Their bare skin was an alarming color – nothing to do with having just taken off the body suits. It was the light from the lurid sunset over the western suburbs – that distant mountain range was a mirage made of a low cloud of risen, suspended dust that turned the slipping sun into a misshapen solitaire the color of dried blood. It lighted their naked bodies with garish blooms of good health and mocked their sterility. Yet most of their friends were infected, and – though it was never simple – those people had found children for themselves. One consequence of having tested positive was that it made the Raths single-minded in their urgent search for a child.

Eight times they had been notified and so the love-making had become a ritual, but each time something had gone wrong. They were more hopeful, even though now the risk was great: it meant a trip across the river over that awful bridge to a neighborhood on the East Bank.

Scowling at the damp body suit that lay crumpled on the bed beside her like the pelt of a gutted animal, Hella brushed it to the floor. In a pious tone that made her nakedness pathetic, she said, 'God, I hope it works out,' adding, like an imploring one-word prayer, 'Please.'

Arvin said, 'We'll be fine.'

Hella knew what he would say next, since he had said it so many times before.

'I can test for anything,' Arvin said.

That was the challenge – one of the challenges. Children were available, but were they healthy? Some had parasites, others had drugs in their system; some were diseased or brain-damaged, some were unbalanced. Many had no papers – twice the Raths had been caught that way, offered smuggled infants by brokers. You could not trust anyone, which was why Arvin had discreetly advertised for his own broker and ignored all the ones who had come to him through the network, having heard that the Raths were desperate.

When Hella told him that it was across the bridge, he did not wince as their friends had at the thought of the East Bank.

Hella said, 'It's one of those neighborhoods.'

Arvin had not said anything, so she knew he had a plan. You needed a plan. The East Bank police were private, but that was only part of the problem. Many of the neighborhoods were sealed, like fortress villages, and were dangerous to outsiders. These days only humans had money value and so some were valuable and some were cheap, and a child might cost anything.

The prospect of getting a child gave the Raths the courage to risk the bridge. They knew that what they were doing was illegal; that what they were planning was an abduction. Yet a child meant everything to them, not only because they were sterile: a child was the future.

They had not told anyone of the broker. Which of their friends knew anything about the East Bank anyway? The previous eight disappointments had been shared and piteously clucked over. Even the persistent party talk – 'We got one in Poland,' 'The Goldstones found one in Mexico,' all that – did not draw them out. You might have thought they were talking about puppies. The Raths, who had had many, were sick of pets and were no longer comforted by warm dogs.

Nor were they dismayed by the adoption stories which had turned out badly – the Bence's Romanian infant girl who had been diagnosed as a vector after a year, and had to be destroyed; the Feericks' boy Ivor, from Russia, who had shot himself in a motel on his twelfth birthday; all the tales of runaways, adoptees who had fled to places like the East Bank and lived like the drifters they called Skells, or the squatters known as Trolls.

'I can test for epilepsy, I can find viruses, I can look into heredity, I can diagnose depression and potential malfunction, I can do brain scans, I can isolate a vector,' Arvin said. 'I can find anything.'

He had confidence in his tests, but where was the child who

could pass them? His sophisticated instruments meant frequent disappointment. Five times he had examined infants in brokers' offices and found dysfunction or systemic problems. And there were the two without papers.

Arvin was a lighting engineer, Hella an architect. Their apartment, an entire floor of a Kingsbury tower, was vast and beautiful, it lacked a child, but that was all. They had the virus but that was no disgrace – it wasn't fatal. Half the people they knew had it. You were inconvenienced by it, you were sterile; you lost your teeth, but the new implants were less trouble.

'What was that?' Arvin asked, hurriedly putting on his robe, an instinctive defense at hearing a noise when he was naked.

Someone was calling, a piercing *peep-peep* filled the room.

'It's my phone,' Hella said and slipped it over her left hand and activated it. 'Hello?'

'Calling the Raths,' the voice said. 'This is Doc.'

The broker, Hella mouthed to Arvin, and then increased the speaker volume and said, 'Is it still on?'

'Sooner than I thought. Can you come first thing tomorrow? Say six?'

That threw them, and Arvin considered this, becoming so engrossed that his face seemed sculpted and pale and doubtful.

'Why so early?' Hella said, prompted by Arvin's suspicious stare.

'The bridge will be clear and it'll be easier for you to find us.'

'We're not finding you,' Arvin said suddenly, facing the tiny phone. 'You find us – in Elmo. The station parking lot. I've got a red van.'

The puzzled voice at the other end said, 'A van?'

'For my instruments. I'm running some tests.'

'You're better off on the surface streets.'

'Elmo,' Arvin said, insisting.

What followed was not so much silence as scarcely audible consternation, like someone mumbling to himself or to another person close by – a lengthy murmuring pause.

'Okay,' the man said at last.

'How do you know Elmo?' Hella asked afterwards.

'I was there about twenty years ago. We had a cleaner who lived in Elmo. It was marginal then. But can it have changed that much?'

*

287

Watching as they drove across the bridge the East Bank seemed greener, denser, less settled to him than it had all those years ago, and they were hopeful again. On the horizon ahead, the sun at dawn was the same dusty solitaire they had seen last evening from the balcony, but inverted, a great lozenge of lighted dust rising in the cloud deck that looked tainted and fatigued. But there were trees here, there was long grass, and the old style of houses, and the fences were low and unthreatening; there were empty streets where they had expected savages and Skells.

'I feel right at home,' Arvin said.

It made her nervous when he tried to be funny, because it meant he wasn't paying attention.

As he spoke they cleared the end of the ramp and the whirring from the echoes of the roadside trees suddenly ceased to drum against the sides of the van, and a different muffled sound began – of the sealed windowless buildings that looked like fortress walls. Then, in a place they least expected it, near an embankment wall, and a sign directing them to Elmo, where the surface streets began, there was a checkpoint, and a policeman. Arvin slowed the car to a crawl as he approached the barrier.

'Howdy,' the policeman said in a friendly way, but still he did not raise the steel barrier. It was mesh. Such barriers had been designed to snare tanks and armored vehicles and rogue trucks.

The policeman smiled and took a step back to see the van's plates. His name-tag was printed *Seely*. He was casual in the way of contract police. His boots weren't shined, his badge was slightly crooked. They were all overworked, nor were they paid as well as the state troopers. But Arvin was reassured by the policeman, particularly when he halted the van and saw the child.

The child, just inside the checkpoint booth, was sitting on a stool, a low one, but even so his feet didn't touch the ground – he was kicking them, driving his heels against the stool's hard legs with a sort of frenzied East Bank vitality as he stabbed at the wall writing RONG DOGZ.

'Where you headed?'

Arvin hesitated, hating the question, but he was still smiling at the scribbling child.

The policeman said, 'I'm asking you for your own good.'

'Elmo. Is there a travel advisory?'

'Not today. But you want to be real careful.' Gesturing with his weapon, he pointed to the back of the van. 'You got a load?'

'We're empty,' Arvin said. 'See you got a little helper.'

Hearing this, the small boy's fleshy lips parted and his face drew tight as he made his teeth protrude. They were new teeth, just grown, and bulked in his mouth looking large and unused.

'Sure do,' the policeman said, and waved them on.

Soon on the surface streets they had their first sight of local people – children, probably kids of Skells and Trolls. But they were not scavenging, as people said. They looked just like the privileged children across the river who played outside, except that these were much younger. There were terrible stories of brokers who had snatched such children, saying, *It's not kidnaping – it's a form of rescue*, and found themselves with vicious, diseased or uncontrollable children who had no papers and had to be impounded.

'Let's make this quick,' Arvin said, when he pulled into the Elmo parking lot and saw the cluster of hurrying people.

A man wearing a khaki shirt and khaki trousers, perhaps an old army uniform, was surrounded by about ten children, mostly boys, none of them more than twelve or thirteen. Several of the children watched Arvin and Hella intently as they drew in and parked the van. The other children were playing. One boy was operating a hand-held instrument and earphones, a game perhaps. The others were shouting much too loudly, and that was how Hella had been able to tell their ages – their voices hadn't broken. And their teeth too were large and ill-fitting and crooked. Nothing about these children was more upsetting to Hella than these adult-sized teeth in their small ten-year-old jaws.

Arvin loathed the sight of the man with these children, the exploiter and the urchins; yet Hella became hopeful seeing the children so closely attentive or else frisking in the way all their small dogs had done.

'I'm Doc,' said the man in khaki, shuffling forward through the crowd of children. 'Can I see your IDs?'

He was older than they had imagined him – too old perhaps to be the father of any of these children; but you never knew.

As Arvin showed his ID, a boy with long, stringy, green-tinted hair crept close to him and looked at the phone on his wrist. His teeth did not fit his mouth; they bulged as he stared at Arvin, who made a point of indicating his phone.

He said, 'I'm on an open channel,' so as to caution them all. And then, 'Can we see the child? I want to run some tests.'

Doc sat down on a bench and tapped his own phone. He was watched intently by several other boys; the one with long hair, perhaps the eldest – thirteen at most – wore big borrowed-looking shoes, probably expensive, though they did not fit, and a shirt that hung to his knees like a dress. A girl walked behind him and, without meeting her eye, the boy reached out and pinched her arm. He turned then and stared as though defying her to scream. But she did not cry out. She pressed her lips together and squinted in dumb suffering.

Surely Doc had seen the boy do this? But the man said nothing.

The children looked bored and impatient and captive – they did not want to be here, Hella could tell. They looked warm and thirsty. She now remembered the child at the checkpoint scribbling RONG DOGZ on the wall of the policeman's booth.

Hella said, 'Are they for sale too?'

She had spoken softly, so that only the man would hear, yet the boy had heard and he gave her a sudden look of scowling malevolence, and he hissed through his clamped-together teeth. Hella was so startled that she could not get her breath.

'Here he is,' Doc said.

Hella was searching among the big-toothed children when she felt her leg being clutched and she turned to see a small bright-eyed child trying to hug her. He was bigger than she expected but still so much younger than any of these other children that he seemed charming and infantile.

'In perfect shape,' Doc was saying. 'Mixed race. Parents couldn't keep him. They need the money. Three isn't old.'

Again she thought: *Who are we taking him from?* and she thought of the nursery, already furnished with a crib, a high chair, a scale, a cupboard of toys, sheets and pillows and stuffed animals, the rocking horse, all the accumulated paraphernalia of their many attempts to find a child. Hella knew she was being sentimental, for part of her yearning to have a child was also her fantasy of cuddling an infant, feeding it, changing it, teaching it to speak and walk. Yet there was a logic in his being three – it was as though this was the child they had begun to search for three years ago, when they discarded their last pets.

'He's very bright. You can give him any test you like,' the man said. 'It'll be easier, you know. Being older he'll be more cooperative.'

Arvin was nodding: he accepted this as reasonable.

'He's got papers,' the man said. 'And if the tests don't work out you can call the whole thing off.'

Arvin made a familiar gesture that meant to Hella: *What have we got to lose?*

The child was clean, he seemed affectionate; he was lightly dressed this warm morning, in a clean shirt and shorts. But he had the teeth too. Arvin stepped forward when the child kissed Hella, as though to protect her, but Hella let him kiss her, and she hugged him. She sorrowed for the child yet she refused to allow herself to feel possessive. If Arvin cleared him, then she would claim him and embrace him.

'What's his name?' Arvin asked.

Before Doc could answer, the child said, 'My name is Corbin' – he had heard, he understood, he was so alert. His mouth was still open, the big teeth gleaming. 'I want to go home with you. I want you to be my mummy.'

Hella plucked his hand away and led him to Arvin. She knew he wanted to begin the tests.

Arvin said, 'He's three? He looks older – six at least.'

'Big for his age,' Doc said. And then, 'I'm going to have to take your phones.'

'Wait a minute,' Arvin said and put his hand over his wrist in a protective reflex.

'Or else how about moving some money into my account?'

'What is this?' Arvin said, and fear strengthened him: something was wrong.

As a small boy gripped his wrist and snagged the phone with his fingers, Arvin turned and saw that Hella was surrounded too, and that Doc was doing nothing except smiling, like a man whose snarling dogs are menacing a stranger.

Hella called out, 'No!' – she was frantic, seeing those mouths and eyes.

Her scream seemed to work: the small, toothy children and their keeper jostled and scattered as a police car skidded towards them on the parking lot.

A voice exploded from a loudspeaker, 'Stand back!'

It was the policeman, Seely, throwing open the doors of his

armored car, and Arvin and Hella scrambled in. Now the policeman seemed scruffier than before, with shiny trouser knees and chipped insignia on the brim of his helmet.

'Didn't I tell you to be careful?'

Arvin said gratefully, 'How did you find us?'

'You think it was hard?'

They were still thanking him as they noticed the small head of a small boy in the front seat, and as though the child knew he was being scrutinized he turned to face Arvin. He was sure when he showed his teeth that he was the boy who had been kicking the stool in the checkpoint booth.

Arvin said, 'Wait. The van's back there.'

But the policeman said nothing. He was driving fast down an alley between two tall buildings.

'Where are you taking us?'

Arvin was still talking as the policeman started to say, 'Listen.'

The small boy beside him interrupted furiously and said, 'Shut up!'

Arvin realized that he was speaking to the policeman, not to him, and he spoke with such anger that the policeman flinched and gripped the steering wheel.

'Sorry,' the policeman said. 'He's the boss.'

He kept driving. The place was blighted. It was not just the decayed buildings and broken streets; there was not a tree, not a single green thing. The trees had been cut but in a random and wasteful way, not for fuel – the limbs were strewn about. The grass had been trampled or poisoned or built over or burned; the place had been mindlessly vandalized, as though by children.

It had the look of violence: broken signs, uprooted poles, smashed windows, the scribbled and misspelled obscenities and big bewildering scrawls: RAT ROOLZ and RONG DOGZ and YUNG-STAZ and DANJAH FREEX and NO MERSI and WORRYERZ.

When Arvin muttered them disgustedly, Hella wanted him to stop.

Ahead was a warehouse, with broken windows, and there seemed to be at least one face at each window, some had more, crowding to see out.

The wide warehouse door swung open to admit the car and inside Arvin could see the broker, Doc. He was seated on a small ridiculous chair, among the children. Doc looked the other way when the policeman entered. The car doors were snatched open and the children crowded forward with steel spears made of sharpened rods and poked at Arvin and Hella. They got out of the car protesting and pleading.

The child with stringy hair and the long dress-like shirt held a weapon and said in a quacking voice to the policeman, 'Why didn't you blindfold them?'

The policeman crouched slightly and, in a tone of respectful explanation, said, 'Because blindfolds spook them.'

'Blindfold them now!' the child said. 'Wrong dogs!'

Doc said softly, as though to calm the children, 'You want me to put out the ransom call?'

'Go away,' the first boy said, and turned to Hella, and as the stinking blindfold went over her eyes she had a last look at the big malevolent teeth that had frightened her back at the parking lot when she had asked *Are they for sale too?*

Another child began to screech, 'Get out! Get out! Leave us alone! No mercy!'

In their darkness, afraid and unable to move, Arvin and Hella heard the two men leaving, muttering as they went out the door, and the large door shutting, an eclipse of light and sound that she could sense through her blindfold. The children came closer. Hella could sense their damp faces and heard them breathing eagerly through their mouths, like warm dogs.

Hella heard a child's voice say, 'This one is mine,' and she cried out as the small fingers touched her.

Part IV

Diplomatic Relations (i): The Consul's File

Part II

Implementation Issues: The Supply Side

The Consul's File

It was a late recessional, one of the last in Asia. The Consulate in that little town had been necessary to the American rubber estates, but the rubber trees were being replaced by oil palms, and most of the Americans had left. It was my job to phase out the Consulate. In other places the consular task was, in the State Department phrase, bridge-building; in Ayer Hitam I was dismantling a bridge – not a difficult job: we had never been very popular with the Malays.

I was unmarried; I had time on my hands. Because I had been told that everything I needed to know was in the files that were kept in the box-room of the Residence, for a long time I avoided looking through them. I had other ideas, and whether it was the annoyance of being known in that place as just another white man or the pointless pressure of the bureaucracy I served, I felt a need to stake a claim, so I might carry a bit of that town away undistorted. In a different age I might have taken a Malay mistress, but in my restless mood – excited by what I saw and yet feeling a little like a souvenir hunter – I decided to write.

The place, people said, was full of stories. One of the first ones I heard – told to me by a member of the Ayer Hitam Club (it concerned a planter on whom a Malay woman had placed a bizarre curse; the planter died of hiccups in Aden, and the man who told me the story claimed he had been in an adjoining stateroom) – I later read in a volume of Somerset Maugham in the club library.

I would write only what I knew to be true, or what I could verify. But the stories were elusive, and I sometimes wondered what another writer would make of them. For example, soon after I arrived there was a grass fire in a nearby village. In itself, this was not remarkable; but the fire had unlikely consequences. The economy of this village was based mainly on the sale of marijuana that grew in tall stalks all around it, a green weed that was made into *bhang*. It was intensively cultivated and nearly all of it was exported by smugglers. A fire had started – no one knew how –

and it burned for days, first in the dry brush that lay under the marijuana, and finally consuming the marijuana itself and turning it into the bittersweet smoke of the narcotic.

The villagers were safe; their houses were surrounded by wide dirt compounds in which nothing grew. Instead of bolting when the fire started, they stayed where they were. And a strange thing happened: for five days, breathing the smoke from the grass fire, they remained high, staggering and yelling, beating gongs and behaving like madmen. They were people who had never tasted alcohol, orthodox Muslims who threw villagers in jail for eating during the daylight hours of Ramadhan. But they inhaled the smoke and forgot their prayers; they rolled in the dust, pounced on each other, ran naked through the *kampong*, and burnt a Chinese shop. Afterwards they were ashamed and stopped growing the weed, and a delegation of them made the *haj* to Mecca to ask Allah's forgiveness.

I thought it was a great story, but I could never make more of it than that. I had only the incident. 'That would make a terrific story,' people said at the Club. But that was the whole of it; to add more would be to distort it; it was extraordinary and so – in all senses – incidental. But stories like that convinced the club members that the town was teeming with 'material.'

They were an odd crowd who treasured their oddity. They thought of themselves as 'characters' – this was a compliment in that place and the compliment was expected to be repaid. They verified each other's uniqueness: Angela Miller's dog had once had a hernia, Squibb had met Maugham at the Sultan's coronation, Alec Stewart often went to work in his pajamas, Strang the surveyor had grown watercress in his gumboots, Duff Gillespie had once owned a Rolls-Royce. But there is something impersonal in the celebration of eccentricity. No one mentioned that Angela had had a nervous breakdown and still, frequently, went into the billiard room to cry, that Alec was married to a Chinese girl half his age, that Squibb – who had a wife in England – was married to a very fat Malay woman, or that Strang's wife, who was pretty and rapacious, danced with every member but her husband; and when *Suzie Wong* was staged at the Club no one commented on the fact that Suzie was played not by a Chinese girl but by a middle-aged and fairly hysterical Englishwoman.

Nor did anyone find it strange that in a place where there were

Hindu *bhajans*, Malay weddings and shadow plays, and Chinese operas, the club members' idea of a night out was the long drive to Singapore to see a British *Carry On* movie, which they would laugh about for weeks afterward. They remarked on the heat: it was hot every day of the year. They didn't notice the insects, how every time a mosquito was slapped it left a smear of blood in your palm; they didn't mention the white ants, which were everywhere and ate everything. Their locutions were tropical: any sickness was a fever, diarrhea was dysentery, every rainfall a monsoon. It wasn't romance, it was habit.

The town was some shops, the Club, the mission, the dispensary, the Methodist school, my Consulate. The Indians lived on the rubber estates, the Malays in neighboring *kampongs*, the Chinese in their shops. The town was flat; in the dry season it was dusty, in the wet season flooded; it was always hot. It had no history that anyone could remember, although during the war the Japanese had used one of its old houses as headquarters for the attack on Singapore. The Club had once had polo-ponies and had won many matches against the Sultan; but all that remained were the trophies – the stables had been converted to staff quarters. Apart from tennis, the Club had no games, and the table in the billiard room where Angela Miller sometimes went to cry was torn and unusable.

After my first week in the town I thought I knew everything there was to know about the place; I had seen it all, I felt, and would not have minded leaving and going back to Africa where I had begun my career in the Foreign Service. The early sunlight saddened me and made me remember Africa; and yet the sun illuminated my mind as well, each dawn lending its peculiar light to my dreams. I had never dreamed much in America, but this tropical sun stirred me and I began to associate it with imagination, like the heat and noise that always woke me with a feeling of my own insignificance.

The unvarying heat, so different from the chilly weather I had known in Africa, had a curious effect on me: I had no sense of time passing – one day was just like another – and I felt puny and very old, as if my life were ending in this hot town in the East that was so small and remote it was like an island.

I had not started writing, since I considered writing my last resort. I would familiarize myself with the town by reading the files, and when I had done that and had no more excuses I would begin writing, if I still felt restless and unoccupied. I would not write much about myself; I would concentrate on the town, this island in which more and more, as they became friendly and candid, so many people said nothing ever happened.

Miss Leong, my secretary, had told me about the files. She had never seen them, but a succession of consuls had referred to them. They were secret; they were the reason my predecessors had chosen to take days off to work undisturbed at the Residence. Miss Leong was confidential, and she gave me the key, which in her loyal Chinese way she had never used. She transmitted this sense of mystery to me, of the secrets that lay in the box-room of the Residence, and it seemed to give my job an importance greater than any I could achieve as a writer of stories. Of the three men in the Foreign Service I knew to be writers, two were failures in their diplomatic duties and the third ended up selling real estate in Maryland.

I gave Ah Wing, my houseboy, the day off; I told Miss Leong that I was working at home; and I opened the box-room. It was very dusty, and when I walked in cobwebs brushed my eyes and trailed down my face. I smelled decayed wood and the peanut-stink of dead insects. The room was small and hot and just being there made me itch. I found some cardboard boxes and, inside, stacks of paper bound with string. I didn't have to untie the string: I lifted it and it broke and I saw that what it had held were ragged yellow papers in which white ants had chewed their way to nest. Many of the ants were dead, but there were still live ones hurrying out of the chewed pages. Another story, dramatic: the consuls' files made illegible by the white ants, because the files were hidden and secret. Well, that was true, but I did not have to look for long to discover that there was little writing on them, and certainly no secrets; in fact, most of the pages were blank.

Dependent Wife

A road, some gum trees, a row of shop-houses, three parked cars: Ayer Hitam was that small, and even after we parked in front of the coffee shop I was not sure we had arrived. But apparently this was all – this and a kind of low dense foliage that gave, in the way it gripped the town, a hint of strangulation. It was to be months before I made anything of this random settlement. It seemed at times as if I was inventing the place. I could find no explanation for its name, which meant 'Black Water.'

The trip had started gloomy with suppressed argument. Flint, number two in the Embassy in Kuala Lumpur, had offered to drive me down and show me around. With no Malay *syce* to inhibit conversation I had expected a candid tour – Flint had been recommended to me as an old Malaysian hand. I needed information to give life to the position papers and the files of clippings I'd studied all summer in Washington. The Political Section had briefed me in KL, but the briefing had been too short, and when finally I was alone with the Press Officer he launched into a tedious monologuing – a clinical dithyramb about his bowel movements since arriving in the country.

Flint also had other things on his mind. As soon as the road straightened he said, 'The Foreign Service isn't what it was. I remember when an overseas post meant some excitement. Hard work, drinking, romance, a little bit of the Empire. I never looked for gratitude, but I felt I was doing a real job.'

'"The White Man's Burden,"' I said.

Flint said, 'That's my favorite poem. Someday I'll get plastered and recite it to you. People think it's about the British in India. It isn't. It's about us in the Philippines. It's a heartbreaking poem – it makes me cry.' He smacked his lips in regret. 'God, I envy you. You're on your own here. The telephone will be out of order half the time, there's a decent club, and no one'll bother you. It's just the kind of job I had in Medan in sixty-two, sixty-three.'

'It doesn't have much strategic value.'

'Never mind that,' said Flint. 'It's a bachelor post.'

I've always hated the presumption in that phrase; like *dirty week-end* it strikes me as only pathetic. I said, 'We'll see.'

'It's no reflection on you,' he said. 'They don't send married men to places like Ayer Hitam anymore. Sure, I'd be off like a shot, but Lois wouldn't stand for it.' He was silent for a while, then he tightened his grip on the steering wheel and said, 'It's in the air, this dependent wife business.'

I said, 'At that party in KL the other night I met a very attractive girl. I asked her what she did. She said, "I'm a wife."'

'See what I mean? I bet she was eating her heart out. Hates the place, hates her husband, bores the pants off everyone with what it means to be a woman.'

'It was a silly question,' I said. 'She seemed happy enough.'

'She's climbing the walls,' said Flint. 'They hate the designation – dependent wife. Lois is going crazy.'

'I'm sorry to hear it.'

He shrugged, bringing his shoulders almost to his ears. 'I've got a job to do. She's supposed to be involved in it, but she refuses to give dinner parties.'

I said, 'They're a lot of work.'

'The hell they are – she's got three goddamned servants!' Flint glowered at the road. For miles we had been passing rubber estates: regular rows of slender trees scored with cuts, like great wilted orchards crisscrossed by perfectly straight paths, a yellowing symmetry that made the landscape seem hot and violated. I had expected a bit more than this. 'And sometimes – I'm not kidding – sometimes she refuses to go to dinner parties with me. We've got one tonight – I'll have to drag her to it.' He squinted. 'I *will* drag her, too. She says I'm married to my job.'

'I can sympathize with some of these wives,' I said. 'They get married right out of college, the husband gets an overseas post and everything's fine – the woman becomes a hostess. Then she sees that what she's really doing is boosting her husband in his job. What's in it for her?'

'I'll tell you what's in it for her,' said Flint, turning angry again. 'She's got three square meals, duty-free booze, a beautiful home, and all the servants she wants. No dishes, no laundry, no house-work. And for that we get kicked in the teeth.'

'I wouldn't know about that.'

'Then listen,' said Flint. 'Lois is upset, but the younger ones are bent out of shape. Sure, they're pleasant when you first meet them, but later on you find out they're really hostile. They want jobs, they want to read the cables, they write letters to *Stars and Stripes* and sign them "Disgusted." Then they corner the Ambassador's wife and start bending her ear.'

'We had a few problems like that in Uganda.'

'This isn't a problem, it's an international incident.' Now Flint was pounding the steering wheel as he spoke. 'The wives in Saigon – you know whose side they were on? The Vietcong! I won't name names but a lot of those gals in Saigon got it into their heads that they were oppressed, and believe me they supported the VC. No, they didn't give speeches, but they nagged and nagged. They talked about "our struggle" as if there was some connection between the guerillas shelling Nhatrang and a lot of old hens in the Embassy compound refusing to make peanut-butter sandwiches. It's not funny. I knew lots of officers who were shipped home – their wives were a security risk.' Then Flint added warily, 'You probably think I'm making this up. I'm not. They don't want to give dinner parties, they don't wear dresses anymore – just these dungarees and sweat-shirts. They hate coffee mornings. "What do you do?" "I'm a wife." Whoever said that to you – I'm not asking – is a very unhappy woman.'

In this way, when he could have been filling me in on Ayer Hitam, Flint ranted for the entire trip from KL. When we arrived at the coffee shop he was a bit breathless and disappointed, as if he wished to continue the journey to continue his rant.

The door of the car was snatched open. Outside was a woman of about thirty, not fat but full-faced, yellow-brown, with thick arms and a tremendous grin. She wore a *sarong kebaya*, and her feet, which were bare, were so dirty I took them at first for shoes. She saw the two of us and let out a cry of gratitude and joy, a kind of welcoming yelp.

It had started to rain, large widely spaced drops going *phut* at the roadside and turning to dust.

She said, 'It's raining! That means good luck!' She ran around to Flint's side of the car, tugged his sleeve and dragged him to a seat on the verandah, repeating her name, which was Fadila.

'Yes, yes,' she said. 'Two coffees and what else? Beer? I got some cold Tiger bottles waiting for you. You want a bowl of Chinese noodles? *Nasi goreng*? *Laksa*? Here, have a cigarette.' She offered us a round can of mentholated cigarettes and muttered for a small Chinese boy to leave us alone. 'Welcome to Ayer Hitam. Relax, don't be stuffy.'

We thanked her and she said something that sounded like 'Hawaii.' We persuaded her to say it more slowly. She said, 'Have you a wife?'

'Not him,' said Flint, slapping me on the arm in what I am sure he meant as congratulation.

'I'm coming,' she said.

She left. Flint said, 'I've never seen her before.'

'Seems very friendly.'

'Typical,' said Flint, full of approval. 'The Malays are fantastic. You get people like this all over the Federation – plenty of time for small talk, very hospitable, give you the shirt off their back. I got this theory. You ask a guy directions in Malaysia. If the guy's Chinese he knows where you want to go but he won't tell you how to get there. If he's Indian he knows and he'll tell you. If he's Malay he won't know the place but he'll talk for ten hours about everything else. It's the temperament. Friendly. No hangups. Outgoing. All the time in the world.'

Fadila was back with the coffees. 'Americans, right?' she said, slopping coffee into the saucers as she set down the cups. 'I know Americans. Just had some here the other day, three of them, going down to Singapore. "Why go to Singapore?" I said. "Why not stay here?" I gave them a good meal, some free beer. Why not? I don't care if the manager gets cross. It's good for business – they'll be back. That's how you get customers.' She grinned at Flint, who had been listening to this with interest. 'Hey, they invited me to visit them in New York City!'

Flint said, 'You wouldn't like New York.'

'Why not? I like KL. I like Johore Bahru. I like Seremban. Why not New York? What's your line of work, mister?'

Ordinarily, someone like Flint would have said 'business' or 'teaching' or made some vague reference to the government service. But Fadila was friendly; Fadila had spooned sugar into his coffee and stirred it; Fadila was snapping her hanky at the flies near the table. So Flint was truthful: 'I'm with the US Embassy in KL. This is your new consul. Mr Rogers's replacement.'

Fadila brightened and became even more voluble. 'Anything you want to know I can tell you.' She winked at me. 'There's something going on here. More than you think. You don't know, mister. I hear everything. Stay here.'

This time she rushed away.

Flint said, 'Jesus, I envy you. This is the real Malaysia. Look how friendly they are!'

'They? You mean *her*.'

'They're all like that in these little towns. And I'm stuck in KL. Maybe Lois is right – I *am* married to my job – but if it wasn't for her I could be in a place like this. And tonight I've got this dinner, another hassle.'

Fadila hurried toward us along the verandah. She was wearing a pair of sunglasses with one cracked lens and carrying two pint bottles of Tiger beer. She placed them on the table and opened them.

'It's rather early for that,' I said.

'It's free,' she said, snorting. 'It's a present. You're my guests. Drink it up.'

Flint was smiling. He drank. I drank. The beer was sweet and heavy, and on top of the coffee fairly nauseating. Fadila talked as we drank; now she was saying something about the Malays – she didn't trust them, they stole, they were lazy, they were sneaky, they lied. She knew they lied: they were always lying about her. The British were good people, but she liked Americans best of all. I listened, but she did not require any encouragement. I concentrated on finishing the bottle of beer and when I had drunk it all I felt dazed, sickened, leaden, no longer hungry, and slightly myopic, as if the beer had been squirted in my eyes.

I said, 'We have to go.'

'What's the rush?' said Flint. 'I'm enjoying myself.'

Fadila said, 'Anyway, the Residence isn't ready.'

Flint looked interested.

'You have to stay at the Club – they're still painting the Residence.'

Flint said, 'They were supposed to have finished that painting last week.'

Fadila shook her head. 'I know the *jaga* – they're not finished. But the Club is nice. I'll see you there, don't worry. I know the Head Boy, Stanley Chee. Tell him Fadila sent you. He'll take good care of you.'

I stood up and thanked her for the beer. Flint said, 'I was just telling my friend here how lucky he is to have a post like this.'

'It's quiet in Ayer Hitam,' she said. 'No rat race here, like KL. You can relax.'

And in the car Flint said, 'Aren't these people fantastic?'

We went to the Consulate, a three-room bungalow made into offices, flying an American flag. It faced directly onto the road, at the beginning of the long driveway which led to the Residence, where another flag flew on a taller pole. I was introduced to my secretary, Miss Leong, to the driver Abubaker, and to the *peon* Peeraswami. They looked apprehensive; they were silent, stiff with worry, seeing their new employer for the first time. I felt sorry for them and tried to relieve their anxiety by staying a while to chat, but this only worried them the more, and indeed the longer I chatted the more their terror of me seemed to increase.

Although it was only a hundred yards away, we drove to the Residence, and Flint – perhaps remembering Medan – said, 'White men don't walk.'

The Residence was blistered and scorched, the columns blackened, the verandah mottled; it had the appearance of having withstood a siege. But it was the workmen, burning off the old paint with blowtorches. They scurried out of broken bushes and set to work as soon as we drove in. Fadila's warning had been accurate: there was a great deal more to do. Bamboo scaffolding had been lashed together around the house, and it tottered as the workmen clung with their flames and scrapers. I could see into and through the house: it was empty but for a figure running out at the back, shooing chickens, slamming doors.

Flint said, 'They should have finished this painting a week ago.'

We turned to go. Fadila was leaning against the car. She was smiling, in her sunglasses, and now I could see how dirty her sarong was, the torn blouse, her grubby feet.

She said, 'I knew where to find you.'

Flint looked pleased, but when he started to talk to her she shouted something quickly in Malay to the painters. She laughed and said, 'I told them to mind their own business and get to work. No fooling and what not. The *Tuans* are watching you. Look, they are afraid.'

'Why, thanks very much,' said Flint.

But I said to her, 'That won't be necessary.'

Flint glanced at me as if to warn me that I'd been too sharp with her.

'We've got work to do,' I said.

Fadila said, 'The Consulate closes for lunch.' She looked at the sun out of the corner of her eye. 'Almost time.'

'Shall we go over to the Club?' said Flint.

'I'll show you where it is,' said Fadila.

I said, 'We'll find it.'

'Look,' she said, pointing at the painters. 'Look at those stupid men. I tell them to work and they don't work. Now they are just sitting.' She screamed at them in Malay and this time they replied, seeming to mock her. It was then that I noticed Fadila's very dirty hair.

Flint said, 'Fadila will keep them on their toes, won't you sweetheart?'

'They are pigs,' she said. 'Malay people are no good.' She spat in their direction. 'They are dirty and lazy. They try to do things to me. Yes! But I don't let them.'

'What kind of things?' asked Flint, savoring the risk in his question.

'With my head.'

I said, 'Let's go.'

But Flint was still talking to Fadila. He said, 'This is a great place. I'd like to be here myself.'

'You stay here,' said Fadila coyly; then she motioned to me. 'He can go back to KL.'

The club dining room was full: men in sports shirts, shorts, and knee socks, women in summer dresses, waiters in stiff jackets and ties carrying trays. It was as if we had stumbled into a lost world, but not an ancient one; here it was eternally 1938. None of the people looked directly at us, and no one had greeted us, but this exaggerated lack of interest made me as uncomfortable as if we were being stared at. A silence had fallen when we entered, then the silence became a rustling of self-consciousness, the clatter of forks, laughter, and loud talking.

Flint said, 'I think I've made a friend.' After we ordered he said, 'I need a friend.'

'I'll keep an eye on her.'

'You were acting pretty funny with her,' he said. 'They're all right, these people. We could learn a lot from them. They look after their menfolk, they know how to run a house, they got a good sense of humor. You won't hear any dependent wife crap from them.'

I said nothing. I continued to eat, and I felt the attention of everyone in the room on me, the pressure of their glances; I sensed them sniffing.

Flint said, 'You won't get anywhere if you take that attitude.'

I looked at him, wishing he'd shut up.

He said, 'That high and mighty attitude, thinking people like Fadila don't matter. They do. And I'll tell you something else – she knows a lot that goes on around here.' He tapped his head. 'She's tuned in.'

'She could use a bath,' I said.

'Uncalled-for,' he said. 'You don't know how lucky we've been. We arrive in town and, bingo, we meet the greatest character in the place. I'll bet everyone knows her.'

He could not have been more right, for five minutes later there was a commotion at the door to the dining room, some shouts, a scuffling, a yell, and the entire room looked up, nodded in recognition, and began muttering. The waiters stiffened at the buffet where a *rijstafel* was set out, then an old Chinese man in a white jacket marched to the door and hissed something in Malay.

Flint got to his feet; the old Chinese man – whom I took to be Stanley Chee, the Head Boy – looked at Flint. Flint said, 'Let that woman through.' The dining room went silent as Fadila walked toward us, adjusting her blouse.

Flint pulled out a chair for her and seated her at our table.

She said, 'That stupid man told me to go away – because of my feet. I said I had to see you.'

'Sure you did,' said Flint.

'It's important,' said Fadila.

Flint looked at me, then frowned at his fingers.

I said, 'We were just about to leave.'

'Want to talk somewhere else?' said Flint.

Fadila said, 'These people hate me. They are bad people. All Malay people are bad, and the Chinese are pigs – they eat pigs – and the Indians always cheat you. That is Ayer Hitam. It is a nasty place. I want to go far away.'

Flint said, 'It seems a nice quiet little place.'

'No,' said Fadila. 'The people take you to the hospital. They want to do things to your head. They make you eat poison. If you refuse they slap you. At night they beat you with a *rotan*. They hide your clothes and make you naked so you cannot run away.' She leaned toward Flint, but instead of whispering she raised her voice. 'I had letters from Mr Battley and Mr Downs. "Fadila is a good *amah*, Fadila speaks English, Fadila is honest." The hospital people destroyed my letters! They cut off my hair! They beat me! I want to be your *amah*.'

Flint said, 'We have to go.'

'Let me be your *amah*. Take me with you.'

Flint's face was fixed in a smile, but his eyes were active. 'Appointments. Business. At the Consulate.'

'The Consulate is closed.'

'*Business*,' he said, and jumped to his feet.

'Take me,' she said. 'You are a good man. He hates me – he thinks I am sick. But you like me. You'll let me be your *amah*.' She took his arm and from the expression on Flint's face I could tell that she must be squeezing him hard. 'I want to go with you.'

'Outside,' said Flint and started for the door with Fadila still holding tightly to his arm.

There were stares, mutters, and one clear voice: *I know what I'd do with her*. Flint hurried from the dining room. I followed, as calmly as I could, and heard, just as I left the room, one word, *Americans*.

Stanley Chee met me at the door; he bowed and made me pause. He said, 'Is she troubling you? If so, I can send her away.'

'Who is she?'

'Last year she was an *amok*. She was given medicine. But she will be an *amok* again soon.'

'Strange,' I said.

'No, not strange. Her husband took another wife, a young girl from Malacca, because Fadila did not give him any children. He went away and Fadila became an *amok*. Her husband was a devil.' He straightened his gold-rimmed glasses and added, 'Sir, all Malays are devils.'

Flint was inside the car, Fadila outside with her face against the window, crying bitterly. I noticed that Flint had locked all the doors. I walked to the other side of the car, but he didn't unlock the door. He rolled the window down a crack and said, 'This is it, old buddy. It's all yours – I've got to run. Lois is expecting me. Dinner party tonight. Keep your fingers crossed. And don't let our friend here get run over.'

Fadila's face hardened as Flint drove away. She turned, limped a few feet, then faced me and said, 'He is a pig and so are you.'

White Christmas

Ah Chiang, the wife of Alec's Chinese cook, had taped bits of holly to the leaves of the potted palm. The mistletoe sprig had been knocked down by the whirling fans and was blowing across the floor under the nose of the cat, but the cotton snowflakes stuck to the mirror of the drawing room were still there. The snowflakes were Mildred's idea. She thought they made the government bungalow look festive, and there was plenty of surgical cotton in the house: Alec was a doctor at the mission hospital. And yet the decorations had a look of tropical exhaustion, shabby and temporary. The snowflakes had wilted, the holly had crinkled shut in the heat, and the mosquito coils that were burning in water-filled dishes around the room gave off a funereal aroma of incense.

It was my first Christmas in Ayer Hitam, and I was too new to the town to be able to turn down Alec's invitation. There were no cars outside when I arrived, and I thought perhaps I had got the time wrong. But I saw people at the windows and, inside, five chatting guests, three Chinese, an Indian, and a large dark woman who wore a Christmas corsage, a plastic Santa bandaged in cotton wool and red ribbon.

The Chinese – two slim girls and Reggie Woo – were whispering together in a corner. The dark woman was talking loudly to Mr Ratnasingham. I recognized him as the pianist who had given a recital in the club lounge in November, when the Sultan had come over for the gymkhana. He was barrel-chested, a cheery Tamil with pomaded hair and an enormous wristwatch, wearing his black recital suit rather uncomfortably in the heat.

It had just rained. The sky was low, and the trees still dripped. The smell of the rain was the smell of the dampened frangipanis, a hot close perfume of muddy blossoms and a cloud of humidity that weighted the bridge of my nose. It was only after a rain that I could smell the flowers, but the rain had brought an oppressive heat to the town that made Christmas seem absurdly distant.

Mr Ratnasingham said, 'We were just talking about Midnight Mass – they have it every year at the mission.'

'I always go,' said the woman. 'Last year there were some Eurasians there. They laughed the whole time. Disgraceful.'

I guessed she had a tincture herself or she would not have mentioned their race.

'This is our American Consul,' said Mr Ratnasingham.

The woman brightened. 'I knew Mr Gilstrap very well.'

Sam P. Gilstrap had been consul in Singapore in the fifties. The woman was an old-timer. I said, 'Sam was half-Indian.'

Mr Ratnasingham smiled. He came close enough for me to hear his watch tick.

'Cherokee,' I said.

Mr Ratnasingham said, 'What was your previous post?'

'Africa – Uganda,' I said. 'One year they deported half a dozen Europeans for singing *White Christmas*.'

Mr Ratnasingham laughed. 'They're just down from the trees. That would never happen in Ayer Hitam.'

'I mustn't drink too much,' said the woman, and I was sure she was Eurasian by her scowl. 'I lose my voice if I drink too much brandy.'

'Miss Duckworth is in the choir,' said Mr Ratnasingham.

'So you're not the only musician, Mr Ratnasingham.'

'Please call me Francis,' he said. 'Actually, I'm a solicitor.'

'I've always been in the Christmas choir,' said Miss Duckworth.

The Chinese girls had drifted over to listen.

'We're talking about Midnight Mass,' said Mr Ratnasingham. 'Are you going?'

They gave that negative cautioning Chinese bark, and one of the girls said, 'Meffidist.'

'Drinks, drinks – who hasn't got one?' It was Alec, with a bottle of Tiger. He pumped my hand. 'I saw that enormous bottle of duty-free whiskey on the table and I knew it must be yours.'

'Season's greetings.'

He made a face. 'I hate Christmas.'

'It's going to be quite a party.'

'We do it for them,' he said.

More guests had begun to arrive, Dr Estelle Lim, the botanist; Squibb and his Malay wife; Mr Sundrum, who, half-Chinese and half-Indian, looked Malay. Alec greeted them, then went on, 'We have a Christmas party every year. It's Mildred's big day.' Mildred, rushing drinks to the newcomers, was a Chinese girl who looked twenty but might have been fifty; Alec had married her after settling in Ayer Hitam to supervise the hospital. 'She keeps it going. They appreciate it.'

I saw who they were. They weren't in the Club; they weren't of the town. Anglicized, a little ridiculous, overneat, mostly Christian, they were a small group with no local affiliations – Methodist Chinese, Catholic Indian, undeclared half-caste – the Empire's orphans. By marriage or inclination they were the misfits of the town for whom the ritual generosity of Christmas was a perfect occasion to declare themselves. From the conversations I heard it sounded as if they had not seen one another since the previous Christmas, here at the Stewarts'.

Alec said, 'When they kick us out what'll they do then?'

I didn't know what to say.

He said, 'There won't be any more Christmas parties.'

Dr Lim came over to where we were standing. I noticed she had a glass of beer, which interested me, because the Chinese aren't drinkers. But the others were drinking beer as well, and Squibb had a large bottle of Tiger and was refilling glasses. Dr Lim was a tall woman with long black hair combed to the small of her back. She had that fine pale Chinese skin that is as tight and unmarked as the membrane on tropical fruit. She handed a small box to Alec and said, 'Merry Christmas.'

'What's this?'

'Just a present-*lah*,' she said.

'I'm going to open it, my dear,' said Alec, who looked slightly embarrassed. He tore off the gift-wrapping – reindeers, Santa Clauses, holly, snow – and took out a green and yellow necktie.

'Batik,' she said.

'Just what I need.' He kissed her on the cheek and she went away smiling. Then he said, 'I haven't worn one of these bloody nooses since nineteen fifty-seven.' He put it on carelessly. He was wearing a blue short-sleeved sports shirt, and the garish colors of the tie made him look as if he were drunk and toppling forward.

Hovering, the others presented their gifts. Mr Ratnasingham gave him a calendar on a stand with a plastic antique car glued to the base; the Methodists gave Mildred some perfume, Miss Duckworth followed up with fancy handkerchiefs, and Mr

Sundrum produced a bunch of white carnations. Everyone took turns sniffing the flowers – they were regarded as quite a prize. In a country where fantastic purple and yellow orchids showed their outlandish ears and whiskers in every garden, the colorless carnation was valued as a great rarity. Dr Lim explained how they grew them up on Fraser's Hill. Not odd, then, that we sweating foreigners should be considered so special by these dainty Malaysians; they were the orchids, we the carnations.

Squibb said, 'Have a little of this,' and poured me a brandy.

'The natives say if you take brandy with durian fruit you die,' said Reggie Woo.

'Codswallop,' said Alec.

'It's what they say,' said Reggie.

'I've never believed that,' said Miss Duckworth.

'Who are the natives?' I asked.

'Malays,' said Reggie.

'We're not natives,' said Hamida Squibb. 'The *sakais* are – Laruts and what not.'

'There was an old man over in the *kampong*,' said Mr Sundrum. 'He took two cups of brandy and then ate durian. He died. His picture was in the *Straits Times*.'

'Absolute rubbish,' said Alec. Mr Sundrum winced and went to find a vase for the carnations. Alec added in a whisper, 'But mind you, I wouldn't try it myself.'

'Drink up, Hamida,' Squibb was saying. He lurched over to me, perspiring, and snatched at my shoulder. Brandy seemed to be percolating out of his eyes. He said, 'She's a Muslim – she only drinks at Christmas.'

Miss Duckworth said, 'I always cry at Christmas. I can't help it.'

Mildred, in her dark blue *cheongsam*, raised a sherry glass: 'Merry Christmas to everyone!' This brought mutters of 'The very best,' 'Here's to you,' and 'Cheers.'

Ah Kwok entered from the kitchen carrying a large varnished turkey on a platter, Ah Chiang behind him with a bowl of potatoes and a gravy boat. Then Mildred flew, got Alec to carve, and set out the rest of the dishes on the long table.

Mr Ratnasingham said, 'That's a big bird.'

'A sixteen-pounder,' said Alec. 'Mildred bought it in Singapore – Cold Storage gets them from Australia.'

'Australia!' said one of the Methodists, clearly overwhelmed.

'And I remembered that you Americans like cranberry sauce,' said Mildred to me.

'I adore cranberry sauce,' said the other Methodist. She turned to me. 'I've always wanted to go to America.'

Mildred made a great show of seating us. Alec stood aside and said, 'I don't care where I sit as long as it's near the gin bottle,' but Mildred pushed and pointed: 'No – it has to be boy-girl-boy-girl.'

Hamida said, 'That's the way it should be. In my *kampong* the men used to eat in one room while the women served!'

'Quite right,' said Squibb. 'I thought I was marrying a Malay and look what I get. Doris Archer.'

'You're the Malay,' said Hamida.

Mildred directed me to sit between Dr Lim and one of the Methodist girls.

Alec said, 'For what we are about to receive may we be truly grateful.'

'Amen' – it chimed assertively in a dozen different voices.

Miss Duckworth said, 'This reminds me of last year.'

'And the year before,' said Alec.

'We used to have such lovely Christmases,' said Miss Duckworth. 'Of course that was in Singapore. Tang's had a Santa Claus on their roof – in a sleigh with all the reindeer. And that week your Chinese provisioner would give you a Christmas basket with tins and fruit all tied in red ribbon. Then there were drinks at the Seaview Hotel and a carol service at the Cathedral. There were so many people there then.'

'There are people there now,' said Reggie Woo.

'I mean English people,' said Miss Duckworth. 'Now it's all Japanese.'

Dr Lim said, 'We used to think white people smelled like cheese.'

'Like corpses,' said Mildred. 'But it was their clothes. After they had been here for a few months they stopped smelling like dead cheese.'

'I like cheese,' said Reggie Woo.

'So do I!' said one of the Methodists, and everyone nodded: cheese was very good, and one day Malays, Indians, and Chinese would realise that.

'Santa Claus is still on Tang's roof, Elsie,' said Mildred. 'I saw it when I picked up the turkey.'

'Cute,' said Hamida.

'Cold Storage was decorated, too. They were playing carols on the loudspeaker system.'

'But there's no one there to appreciate it,' said Miss Duckworth. 'No, they don't have Christmases like years ago.'

'Christmas in England,' said Mr Sundrum. 'That's a real white Christmas.'

'Horrible,' said Squibb. 'You have no idea. We had a council house outside Coventry. All I remember is expecting something to happen that never happened. I didn't know my old man had been laid off.'

'But the snow,' said Mr Sundrum.

'Hate it,' said Squibb. 'Freezes the pipes.'

'I'd like to see snow,' said Mr Sundrum. 'Just once. Maybe touch it.'

'Ah Kwok, show Sundrum to the fridge,' said Alec. 'He wants to stick his hand in the freezing compartment.'

Ah Kwok cackled and brought second helpings.

Dr Lim said, 'Listen – it's starting to rain.'

It was; I could see the palm fronds nodding at the window, and then it began on the roof, a light patter on the tiles. It encouraged talk, cheerless and regretful, of other Christmases, of things no one had ever seen, of places they had never visited; phrases heard secondhand and mispronounced. They were like children with old inaccurate memories, preparing themselves for something that would never occur.

In that same mood, Dr Lim said, 'I had a dream last night about my father.'

'I like hearing people's dreams,' said Mildred.

'My father is dead,' said Dr Lim, and she gave her plate a nudge. She lit a cigarette.

'I don't think I want to hear,' said one of the Methodists.

'Go on, Estelle,' said Alec. 'You've got us all in suspense.'

'He came into my room,' she said. 'But he was dressed in white pajamas – Chinese ones, with those funny buttons. He was buried in clothes like that. He had something in his hand and I could tell he was very cross. Then I saw what he was holding – an opium pipe. He showed it to me and came so close I could see the tobacco stains on his teeth. I said to him, "What do you want?" He didn't reply, but I knew what he was thinking. Somehow, he was thinking, *You're not my daughter anymore.*'

'That gives me the shivers,' said Mildred.

'Then he lifted up the opium pipe and broke it in half,' said Dr Lim. 'He just snapped it in my face. He was angry.'

'And you woke up,' said Mr Ratnasingham.

'Yes, but that was the strange part. When I woke up he was still there in my room. The white pajamas were shining at me. I looked harder and he backed out the door.'

Everyone had stopped eating. Dr Lim puffed her cigarette, and though her face was fixed in a smile I could see no pleasure in it.

'White is the Chinese color for death,' said Mr Sundrum.

'That's what I mean,' said Dr Lim.

'Like black is for us,' said Reggie Woo.

Mildred said, 'I think it's time for the Christmas pudding. Alec, get your brandy butter.'

Hamida said, 'I don't believe in ghosts. Do you, Francis?'

'I'm a Catholic,' said Mr Ratnasingham.

Miss Duckworth had begun to cry. She cried without a sound, terribly, shaking her shoulders as if she were trying to stand up.

'Can I get you anything?' said one of the Methodists.

'No,' whispered Miss Duckworth, sobbing hoarsely. 'I always cry at Christmas.'

The girl said, 'I wasn't here last year.'

Squibb said, 'I used to dress up as Santa Claus. But you're all getting old now, and besides I'm drunk.'

The Christmas pudding was carried alight from the kitchen by Ah Kwok, and Ah Chiang brought the cheese board. I finished my pudding quickly, and seeing me with an empty bowl, Dr Lim passed me the cheese. She said, 'You must have some of this.'

'Just a slice of the Brie,' I said.

'That's not Brie – it's Camembert,' said Dr Lim.

'He doesn't know the difference!' cried Reggie Woo.

Mr Ratnasingham said, 'How about a Christmas song?' He began to sing 'White Christmas' in his harsh Tamil voice. The others joined in, some drunkenly, some sweetly, drowning the sound of the rain on the bungalow roof.

'You're not singing,' muttered Dr Lim to me.

So I did, but it was awkward because only I knew the last verse, and I was obliged to sing it alone like a damned fool while the others hummed.

Pretend I'm Not Here

Even an amateur bird-watcher knows the bird from the way the empty nest is woven on a limb; and the wallpaper you hate at your new address is a pattern in the former tenant's mind. So I came to know Rogers, my predecessor at the Consulate, from the harsh-voiced people who phoned for him at odd hours and the unpaid bills that arrived to reveal his harassments so well. That desk drawer he forgot to empty told me a great deal about his hoarding postcards and the travels of his friends (Charlie and Nance in Rome, Tom and Grace in Osaka – interesting, because both couples reported 'tummy-aches'). But I knew Rogers best from the habits of Peeraswami, the Indian clerk, and the descent of Miss Harbottle.

Peeraswami said, 'I see European lady today morning, *Tuan*,' and I knew he had no letters. Rogers had allowed him to take credit for the mail: he beamed with an especially important letter and handed it over slowly, weighing it in his brown hand like an award; if there were no letters he apologized and made conversation. Rogers must have found this behavior consoling. It drove me up the wall.

'Thank you.' I went back to my report.

He hesitated. 'In market. With camera. Taking snaps of City Bar's little girl.' Woo Boh Swee, who owned the establishment, was known locally as City Bar, though his elder child was always called Reggie. 'European from America.'

'An American?' I looked up. 'How do you know?'

'Wearing a hat,' he said. 'Carrying her own boxes.'

'That doesn't mean she's an American.'

'Riding the night bus.' He smiled. 'American.'

A show of contempt from the barefoot mail-boy. Americans, once thought of as free-spenders and luxury travelers, were now considered cheapskates. What he said was partly true: the night bus from Kuala Lumpur was used mostly by American students and Tamil rubber tappers. But Peeraswami was such a know-it-all; I hoped he was wrong.

I saw her after lunch. She was sitting on the front steps of the Consulate, fiddling with her camera. Her suitcases were stacked next to her. I recognized her from the hat. It was a Mexican model, and the wide brim was tied at the sides by a blue ribbon, making it into a silly bonnet with a high conical crown.

She said, 'I shouldn't be doing this in broad daylight.'

She was juggling little yellow capsules, changing the film in her camera. I stepped past her and unlocked the front door.

'Are you open now?' She looked up and made a horrible face at the sun.

'No,' I said. 'Not until two. You've got a few minutes more.'

'I'll just sit right here.'

I went inside, and reflecting on that hat, considered leaving by the back door. But it was too hot for tennis, too early for a drink; and I had work to do. I turned on the fan and began signing the letters I'd dictated that morning. I had signed only three when the door burst open.

'Hey!' She was at the door, undoing her bonnet. 'Where's Mr Rogers?'

'I'm the new Consul.'

'Why didn't you say so out there?'

'I only admit to it during office hours,' I said. 'It cuts down on the work.' I showed her my pen, the letters on my blotter.

'Well, I've got a little problem,' she said. Now her bonnet was off, and I could see her face clearly. She was sunburned, plump, and not young; her hands were deeply freckled and she stood leaning one fist on my desk, talking to me as if at an employee. 'It's to do with accommodation. I don't have any, and I was counting on Rogers. I know him from Riyadh.'

'He's in Turkey now,' I said. 'But there's a rest house in town.'

'It's full.'

'There are two Chinese hotels.'

She leaned still further on her fist: 'Did you ever spend a night in a Chinese hotel?'

'There's a campsite,' I said. 'If you know anything about camping.'

'I camped my way through the Great Nafud. That's where I met Rogers,' she said. 'I wrote a book about it.'

'Then Ayer Hitam shouldn't bother you in the least.'

'My tent was stolen yesterday in KL, at the bus depot.'

'You have to be careful.'

'It was stolen by an American.'

She looked as if she was holding me responsible. I said, 'I'll keep an eye out for it. In the meantime –'

'All I want is a few square feet to throw my sleeping bag,' she said. 'You won't even know I'm there. And don't worry – I'll give you an acknowledgment in my book.'

'You're writing another one, are you?'

'I always do.'

It might have been the heat or the fact that I had just noticed she was a stout woman in late middle age and looked particularly plain and vulnerable in her faded cotton dress, with her sunburned arms and peeling nose and a bulbous bandage on her thumb. I said, 'All right then. Be at my house at six and I'll see what I can fix up for you.'

Ah Wing met me in the driveway as Abubaker swung the car to a halt. Ah Wing had been Rogers's cook, and he was old enough to have been cook for Rogers's predecessor as well; he had the fatigued tolerance of the Chinese employee who treats his employers as cranky birds of passage. He said, 'There is a *mem* in the garden.'

'Wearing a hat?'

'Wearing.'

She had spread a ground sheet on the grass and opened one of her suitcases. A half-rolled sleeping bag lay on the ground sheet, and she was seated on the second suitcase, blowing up a rubber air mattress. She took the nozzle out of her mouth and said, 'Hi there!'

'You're not going to sleep here, are you?'

'This suits me fine,' she said. 'I'm no sissy.' The implication being that I was one for using a bed. 'Now you just leave me be and pretend I'm not here. Don't worry about me.'

'It's the grass I'm worried about,' I said. 'New turf. Rather frail.'

She allowed herself to be persuaded, and gathered up her camping equipment. Inside the house she said, 'You live like a king! Is this all yours?'

'It's rented from the Sultan.'

'Taxpayers' money,' she said, touching the walls as she went along.

'This is considered a hardship post by the State Department.'

'I haven't seen any hardships yet,' she said.

'You haven't been in town very long,' I said.

'Good point,' she said.

She was in the bedroom; she dropped her suitcases and sat on the bed and bounced. 'A real bed!'

'I suppose you'll be wanting dinner?'

'No, sir!' She reached for her handbag. 'I've got all I need right here.' She took out a wilted branch of rambutans, half a loaf of bread, and a tin of Ma-Ling stew.

'That won't be necessary,' I said.

'Whatever you say.' On the verandah she said, 'You do all right for yourself,' and punished the gin bottle; and over dinner she said, 'Golly, do you eat like this every day?'

I made noncommittal replies, and then I remembered. I said, 'I don't even know your name.'

'Harbottle,' she said. 'Margaret Harbottle. Miss. I'm sure you've seen my travel books.'

'The name rings a bell.'

'The Great Nafud was the toughest one. Rogers didn't have a place like this!'

'It must be very difficult for a woman to travel in Saudi Arabia.'

'I didn't go as a woman,' she said.

'How interesting.'

'I went as a man,' she said. 'Oh, it's really quite simple. I'm ugly enough. I cut my hair and wore a burnous. They never knew the difference!'

She went on to tell me of her other travels, which were stories of cheerful privations, how she had lived on dates and Nile water for a week in Juba, slept in a ditch in Kenya, crossed to Lamu by dhow. She was eating the whole time she spoke, jabbing her fork in the air as if spearing details. 'You won't believe this,' she said, 'but I haven't paid for a meal since Penang, and *that* was a misunderstanding.'

'I believe it.'

She looked out the window at the garden. 'I'm going to paint that. Put it in the book. I always illustrate my own books. "With illustrations by the author."'

We finished dinner and I said, 'I usually read at this time of day.'

'Don't let me interrupt your routine,' she said.

We had coffee, and then I picked up my novel. She sat in the lounge with me, smoking a Burmese cheroot, looking around the room. She said, 'Boy, you do all right!' I glanced up in annoyance. 'Go ahead – read,' she said. 'Pretend I'm not here.'

Days later she was still with me. Ah Wing complained that her food was stinking up the bedroom. There was talk of her at the Club: she had been seen sniffing around the Sultan's summer house, and then had come to the club bar and made a scene when she was refused a drink. She got one eventually by saying she was my houseguest. I signed the chits the next day: five gins and a port and lemon. It must have been quite an evening.

Her worst offense was at the river. I heard the story from Peeraswami. She had gone there late one afternoon and found some men bathing, and she had begun photographing them. They had seen her but, stark naked, they couldn't run out of the water. They had shouted. She photographed that. It was only when she started away that the men wrapped themselves in sarongs and chased her, but she had taken one of their bicycles and escaped.

'They think I haven't seen a man before,' she said, when I asked her about it.

'Malay men are modest,' I said.

'Believe me, they've got something to be modest about!'

I decided to change the subject. I said, 'I'm having some people over tomorrow for drinks.'

'I don't mind,' she said.

'I was hoping you wouldn't.'

'And don't worry about me,' she said. 'Just pretend I'm not here.'

I was tempted to say, 'How?' I resisted and said, 'You don't do much painting.'

'The light's not right.'

The next evening she had changed into a clean dress. I could not think of a polite way of getting rid of her. She stayed, drank more than anyone, and talked nonstop of her travels. When the guests left, she said, 'They were nice, but kind of naive, you know what I mean?'

'Miss Harbottle,' I said, 'I'm expecting some more people this weekend.'

She smiled. 'Pretend I'm not here.'

'That is not a very easy thing to do,' I said. 'You see, they're staying overnight, and I was planning to put them in your room.'

'But you have lots of rooms!'

'I expect lots of guests.'

'Then I'll sleep on the grass,' she said. 'I intended to do that anyway. You won't even know I'm there.'

'But if we decide to play croquet we might disturb that nap you always have after lunch.'

'It's your meals,' she said. 'I usually don't eat so much. But I hate to see food go to waste.'

That was Thursday. On Friday I had a visit from Ali Mohammed. 'It is about your houseguest,' he said. 'She took some cloth from my shop and has not paid for it.'

'She might have forgotten.'

'That is not all. The men she photographed at the river are still cross. They want very much to break up her camera. And Mekmal says she scratched his pushbike.'

'You'll have to see her about it.'

'This is serious,' he said, glowering and putting on his *songkok*. 'She is your houseguest.'

'She won't be much longer.'

I can't say I was sorry her inconvenience extended to Ali Mohammed; he had been in the habit of saying to me, 'When is *Tuan* Rogers coming back?' And then it occurred to me that an unwelcome guest is like a weapon. I could use Miss Harbottle quite blamelessly against Ali or Peeraswami, both of whom deserved her. An unwelcome guest could carry annoyance to your enemy; you only had to put them in touch.

'Ali Mohammed was in the office today,' I said over lunch. 'He says you took some cloth from him without paying for it.'

'I thought it was a present.'

'He didn't think so.'

'When I go to a country,' said Miss Harbottle, with a note of instruction in her voice, 'I expect to be given presents. I'm writing a book about this place. I'm *promoting* these people.'

'That reminds me,' I said. 'I've decided to charge you rent.'

Miss Harbottle's face fell. 'I never pay,' she said. 'I don't carry much cash.' She squinted at me. 'That's pretty unfair.'

'I don't want money,' I said.

She said, 'You should be ashamed of yourself. I'm fifty-two years old.'

'And not that either,' I said. 'Your payment will be a picture. One of your water colors for every night you stay here from now on.'

'I can't find my brushes.'

'I'll buy you some new ones.'

'I see,' she said, and as soon as we finished eating she went to her room.

Late that same night the telephone rang. It was Peeraswami. He had just come from a meeting outside the mosque. Ali Mohammed was there, and Mekmal, and City Bar, and the men from the river, the rubber tappers – everyone with a grievance against Miss Harbottle. They had discussed ways of dealing with the woman. The Malays wanted to humiliate her; the Chinese suggested turning the matter over to a secret society; the Indians had pressed for some expensive litigation. It was the first time I had seen the town united in this way, their single object – the plump Miss Harbottle – inspiring in them a sense of harmonious purpose. I didn't discourage Peeraswami, though he reported the proceedings with what I thought was uncalled-for glee.

'I'm afraid there's nothing I can do,' I said. She was Rogers's guest, not mine; Rogers's friends could deal with her.

'What to do?' asked Peeraswami.

'Whatever you think best,' I said. 'And I wouldn't be a bit surprised if she was on the early bus tomorrow.'

In the morning, Ah Wing woke me with tea and the news that there were twenty people in the garden demanding to see me. I took my time dressing and then went out. They saw me and called out in Malay, 'Where is she? Where is the *orang puteh*?'

Ah Wing shook his head. He said, 'Not here.'

'Liar!' Peeraswami yelled, and this cry was taken up by the others.

Ah Wing turned to me and said, 'She left early – on the Singapore bus.'

'Liar!' said Peeraswami again. 'We were at the bus station!'

'Yes,' said Ali Mohammed. 'There was no woman at the station.' He had a stick in his hand; he shook it at me and said, 'We want to search your house.'

'Wait,' I said. 'Did you see a European?'

'A man only,' said Ali Mohammed.

'A fat one,' said Peeraswami with anger and disgust. 'He refused Mekmal to carry his boxes.'

I'm sure my laughter bewildered them; I was full of gratitude for Miss Harbottle. I loved her for that.

Loser Wins

The insects warbled at the windows, and on the wall a pale gecko chattered and flicked its tail. It was one of those intimate late-night pauses – we had been drinking for two hours and had passed the point of drunken chitchat. Then, to break the silence, I said, 'I've lost my spare pair of glasses.'

'I hadn't noticed,' said Strang. A surveyor, he had the abrupt manner of one who works alone. He was mapping this part of the state and he had made Ayer Hitam his base. His wife, Milly, was devoted to him, people said; it seemed an unusual piece of praise. Strang picked up his drink. 'You won't find them.'

'It's an excuse to go down to Singapore for a new pair.'

Strang looked thoughtful. I expected him to say something about Singapore. We were alone. Stanley Chee had slammed the door for the last time and had left a tray of drinks on the bar that we could sign for on the chit-pad.

Still Strang didn't reply. The ensuing silence made my sentence about Singapore a frivolous echo. He walked over and poured himself a large gin, emptied a bottle of tonic into the tall glass and pinched a new slice of lemon into it.

'I ever tell you about the Parrishes?'

A rhetorical question: he was still talking.

'Married couple I met up in Kota Bharu. Jungle bashers. Milly and I lived there our first year – looked like paradise to us, if you could stand the sand flies. Didn't see much of the Parrishes. They quarreled an awful lot, so we stayed as far away as possible from their arguments. Seemed unlucky. We'd only been married a few months.' He smiled. 'Old Parrish took quite a shine to Milly.'

'What did the Parrishes argue about?' Was this what he wanted me to ask? I hoped he was not expecting me to drag the story out of him. I wanted him to keep talking and let it flow over me. But even at the best of times Strang was no spellbinder; tonight he seemed agitated.

'See, that shows you've never been spliced,' he said. 'Married people argue about everything – anything. A tone of voice, saying please, the color of the wallpaper, something you forgot, the speed of the fan, food, friends, the weather. That tie of yours – if you had a wife she'd hate you for it. A bone of contention,' said Strang slowly, 'is just a bone.'

'Perhaps I have that in store for me.' I filled my own drink and signed for that and Strang's.

'Take my advice,' he said. 'No – it was something you said a minute ago. Oh, you lost your specs. That's what I was going to say. The Parrishes argued about everything, but most of all they argued about things they lost. I mean, things *she* lost. She was incredible. At first he barely noticed it. She lost small things, lipstick, her cigarettes, her comb. She didn't bother to look for them. She was very county – her parents had money, and she had a kind of contempt for it. Usually she didn't even try to replace the things she lost. The funny thing is, she seemed to do it on purpose – to lose things she hated.

'He was the local magistrate. An Outward Bound type. After a week in court he was dead keen to go camping. Old Parrish – he looked like a goat, little pointed beard and those sort of hairy ears. They went on these camping trips and invariably she lost something en route – the house keys, her watch, the matches, you name it. But she was a terrific map-reader and he was appalling, so he really depended on her. I think he had some love for her. He was a lot older than she was – he'd married her on a long leave.

'Once, he showed how much he loved her. She lost fifty dollars. Not a hard thing to do – it was a fifty-dollar note, the one with the mosque on it. I would have cried, myself, but she just shrugged, and knowing how she was continually losing things he was sympathetic. "Poor thing," he says, "you must feel a right charlie." But not a bit of it. She had always had money. She didn't take a blind bit of notice, and she was annoyed that he pitied her for losing the fifty sheets. Hated him for noticing it.

'They went off on their camping trips – expeditions was more like it – and always to the same general area. Old Parrish had told me one or two things about it. There was one of these up-country lakes, with a strange island in the middle of it. They couldn't find it on the map, but they knew roughly where it was supposed to be – there's never been a detailed survey done of the Malaysian interior. But that's where the Parrishes were headed every weekend during that dry season. The attraction was the monkeys. Apparently, the local *sakais* – they might have been Laruts – had deported some wild monkeys there. The monkeys got too stroppy around the village, so being peace-loving buggers the *sakais* just caught them and tied them up and brought them to the island where they wouldn't bother anyone. There were about a dozen of these beasts, surrounded by water. An island of wild monkeys – imagine landing there on a dark night!

'In the meantime, we saw the Parrishes occasionally in the compound during the week and that's where I kept up to date with the story. As I say, his first reaction when she lost things was to be sympathetic. But afterward, it irritated him. She lost her handbag and he shouted at her. She lost her watch – it was one he had given her – and he wouldn't speak to her for days. She mislaid the bathplug, lost some jewelry, his passport disappeared. And that's the way it went – bloody annoying. I don't know what effect this had on her. I suppose she thought she deserved his anger. People who lose things get all knotted up about it, and the fear of losing things makes them do it all the more. That's what I thought then.

'And the things she lost were never found. It was uncanny, as if she just wished them away. He said she didn't miss them.

'Then, on one of these expeditions she lost the paraffin. Doesn't seem like much, but the place was full of leeches and a splash of paraffin was the only thing that'd shake them loose from your arms or legs. They both suffered that weekend and didn't find the island either. Then, the next weekend, she lost the compass, and that's when the real trouble started. Instead of pitying her, or getting angry, or ignoring it, old Parrish laughed. He saw how losing the compass inconvenienced her in her map-reading, and she was so shaken by that horrible laugh of his she was all the more determined to do without it. She succeeded, too. She used a topographical map and somehow found the right landmarks and led them back the way they'd come.

'But Parrish still laughed. I remember the day she lost the car keys – *his* car keys, mind you, because she'd lost practically everything she owned and now it was his stuff up the spout. You could hear old Parrish halfway to Malacca. Then it was the malaria tablets. Parrish laughed even harder – he said he'd been in the Federation so long he was immune to it, but being young and new to the place she'd get a fever, and he found that screamingly funny.

This was too much for her, and when his wedding ring went missing – God only knows how *that* happened – and Parrish just laughed, that was the last straw. I suppose it didn't help matters when Parrish set off for the courthouse in the morning saying, "What are you going to lose today, my darling?"

'Oh, there was much more. He talked about it at parties, laughing his head off, while she sulked in a corner, and we expected to find him dead the next morning with a knitting-needle jammed through his wig.

'But, to make a long story short, they went off on one of their usual expeditions. No compass, no Paludrine, no torch – she'd lost practically everything. By this time, they knew their way, and they spent all that Saturday bushwhacking through the *ulu*. They were still headed in that deliberate way of theirs for the monkey island, and now I remember that a lot of people called him "Monkey" Parrish. She claimed it was mythical, didn't exist, except in the crazy fantasies of a lot of *sakais*; but Monkey said, "I know what you've done with it, my darling – you've lost that island!" And naturally he laughed.

'They were making camp that night in a grove of bamboos when it happened. It was dusk, and looking up they saw one of those enormous clouds of flying foxes in the sky. Ever see them? They're really fruit-bats, four feet from tip to tip, and they beat the air slowly. You get them in the *ulu* near the coast. Eerie, they are – scare the wits out of you the way they fly, and they're ugly as old boots. You can tell the old ones by the way they move, sort of dropping behind and losing altitude while the younger ones push their noses on ahead. It's one of the weirdest sights in this country, those flying foxes setting off in the twilight, looking so fat and fearsome in the sky. Like a bad dream, a kind of monster film – they come out of nowhere.

'She said, "Look, they're heading for that island."

'He said, "Don't be silly – they're flying east, to the coast."

'"There's the light," he said, "that's west." She claimed the bats preferred islands and would be homing in on one where there was fruit – monkey food. The wild monkeys slept at night, so they wouldn't bother the bats. She said, "I'm going to have a look."

'"There's no torch," he says, and he laughs like hell.

'"There's a moon," she says. And without another word she's crashing through the bamboos in the direction the foxes are flying.

Parrish – Monkey Parrish – just laughed and sat down by the fire to have a pipe before bed. Can you see him there, chuckling to himself about this wife of his who loses everything, how he suddenly realizes that she's lost herself and he has a fit of laughter? Great hoots echoing through the jungle as old Parrish sees he's rid of her at last!

'Maybe. But look at it another way. The next morning he wakes up and sees she's not there. She never came back. At first he slaps his thigh and laughs and shouts, "She's lost!" The he looks around. No map, no compass, no torch – only that low dense jungle that stretches for hundreds of miles across the top of the country, dropping leeches on anyone who's silly enough to walk through it. And the more he thinks about it the more it becomes plain to him that *he*'s the one who's lost – she's wished him away, like the wedding ring and the torch and the fifty-dollar bill. Suddenly he's not laughing anymore.

'I'm only guessing. I don't really know what he was thinking. I had the story from her, just before she left the country. She said there were only two monkeys on the island, a male and a female, bickering the whole time, like her and her late husband. Yes, *late* husband. No one ever found him – certainly not her, but she wouldn't, would she?'

The Flower of Malaya

'Is she one of yours?' they'd ask on the club verandah when a white girl went past. Nothing salacious intended: they were just wondering if she was American. It was in this way – a casual inquiry to which I did not have an answer – that I discovered Linda Clem. We assigned names to strangers, a tropical pastime, nicknaming them at a distance; she was 'The Flower of Malaya.' For a brief period I found it hard to think of her and not be reminded of that disappointed ghost the Malays believe in, who is known simply as Pontianak, 'The Ghost.' Pontianak has a pretty face and is always alone. She takes a trishaw, but when it arrives at the destination and the driver asks for the fare, the seat is empty, Pontianak is gone. Or she stops a man on a jungle path – something Malay women never do – and asks the man to follow her. The offer is not usually refused, but when she turns to go the man sees she has an enormous hole in her back. Then she melts away. At night, before heavy storms, she can be heard weeping in the banana groves. Pontianak is the ghost of a woman who died in childbirth and she has been sighted from Kota Bharu on the north coast to Kukup in the south; the Javanese know her, so do the Sumatrans. She gets around, but what does she want?

Linda Clem got around, and she had Pontianak's melancholy. It seems to come easily to most women – there is a kind of sisterhood in sadness. She was a teacher. That word, so simple at home, spells disaster in the East. They have such hopes, and it always ends so badly. She taught English, most of them do, never asking themselves what happens when a half-starved world is mumbling in heavily accented English, 'I want –.' She struck me as accident-prone, but I suppose that was her job, her nationality, her boy friend.

She was a plump graceless soul who hated her body. She had fat legs and a bottom only a Chinese upholsterer could have admired. But she had a pretty face with slightly magnified features, and she had long beautiful hair. Within a week of arriving she was in a sarong – ill-fitting, but it took care of those legs. Within a month she was on the arm of a boy vaguely related to the Sultan, a cousin of a cousin, known locally (but inaccurately) as 'Tunku,' The Prince. He was a charming idle fellow who owed money at every Chinese shop in town.

A hopeless liaison: he wanted to be American, she aimed at being Malay – the racial somersault often mistaken for tolerance. It was usually inverted bigotry, ratting on your own race. I saw their determined effort at affection, strolling hand-in-hand across the maidan, or at the club social evenings – evidently she thought she was teaching us a thing or two about integration; and at City Bar, smooching under the gaze of the Chinese secret society that congregated there. I guessed The Prince was using her money – she looked credulous enough to loan it to him. How pathetic to watch the newcomer, innocent to the deceits of the East, making all the usual mistakes.

I waited for the eventual break-up, but it happened sooner than I expected. One morning she appeared at the Consulate just after we opened. She pushed Peeraswami aside, ignored the secretary's squawk, and flung open my office door.

'I'm looking for the Consul,' she said.

'Do you have an appointment?' I asked.

'The secretary already asked me that,' she said. 'Look, this is an emergency.'

She sat down and threw her shoulder bag on a side table. Is it only Americans who treat consulates as their personal property, and diplomatic personnel as their flunkies? 'They move in and walk all over you,' a colleague used to say – he kept his door locked against American nationals demanding service. It earned us, in Ayer Hitam, the contemptuous pity of the European consulates.

Miss Clem said, 'I want to report a break-in.'

'I'm afraid that's a matter for the police.'

'This is confidential.'

'They can keep a secret,' I said.

'You're my consul,' she said rather fiercely. 'I'm not going to any Malay cop.' She was silent a moment, then she said, 'A man's been in my room.'

I said nothing. She glared at me.

'You don't care, do you?'

'I find it hard to understand your alarm, Miss Clem.'

'So you know my name.' She frowned. 'They told me you were like that.'

'Let's try to be constructive, shall we?' I said. 'What exactly did the man do?'

'You want details,' she said disgustedly.

'Isn't that why you came here?'

'I told you why I came here.'

'You'll have to be specific. Are you reporting a theft?'

'No.'

'Assault?'

'Kinda.'

'Miss Clem,' I said, and I was on the point of losing my temper, 'I'm very busy. I can't read your mind and I'd rather you didn't waste my time. Now play ball!'

She put her face in her hands and began to blubber, clownish notes of hooted grief. She had that brittle American composure that breaks all at once, like a windshield shattered with a pebble. A fat girl crying is an appalling sight, in any case, all that motion and noise. Finally she spoke up: 'I've been raped!'

I closed the door to the outer office, and said, 'Do you know who did it?'

She nodded sadly and pushed her hair out of her eyes. She said, 'Ibrahim.'

'The Prince?'

'He's no prince,' she said. Then plaintively, 'After all I did for him.'

'You'll have to go to the police and make a statement.'

'What will I say?' she said in a small voice.

'Just tell them what happened.'

'Oh, God, it was really awful,' she said. 'He came through the window with no clothes on – just like that. I was up combing my hair and I saw him in the mirror. He turned off the light and grabbed me by the arm. I tried to push him away, but you know, it was really strange – he was all slippery. His skin was covered by some kind of oil. "Cut it out," I said. But he wouldn't. He didn't say anything. He just lifted me up by the legs like a wheel-barrow, and – I'll never forgive him for this. I was giving him English lessons!'

'Tell that to the police. I'll send you in my car. They'll want to know the times and that sort of thing.'

'What'll they do?'

'I imagine they'll arrest him, if they can find him.'

'They'll find him,' she said bitterly. 'I just saw him in town.'

So Ibrahim, The Prince, was picked up, and Miss Clem pressed charges. Only the younger members of the Club wondered why The Prince had stayed around. The rest of us knew how Miss Clem had ventured into danger; she had led him on and the poor dumb Malay had misread all her signs. Miss Clem had discovered how easy it was, after all, to be a Malay. It was typical enough for farce.

Squibb said, 'She got just what she deserved. She was asking for it.'

'She doesn't know the first thing about it,' said Strang.

Squibb squinted maliciously: 'She knows now. The Flower of Malaya's been deflowered.'

I said I agreed with them – it was fatal to disagree with anyone in such a small post – but I sympathized with the girl. She knew nothing of the country; she had fallen in headfirst. All you had to do to survive was practice elementary caution. In one sense she deserved what she got, but it was a painful lesson. I had some sympathy for The Prince, too; he was not wholly to blame. He had mistaken her for one of his own. But how was he to know? They were all beginners, that was the worst of these interracial tangles: how infantile they were!

Predictably, Miss Clem stopped wearing her sarong. She tied her hair differently, and she began dropping into the Club alone. The members were kind to her – I noticed she usually had a tennis partner, and that was truly an act of kindness, since she was such a dreadful player. Overnight, she acquired the affectations of a memsahib; a bit sharp with the waiters and ball-boys, a common parody of hauteur in her commands, that odd exaggerated play-actor's laugh, and a posture I associate with a woman who is used to being waited on – a straight-backed rigidity with formal, irritated hand signals to the staff, as if her great behind was cemented to a plinth. Then I disliked her, and I saw how she was patronized by the club bores, who rehearsed their ill-natured stories with her. She encouraged them in racial innuendo; the memsahib lapping at the double peg in her glass. A month before she had been sidling up to a Malay and probably planning to take out citizenship; now she was in a high-backed Malacca chair under a fan calling out, 'Boy!'

There was, so far, no trial. Ibrahim the Prince was languishing in the Central Jail, while the lawyers collected evidence. But they hadn't extracted a confession from him, and that was the most unusual feature of the whole business, since even an innocent man would own up simply to get a night's sleep. The Ayer Hitam police were not noted for their gentleness with suspects.

One night at the Club Miss Clem spoke to me in her new actressy voice. 'I want to thank you for all you've done. I'm glad it's over.'

'You're welcome,' I said, 'but I'm afraid it's not over yet. There's still the trial. You won't like that.'

'I hope you'll be there to give me moral support.'

'I don't like circuses,' I said. 'But if there's anything useful I can do, let me know.'

The following week she had a different story, a different voice. She entered the Consulate as she had that first time, pushing my staff aside and bursting into my office. She had been crying, and I could see she was out of breath.

'You're not going to believe this,' she said. Not the memsahib now, but that other voice of complaint, the innocent surprised. She sat down. 'It happened again.'

'Another break-in?'

'I was raped,' she said softly.

'The Prince is in jail,' I said in gentle contradiction.

'I'm telling you I was raped!' she shouted, and I was sure she could be heard all the way to the Club.

'Well, who do you suppose could have done it?'

She said nothing; she lowered her eyes and sniffed.

'Tell me, Miss Clem,' I said, 'does this sort of thing happen to you often?'

'What do you mean "often"?'

'Do you find that when you're alone, in a strange place, people get it in their heads to rape you? Perhaps you have something that drives men wild, some hidden attraction.'

'You don't believe me. I knew you wouldn't.'

'It seems rather extraordinary.'

'It happened again. I'm not making it up.' Then she pulled the top of her dress across one shoulder and showed me, just below her shoulder bone, a plum-colored bruise. I looked closer and saw circling it were the stitch-marks of a full set of teeth.

'You should have that seen to,' I said.

'I want that man caught,' she insisted.

'I thought we *had* caught him.'

'So did I.'

'So it wasn't The Prince?'

'I don't know,' she said.

'Was it the same man as before?'

'Yes, just like before. He was terrible – he laughed.'

And her story was the same, even the same image as before, about him picking her legs up 'like a wheelbarrow,' a rather chilling caricature of sexuality. Truth is not a saga of alarming episodes; it is a detail, a small clear one, that gives a fiction life. Hers was that horrible item, unusual enough to be a fact and too bizarre to be made up, about the slippery skin of the rapist. He was greasy, slimy – his whole body gleamed. She couldn't fight against him; she couldn't get a grip on him. He had appeared in her room and pounced on her, and she was helpless. This time she said she had resisted and it was only by biting on her that he held on.

I said, 'You'll have to drop your charges against The Prince.'

'I'm afraid to.'

'But don't you see? He's in jail, and if it was the same man as before then it couldn't have been The Prince.'

'I don't know what to do.'

'I suggest you get a telephone installed in your house. If you hear any suspicious noises, ring me or the police. Obviously it's some local person who fancies you.'

But The Prince was not released. Somehow the police had extracted a confession from him, a date was set for the trial and Miss Clem was scheduled to testify. That was weeks away. In the meantime, Miss Clem had her telephone put in. She rang me one evening shortly afterward.

'Is there anything wrong?' I asked, hearing her voice.

'Everything's fine,' she said. 'I was just testing it.'

'From now on only ring me in the event of an emergency,' I said.

'I think I'm going to be all right,' she said, and rang off.

For a brief period I forgot about Miss Clem, the Flower of Malaya. I had enough to keep me busy – visa matters were a continual headache. It was about this time that the Strangs got their divorce – which is another story – but the speculation at the

Club, up to then concerned with Miss Clem, was centered on what Milly Strang could possibly be doing in Bali. She had sent a gleeful postcard to Angela, but nothing to Lloyd. Miss Clem dropped from view.

My opposite number came down from Penang on a private visit and we had a little reception for him. The invitation specified 'drinks 6–8 P.M.' but at eleven there were still people on the verandah badgering the waiters for fresh drinks. My reaction was tactical: I went into my study and read the cables. Usually it worked – when the host disappears the guests are at sea; they get worried and invariably they take the hint.

The telephone rang. I was not quick and when I picked up the receiver the line went dead. At first I did nothing; then I remembered and was out the door.

Peeraswami had been helping out at the party. As I rushed out the back door I noticed him at the edge of the courtyard, chatting to the kitchen staff. I called to him and told him to get into the car. On the way I explained where we were going, but I did not say why.

Miss Clem's house was in the teachers' compound of the mission school. It was in darkness. I jammed on the brakes and jumped out. Peeraswami was right behind me. From the bungalow I could hear Miss Clem sobbing.

'Go around back,' I said to Peeraswami. 'In those trees. If you see anyone, catch him!'

Peeraswami sprinted away. I went into the house and stumbled in the direction of the sobbing. Miss Clem was alone, sitting on the edge of the bed. I switched on the light and saw her sad fat body on the rumpled bedclothes. She had an odd shine, a gloss on her skin that was lit like a snail's track. But it covered her stomach; it was too viscous to be perspiration and it had the smell of jungle. She was smeared with it, and though she seemed too dazed to notice it, it was like nothing I had ever seen before. She lay down sobbing and pulled a sheet over her.

'It was him,' she said.

'The Prince?'

'No, no! Poor Ibrahim,' she sobbed.

'Take a bath,' I said. 'You can come back to my house when you've changed.'

'Where are you going?'

'I've got to find my *peon*.'

I found him hurrying back to the house. In the best of times he had a strange face, his dark skin and glittering teeth, his close-set eyes and on his forehead a thumbprint of ashes, the Eye of God. He was terrified – not a rare thing in Peeraswami, but terror on that Tamil face was enough to frighten anyone else.

'*Tuan*!' he cried.

'Did you see him?'

'Yes, yes,' he said. 'He had no clothings, no shirtings. Bare-naked!'

'Well, why the hell didn't you catch him?' I snapped.

'*Tuan*,' said Peeraswami, 'no one can catch *Orang Minyak*.'

'You knew him?'

'Everyone know him.'

'I don't understand,' I said. '*Orang* is man. But *Minyak* – is that a name?'

'It his name. *Minyak* – oily, like ghee butter on his body. You try but you cannot catch hold. He trouble the girls, only the girls at night. But he Malay spirit – not Indian, *Malay*,' said Peeraswami, as if disclaiming any responsibility for another race's demons.

An incubus, I thought. What a fate for the Flower of Malaya. Peeraswami lingered. He could see I was angry he hadn't caught *Orang Minyak*. And even then I only half-believed.

'Well, you did your best,' I said, and reached out to shake his hand. I squeezed and his hand shot away from mine, and then my own hand was slippery, slick, and smelling of jungle decay.

'I touch, but I do not catch,' said Peeraswami. He stooped and began wiping his palms on the grass. 'You see? No one can catch *Orang Minyak*.'

The Autumn Dog

'Mine used to sweat in his sleep,' said the woman in the white dress, a bit drunkenly. 'It literally poured off him! During the day he'd be dry as a bone, but as soon as he closed his eyes, bingo, he'd start percolating.'

Her name was Maxine Stanhope and practically the first thing she had said to the woman who sat opposite was, 'Please call me Max, all my friends do.' They sat on the verandah of a hotel outside Denpasar, in Bali, in the sun the other tourists avoided. They had dark reptilian tans and slouched languorously in the comfortable chairs like lizards sunning themselves on a rock. Lunch was over, the wine was gone, their voices were raised in emphatic friendliness. They had known each other for only three hours.

'Mine didn't sweat that much, but he made the most fantastic noises,' said Milly Strang. 'He carried on these mumbling monologues, using different voices, and groaning and sort of swallowing. Sometimes I'd wake up and just look at him and laugh.'

'It's not funny,' said Maxine. But she was laughing; she was the larger of the two, and sharp-featured, her hair tugged back and fitting her head closely. There was a male's growl of satisfaction in her laugh, not the high mirth you would have expected from that quick, companionable mouth. 'When I remember the things he put me through, I think I must have been crazy. Mine made me warm his cup. I should have broken it over his head.'

'Mine had this way of pawing me when he was feeling affectionate. He was really quite strong. He left bruises! I suppose he thought he was – what's the expression? – turning me on.'

'They always think that,' said Maxine. She held the empty wine bottle over the other's glass until a drop fell out. 'Let's have another – wine makes me honest.'

'I've had quite enough,' said Milly.

'You're the boss,' said Maxine. Then she said, 'Mine weighed two hundred pounds.'

'Well, mine was at least that. I'm not exaggerating. When I think of him on top of me – it's ludicrous.'

'It's obscene. Mine kept gaining weight, and finally I said to him, "Look, if this goes on anymore we won't be able to make love." Not that *that* worried me. By then I'd already taken a lover – not so much a lover as a new way of life. But Erwin said it didn't matter whether you were fat or thin. If you were fat you'd just find a new position.'

'The fat man's position!'

'Exactly. And he got this – this manual. All the positions were listed, with little diagrams and arrows. Arrows! It was like fitting a plug, an electrical manual for beginners. "Here," he said, "I think that one would suit us." They all had names – I forget what that one was, but it was the fat man's position. Can you imagine?'

'Mine had manuals. Well, he called them manuals. They were Swedish I think. You must have seen them. Interesting and disgusting at the same time. He didn't want me to see them – I mean, he hid them from me. Then I found them and he caught me going through them. Honestly, I think I gave him quite a shock. He looked over my shoulder. "Ever see anything like it?" he said. I could hear him breathing heavily. He was getting quite a thrill!'

'Did yours make a fuss over the divorce?'

'No,' said Milly, 'what about yours?'

'*He* divorced *me*. Nothing in particular – just a whole series of things. But, God, what a messy business. It dragged on for months and months.'

'Mine was over before I knew it.'

'Lucky,' said Maxine.

'Up till then we'd been fairly happy.'

'Happy marriages so-called turn into really messy divorces,' said Maxine.

'I think not,' said Milly. 'The best marriages end quickly.'

Theirs, the Strangs', had gone on serenely for years, filling us with envious contempt. It fell to pieces in an afternoon of astonishing abuse. They had pretended politeness for so long only an afternoon was necessary. Then we were friendlier toward the couple, no longer a couple, but Milly alone in the house and Lloyd at the Club. The marriages in Ayer Hitam were no frailer than anywhere else, but we expatriates knew each other well and enjoyed a kind of kinship. A divorce was like a death in the family. Threatened with gloom, we became thoughtful. The joking was nervous: Milly had burned the toast; Lloyd had made a pass at the *amah*. Afterward, Lloyd clung to the town. He was overrehearsed. One of his lines went, 'It was our ages. Out of the horse latitudes and into the roaring forties.' He was no sailor; he was taking it badly.

Milly, unexpectedly cheerful, packed her bags and left the compound. Within a week she was in Indonesia. Before she left she had said to Angela Miller, 'I always wanted to go to Bali. Lloyd wouldn't let me.' She went, Lloyd stayed, and it looked as if he expected her back: her early return to Ayer Hitam would have absolved him of all blame.

It did not happen that way. Before long, we all knew her story. Milly saw friends in Djakarta. The friends were uneasy with this divorced woman in their house. They sent their children out to play and treated her the way they might have treated a widow, with a mixture of somberness and high spirits, fearing the whole time that she'd drink too much and burst into tears. Milly found their hospitality exhausting and went to Djokjakarta, for the temples. Though tourists (seeing her eating alone) asked her to join them, she politely refused. How could she explain that she liked eating alone and reading in bed and waking when she wished and doing nothing? Life was so simple, and marriage only a complication. Marriage also implied a place: you were married and lived in a particular house; unmarried, you lived in the world, and there were no answers required of you. Milly changed her status slowly, regaining an earlier state of girlishness from the widowhood of divorce. Ten years was returned to her, and more than that, she saw herself granted a valuable enlightenment, she was wiser and unencumbered, she was free.

The hotel in Bali, which would have been unthinkably expensive for a couple with a land surveyor's income, was really very cheap for one person. She told the manager (Swiss, married – she could tell at a glance) she would stay a month. There was a column in the hotel register headed *Destination*. She left it blank. The desk clerk indicated this. 'I haven't got one,' she said, and she surprised the man with her natural laugh.

The tourists, the three-day guests at the hotel, the ones with planes to catch were middle-aged; some were elderly, some infirm, making this trip at the end of their lives. But there were other visitors in Bali and they were mostly young. They looked to Milly like innocent witches and princelings. They slept on the beach, cooked over fires, played guitars; she saw them strolling barefoot or eating mountains of food or lazing in the sand. There was not a sign of damage on them. She envied them their youth. For a week Milly swam in the hotel's pool, had a nap after lunch, took her first drink at six and went to bed early: it was like a spell of convalescence, and when she saw she had established this routine she was annoyed. One night, drinking in the bar, she was joined by an Australian. He talked about his children in the hurt remote way of a divorced man. At midnight, Milly stood up and snapped her handbag shut. The man said, 'You're not going, are you?'

'I've paid for my share of the drinks,' she said. 'Was there something you wanted?'

But she knew, and she smiled at the fumbling man, almost pitying him.

'Perhaps I'll see you tomorrow,' she said, and was gone.

She left the hotel, crossed by the pool to the beach, and walked toward a fire. It was the makeshift camp of the young people and there they sat, around the fire, singing. She hesitated to go near and she believed that she could not be seen standing in that darkness, listening to the music. But a voice said, 'Hey! Come over here, stranger!'

She went over, and seating herself in the sand, saw the strumming boy. But her joining the group was not acknowledged. The youths sat crosslegged, like monks at prayer, facing the fire and the music. How many times, on a beach or by a roadside, had she seen groups like this and, almost alarmed, looked away! Even now she felt like an impostor. Someone might ask her age and laugh when she disclosed it. She wished she was not wearing such expensive slacks; she wished she looked like these people – and she hoped they would not remind her of her difference. She was glad for the dark.

Someone moved behind her. She started to rise, but he reached out and steadied her with his arm and hugged her. She relaxed and let him hold her. In the firelight she saw his face: twenty years old! She put her head against his shoulder and he adjusted his grip to hold her closer. And she trembled – for the first time since leaving Ayer Hitam – and wondered how she could stop herself from rolling him over on the sand and devouring him. Feeling that hunger, she grew afraid and said she had to go: she didn't want to startle the boy.

'I'll walk you back to the hotel,' he said.

'I can find the way.' Her voice was insistent; she didn't want to lose control.

The boy tagged along, she heard him trampling the sand; she wanted him to act – but how? Throw her down, fling off her clothes, make love to her? It was mad. Then it was too late, the hotel lights illuminated the beach; and she was relieved it had not happened. *I must be careful* – she almost spoke it.

'Will I see you again?'

'Perhaps,' she said. She was on her own ground: the white hotel loomed behind the palms. Now – here – it was the boy who was the stranger.

'I want to sleep with you.' It was not arrogant but imploring.

'Not now.'

Not now. It should have been *no*. But marriage taught you how to be perfunctory, and Milly had, as a single woman, regained a lazy sense of hope. *No* was the prudent answer, *Not now* was what she had wanted to say – so she had said it. And the next day the boy was back, peering from the beach at Milly, who lounged by the pool. In the sunlight he looked even younger, with a shyness that might have been an effect of the sun's brightness, making him hunch and avert his eyes. He did not know where to begin, she saw that.

Milly waved to him. He signaled back and like an obedient pet responding to a mistress's nod came forward, vaulted the hibiscus hedge, smiling. Instead of taking the chair next to her he crouched at her feet, seeming to hide himself.

'They won't send you away,' said Milly. 'You can say you're my guest.'

The boy shrugged. 'At night – after everyone clears out – we come here swimming.' He was silent, then he said, 'Naked.'

'How exciting,' said Milly, frowning.

Seeing that it was mockery, the boy did not reply. He got to his feet. For a moment, Milly thought he was going to bound over the hedge and leave her. But in a series of athletic motions he strode to the edge of the pool, and without pausing tipped himself into it. He swam under water and Milly followed his blue shorts to the far end of the pool where he surfaced like a hound, gasping and tossing his head. He returned, swimming powerfully, flinging his arms into the water. But he did not climb out of the pool; he rested his forearms on the tiles and said, 'Come in. I'll teach you how to swim.'

'I was swimming before you were born.' She wished she had not said it, she wished it was not true. She picked up a magazine from her lap and plucked at a page.

The boy was beside her, dripping.

'Take this,' she said, and handed him a towel. He buried his face in it with an energy that aroused her, then he wiped his arms and threw it aside.

'Time for lunch,' said Milly.

'Let me treat you,' said the boy.

'That's very thoughtful of you,' said Milly, 'but I'm afraid they won't let you in the dining room like that.'

'They have room service. We can have it sent up – eat on the balcony.'

'You seem to be inviting yourself to my room,' said Milly.

'No,' said the boy, 'I'm inviting you to mine.'

Milly almost laughed. She said, '*Here?*'

'Sure. I've been here for about six weeks.'

'I've never seen you at breakfast.'

'I never eat breakfast,' said the boy. 'And I've only used my room a few times in the past week or so. I met a girl over on the beach – they have a house there. But my stuff is still in my room. My money, camera, passport, watch – the rest of it. I don't want it stolen.'

'It must be fearfully expensive.'

'My mother pays.'

'How very American.'

'She's on a tour – in Hong Kong,' said the boy. 'I thought we were talking about lunch.'

'If you're a guest at this hotel, then you must have other clothes here. I suggest you dress properly, and if there's an empty chair at my table I have no objection to your joining me.' Her voice, that fastidious tone, surprised and appalled her.

The boy's name was Mark. He told her that over lunch, but he said very little else. He was so young there was practically nothing he could say about himself beyond his name, and it was for Milly to keep the conversation going. It was not easy in her new voice. She described her trip through Indonesia, everything that had happened to her since leaving Ayer Hitam, but after that she was stumped. She would not speak about Lloyd or the divorce, and it angered her that it was impossible to speak about her life without discussing her marriage. Nearly twenty years had to be suppressed, and it seemed as if nothing had happened in those years that could matter to this young boy.

To his timid questions she said, 'You wouldn't understand.' She was hard on him. She knew why: she wanted him in the simplest way, and she resented wanting him. She objected to that desire in herself that would not allow her to go on alone. She did not want to look foolish – the age difference was ridicule enough – and wondered if in shrinking from an involvement she would reject him. She feared having him, she feared losing him. He told her he was nineteen and eagerly added the date of his next birthday.

Milly said, 'Time for my nap.'

'See you later, then,' said Mark. He shook her hand.

In her room, she cursed herself. It had not occurred to her that he might not be interested. But perhaps this was so. He had a girl, one of the innocent witches; but her fate was the Australian who, late at night, rattled the change in his pocket and drawled for a persuasive way to interest her. She pulled the curtains, shutting out the hot sun, and for the first time since she arrived lay down on her bed wondering not if she should go, but where.

She closed her eyes and heard a knock on the door. She got out of bed, sighed, and opened the door a crack. 'What is it?'

'Let me come in,' said Mark. 'Please.'

She stared and said nothing. Then she moved aside and let the boy swing the door open. He did this with unnecessary force, as if he had expected her to resist.

Milly had not written any letters. A few postcards, a message about the weather. Letters were an effort because letters required either candor or wit, and her solitary existence had hardened her to both. What Milly had done, almost since the hour she had left Ayer Hitam, was rehearse conversations with an imaginary friend, a woman, for whom in anecdote she would describe the pleasures of divorce. Flying alone. The looks you got in hotels. The Australian. A room of one's own. The witches and princelings on the beach. Misunderstandings. The suspicious eyes of other men's wives. The mystery and the aroma of sexuality a single woman carried past mute strangers.

Listen, she imagined herself saying; then she reported, assessed, justified. It was a solitary traveler's habit, one enforced by her separation from Lloyd. She saw herself leaning over a large menu, in the racket of a restaurant – flowers on the table, two napkin cones, a dish of olives – and she heard her own voice: *I think a nineteen-year-old boy and a woman of – let's be frank – forty-one – I think they're perfectly matched, sexually speaking. Yes, I really do. They're at some kind of peak. That boy can have four or five orgasms in a row, but so can a middle-aged woman – given the chance. It's the middle-aged man with all his routines and apologies that makes the woman feel inadequate. Sex for a boy, granted, is usually a letdown because he's always trying himself out on a girl his age, and what could be duller? It hurts, Jim, and hurry up, and what if my parents find out? What I'm saying, and I don't think it's anything to be ashamed of, is Mark and I were well-matched, not in spite of our ages, but on the contrary, on the contrary. It was like coaching a champion. I know I was old enough to be his mother, but that's just the point. The age ratio isn't insignificant. Don't laugh – the boy of a certain age and his mother would make the best of lovers –*

But lovers was all they'd make. Conversation with Mark was impossible. He would say, 'I know a guy who has a fantastic yacht in Baltimore.'

A yacht. At the age of twenty-three, when Mark was one, Milly had driven her own car to the south of France and stayed with her uncle, a famous lawyer. That handsome man had taken her on his yacht, poured her champagne, and tried to seduce her. He had failed, and angrily steered the yacht close to the rocky shore, to scare her. Later he bought her an expensive ring, and in London took her to wonderful restaurants, treating her like his mistress. He renamed his yacht *Milly*. Lloyd knew part of the story. To Mark Milly said, 'I was on a yacht once, but I was much younger then.'

For three weeks, in her room, in his, and twice on the beach, they made love. They kissed openly and made no secret of the affair. The guests at the hotel might whisper, but they never stayed longer than a few days, and they took their disapproval away with them. Milly herself wondered sometimes what would happen to her when Mark left, and she grew anxious when she remembered that she would have to leave eventually. She had no destination; she stayed another month: it was now November, and before Christmas she would exhaust herself of this boy. She was not calculating, but she saw nothing further for him. The affair, so complete on this bright island, would fail anywhere else.

Mark spoke of college, of books he planned to read, of jobs he'd like to have. It was all a hopeful itinerary she had traced before: she'd made that trip years ago, she'd read the books and known all the stops. She felt – listening to him telling her nothing new – as if she'd returned from a long sojourn in the world, one on which he, encumbered with ambition, was just setting out. She smiled at his innocent plans, and she gave him some encouragement; she would not disappoint him and tell him he would find nothing. He never asked for advice; he was too young to know the questions. She could tell him a great deal, but youth was ignorance in a splendid body: he wouldn't listen.

'I want to marry you,' he said one day, and it sounded to Milly like the expression of a longing that could never be fulfilled, like saying, *If only I could marry you!*

'I want to marry you, too,' she said in the same way.

He kissed her and said, 'We could do it here, the way the Balinese do – with a feast, music, dancing.'

'I'll wear flowers in my hair.'

'Right,' he said. 'We'll go up to Ubud and –'

'Oh, God,' she said, 'you're serious.'

His face fell. He said, 'Aren't you?'

'I've been married,' she said, without enthusiasm, as she had once said to him, 'I've been to Monte Carlo,' implying that the action could not possibly be repeated.

'I've got lots of money,' he said.

'Spend it wisely.' It was the closest she had ever come to giving him advice.

'It would make things easier for us.'

'This is as easy as it can ever be,' she said. 'Anyway, it's your mother's money, so stop talking this way. We can't get married and that's that.'

'You don't have to marry me,' he said. 'Come to the States – we'll live together.'

'And then what?

'We'll drive around.'

'What about your college – all those plans of yours?'

'They don't matter.'

'Drive around!' She laughed hard at the thought of them in a car, speeding down a road, not stopping. Could anything short of marriage itself be a more boring exertion than that? He looked quite excited by the prospect of driving in circles.

'What's wrong?'

'I'm a bit old for that sort of thing.'

'We can do anything you want – anything,' he said. 'Just live with me. No strings. Look, we can't stay here forever –'

It was true: she had nowhere to go. Milly was not fool enough to believe that it could work for any length of time, but for a month or two it might be fun. Then somewhere else, alone, to make a real start.

'We'll see,' she said.

'Smile,' he said.

She did and said, 'What would you tell your mother?'

'I've already told her.'

'No! What did she say?'

'She wants to meet you.'

'Perhaps – one day.' But the very thought of it filled her with horror.

'Soon,' he said. 'I wrote to her in Hong Kong. She replied from Bangkok. She'll be here in a week or so.'

'Mine was so pathetic when I left him,' Milly was saying. 'I almost felt sorry for him. Now I can't stand the thought of him.'

'As time goes on,' said Maxine, 'you'll hate him more and more.' Abstractedly, she said, 'I can't bear them to touch me.'

'No,' said Milly, 'I don't think I could ever hate –'

Maxine laughed. 'I just thought of it!'

'What?'

'The position my husband suggested. It was called "The Autumn Dog." Chinese, I think. You do it backward. It was impossible, of course – and grotesque, like animals in the bushes. He accused me of not trying – and guess what he said?'

'Backward!'

'He said, "Max, it might save our marriage"!'

It struck Milly that there were only a few years – seconds in the life of the world – when that futile sentence had meaning. The years had coincided with her own marriage, but she had endured them and, like Maxine, earned her freedom. She had borne marriage long enough to see it disproved.

'But it didn't save it – it couldn't,' said Maxine. Her face darkened. She said, 'He was evil. He wanted Mark. But Mark wouldn't have him – he was devoted to me.'

'Mark is a nice boy.'

Maxine said, 'Mark is lovely.'

'At first I was sorry he told you about me. I was afraid to meet you. I thought you'd dislike me.'

'But you're not marrying him, are you?'

'I couldn't,' said Milly. 'Anyway, I'm through with marriage.'

'Good,' said Maxine. 'The Autumn Dog.'

'And Max,' said Milly, using the woman's name for the first time, 'I don't want you for a mother-in-law!'

'No – we'll be friends.'

'What a pity I'm leaving here.'

'Then we must leave together.'

And the other woman's replies had come so quickly that Milly heard herself agreeing to a day, a flight, a destination.

'Poor Mark,' said Milly at last.

'He's a lovely boy,' said Maxine. 'You have no idea. We go to plays together. He reads to me. I buy all his clothes. I like to be seen with him. Having a son like Mark is so much better than having a husband.'

Milly felt the woman staring at her. She dropped her eyes.

'Or a friend like you,' said Maxine. 'That's much better. He told me all about you – he's very frank. He made me jealous, but that was silly, wasn't it? I think you're a very kind person.'

She reached across the table. She took Milly's fingers and squeezed.

'If you're kind to me we'll be such good friends.'

'Please stop!' Milly wanted to say. The other woman was hurting her hand with the pressure of her rings, and she seemed to smile at the panic on Milly's face. Finally, Milly said it, and another fear made the demand into a plea. Maxine relaxed her grip, but she held on, even after Mark appeared at the agreed time, to hear the verdict.

Dengué Fever

There is a curious tree, native to Malaysia, called 'The Midnight Horror.' We had several in Ayer Hitam, one in an overgrown part of the Botanical Gardens, the other in the front garden of William Ladysmith's house. His house was huge, nearly as grand as mine, but I was the American Consul and Ladysmith was an English teacher on a short contract. I assumed it was the tree that had brought the value of his house down. The house itself had been built before the war – one of those great breezy places, a masterpiece of colonial carpentry, with cement walls two feet thick and window blinds the size of sails on a Chinese junk. It was said that it had been the center of operations during the occupation. All this history diminished by a tree! In fact, no local person would go near the house; the Chinese members of the staff at Ladysmith's school chose to live in that row of low warrens near the bus depot.

During the day the tree looked comic, a tall simple pole like an enormous coatrack, with big leaves that looked like branches – but there were very few of them. It was covered with knobs, stark black things; and around the base of the trunk there were always fragments of leaves that looked like shattered bones, but not human bones.

At night the tree was different, not comic at all. It was Ladysmith who showed me the underlined passage in his copy of Professor Corner's *Wayside Trees of Malaya*. Below the entry for *Oroxylum indicum* it read, 'Botanically, it is the sole representative of its kind; aesthetically, it is monstrous . . . The corolla begins to open about 10 P.M., when the tumid, wrinkled lips part and the harsh odour escapes from them. By midnight, the lurid mouth gapes widely and is filled with stink . . . The flowers are pollinated by bats which are attracted by the smell and, holding to the fleshy corolla with the claws on their wings, thrust their noses into its throat; scratches, as of bats, can be seen on the fallen leaves the next morning . . .'

Smelly! Ugly! Pollinated by bats! I said, 'No wonder no one wants to live in this house.'

'It suits me fine,' said Ladysmith. He was a lanky fellow, very pleasant, one of our uncomplicated Americans who thrive in bush postings. He cycled around in his bermuda shorts, organizing talent shows in *kampongs*. His description in my consulate file was 'Low risk, high gain.' Full of enthusiasm and blue-eyed belief; and open-hearted: he was forever having tea with tradesmen, whose status was raised as soon as he crossed the threshold.

Ladysmith didn't come round to the Club much, although he was a member and had appeared in the Footlighters' production of Maugham's *The Letter*. I think he disapproved of us. He was young, one of the Vietnam generation with a punished conscience and muddled notions of colonialism. That war created dropouts, but Ladysmith I took to be one of the more constructive ones, a volunteer teacher. After the cease-fire there were fewer; now there are none, neither hippies nor do-gooders. Ladysmith was delighted to take his guilt to Malaysia, and he once told me that Ayer Hitam was more lively than his home-town, which surprised me until he said he was from Caribou, Maine.

He was tremendously popular with his students. He had put up a backboard and basketball hoop in the playground and after school he taught them the fundamentals of the game. He was, for all his apparent awkwardness, an athletic fellow, though it didn't show until he was in action – jumping or dribbling a ball down the court. Perhaps it never does. He ate like a horse, and knowing he lived alone I made a point of inviting him often to dinners for visiting firemen from Kuala Lumpur or Singapore. He didn't have a cook; he said he would not have a servant, but I don't believe he would have got any local person to live in his house, so close to that grotesque tree.

I was sorry but not surprised, two months after he arrived, to hear that Ladysmith had a fever. Ayer Hitam was malarial, and the tablets we took every Sunday like communion were only sup-pressants. The Chinese headmaster at the school stopped in at the Consulate and said that Ladysmith wanted to see me. I went that afternoon.

The house was empty; a few chairs in the sitting room, a shelf of paperbacks, a short-wave radio, and in the room beyond a table holding only a large bottle of ketchup. The kitchen smelled of peanut butter and stale bread. Bachelor's quarters. I climbed the stairs, but before I entered the bedroom I heard Ladysmith call out in an anxious voice, 'Who is it?'

'Boy, am I glad to see you,' he said, relaxing as I came through the door.

He looked thinner, his face was gray, his hair awry in bunches of standing hackles; and he lay in the rumpled bed as if he had been thrown there. His eyes were sunken and oddly colored with the yellow light of fever.

'Malaria?'

'I think so – I've been taking chloroquine. But it doesn't seem to be working. I've got the most awful headache.' He closed his eyes. 'I can't sleep. I have these nightmares. I –'

'What does the doctor say?'

'I'm treating myself,' said Ladysmith.

'You'll kill yourself,' I said. 'I'll send Alec over tonight.'

We talked for a while, and eventually I convinced Ladysmith that he needed attention. Alec Stewart was a club member Ladysmith particularly disliked. He wasn't a bad sort, but as he was married to a Chinese girl he felt he could call them 'Chinks' without blame. He had been a ship's surgeon in the Royal Navy and had come to Ayer Hitam after the war. With a young wife and all that sunshine he was able to reclaim some of his youth. Back at the office I sent Peeraswami over with a pot of soup and the latest issue of *Newsweek* from the consulate library.

Alec went that night. I saw him at the Club later. He said, 'Our friend's pretty rocky.'

'I had malaria myself,' I said. 'It wasn't much fun.'

Alex blew a cautionary snort. 'He's not got malaria. He's got dengué.'

'Are you sure?'

'All the symptoms are there.'

'What did you give him for it?'

'The only thing there is worth a docken – aspirin.'

'I suppose he'll have to sweat it out.'

'He'll do that all right.' Alec leaned over. 'The lad's having hallucinations.'

'I didn't know that was a symptom of dengué,' I said.

'Dengué's a curse.'

He described it to me. It is a virus, carried by a mosquito, and begins as a headache of such voltage that you tremble and can't stand or sit. You're knocked flat; your muscles ache, you're doubled-up with cramp and your temperature stays over a hundred. Then your skin becomes paper-thin, sensitive to the slightest touch – the weight of a sheet can cause pain. And your hair falls out – not all of it, but enough to fill a comb. These severe irritations produce another agony, a depression so black the dengué sufferer continually sobs. All the while your bones ache, as if every inch of you has been smashed with a hammer. This sensation of bruising gives dengué its colloquial name, 'breakbone fever.' I pitied Ladysmith.

Although it was after eleven when Alec left the Club, I went straight over to Ladysmith's house. I was walking up the gravel drive when I heard the most ungodly shriek – frightening in its intensity and full of alarm. I did not recognize it as Ladysmith's – indeed, it scarcely sounded human. But it was coming from his room. It was so loud and changed in pitch with such suddenness it might easily have been two or three people screaming, or a dozen doomed cats. The Midnight Horror tree was in full bloom and filled the night with stink.

Ladysmith lay in bed whimpering. The magazine I'd sent him was tossed against the wall, and the effect of disorder was heightened by the overhead fan which was lifting and ruffling the pages.

He was propped on one arm, but seeing me he sighed and fell back. His face was slick with perspiration and tear-streaks. He was short of breath.

'Are you all right?'

'My skin is burning,' he said. I noticed his lips were swollen and cracked with fever, and I saw then how dengué was like a species of grief.

'I thought I heard a scream,' I said. Screaming takes energy; Ladysmith was beyond screaming, I thought.

'Massacre,' he said. 'Soldiers – killing women and children. Horrible. Over there –' He pointed to a perfectly ordinary table with a jug of water on it, and he breathed, 'War. You should see their faces, all covered with blood. Some have arms missing. I've never –' He broke off and began to sob.

'Alec says you have dengué fever,' I said.

'Two of them – women. They look the same,' said Ladysmith, lifting his head. 'They scream at me, and it's so loud! They have no teeth!'

'Are you taking the aspirin?' I saw the amber jar was full.

'Aspirin! For this!' He lay quietly, then said, 'I'll be all right. Sometimes it's nothing – just a high temperature. Then these Chinese . . . then I get these dreams.'

'About war?'

'Yes. Flashes.'

As gently as I could I said, 'You didn't want to go to Vietnam, did you?'

'No. Nobody wanted to go. I registered as a CO.'

Hallucinations are replies. Peeraswami was always seeing Tamil ghosts on his way home. They leaped from those green fountains by the road the Malays call *daun pontianak* – 'ghost leaf' – surprising him with plates of hot samosas or tureens of curry; not so much ghosts as ghostesses. I told him to eat something before setting out from home in the dark and he stopped seeing them. I took Ladysmith's visions of massacre to be replies to his conscientious objection. It is the draft-dodger who speaks most graphically of war, not the soldier. Pacifists know all the atrocity stories.

But Ladysmith's hallucinations had odd highlights: the soldiers he saw weren't American. They were dark orientals in dirty undershirts, probably Vietcong, and mingled with the screams of the people with bloody faces was another sound, the creaking of bicycle seats. So there were two horrors – the massacre and these phantom cyclists. He was especially frightened by the two women with no teeth, who opened their mouths wide and screamed at him.

I said, 'Give it a few days.'

'I don't think I can take much more of this.'

'Listen,' I said. 'Dengué can depress you. You'll feel like giving up and going home – you might feel like hanging yourself. But take these aspirin and keep telling yourself – whenever you get these nightmares – it's dengué fever.'

'No teeth, and their gums are dripping with blood –'

His head dropped to the pillow, his eyes closed, and I remember thinking: everyone is fighting this war, everyone in the world. Poor Ladysmith was fighting hardest of all. Lying there he could have been bivouacked in the Central Highlands, haggard from a siege, his dengué a version of battle fatigue.

I left him sleeping and walked again through the echoing house. But the smell had penetrated to the house itself, the high thick stink of rotting corpses. It stung my eyes and I almost fainted with the force of it until, against the moon, I saw that blossoming coatrack and the wheeling bats – The Midnight Horror.

'Rotting flesh,' Ladysmith said late the next afternoon. I tried not to smile. I had brought Alec along for a second look. Ladysmith began describing the smell, the mutilated people, the sound of bicycles, and those Chinese women, the toothless ones. The victims had pleaded with him. Ladysmith looked wretched.

Alec said, 'How's your head?'

'It feels like it's going to explode.'

Alec nodded. 'Joints a bit stiff?'

'I can't move.'

'Dengué's a curse.' Alec smiled: doctors so often do when their grim diagnosis is proved right.

'*I can't* –' Ladysmith started, then grimaced and continued in a softer tone. 'I can't sleep. If I could only sleep I'd be all right. For God's sake give me something to make me sleep.'

Alec considered this.

'Can't you give him anything?' I asked.

'I've never prescribed a sleeping pill in my life,' said Alec, 'and I'm not going to do so now. Young man, take my advice. Drink lots of liquid – you're dehydrating. You've got a severe fever. Don't underestimate it. It can be a killer. But I guarantee if you follow my instructions, get lots of bed rest, take aspirin every four hours, you'll be right as ninepence.'

'My hair is falling out.'

Alex smiled – right again. 'Dengué,' he said. 'But you've still got plenty. When you've as little hair as I have you'll have something to complain about.'

Outside the house I said, 'That tree is the most malignant thing I've ever seen.'

Alec said, 'You're talking like a Chink.'

'Sure, it looks innocent enough now, with the sun shining on it. But have you smelled it at night?'

'I agree. A wee aromatic. Like a Bengali's fart.'

'If we cut it down I think Ladysmith would stop having his nightmares.'

'Don't be a fool. That tree's medicinal. The Malays use it for potions. It works – I use it myself.'

'Well, if it's so harmless why don't the Malays want to live in this house?'

'It's not been offered to a Malay. How many Malay teachers do you know? It's the Chinks won't live here – I don't have a clue why that's so, but I won't have you running down that tree. It's going to cure our friend.'

I stopped walking. 'What do you mean by that?'

Alec said, 'The aspirin – or rather, not the aspirin. I'm using native medicine. Those tablets are made from the bark of that tree – I wish it didn't have that shocking name.'

'You're giving him *that*?'

'Calm down, it'll do him a world of good,' Alex said brightly. 'Ask any witch doctor.'

I slept badly myself that night, thinking of Alec's ridiculous cure – he had truly gone bush – but I was tied up all day with visa inquiries and it was not until the following evening that I got back to Ladysmith's. I was determined to take him away. I had aspirin at my house; I'd keep him away from Alec.

Downstairs, I called out and knocked as usual to warn him I'd come, and as usual there was no response from him. I entered the bedroom and saw him asleep, but uncovered. Perhaps the fever had passed: his face was dry. He did not look well, but then few people do when they're sound asleep – most take on the ghastly color of illness. Then I saw that the amber bottle was empty – the 'aspirin' bottle.

I tried to feel his pulse. Impossible: I've never been able to feel a person's pulse, but his hand was cool, almost cold. I put my ear against his mouth and thought I could detect a faint purr of respiration.

It was dusk when I arrived, but darkness in Ayer Hitam fell quickly, the blanket of night dropped and the only warning was the sound of insects tuning up, the chirrup of geckoes and those squeaking bats making for the tree. I switched on the lamp and as I did so heard a low cry, as of someone dying in dreadful pain. And there by the window – just as Ladysmith had described – I saw the moonlit faces of two Chinese women, smeared with blood. They opened their mouths and howled; they were toothless and their screeches seemed to gain volume from that emptiness.

'Stop!' I shouted.

The two faces in those black rags hung there, and I caught the whiff of the tree which was the whiff of wounds. It should have scared me, but it only surprised me. Ladysmith had prepared me, and I felt certain that he had passed that horror on. I stepped forward, caught the cord, and dropped the window blinds. The two faces were gone.

This took seconds, but an after-image remained, like a lamp switched rapidly on and off. I gathered up Ladysmith. Having lost weight he was very light, pathetically so. I carried him downstairs and through the garden to the road.

Behind me, in the darkness, was the rattle of pedals, the squeak of a bicycle seat. The phantom cyclists! It gave me a shock, and I tried to run, but carrying Ladysmith I could not move quickly. The cycling noises approached, frantic squeakings at my back. I spun round.

It was a trishaw, cruising for fares. I put Ladysmith on the seat, and running alongside it we made our way to the mission hospital.

A stomach pump is little more than a slender rubber tube pushed into one nostril and down the back of the throat. A primitive device: I couldn't watch. I stayed until Ladysmith regained consciousness. But it was useless to talk to him. His stomach was empty and he was coughing up bile, spewing into a bucket. I told the nursing sister to keep an eye on him.

I said, 'He's got dengué.'

The succeeding days showed such an improvement in Ladysmith that the doctors insisted he be discharged to make room for more serious cases. And indeed everyone said he'd made a rapid recovery. Alec was astonished, but told him rather sternly, 'You should be ashamed of yourself for taking that overdose.'

Ladysmith was well, but I didn't have the heart to send him back to that empty house. I put him up at my place. Normally, I hated houseguests – they interfered with my reading and never seemed to have much to do themselves except punish my gin bottle. But Ladysmith was unobtrusive. He drank milk, he wrote letters home. He made no mention of his hallucinations, and I didn't tell him what I'd thought I'd seen. In my own case I believe his suggestions had been so strong that I had imagined what he had seen – somehow shared his own terror of the toothless women.

357

One day at lunch Ladysmith said, 'How about eating out tonight? On me. A little celebration. After all, you saved my life.'

'Do you feel well enough to face the club buffet?'

He made a face. 'I hate the Club – no offense. But I was thinking of a meal in town. What about that *kedai* – City Bar? I had a terrific meal there the week I arrived. I've been meaning to go back.'

'You're the boss.'

It was a hot night. The verandah tables were taken, so we had to sit inside, jammed against a wall. We ordered *meehoon* soup, spring rolls, pork strips, fried *kway-teow*, and a bowl of *laksa* that seemed to blister the lining of my mouth.

'One thing's for sure,' said Ladysmith, 'I won't get dengué fever again for a while. The sister said I'm immune for a year.'

'Thank God for that,' I said. 'By then you'll be back in Caribou, Maine.'

'I don't know,' he said. 'I like it here.'

He was smiling, glancing around the room, poking noodles into his mouth. Then I saw him lose control of his chopsticks. His jaw dropped, he turned pale, and I thought for a moment that he was going to cry.

'Is anything wrong?'

He shook his head, but he looked stricken.

'It's this food,' I said. 'You shouldn't be eating such strong –'

'No,' he said. 'It's those pictures.'

On the whitewashed wall of the *kedai* was a series of framed photographs, old hand-colored ones, lozenge-shaped, like huge lockets. Two women and some children. Not so unusual; the Chinese always have photographs of relations around – a casual reverence. One could hardly call them a pious people; their brand of religion is ancestor worship, the simple display of the family album. But I had not realized until then that Woo Boh Swee's relations had had money. The evidence was in the pictures: both women were smiling, showing large sets of gold dentures.

'That's them,' said Ladysmith.

'Who?' I said. Staring at them I noticed certain wrinkles of familiarity, but the Chinese are very hard to tell apart. The cliché is annoyingly true.

Ladysmith put his chopsticks down and began to whisper: 'The women in my room – that's *them*. That one had blood on her hair, and the other one –'

'Dengué fever,' I said. 'You said they didn't have any teeth. Now I ask you – look at those teeth. You've got the wrong ladies, my boy.'

'No!'

His pallor had returned, and the face I saw across the table was the one I had seen on that pillow. I felt sorry for him, and as helpless as I had before.

Woo Boh Swee, the owner of City Bar, went by the table. He was brisk, snapping a towel. 'Okay? Anything? More beer? What you want?'

'We're fine, Mr Woo,' I said. 'But I wonder if you can tell us something. We were wondering who those women are in the pictures – over there.'

He looked at the wall, grunted, lowered his head, and simply walked away, muttering.

'I don't get it,' I said. I left the table and went to the back of the bar, where Boh Swee's son Reggie – the 'English' son – was playing mahjong. I asked Reggie the same question: who are they?

'I'm glad you asked me,' said Reggie. 'Don't mention them to my father. One's his auntie, the other one's his sister. It's a sad story. They were cut up during the war by the dwarf bandits. That's what my old man calls them in Hokkien. The Japanese. It happened over at the headquarters – what they used for headquarters when they occupied the town. My old man was in Singapore.'

'But the Japanese were only here for a few months,' I said.

'Bunch of thieves,' said Reggie. 'They took anything they could lay their hands on. They used those old ladies for house girls, at the headquarters, that big house, where the tree is. Then they killed them, just like that, and hid the bodies – we never found the graves. But that was before they captured Singapore. The British couldn't stop them, you know. The dwarf bandits were clever – they pretended they were Chinese and rode all the way to the Causeway on bicycles.'

I looked back at the table. Ladysmith was staring, his eyes again bright with fever, staring at those gold teeth.

The South Malaysia Pineapple
Growers' Association

They had a drama society, but it was not called the South Malaysia Pineapple Growers' Drama Society; it was the Footlighters, it met on Wednesday evenings in the club lounge, and the official patron was the Sultan. He seldom came to the plays and never to the Club. It was just as well, the Footlighters said; when the Sultan was at the theater you couldn't drink at the bar between the acts, which was why most of the audience came, the men anyway. Angela Miller, who drove down from Layang Layang every Wednesday, said the Sultan was a frightful old bore whose single interest was polo.

An effortlessly deep-voiced woman, much more handsome at forty-five than she had been pretty at twenty, Angela had played a Wilde heroine six years before – that was in Kota Bharu – and found the role so agreeable, so suited to her temper, that in moments of stress she became that heroine; telling a story, she used the heroine's inflections and certain facial expressions, especially incredulity. Often it allowed her to manage her anger.

It was Angela who told the story of Jan's first visit to the Club. Jan had looked at the photographs on the wall of the bar and then sat in a lounge chair sipping her gimlet while the other members talked. Only Angela had seen Jan rush to the window and exclaim, 'What a *lovely* time of day!'

'All I could see were the tennis courts,' said Angela later, 'but little Jan said, "Look at the air – it's like *silk*."'

Jan Prosser was new, not only to the Club and the Footlighters, but to Ayer Hitam, where her husband, Rupert, had just been posted to cut down a rubber estate and oversee the planting of oil palms.

'Anyone,' said Angela, 'who spends that long looking out the window *has* to be new to Ayer Hitam. I look out the window and don't see a blessed thing!'

It had happened only the previous week. Already it was one of

Angela's stories; she had a story to explain the behavior of every Footlighter and, it was said, most planter families. That exclamation at sundown was all the Footlighters knew of Jan on the evening they met to pick a new play. She was a pale girl, perhaps twenty-six, with a small head and damp nervous eyes. Some of the male Footlighters had spoken to Jan's husband; they had found him hearty, with possibilities backstage, but mainly interested in fishing.

Angela was chairing the meeting; they had narrowed the selection to *Private Lives* and *The World of Suzie Wong*, and before anyone asked her opinion, Jan said, 'We did *Private Lives* in Nigeria.' It was an innocent remark, but Jan was slightly impatient and gave it a dogmatic edge, which surprised the rest into silence.

'Oh, really?' said Angela in her intimating bass after a pause. She trilled the *r* as she would have done on stage, and she glared at Jan.

'Yes, um,' said Jan, 'I played Amanda. Rupert helped with the sets.' She smiled and closed her eyes, remembering. 'What a night that was. It rained absolute *buckets*.'

'Maybe we should put it on here,' said Duff Gillespie. 'We need some rain over at my place.'

Everyone laughed, Angela loudest of all, and Jan said, 'It's a very witty play. Two excellent women's parts and lots of good lines.'

'Epicene,' said Tony Evans.

'I've noticed,' said Henry Eliot, a white-haired man who usually played fathers, 'that when you use a big word, Tony, you never put it in a sentence. It's rather cowardly.'

'That's who we're talking about,' said Tony, affecting rather than speaking in the Welsh accent that was natural to him. 'Noel Coward.'

'Too-bloody-shay,' said Duff, 'pardon my French.'

Jan looked from face to face; she wondered if they were making fun of her.

'That settles it,' said Angela. '*Suzie Wong* it is.'

'When did we decide that?' asked Henry, making a face.

'You didn't,' said Angela, '*I* did. We can't have squabbling.' She smiled at Jan. 'You'll find me fantastically dictatorial, my dear. Pass me that script, would you, darling?' Angela took the gray booklet that Tony Evans had been flipping through. She put it on the table, opened it decisively to *Cast, in Order of Their*

Appearance, and ran the heel of her hand down the fold, flattening it. She said, 'Now for the cast.'

At eleven-thirty, all the main parts had been allotted. 'Except one,' said Jan.

'I beg your pardon,' said Angela.

'I mean, it's all set, isn't it? Except that we haven't –' She looked at the others ' – we haven't decided the biggest part, have we?'

Angela gave Jan her look of incredulity. She did it with wintry slowness, and it made Jan pause and know she had said something wrong. So Jan laughed, it was a nervous laugh, and she said, 'I mean, who's Suzie?'

'Who indeed?' said Henry in an Irish brogue. He took his pipe out of his mouth to chuckle; then he returned the pipe and the chuckling stopped. He derived an unusual joy from watching two women disagree. His smile showed triumph.

'You've got your part,' said Angela, losing control of her accent. 'I should say it's a jolly good one.'

'Oh, I know that!' Jan said. 'But I was wondering about –' She looked at the table and said, 'I take it you're going to play Suzie.'

'Unless anyone has any serious objections,' said Angela. No one said a word. Angela addressed her question to Jan, 'Do you have any serious objections?'

'Well, not *serious* objections,' said Jan, trying to sound good-humored.

'Maybe she thinks –' Duff started.

Angela interrupted, 'Perhaps I'm too old for the part, Jan, is that what you're trying to say?'

'God, not that,' said Jan, becoming discomposed. 'Honestly Angela, I think you're perfect for it, really I do.'

'What is it then?'

Jan seemed reluctant to begin, but she had gone too far to withdraw. Her hands were clasped in her lap and now she was speaking to Duff, whose face was the most sympathetic. 'I don't want to make this sound like an objection, but the point is, Suzie is supposed to be, well, *Chinese* . . . and, Angela, you're not, um, Chinese. Are you?'

'Not as far as I know,' said Angela, raising a laugh. The laughter subsided. 'But I am an actress.'

'I know that,' said Jan, 'and I'm dead sure you'd do a marvelous

Suzie.' Jan became eager. 'I'm terribly excited about this production, really I am. But what if we got a Chinese girl from town to play Suzie. I mean, a *real* Chinese girl, with one of those dresses slit up the side and that long black hair and that sort of slinky –'

Angela's glare prevented Jan from going any further.

'It's a challenging role,' said Angela, switching her expression from one of disapproval to one of profound interest. 'But so are they all, and we must be up to it. Henry is going to play the old Chinese man. Would you prefer that Stanley did it?'

Stanley Chee, a man of sixty, with gold-rimmed glasses and a starched uniform, was Head Boy of the Club, and at that moment he could be seen – all heads turned – through the bar door, looking furtive as he wiped a bottle.

Jan shook her head from side to side.

'It's going to be a hard grind,' said Angela, and she smiled. 'But that's what acting is. Being someone else. Completely. That's what I tell all the new people.'

The Butterfly of the Laruts

The people in Ayer Hitam stopped referring to her as Dr Smith as soon as they set eyes on her. She was 'that woman,' then 'our friend,' and only much later, after she had left the district and when the legend was firmly established, was she Dr Smith again, the title giving her name a greater mockery than anyone there could manage in a tone of voice. She didn't have much luck with her simple name; as everyone knew, even the man she married could not pronounce it. But that was not surprising: a narrow ornament, a sliver of ivory he wore in his lower lip, prevented him from saying most words clearly.

She flitted into town that first day in a bright, wax-print sarong, and with a loose pale blouse through which you could see her breasts in nodding motion. She might have been one of those ravished American women, grazing the parapet of middle age, with a monotonous libido and an expensive camera, vowing to have a fling at the romance travel was supposed to provide. But she was far from frivolous, and she had not been in the district long before it became apparent that she was anything but typical.

A typical visitor stayed at the Government Rest House or the Club, but Dr Smith never went near either of them, nor did she stay at the Chinese hotels. Her few days in Ayer Hitam were passed at a Malay *kedai*, a flyblown shop on a back road. It was assumed she shared a room. You can imagine the speculation. But she had the magic travelers sometimes have, of finding in a place something the residents have missed and giving it a brief celebrity.

So, after she had gone into the jungle, some of us used this *kedai* and we discovered that it employed as sweepers several men from a small tribe of *orang asli* who lived sixty miles to the north, in an isolated pouch of jungle near one of Fred Squibb's timber estates. Their looks were unmistakable. That should have been our first clue: we knew she was an anthropologist, we heard she had taken a taxi north, and Squibb, the timber merchant, said the taxi had dropped her at the bush track which met the main road and extended some fifteen miles to the *kampong*. There had been, he said, half a dozen tribesmen – Laruts, they were called – squatting at the trampled mouth of the path. Squibb said they were waiting for her and that they might have been there, roosting like owls, for days.

We had seen anthropologists before. Their sturdy new clothes and neatly packed rucksacks, tape recorders and parcels of books and paper, gave them away immediately. But Dr Smith caused a local sensation. No one since Sir Hugh Clifford had studied the Laruts; they were true natives, small people with compressed negroid features, clumsy innocent faces, and long arms, who had been driven into the interior as the Malays and Chinese crowded the peninsula. There were few in the towns. You saw them unexpectedly tucked in the bends of bush roads, with the merchandise they habitually sold – red and yellow parrots, flapping things snared in the jungle, unused to the ingeniously woven Larut cages; and orchids harvested from the trunks of forest trees; and butterflies, as large as those orchids, mounted lopsidedly in cigar boxes. The Laruts were our savages, proof we were civilized: Malays especially measured themselves by them. Their movements, jinking in the forest, were like the flights of the butterflies they sold on the roadsides with aboriginal patience. Selling such graceful stuff was appropriate to this gentle tribe, for as was well known, they were nonviolent: they did not make weapons, they didn't fight. They had been hunted for sport, like frail deer, by early settlers. As the Malays and the Chinese grew more quarrelsome and assertive, the Laruts responded by moving further and further inland, until they came to rest on hillsides and in swamps, enduring the extremes of landscape to avoid hostile contact.

Bur Dr Smith found them, and a week later there were no Laruts on the road, no butterflies for sale, only the worn patches on the grassy verge where they had once waited with their cages and boxes, smoking their oddly shaped clay pipes.

At the Club, Angela said, 'I expect we'll see her in town buying clothes.' But no one saw her, nor did we see much of the Laruts. They had withdrawn, it seemed, to the deepest part of the forest, and their absence from the roads made those stretches particularly cheerless. We guessed at what might be going on in the Larut *kampong*, and with repetition our guesses acquired all the neatness and authority of facts. Then we had a witness.

Squibb went to the area; he brought back this story. He had borrowed a motorbike at one of his substations and had ridden it over the bush track until at last he came to the outskirts of the *kampong*. He saw some children playing and asked them in Malay if 'the white queen' was around. They took him to her, and he said he was astonished to see her kneeling in the dust by a hut, pounding some food in a mortar with several Larut women. They were stripped to the waist and chanting.

'You could have knocked me over with a feather,' Squibb said. He spat in disgust and went on to say how dirty she was; her sarong was in tatters, her hands filthy. Apparently he went over to her, but she ignored him. Finally, she spoke.

'Can't you see I'm busy?' She went on heaving the pestle.

Squibb was persistent. She said (and this was the sentence I heard Squibb repeating in the club lounge for days afterward): 'We don't want you here.'

There were other stories, but most of them seemed to originate with Squibb: the Ministry of Tourism was angry that the Laruts had stopped selling butterflies on the road; the missionaries in the area, Catholic fathers from Canada, were livid because the Larut children had stopped going to the mission school, and for the first time in many years the mission's dispensary – previously filled with snakebite victims and Laruts with appendicitis and strangulated hernias – was nearly empty. There was more: the Laruts had started to move their *kampong*, putting up huts in the heavily forested portion of jungle that adjoined Squibb's timber estate.

'She's a menace,' Squibb said.

He came to me at the Consulate and sat, refusing to leave until I listened to the last of his stories.

'There's nothing I can do,' I said.

'She's an American – you can send her home.'

'I don't see any evidence of treachery here,' I said.

'She's sticking her nose in where she's not wanted!'

'That's a matter for the Malaysians to decide.'

'They're as browned-off as I am,' Squibb said. He became solicitous about the Laruts; odd – he had always spoken of them as a nuisance, interrupting the smooth operation of his lumber mills with their poaching and thieving.

A day or two later, the District Commissioner dropped in. He was a dapper, soft-spoken Malay named Azhari, educated in

London; he had a reputation as a sport, and his adventures with various women at the Club were well known. There were 'Azhari stories.' He informed me politely that he was serving a deportation order on Dr Smith.

'What for?'

'Interfering in the internal affairs of our country,' he said. I wondered if she had turned him down.

'You've been talking to Squibb,' I said. He smiled; he didn't deny it.

It was Azhari's assistant who cycled to the village with the deportation order; it was he who brought us the news of the marriage.

At the Club, people said to me, 'You Americans,' and this was the only time in all my years at the Consulate there that Ayer Hitam was ever mentioned in the world's press. It was so unusual, seeing the town in the paper, mentions of the Club, City Bar, the *kedai* where Dr Smith had stayed, each one shabbily hallowed to a shrine by the coarse prose of journalists. They attempted a description of our heat, our trees, our roads, our way of life; struggling to make us unique they only succeeded in making us ridiculous (I was the 'youthful American Consul'). They spelled all our names wrong.

There were photographs of Dr Smith and the chief. She wore a printed scarf across her breasts in a makeshift halter, her hair knotted, and around her neck a great wooden necklace. He had headgear of parrot feathers, leather armlets on his biceps, and heavy earrings; he was a small man of perhaps fifty, with a worried furrowed face and tiny ears. In the photographs he looked cross-eyed, but that might have been his worry distorted in the strong light. She towered over him, triumphant, wistful. His arm was awkwardly crooked in hers. Around them were many blurred grinning faces of Larut wellwishers.

'We are very much in love,' she was reported to have said. 'We plan to have lots of children. I know my duties as a Larut wife.'

It was not simple. The Laruts, idle and good-hearted, were polygamous. The chief had eight wives. Dr Smith was the ninth.

This was the last we heard of her for several months.

Father Lefever from the mission came to see me one afternoon. He was circumspect; he asked permission to smoke and then set fire to a stinking cheroot. In the middle of casual remarks about the late monsoon he said, 'You must do something about that woman.'

'So what Squibb said about the dispensary is true.'

'I don't know what he said, but I think this woman could do a great deal of harm. The Laruts are a simple people – like children. They are not used to this attention.'

'I haven't heard anything lately, though Squibb said they're treating themselves with native medicine – they've stopped coming to your dispensary.'

The priest looked down. 'And to church.'

'That's their choice, one would guess.'

'No, it's her. I know it. Not the Laruts.'

'But *she's* a Larut,' I said.

Azhari was firmer. He came demanding information on her background, by which he meant her past. I guessed his motive to be resentment: a man he regarded as a savage had become his sexual competitor. But the whole affair was beginning to annoy me. I told him it was none of my business, her marriage had given her Malaysian citizenship, and as far as I was concerned she was no longer an American subject. I said, 'I don't see what all the fuss is about.'

'You don't know these chaps,' said Azhari. 'They are special people in this country. They don't pay taxes, they don't vote, they can go anywhere they wish. And since that woman came there's been a lot of loose talk.'

'Of what sort?'

'She's stirring them up,' he said. But he didn't elaborate. 'If you won't help me I'll go over your head to the Ambassador.'

'Nothing would please me more.'

All this interest in the Laruts, who until then had only sold butterflies, and were famous because they did not use violence.

Late one night, there was a loud rapping at the front door. Ah Wing answered it and seeing the visitors, said '*Sakais*,' with undisguised contempt.

A boy and an old man, obviously the chief. They came in and sat on the floor, the old man quite close, the boy – who was about twelve or thirteen – some distance away. They must have walked all the way from the village; their legs were wet and they had bits of broken leaf in their hair. They had brought the smell of the jungle into the room. The chief looked troubled; he nodded to the boy.

The boy said, 'He wants you to take her away.'

'His wife?' The boy jerked his head forward. 'I can't do that. Only he can do that. Tell him he is her husband.'

This was translated. The old man winced, and the scars beside his eyes bunched to tiny florets. He said something quickly, a signaling grunt. They had rehearsed this.

'He has money,' the boy said. 'He will pay you.'

'Money doesn't matter,' I said. I felt sorry for the old man: what had happened? Bullying, I imagined, threats of violence from Dr Smith; what pacifist tribe could contain an American academic, a woman with a camera? I said, 'There's a way. It's very simple – but he must be absolutely sure he never wants to see her again.'

'He is sure.' The boy didn't bother to translate. He knew his orders. He listened to what I said.

And it was so strange, the boy translating into the Larut language the process of divorce, the old man shaking his head, and the word for which there could not have been a Larut equivalent, recurring in the explanation as *vuss . . . vuss*. The old chief looked slightly shocked, and I was embarrassed; he was having this new glimpse of us, a revelation of a private cruelty of ours, a secret ritual that was available to him. At the end he wanted to give me money. I told him to save it for the lawyer.

The newspapers were interested; there was another influx of journalists from Singapore, but Dr Smith left as soon as the chief engaged a lawyer, and this time she didn't pass through Ayer Hitam. The journalists caught up with her in Tokyo – or was it Los Angeles? I forget. The pity of it was that they took no notice of what followed, the Laruts' new village (and prosperity for the chief) in the remotest part of the state, the closing of the mission, and Squibb's timber operation, which, it was said, made that little bush track into a road wide enough for huge timber trucks to collect the trees that were felled in and around the derelict village.

The Tennis Court

Everyone hated Shimura; but no one really knew him: Shimura was Japanese. He was not a member of the Club. About every two weeks he would stop one night in Ayer Hitam on his way to Singapore. He spent the day in Singapore and stopped again on the way back. Using us – which was how Evans put it – he was avoiding two nights at an expensive hotel. I say he wasn't in our club; yet he had full use of the facilities, because he was a member of the Selangor Club in Kuala Lumpur and we had reciprocal privileges. Seeing his blue Toyota appear in the driveway, Evans always said, 'Here comes the freeloader.'

Squibb said, 'I say, there's a nip in the air.'

And Alec said, 'Shoot him down.'

I didn't join them in their bigoted litany. I liked Shimura. I was ashamed of myself for not actively defending him, but I was sure he didn't need my help.

That year there were hundreds of Japanese businessmen in Kuala Lumpur selling transistor radios to the Malays. It seemed a harmless enough activity, but the English resented them and saw them as poaching on what they considered an exclusively British preserve. Evans said, 'I didn't fight the war so that those people could tell us how to run our club.'

Shimura was a tennis player. On his fifth or sixth visit he had suggested, in a way his stuttering English had blunted into a tactless complaint, that the ball-boys moved around too much.

'They must stand quiet.'

It was the only thing he had ever said, and it damned him. Typical Japanese attitude, people said, treating our ball-boys like prisoners of war. Tony Evans, chairman of the tennis committee, found it unforgivable. He said to Shimura, 'There are courts in Singapore,' but Shimura only laughed.

He seemed not to notice that he was hated. His composure was perfect. He was a small dark man, fairly young, with ropes of muscle knotted on his arms and legs, and his crouch on the court made him seem four-legged. He played a hard darting game with a towel wound around his neck like a scarf; he barked loudly when he hit the ball.

He always arrived late in the afternoon, and before dinner played several sets with anyone who happened to be around. Alec had played him, so had Eliot and Strang; he had won every match. Evans, the best player in the Club, refused to meet him on the tennis court. If there was no one to play, Shimura hit balls against the wooden backboard, barking at the hard ones, and he practiced with such determination you could hear his grunts as far as the reading room. He ate alone and went to bed early. He spoke to no one; he didn't drink. I sometimes used to think that if he had spent some time in the bar, like the other temporary members who passed through Ayer Hitam, Shimura would have no difficulty.

Alec said, 'Not very clubbable.'

'Ten to one he's fiddling his expenses,' said Squibb.

Evans criticized his lob.

He could not have been hated more. His nationality, his size, his stinginess, his laugh, his choice of tennis partners (once he had played Eliot's sexually browsing wife) – everything told against him. He was aloof, one of the worst social crimes in Malaysia; he was identified as a parasite, and worst of all he seemed to hold everyone in contempt. Offenses were invented: he bullied the ball-boys, he parked his car the wrong way, he made noises when he ate.

It may be hard to be an American – I sometimes thought so when I remembered our beleaguered Peace Corps teachers – but I believe it was even harder to be a Japanese in that place. They had lost the war and gained the world; they were unreadable, impossible to know; more courtly than the Chinese, they used this courtliness to conceal. The Chinese were secretive bumblers and their silences could be hysterical; the Japanese gave nothing away; they never betrayed their frenzy. This contempt they were supposed to have: it wasn't contempt, it was a total absence of trust in anyone who was not Japanese. And what was perhaps more to the point, they were the opposite to the English in every way I could name.

The war did not destroy the English – it fixed them in fatal attitudes. The Japanese were destroyed and out of that destruction came different men; only the loyalties were old – the rest was new. Shimura, who could not have been much more than thirty, was one of these new men, a postwar instrument, the perfectly calibrated Japanese. In spite of what everyone said, Shimura was an excellent tennis player.

So was Evans, and it was he who organized the club game: How to get rid of Shimura?

Squibb had a sentimental tolerance for Malays and a grudging respect for the Chinese, but like the rest of the club members he had an absolute loathing for the Japanese. When Alec said, 'I suppose we could always debag him,' Squibb replied fiercely, 'I'd like to stick a *kukri* in his guts.'

'We could get him for an infraction,' said Strang.

'That's the trouble with the obnoxious little sod,' said Squibb. 'He doesn't break the rules. We're lumbered with him for life.'

The hatred was old. The word 'Changi' was associated with Shimura. Changi was the jail in Singapore where the British were imprisoned during the war, after the fall of the city, and Shimura was held personally responsible for what had gone on there: the water torture, the *rotan* floggings, the bamboo rack, the starvation and casual violence the Japanese inflicted on people they despised because they had surrendered.

'I know what we ought to do,' said Alec. 'He wants his tennis. We won't give him his tennis. If we kept him off the courts we'd never see his face here again.'

'That's a rather low trick,' said Evans.

'Have you got a better one?' said Squibb.

'Yes,' said Evans. 'Play him.'

'I wouldn't play him for anything,' said Squibb.

'He'd beat you in any case,' said Alec.

Squibb said, 'But he wouldn't beat Tony.'

'Not me – I'm not playing him. I suggest we get someone else to beat him,' said Evans. 'These Japs can't stand humiliation. If he was really beaten badly we'd be well rid of him.'

I said, 'This is despicable. You don't know Shimura – you have no reason to dislike that man. I want no part of this.'

'Then bugger off!' shouted Squibb, turning his red face on me. 'We don't need a bloody Yank to tell us –'

'Calm yourself,' said Alec. 'There's ladies in the bar.'

'Listen,' I said to Squibb, 'I'm a member of this Club. I'm staying right here.'

'What about Shimura?' said Alec.

'It's just as I say, if he was beaten badly he'd be humiliated,' said Evans.

Squibb was looking at me as he said, 'There are some little fuckers you can't humiliate.'

But Evans was smiling.

The following week Shimura showed up late one afternoon, full of beans. He changed, had tea alone, and then appeared on the court with the towel around his neck and holding his racket like a sword. He chopped the air with it and looked around for a partner.

The court was still except for Shimura's busy shadow, and at the far end two ball-boys crouched with their sarongs folded between their knees. Shimura hit a few practice shots on the backboard.

We watched him from the rear verandah, sitting well back from the railing: Evans, Strang, Alec, Squibb, and myself. Shimura glanced up and bounced the racket against his palm. A ball-boy stood and yawned and drew out a battered racket. He walked toward Shimura, and though Shimura could not possibly have heard it there were four grunts of approval from the verandah.

Raziah, the ball-boy, was slender; his flapping blue sports shirt and faded wax-print sarong made him look careless and almost comic. He was taller than Shimura and, as Shimura turned and walked to the net to meet him, the contrast was marked – the loose-limbed gait of the Malay in his rubber flip-flops, the compact movements of the Japanese who made his prowl forward into a swift bow of salutation.

Raziah said, 'You can play me.'

Shimura hesitated and before he replied he looked around in disappointment and resignation, as if he suspected he might be accused of something shameful. Then he said, 'Okay, let's go.'

'Now watch him run,' said Evans, raising his glass of beer.

Raziah went to the baseline and dropped his sarong. He was wearing a pair of tennis shorts. He kicked off his flip-flops and put on white sneakers – new ones that looked large and dazzling in the sunlight. Raziah laughed out loud; he knew he had been transformed.

Squibb said, 'Tony, you're a bloody genius.'

Raziah won the toss and served. Raziah was seventeen; for seven

373

of those years he had been a ball-boy, and he had learned the game by watching members play. Later, with a cast-off racket, he began playing in the early morning, before anyone was up. Evans had seen him in one of these six o'clock matches and, impressed by Raziah's speed and backhand, taught him to serve and showed him the fine points of the game. He inspired in him the psychic alertness and confidence that makes tennis champions. Evans, unmarried, had used his bachelor's idleness as a charitable pledge and gave this energy and optimism to Raziah, who became his pet and student and finally his partner. And Evans promised that he would, one of these years, put Raziah up for membership if he proved himself; he had so far withheld club membership from the Malay, although the boy had beaten him a number of times.

Raziah played a deceptively awkward game; the length of his arms made him appear to swing wildly; he was fast, but he often stumbled trying to stop. After the first set it was clear that everyone had underestimated Shimura. Raziah smashed serves at him, Shimura returned them forcefully, without apparent effort, and Shimura won the first two sets six love. Changing ends, Raziah shrugged at the verandah as if to say, 'I'm doing the best I can.'

Evans said, 'Raziah's a slow starter. He needs to win a few games to get his confidence up.'

But he lost the first three games of the third set. Then Shimura, eager to finish him off, rushed the net and saw two of Raziah's drop shots land out of reach. When Raziah won that game, and the next – breaking Shimura's serve – there was a triumphant howl from the verandah. Raziah waved, and Shimura, who had been smiling, turned to see four men at the rail, the Chinese waiters on the steps, and crouching just under the verandah, two Tamil gardeners – everyone gazing with the intensity of jurors.

Shimura must have guessed that something was up. He reacted by playing angrily, slicing vicious shots at Raziah, or else lifting slow balls just over the net to drop hardly without a bounce at Raziah's feet. The pretense of the casual match was abandoned; the kitchen staff gathered along the sidelines and others – mostly Malay – stood at the hedge, cheering. There was laughter when Shimura slipped, applause when the towel fell from his neck.

What a good story a victory would have made! But nothing in Ayer Hitam was ever so neat. It would have been perfect revenge, a kind of romantic battle – the lanky local boy with his old racket, making a stand against the intruder; the drama of vindicating not only his own reputation as a potentially great tennis player, but indeed the dignity of the entire club. The match had its charms: Raziah had a way of chewing and swallowing and working his Adam's apple at Shimura when the Japanese lost a point; Raziah talked as he played, a muttering narration that was meant to unnerve his opponent; and he took his time serving, shrugging his shoulders and bouncing the ball. But it was a very short contest, for as Evans and the others watched with hopeful and judging solemnity, Raziah lost.

The astonishing thing was that none of the club staff, and none of Raziah's friends, seemed to realize that he had lost. They were still laughing and cheering and congratulating themselves long after Shimura had aced his last serve past Raziah's knees; and not for the longest time did the festive mood change.

Evans jumped to the court. Shimura was clamping his press to his racket, mopping his face. Seeing Evans he started to walk away.

'I'd like a word with you,' said Evans.

Shimura looked downcast; sweat and effort had plastered his hair close to his head, and his fatigue was curiously like sadness, as if he had been beaten. He had missed the hatred before, hadn't noticed us; but the laughter, the sudden crowd, the charade of the challenge match had showed him how much he was hated and how much trouble we had gone to in order to prove it. He said, 'So.'

Evans was purple. 'You come to the Club quite a bit, I see.'

'Yes.'

'I think you ought to be acquainted with the rules.'

'I have not broken any rules.'

Evans said curtly, 'You didn't sign in your guest.'

Shimura bowed and walked to the clubhouse. Evans glared at Raziah; Raziah shook his head, then went for his sarong, and putting it on he became again a Malay of the town, one of numerous idlers who'd never be members of the Ayer Hitam Club.

The following day Shimura left. We never saw him again. For a month Evans claimed it as a personal victory. But that was short-lived, for the next news was of Raziah's defection. Shimura had invited him to Kuala Lumpur and entered him in the Federation Championship, and the jersey Raziah wore when he won a respectable third prize had the name of Shimura's company on it, an electronics firm. And there was to be more. Shimura put him up for membership in the Selangor Club, and so we knew that it was only a matter of time before Raziah returned to Ayer Hitam to claim reciprocal privileges as a guest member. And even those who hated Shimura and criticized his lob were forced to admire the cleverness of his Oriental revenge.

Reggie Woo

His father, Woo Boh Swee, had chased after the English in that shy, breathless Chinese way, hating the necessity of it and making his embarrassment into haste. He had gone from Canton to Hong Kong to work on an English ship and later had come to Ayer Hitam to supply the rubber estates with provisions. But the rubber price had fallen, many English and American families left the town, and the Chinese who replaced them imported or grew their own food; so he started City Bar.

It was the biggest coffee shop in town, the meeting place for a secret society – but the gang was only dangerous to other Chinese and did not affect Woo's regular trade, the remaining English planters, and the Tamil rubber tappers. Woo – or 'City Bar' as he was known – was thoroughly Chinese; he was a chain smoker, he played mahjong on a back table of the shop, he observed all the Chinese festivals with *ang pows*. The shop smelled of dusty bottles and bean curd, and dark greasy ducks and glazed pork strips hung on hooks in the front window. He and his wife were great gamblers, and they had two children.

The children went to different schools. It was as if, this once, the Woos were hedging, making an each-way bet. The girl, Jin Bee, was at the Chinese primary school; the boy, Reggie, had been to the Anglo-Chinese school, then to Raffles Institution and the University of Singapore. He was the English child; he played cricket and tennis and was a member of the Ayer Hitam Club. He had distinguished himself by appearing in the Footlighters' production of Maugham's play, *The Letter*. It was the first play to attract a local audience; it ran for a week, and Reggie's picture was in the *Johore Mail*. That picture, bright yellow with age, was taped to the wall of City Bar. Everyone had hopes for Reggie. He was that odd figure you sometimes see in the East, the person who leaves his race behind, who goes to school and returns home English. Ayer Hitam was not an easy place to be English, but Reggie, an actor, had certain advantages. He was right for the part. And though drinks at the Club were more expensive than at City Bar, Reggie was at the Club, drinking, nearly every evening.

One night I saw him alone in the lounge. He looked like an actor who hadn't been warned that his play was canceled; dressed up, solitary, he was a figure of neglect, and his expectant look was changing into one of desolation. I joined him, we talked about the heat, and after a while I told him he ought to get a scholarship to study overseas.

'I wouldn't mind!' He brushed his hair out of his eyes. 'How do I go about it?'

'That depends,' I said. 'What's your field?'

'Philosophy.'

I was prepared to be surprised, but I was unprepared for that. It was his clothes, narrow trousers, pointed shoes, a pink shirt, and a silk scarf knotted at his throat. 'It would be strange,' I said. 'A Chinese from Malaysia going to the States to study Oriental philosophy.'

'Why do you say Oriental philosophy?' He looked offended in a rather formal way.

'Just a wild guess.'

'A bad guess,' he said. 'Whitehead, Russell, Kant.' He showed me three well-manicured fingers. Then a fourth. 'Karl Popper.'

'You're interested in them, are you?'

'I studied them,' he said. 'I wrote on the mind–body problem.'

'I'll see what I can do.'

The Fulbright forms had to come from Kuala Lumpur, so it was a week before I looked for him again, and when I looked he wasn't there – not at the Club and not at City Bar. 'In Singapore,' his father said. 'Got business.'

There were eight or ten people at the Club the night Reggie came back. I noticed they were all Footlighters. I waited until they left him – they had been gathered around him, talking loudly – and then I told him I had the forms.

'Something's come up,' he said. He grinned. 'I'm going to be in a film. That's why I was in Singapore. Auditioning. And I got the part-*lah*.'

'Congratulations,' I said. 'What film is it?'

'*Man's Fate*,' he said. 'I'm playing Ch'en. I've always adored Malraux and I love acting. Now I can draw on my philosophy background as well. So you see, it's perfect.'

'What does your father think about it?'

'It's a job – he's keen,' said Reggie. 'It's my big chance, and it could lead to bigger parts.'

'Hollywood,' I said.

He smiled. 'I would never go to Hollywood. False life, no sense of values. I plan to make London my base, but if the money was good I might go to the States for a few weeks at a time.'

'When are they going to make *Man's Fate*?'

'Shooting starts in Singapore in a month's time.'

And the way he said *shooting* convinced me that the Fulbright forms would never be used.

After that I heard a lot about Reggie at the Club. Ladysmith, the English teacher, said, 'City's Bar's son's done all right for himself,' and Reggie was always in sight, in new clothes, declining drinks. Squibb said, 'These things never come off,' and some people referred to Reggie as 'that fruit.' But most were pleased. The Footlighters said, 'I can say I knew you when,' and cautioned him about the small print in contracts, and when they filed in at dusk for the first drink they greeted him with, 'How's our film star?'

Reggie's reply was, 'I had a letter just the other day.' He said this week after week, giving the impression of a constant flow of mail, keeping him up to date. But I realized, as his manner became more abrupt and diffident, that it was always the same letter.

Then a job came up at the Anglo-Chinese school: a history teacher was needed. Reggie's name was mentioned, it was his old school, he was out of work. But he turned it down. 'I can't commit myself to a teaching post with this film in the pipeline!' He lost his temper with the Chinese barman who mistook tonic for soda. He shouted at the ball-boys on the tennis courts. Like a film star, people said.

Twice a week, when the program changed at the Capitol Cinema in Johore Bahru, Reggie made the sixty-mile drive in his father's van, usually with an English girl from the Club. There were rumors of romance, even talk of marriage; names were mentioned, Millsap's daughter, Squibb's niece. Reggie spoke of going to London.

One day he was gone. I noticed his absence because the Club was holding rehearsals for a new play, and Reggie, who had not missed a major production since *The Letter*, was not in the cast.

It was said he was in Singapore, and I assumed they were shooting *Man's Fate*.

Sometime later, the glimpse of a face being averted in a post office crowd reminded me of Reggie. I mentioned him to my *peon*, Peeraswami.

'At City Bar,' said Peeraswami.

'Then he *is* back.'

I remember the night I went over to offer my congratulations, and I could find it on a calendar even now, because there was a full moon over a cloud that hung like a dragon in the sky. The usual nighttime crowd of drinkers and idlers was at City Bar. I looked for the figure in the scarf and sunglasses I had seen so many times in the Club, but all I saw were Chinese gesturing with coffee cups and Tamils drinking toddy – everyone in short-sleeved white shirts. A hot night in a Malaysian town has a particular bittersweet taste; the chatter and noise in that place seemed to make the taste stronger. I fought my way into the bar and saw Woo Boh Swee, scowling at the cash register.

'Where's Reggie?'

He jerked his thumb inside but stared at me in an excluding way. When I saw Reggie in the back, hunched over the mahjong table in the short-sleeved shirt that made him anonymous, his legs folded, kicking a rubber sandal up and down, I knew it would be an intrusion to go any further. I heard him abuse his opponent in sharp, unmistakably Cantonese jeers as he banged down a mahjong tile. I left before he caught sight of me and went back to the Club, crossing the road with that sinking feeling you get at a national boundary or an unguarded frontier.

Conspirators

Not one person I had known in Africa was my age – they were either much older or much younger. That could hardly have been true, and yet that was how it appeared to me. I was very young.

The Indian seemed old; I had never spoken to him; I did not know his name. He was one of those people, common in small towns, whom one sees constantly, and who, like a feature of the landscape, become anonymous because they are never out of view, like a newspaper seller or a particular cripple. He was dark, always alone, and threadbare in an indestructible way. He used to show up at the door of the Gujarati restaurant where I ate, The Hindu Lodge, an old man with a cardboard box of Indian sweets, and he said – it was his one word of English – 'Sweetmeats.'

In my two-year tour in Uganda I saw him hundreds of times, in that open doorway, blinking because of the flies near his face. No one bought the food he had in the dirty cardboard box. He showed the box, said his word, and then went away. It was as if he was doing it against his will: he had been sent by someone conspiring to find out what we would do with him, a test of our sympathy. We did nothing. If anyone had asked me about him at the time I think I would have said that I found him terribly reassuring. But no one asked; no one saw him.

Ayer Hitam, half a world away, had her Indian conspirators, but being political, they had names. Rao had been arrested on a political charge. It was said that he was a communist. I found the description slightly absurd in that small town, like the cheese-colored building they called the Ministry of Works or the bellyache everyone referred to as dysentery. In Malaysia a communist meant someone either very poor or very safe, who gathered with others in a kind of priestly cabal, meeting at night over a table littered with boring papers and high-minded pamphlets to reheat their anger. I could imagine the futile talk, the despair of the ritual which had its more vulgar counterpart in the lounge of the Ayer Hitam Club. It was said that the communists wanted to poison the Sultan's polo-ponies and nationalize the palm-oil estates. They were people seeking to be arrested. Arrest was their victory, and in that sense they were like early Christians, needing to be persecuted because they wished to prove their courage. They were conspirators; they inspired others in conspiracy against them. Most Malays were superstitious about them. To speak too much of the communists was to give their faith an importance it didn't deserve. But when they were caught they were imprisoned.

Rao had been in prison for some time. The Embassy told me of his release and how he had returned to Ayer Hitam. I was ashamed to admit that I had never heard of him. My people gave me a few facts: Rao had been a real firebrand; he had given public speeches; he had started a cell in the mission school; he was a confidant of the Chinese goldsmiths who were, somehow, Maoists; he had caused at least two riots in town. I was skeptical but interested: large affairs, wild talk – but the town looked small and tame and too sparsely populated to support a riot. An unlawful assembly, perhaps, but not a riot.

Virtually everyone I knew suspected me of being a spy. I was seen as a legitimate conspirator. In a small way I suppose I was. My information was negligible: I was sorry it mattered so little. It would have been encouraging to know that my cables were eagerly awaited and quickly acted upon. But what I sent was filed and never queried, never crucial. I was in the wrong place. I could have reported on the Chinese goldsmiths, but I knew better. Theirs was a sentimental attachment to China, their nationalism the nostalgia of souvenirs, like calendar pictures of Tien-An-Men Square in Peking. I reminded myself that an Italian in the United States would have a feeling for Italy no matter who governed. It was the same with the Chinese. My cables were as eventless as the town. I knew I didn't count.

I was surprised when the Political Section asked me to see Rao privately and find out what he was up to. I assumed that if I approved him he might be offered a scholarship to study in the States. There was no better catch than an ex-communist. People would listen to him, and he could always have the last word. He knew the other side: he had been there. If I flunked him, I knew – it was the system – he would be unemployable.

Rao worked, I found out, in the office of the town's solicitor, Francis Ratnasingham. I spoke to Francis and he said that he had no objection to my talking to Rao during office hours: 'He will be flattered by your interest.'

Rao came into the room carrying a tray of papers. It looked for a moment like a shallow box of food. He held it out and gave me a wan smile.

'They said you wanted to talk to me.'

His voice was flat and had a hint of defeat in it, which contradicted what I had heard about him, the speeches, the riots he'd caused. He was heavy – jail weight, like the useless bulk of a farm turkey. He looked underexercised and slow.

I said, 'I don't want to take you away from your work.'

'It doesn't make any difference.'

I tried not to stare at his big soft face. This was a firebrand! He looked at the tray, as if surprised to see it in his hands, then placed it on a desk.

'I hope you're not busy.'

He said, 'Francis told me to expect you.'

Ratnasingham's office was in Victoria Chambers on the main street, Jalan Besar. I said we could have a drink at the Club. Rao suggested tea at City Bar, and it was there that he said, 'I reckon you saw me on television in KL.'

'No,' I said. 'When was that?'

'Two months ago.'

'What did you do?'

'I recanted.' He smiled.

I stared: *recanted?*

He said, 'I had to do it twice. They didn't like my first try – they said I didn't sound sincere enough.'

I had heard that political prisoners had been made to recant, but I didn't realize the government televised it. Rao said it was one of the conditions of release.

'How long were you in jail?'

'Seven years.'

I couldn't hide my astonishment. And I put it in personal terms – seven years was the length of my whole Foreign Service career. So Rao and I were the same age, conspiring differently.

He said, 'You don't believe me.'

'It's a hell of a long time to be in jail.'

'Yes.' He stirred his tea. 'But I took lessons. I did correspondence courses. I studied. It helped the time pass.' He shrugged. 'How do you like Malaysia?'

'I'm enjoying myself.' This sounded frivolous. 'Maybe I shouldn't be.'

'Why not? It's a nice country. We have our problems. But –' He shrugged again, and laughed. This time his amusement seemed real.

'What were you studying in prison?'

'Law – an external degree from London University. They sent me books and lessons. They were very good about it. They didn't charge me anything.'

'You got the degree?'

'Oh, no,' he said, and he sighed. 'There were too many interruptions. I couldn't keep the written material in my cell without permission. I had to request it from the warders and they needed a chit from the prison governor. One day they would give me a book but no paper. The next they'd give me paper but no pencil or book. I'd ask for a pencil. They'd give it, but take away the paper.'

'That's torture,' I said.

'Maybe,' he said. 'It was a problem.'

'But they were doing it deliberately!'

He nodded. I searched for anger on his face. There was only that dull look of amusement. He said, 'It made the time pass.'

'I can see why you didn't get the degree in prison. What a relief it must be to have your own paper and pens and books and make your own rules for a change.'

'I don't make any rules,' he said, and sounded defensive.

'I mean, about studying,' I said quickly.

'I don't study.'

'But you said you were working for a degree.'

'In prison,' he said. 'It was important at the time, even that business about paper but no pencil. When I was released, I stopped. I didn't need it.'

I said, 'You could continue your studies in the States.'

He shook his head.

'Don't you want to leave the country?'

'It's them. They wouldn't give me a passport.'

'You could get a traveling document. I might be able to help you with that.'

He smiled, as if he had been told all of this before.

'Why don't you leave?'

He said, 'Because they wouldn't let me back into the country.'

'So you can never leave?'

'I don't say never. I don't think about time anymore.'

'Do you mind me asking you these questions?'

He said softly, 'I know who you are.'

'I would genuinely like to help you.'

He laughed again, the authentic laugh, not the mechanical one. 'Maybe you could have helped me, seven years ago. Now, no.'

'What are the other conditions of your release? You had to recant, you're forbidden to leave the country –'

'You don't understand,' he said. 'I recanted voluntarily. I don't want to leave the country. It's my choice.'

'But the alternative was staying in jail.'

'Let's say it took me seven years to make up my mind.' He stared at me and frowned. 'It wasn't a hasty decision.'

He was impenetrable. And he looked it, too. He was not tall, but he was large, square-headed, and had a thickness of flesh that wasn't muscle. I could not help thinking that he had deliberately become like this as a reproach to all action; it was his way of sulking.

He said, 'I know some chaps who were in even longer than me, so I don't complain.'

This was news. 'You keep in touch with other prisoners?'

'Oh, yes,' he said lightly. 'We're members of the Ex-Detainees Association.'

'You have a club?'

He nodded. 'I'm the secretary.'

I might have known. Ayer Hitam was full of clubs – Chinese clan associations, secret societies, communist cells, Indian sports clubs, the South Malaysia Pineapple Growers' Association, the Muslim League, the Legion of Mary, the Methodist Ramblers; and I was in one myself. No one lived in the town, really; people just went to club meetings there.

Rao looked at his watch. He said, 'Five o'clock.'

'I've kept you.'

'It doesn't matter. I don't have any work to do. I'm just a file clerk. They won't sack me.'

'Have another cup of tea. Or what about splitting a large Anchor?'

'I don't drink beer,' he said. 'I learned to do without it.'

I couldn't ask him the other thing, how he had gone so long without a woman. But I was curious, and when he said 'I should be heading home,' I offered him a ride.

In the car he spoke to Abubaker gently in Malay, and Abubaker laughed. For a moment they looked like conspirators sharing a secret. But Rao, as if guessing at my interest, said, 'I told him I wanted to buy his posh car.'

'Do you?'

'Not at all.'

We drove for several miles in silence.

Rao said, 'It was a joke, you see.'

His house, a small two-room bungalow, unfenced, exposed to the sun, was directly on the road – an odd place to be in so empty a landscape.

Rao said, 'Will you come in?'

He was being polite. He didn't want me.

I said, 'All right. But just for a minute.'

After the business of making tea and his carefully setting out a dish of savories that were like macaroni coated with hot pepper, there seemed nothing to say. The room was bare. It did not even have the calendar most of the houses in Ayer Hitam displayed. It had no mirror, no pictures. It was, surprisingly, like a jail cell. He lived alone; there was no sign of a woman, no servants' quarters, no books.

A timber truck went by and shook the windows.

'I like it here,' said Rao, almost defiantly.

He left the room and came back with a large plastic-covered book with thick pages, a photograph album. He showed me an old blurred snapshot of a dark schoolboy in white shorts. He said, 'That's me.' He showed me a picture of a Chinese man. 'He was one of the warders.' A palm tree. 'That's Mersing. There are beautiful islands there. You should visit.' A battered car. 'That belonged to my uncle. He died.' There were no more pictures. Rao said, 'When I have some free time I take out this album and look at the pictures.'

But they were pictures of nothing. He had no fire. I had suspected him of keeping something from me; but he hadn't, he was concealing nothing, he had been destroyed.

He said, 'I told you I couldn't help you.'

And I left. I was driving back when I remembered that poor

Indian in Kampala. I hadn't thought of him for years. I was sad, sadder than I had been for a long time, because I knew now he was dead.

It took me weeks to write my report on Rao. I had to suppress the implications of what I'd seen. I put down the obvious facts, and – saying that he'd returned to normal life – invented a happy man, whom prison had cured of all passion. The conspiracy was complete. But I was glad he had showed no interest in a scholarship or a travel grant, because when I reflected on Rao I saw his transformation as the ultimate deceit. I knew I would not have trusted him an inch.

The Johore Murders

The first victim was a British planter, and everyone at the Club said what a shame it was that after fifteen years in the country he was killed just four days before he planned to leave. He had no family, he lived alone; until he was murdered no one knew very much about him. Murder is the grimmest, briefest fame. If the second victim, a month later, had not been an American I probably would not have given the Johore murders a second thought, and I certainly would not have been involved in the business. But who would have guessed that Ismail Garcia was an American?

The least dignified thing that can happen to a man is to be murdered. If he dies in his sleep he gets a respectful obituary and perhaps a smiling portrait; it is how we all want to be remembered. But murder is the great exposer: here is the victim in his torn underwear, face down on the floor, unpaid bills on his dresser, a meager shopping list, some loose change, and worst of all the fact that he is alone. Investigation reveals what he did that day – it all matters – his habits are examined, his behavior scrutinized, his trunks rifled, and a balance sheet is drawn up at the hospital giving the contents of his stomach. Dying, the last private act we perform, is made public: the murder victim has no secrets.

So, somewhere in Garcia's house, a passport was found, an American one, and that was when the Malaysian police contacted the Embassy in Kuala Lumpur. I was asked to go down for the death certificate, personal effects, and anything that might be necessary for the report to his next of kin. I intended it to be a stopover, a day in Johore, a night in Singapore, and then back to Ayer Hitam. Peeraswami had a brother in Johore; Abubaker, my driver, said he wanted to pray at the Johore mosque; we pushed off early one morning, Abubaker at the wheel, Peeraswami playing with the car radio. I was in the back seat going over newspaper clippings of the two murders.

In most ways they were the same. Each victim was a foreigner, unmarried, lived alone in a house outside town, and had been a resident for some years. In neither case was there any sign of a forced entry or a robbery. Both men were poor, both men had been mutilated. They looked to me like acts of Chinese revenge. But on planters? In Malaysia it was the Chinese *towkay* who was robbed, kidnaped, or murdered, not the expatriate planters who lived from month to month on provisioner's credit and chit-signing in bars. There were two differences: Tibbets was British and Ismail Garcia was American. And one other known fact: Tibbets, at the time of his death, was planning to go back to England.

A two-hour drive through rubber estates took us into Johore, and then we were speeding along the shore of the Straits, past the lovely casuarina trees and the high houses on the leafy bluff that overlooks the swampland and the marshes on the north coast of Singapore. I dropped Peeraswami at his brother's house, which was in one of the wilder suburbs of Johore and with a high chain-link fence around it to assure even greater seclusion. Abubaker scrambled out at the mosque after giving me directions to the police headquarters.

Garcia's effects were in a paper bag from a Chinese shop. I signed for them and took them to a table to examine: a cheap watch, a cheap ring, a copy of the Koran, a birth certificate, the passport.

'We left the clothes behind,' said Detective-Sergeant Yusof. 'We just took the valuables.'

Valuables: there wasn't five dollars' worth of stuff in the bag.

'Was there any money?'

'He had no money. We're not treating it as robbery.'

'What *are* you treating it as?'

'Homicide, probably by a friend.'

'Some friend.'

'He knew the murderer, so did Tibbets. You will believe me when you see the houses.'

I almost did. Garcia's house was completely surrounded by a high fence, and Yusof said that Tibbets's fence was even higher. It was not unusual; every large house in Malaysian cities had an unclimbable fence or a wall with spikes of glass cemented on to the top.

'The lock wasn't broken, the house wasn't tampered with,' said Yusof. 'So we are calling it a sex crime.'

'I thought you were calling it a homicide.'

Yusof smirked at me. 'We have a theory. The Englishmen who

live here get funny ideas. Especially the ones who live alone. Some of them take Malay mistresses, the other ones go around with Chinese boys.'

'Not Malay boys?'

Yusof said, 'We do not do such things.'

'You say Englishmen do, but Garcia was an American.'

'He was single,' said Yusof.

'I'm single,' I said.

'We couldn't find any sign of a mistress.'

'I thought you were looking for a murderer.'

'That's what I'm trying to say,' said Yusof. 'These queers are very secretive. They get jealous. They fight with their boy friends. The body was mutilated – that tells me a Chinese boy is involved.'

'So you don't think it had anything to do with money?'

'Do you know what the rubber price is?'

'As a matter of fact, I do.'

'And that's not all,' said Yusof. 'This man Garcia – do you know what he owed his provisioner? Eight hundred-over dollars! Tibbets was owing five hundred.'

I said, 'Maybe the provisioner did it.'

'Interesting,' said Yusof. 'We can work on that.'

Tibbets was English, so over lunch I concentrated on Garcia. There was a little dossier on him from the Alien Registration Office. Born 1922 in the Philippines; fought in World War II; took out American citizenship in Guam, came to Malaysia in 1954, converted to Islam and changed his name. From place to place, complicating his identity, picking up a nationality here, a name there, a religion somewhere else. And why would he convert? A woman, of course. No man changed his religion to live with another man. I didn't believe he was a homosexual, and though there was no evidence to support it I didn't rule out the possibility of robbery. In all this there were two items that interested me – the birth certificate and the passport. The birth certificate was brown with age, the passport new and unused.

Why would a man who had changed his religion and lived in a country for nearly twenty years have a new passport?

After lunch I rang police headquarters and asked for Yusof.

'We've got the provisioner,' he said. 'I think you might be right. He was also Tibbet's provisioner – both men owed him money. He is helping us with our inquiries.'

'What a pompous phrase for torture,' I said, but before Yusof could reply I added, 'About Garcia – I figure he was planning to leave the country.'

Yusof cackled into the phone. 'Not at all! We talked to his employer – Garcia had a permanent and pensionable contract.'

'Then why did he apply for a passport two weeks ago?'

'It is the law. He must be in possession of a valid passport if he is an expatriate.'

I said, 'I'd like to talk to his employer.'

Yusof gave me the name of the man, Tan See Leng, owner of the Tai-Hwa Rubber Estate. I went over that afternoon. At first Tan refused to see me, but when I sent him my card with the Consulate address and the American eagle on it, he rushed out of his office and apologized. He was a thin evasive man with spiky hair, and though he pretended not to be surprised when I said Garcia was an American national I could tell this was news to him. He said he knew nothing about Garcia, apart from the fact that he'd been a good foreman. He'd never seen him socially. He confirmed that Garcia lived behind an impenetrable fence.

'Who owned the house?'

'He did.'

'That's something,' I said. 'I suppose you knew he was leaving the country.'

'He was not leaving. He was wucking.'

'It would help if you told me the truth,' I said.

Tan's bony face tightened with anger. He said, 'Perhaps he intended to leave. I do not know.'

'I take it business isn't so good.'

'The rubber price is low, some planters are switching to oil palm. But the price will rise if we are patient.'

'What did you pay Garcia?'

'Two thousand a month. He was on permanent terms – he signed one of the old contracts. We were very generous in those days with expatriates.'

'But he could have broken the contract.'

'Some men break.'

'Up in Ayer Hitam they have something called a "golden hand-shake." If they want to get rid of a foreigner they offer him a chunk of money as compensation for loss of career.'

'That is Ayer Hitam,' said Tan. 'This is Johore.'

'And they always pay cash, because it's against the law to take that much money out of the country. No banks. Just a suitcase full of Straits dollars.'

Tan said nothing.

I said, 'I don't think Garcia or Tibbets were queer. I think this was robbery, pure and simple.'

'The houses were not broken into.'

'So the papers say,' I said. 'It's the only thing I don't understand. Both men were killed at home during the day.'

'Mister,' said Tan. 'You should leave this to the police.'

'You swear you didn't give Garcia a golden handshake?'

'That is against the law, as you say.'

'It's not as serious as murder, is it?'

In the course of the conversation, Tan had turned to wood. I was sure he was lying, but he stuck to his story. I decided to have nothing more to do with the police or Yusof and instead to go back to the house of Peeraswami's brother, to test a theory of my own.

The house bore many similarities to Garcia's and to what I knew of Tibbets's. It was secluded, out of town, rather characterless, and the high fence was topped with barbed wire. Sathya, Peeraswami's brother, asked me how I liked Johore. I told him that I liked it so much I wanted to spend a few days there, but that I didn't want the Embassy to know where I was. I asked him if he would put me up.

'Oh, yes,' he said. 'You are welcome. But you would be more comfortable in a hotel.'

'It's much quieter here.'

'It is the country life. We have no car.'

'It's just what I'm looking for.'

After I was shown to my bedroom I excused myself and went to the offices of the *Johore Mail*, read the classified ads for the previous few weeks and placed an ad myself. For the next two days I explored Johore, looked over the Botanical Gardens and the Sultan's mosque, and ingratiated myself with Sathya and his family. I had arrived on a Friday. On Monday I said to Sathya, 'I'm expecting a phone call today.'

Sathya said, 'This is your house.'

'I feel I ought to do something in return,' I said. 'I have a driver and a car – I don't need them today. Why don't you use them?

Take your wife and children over to Singapore and enjoy yourself.'

He hesitated, but finally I persuaded him. Abubaker, on the other hand, showed an obvious distaste for taking an Indian family out for the day.

'Peeraswami,' I said. 'I'd like you to stay here with me.'

'*Tuan*,' he said, agreeing. Sathya and the others left. I locked the gate behind them and sat by the telephone to wait.

There were four phone calls. Three of the callers I discouraged by describing the location, the size of the house, the tiny garden, the work I said had to be done on the roof. And I gave the same story to the last caller, but he was insistent and eager to see it. He said he'd be right over.

Rawlins was the name he gave me. He came in a new car, gave me a hearty greeting, and was not at all put off by the slightly ramshackle appearance of the house. He smoked a cheroot which had stained his teeth and the center swatch of his mustache a sticky yellow, and he walked around with one hand cupped, tapping ashes into his palm.

'You're smart not to use an agent,' he said, looking over the house. 'These estate agents are bloody thieves.'

I showed him the garden, the lounge, the kitchen.

He sniffed and said, 'You like curry.'

'My cook's an Indian.' He went silent, glanced around suspiciously, and I added, 'I gave him the day off.'

'You lived here long?'

'Ten years. I'm chucking it. I've been worried about selling this place ever since I broke my contract.'

'Rubber?' he said, and spat a fragment of the cheroot into his hand.

'Yes,' I said. 'I was manager of an estate up in Kluang.'

He asked me the price and when I told him he said, 'I can manage that.' He took out a checkbook. 'I'll give you a deposit now and the balance when contracts are exchanged. We'll put our lawyers in touch and Bob's your uncle. Got a pen?'

I went to the desk and opened a drawer, but as I rummaged he said, 'Okay, turn around slow and put your hands up.'

I did as I was told and heard the cheroot hitting the floor. Above the kris Rawlins held his face was fierce and twisted. In such an act a man reverts; his face was pure monkey, threatening teeth and eyes. He said, 'Now hand it over.'

'What is this?' I said. 'What do you want?'

'Your money, all of it, your handshake.'

'I don't have any money.'

'They always lie,' he said. 'They always fight, and then I have to do them. Just make it easy this time. The money –'

But he said no more, for Peeraswami in his bare feet crept behind him from the broom cupboard where he had been hiding and brought a cast-iron frying pan down so hard on his skull that I thought for a moment I saw a crack show in the man's forehead. We tied Rawlins up with Sathya's neckties and then I rang Yusof.

On the way to police headquarters, where Yusof insisted the corpse be delivered, I said, 'This probably would not have happened if you didn't have such strict exchange control regulations.'

'So it was robbery,' said Yusof, 'but how did he know Tibbets and Garcia had had golden handshakes?'

'He guessed. There was no risk involved. He knew they were leaving the country because they'd put their houses up for sale. Expatriates who own houses here have been in the country a long time, which means they're taking a lot of money out in a suitcase. You should read the paper.'

'I read the paper,' said Yusof. 'Malay and English press.'

'I mean the classified ads, where it says, "Expatriate-owned house for immediate sale. Leaving the country. No agents." Tibbets and Garcia placed that ad, and so did I.'

Yusof said, 'I should have done that. I could have broken this case.'

'I doubt it – he wouldn't have done business with a Malay,' I said. 'But remember, if a person says he wants to buy your house you let him in. It's the easiest way for a burglar to enter – through the front door. If he's a white man in this country no one suspects him. We're supposed to trust each other. As soon as I realized it had something to do with the sale of a house I knew the murderer would be white.'

'He didn't know they were alone.'

'The wife and kids always fly out first, especially if daddy's breaking currency regulations.'

'You foreigners know all the tricks.'

'True,' I said. 'If he was a Malay or a Chinese I probably wouldn't have been able to catch him.' I tapped my head. 'I understand the mind of the West.'

The Tiger's Suit

Almost the worst corpse I've ever seen was that of a Malay woman, an epileptic, who, out planting rice in a field, had had a fit and tumbled into a flooded ditch. She was alone, and as soon as she was submerged the horseleeches swarmed beneath her loose blouse and over her legs and face. She hadn't drowned; she died from loss of blood, it had been sucked by those fattened leeches. They still clung to her, black with her blood, after she was hauled out. Her color was the most awful gray, like a dead sea creature with salt in her veins. Then the leeches were struck by the air and they peeled off and sank in the ditch, leaving the woman covered with welts the shape of watchstraps. It gave Ayer Hitam a week of fame. People came from all over to look at the ditch, and even now you can see the spot clearly because no one would plant rice near it after the tragedy. It had the makings of a horror story: the corpse found with its blood sucked, an investigation, some detective work, the news that she was an epileptic, and the chilling truth – leeches.

I never thought I would see anything worse; then the corpse of the child turned up, Aziza binte Salim. I suppose what made it particularly dreadful was her age – not more than seven – and the fact that she was a girl. Most people are apprehensive about their daughters; Malays turn this apprehension into paranoia, or at least underpin it with the ferocity of Islamic suspicion. Aziza was a prize, a cute round-faced girl with jet-black hair. She lived in the *kampong* at the northern end of the town, which bordered on the derelict rubber estate. The Malays there had repossessed the huts of the Tamil rubber tappers, shading them with banana groves. I often used to walk out that way in the late afternoon when the Consulate closed, to limber up for tennis. My walks were a displacement activity: I would have had a drink if I had gone to the Club after work; then another drink, and another, and no tennis. Though I never knew her name, I went through the *kampong* afterward and – how shall I put it? – I noticed she was missing. Then I remembered her laughing face.

The monsoon was late that year, so late it looked as if the rice shoots would never be planted. The fields had been prepared in that clumsy traditional way, by buffaloes dragging the metal ploughs through the water, stirring the mud. But weeks later there was still no rain, and the paddy fields were beginning to show the ridges of the empty furrows as the water level dropped. The ditches dried and the embankments came apart as the grass that knitted them together died. A sad sight: the quilt of drying fields that had been so green in the previous planting, the sun's slow fire bringing death.

While the agricultural officers were deliberating over their clipboards (one American-trained Malay used to come to the Club and say, 'These guys haven't got a chance' – I wanted to sock him in the jaw), the *kampong* was deciding things its own way.

I had the story from Peeraswami. As soon as it became clear that the situation was desperate, the Malay rice farmers met and decided to bring their problem to a *bomoh* – a medicine man – whose hut was deep in the bush, not far from the village of aboriginal Laruts who acted as his messengers. It was a part of the jungle where not even the Sultan's tax collectors showed their faces. This *bomoh*, Noor, had a reputation. Later when I saw him in court he looked a most mild man, somewhat comic in his old-fashioned wire spectacles.

But he scared the life out of Peeraswami, who said that the Malays from the *kampong* had sworn that no one should reveal their identities – they took a vow of secrecy before they set out. Most of the stories about the *bomoh* Noor came from the Laruts, who spoke of goats that had disappeared and odd howlings from the *bomoh*'s hut. The Laruts had never engaged him, but the reason was simple: Noor was expensive. He asked the visiting Malays to make a contribution before he allowed them in.

The next thing he said was that the *kampong* was cursed: the curse was keeping the monsoon away.

They expected to hear that. They would have been surprised if he had said anything else. But how to cure it?

'There is always a cure,' said the *bomoh* Noor. 'Can you afford it?'

They said yes, of course, but when the *bomoh* only smiled and said nothing else for several minutes they began wondering if their answer should have been no.

'Three hundred dollars,' said Noor, finally.

At that time, the exchange rate was three to one, Straits dollars to American green. But this was quite a sum to simple rice farmers who, long before the next harvest, would be living on credit from the Chinese shops. They had a fear, common in agricultural societies, of being uprooted and driven to a hostile part of the country to begin again. They asked the *bomoh* his terms.

'Half the money now, the balance when it is finished.'

'When the rain falls,' said one man.

'When it is finished there will be rain.'

The strange distancing construction of the Malay verbs made them inquire further: 'You're going to do it yourself?'

'It will be done,' said the *bomoh*, using the same courtly remoteness.

'By you?'

'It is tiger's work,' said the old man. He smiled and showed his black teeth. Even the most menacing *bomoh* had an access of comedy – it could be as effective a curative as fear. The ramshackle hut, the clay bowls of beaks and feathers, the stink of decayed roots had, mingled with the riddle of their threat, an element of the clownish. But according to Peeraswami no one laughed. The old man said, 'The money.'

They handed over the hundred and fifty. The bills were counted and put in a strong-box. The old man gestured for them to sit down.

The sun continued hot, wilting the foliage of the elastic figs; the frangipanis lost their leaves, and the bougainvillaeas at the Club took on a frail drooping look, rusted blossoms and slack leaves hanging from brittle branches. The dust was everywhere. The grass courts behind the Club were impossible, and I recall how an especially hard backhand shot would send the ball bouncing into my opponent's face with a great puff of red dust. This was bad, and most people said it would get worse. It was a suffocating business to take the shortest walk. I worked late just to be away from the Club and the temptation to drink heavily. The other members wilted visibly at tables, cursing the heat over glasses of beer. Ayer Hitam was parched, changed in color from the yellow stucco to the deep red of the risen dust, and the tires of the trishaws left marks in the sun-softened tar.

After another week I was drinking – my habitual anesthetic of gin. One lunchtime, on the club verandah, I heard a commotion – whoops, shouts, a great gabbling. Odd sounds in such exhausting weather. On the road beyond the Club's cricket ground were running people, twenty or more. They were gibbering and crying out, beating their way from a banana grove. The cries reached us, '*Matjan! Matjan!*'

At the next table Squibb said, 'Something's up.'

We went to the rail. The elderly Chinese Head Boy, Stanley Chee, crossed the verandah with a tray and towel. He peered at the road and cocked his head.

'It's a tiger,' he said.

'Balls,' said Squibb. 'There hasn't been a tiger here for twenty years. Sure, you get them in Tapah, the Cameron Highlands, those places. They can feed there. But you never get them as far south as this. There's nothing for them to eat, and they've all been poached away.'

'*Matjan!*' The word was clear.

'If it is a tiger,' said Angela Miller, 'I'd love to see it. But an Ayer Hitam tiger would probably look like the one in that Saki story – toothless and frightened.'

Stanley Chee was still studying the mob in the road. He said, 'This tiger killed someone.'

'No,' said Angela, touching her throat.

'They have the body – there, you can see them carrying it.'

If it had been a car accident none of us would have gone near. Malays have been known to overturn a vehicle and kill the driver at the scene of an accident. But with Stanley's assurance that it was a tiger we left the verandah and met the procession.

And that is when I saw the corpse, which as I say was much worse than that poor epileptic's. It was clearly a small girl. She had been torn open, partially eaten – or at least frantically chewed – and flayed like a rabbit. Her blood stained the sheets they were carrying her in: red blossoms soaked it. Nor was that all, for just behind the first group there was another group, with a smaller sheet, and this bundle contained Aziza's head.

People were running from all directions, the Chinese from the shops, Peeraswami and his Tamil pals from the post office; and the Malays continued to shout while the impassive Stanley said, 'They found her in the *lallang* like that – they think it was a tiger. She is the daughter of Salim the carpenter.'

While we were standing there I got a sudden chill that made me hunch my shoulders. I thought it was simple fear and did not notice the sky darkening until it had gone almost black. Bizarre: but the monsoon is like that, brining a dark twilight at noon. The bamboos started cracking against each other, the banana leaves turned over and twisted in the wind, the grass parted and flattened – pale green undersides were whipped horizontal. And there was that muffled announcement of a tropical storm, the distant weeping of rain on leaves. I looked up and saw it approaching, the gray skirt of the storm being drawn towards us. The Malays began running again with their corpse, but they had not gone thirty yards when the deluge was upon us, making a deafening crackle on the road and gulping in the nearby ditches.

The rice was planted. The rain continued.

It was about a month after this that we heard the news of the lawsuit. It was Peeraswami who explained it to me, and I am ashamed to say I didn't believe him. I needed the confirmation of Squibb and the others at the Club, but they didn't know half as much as my *peon*. For example, Peeraswami not only knew the details of the lawsuit but all that background as well – the arrangement that had been made in the *bomoh*'s hut and that tantalizing scrap of dialogue, 'It is tiger's work.'

What happened was this. After the death of little Aziza – after the first of the rain – the *kampong* held a meeting. Salim was wretched: the rain was proof of his daughter's curse. And yet it was decided that the remainder of the money would not be paid to the *bomoh*. Salim said that whoever paid it would be regarded as the murderer of Aziza – and that man would be killed; also, the *Penghulu*, the headman, pointed out that the fields were full, the rice was planted, and even if it did not rain for another six months it would be a good harvest. The *bomoh* had brought the rain, but he could not take it away. A Larut boy – in town selling butterflies to tourists – was given the message. There was no response from the *bomoh*. None was expected: it was unanswerable, the matter settled.

Then the *bomoh* acted. Astonishing! He was suing the *kampong*'s headman for nonpayment of the debt, a hundred and fifty Straits dollars plus costs. Peeraswami had the news before anyone. A day later the whole of Ayer Hitam knew.

'Apart from anything else,' said Squibb, 'they'll tear him apart as soon as they set eyes on him.'

'He's a monster,' said Angela.

'He must be joking,' said Lloyd Strang, the government surveyor.

'If the *kampong* don't kill him, the court will,' said Alec Stewart.

We consulted Stanley Chee.

'You don't know these Malay boys,' he said. 'They are very silly.'

I had to ask him to repeat that. The rain made a clatter on the roof, like a shower of tin discs. Now we were always shouting, and the monsoon drains, four feet deep, were filled to the brim.

The *bomoh* was taken into protective custody and a magistrate was sent from Seremban to hear the case. The week of the trial no one worked. It was like Ramadhan: a sullenness came over the town, the streets were empty and held a damp still smell of desertion. Down by the jail a group of Malays sheltered under the eaves from the rain and called out abuse to the upper window.

I knew the court would be jammed, so the morning of the trial I drove in my official car with the CC plates and parked conspicuously by the front steps. A policeman opened the door and waving the crowd aside showed me in. I saw the *bomoh*, sitting at a side table with an Indian lawyer. At a table opposite were the gloomy Malays, the headman, Salim, some others, and their Chinese lawyer. Two fans were beating in the courtroom, and yet it was terribly hot; the windows were shut to keep the rain out, sealing the sodden heat in.

The *bomoh* took his spectacles off and polished them in his shirt-tail. He had looked like a petty clerk; now he looked only frail, with close-set eyes and a narrow head. He replaced his glasses and laid his skinny arms on the table. The Indian lawyer, whose suit was stained with dark patches of sweat, leaned over and whispered to him. The *bomoh* nodded.

'The court will now rise.'

The magistrate entered, a Chinese man in a black robe and ragged wig. He sat – dropped behind the tall bench until only his head showed – and fussed with papers. He called upon the *bomoh*'s lawyer to present the case, which, flourishing a truncheon of rolled foolscap, the Indian did. 'My client is owed the sum –'

The headman was called. The Chinese lawyer squawked something about 'blood money' and was silenced by the magistrate.

Twenty minutes of wrangling, then the magistrate said, 'I have heard both sides of this unusual case. I order that *Penghulu* Ismail pay within thirty days the sum of one hundred and fifty –'

There were shouts, screams, stampings, and a woman's wail briefly drowned the rain.

'Silence or I'll clear the court!'

The magistrate continued with his verdict. So it was settled. The *kampong* had to pay the debt and the court costs. When the magistrate had finished, the clerk of the court stood and shouted above the hubbub, 'The court will now adjourn.'

'What happens now?' I said.

A fat Tamil in a light seersucker suit next to me said, 'They are going to try the blighter for murder.'

I was afraid that if I left the court I'd lose my seat, so I stayed and talked to this Indian. He had come all the way from Singapore. He was a lawyer there in a firm that handled mostly shipping cases – 'but I'm on the criminal side myself.' This was a celebrated case: he knew the *bomoh*'s lawyer and he explained the defense.

'Well, it's a fine point. A British court would have thrown the book at him, but these Malay chaps are trying to do things their own way.' He grinned, displaying a set of rusted betel-stained teeth. 'Justice must be seen to be done. It's not so simple with these witch doctors. They're always giving trouble. Traditional law – it's a big field – they're going into it in KL. In a nutshell, this silly blighter *bomoh* is claiming he did not do the murder. Yes, there *was* a murder, but a tiger did it. You see?'

'But he won the other case – he got his money. So he must be guilty.'

'Not necessarily. Contract was made with him. Breach was proven – you heard it.'

'Which means he killed the girl.'

'No, tiger killed girl.'

'But he's the tiger.'

'No, he is man. Tiger is tiger.'

'I don't get it,' I said.

The Indian sighed. 'Man cannot be tiger. If tiger killed girl, tiger must be brought to trial. If tiger cannot be found, man must be released.'

I said sharply, 'It's the same damned person!'

'Listen, my friend. I will explain you for the last time. Tiger killed girl and *perhaps* man became tiger. *But*, if such is the case, he was not man when he killed girl and *therefore* man cannot be held responsible for crime. He can change shape, into monkey or tiger or what not. He can work magic. So traditional law applies.'

'Has he got a chance?'

'No, but it will be interesting all the same.'

The magistrate returned. The *bomoh*'s lawyer outlined the facts of the case, arguing along the lines the Indian next to me had suggested, and he concluded, 'I submit, m'lud, that my client is innocent of this deed. He has never been to the *kampong* in question, he has never seen the girl.'

The *bomoh* was put in the witness box and cross-examined through a translator. He sat with his head slightly bowed, answering softly in Malay. The prosecuting lawyer charged him, flung his arms about, rounded on him with accusations. But the *bomoh* said, 'Yes, I took the money – half of it – but I did not kill the girl. A tiger did that.'

'I am putting it to you that you are the tiger,' said the furious lawyer.

The *bomoh* spoke, then smiled. It was translated. 'I think that someone like you who has been to a school can tell the difference between a tiger and a man.'

There was little more. An adjournment, the sound of rain, the suffocating heat. Then the verdict: guilty. The magistrate specified the punishment: the *bomoh* Noor was to be hanged.

People stood and howled and shook their fists, and I saw the *bomoh* being led away, a small foolish man in a faded shirt, handcuffed to two hurrying policemen.

It was difficult not to feel sorry for the deluded witch doctor who had sued the *kampong* for breach of contract and delivered himself into the hands of the police. He was a murderer, undoubtedly, but my sympathy for him increased when his appeal was turned down. The people at the Club, some of them, asked me if I could use my influence as a member of the diplomatic corps and get them into the hanging at the Central Jail.

There were some stories: Father Lefever from the Catholic mission had visited him, to hear his confession – what a confession *that* would have been! – but the *bomoh* sent him away; in another version of that story, the *bomoh* was baptized and converted to Catholicism. Food was brought to the *bomoh* by a group of Larut tribesmen, and it was said that attempts had been made to poison it.

The failure of his appeal met with general satisfaction. Squibb said, 'I'd hang him myself if they gave me a chance. I've got the rope, too.'

The night before the hanging I heard a cry, a low continual howl. I had just come back from the Club and was having a brandy alone on my upstairs verandah. I closed my eyes and listened very carefully. I had not imagined it: it had roused the village dogs, who replied with barks.

I gasped and had to put my glass down. For a moment I felt strangled – I couldn't breathe. My mind hollowed and in its emptiness was only the sound of crickets and a solitary gecko. I had never experienced such frightful seconds of termination. But it was the rain: I had become so accustomed to the regular sprinkle it was like a sound within me. Now there was no rain, and it was as if my heart had stopped.

The sun – the first for many weeks – woke me the following morning, and hearing excited voices from the road, I rose and instead of having breakfast, took the car into town. There was a great mob gathered at the Central Jail, mostly Malays. I parked the car and pushed to the center of the mob, where there were half a dozen policemen holding the crowd back. A police guard in a khaki uniform lay in the mud, his arms stretched out, one puttee undone and revealing not a leg but the bone of a leg. And his face had been removed: he wore a mask of dark meat.

Fifty feet away the jail door was open. The hasp of the lock dangled – it had obviously received a tremendous blow. The Malays' interest was all in the dead man, stinking in that bright dawn, but what interested me was not the twisted hasp or even the disorder that led to the cells, the smashed bench, the overturned chair, but rather the door itself, which was painted that Ministry of Works yellow. It had been raked very deeply with claws.

'*Tuan!*'

I turned. It was Peeraswami, all eyes and teeth, and he hissed at me, '*Matjan!*'

Coconut Gatherer

'Welcome, welcome,' said Sundrum, tightening his sarong and showing me to a chair. He had raised his voice; there were children playing under the window, shouting and thumping against the frail wall of the house.

'I'm surprised you get any work done, with that racket.'

'Children,' said Sundrum. 'I love them. Their voices are music.'

It was my first visit to Sundrum's. I had met him at Alec's Christmas party, where he'd talked about the snow he had always wanted to see. Sundrum had been introduced to me as a teacher. I discovered later that he was a writer as well, Ayer Hitam's only novelist. And I was moved by that description: the Chekhovian character stifling in an airless provincial town, comforted by his books, puffing his pipe, casting ironic glances at his neighbors and keeping his diary up to date.

'So you have this symphony every day?' The children were still at it, yelling and banging.

'How else could I work?' said Sundrum. He was half-Chinese, half-Indian and so looked Malay, with a potbelly and a grin. It was a Malaysian grin, the result of the heat, and it seemed cooked into his face. 'Foreigners say this is a noisy country. I never notice it – perhaps it is because I am so busy.'

'I'd be embarrassed to tell you how little I have to do.'

'Writing is my life,' he said. 'I realized when I was in jail that life is short. I've had to make up for lost time.'

'You don't seem the criminal type.'

'I was imprisoned for my views. It was during the Emergency.'

'You must have had strong views.'

'I was held a month and then released.'

'I see.' A month's imprisonment: people got that for letting mosquitoes breed in their back yard. But I was angry with myself for ridiculing his jail sentence.

Sundrum said, 'I didn't suffer. I listened to the birds. It is a matter of perspective. Perspective is everything, don't you agree?'

'Absolutely.'

'People come here and write about Ayer Hitam. They are tourists – what do they know?' He threw open his arms and said, 'But if you live here it's different! You have perspective. You don't hear children screaming – you hear the voices of the future. Music.'

I was sorry I'd mentioned the children. Was he trying to rub it in?

'This is quite a library,' I said, indicating the bookshelves, a rare sight in a Malaysian household. A pedestal held a dictionary, which was open in the middle.

'My books,' said Sundrum. 'But what do they matter? Life is so much more important than books. I write, but I know I am wasting my time. Do you know what I always wanted to be?'

'Tell me.'

'A gatherer of coconuts,' he said. 'Not a farmer, but a laborer – one of these men who climbs the trees. Have you seen them? How they scramble up the vertical trunks? They cling to the tops of the trees and hack at the coconuts.' He motioned with his hands, illustrating. 'They defy gravity. And they see more from the tops of those palm trees than anyone on the ground. I have spoken to those men. Do you know what they say? Every coconut is different.'

'Is that so?'

'Every coconut is different!' He said it with surprising energy. 'They are the true poets of this country. They have perspective. I must say I envy them.'

Coconut gathering didn't seem much of an ambition. I had seen trained monkeys do it in Ayer Hitam. But Sundrum had spoken with enthusiasm, and I was almost persuaded. I thought: At last, a Malaysian who doesn't want a car, a passport, a radio, his airfare to New York. He was the first really happy man I had met in the country.

'I can't climb the coconut trees,' he said. 'So I do the next best thing. I write about it. You see?'

He raised his foot to the low wicker table and with his toe pushed a book towards me. The title in green was *The Coconut Gatherer*. He said, 'This is my tree.'

'I'd love to read it,' I said.

'Take it with my compliments,' he said. 'It is about a boy who lives in a *kampong* like this. He is a sad boy, but one day he climbs a coconut tree and sees the town of Ayer Hitam. He leaves home, and the book is a record of his many unfortunate adventures in the town. He is bitterly disappointed. He loses his money. He is starving. He climbs a coconut tree in Ayer Hitam and sees his *kampong*. He goes home.' Sundrum paused, then said, 'I am that boy.'

A Malay woman entered the room with a tray of food. She set the tray down on a table and withdrew, self-conscious as soon as her hands were empty.

'I hope you're hungry,' said Sundrum.

'It looks good,' I said.

He urged me to fill my plate. It was *nasi padang*, prawns, mutton chops, chicken, curried vegetables, and a heap of saffron rice; we finished with *gula malacca*, a kind of custard with coconut milk and sweet sauce. Sundrum ate greedily, wiping his hands on his sarong.

'I wish I had your cook,' I said.

'I have no cook. I made this myself. That girl you saw – she is just the *amah*.'

'You're not married?'

'I will marry when my work is done,' he said.

'You should open a restaurant.'

'Cooking is a creative activity,' he said. 'I would rather cook than write. I would rather do almost anything than write. For me, enjoyment is going down to the *jelutong* tree where the old men gather, to listen to the stories of the old days. They are much wiser than I am.'

I couldn't mock him; he spoke with feeling; I believed his humility to be genuine. And again I was ashamed, for what did I know of the town? I had never spoken to those old men. Indeed, my life seemed to be centered around the Club and the Consulate, the gossip of members, the complaints of Americans. Sundrum said he envied the coconut gatherers, but I envied Sundrum his peace of mind in this green clearing. It was an aspect of life that was so often overlooked, for there was contentment here, and just admitting that made me feel better, as if somehow Sundrum represented the soul of the people.

After lunch he took me around the *kampong* and introduced me. My Malay was no good then; I let him do all the talking and I barely understood what he was saying. I was impressed by the familiar way he greeted the old men and by their respectful attitude toward him. And I think that if I could have traded my life for his I would have done so, and changed into a sarong and spent the rest of my days there, swinging in a hammock and peeling prawns.

'Don't forget the book,' he said, when I told him I had to go. He rushed back to the house to get it, and he presented it in a formal, almost courtly way. 'I hope you enjoy it.'

'I'm sure I will.'

'You were very kind to come out here,' he said. 'I know it is not very exciting, but it is important for you to see the whole of Malaysia, the great and the small.'

'The pleasure is mine.'

He took my hand and held it. 'Friendship is more important than anything else. I tell my students that. If people only realized it, this would be a happier world.'

I hurried away and almost hated myself when I remembered that I was hurrying to a cocktail party at Strang's. Now it was clear that Milly Strang wasn't coming back, and Strang was behaving like a widower. He needed cheering up; he would have taken my absence to mean moral disapproval.

That night, after the party, to recapture the mood of my visit to Sundrum's I took up *The Coconut Gatherer*. I read it in disbelief, for the story was mawkish, the prose appalling and artless, simply a sludge of wrongly punctuated paragraphs. It went on and on, a lesson on every page, and often the narrative broke down and limped into a sermon on the evils of society. The main character had no name; he was 'Our Hero.' I was surprised Sundrum had found a publisher until I looked at the imprint and saw that it was the work of our local Chinese printer, Wong Heck Mitt.

I soon forgot the book, but Sundrum himself I thought of often as a good man in a dull place. He was a happy soul, plump and brown in his little house, and I was glad for his very existence.

It was a year before I saw him again. The intervening time had a way of making Ayer Hitam seem a much bigger place, not the small island I knew it to be, but a vastness in which people could change or disappear.

I had expected to see him at Alec's Christmas party. He was not there, though the party was much the same as the first one. I arrived at Sundrum's house one day in early January, and he looked at me half in irritation, half in challenge, the kind of hasty recognition I had become accustomed to: he saw my race or nationality and there his glance ended. He didn't remember my name.

'I hope I'm not disturbing you,' I said.

'Not at all. It's just that I've had so many visitors lately. And I've been on leave. Singapore. The *Straits Times* was doing a piece about me.'

His tone was cold and self-regarding, but the room was as before – bizarrely so. The same arrangement of books, the open dictionary, *The Coconut Gatherer* on the low wicker table, and at the window the children's laughter.

Sundrum offered me Chinese tea and said, 'Listen to them. Some people call that noise. I call it music.'

'They seem pretty excited.'

'They caught a python in the monsoon drain yesterday. That's what they're talking about. The whole *kampong* is excited. They've probably killed it already.' He listened at the window, then said, 'They have no idea what I do.'

'How is your writing?'

'Writing is my life,' he said. 'I learned that in jail when I had no pencil or paper. But I make up for lost time.'

I said, 'It must have been the worst month of your life.'

'Month?' His laugh was mocking and boastful. 'It was closer to a year! I'll never forgive them for that. And I know who was behind it – the British. It was during the Emergency – they couldn't tell us apart. If you were so-called native you were guilty. You people have a lot to answer for.'

'I'm not British,' I said.

'You're white – what's the difference? The world belongs to you. Who are we? Illiterates, savages! What right do we have to publish our books – you own all the printeries. You're Prospero, I'm Caliban.'

'Cut it out,' I said. 'I'm not an old fool and your mother isn't a witch.'

'I'll tell you frankly,' said Sundrum. 'When the Japanese occupied Malaysia and killed the British we were astonished. We didn't hate the Japanese – we were impressed. Orientals just like us drove out these people we had always feared. That was the end; when we saw them fall so easily to the Japanese we knew we could do it.'

'Really?' I said. 'And what did you think when the Japanese surrendered?'

'I wept,' he said. 'I wept bitterly.'

'You should write about that.'

'I have, many times, but no one wants to hear the truth.'

'I take it you're having some difficulty being published.'

'Not at all,' he said. 'I've just finished a book. Here.' He picked up *The Coconut Gatherer* and handed it to me. 'Just off the presses. It's coming out soon.'

I turned the pages to verify that it was the same book and not a sequel. It was the one I had read. I said, 'But this isn't about the Japanese.'

'It is about self-discovery,' he said. 'Do you know what I always wanted to be?'

'A coconut gatherer?'

He looked sharply at me, then said, 'I'm not ashamed of it. I can't climb coconut trees, so I do the next best thing. I write about it.'

I handled the book, not knowing what to say.

'Take that book,' he said. 'See for yourself if I'm not telling the truth.'

It was too late to say that I had already read it, that he had given me a copy on my last visit. I said, 'Thank you.'

'I'm sorry I can't offer you anything but this tea. My cook is ill. She is lying, of course – helping her husband with the rice harvest. I let her have her lie.'

'This tea is fine.'

'Drink up and I will show you the *kampong*,' he said.

The old men were seated around the great tree; a year had not changed their features or their postures. Seeing Sundrum they got to their feet, as they had done the previous year, and they exchanged greetings. On my first visit my Malay had been shaky, but now I understood what Sundrum was saying. He did not tell the old men my name; he introduced me as someone who had come 'from many miles away, crossing two oceans.' 'How long will he stay?' asked one old man. Sundrum said, 'After we discuss some important matters he will go away.' The men shook my hand and wished me a good journey.

'What a pity you don't understand this language,' said Sundrum, as we walked back to the house. 'It is music. Foreigners miss so much. But they still come and write about us. And their books are published and ours are not!'

'What were you talking about to those old men?' I asked.

'About the snake,' he said, and walked a bit faster.

'The snake?' No snake had been mentioned.

'The python that was caught yesterday. It is going to be killed. They think it is a bad omen, perhaps it means we will have a poor harvest. I know what you think – a silly superstition! But I tell you I have known these omens to be correct.'

I said, 'Have you known them to be wrong?'

'To you, this must seem a poor *kampong*,' said Sundrum. 'But a great deal happens here. This is not Ayer Hitam. Every year is different here. I could live anywhere – a schoolmaster can name his price – but I choose to live here.'

I looked again at the *kampong* and it was less than it had seemed on my previous visit, smaller, dirtier, a bit woebegone, with more naked children, and somewhere a radio playing a shrill song. I wanted to leave at once.

'I have to go,' I said.

'Europeans,' he said. 'Always in a hurry.'

'I've got work to do.'

'Look at those old men,' he said, and turned and looked back at the *jelutong* tree. 'They have the secret of life. They sit there. They don't hurry or worry. They are wiser than any of us.'

'Yes.' But I thought the opposite and saw them as only old and baffled and a bit foolish, chattering there under their tree year after year, meeting their friends at the mosque, facing the clock-tower to face Mecca, talking about the *haj* they would never take and going home when it got dark. Islanders.

Sundrum said, 'When I was in jail I used to hear the birds singing outside my window and sometimes I dropped off to sleep and dreamed that I was back here on the *kampong*. It was a good dream.'

'You're happy here.'

'Why shouldn't I be?' he said. 'I'm not like some people who write their books and then go to Singapore or KL to drink beer and run around with women. No, this is my life. I have my books, but what do they matter? Life is so much more important than books. I have no wish to live in Ayer Hitam.'

Ayer Hitam could be seen from the top of a palm tree; for Sundrum it was a world away, a distance that could scarcely be put into words. A year before I had seen him as a solitary soulful man, who had found contentment. Now he seemed manic; another visitor might find him foolish or arrogant, but his arrogance was fear. He had that special blindness of the villager. How cruel that he had turned to writing, the one art that requires clear-sightedness.

I said, 'You weren't at the Christmas party this year.'

'I went last year.'

'I know.'

'Were you there? I didn't know the people well. I went to gather material. I've finished with Christmas parties, but I still need perspective – perspective is everything. From the ground, all coconuts look the same, but climb the tree and you will see that each one is different – a different shape, a different size, some ripe, some not. Some are rotten! That is the lesson of my novel.'

We had reached his house. I said, 'It's late.'

'I promised you my book,' he said. 'Let me get it for you.'

I heard him crossing the floor of his house, treading the worn planks. No, I thought: every coconut is the same. It takes time to decide that your first impression, however brutal, was correct.

There was no party that night. After dinner I sat down with *The Coconut Gatherer*. The book was identical to the one he had given me the previous year, the friendly flourish of his inscription on the flyleaf exactly as it was in the other copy. But I read it again, this time with pleasure. I admired his facility, the compactness of his imagery, the rough charm of his sermonizing. It was clumsy in parts: he had no gift for punctuation. But I could not fault him for these mechanical lapses, since beneath the husk and fiber of his imitative lyricism so much of what he described was recognizably true to me.

The Last Colonial

The planter Gillespie swore he'd never leave. Though he remained embattled – one of the last colonials – the changeover from rubber to palm oil continued on the larger estates. After eighteen months of it, I saw a time, not very far off, when I would gladly close the Consulate – or what was more likely, sell the remainder of my lease to the Arabs or the Japanese. Gillespie wanted me to dig my heels in and stay; he typified the older sort of expatriate, his attitude was a definition of that exile – home was defeat. Estate managers who went home caught cold, drove buses, and lived an *amah*'s life, cooking and doing dishes.

And then, like deliverance, Gillespie was ambushed, killed on the road to Kluang. His *syce* was handed pamphlets and allowed to go free, so we knew it was political. But even that aspect did not shake the others at the Club; they said that sudden burst of gunfire on the lonely road was preferable to a slow death in Baltimore – Gillespie was an American – and they took the view that he was luckier than some who, hacked by *parangs*, had gone home maimed.

I had been told to expect it as the natural result of our collapse in Vietnam, more guerilla activity in Malaysia, a resurgence of revolutionary zeal. I was not surprised to hear of incidents in the northern states, where there were borders and concealing jungle. But here, in Ayer Hitam? It seemed unthinkable. And I couldn't imagine why anyone here would kill to make a political point or want to repeat the old cycle of taking power just to give another group its turn in purgatory. Yet it had started, and one of the pamphlets handed to Gillespie's *syce* was titled *Sejauh Mana Kita Bersabar? – How Long Must We Be Patient?* It could have been the complaint of any political group – of anyone who wanted power. But in the circumstances it was a threat. If this was patience I trembled to think what a loss of temper might mean.

Seeing that the recessional might be bloodier than I'd expected, I decided to stick my neck out and see the Sultan about it – not in my official capacity, but informally, to find out, before State Department representations were made, what steps were being taken to deal with terrorists. Unofficially, I had been told that the Malaysian government expected American military support. Though they had not been turned down, Flint in the Embassy in Kuala Lumpur had told me, 'They're whistling in the dark, but if it makes things easier for you tell them we're thinking of giving them air cover.'

The American position was: we'll help if the casualties are yours. I decided to hint this to the Sultan in the Oriental – or at least Malaysian – way. My opportunity came a few weeks after Gillespie's murder when talking with Azhari, the District Commissioner, at the ceremonial opening of a palm-oil estate, I asked if the Sultan was going to be there.

'He doesn't travel,' said Azhari, as if the Sultan were some rare wine. He searched my face suspiciously: had I meant my question as criticism?

I said that I had been longing to meet him; that I might be leaving soon. 'I'd hate to leave without having had a chat with him.'

'I can arrange that,' said Azhari.

I felt I had gone about it in the right way. The Sultan might get in touch with me, or Azhari might give me the go-ahead. I'd write a personal note and wouldn't mention security – I didn't want to talk to a general. But nothing happened. It was so often the case with the Oriental approach: one needed Oriental patience, like Gillespie.

It was a sign of our diminishing numbers, perhaps a siege mentality, that we began meeting together for lunch, Alec, Squibb, Evans, Strang, and sometimes Prosser. A club within the Club, for since I had arrived many expatriates had left and the membership committee started encouraging locals to join. It looked like tolerance; it was a way of paying the bills. Our lunches might have been a reaction to the Chinese tables, the Malay tables, the Indian tables. A multiracial club seemed to mean nothing more than a dining room filled with tables at which the various races asserted their difference by practicing exclusion.

At one of those lunches I noticed Alec carrying an odd familiar stick that I recognized and yet could not name.

'A shooting stick,' he said when I asked. 'You sit on it, like so.' He opened it, stuck it into the dining-room carpet and sat. There were some stares; the local members had not progressed to the point where they were allowed this sort of eccentricity.

'Going shooting?' asked Evans.

'Polo,' said Alec. 'I'm driving down to the Sultan's. This is the last day of the festival.'

'Hari Raya Haji's months away,' I said.

'Not that festival, you idiot. The Sultan's not a complete barbarian.' He winked at me. 'Polo festival. It's been going on for a week. This will be the best day – Pahang's playing. And tonight the Sultan awards his cup. But I shan't stay for that hoo-hah.'

'Do you mind if I come along with you?'

Alec spoke to Squibb. 'Hear that? I told you we'd make a gentleman out of this Yank.'

And Alec even found me a shooting stick in one of the Club's storerooms. 'Remember,' he said, 'pointed end in the ground. Got it?'

There were flags flying at the gateway of the Sultan's mansion, the flags of all the states, and colored pennants fluttering on wires. Across the driveway were the Christmas lights the Malays dragged out for special occasions. The day was overcast and sultry and the spectators looked subdued in the heat – a crowd of Malays standing on the opposite side, some still figures on our side, surrounded by many empty chairs. As we passed behind the awnings of the Royal Pavilion Alec said, 'Just follow me and set your stick up. Don't turn around. Concentrate on the match.'

'What's wrong?'

'He's here,' said Alec. 'I was hoping he wouldn't be. Worse luck.'

'Who?'

'Buffles,' said Alec.

'The Sultan?'

'Buffles. And if I catch you calling him "Your Highness" I'll never give you lunch again.'

We were not at the sidelines – Alec said we'd be trampled there. We had set up our sticks about thirty feet from the margin of the field, our backs to the pavilion.

It was to me an unexpectedly beautiful sport, graceful horses leaping back and forth on a field of English grass; like mock warfare, a tournament, chargers in the colors of chivalry, green and gold. No shouts, only the hoof beats, the occasional crack of sticks, and the small white ball flying from the scrimmage of snorting horses.

'Third chukka,' said Alec. 'There's Eddie Pahang – awfully good player. Get him!' Alec lurched with such excitement he drove his shooting stick deeper into the ground.

'I say, aren't you playing, Stewart?'

It was a high querulous voice. Alec sighed and said, 'Buffles.' But he turned smiling towards the striped awning. 'Not today!'

I had not taken a good look at the Sultan when we entered the polo ground. Now I saw him and, seated next to him, Angela Miller in her garden-party outfit, white gloves and a long dress and a wide-brimmed hat. The Sultan wore a batik sports shirt and dark glasses; his head came to Angela's shoulder, her hat shielding him like an umbrella.

'Sit here, Stewart,' he said, patting an armchair in front of him. 'Join us – bring your friend.'

Alec smiled rather coldly at Angela, as at a betrayer, then introduced me.

The Sultan said, 'I didn't know there was still a consulate in Ayer Hitam. Why don't my people tell me anything?'

'It's really a small affair,' I said.

'Ayer Hitam is lovely. Like those villages in the Cotswolds one sees. One drives through and always wishes one could stop. But one never does. Stewart, what do you think of the game?'

The Sultan was about seventy, with the posture and frown of an old toad. I had never seen a Malay who looked quite like him, certainly none as fat. And there was a greater difference – his skin was unmistakably freckled and in places blotchy, crushed, and oddly pigmented: strange for the ruler of such sleek unwrinkled people.

'– spirited,' Alec was saying.

'Yes, spirited, spirited,' said the Sultan. 'That's just what I was telling Angela.' He peered again at me, so that I could see my face in each of the lenses of his glasses. 'Did you say you were a writer?'

'Consul,' I said.

'But you know Beverley Nichols.'

'I've heard of him.'

'English,' said the Sultan. 'Frightfully clever. Wrote a book –' The Sultan fidgeted, trying to remember.

'*The Sun in My Eyes*, Your Highness,' said Angela.

'That's it. Frightfully good book.'

'His Highness appears in the book,' said Angela.

'We must get it for the club library,' I said.

'It's there,' said Alec. 'Nichols stopped for the night a few years ago. Gave us a signed copy. Bit of an old woman actually.'

Angela said, 'Literary gossip! It makes me homesick.'

'He stayed with me a fortnight,' said the Sultan. 'I had a letter from him yesterday. His book was a best-seller.' He turned to Angela. 'Someone's coming to stay. Lord – who is it?'

'Elsynge, Your Highness.'

'Elsynge is coming, yes. Elsynge. Had a letter from him. Here,' he said, 'you two sit here. Do put those sticks away. You'll be more comfortable.' He motioned to the armchairs in front of him and after we sat down he touched me on the shoulder. 'Somerset Maugham – did you know him?'

'I never had the pleasure,' I said.

'He visited,' said the Sultan. 'With his friend Earl, of course. Had to have Earl.'

'He came to your coronation, Your Highness.'

'Yes, he came to my coronation. He was here a week. But he stayed at Raffles Hotel. He liked Raffles. If he was alive to see it now he'd die!'

Alec said, 'He's away!'

A pack of horses galloped down the field after one rider who had broken away swinging his mallet. The handle curved as he hit the ball, which rose toward the goal. There was a great cheer from the Pahang side. The horses trotted away to regroup on the field.

The Sultan said, 'Was that a goal?'

'No, Your Highness, but very nearly,' said Angela.

'Very nearly, yes! I saw that, didn't I?'

'Missed by a foot,' said Alec.

'Missed by a foot, yes!' said the Sultan and wiped his face.

'They're beautiful horses,' I said. 'I had no idea it was such a graceful sport.'

The Sultan said, 'Did you say you're a Canadian?'

'American.'

'Do you know what a Canadian told me once? He said horsemeat is very good. This Canadian had pots of money – he owned all the cinemas in Canada. He went on safaris and shot grizzly bears in Russia and what not. He said to me, "Bearmeat is the best, but the second best is horsemeat." He said that. Yes, he did!'

Alec looked at me slyly and said, 'That Canadian never tasted haggis.'

'The *syces* here eat it,' said the Sultan.

'Haggis?' said Alec.

But the Sultan hadn't heard. 'My father was a sportsman. Oh, he was a great hunter. He shot everything, too, elephants, lions. He shot the last tiger in Malaya – the very last one! You might like to see his trophies after the match.'

'We'll have to be heading back,' said Alec.

'My father said horsemeat was good to eat. Yes, indeed. But it's very heating, he said.' The Sultan placed his freckled hands on his belly and tugged. 'You can't eat too much of it. It's too heating.'

'You've tried it then?' I said.

He looked disapproving. 'My *syces* eat it.'

There was a shout from the Malays at the periphery of the field.

'What was that? A goal?'

'A foul, Your Highness,' said Angela.

'A foul? What did he do?'

'Crossed over, Your Highness.'

'Is that a foul?'

'Yes, Your Highness.'

The Sultan grimaced in boredom. 'Stewart, I was in Singapore yesterday. They gave me an escort and then they cleared Bukit Timah Road for me. Just closed the road. Too bad, chaps, they said. Took me fifteen minutes to get back from the Seaview.'

'Fancy that,' said Alec.

'The Bird Park's open,' said the Sultan. 'It's full of chickens, they say. Chickens of various kinds. They wanted me to see them. Know what I told them? I said, "*I have penguins.*" I do – eight or ten. Perhaps your friend would like to see them after the match.'

'We're expected back in Ayer Hitam when the match is over,' said Alec. He scowled at his watch. 'Which should be any minute now.'

'I won't let you go,' said the Sultan. He spoke to Angela. 'I won't let them go.'

'No, Your Highness.'

The match ended soon after she spoke. The Sultan said, 'Come,

Stewart,' and he took Angela's arm. 'If you don't come I shall never speak to you again.'

Alec whispered, 'He's not joking.'

We were in the Sultan's ballroom. The lights of the chandeliers were on, and the fans rattled their glass. But it was not yet dark outside; the setting sun ridiculed these lights and made them look cheap, like the garish illuminations of an arcade. Some of the glass hangings were missing or broken; the wall mirrors were imperfect and had that tropical decay that showed as gray blistered smears on their undersides. I saw the Sultan's flowered shirt in one of the mirrors; it passed into a smear and he was gone.

The room was filled with people – women dressed like Angela, men in white suits, waiters carrying trays of drinks. The polo players were still in their uniforms, much grimier than they had looked on their horses, with mud-spattered boots. It was their celebration: they wore their mud proudly like a badge of combat.

'Have a drink,' said a Malay polo player. He handed me a large gold cup.

The metal was warm and sticky, and I hesitated again when I saw the sloshing liquid, faintly yellow under a spittly froth. I tried to pass it back to him.

'Drink,' he said. 'It's champagne. We won!'

'Congratulations,' I said, and made a show of drinking.

'It's solid gold,' he said. 'From Asprey's.'

The cup was taken from me by a fat Malay girl who raised it to her mouth so quickly it splashed down her dress.

'That's okay,' she said, and brushed at her dress. 'It's just a cheap thing I got in London.'

'Very pretty,' I said.

'Do you like it? It's from a boutique. 'Che Guevara' on Carnaby Street.'

'The Che Guevara boutique,' I said. 'That sums up the past fifteen years, doesn't it?'

She said, 'The cup's from Asprey's. It cost three thousand dollars.'

The polo player smiled. 'Three thousand eight hundred.' As he spoke his teeth snagged on his lip.

I was relieved to see Alec making his way toward us. He greeted the girl, 'How's my princess? You're looking fit.'

'I'm not,' she said. 'It's this stinking climate. Daddy insists I spend my hols here. He knows I hate it, so he bought me a car this time. Red. Automatic transmission. It's the only one in the country.'

'Drive up and see us some time,' said Alec.

'You'd like that, wouldn't you?' she said. 'Excuse me, I need a drink.' She wandered into the crowd.

'The princess,' said Alec. 'She's a hard lass. Her tits are solid gold.'

'Who are all these people?'

'Royalty of various kinds,' said Alec. 'They're all in the stud book. Try to look interested – we won't be here long.'

'I was hoping to talk to the Sultan.'

'I thought you'd had your fill of that.'

'Political questions,' I said. But I didn't want to ask them. I knew the answers, and I was certain it would only make me angrier to hear him say them.

Alec said, 'It doesn't matter. Whatever you ask him, he'll turn the conversation to Beverley Nichols and Willie Maugham. Here he comes.'

The Sultan entered the room. He had changed into a buff-colored military uniform that resembled a Masonic costume. None of the medals and ribbons thatched on his breast pocket were as striking as the buttons down the front of his jacket, which turned the dim light from the chandeliers into a dazzle. There was some applause as he took his seat at the head table.

'Those buttons are something,' I said.

'Diamonds,' said Alec. 'That's how we kept these jokers on our side, you know. We let them design their own uniforms. Buffles is one of the better ones. True, he barely speaks Malay, he's half gaga and he thinks Beverley Nichols is Shakespeare. But I tell you, Buffles is one of the better ones.'

'Isn't this rather an expensive farce?' I said. I looked around and thought: Gillespie died for them. But Gillespie had been a polo player.

'It's your farce from now on. You Americans will pay for it.'

'No,' I said. 'They're whistling in the dark.'

'We're being summoned,' said Alec. 'Here comes the princess. What did I tell you? Now we have to stay.'

'No,' I said. 'I'm not hungry anymore.'

The princess said, 'Daddy wants you to sit down.'

The Sultan had already begun eating. He was hunched biliously over his food and appeared to be spitting into his plate.

'We'll be right over,' said Alec.

'I'm expected in Ayer Hitam,' I said.

'Daddy said you're to stay.'

'I'm afraid that's out of the question,' I said.

Alec tried to soothe her, but she stepped in front of him and said crossly, 'Daddy said so.' She went back to the Sultan and whispered in his ear. The old man looked up, trying to focus on me. He looked blackly furious, and then his cheeks bulged with a bone which he spat on the table-cloth.

'Now you've done it,' said Alec.

The princess returned to us. 'Go, if you want to,' she said. 'Daddy doesn't care. But I do. You have no right to treat him that way. You know what I think of you? I think you're a typical rude American.'

'If you believe that,' I said, 'then it won't surprise you if I tell you that I think you're a fat overprivileged little prig.'

Her eyes widened at me. I thought she was going to scream, but all she said was, 'I'm telling Daddy.'

'Please do.'

Alec said, 'Are you off your head?' He rushed over to the Sultan and spoke to him, and he did not leave until he had the Sultan laughing, agreeing, sharing whatever story he had concocted to excuse himself for my bad manners.

'What were you telling the Sultan?' I asked on the way back to Ayer Hitam.

'Nothing,' he said. Then suddenly, 'You don't have to live here – I do.'

The road was dark; we drove in silence for a while past the ruined rubber estates. At one, there was a shack at the roadside. I heard a child bawling. I said, 'Poor Gillespie.'

Alec grunted. He said, 'Gillespie would have stayed.'

He was right, of course. Gillespie would have stayed and charmed the Sultan and complimented the princess. I had overreacted – my squawk was ineffectual. But Gillespie didn't matter much. He was just another Maugham hero whose time was up. Only the night mattered, and those feebly lighted shacks, and the cry of that child in the darkness, and the danger that all of us deserved. We drove down the road which was made cavernous by hanging branches, and there was no sound but the pelting insects smashing against the windshield.

Triad

We rather disliked children; we had none of our own, but that was seldom noticed because the local kids were everywhere. They strayed from the staff quarters and the *kampong* into the club grounds, meeting in threes – three Tamils, three Malays, three Chinese, as if that was the number required for play. They usually quarreled: it was an impossible number – one was invariably made a leper, victimized, and finally rejected. Alec called them villains. He blamed the theft of his camera on one particular threesome who played their own version – no teams, no net – of the Malay game of *sepak takraw*, kicking a raffia ball the size of a grapefruit back and forth at the side of the clubhouse.

There was a solitary one, perhaps Malay. It was hard to tell how dark she was beneath her dirt. She had uncombed hair and bruised legs and elbows and she wore a soiled waistless dress of the sort sent in bales from America and England and distributed by bush missionaries. She was not tall, but neither was she very young. The dirt gave her skin the texture of greasy fabric. Her feet were cracked like an adult's, she was solemn, she did not play. She squatted on the grass with her arms folded on her knees, her tangled hair drooping, and she watched the other children taking possession of the parking lot, the gardens, the old bowling green. She looked upon them with a witchy aloofness. She was, for all her dirt, free.

All this I remembered after she joined us.

Late one night, over drinks, Tony Evans was describing how a tennis ball should strike the racket if it was to have maximum top-spin. There were three of us in the lounge – Tony, Rupert Prosser, and myself – and it was October, just before the second monsoon. Tony was still in his white tennis outfit, having made a night of his after-game drinks; there were spills of pink Angostura down the front of his Fred Perry shirt.

'You should concentrate on your game now that the Footlighters have folded,' he said to Prosser, the pink gins giving what was meant as a casual remark a leaden pedantry. 'Jan's got a weak serve – she should be working on that.' He sipped his drink. 'Now, top-spin. Ideally, the ball should hit the racket at this angle.'

He touched the ball to the strings and then with a sudden hilarity hit the ball hard. It shot out of the window and made a dark thump in the grass.

'You weren't paying attention.'

Prosser said, 'You're drunk.'

But Evans was heading for the door. He said, 'Now I've got to find my bloody ball.'

We heard him stamping around the lawn and swishing through the flowers under the window. He cursed; there was a cry – not his – like a cat's complaint. The next we knew he was at the door and saying, 'Look what I found!'

He did not hold the girl in his arms – she was too big for that. He held her wrist, as if he was abducting her, and she was trying to pull away. She had the haggard, insolent look of someone startled from sleep. She did not seem afraid, but rather contemptuous of us.

'She was at the door,' said Evans. 'I saw her legs sticking out. These people can sleep anywhere.'

'I've seen her around,' said Prosser. 'I thought she was from the *kampong*.'

'Could use a bath,' said Evans. He made a face, but still he held her wrist.

In Malay, I asked her what her name was. She scowled with fear and jerked her head to one side. Her thin starved face allowed her teeth and eyes to protrude, and she smelled of dust and damp grass. But she was undeniably pretty, in a wild sort of way, like a captive bird panting under its ragged feathers, wishing to break free of us.

'Call the police,' said Evans. 'She shouldn't be sleeping out there.'

Then he said with unmistakable lechery, 'She doesn't look like much, but believe me she's got a body under all those rags. I felt it! Give her a bath and you might be surprised by what you find. All she wants is a good scrub.'

I said, 'We ought to call the mission.'

'They'll be asleep – it's nearly midnight,' said Prosser. 'I'll ring Jan. We can put her in the spare room.'

Prosser went to the phone. Evans picked up the bowl of peanuts from the bottle-cluttered table. He showed her the peanuts and said, '*Makan?*'

At first she hesitated, then seeing that she was being encouraged she took a great handful and pushed it into her mouth. She turned away to chew and I could hear her hunger, the snappings and swallowings.

Evans nudged me. 'Listen to him' – Prosser was drunkenly shouting into the phone in the next room – 'I'll bet Jan thinks he's picked up some tart!'

A week later the girl was still with the Prossers.

'She's landed on her feet,' said Evans. 'Couple of bleeding hearts. They always wanted a kid.'

'She's no kid,' I said. 'Has Prosser told the police? Her parents might be looking for her. Who knows, she might have had amnesia.' Evans was shaking his head. 'She might be a bit simple.'

'Not according to Jan. They're thinking of taking her on as an *amah*. She learns fast, they say. The only thing is, she hasn't said a blessed word!'

'Suppose she's not Malay? Suppose she's Chinese? We should get someone to talk to her in Cantonese or Hokkien. Father Lefever could do it.'

'You don't want a mish for this,' said Evans. 'My provisioner's just the man. I'll put him onto it. You're in for a treat. Pickwick's a real character.'

That afternoon, as I was walking into town, a car drew up beside me, the Prossers' Zephyr.

'Give you a lift?' said Rupert.

I thanked him, but said I'd walk. Then I saw the girl. She was in the back seat, in a beautiful sarong, with a blouse so starched it was like stiff white paper enfolding her dark shoulders. She smiled at me shyly, as if ashamed to be seen this way. The blouse was crushed against her breasts, the sarong tightened on her curve of belly. Cleaned up she looked definitely Chinese; her face was a bit fuller, her eyes deep and lacking the dull shine her hunger had given them. She was a beauty in tremulous trapped repose, and the Prossers in the front seat were obviously very proud of her.

'We're taking Nina into town to buy some clothes,' said Jan. 'She doesn't have a stitch, poor thing.'

'We had to burn her dress,' said Rupert, grinning. 'It stank!'

'Filthy! She was caked with it,' said Jan, who like Rupert seemed to relish their transformation of the girl.

Rupert glanced back admiringly. 'We gave her a good scrub. Jan wouldn't let me help.'

Jan was coy. 'She's hardly a child.'

The girl hid her face against her shoulder: she knew she was being discussed.

I said, 'What does she have to say?'

'Not much,' said Jan. 'Nothing actually. We think she'll open up when she gets used to us.'

I told them my idea of asking someone to speak to her in Chinese and how Evans had suggested his provisioner.

'Wonderful,' said Rupert. 'Send him around. We're dying to find out about her.'

'You know her name at least.'

'Nina? That was Jan's idea. We always said if we had a girl we'd call her Nina.'

And they drove away, like a couple who've rescued a stray cat. They looked happy, but I was struck by the sight of their three odd heads jogging in the car's rear window. If the girl had been younger, if she had not looked so changed by that hint of shame, I think I would have let the matter rest. There would have been little to describe: a lost child – and children look so much alike. But she was different, describable, almost remarkable in her looks, perhaps fifteen or sixteen, all her moles uncovered, a person. Someone would remember her. I knew Jan and Rupert wouldn't forgive me for going to the police, so the first chance I had I rang Father Lefever at the mission and asked him if he could find out anything about her. The mission net was wide: Johore was a parish.

Evans's provisioner was that unusual person in Malaysia, a fat man. I distrusted him the moment I saw him. He had an obscure tattoo on the back of his hand, three linked circles, and he had that wholly insincere jollity the Chinese affect when they are among strangers.

Evans introduced him as Pickwick and the fat man laughed and said his name was Pei-Kway. He said, 'Too hard for Europeans to say.'

I stared at him, pursed my lips, and said crisply, 'Pei-Kway.'

Prosser was leading the girl into the room. She was even prettier than she had seemed in the car, but her look of wildness was gone; she was slow, uncertain, domesticated. She watched the floor.

'Ask her how old she is,' said Jan.

'Go on, Picky, do your stuff,' said Evans.

Pei-Kway spoke to the girl, and getting no reply he repeated his question in a slightly different tone, licking at the words and gulping as he spoke.

The girl's answer was little more than a sigh.

'Hokkien,' said Pei-Kway. 'She is sixteen years.'

'Amazing,' said Evans. 'Small for her age.'

'Not really,' said Rupert. 'Ask her where she's from.'

This time the girl seemed reluctant to speak, and I could see that Pei-Kway was urging her. He was certainly challenging her, and he could have been uttering threats, his tone was so nasty. He did most of the talking, with greedy energy. The girl replied in monosyllables to his squawks. None of us interrupted; we stood by, lending Pei-Kway authority in what was by the minute becoming an inquisition. Though instead of going closer and bearing down on her, Pei-Kway inched back as he kept up this flow of questions.

He stopped. After all that talk all he said was, 'She's not from Ayer Hitam.'

'I could have told you that,' said Evans.

'Doesn't she have parents?' asked Jan.

'Dead,' said Pei-Kway. He made a vague gesture with his tattooed hand. He seemed satisfied, almost subdued. He had become as laconic as the girl; his grin was gone.

Now, unprompted, the girl spoke.

Pei-Kway said, 'She wants to stay here. She is saying thank you.' He said something to the girl in a harsh growl and I saw her react as if he'd given her a push.

I said, 'What did you just say to her?'

Pei-Kway gave me a vast empty smile, simply a stiffening of his face. 'I say, this is not your place.' To Evans he said, '*Tuan*, I'm going.'

But Jan had put her arm around the girl. 'Wait a minute,' she said. 'Why is it she doesn't speak Malay? I thought everyone in this country knew Malay.'

'They speak Hokkien in her village.'

Rupert said, 'Where is this village?'

'Batu Pahat,' said Pei-Kway, who no longer looking at the girl was replying without referring to her. He appeared restless. He had announced his intention to go, but was kept at the door by the questions.

Jan said, 'But what's her name?'

Angrily, Pei-Kway addressed the girl. Her mutter sounded familiar.

'Nina,' said Pei-Kway.

For several days I saw nothing of the Prossers, but as usual when someone stayed away from the Club he became all the more present in conversation. Gossip and hearsay made absentees interesting and gave them a uniqueness that was dispelled only when they showed up.

'Prosser's got his hands full,' said Evans one day. 'Nina tried to do a bunk last night. Found her sneaking out of the house. Scared rigid, she was. Had to carry her back bodily and lock her in her room.'

'Lucky he caught her in time,' I said.

'Very lucky, I'd say.' Evans laughed loudly. 'Imagine old Prosser, who's in bed by midnight – and he sleeps like a bloody log – imagine him catching the girl leaving his house at four in the morning.'

'You're sure of the time, are you?'

'Jan heard him. Maybe he was up splashing his boots,' said Evans. 'But she's pretty, that girl.'

I had not heard from Father Lefever. I rang him when Evans left, and he apologized for not getting in touch with me. He said he had found out nothing – he had completely forgotten about the girl.

'But now that you've reminded me,' he said, 'I will get down to business.'

I told him to try Batu Pahat.

And yet I began to feel that I was prying. The Prossers seemed happy, and Evans's gossip I was sure was full of malicious envy. The girl had to be given a chance. If what Evans had said was true – that she had tried to get away – then it was only the fact of the odd numbers, the three of them. I pictured them in their bungalow on the oil-palm estate, playing at being a family, as the children in threes played their games on the Club's grounds. And I began to think they had succeeded with the girl in creating one of those outposts of intimacy so rare in the tropics, a happy family. They had left us.

There followed a period of dateless time, the hiatus of the delayed monsoon, hot and lacking any event; only the whine of the locusts, the occasional roar of a timber truck, the sound of the thin breeze rattling the palms, the accumulation of dust on the verandah that was more like sand or silt, bulking against my house. Silence and the meaningless chirp of birds, the scraw of lizards behind the pictures on the wall. I wished that I had, like Rupert Prosser, found a child in a garden at midnight that I could treat as my pet.

The mood was broken one afternoon by Prosser's voice saying, 'Come over quick. I can't leave the house. Hurry, it's important. Evans is on his way.'

'If anyone rings,' I told Miss Leong, 'I'm at the Prossers'. But I'm not expecting any calls.'

Jan and Nina were on the sofa when I arrived. Nina was pale and held her face with the tips of her thin fingers; Jan was comforting her. Nina's face was shining with fear. Rupert was almost purple, and before I could speak he shouted, 'They had her in a bag!'

Hearing this, Jan hugged the girl so tightly I thought she'd break. But the girl only drew her arms together, contracting in grief and closing her fingers to hide her face.

Evans's car drew up to the verandah. Rupert paused until he entered the room, then said again, 'They had her in a bag!'

'Chinese?' said Evans.

'Three of them,' said Rupert. 'They must have been watching the house, because as soon as Jan left for her tennis they stepped in.'

'Rupert found them –'

'I had an inkling something was wrong,' said Rupert, and he swallowed hard, trying to resume. 'I was at the estate stores and had this inkling. As soon as I saw their car I was on my guard, then three blokes came out of the house struggling with this bag. It shook me. I ran back to the car and got my pistol. They took one look at it and dropped the bag and drove off. They had *parangs*, but they're no match for a bullet. I thought it was a break-in – reckoned they had my hi-fi and Jan's jewelry in the bag. When I saw Nina crawling out you could have knocked me over with a feather.'

Evans, with just the trace of a smile, said, 'Lucky you came back when you did.'

Rupert bent over and tugged his knee socks straight.

'I didn't know you had a gun,' I said.

'I was in Nigeria,' he said. 'I would have shot the bastards too, but they dropped the bag. I don't want any trouble with the police. You can get a jail sentence for shooting burglars in this bloody country. Burglars! But these were kidnapers.'

'Probably political,' said Evans.

'Sure,' said Rupert. 'Communists. They want to hold the estate to ransom.'

'That sort of thing doesn't happen around here,' I said. 'This isn't Kedah. It might have been her relatives. Anyway, she's sixteen. You don't know much about her. She might be married. Her husband –'

Rupert said, 'She's not married,' and cleared his throat. 'Dead scared, she was,' and coughed, 'I got their license number. But I don't want to go to the police because they'll start asking a lot of questions about who she is.'

'The kidnapers might try again,' said Evans.

'I'll shoot them next time,' said Rupert hoarsely. 'We'll move, get a transfer. But you've got to help me.'

'I'd go to the police,' I said.

'Don't you understand anything?' said Rupert. 'We're keeping her.'

Jan said, 'We're determined now,' and jumped as the telephone jangled.

'That'll be my wife,' said Evans.

But it was Miss Leong. Father Lefever had called the Consulate. He wanted to see me immediately.

'I'm going over to the mission,' I said to Rupert.

'I'll give you a lift,' said Evans.

'I was hoping you'd stick around,' said Rupert.

'You'll be all right,' said Evans, giving Rupert a matey slap on the back.

In the car Evans said, 'He thinks we're stupid. People come here from tin-pot places like Nigeria and they think they have all the answers.'

'What are you talking about?'

'He discovered her trying to leave. He discovered some kidnappers. It's rubbish!' said Evans with greater outrage than I thought he was capable of. 'He's knocking her off. He's setting the whole thing up. There was no kidnaping attempt. In a few weeks there'll be another disappearance, but this time it'll be the two of them doing a bunk, mark my words. Then you'll hear they're in North Borneo playing housie. Prosser's screwing her, the lucky sod.'

At the mission I thanked him and started to get out of the car. He stopped me with his hand and said, 'Who do you believe, him or me?'

'I believe the girl,' I said, and saw that frightened face again.

Evans said, 'She's not talking.'

Across the courtyard, Father Lefever watched from his office door-way, and as I drew nearer I could see on his cassock – so white at a distance – grease marks and stains. A French Canadian, he had the grizzled appearance that dedicated missionaries acquire in the tropics; he usually needed a shave, his house boy cut his hair. His sandals had been clumsily resewn, and yet these like the stains on his cassock seemed proof of his sanctity. Eager to talk he put his arm around me and hurried me inside.

'The girl,' he said. 'I think I know who she is.'

I told him I had just seen her.

'Is she well?'

'She's rather upset.'

'I didn't mean that. Is she in good health?'

'Father Lefever, someone tried to kidnap her today.'

'Yes,' he said, and shook his head. 'I was also afraid of that.'

'It was pretty serious. Three men came to Prosser's and put her in a sack. Prosser arrived just in time to stop them kidnaping her.'

'He saved her life – they meant to kill her.' Father Lefever fingered the knots on the rope that was tied around his waist. 'It's the Triad,' he said. 'Probably the Sa Ji – they're the fellows who keep order around here.'

Triad: the word was new to me. I told him so.

He said, 'A Chinese secret society.'

'Then it's not political,' I said. 'But Prosser doesn't have any money.'

'Triads don't kidnap only for money,' he said. He showed me the three knots on his rope belt. 'It is like a religious order,' he said, grasping one thick knot. 'This obsesses them. Purity – but their kind of purity. And they punish impurity their own cruel way.

A person is taken and put in a sack and drowned. They call it "death by bath."'

I saw Evans's point. He had guessed that Rupert had been to bed with her; and he had a good case – fortuitous finding of the girl about to escape, the visit home in the middle of the day: adulterer's luck. And now I understood Pei-Kway's tattoo.

'I suppose if the Triad thought she was Prosser's mistress they'd do that. Punishing the adultery.'

'I didn't say anything about adultery,' said Father Lefever. 'They don't want her here, that's all.'

'Batu Pahat's not far away.'

'She doesn't live in Batu Pahat. Quite a bit off the road, in fact, at our mission hospital. I doubt that you've ever seen it. No one goes there willingly.'

'A hospital?'

'A leprosarium,' he said.

'She's a leper.' I could not conceal my shock.

But Father Lefever was smiling. 'You see your reaction? You're as bad as the Triad. It's not the girl, but her parents. Both have what we now call Hansen's disease. It's not so much a hospital as a village – very isolated, because people have such a horror of the disease. The girl probably doesn't have it, but what can she do? Her parents want her near them. She ran away six weeks ago. The priests were very reassured to know that she is safe here.'

'What happens now?'

'You should tell your friends something of the girl's background. I'll put them in touch with the leprosarium and they can take it from there.'

'They'll be horrified.'

'Tell them not to worry. Even if she's a carrier it's only infectious if contact has been extensive. She's merely a house guest – there's no problem.'

Walking out to the courtyard, Father Lefever said, 'They are doing great work at Batu Pahat. Why, do you know that two years ago your Mr Leopold visited? He was much impressed. He's made a study of the disease.'

'I don't know him,' I said.

'Yes, you do. Leopold – he and his friend murdered that poor child in Chicago about fifty years ago. It was a celebrated case.'

I delivered the news as tactfully as possible and withdrew,

wondering what would happen. Though I had said nothing to Evans he knew all about it within a week – not from Prosser but from Pei-Kway. And Pei-Kway had the news that the girl had been sent back. I never found out what had gone on at the Prossers', among those three people; and the Triad was not charged with attempted murder. The only victim was that waif, who was made a leper, and each time I thought of her I saw her radiant, captive, in a new dress entering the leper village to join those two ruined people.

Jan stopped coming to the Club; Rupert was there every night until the bar closed. One weekend he went down to Batu Pahat. We didn't know whether he was seeing the girl or taking a cure, or both. He came back alone and seemed much happier; he talked of his great luck. Evans became fond of saying, 'I give that marriage six months.'

Diplomatic Relations

I imagine that couples often forget they're married; I know that a person who is single remembers it every day, like a broken promise, that dwindling inheritance he is neglecting to spend. The married ones remind him of his condition – children do, too. He feels called upon to apologize or explain. He resists saying that he has made a choice. Where is his act? Bachelorhood looks like selfish delay, and the words are loaded: bachelor means queer, spinster means hag.

The hotel elevator stopped at every floor, filling with witnesses who brought me back to myself, to Jill's note. She was planning to stop in Ayer Hitam on her way to Djakarta – would I mind if she stayed a few days? She had specified the dates, her time of arrival, the telephone number and contact address in Kuala Lumpur where she could be reached. The flat belonged to her friend who was, like Jill, a secretary: the Embassy's sorority sisters. She told me how many suitcases she had. She was methodical, decisive; she had typed the note neatly. Several weeks later she sent a postcard repeating the information. She wasn't pestering. It was secretarial work.

And the only indication I had of her present state of mind was the form in which she sent the messages. The letter came in a 'Peanuts' envelope – a cartoon of Snoopy on the flap; her neatly typed note was from a joke note-pad titled *Dumb Things I Gotta Do*. The postcard was of a square-rigger and she had mailed it from Miami. I guessed that she had taken the windjammer cruise advertised on the front.

We had met in Kampala during my first overseas tour. As she was the Ambassador's secretary and I was a junior political officer she knew a great deal more than I did about the running of the Embassy. She showed me how to work the shredder, she alerted me to important cables. The fact that I was seeing her caused a certain amount of talk, embassy gossip, more class snobbery than a concern for security. The way she reacted to it made me like her the more: she never referred to her boss except by calling him 'the Ambassador,' she was discreet, she did not betray the smallest confidence. It was as if she had taken vows, and though celibacy was not one of them, secrecy was. She was so tactful about other people, I knew she would be tactful when my name came up. On the weekends we went to the loud dirty African night-clubs and danced to Congolese bands. I had made love to her on nine occasions – I kept count as if preparing a defense for myself, because I was sure we were watched. Eight of the occasions were after these dances; the ninth was the night before she left the country on transfer – I remember her suitcase in the living room and the stack of tea-chests awaiting the embassy packers. I was left with the sense that we had been deliberately separated.

She was sent to Vietnam, a promotion of sorts since her salary was practically doubled with hardship pay. There she stayed, in Saigon, while I finished in Kampala and was reassigned to Ayer Hitam. At first she had written to me often; the letters became fewer, and finally they stopped altogether. I thought I had heard the last of her, then the 'Peanuts' envelope came, and the windjammer postcard, the news that she was being sent to Djakarta. Knowing that I was going to meet her again I felt a thrill and a slight ache, the mingled sense of freedom and obligation at seeing a former lover.

Ayer Hitam was a considerable detour for her. I was flattered by her willingness to put up with the inconvenience. I looked forward to her visit. But I did not answer her letter immediately. Instead, I tried to recall in as much detail as possible the times we had spent together, and almost unexpectedly I discovered the memories to be tender. We had been alone, private, complete, for the short time we'd known each other, and she had shown me by example how to manage such affairs.

But the mind is thorough: seeking the past it casts us images of the future. I saw Jill in Ayer Hitam being joshed at the Club by Alec and leered at by Squibb and hearing how Strang grew watercress in his gumboots. At City Bar and at the mission she would look for more and see nothing more. In the town and at my house, trying to praise, she would miss what it took a year of residence to see, as if your eyes had to become accustomed to the strong light to perceive that the place had features, that the club members' ghastly jollity was a defense against strangers, that the weather was not as harsh in November as it was in June, or the aspect of the town – its dust and junk – as unimportant as it seemed. I would not be able to prove that events had taken place in Ayer Hitam; where was the proof? The past in the tropics is just the green erasures of wild plants. Jill was a kind person, but even her kindness would not prevent her, on a short visit to the town, from seeing the place as a backwater.

I wrote saying that I would be in Singapore on the dates she mentioned. Perhaps we could meet there? The letter went to her contact address in KL. She phoned me when she arrived in the capital, said she understood and that Singapore was perfect. She was planning to fly from there to Djakarta to start her new job.

'What about Raffles Hotel – romantic!'

'It's not what it was,' I said. 'I generally stay at one of the plastic ones, the Mandarin.'

'You're the mandarin,' she said. 'I'll see you there, Thursday at three.'

'Will I recognize you?'

She laughed. 'Probably not. I'll be the fat blonde in the lobby.'

Everyone in the elevator was staring at the lighted numbers. For part of the descent I was giving myself reasons why I should not sleep with Jill; for the rest, reasons why I should make an attempt; and then we were at the lobby. She had not been fat before, and her hair had been dark, but she was partly right – she had put on a few pounds and her hair was now streaked gray-blonde. She looked, when I saw her sitting by the fountain, like a woman waiting for her lover – not me, someone older, richer, whom she would describe as a snappy dresser, a riot, a real card. She was sensible enough to know that she looked her best in a light suit, with make-up. She was of the denim and T-shirt generation, but in matters of dress State Department employees are twenty years behind the times. She had obviously just had her hair done, she wore beautiful shoes, and her jewelry – four bracelets on each wrist, a necklace, a brooch – gave her the appearance of being bigger than she was, and slightly vulgar. Jewelry represents in its glitter a kind of smug self-esteem, cold and protective, like queenly armor. She looked safe and unassailable wearing her jewels.

She saw me and sat forward to let me kiss her, and she lingered a fraction as if posing a question with that pressure. Perfume – a familiar scent, but much more of it, so much that it clung to my mouth, and each time she moved she created drafts of it against my eyes.

We did not speak until we were in the bar and touching glasses. She said, 'You haven't changed. I know I have – let's not mention it here. I'm out of my element. How do you manage to keep so thin?'

'Dysentery. I've got the worst cook in Malaysia.'

'Be glad you don't have me – I can't cook to save my life! Hey, the gal I was staying with in KL said you've got just the prettiest little Consulate. And you must like it because she says you never set foot out of it.'

'I do, but I don't tell anyone.'

'I forgot you were so young!' I saw in her smile and that wink – as obvious as a shade being drawn – pure lust. She was counting on me.

She said, 'Did I tell you I was robbed?'

'You didn't mention it, no.'

'I thought I told you on the phone. I've told everyone else. It was at that gal's flat when I arrived. My bags were on the landing. She let me in and when I went out for my bags the small case was gone. It couldn't have been there more than two minutes. They think a child did it. They've had other incidents. Of course, they haven't found it.'

She did not look in the least distressed. She had lost her bag but now she had a good story.

'Was there anything valuable in it?'

'My watch. One I had made in Bangkok when I was getting Saigon out of my system. It's not the money – it was specially made for me. Sentimental value.'

'If it was custom-made it must have been worth something.'

She faced me. 'It cost two thousand dollars. It had a jade face, diamond chips, and a gold strap. That was two years ago. It's probably worth more now. But it's not the money.'

'I'd be in mourning if I were you.'

'You're lying,' she said. Her tone was affectionate. 'But thanks – it's a nice lie.'

I said, 'Maybe they'll find the thief.'

'I can always buy another one. But it won't be the same.'

'A watch,' I said. 'Worth two grand.'

'More like three. But friends are much more important than things like that.' She met my gaze. 'Don't you think so?'

I wanted to say no. I felt slightly blackmailed by the sentiments her loss required of me. But I said, 'Sure I do.'

'I was looking forward to seeing you.'

This all came so neatly that I suspected a trick; she had baited the trap with something pathetic to arouse my sympathy and make me pause. Then she'd pounce. And yet I felt a futile indebtedness. We had been lovers – we were no longer. There was no way I could repay her except by a show of that same love, and that was gone. I did not feel the smallest tug of lust, only a foolish reflex, as if I'd seen two youngsters kissing and had to turn away to spare them embarrassment, to save myself from judging them.

I said, 'I've thought about you a lot. Those terrible nightclubs. What a dreadful place Uganda was. But I didn't notice. You had such a cozy apartment.'

'You should have seen it with the lights on. A mess. But I had a nice one in Saigon. It was in the compound – they all were – but on the top floor, air-conditioned, a guest room. I bought one of those waterbeds. They're fun, even if you're alone.'

'Waterbeds in Saigon,' I said. 'No wonder we lost the war.'

She winced, and all her make-up exaggerated this pained face as it had exaggerated her smiling one. She said, 'I hated to leave. Sometimes I think of the others, the local staff, those telex operators and code clerks we left behind, and I want to weep. You never came to Vietnam.'

'I was offered a trip, a fact-finding tour. I knew the facts, so I refused.'

'You could have seen me. I'd have shown you around. I was hoping you'd visit. When you didn't I knew you'd thought about it and decided not to – you'd made a choice.'

I wondered if she was being gentle with me by describing this missed opportunity: if I had gone, if she had shown me around, if I had made a gesture then, things would be different now.

I said, 'Maybe we'll both be posted to Hanoi when we open our embassy there. It won't be long.'

Jill said, 'They shoot dogs in Hanoi. They won't shoot my Alfie.'

'You have a dog?'

'Upstairs. Wouldn't travel without him. A cocker spaniel.'

'You didn't have a dog in Kampala.'

'I inherited him in Saigon,' she said. 'He changed my life. I took him back to the States after the pull-out. I'm taking him to Djakarta.'

'He's a well-traveled dog.'

'You'd better believe it. In the States we crossed the country. We went all the way to Arizona together.'

'I thought you were from Ohio.'

'I bought some land in Arizona.' She saw my interest and added, 'Twenty acres.'

This, like the expensive watch, baffled me. She had told me once how after her father had died she'd gone to secretarial school in Cleveland, because it was cheaper than college. She had worked for three years supporting her mother: the single person always has a significant parent, inevitably a burden. But her mother had died, and Jill had joined the Foreign Service, to leave Ohio.

She said, 'It's outside Tucson – it's good land. When I left Saigon I had so much money! We had all that hardship pay, those bonuses – everyone made money in Vietnam except the GIs. I thought I'd invest it, so we looked around, Alfie and me, and we settled on Arizona. It's sunny, it's clean, I can go there when I retire. I'll sell the land off in lots. Actually, I was thinking I'd sell half and use the money to build some houses on the rest, then sell those houses and buy myself a really nice one.'

It was an ingenious scheme, and at once it all fitted together, the watch, the dog, the vacations, the jewelry, the land. She had made a choice. Once, perhaps, she had needed me; no longer. I could not be her life – this was her life. And seeing how she was managing – that however much she might have needed me she had never counted on me – I felt tender towards her and slightly saddened by the complicated arrangements that are necessary when we can't depend on each other. What precautions had I taken?

This security of hers was, if not an aphrodisiac, an encouragement. I had had two drinks, but seeing how safe and contented she was made me happy. She was managing; she wouldn't make demands. She was like that fabulous mistress, the older woman, either divorced or happily married who, with free afternoons, finds a man she likes and sleeps with him because she is energetic and resourceful and likes his dark eyes and believes that as long as she is happy she is blameless.

Land in Arizona: it reassured me.

I said, 'How do you like this hotel?'

'The drinks are too expensive down here,' she said. 'I've got a bottle in my room. Shall we economize?'

'Whatever you say.'

'It's time I fed Alfie. He's probably tearing the room apart.'

Her room was on the fifteenth floor, and from the window I could see the sprawling island, the tiny red-roofed houses and the high-rise horrors. The hotel in the underdeveloped country is like a view from a plane. You are passing overhead and you know that if those people down there had this view they would overthrow their government.

I looked out the window so as to avoid staring at the room. The dog had been sleeping on the unmade bed, and as we entered he had woken and bounded toward us, whimpering at Jill, barking at me.

'You're all excited, aren't you? Yes, you are!' Jill was scratching him affectionately. 'He's very possessive. Look at him.'

The dog was shaking with excitement and rage. I thought he might sink his teeth into me.

Jill said, 'That's pure jealousy.'

There were shoes on the bed. One dress lay over the back of a chair, another over a door to the closet. Three suitcases were open on the floor and it looked as if the dog had pulled the clothes out. Jill's short-wave radio was on the bedside table with a copy of *Arizona Highways* and a Doris Lessing paperback.

She saw me looking at the novel and said, 'Airplane reading. I picked it up in London. That gal has problems.'

'Don't most gals?'

She looked hurt. 'Don't most people?'

She had seemed so cool in the bar. Up here, in this cluttered room, it was as if I was seeing the contents of her mind, all of it shaken out. And I had known the moment I saw the dog that I couldn't do anything here – certainly not make love. There was no room for me; she could not have all this and a lover – she had made her choice.

'Is your room like this?' she asked.

I nodded. One suitcase, my pipe, my drip-dry suit. The opposite of this, and yet I envied her the completeness of her mess and saw in it a recklessness I could never manage.

'I love these little refrigerators. They must be Japanese.' She walked towards the squat thing and the rubber around the door made a sucking noise as she pulled it open. 'Same again? Here's the tonic, here's the ice, and here's the anesthetic.' She had brought an enormous bottle of gin from the bathroom. 'This was supposed to be your present for letting me stay at your house. Five bucks at the duty-free shop in Bangkok.'

'I'm sorry about that.'

'No, no,' she said. 'This is fine, a real reunion – I'm out of my element.' She made herself a drink and crawled on to the bed. I noticed she was still wearing her shoes. She sat with her legs crossed, stroking the dog. She had moved through the clutter without seeing it; this disorder was her order.

I touched her glass. 'To your new job.'

'Same job, new place,' she said. 'And here's to your new place.'

'I'm leaving Ayer Hitam in two months,' I said.

'That's what I mean.'

'So you knew.'

She said, 'I saw a cable.'

'Where am I going?'

She said, 'I forget.'

Was this why she had come? Because no matter what happened it wouldn't last; we would be parted, as we had been in Kampala. She had known she was leaving there – how wrong I had been to think I was the cause of her transfer to Saigon. That was her element, diplomatic relations, the continual parting. She was stronger than I had guessed.

I said, 'Well, it's not Djakarta.'

'No.'

'It's far.'

'They told you.'

'No,' I said. 'You did.'

She laughed. 'If I knew you,' she said, 'I think I'd really like you a lot.'

'Maybe you should have come to Ayer Hitam.'

'I'm glad I didn't,' she said. 'What if I had liked it? It might be nice – flowers, trees, friendly people. I guessed you had one of those big shady houses, very cool, with gleaming floors and everything put away and a little Chinese man making us drinks.'

I said nothing: it was as she had described it.

'Then I wouldn't have wanted to go. I'd have been sad, crying all the way to Djakarta. You've never seen me cry. I'm scary.'

'You're not sad now.'

'No,' she said. 'This is the place for us. A hotel room. Our own bottle of gin. Glasses from the bathroom. Couldn't be better.'

I must have agreed rather half-heartedly – I was still thinking of her calculation in seeking me out just before I was to be transferred – because the next thing I heard her say was, 'I suppose I should be sightseeing. Sniffing around. Every country has its own cigarette smell. Funny, isn't it? You know where you are when someone lights up.'

I said, 'I could take you sightseeing. There's only the Tiger Balm Gardens, a few noodle stalls, and the harbor.'

'I'd hate you to do that,' she said. 'Anyway, this is a business trip for you. I don't want to be in your way.' She winked as she had before. 'Diplomatic relations.'

As I raised my glass to her the dog growled.

'You don't think it's tacky, retiring to Arizona?'

'You're not retiring yet.'

'So you do think it's tacky. But you're right – there'll be lots of assignments between now and then.'

'Hanoi.'

She said, 'I'll hide Alfie in the pouch. I'll be your secretary. I'm out of my element here, but I'm a damned good secretary.'

'Perfect.'

She said, 'It's a date. Can I freshen your drink?'

How appropriate those phrases were to her fifties chic, the girdle, the beautiful shoes, the lipstick, the jewels.

'Business,' I said, and put my empty glass down out of her reach. 'I have an appointment. You understand.'

She did: I had reminded her that she was a secretary. She said, 'Maybe I'll see you at breakfast.'

'I'll be on the road before seven.'

'Whatever you do, don't call me at seven!' She smiled and said, 'Hanoi, then.'

She knew she was absurd and insincere; she had no idea how brave I thought she was. She stood between me and the barking dog and let me kiss her cheek.

'Diplomatic relations,' she said. 'Off you go.'

I went to my room and drew the curtains, cutting off the aching late-afternoon sun. I lay on my bed and tried to sleep, but it was no good. I felt I had revealed more to Jill in my reticence than if I had been stark naked and drunk. This thought was like a bump in the mattress. I did not wait for morning. That night I checked out of the hotel, roused Abubaker and went home. And now I knew why I hadn't let her visit Ayer Hitam: I didn't want her to pity me.

Dear William

For the past week or so, I have been putting off writing my report to the State Department – three pages to sum up my two years in Ayer Hitam – and then, this morning, your letter came. A good letter – what interesting things happen to people your age! You're game, impatient, unsuspicious: it is the kind of innocence that guarantees romance. I'm not mocking you. The woman sounded fascinating. But I advise you to follow your instinct and not see her again. It is possible to know too much. A little mystery is often easier to bear than an unwelcome fact; leave the memory incomplete.

Forgive my presumption. I haven't done my report, and here I am lecturing you on romance. I do think you'll be all right. You had quite a scare in Ayer Hitam – your bout of dengué fever has become part of the town's folklore. Isn't it amazing? What happens after the ghostly episode in the tropical place – the haunting, the shock? Of course – the victim picks himself up and leaves, meets a woman on the plane, and has another experience, totally unrelated to the ghost. Stories have no beginning or end; they are continuous and ragged. But the sequel to the ghost story must be something romantic or ordinary or even banal. I have never believed that characters in fiction vanish after the last page is turned – they have other lives, not explicit or remarkable enough for fiction, and yet it would be sad to think they were irrecoverable.

You mention getting 'culture shock' when you arrived home. I know the feeling. You certainly didn't have it in Ayer Hitam. I'm sure you'll be back here sooner or later, as a contract teacher or whatever. It's fairly easy to get to countries like this; it's very hard to leave, which is why all of us who don't belong must leave. We crave simple societies, but they're no good for us. Now I understand why these rubber planters stayed so long – overstayed their visit, wore out their welcome. We have no business here. Up to a point – if you're young enough or curious enough – you can grow here; but after that you must go, or be destroyed. Is it possible to put down roots here? I don't think so. The Chinese won't, the Tamils can't, the Malays pretend they have them already, but they don't. Countries like this are possessed on the one hand by their own strangling foliage, and on the other by outside interests – business, international pressures (as long as the country has something to sell or the money to buy). Between jungle and viability, there is nothing – just the hubbub of struggling mercenaries, native and expatriate, staking their futile claims.

You asked about Squibb and the others. The others are fine. Squibb is another story. It was he who said, 'I came here for two weeks and I stayed for thirty-five years.' I didn't say anything, but I thought: Those first two weeks must have been the only ones he spent in this country that mattered.

He is so strange. I found it impossible to read his past; I have no idea what will happen to him. He told me that he had been in the Club dining-room when I entered, my first day in Ayer Hitam. He took credit for recognizing me – he discovered me – and some-time later he gave me the lowdown on the other members. He told me about Angela Miller's breakdown and how Gillespie used to drive an old Rolls. He filled me in on the Club's history – the polo, the cricket, the outings they made to Fraser's Hill just after the war. 'Your people are all over the place,' he said. And they were, too – though now, apart from missionaries and teachers, there isn't an American between here and the Thai border. 'Gillespie's an old-timer,' he said. 'Plays polo. An American who plays polo is compensating for something. I've got no time for him.' And yet Gillespie's murder shook him.

'Bachelor,' he said, when I told him I wasn't married. 'But you're too young to be a *confirmed* bachelor. Singapore's the place for a dirty weekend, by the way. Evans goes down now and again. Strang used to go, when his wife was on leave. His wife's devoted to him – you won't get anywhere with her. The Prossers are about your age, but they're new, and dead keen on the drama group. The locals are thick as two planks, the Sultan's a bloody bore, the missionaries don't speak to me, Angela's a rat-bag, and Alec Stewart's an odd fish. Yes, he's an odd one, he is.'

I looked at Squibb.

He said, 'He likes the lash.'

I must have made a face, but he went on talking. Already he had taken me over. He had put it this way: if the people didn't like him, they would not take to me; if he found them odd, so would I. He wanted me on his side.

I hesitated, hung fire, or whatever the word is. I made him understand that I'd see for myself. And all this time, in the way a person offers information in order to get a reaction, he was searching my face, listening hard. He wanted to know what I was up to. What were my weaknesses? Did I drink, whore around, do my job? And, of course, was I queer?

I'm afraid I disappointed him, and perhaps many others. Typically, the Consul is a character: a drinker, a womanizer, reckless, embittered, a man with a past, an extravagant failure of some sort with a certain raffish charm. I wasn't a character. I didn't drink much. I was calm. I thought I might make an impression on him, but if I did – on him or the others – it was not because I was a bizarre character, but because I was pretty ordinary, in a place that saw little of the ordinary.

I tried to be moderate and dependable, for the fact is that colorful characters – almost unbearable in the flesh – are colorful only in retrospect. But Squibb was angling. He wanted me on his side, and he searched me for secrets. He saw nothing but my moment of revulsion when he told me about Alec: 'He likes the lash.' I listened attentively: the Club Bore, that first hour, strikes one as a great raconteur.

He was what some people call a reactionary; he was brutal and blind, his fun was beer. It had swollen his little body and made him grotesque, a fat red man who (the memory is more tolerable than the experience) sat in the Club at nine in the morning with a pint of Tiger and a can of mentholated Greshams, drinking and puffing. Smoke seemed to come out of his ears as he grumbled over the previous day's *Straits Times*.

I used to wonder why he stayed, when others had gone. Like many so-called reactionaries he had no politics, only opinions, pet hates, grudges, and a paradoxical loathing for bureaucracy and trust in authority. He wanted order but he objected to the way in which order was established and maintained. If he'd had power he would have been a dictator – it was true of several other expatriates in Ayer Hitam – but weak, he was only a bore.

He wanted my friendship. He shared his experience with me: don't wear an undershirt, take a shower in the morning when the pipes are cold, keep drinking water in an old gin bottle, have a curry once a week, don't drink brandy after you've eaten a durian.

That kind of thing; and as for unresponsive people, 'Beat them,' he said, 'just beat them with barbed wire until they do what you want.'

It was so simple with Squibb – you punished people and they obeyed. He had a theory that most people were glad to be dominated: it was the tyrant's contempt. 'They like to be kicked,' he'd say, and his mouth would go square with satisfaction. 'Like Alec.'

You know some of this. Wasn't it odd that he didn't like anyone – not anyone? That should have told us something about him. And he had failed at being a person, so he tried to succeed at being a character – someone out of Maugham. What tedious eccentricity Maugham was responsible for! He made heroes of these time-servers; he glorified them by being selective and leaving out their essential flaws. He gave people like Squibb destructive models to emulate, and he encouraged expatriates to pity themselves. It is the essence of the romantic lie.

Fiction is so often fatal: it hallows some places and it makes them look like dreamland: New York, London, Paris – like the label of an expensive suit. For other places it is a curse. Ayer Hitam seemed tainted, and it was cursed with romance that was undetectable to anyone who was not sitting on the club verandah with a drink in his hand.

'He likes the lash,' Squibb had said, about Alec, and he looked for my reaction.

I couldn't hide it. I was shocked. I made a face.

'The whip,' he said, giving a little provisional chuckle of mockery. 'His missus beats him. The *rotan*. Pain. Why else would he be here? He was cashiered from the Royal Navy for that.'

I didn't believe it, and yet what Squibb had said frightened me: it was cruel, pitiful, lonely agony. I could almost picture it. What if it was true? We lead lives that even the best fiction can't begin to suggest. Angela: was she the person who had a nervous break-down, the queen of the Footlighters, or the Sultan's mistress? She was all three and much more, but no story could unify those three different lives; they were not linked. The truth is too complicated for words: truth is water.

Squibb was animated that day, revealing secrets, trying to oblig-ate me with his own rivalries. What more damaging fact could one learn about a doctor than that he was engrossed by pain and had another life as the victim in some strange sexual game?

I had said, 'What will you say about me?'

'Ever tried it – the lash?'

I closed my eyes.

He said, 'Don't take it so hard,' and he gave me a gloating, rueful laugh.

It was a brief conversation; it initiated me, it disturbed me deeply, and it affected everything that happened after that. I was circumspect with Alec, and Squibb went his own way. Because of what Squibb had said, I never got to know Alec very well. If Alec had a secret it was better left with him. And we got on fine because I never inquired further. He must have thought I was rather distant with him, and there were times – when he looked after you, for example – that I thought he was unnecessarily hard, confusing pleasure with its opposite and seeing pain as a cure, or at least a relief.

The person who appears to have no secret seems to be hiding something; and yet there is a simpler explanation for this apparent deception – there probably isn't any secret. We tend to see mystery in emptiness, but I knew from Africa that emptiness is more often just that: behind it is a greater emptiness.

I didn't like Squibb well enough to look for more in him. I liked Alec too much to invade his privacy. For the most part they stayed on the fringes of my life in Ayer Hitam. I didn't depend on them. I never felt that I had been admitted to the society here, but I began to doubt that society of that kind – ambitious order – really existed.

Sometimes, after a session at the Club, Alec would say, 'I've got to be off. My missus is waiting.' And I would get a dull ache in my soul imagining that he was going back to his bungalow to be whipped. It made me wince. I didn't want to think about it. But the one fact that I had been told made me suspicious of everyone I met, and when I realized the sort of double life that people led – and had proof of it – I felt rather inadequate myself. What was my life? My job, my nationals, my files: hardly enough. I wasn't a character; it was the other people who mattered, not me. I've always been rather amused by novelists who write autobiographically: the credulous self-promotion, the limited vision, the display of style. Other people's lives are so much more interesting than one's own. I am an unrepentant eavesdropper and I find anonymity a consolation.

So I have had an interesting two years. And it looks even better – more full – now that it's nearly over: teeming with incident. Those were hours and days. I've already forgotten the months and months when nothing happened but the humdrum hell of the tropical world, the sun directly overhead and burning dustily down; steam and noise; the distant shouting that might have been some deaf man's radio, the fans blowing my papers to the floor and my sweaty hand losing its grip and slipping down the shaft of my ballpoint pen. Who wouldn't reminisce about ghosts, and even miss them a little?

I never made a friend here. If I had I think I would have seen much less of this place. I am old enough now to see friendship as a constraint. Perhaps, as you say, we will meet again. But I'm rambling – I was telling you about Squibb. Is there more? Yes, if you stay long enough, 'look on and make no sound,' and if you're patient enough, truth – colorless, odorless, tasteless – comes trickling out. Because no one forgets what he has said more quickly than the liar.

'You'll have to have a party,' said Squibb, when he heard I was being posted back to Washington. Need I say our numbers have been substantially reduced? For Squibb, a party these days is a way of excluding the locals – he doesn't count his Malay wife. Remember, I barely know the man.

The party at his house was his idea – drinks. I had never been to his place before. Strang, the Prossers, Evans (he's off to Australia at the end of the month), the Stewarts. Squibb had the good grace to invite Peeraswami, but the poor fellow didn't know which way to turn – he looked at the little sandwiches, the spring rolls, the *vol-au-vents*. 'This is having meat in it, *Tuan*?' he whispered. The shapes threw him a bit. Instead of eating, he drank; and he started talking loudly about the merits of Indian toddy. Then: 'What will happen to me when you go?' Perhaps I have made a friend. Poor Peeraswami.

Stewart made a speech: 'Our American colleague' – that kind of thing. Jokes: 'I approve of nudity – in the right places,' 'Keep that bottle up your end,' 'How can you be an expert in Asian affairs unless you've had one?' After this, several embarrassing minutes of Alec's personal history, begun – as such stories so often are – by Alec shouting, 'And I'm not ashamed to say –'

Peeraswami took out his hanky and vomited noisily into it. Then he ran out of the room.

As guest of honor, I could not leave until the others made a move. Without realizing it, I was wandering from room to room. Squibb has a library! Military histories, bad novels, Wallace's *The Malay Archipelago*, blood and thunder, and the usual bird and flower books one finds in every expatriate household. And souvenirs: sabers, spears, a samurai sword, bows, arrows, hatchets, Dyak weapons, Chinese daggers, a jeweled kris, and a rack of blowpipes that might have been flutes.

Squibb followed me in and boasted about how he'd stolen this and paid fifty cents for that. I saw a similar assortment on the wall of an adjoining room.

'More treasures,' I said, and went in.

Squibb cleared his throat behind me as I ran my eye along the wall: bamboo rods, *rotans*, flails, birches of various kinds, handcuffs. They were narrow, shiny, cruel-looking implements, some with red tassels and leather handles, all on hooks, very orderly, and yet not museum pieces, not gathering dust. They had the used scratched look of kitchenware and – but I might have been imagining it – a vicious smell.

How was I to know I was in his bedroom? The bed was not like any other I had ever seen – a four-poster, but one of those carved and painted affairs from Malacca, probably a hundred years old, like an opium platform or an altar. I stared at it a long time before I realized what it was.

I said, 'Sorry,' and saw the straps on each post.

'No,' said Squibb.

If I had left the room just then I think it would have been more embarrassing for him. I waited for him to say something more.

He picked up a bamboo rod and flexed it, like a Dickensian schoolmaster starting a lesson. He tapped one of the bedposts with it. The headboard was inlaid with oblong carvings: hunting scenes, pretty bridges, and pagodas. He said, 'It's a Chinese bridal bed,' and whacked the post again.

Something else was wrong: no mosquito net. I was going to comment on that. I heard the hilarity of the party, so joyless two rooms away.

Squibb, puffing hard on a cigarette, started to cough. The whips on the wall, the flails, the rods, black and parallel on their hooks; the heavy blinds; the dish of sand with the burned ends of joss sticks. I had discovered the source of his old lie, but this was not a truth I wanted to know in detail. If he had said, 'Forget it,' I would have gladly forgotten; but he was defiant, he lingered by the bed almost tenderly.

He said, 'And this is where we have our little games.'

Straps, whips, stains: I didn't want to see.

He laughed, his old gloating and rueful laugh. Two years before he had prepared me; and I had been shocked, I'd failed the test. Now I didn't matter: I was leaving in a few weeks. We were strangers once more, and he might not even have remembered how he'd made this all Alec's secret.

He put the bamboo rod back on the wall and glanced around the room. He seemed wistful now. What could I say?

'It's time I went,' I said. He nodded: he released me.

This was a week ago. Since then he has treated me with sly and distant familiarity. I know his secret; it is not one I wished to know, but it makes many things clear.

So much for Squibb. Are you sorry you asked? There is no scandal. Apparently, I was the only one who didn't know. The scandal is elsewhere – the language barrier once more: I'm accused of calling the Sultan's daughter a pig. Being a Muslim, she objects. Actually, I called her a prig. It's all I'll be remembered for here. But that's another story.

My bags are packed, my *ang pows* distributed. As soon as it became known that I was leaving I was treated as if I didn't exist: I was a ghost, but a rather ineffectual one. Once a person signals that he is leaving he ceases to matter: he's seen as disloyal; his membership has ended, conviviality dies. But Peeraswami is still attentive: he covets my briefcase. I think I'll give it to him if he promises to look after my casuarina tree. I've already recommended him for a promotion; I'll deal with the others later, in my own way.

Now I must write my report.

Part V

Diplomatic Relations (ii): The London Embassy

Volunteer Speaker

It annoyed me when people asked, because I had to tell them I had just been in Southeast Asia. That was a deceptively grand name for the small dusty town where I was American Consul. But who has heard of Ayer Hitam? Officially, it was a hardship post – the designation meant extra money, a hardship allowance I could not spend. There was no hardship, but there was boredom, and nothing to buy to relieve me of that. With a free month before I was due in Washington to await reassignment, I decided to finance a private trip to Europe – another grand name. One town on my route was Saarbrücken, where the river formed the French–German border. It looked like magic the day I arrived; at dinner it seemed like a version of the town I had left in Malaysia.

My choice of Saarbrücken was not accidental. The Flints, Charlie and Lois, had been posted here after their stint in Kuala Lumpur. They had been urging me to visit them: the single man and the childless couple are natural allies, in an uncomplicated way. Charlie had accepted this minor post because he had refused to spend the usual two deskbound years in Washington. He had not lived in Washington for fifteen years. It was his boast – no good telling him that Washington had changed – and it meant that he had to keep on the move. A little patience and politicking would have earned him promotions. 'Next stop Abu Dhabi,' he used to say. That was before Abu Dhabi became important. At dinner, he said, 'Next stop Rwanda. I don't even know the capital.'

'Kigali,' I said. 'It's a hole.'

'I keep forgetting you're an old Africa hand.'

Lois said, 'One of these days, the State Department's going to send us to a really squalid place. Then Charlie will have to admit it's worse than Washington.'

'I didn't squawk in Medan,' said Flint. 'I didn't squawk in KL. I actually liked Bangalore. They once threatened me with Calcutta. The idiots in Washington don't even know that Calcutta morale is the highest in the Foreign Service. The housing's fantastic and you can get a cook for ten bucks. That's my kind of place. Only squirts want Paris. And the guys on the third floor – they like Paris, too.'

'Who are the guys on the third floor?'

'The spooks,' said Flint. 'That's what they call them here.'

Lois winked at me. 'He's been squawking here.'

'I didn't think anyone complained in Europe,' I said.

'This isn't Europe,' said Flint. 'It's not even Germany. Half the people here pretend they're French.'

'I like these border towns,' I said. 'The ambiguity, the rigmarole at the customs post, the rumors about smugglers – it's a nice word, smugglers. I associate borders with mystery and danger.'

'The only danger here is that the Ambassador will cable me that he wants to go fishing. Then I have to waste a week fixing up his permits and finding his driver a place to stay. And all the other security – antikidnap measures so he can catch minnows. Jesus, I hate this job.'

Flint had turned grouchy. To change the subject, I said, 'Lois, this is a wonderful meal.'

'You're sweet to say so,' Lois said. 'I'm taking cooking lessons. Would you believe it?'

'It's a kind of local sausage,' said Flint, spearing a tube of encased meat with his fork. 'Everything's kind of local sausage. You'd get arrested for eating this in Malaysia. The wine's drinkable, though. All wine-growing countries are right-wing – ever think of that?'

'Charlie still hasn't forgiven me for not learning to cook,' Lois said. She stared at her husband, a rather severe glaze on her eyes that fixed him in silence; but she went on with what seemed calculated lightheartedness, 'I can't help the fact that he made me spend my early married life in countries where cooks cost ten dollars a month.'

'Consequently, Lois is a superb tennis player,' said Flint.

A certain atmosphere was produced by this remark, but it was a passing cloud, a blade of half-dark, no more. It hovered and was gone. Lois rose abruptly and said, 'I hope you left room for dessert.'

Charlie did not speak until Lois was in the kitchen. I see I have written 'Charlie' rather than 'Flint'; but he had changed, his tone grew confidential. He said, 'I'm very worried about Lois. Ever since we got here she's been behaving funnily. People have mentioned it to me – they're not used to her type. I mean, she cries a lot. She might be heading for a nervous breakdown. You try doing a job with a sick person on your hands. It's a whole nother story. I'm glad you're here – you're good for her.'

It was unexpected and it came in a rush, the cataract of American candor. I murmured something about Lois looking perfectly all right to me.

'It's an act – she's a head case,' he said. 'I don't know what to do about her. But you'd be doing me a big favor if you made allowances. Be good to her. I'd consider it a favor –'

Lois entered the room on those last words. She was carrying a dark heap of chocolate cake. She said, 'You don't have to do something just because Charlie asks you to.'

'We were talking about the Volunteer Speakers Program,' said Flint, with unfaltering coolness and even a hint of boredom: it was a masterful piece of acting. 'As I was saying, I'm supposed to be lining up speakers, but we haven't had one for months. The last time I was in Bonn, the Ambassador put a layer of shit in my ear – what am I doing? I told him – bringing culture to the Germans. The town's a thousand years old. There were Romans here! He didn't think that was very funny. It would help if you gave a talk for me at the Center.'

Lois reached across the table and squeezed my hand. There was more reassurance than caution in the gesture. She said, 'Pay no attention to him. He could have all the volunteer speakers he wants. He just doesn't ask them.'

'Herr Friedrich on Roman spittoons, Gräfin von Spitball on the local aristocracy. That's what Europe's big on – memories. It hasn't got a future, but what a past! There's something decadent about nostalgia – I mean, really diseased.'

'Charlie doesn't like Germans,' said Lois. 'No one likes them. For fifteen years, all I've heard is how inefficient people are in tropical countries. Guess what the big complaint is here? Germans are efficient. They do things on time, they keep their word – this is supposed to be sinister!'

Flint said, 'They're machines.'

'He used to call Malays "superslugs,"' said Lois.

'And Germans think we're diseased,' said Flint. 'They talk about German culture. What's German culture? These days it's American culture – the same books, the same music, the same movies, even the same clothes. They've bought us wholesale, and they have the nerve to sneer.' His harangue left him gasping. With a kind of mournful sincerity he said, 'I'd consider it a favor if you did a lecture. We have a slot tomorrow – there's a sewing circle that meets on Thursdays.'

He was asking me to connive at his deception, and he knew I could not decently refuse him such a simple request. I said, 'Doesn't one need a topic?'

'The white man's burden. War stories. Life in the East. Like the time the locals besieged your consulate and burned the flag.'

'All the locals did was smile and drink my whiskey.'

'Improvise,' he said, twirling his wineglass. 'Ideally, I'd like something on "America's Role in a Changing World" – like, What good is foreign aid? What are the responsibilities of the super-powers? The oil crisis with reference to Islam and the Arab states. Are we at a crossroads? Look, all they want is to hear you speak English. We had to discontinue the language program after the last budget cuts. They'll be glad to see a new face. They're pretty sick of mine.'

Lois squeezed my hand again. 'Welcome to Europe.'

The next morning, trying sleepily to imagine what I would say in my lecture – and I hated Flint for making me go through with this charade – I was startled by a knock at the door. I sat up in bed. It was Lois.

'I forgot to warn you about breakfast,' she said, entering the room. Her tone was cheerfully apologetic, but her movements were bold. At first I thought she was in her pajamas. I put on my glasses and saw she was in a short pleated skirt and a white jersey. The white clothes and their cut gave her a girlish look, and at the same time contradicted it, exaggerating her briskness. Tennis had obviously kept her in shape. She was in her early forties – younger than Charlie – but was trim and hard-fleshed. She had borne no children – it was childbirth that left the marks of age on a woman's body. She had a flat stomach, a server's stride, and as she approached the bed I noticed the play of muscles in her thighs. She was an odd apparition, but a woman in a tennis outfit looks too athletic in a businesslike way to be seductive.

She was still talking about breakfast, not looking at me, but pacing the floor at the foot of the bed. Charlie didn't normally have more than a coffee, she said. There was grapefruit in the fridge and cereal on the sideboard. The coffee was made. Did I want eggs?

'I'll have a coffee with Charlie,' I said.

'He's gone. He left the house an hour ago.'

'Don't worry about me. I can look after myself.'

Lois's tennis shoes squeaked as she paced the polished floor. Then she stopped and faced me. 'I'm worried about Charlie,' she said. 'I suppose you thought he was joking last night about the Ambassador. It's serious – he hasn't accomplished anything here. Everyone knows it. And he doesn't care.'

Almost precisely the words he had used about her: I wondered whether they were playing a game with me.

'I'm his volunteer speaker,' I said. 'That's quite a feather in his cap.'

'You don't think so, but it is. He's in real trouble. He told the Ambassador he was thinking of taking early retirement.'

'Might not be a bad idea,' I said.

'He said, "I can always sell second-hand cars. I've been selling second-hand junk my whole Foreign Service career." That's what he told the Ambassador! I was flabbergasted. Then he told me it was a joke. It was at a staff meeting – all the PAOs were there. But no one laughed. I don't blame them – it's not funny.'

I wanted to get out of bed. I saw that this would not be simple while she was in the room. I could not think straight, sitting up, with the blankets across my lap, my hair in my eyes.

Lois said, 'Can I get in?'

I have always felt that if a person wants something very badly, and if it is not unreasonable, he should have it, no matter what. I usually feel like supplying it myself. Once, I gave my hunting knife to a Malay. He admired it; he wanted it; he had some use for it. Generosity is easy to justify. I always lose what I don't need.

I considered Lois's question and then said, 'Yes – sure,' convinced that Charlie had not misled me: something was wrong with her.

She got in quickly, without embarrassment. She said, 'He's mentally screwed up, he really is.'

'Poor Charlie.'

We lay under the covers, side by side, like two Boy Scouts in a big sleeping bag, sheltering from the elements in clumsy comradeship. Lois had not taken off her tennis shoes: I could feel the canvas and rubber against my shins. Her shoes seemed proof that Charlie had not exaggerated her mental state.

'He thinks it's funny. It's me who's suffering. People pity mental cases – it's their families they should pity.'

'That's pitching it a bit strongly, isn't it?' I tried to shift my hand from the crisp pleats of her skirt. 'Charlie may be under a little strain, but he hardly qualifies as a mental case.'

'A month ago we're at a party. It was endless – one of these German affairs. They really love their food, and their idea of fun is to get stinking drunk and sing loud. There's no social stigma attached to drunkenness here. So everyone was laughing stupidly and the men were behaving like jackasses. One of them took my shawl and put it over his head and did a Wagner bit. And there was this Italian – just a hanger-on, he wasn't a diplomat. He suggested they all go to a restaurant. It's two in the morning, everyone's eaten, and he wants to go to a restaurant! There was a sort of general move to the door – they're all yelling and laughing. I said to Charlie, "Count me out – I'm tired."

"You never want to do anything," he said.

'I told him he could go if he wanted to. He gave me the car keys and I went home alone. I was asleep when he came back. There was a big commotion at the front door – it was about five. I go to the door and who do I see? Charlie. And the Italian. They're holding hands.'

I almost laughed. But Lois was on the verge of tears. I felt her body stiffen.

'It was awful. The Italian had this guilty, sneaky look on his face, as if he'd been caught in the act. I saw that he wanted to drop the whole thing. He wouldn't look at me. Charlie was gray – absolutely gray. He wasn't even drunk – he looked sick, crazy, and he kept holding this Italian by the hand. He told me to go back to bed.

'"I'm not going back to bed until he leaves," I said.

'"This is my friend," he said. His friend! They're holding hands! He dragged the Italian into the house and I really wanted to hit both of them. Charlie said, "We're staying."

'"Not him," I said. "He's not staying in my house."

'"You never let me have any friends," said Charlie, and he starts staggering around with this other guy. I thought I was dreaming, it was so ridiculous.

"I don't care what you do," I said, "but you're not taking this creep into my house." Then I got hysterical, I started screaming, I hardly knew what I was saying.

'Charlie said, "All right, then, let's go." And off they went, hand in hand, out the door. I don't know where they went. I didn't see Charlie until that night. He looked terrible – I don't even think he'd been to work. He hasn't mentioned it since. And you deny he's a mental case.'

Listening to her story, it struck me that I hardly knew Charlie Flint. He was as frenzied as anyone in the Embassy, and he had a theory that the Embassy wives were going to start an insurrection, but our relationship was mainly professional. I knew nothing of his personal life beyond the fact that he drank too much; that fact applied to everyone I met in the Foreign Service. I regarded his determination to stay out of Washington as a worthy aim. He wasn't ambitious. And he had prepared me for his wife's oddness.

I replied to her in platitudes: Don't jump to conclusions, things will settle down, and so forth. What else could I offer? I did not know her well, and I was in bed with her. I said, as an afterthought, 'You're not suggesting he's gay, are you?'

'Do you think I'd care about that?' she said. 'You've been in the bush for two years, so you don't know. But being bisexual is the big thing in Europe these days. Everyone's gay. The men think it's fashionable, almost masculine – proof that you don't have any hang-ups. They're always hugging each other, holding hands – God only knows what else they do, though I have a pretty good idea. I'm telling you, Europe makes Southeast Asia look civilized. I get propositioned about once a week – by women!'

'Are you tempted?'

'No,' Lois said, 'I tried it.'

'With a woman?'

She nodded; her whole body moved, and she wore a curious half-smile. 'A German chick. About nineteen. Very pretty. It didn't work out.' She made a face. 'Charlie wanted me to. That's why I didn't take it seriously. I thought it would encourage him in his craziness. Now, when I think about it, I just laugh.' She shifted sideways on the bed, propped herself up on one arm and said, 'How come you're so normal?'

'Everything is human.'

'You're making excuses for Charlie.'

'Charlie has a conscience.'

'Don't you?'

'I don't know. But I know that the lack of it can make some people look fairly serene, even harmless and normal. Charlie hasn't hurt anyone.'

'He's hurt me!' Lois cried, and I felt her shoe. 'I'm sorry,' she said. 'I didn't mean to kick you. But what good is it saying, "Everything's human and everything's normal"? We were in Indonesia, India, Malaysia – yes, things were normal in those places. But Europe's different. And I'm telling you, I can't handle it.'

I felt sure she was mistaken, but I didn't want to contradict her, since she appeared to take everything as a personal attack. She saw Charlie's drunken hand-holding as an affront to her, but this casual mention of *a German chick* – wasn't that equally odd? She didn't appear to think so. I understood why she was lying to me, though it was not in character for her to belittle Charlie. Adultery is a great occasion for lying; the wife in another man's bed usually talks about her husband.

I said, 'I'm glad I came to Europe. I had no idea it was so lively. It makes Ayer Hitam seem rather tame.'

'Where are you going after this?'

'Up the Rhine. I'm leaving tonight, after my talk. I'll be in Düsseldorf for a few days.'

'Are you staying with Murray Goldsack?'

'Charlie gave me his name. But I'll probably stay in a hotel.'

'Charlie gave you his name,' Lois said bitterly. 'He would. We were up there three weeks ago. Another disaster.'

I didn't want to hear it, but she had already begun.

'The Goldsacks have been there about a year. She writes poetry, he's big on painting – he'll show you the gallery he opened. It's full of pretentious crap – stupid, simple, neurotic blurs. Doesn't anyone paint people anymore? The Goldsacks don't have any children. In fact, when they got married they signed a contract saying they wouldn't have any kids and deciding who'd get what when they split up. They assumed they'd split up eventually – Murray will give you all the statistics. They're very modern laid-back people with a house full of crap art and heads full of crap opinions. Over dinner, they told us how they keep their marriage alive.

'Get this. They play games. Like "White Night." Sue puts on a white dress, white slippers, white everything. Then she cooks a white meal – mashed potatoes, steamed fish, cauliflower, Chablis. Murray wears a white suit. Then they get drunk and go to it.'

'That doesn't sound so odd,' I said. She was not lying, but repeating a lie.

'They also have Black Night, Red Night. Or Indian Night. She puts on a sari, cooks a curry, they burn incense and run through the *Kamasutra*.'

'Tell me about Eskimo Night. Do they rub noses?'

'Be serious, will you? Murray was telling me about it – we were in his living room. As he was describing these dressing-up games I noticed he was filling my glass. This little squirt was trying to get me drunk! I was feeling pretty rotten, and he was annoyed that I wasn't drinking fast enough. So he pulled out some pot and rolled me a joint. I once tried some in KL, but it wasn't anything like this. My brain turned into oatmeal. Then I looked around and didn't see Charlie. I was panicky. "Where's Charlie?" I said. Murray looked at me. "Oh, he's with Sue."

'"Where are they?" I said.

'He pointed to a door – the door was closed. I said, "I've got to talk to him" – I don't know why I said it. Maybe it was that stuff I had just smoked.

'Murray said, "Don't go in there. They don't want you to."

'"How do you know what they want?" I said. He sort of chuckled. I said, "Hey, what's going on?"

'He had a really evil look on his face. He said, "You really want to know?"

'Then I knew. I wanted to cry. I said, "My husband's in that room with your wife!" He said something like, "So what?" and put his arm around me. I pushed him away and stood up. He got mad at me – he was really peeved. He tried to grab me again, and I hit him. He said, "Hey, what's wrong with you?"

'What's wrong with *me*? This man's a cultural affairs officer in the United States Embassy. He's supposed to be a diplomat, he gives lectures, he makes statements to the press, he writes reports – or whatever they do. And he's peeved because I won't cooperate with his wife-swapping! It was too much. After an hour or so, Charlie and Sue came out looking pretty pale and pushing their clothes back in place. We all had a drink and talked about – Jesus, we talked about Jimmy Carter and the budget cuts. The next day we left. Charlie wouldn't talk about the other thing – the monkey business.'

Lois was silent for a while. Then she turned over onto her side, her back to me. I got up on one elbow and, seeing that she was crying, I put my arm around her to comfort her.

She said, 'Hold me tight – please.' I did. She murmured, 'That's nice.'

What now? I thought.

She said, 'Charlie never pays any attention to me.'

'I can't help liking him,' I said.

Lois said, 'I'm married to him,' and then, 'Don't let go.'

'I feel a bit silly,' I said. 'Should we be doing this?'

'I get nothing,' she said. 'Nothing, nothing. This isn't a life.'

'You're going to miss your tennis.'

She twisted away from me and heaved her legs up.

'What are you doing, Lois?'

'Getting these damn shoes off.'

I said, 'I'm supposed to be having lunch with Charlie. I couldn't face him. Please don't take your shoes off.'

'He doesn't care,' she said.

Another lie: for all his frenzy and occasional deceit, there was no man who would have cared more about his wife's infidelity. Remember, they had no children to encumber their intimacy, so they were like children themselves – such couples so often are.

'That seems worse,' I said, resenting her ineptness.

She pressed her back against me, moving her skirt sinuously on my thighs; and still facing away she uttered a despairing groan.

'Then just hold me,' she said. 'I'll be all right in a minute.'

When she got out of bed her pleated skirt was crushed and her socks had slipped down. She brushed herself off, adjusted her socks, and tucked in her jersey. She looked as if she had just played her match and been defeated.

She said, 'I feel very virtuous.'

'I don't,' I said. Then she was out the door. I thought: *She is insane.*

Charlie was late for lunch. When he arrived, I looked for indications of the craziness Lois had attributed to him. But there were none. She needed to believe he was crazy, in order to make excuses for herself.

He said, 'Do you really have to go to Düsseldorf after the lecture?'

'The lecture was your idea,' I said. 'If it wasn't for that I'd be on the train now.'

'You're welcome to stay as long as you like. Lois was hoping you would.'

I said, 'I don't think there's much I can do for her.'

'Fair enough.' He seemed gloomy and almost apologetic, as if he had guessed at what had gone on that morning between Lois and me. I did not want to upset him further by telling him her wild stories. He said, 'I'd leave this place tomorrow except for one thing. This is the first place Lois can live a normal life. I'm staying for her sake. Believe me, it's a sacrifice. But there are good doctors here. The best medical care. That's what she needs.'

'I understand.' I could not say more without revealing that I pitied him.

'You'll like Düsseldorf. Goldsack's a live wire. A very bright guy – he's got a big future in the Foreign Service. He'll make Ambassador as sure as anything. His wife's fun, and I think I should tell you – she's an easy lay.'

That was the first clue I had that Lois might not have been completely wrong about Charlie. And it made me all the more eager to meet the Goldsacks. I left immediately after my lecture, and two days later was in Murray Goldsack's office.

'Flint cabled me that you were coming,' he said. 'I've been looking over your bio. It's really impressive.' Goldsack was small and dark, in his early thirties, and he looked me over closely, giving me the strong impression that I was being interviewed and appraised. He said, 'I wish I had your Southeast Asia experience. My wife keeps saying we should put in for a tour there.'

'You might be disappointed.'

'I'm never bored,' he said, and made it sound like a reproach. 'Flint said you might be available as a volunteer speaker.'

'Other people do it so much better,' I said.

'Give us a chance to entertain you at least,' he said. 'We'd like to have you and your wife over for a meal. I hope you'll both be able to make it.'

'If my bio says I'm married, you've been misinformed.'

Goldsack laughed. 'What I mean is, I'd rather you didn't come alone.'

I said, 'I know an antique dealer in town. He's a lovely fellow.

Now, he's someone you might like to consider as a volunteer speaker.'

'Wonderful,' said Goldsack. He jumped up and shook my hand to signal the meeting was over. 'I'll leave a message at your hotel with the details.'

That was the last I saw of Goldsack. There was no message, which was just as well, because there was no antique dealer. I thought: *Poor Lois*.

Reception

The best telegram I ever had said this: CALL ME TOMORROW FOR WONDERFUL NEWS. I had twenty hours to imagine what the news might be. And I delayed for a few hours more. I wanted to prolong the pleasure. I loved the expectation. How often in life do we have the bright certainty that everything is going to be fine?

Traveling alone through Europe, I had just left Germany for Holland, where the telegram awaited me. I liked the Dutch. They were sensible; they had been brave in the war. They still tried to understand the world, and their quaint modernism had made them tolerant. They behaved themselves. It was a church-and-brothel society in which there were neither saints nor sinners, only at worst a few well-meaning hypocrites. Vice without passion, theology without much terror; they were even idealistic in a practical way. They were unprejudiced and open-minded without being naively enthusiastic. They had nice faces. Their pornography was ridiculous, and I think it embarrassed them, but they knew that left to its impotent spectators and drooling voyeurs it was just another sorry prop in sex's sad comedy.

In Amsterdam, where I could have chosen anything, I chose to be idle. I smoked a little hash, talked to Javanese in quacking Bahasa, and was reminded how the 'colonial' and the 'bourgeois' are full of the same worthy illusions, like the solidity and reassurance of plump upholstered armchairs in a warm parlor. I sat and read. I ate Eastern food and slept soundly in a soft Dutch bed. Each night I dreamed without waking – it had never happened in Ayer Hitam, where nights were rackety and hot.

It was winter. The canals froze. Some people skated, as they did in the oldest oil paintings on earth – moving so fast that the swipes of the speed-skaters' blades made a sound like knives being sharpened. Gulls dived between the leaning buildings and gathered on the green ice. The small frosty city smelled of its river and its bakeries, and beer. I went for long ankle-twisting walks down cobblestone streets.

At last, almost sad because it meant the end of a joyous wait, I made my phone call. The telegram had been informal – a friend in the State Department. I had tried to avoid guessing the news: expect nothing and you're never disappointed.

She said, 'You've got London.'

This was London, this reception. A month had passed since the telegram. The party invitations had my name on them ('*To Welcome . . .*'). The guests had been carefully selected – it was pleasure for them, a night out. For us, the Embassy staff, it was overtime. I did not mind. I had wanted London. In London I could meet anyone, do anything, go anywhere. It was the center of the civilized world, the best place in Europe, the last habitable big city. It was the first city Americans thought of traveling to – funny, friendly, and undemanding; it was every English-speaker's spiritual home. I had been intending to come here for as long as I could remember.

And this was also a promotion for me: from FSO-5, my grade as Consul in the Malaysian town of Ayer Hitam, to FSO-4, Political Officer. My designation was POL-1, not to be confused with POL-2, the CIA – 'The boys on the third floor,' as we called them at the London Embassy. I was a spy only in the most general and harmless sense of the word.

It had been a mistake to walk from my hotel to this reception. My hotel was in Chelsea, near the Embankment; the party was at Everett Horton's Briarcliff Lodge, in Kensington. London is not a city. It is more like a country, and living in it is like living in Holland or Belgium. Its completeness makes it deceptive – there are sidewalks from one frontier to the other – and its hugeness makes it possible for everyone to invent his own city. My London is not your London, though everyone's Washington, DC, is pretty much the same. It was three miles from my hotel to Horton's, and this was only a small part of the labyrinth. A two-mile walk through any other city would take you inevitably through a slum. But this was unvarying gentility – wet narrow streets, dark housefronts, block upon block. They spoke of prosperity, but they revealed nothing very definite of their occupants. They were sedate battlements, fortress-walls, with blind windows or drawn curtains. I imagined, behind them, something tumultuous. I had never felt more solitary or anonymous. I was happy. The city had been built to enclose secrets, for the British are like those naked Indians who hide in the Brazilian jungle – not timid, but fanatically private and untrusting. This was a mazy land of privacies – comforting to a secretive person, offering shelter to a fugitive, but posing problems to a diplomat. It was my job to know its secrets, to inform and represent my government, to penetrate the city and make new maps.

That walk through London humbled me. I began to feel less like an adventurer – a grand cartographer – than someone in a smaller role. I played with the idea that we were like gardeners. We were sent to maintain this garden, to keep the grass cut and the weeds down, to dead-head the roses, encourage the frailer blossoms. We could not introduce new plants or alter it. We watched over it, kept it watered; we dealt with enemies and called them pests. But our role was purely custodial. Each of us, in time, would go away. It was the image of a harmless occupation.

But of course in London there was a difference. It was a city without front yards. This was not America, with a low-maintenance lawn around every house. The garden was not a boasting acre here to advertise prosperity to passersby. In London, all gardens were behind the houses. They were hidden. 'Plots' was the word.

Briarcliff Lodge had once belonged to a duke. It rose up from its surrounding hedge, a graceful monument of creamy floodlit walls and tall windows. What an earlier age had managed with stone, we had with light – floodlights, spot-lights, bulbs behind cornices and buried in the ground, wrapped in vines and under water. It was beauty as emphasis, but it also afforded protection. Inside and out, Everett Horton had restored Briarcliff Lodge at Embassy expense. He had hired six waiters tonight, and two front-door functionaries. I handed the first my raincoat – apologizing for its being wet – and gave my name to the second man. But I was not announced. I was early and, after all, I was the guest of honor.

'Mr Horton will be down shortly.'

'Excuse me, where's the –?'

'Just behind you, sir. One flight up.'

In such circumstances the British are telepathic.

Then I heard a child's voice from the upper floor.

'Are the people here yet, Dad?'

'Not yet, but they will be soon. Better make it snappy.' It was

Horton's voice. He cleared his throat and said, 'Now, do you want to do a tinkle or a yucky?'

I began to back away.

'Both,' the child said.

'All right,' the diplomat said patiently. 'Take your time.'

All happy families have a private language. The Hortons' was just about as useful and ludicrous-sounding as any other. But if Horton could be that patient with his child, I had little to worry about; and if he was happy, he was more than human.

The rooms in this house were enormous – a gym-size drawing room (perhaps once the ballroom), a library, the dining room to the right, and behind it the morning room and conservatory. A foyer, a cloakroom, a wide staircase. And this was only the ground floor. It was ducal splendor, but Horton was no duke. He lived, I knew, with his wife and child in an apartment on the third floor, at the back of the house. Servants' quarters, really – their little yellow kitchen, microwave oven, dishwasher, toaster, Bloomingdale's furniture, their TV, and five telephones. Horton had not taken possession of the house – he was its custodian. He lived like any janitor, like any gardener. Such is the fate of a career diplomat.

Some minutes later, he came downstairs.

'We've got rather a mixed bag tonight,' he said. He was formal, a bit stiff-faced. He had a reputation for affecting British slang, and it was hard for me now to think of him as the same man who had just said *a tinkle or a yucky*.

The front door thumped shut.

'Mr and Mrs Roger Howlett,' said the functionary from the hall. There was both dignity and strain in his announcing voice.

'The publisher,' I said.

'Good show,' Horton said. 'I'm glad you had a chance to swot up the guest list.'

He was being tactful – I had done little else for the past week. It had been, so far, the whole of my job, that guest list with its fifty names – and more: occupations, ages, addresses, and (if applicable) political leanings. It was a comprehensive list, like 'Cast of Characters' at the opening of a Victorian novel. Learning it was like cramming a vocabulary list for a language exam. The only danger at such a reception was in knowing too much – startling the innocent guest by seeming overfamiliar with him.

Until then, my overseas experience had been in Uganda and

Malaysia. Prudence, but not much subtlety, had been required of me in those places. Uganda wanted money from us; Malaysia wanted political patronage. Both deviously demanded that we be explicit and suspected us of being spies. Here in London we were regarded as high-living and rather privileged diplomats, a bit spoiled and unserious. But in fact every officer at the London Embassy was in his own way an intelligence gatherer. There were too many secrets here for any of us to be complacent. This garden was not ours, and it contained some strange blooms. And maybe all good gardeners are at heart unsentimental botanists.

Horton's drawing room was soon filled. I stood at the door to the foyer. In this, the most casual setting imaginable, no one could be blamed for thinking that mine was the easiest job in the world. But every American in that room was hard at work, and only the British people here were enjoying themselves. Once again it struck me how cooperative party guests were – it was perhaps the only reason Embassy receptions were ever given, to enlist the help of unsuspecting people, to find out whether the natives were friendly, to take soundings, to listen for gossip.

I entered the room – penetrated London for the first time – and set to work.

'Hello. I don't think we've met,' I said to a young woman.

It was Mrs Sarah Whiting, second wife of Anthony Whiting, managing director of the British subsidiary of an American company that made breakfast cereal. Whiting himself was across the room, talking to Margaret Duboys from our Trade Section. The Whitings had no children of their own, though Mr Whiting had three by a previous marriage to an American woman still resident in Britain and still referred to by Vic Scaduto, our CAO, as 'Auntie Climax.' Sarah Whiting was something of a mystery to the Embassy; she had been married only a year to the managing director. She was still full of the effortful romance of the second marriage – or so it seemed. I got nowhere by inquiring about her husband's business. Second wives are usually spared the details: the husband's affairs were determined by another woman, long ago. Anyway, I knew the answers before I asked the questions.

She said, 'You're an American.'

'How did you guess?'

'You look as if you belong here.'

'Seeing as how I've been here only a week, I'm deeply flattered.'

'Then you must be the guest of honor,' she said. 'Welcome to London.'

We chatted about the weather, the high price of apartments – I told her I was looking for a place – and the décor of this room. She spoke knowledgeably about interior decoration ('I would have done that fascia in peach'), and when I complimented her, she said that she was interested 'in a small way.' I was soon to find out how small.

'I make furniture,' she said.

'Design it or build it?'

'I do everything.'

I was impressed. I said, 'You upholster it, too?'

'Not much upholstery is necessary,' she said. 'Most of my furniture is for dollhouses.'

I thought I had misheard her.

'You mean' – I measured a few inches with my fingers – 'like this?'

'It depends on the house. Some are smaller, some bigger. I make cutlery, as well.'

'For dollhouses?'

'That's right,' she said.

'Very tiny knives and forks?'

'And spoons. And tea strainers. Why are you smiling?'

'I don't think I've ever met anyone in your line of work.'

She said, 'I quite enjoy it.'

'Your children' – yes, I knew better, but it was the obvious next remark – 'your children must be fascinated by it.'

'It's not really a child's thing. Most of the collectors are adults. It's a very serious business – and very expensive. We export a great deal. In any case, I don't have any children of my own. Do you have kids?'

'I'm not married,' I said.

'We'll find you a wife,' she said.

I hated that – it was the tone of a procuress. I may have showed a flicker of disapproval, because she looked suddenly uneasy. Maybe I was queer! Bachelor means queer!

I said, 'Please do.'

She turned to the woman next to her and said, 'Sophie, this is the guest of honor,' and stepped aside to make room.

'Sophie Graveney,' Sarah Whiting said, and introduced us.

Miss Graveney, thirty, was an Honorable, her late father a lord. Her brother had succeeded to the title. We knew little about her, except for the fact that she had spent some time in the States.

I said, 'We were just talking about dollhouses.'

'Sarah's passionate about them.'

'If things go on like this, I'll have to get Sarah to rent me one to live in.'

'You're looking for a place, are you?'

'Yes. Just an apartment – a flat.'

'What location?'

'I'm near the river at the moment, near Chelsea Embankment. I think I'd like to stay down there.'

'Chelsea's very nice. But it's pricey. You might find something in Battersea. It's not as fashionable, but it's just across the bridge – South Chelsea, the snobs call it. There are some beautiful flats on Prince of Wales Drive, overlooking the park.'

'I'll consider anything except the sort of place that's described as "delightfully old-fashioned." That always means derelict.'

'Those are lovely,' she said. 'Do you jog? Of course you don't, why should you?' And she gave me an appraising stare. She had soft curls and wore lip gloss and I could see her body move beneath her loose black dress. She was also very tall and had large feet. Her shoulders were scented with jasmine. 'I do jog, though. For my figure. Usually around Battersea Park at the crack of dawn.'

Sarah Whiting laughed and said, 'Tell him your story about that man.'

'Oh, God,' Sophie said. 'That man. Last summer I was out jogging. It was about seven in the morning and I'd done two miles. I was really mucky – pouring with sweat. An old man stepped in front of me and said, "Excuse me, miss, would you care for a drink?" I thought he meant a drink of water. I was out of breath and sort of steaming. I absolutely stank. I could barely answer him. Then he sort of snatched at my hand and said, "I've got some whiskey in my car."'

Her eyes were shining as she spoke.

'Do you get it? There I am in my running shoes and track suit, drenched with sweat, my hair hanging in rat tails, and this foolish old man is trying to pick me up! At seven o'clock in the morning!'

'Incredible!' Sarah said.

'Then he said, "I want to be your bicycle seat," and made a

hideous face. I jogged away,' Sophie said innocently. 'I didn't fancy him one little bit.'

'If I get a flat near Battersea Park I can watch you jogging,' I said.

'Yes. If you get up early. Isn't that thrilling?'

A waiter passed by with a tray of drinks. Sophie took another glass of white wine and, seeing that I did not take any, she looked somewhat disapproving.

'Oh, God, are you one of those people who don't drink?'

I said, 'I'm one of those people who're cutting down.'

'Oh, God, you don't smoke either – how boring! I smoke about two packs a day.'

'Do you?' I said. 'Now that's really interesting.'

'Is that funny?' she said, and blinked at me. 'I never know when people are joking.'

There was a dim suspicion in her voice and a moment of stillness, as if she had just realized that I was a perfect stranger, who might be mocking her. She looked around and smiled in relief.

'Terry!' she said, as if calling for help.

She had seen a friend. She introduced him to me as Lord Billows, though he insisted I call him Terry. I recognized him from the guest list – he ran a public relations firm that had a New York office. We talked for the next ten minutes about smoking, its hazards and pleasures: he represented a tobacco company and was very defensive about its sponsorship of mountain-climbing competitions – teams of climbers racing up mountainsides, a sport I had never heard of. To change the subject, I told him I had spent the past two years in Malaysia. He said he knew 'Eddie Pahang.' Very chummy: he was referring to the Sultan of Pahang.

Lord Billows said, 'Your Ambassador in KL gave marvelous parties.'

'So they said. I seldom got to KL. I was in Ayer Hitam, with the stinking durians and the revolting rubber tappers. You've never heard of it. Nobody has. On the good days it was paradise.'

'Who was your sultan?'

'Johore.'

'Buffles – I knew him well. Buffles was a real old trooper. A magnificent polo player in his time, you know. And a greatly mis-understood man.'

'He used to come to our club once a year,' I said. 'One of his mistresses was in the drama society. She was a Footlighter. That's what they called themselves. They loved being in plays.'

Lord Billows had been grinning impatiently at me through all this. Then he said, 'I'm going to ask you a very rude question,' and fixed his face against mine. 'But you probably won't consider it rude. You Americans are so straight forward, aren't you?'

'That is rather a rude question,' I said.

Lord Billows said, 'That's not the question.'

'Ask him,' Sophie said. 'I'm all ears.'

'The question is, are you in fact a member of a club in London?' Lord Billows turned aside to Sophie and said, 'You see, in the normal way one would never ask an Englishman that.'

I said, 'I think the Ayer Hitam Club has a reciprocal arrangement with a London club.'

'I doubt that very much,' Lord Billows said. 'I have three clubs. The Savile might suit you – we have some Americans. I'm not as active as I'd like to be, but there it is. I put your chap Scaduto up for the Savile. I could do the same for you. Let me give you lunch there. You could look it over. I think you'd find it convivial.'

'Is it delightfully old-fashioned?' Sophie asked.

'Exactly,' Lord Billows said.

Sophie said, 'He'll detest it.'

'When applied to houses, delightfully old-fashioned means a drafty ruin. When applied to clubs, it means bad food and no women.'

'The Savile has quite decent food,' Lord Billows said. 'And most of the staff are women.'

'I was in a club like that once,' I said.

'In London?'

'The States. When I was eleven years old,' I said. 'No girls. That was the rule.'

Lord Billows stared at me for several seconds, as if translating what I had said, and then he said coldly, 'You'll excuse me?' He walked away.

'You shouldn't have said that to him,' Sophie said. 'Why make a fuss about men's clubs? I don't object. I hate all this women's lib stuff, don't you?'

She had not addressed the question to me, but to Mrs Howlett – Diana – wife of Roger, the publisher, who was standing next to her. The two women began laughing in a conspiratorial way, and

Roger Howlett told me several stories about Adlai Stevenson, and I gathered Horton had briefed him about me, because Howlett finished his Stevenson stories by saying, 'Adlai was enormously good value – single, like yourself.'

'Meet Walter Van Bellamy,' Roger Howlett said, and tapped a tall rangy white-haired man on the arm. 'One of your fellow countrymen.'

Bellamy showed me his famous face and celebrated hair, but his eyes were wild as he said, 'You and I have an awful lot in common, sir.' Then he moved away, pushing through the crowd with his arms up, like a sleepwalker.

'He won all the pots and pans last year,' Howlett said. 'And here is one of our other authors.' He took hold of a large pink man named Yarrow.

'I've written only one book for Roger,' Yarrow said. 'It was political. About land reform. I was a Young Communist then. You didn't blink. That's funny – Americans usually do when I say that. It was a failure, my literary effort.'

'I've found,' Howlett said, 'that some of my authors actually get a thrill when their books fail. I've never understood it. Is it the British love of amateurism?'

I knew from the guest list that Yarrow was a Member of Parliament, but to be polite I asked him what his business was.

He hooked his thumb into his waistcoat pocket and sipped his drink and said, 'I represent a squalid little constituency in the West Midlands.'

The way he said it, with a smirk on his smooth pink face and a glass in his hand and his tie splashed – he had sloshed his drink as he spoke – I found disgusting. If he meant it, it was contemptible; if he had said it for effect, it was obnoxious.

I said, 'Maybe you'll be lucky and lose your seat at the next election.'

'No fear. It's a safe Tory seat. Labour haven't got a chance. The working class don't vote – too lazy.'

'I want him to do me a book about Westminster,' Howlett said.

'Europe – that's the subject. We're European,' Yarrow said. 'That's where our future is. In a united Europe.'

'What actually *is* a European?' I asked. 'I mean, what language does he speak? What flag does he salute? What are his politics?'

'Don't ask silly questions,' Yarrow said. 'I must go. There's a vote in the Commons in twenty minutes. Rather an important bill.'

'Are you for it or against it?'

'Very much against it!'

'What is the bill?'

'Haven't the faintest,' Yarrow said. 'But if I don't vote, there'll be hell to pay.'

He left with two other MPs. Howlett went to the buffet table, and I walked around the room. I saw Miss Duboys talking to Lord Billows, and Vic Scaduto to Walter Van Bellamy, the poet. A black American, named Erroll Jeeps, from our Economics Section, looked intense as he stabbed his finger into the transfixed face of a woman. Jeeps saw me passing and said, 'How are you holding up?'

'Fine,' I said.

'This is our main man,' Jeeps said, 'the guest of honor.'

I said, 'I'd almost forgotten.'

'It's a very jolly party,' the woman said. 'I'm Grace Yarrow.'

'I just met your husband.'

'He's gone to vote. But he'll be back,' she said.

'The third reading of the finance bill,' Jeeps said. 'It's going to be close.'

'You Americans are so well informed,' Mrs Yarrow said.

Horton stepped over and said, 'I'm going to drag our guest of honor away,' and introduced me to a *Times* journalist, an antique dealer named Frampton, and a girl who did hot-air ballooning. The party had grown hectic. I stopped asking for names. I met the director of a chain of hotels, and then a young man who said, 'Sophie's been telling me all about you' – as if a great deal of time had passed and I had grown in reputation. A party was a way of speeding friendship and telescoping time. It was a sort of hot-house concept of forced growth. We were all friends now.

Someone said, 'It rains every Thursday in London.'

'We bought our Welsh dresser from a couple of fags,' someone else said.

The man named Frampton praised one of Horton's paintings, saying, 'It's tremendous fun.'

At about eleven, the first people left, and by eleven-thirty only half the guests remained. They had gathered in small groups. I met a very thin man who gave his name as Smallwood, and I could hardly match him to the man on the guest list who appeared as Sir Charles Smallwood. And I assumed I had the wrong man, because this fellow had a grizzled, almost destitute look and was wearing an old-fashioned evening suit.

Edward Heaven, a name that appeared nowhere on the guest list, was a tall white-haired man with large furry ears, who vanished from the room as soon as he told me who he was, on the pretext of giving himself an insulin injection in the upstairs toilet. 'Puts some people off their food, it does,' he said, but he made for the front door, and the next moment he was hurrying down the street in the drizzle, without a coat.

The party was not quite over, I thought. But it was over. Of the nine people remaining in the room, seven were Embassy people, and when the last guests left – the *Times* man and the antique dealer – Horton said to us, 'Now, how about a real drink?'

He then went out of the room and told the hired help they could go home. In his dark suit, and carrying a tray, Horton looked like a waiter. On the tray was a bottle of whiskey and some glasses. He poured himself a drink, urged us to do the same, and said, 'Please sit down – this won't take long.'

I assumed this was one for the road. But it occurred to me, sitting among my Embassy colleagues, that I had said very little to them all evening. In a sense, we were meeting for the first time. Their party manner was gone, and although they were tired – it was well past midnight – they seemed intense, all business. This impression was heightened by the fact that Debbie Horton, Everett's wife, had disappeared upstairs in the last hour of the party. Neither Miss Duboys nor I was married, and none of the others' wives were present. We had all come to the reception alone.

Horton sat in the center of the circle of chairs, like a football coach after an important game. Scaduto had told me that he liked to be called 'coach.' He looked the part – he was a big fleshy-faced man, who used body English when he spoke.

He said, 'To tell the truth, I didn't expect to see Lord Billows here tonight. We were told he was going through a rather messy divorce.'

'They've agreed on a settlement,' Al Sanger said. Sanger had dark hair and a very white face and a bright, almost luminous, scar on his forehead. He was, like me, a political officer, but concerned with legal matters. 'His wife gets custody of the children.'

Miss Duboys said, 'What happens to her title?'

'She stays Lady Billows,' Erroll Jeeps said. 'If she remarries, she loses it.'

'Find out what she's styling herself now,' Horton said to Jeeps. 'We don't want to lose touch with her. If we do, there goes one of our most persuasive strings.' He turned to me and said, 'I noticed our guest of honor chatting up Lord Billows. Did you make any headway?'

'He wanted to put me up for a club,' I said.

'Jolly good,' Horton said.

'I told him I wasn't interested.'

'That was pretty stupid,' Sanger said. 'He was trying to do you a favor.'

I could tell from Horton's expression that he was in sympathy with Sanger's remark.

Sanger still faced me. I said, 'So you approve of discrimination against people on the grounds of sex?'

'It's a London club,' he said.

'They don't allow women to join.'

Sanger said, 'Are you afraid they'll turn you down?'

Horton and the others looked shocked, and Margaret Duboys said, 'I don't want to get drawn into this discussion.'

I said, 'Tell me, Sanger, is that remark characteristic of your tact? Because if it is, I'd say your mouth is an even greater liability than your face.'

'Gentlemen, please,' Horton said, in his coach's voice. 'Before this turns into a slanging match, can we move on to something less controversial? I need something on Mrs Whiting – the second Mrs Whiting. Did anyone have a word with her?'

Scaduto said, 'I didn't get anywhere.'

'She makes furniture,' I said. 'Very small furniture. For dollhouses.'

Sanger said, 'You dig deep.'

'And cutlery,' I said. 'Very tiny forks and knives. If you wanted to stab someone in the back' – here I looked at Sanger – 'I don't think you'd use one of Mrs Whiting's knives.'

Horton smiled. 'Debbie wants her on a committee. We had no idea what her interests were. That's useful. What about our MPs?'

Jeeps said, 'The finance bill passed with a government majority of sixteen. I've just had a phone call. There were eight abstentions.'

'Good man,' Horton said. 'Were any of those abstentions ours?'

'Six Labour, two Liberal. The Tories were solid.'

Miss Duboys said, 'Derek Yarrow filled me in on the antinuclear lobby. It seems to be growing.'

Jeeps said, 'I did a number on Mrs Yarrow.'

'What did you make of Mr Yarrow?' Horton asked me, and I realized that in spite of the crowded party my movements had been closely monitored.

'Blustery,' I said. There was no agreement. 'Contemptuous. Probably tricky.'

'He's given us a lot of help,' Sanger said.

'He seemed rather untrustworthy to me. He described his constituency as "squalid." I didn't like that.'

'That's a snap judgment.'

'Precisely what I felt,' I said, and Sanger scowled at me for deliberately misunderstanding him. 'He's a born-again Tory. He lectured me on Europe. You realize of course that he was a Communist.'

'That's not news to us,' Scaduto said.

'I intend to read his book,' I said.

Sanger appeared to be speaking for the others when he said, 'Yarrow doesn't write books.'

'He wrote one. It didn't sell. It was political. Howlett published it.'

'Yarrow's a heavy hitter,' Sanger said.

'Thank you,' I said, scribbling. 'I collect examples of verbal kitsch.'

Horton said, 'Do me a memo on Yarrow's book after you've read it.' Then, 'Was Sophie Graveney alone?'

'Yes,' Steve Kneedler said. It was his one offering and it was wrong.

'No,' Jeeps said. 'She left with the BBC guy – the one with the fake American accent. I think she lives with him.'

'That would be Ramsay,' Horton said.

'She doesn't live with Ramsay,' I said.

'How do you know that?' Jeeps said.

I said, 'Ramsay's address is given as Hampstead. Sophie Graveney doesn't live in Hampstead.'

'Islington,' Jeeps said. 'It's not far.'

'Then why is it,' I said, 'that she jogs around Battersea Park every morning?'

The others stared at me. Horton said, 'Maybe you can put us in the picture. If she's living with someone there, we ought to know about it.'

Scaduto said, 'Her mother's Danish.'

'So was Hamlet's,' Sanger said.

'I've just realized what it is that I don't like about the English aristocracy,' Scaduto said. 'They're not English! They're Danes, they're Germans, they're Greeks, Russians, Italians. They're even Americans, like Lady Astor and Churchill's mother. They're not English! My charlady is more English than the average duke in his stately home. What a crazy country!'

Margaret Duboys said, 'The Greek royal family is Swedish,' and this seemed to put an end to that subject.

But there was more. The guest list was gone through and each guest discussed so thoroughly that it was as if there had been no party but rather an occasion during which fifty British people had passed in review for us to assess them. Miss Duboys said that she had found out more on the Brownlow merger, and Jeeps said that he had more on his profile about the printing dispute at the *Times*, and Sanger said, 'If anyone wants my notes on export licensing, I'll make a copy of my update. Tony Whiting gave me a few angles. He's got a cousin in a Hong Kong bank.'

I said, 'No one has mentioned that fidgety white-haired fellow.'

'Howlett,' said Scaduto.

'No. I met Howlett,' I said. 'The one I'm talking about said his name was Edward Heaven. He wasn't on the guest list.'

'Everyone was on the guest list,' Horton said.

'Edward Heaven wasn't,' I said.

No one had any idea who this man was; no one had spoken to him or indeed seen him. But there was no mystery. Before we left Briarcliff Lodge, Horton called the Embassy and got the telex operator, a young fellow named Charlie Hogle. Hogle took the name Edward Heaven and had the duty officer run it through the computer. The reply came quickly. Two years previously, Edward Heaven had been Horton's florist. He was probably still associated with the florist and had found out about the party because of the flowers that had been delivered. Mr Heaven had crashed the party. Horton said that he would now get a new florist and would try to tighten security. You couldn't be too careful, he said. They were kidnaping American diplomats in places like Paris.

'I think we can adjourn,' he said, finally. 'It's been a long day.'
At the door, he said, 'You look tired, fella.'

'I'm not used to working overtime,' I said.

'You've been spoiled by the Far East,' he said. 'But you'll learn.'
He clapped me on the shoulder. 'I know it's expecting a lot – after
all, you're new here. But I like to start as I mean to go on.'

Namesake

Erroll Jeeps was a great talker and lively company; but his jokes could be savage. It was he who first told me the story about the truck with the load of bowling balls that overturns on the expressway outside Chicago. The police arrive and see a Polish workman slamming the bowling balls with a hammer and breaking them into pieces. They ask him what he's doing and he says, 'I'm trying to kill some of these niggers before they hatch!'

He told these stories with the best of humor, but I could not repeat them without feeling guilty and bigoted. In any case, I saw a lot of Jeeps. Every day after lunch, which was usually a cheese sandwich in the Embassy cafeteria with him, I went for a walk in Hyde Park. They were long walks, but I timed them: I could quick-march down Rotten Row or around the Serpentine and be back at my desk in under an hour. When Jeeps came along, I took longer – I could justify it. Wasn't this part of my job?

He said that because he was black, he was treated as if he had an affliction. He had been at the London Embassy for three years and knew everyone. Some people behaved toward him as if he were an invalid – they were solicitous; others acted as if he had something contagious.

'Then there's people who think they understand me because they just spent four years in Mozambique!' He deliberately mispronounced the name. 'Mozam-bee-que,' he said. It rhymed with 'barbeque.'

'You've got high visibility, Erroll,' I said.

'There's all kinds of names for it,' he said. 'I used to be colored, right? Then I was a Negro. And then I turned into an Afro-American. After that, I was just a member of a Minority Group. Now, I'm black. Listen, when I joined the Foreign Service everyone figured I'd put in for Africa – that's where blacks are supposed to go – like people with names like Scaduto angle for the Rome embassy.'

'My first overseas post was Kampala,' I said.

'Better you than me. They've got tails there. I asked for New Zealand. I did my graduate work in economics – the effects on the labor force in depressed capital-intensive economies. New Zealand's a good model – it's going broke. I figured I could get some research done. Instead, I was posted here. England's a good model, too. Three million unemployed, galloping inflation – hey, this place is mummified!'

It was March, but spring comes early to London. The daffodils looked like flocks of slender-necked ducks in pale poke-bonnets, and the crocuses, bright as candy, dappled the ground purple and white. The sky was clear – bluer than any in Malaysia. Girls in riding coats and black velvet hats trotted along the bridleway.

Hyde Park is a series of meadows, big enough so that the habitual park-users – dog-owners, kite-fliers, lovers, and tramps – have plenty of room. They need it. There was heavy traffic in Kensington Road; I mentioned to Jeeps that in three weeks I had yet to hear anyone blow his horn here.

'They know it's no use,' he said. 'Look at all those cars. It's worse than Chicago. And the price of gas! Those people are paying almost four bucks a gallon to sit there in that jam. Hey, life can be kind of abrasive here. I wouldn't stay, except that from an economist's point of view this is the front lines. This is where all the casualties are.'

'You'd hardly know it here. It's very peaceful.'

'People have been mugged in Hyde Park,' Jeeps said. He spoke with satisfaction and now he had a spring in his step.

We had walked along the margin of the park. Jeeps had pointed out the Iranian Embassy at Princes Gate, where the siege had taken place; he had shown me the scorch marks on the windows. We walked farther. At the Albert Memorial he stopped. He smiled at me.

'Hey, some people have had even worse experiences.'

'Killed?'

'Maimed for life,' he said.

He was still smiling.

'That's hilarious,' I said. But my sarcasm had no effect on him.

'I'm thinking of a particular case,' he said, and went on chuckling. Then he turned to the Albert Memorial; the exaggerated grief in the monument, and all that expensive sculpture, only cheapened it and made it more pompous. I looked at it – it was frantic gazebo – and thought of money.

Jeeps was saying, 'England is a terrible place for Anglophiles. This post attracts snobs, you know. They end up so disappointed.'

I said, 'I've never known a snob who wasn't also a liar.'

'Right,' he said. 'Baldwick was a liar.'

'Baldwick – is that a name?'

'Baldwick is *only* a name. He was CAO before Vic Scaduto took over. It was the only interesting thing about him – his name. He was really proud of it. It was an old English name, he said, one of the great English families, the Baldwicks of Somewhere – he wasn't sure where. He was about forty-five or so; he'd been posted around the world. He kept asking for London and getting a negative. Like these people who want Africa so they can find their roots – he wanted to find his roots in England. Someone – was it his grandfather? – anyway, someone had told him there was a family estate, a castle, property, shields, suits of armor, all the rest of it. The Baldwicks were in the Domesday Book, the old man said, only where do you find the Domesday Book? Certainly not in Dacca, which was Baldwick's first post. Not in La Paz, not in Addis, not in Khartoum – his other posts. All he found were telephone books.

'That was it, see? Wherever he went, even if it was Baltimore, he picked up the telephone book and looked for his name. It's probably not so strange. I've done it myself. But the world is full of people called Jeeps – although you might not think so – and it is not exactly crawling with Baldwicks. He never found one! He found Baldwins and Baldicks and even Baldwigs – I love that one – but he couldn't find Baldwick. Was he discouraged? No, sir – it made him real proud, because this meant he was the only claimant to the family fortune.

'And it also made him a little obsessive. He wanted to find another Baldwick, but he didn't want to hear that there were a million of them running around the place. He kept looking in telephone books wherever he was posted. No luck – but he had hopes. After all, the Baldwicks were supposed to be in England. By this time he had worked himself up to public affairs officer. It was a pretty glorious job for a guy who wasn't very bright and whose field was visual aids. But that's what happens when you go to Dacca and Khartoum.

'He was finally posted to London. In order to swing it, he took a cut in salary and agreed to be demoted to CAO. Was he eager, or what? They say his wife threatened to leave him, but this was what he had always wanted. At last, a chance to climb the family tree! His wife never forgave him. She was the one who told me this story. She was really bitter – she didn't leave anything out.

'The first thing Baldwick did in London was get a telephone book. He looked up his name, and bingo! He found one – only one, so that was perfect. It was a John Baldwick, living in some armpit in East London. But then, having found the name, he really didn't know what to do. Should he tell him he was a long-lost relative? The man might not believe him. And what if the family fortune was in dispute? What if the will was being probated? He figured they might make it tough for him – cut him out of it altogether. And the last thing he wanted to do was reveal that he – one of the noble Baldwicks – was doing a fairly humdrum job at the American Embassy.

'He knew he had to get his act together. He decided to pose as a tourist. He would say that he was just passing through and that, seeing as how this fellow and he had the same unusual name, would he be interested in meeting for a drink? Completely innocent, see? Very casual.

'He phoned the number and got no answer. He kept trying. One day he got a funny noise – not a busy signal, but something that sounded like a bumblebee. He phoned the operator and was told that the line had been disconnected.

'A few weeks went by. He considered writing a letter. Do tourists passing through London write letters to people in London? Baldwick didn't think so. He stuck to the casual approach. He called again. It rang this time. It was the other Baldwick! The guy had a funny accent – probably upper class, he thought. I mean, upper-class accents are really strange, hardly English at all, German or "mew-mew" or a bad case of adenoids. Half these so-called aristocrats sound like they have sinus trouble.

'Baldwick barely understood his namesake. This pleased him – the guy was genuine! He did his routine. Just passing through. Same name. Wonder if you'd care for a drink? The guy was a little leery – wouldn't you be? – but it worked. They agreed to meet. Now, here's the interesting part. Being new to London, Baldwick didn't know where to meet him. The man didn't invite him to his house – English people never do until they've known you about ten years. So our Baldwick says, "Let's meet in Piccadilly Circus."

'Would a New Yorker say, "I'll meet you in Times Square"? You know he wouldn't, but Baldwick had every hope of actually finding this guy in Piccadilly Circus in the middle of June. "By the fountain," he said. "Six o'clock."

'Naturally, it didn't work. There were hundreds of people there. Baldwick paced up and down for an hour and then went home. Later, he called the guy. "Why weren't you there?" he says. The other man swore he had been there, but how could he find him with a thousand people milling around?

'"What about a quieter place?" our Baldwick says. "What about a pub?" The other guy says okay and the place they fixed on was the Bunch of Grapes in Knightsbridge. Baldwick said he was staying at a hotel nearby. Actually he had an apartment near there, in Egerton Gardens, but he didn't want the guy to know.

'The night they agreed to meet, there was something doing here in Hyde Park – one of those free-for-all races. And the Bunch of Grapes, which usually wasn't very busy, was packed with people. And yet Baldwick had arrived early. He sat by the main door in the saloon bar and watched every person come in. Every single one. He stared at each one, but no one came up to him and said, "Mr Baldwick – my name is Baldwick, too!" He sat there until closing time. He got pretty drunk, because by now he figured the other guy had his number – suspected him of trying to horn in on the family fortune. Here's this lousy American claiming to be a member of this great English family – castle, swords, paintings, suits of armor, et cetera. Before he left the Grapes he looked into the public bar, stared in each man's face. No takers. He went home.

'The next day he called the guy again. The guy was furious and so was he. Each accused the other of having let him down; each one said it was a pretty rotten trick, a waste of time, and what did he think he was trying to pull? They argued for a while, and then it came out. Our Baldwick said he had been in the saloon bar, the other guy had spent the whole evening in the public bar. "I always use the public bar," the guy says.

'Our Baldwick didn't know the difference. If he had, he might have left it there. He might have hung up and stopped looking for his long-lost relatives. He might have just quietly sized the whole

485

thing up and stopped chasing around for his namesake. I'll tell you one thing – if he had stopped looking then, he would have died a happy man. Not fulfilled, but happy. Aren't people better off with an illusion? The truth is pretty awful sometimes, and illusions can make a nice pillow.

'Baldwick told him he had looked into the public bar, but he admitted that by then he had been in a hurry. The other guy started arguing again. Our Baldwick said he had to leave London in a few days and that he would probably never be back. It was now or never. "And I've got a little present for you." He had to say that. Things were getting a little spooky.

'The other Baldwick cheered up. But still he did not offer our man an invitation to drop in for tea. Somehow, this made our man imagine an even greater house, an even grander estate, even shinier armor, and a fat legacy. He says, "Do you know the Albert Memorial?"

'The other guy says, "No." *No*!

'Our Baldwick still isn't suspicious. "It's near the Albert Hall," he says. "Across the street."

'"Oh, I went to a boxing match there once," the guy says. They actually have boxing matches in that beautiful building. It's a kind of bullring! Incongruous, isn't it? But listen, here is our man, Baldwick, explaining to the Londoner where the Albert Memorial is, and if that's not incongruous I don't know what is.

'"I'll meet you on the top platform of the Albert Memorial at exactly two o'clock tomorrow," our man says. "We'll be the only people there. It's foolproof. And then I can give you the present I mentioned."

'It was right here,' Jeeps said.

We were on the steps of the Albert Memorial – he had walked as he told the story – and now it was just before two o'clock. I wondered whether Jeeps had planned all this – rehearsed the story, dramatized it for my benefit, so that it was the right place and time. We were alone at the monument. The traffic flowed toward Kensington Gore and streamed through the park.

Jeeps said, 'Baldwick came from down there,' and pointed past the Albert Hall. 'He walked to one of those archways and waited until about one minute to two. At exactly two, he saw a guy running across the road, dodging cars, coming lickety-split. Up the walkway, up all these steps, to here –'

Jeeps had been walking up the stairs. He stopped; he stood still; he squinted at the path.

I said, 'Then what happened?'

'Our Baldwick almost cried. He stayed right where he was, over there at the Albert Hall. I mentioned that he was a snob. He was a roaring snob. The kind you want to punch in the face. But now all his dreams about his old family and his name –'

'Was the other guy wearing old clothes?'

'No, he was fairly well dressed – even carried an umbrella.' Jeeps had an umbrella. He tucked it under his arm and went on squinting. 'He was completely respectable. So that wasn't the matter. That wasn't why our Baldwick turned away and hid behind a pillar and went home to his wife.'

'He went home?' I said. 'He didn't talk to this guy, after all that trouble?'

'Nope.'

'I don't understand why, Erroll. They could have been related!'

'Look. Stand down there a little, and look.'

I moved down the stairs and did so.

'What our Baldwick saw, you see now. The other guy was right here, at just this time of day. Get it?'

'His namesake was where you are now,' I said.

'Right. But that's all they had in common, that funny name. The rest was what you see. Look! If your name was Jeeps would you think you were related to me?'

He began laughing very hard in a mocking way, as if jeering at me for not having guessed sooner about Baldwick's namesake. His laughter was humorless. It was merely a harsh noise, challenging me to look at his black face.

An English Unofficial Rose

The fashion in London that year was rags – expensive ones, but rags all the same. Women wore torn blouses and patched jeans, and their shoes were painted to make them looked scuffed and wrongly paired. Their hair was cut in a raggedy way – front hanks of it dyed pink and green and bright orange and blue. They wore plastic badges and safety pins, and they called themselves punks. The idea was for them to seem threadbare. It was a popular look, but it was not easy to achieve. It took imagination, and time, and a great deal of money for these spoiled wealthy girls to appear down and out.

But Sophie Graveney wore a smooth blouse of light silk the texture of skin, and a close-fitting skirt slit all the way to her hip, and steeply pitched spike-heeled shoes. The weather was uncertain, but most days were warm enough for a jacket. Sophie's was bottle-green velvet, with two gold clasps where there might have been buttons. She said she could not bear to be mistaken for someone poor, and was willing to risk being called unfashionable for her rich clothes. Styles change, but beauty is never out of fashion – I told her that. And no one expected this rag business and colored hair to last very long. People stared at Sophie. She was no punk. Horton, my boss at the London Embassy, had called her 'an English rose.'

I find it impossible to see a well-dressed woman without thinking that she is calling attention to her charms. Isn't that lady with the plunging neckline and that coin slot between her squeezed breasts – isn't she declaring an interest? Certainly that attractive woman in the tight skirt is making a general promise. At the same time, such women are betraying a certain self-love. Narcissism is necessary to that kind of beauty. It is the aspect that maddens lovers, because it is unreachable. Sophie's self-possession was a kind of inaccessible narcissism. In her beauty there was both effort and ease. Her hair had been softly curled, her eyes and mouth delicately painted, but beneath her make-up and under her lovely clothes was a tall strong girl in the full bloom of thirty, who jogged four miles before breakfast. She was healthy; she was reliable; she dressed as if she was trying to please me. I was flattered, and grateful. So far, I had no friends in London who weren't connected with the Embassy. I liked the promises of her clothes. I needed someone like Sophie.

After a month here I had a routine. It was a bachelor's consolation – my job, my office, my hotel room – and I hated it. It made everything serious and purposeful, and I suppose I began to look like one of those supersolemn diplomats, all shadows and monosyllables, who carry out secret missions against treacherous patriots in the (believe me) laughably false plots of political thrillers. It seemed pointless, this austerity, and I did not believe in my own efficiency. I wanted to break free of it, to prove to myself that my job did not matter that much. I hated the implied timidity, the repetition, the lack of surprise in this routine. In a poor country – a hardship post – I could have justified these dull days by telling myself that I was making a necessary sacrifice. It is some comfort, when one is braving tedium, to know that one is setting a good example. But in London I wanted to live a little. I knew I was missing something.

No longer: Sophie and I were dining at Le Gavroche, having just seen a spirited *Hamlet* at the Royal Court. She smiled at me from across the table. There was a flicker of light in her eyes, a willingness to agree, good humor, a scent of jasmine on her shoulders, and a certain pressure of her fingers on my hand that offered hope and a promise of mildly rowdy sex. I was happy.

She talked the whole time, which was fine with me. By habit and inclination I never discussed my work with anyone outside the Embassy. I listened gladly to everything she said; I was grateful that I did not have to ask my ignorant questions about London. And yet, though she talked mostly about herself, she revealed very little. She told me her plans – she wanted to travel, see Brazil ('again') – she had friends in Hong Kong and New York. She was vague about what she was doing at the moment. She seemed surprised and a little annoyed that I should ask.

'"What do you do for a living?"' Her accent was the adenoids-and-chewing-gum American drawl that the British put on when they are feeling particularly skittish, which, thank God, is seldom. She went on, 'It's not a question people ask in England.'

'It wasn't my question. I didn't say, "What do you do for a living?" I said, "What are you doing at the moment?"'

'I know what you meant, and you shouldn't have asked.'

'I wonder why.'

'Because it's bloody rude, that's why,' she said softly, and seemed pleased with herself. 'Anyway, why should one do anything? I know plenty of people who don't do anything at all – absolutely nothing.'

'You like that, do you?'

'Yes, I think there's something really fantastic about pure idleness.'

' "Consider the lilies of the field," et cetera, et cetera.'

'Not only that. If a person doesn't really do anything, you have to take him for what he is rather than what he does. Your asking me what I'm doing is just a cheap way of finding out what sort of person I am. That's cheating.'

I said, 'I don't see why.'

She shrugged and said, 'Daddy didn't do much, but Daddy was a gentleman. You probably think I'm a frivolous empty-headed girl who sits around the house all day varnishing her nails, waiting for parties to begin.' She worked her tongue against her teeth and said, 'Well, I am!'

'It's been the ruin of many a Foreign Service marriage – I mean, the wife with nothing to do but advance her husband's career. All that stage-managing, all those tea parties, all that insincerity.'

'I'd love it. I wouldn't complain. My headmistress used to say "Find a husband who'll give you a beautiful kitchen, and lovely flowers to pick, and lots of expensive silver to polish." That sort of thing's not fashionable now, is it? But I don't care. I like luxury.'

And although this was only the second time I had seen her, I began seriously to calculate the chances of my marrying her. She was glamorous and intelligent; she was good company. Men stared at her. She had taste, and she was confident enough in her taste so that she would never be a slave to fashion.

I was turning these things over in my mind when she said, 'What do I do? A bit of modeling, a little television, some lunchtime theater. You probably think it's all a waste of time.'

'You're an actress,' I said.

'No,' Sophie said, 'I just do a little acting. It's not what you'd call a career. Everyone criticizes me for not being ambitious. Crikey, of course I spend time, but I don't waste time – are you wasting time if you're enjoying yourself?' She did not wait for my reply. She said, 'I'm enjoying myself right now.'

'Shall we do this again sometime?'

'Again and again,' she said slowly, in a kind of heated contentment. 'Would you like that?'

'Yes,' I said, 'I really would.'

She reached over and touched my face, brushed the aroma of jasmine on my cheek – it was the most intimate, the most disarming gesture – and said, 'It's getting late –'

I kissed her in the taxi going back to her house. She did not push me away. But after a few minutes she lifted her head.

'What's wrong?'

'This is Prince of Wales Drive,' she said. 'Aren't those mansion blocks fantastic?' She kissed me again, then she took my arm and said, 'Wouldn't you like to live there?'

They were not my idea of mansions, but I found myself agreeing with her: yes, I said, and looked through the taxi window at the balconies. It was as if we were choosing a location for a love nest. Sophie squeezed my arm and said, 'That one's fun.'

I saw dark windows.

'Wouldn't it be super to live here?' she said. And it seemed as if she were speaking for both of us.

I said, 'It sure would.'

'Are you looking for a place to rent? Your hotel must be rather cramped.'

'I'm moving the first chance I get. I'm going to buy a place – renting is pointless, and anyway I've got two years' accumulated hardship allowance to spend.'

She kissed me then, and we were still kissing as the taxi sped on, turned into a side street, and came to rest on Albert Bridge Road in front of a tall terrace of narrow houses. I paid for the taxi, then walked with her to the front gate.

She said, 'Your taxi's driving away.'

'I've paid him. I told him to go.'

'That was silly. You'll never get another one around here – and the buses have stopped running.'

I said, 'Then I'll walk,' and clung to her hand, 'although I don't want to.'

'It's not far to your hotel.'

'I didn't mean that. I just meant I'd rather stay here with you.'

'I know,' she said. 'You're sweet.'

The English are frugal. They can even economize on words. Sophie gave nothing away. She planted a rather perfunctory kiss on my cheek, and when I tried to embrace her she eased out of my grasp and said comically, 'Do you *mind*?' and took out her door key.

'You're beautiful,' I said.

'I'm tired,' she said. 'I must get some sleep. I have a big day tomorrow – a screening – and I have to be up at the crack of dawn.' She gave me another brisk kiss and said lightly, 'Otherwise I'd invite you in.'

I said, 'I want to see you again soon.'

'I'd like that,' she said.

I was half in love with her by then, and in that mood – half-true, half-false – I strolled home whistling, congratulating myself on my good luck. London is kind to lovers – it offers them privacy and quiet nights and spectacles. Albert Bridge was alight. In the daytime it is a classic bridge, but at night all its thousands of yellow light bulbs and its freshly painted curves give it the look of a circus midway suspended in the sky. The lights on its great sweeps are very cheering at midnight over the empty river.

The next day I wanted to call her, but a long meeting with Scaduto held me up. It was eight o'clock before I left the office. Scaduto furiously preened himself in the elevator mirror as we descended to Grosvenor Square. He said he had called his wife to tell her he'd be late. She had screamed at him.

'Get this,' he said. 'She says to me, "You never listen." That's interesting, isn't it? What does it mean, "You never listen"? Isn't it a paradox, or some kind of contradiction? Tell me something – has anyone ever said that to you? "You never listen"?'

I said no.

'Right. Because you're not married,' Scaduto said. 'You've got to be married to hear things like that. Isn't that terrible?' He began to laugh, and said, 'You wouldn't believe the things married people say to each other. You can't imagine the hostility. "You never listen" is nothing. The rest is murder.'

'Awful things?'

'Horrendous things,' he said. 'What are you smiling for?'

'What does it matter what people say, if you never listen?'

Steam came out of Scaduto's nose – the sound of steam, at any rate. Then he said, 'I've seen guys like you – nice, happy, single guys. They get married. They get ruined. Unhappy? You have no idea.'

I was indignant at this, because I took everything he said to be a criticism of Sophie. His conceited and miserable presumption belittled her. I thought: *How dare you* – because his cynicism was about life in general, the hell of marriage, the tyranny of women. He was cheating me out of my pleasant mood, the afterglow of having met someone I genuinely liked and wanted to be with. I hated his sullen egotism: his marriage was all marriages, his wife was all women, he and I were brothers. *Ain't it awful* was the slogan of this fatuous freemasonry of male victims.

I said, 'I pity you.'

'Keep your pity,' Scaduto said. 'You'll need it for yourself.'

His voice was full of fatigue and experience – and ham. The married man so often tries to sound like a war veteran, and the divorced one like a man discharged because of being wounded in action.

I met Sophie for a drink a few days later. We went out to eat again the following week. On our first date I had wanted to go to bed with her. That desire had not passed, and yet another feeling, a deeper one, like loyalty and trust, asserted itself. It was compatible with lechery – in fact, it gave lechery an honorable glow.

And now she called me occasionally at work. She had a touching telephone habit of saying, 'It's only me –' What could be easier or more intimate? She liked to talk on the phone. It was fun, she said, whispering into my ear.

About two weeks after *Hamlet* she called and said, 'Are you free this evening?'

'Yes,' I said, and thought of an excuse to dispose of the appointment I had – a journalist that Jeeps had urged me to meet. I could meet him any time, but Sophie –

'It's a flat,' she said.

What was she talking about?

'Just what you've been looking for,' she said. 'Bang on Prince of Wales Drive. Overstrand Mansions. It's at the front, with that lovely view.'

'That's wonderful – shall we meet there?'

'I'm afraid I can't make it. I've got a screening on. But you should go. I'll give you the owner's number. It's a friend of a friend.'

'I was hoping to see you,' I said, interrupting her as she told me the price. 'What about going with me tomorrow?'

'This flat might not be available tomorrow,' she said.

'I'll look at it this evening then.'

'Super.'

'Will you be available tomorrow?' I said.

'Quite available.' She said that in what I thought of as her actress's voice. Whenever she said anything very serious or very definite, she used this voice, and sometimes an American accent.

I went to see the flat. Its balcony was the brow of this red brick mansion block, and from it I could see my own hotel beyond the park and the river. This pleased me – my own landmark, in this enormous city, among the slate roofs and steeples and treetops.

The flat was larger than I wanted, but I thought of Sophie and began to covet it for its extra rooms. The owner, a friendly German, offered me a drink.

He said, 'As you probably gathered, my wife and I decided to split up.'

I told him I had gathered no such thing, that it was none of my business, but the longer I sat there trying to stop him telling me about his divorce (it seemed to cast a blight on the place), the more I felt I was sitting in my own room, enclosed by my own walls, the crisp shadow spikes of my balcony's grillwork printed on my own floor.

'She is now back in Germany,' he said. 'She is an extremely attractive woman.'

Because I felt it was already mine, and because I knew it was a sure way of getting him off the subject of his wife, I said, 'I want it – let's make a deal.'

Later I gave him the name of the Embassy lawyer and said I wanted to move quickly. By noon the next day my deposit was down and a surveyor was on his way to Overstrand Mansions. Within a week papers were examined and contracts exchanged. It was the fastest financial transaction I had ever made, but I was paying cash – my accumulated hardship allowance from my Malaysian post, and the rest of my savings. It was my first property deal, but I felt in my heart that I was not in it alone and not acting solely for myself.

I had called Sophie the day after visiting the flat. I was, I realize, intent upon impressing her. Would she want me if she saw I was powerful and decisive? When I finally found her, she was pleased but said she couldn't meet me. 'Quite available' meant busy. She had a 'sitting' or perhaps a 'shooting' or a 'screening' or a 'viewing' or an 'opening' or a 'session.' What did she mean? I had never come across these obscure urgencies before. Language is deceptive; and though English is subtle it also allows a clever person − one alert to the ambiguities of English − to play tricks with mock precision and to combine vagueness with politeness. English is perfect for diplomats and lovers.

Some days later I was making Sophie a drink in my hotel room − a whiskey. I had the bottle in my hand.

'It should be champagne,' I said. 'We're celebrating − I've exchanged contracts.'

'Whiskey's warmer than champagne,' she said, and sat down to watch me.

'How do you like it?'

'Straight,' she said. She was not looking at the glass. 'As it comes.'

'How much?'

'Filled,' she said, and showed me her teeth.

'How many inches is that?'

'Right up,' she said, and sighed and smiled. She had said that in her actress's voice.

There was no hitch, the survey encouraged me, and Horton − as if praising my on-the-job initiative − said that London property was a great investment. I was more than hopeful; I had, mentally, already begun to live at Overstrand Mansions. In this imagining Sophie was often standing at the balcony with a drink in her hand, or in her track suit, damp with dew and effort (running raised her sexual odors, the mingled aroma of fish and flowers), and she was laughing, saying, 'Do you *mind*?' as I tried to hold her, and driving me wild.

I had to be reassured that she needed me as much. We had not so far used the word 'love.' We pretended we had an easygoing, trusting friendship. I think I joked with her too much, but I was very eager − foolishly so. Instead of simply saying that I wanted to see her and making a date with her, I said, 'Sophie, you're avoiding me.'

It was facetious. I could not blame her for missing the feeble joke. But, unexpectedly, it made her defensive. She took it as an accusation, and explained carefully that she had very much wanted to see me but that she was busy with – what? – a 'shooting' or a 'viewing.' Then I was sorry for what I'd said.

The arrival of my sea freight a day later gave me an excuse to call her. She was excited. She said, 'You've got the key!'

'Not yet.'

She made a sympathetic noise. She sounded genuinely sorry I hadn't moved in. And then, 'What if something goes wrong with the deal?'

'I'll find something else.'

'No, no,' she said. 'Nothing will go wrong. Actually, I can quite see you there in Overstrand Mansions –'

She didn't say *us*, she excluded herself; but this talk of me and my flat bored me. And I was a little disappointed. I listened dimly, then hung up, having forgotten to tell her my real reason for calling – that my sea freight had passed through customs and was at the warehouse.

It was my furniture, my Malaysian treasures, my *nat* from Burma, a temple painting from Vietnam, Balinese masks, *wayang* puppets, and my Buddha and the assortment of cutthroat swords and knives (a *kris* from the sultan, a *kukri* from the DC) I had been given as going-away presents. I had bought the furniture in Malacca. It was Chinese – an opium-smoker's couch, and a carved settee with lion's head legs. The bed had carved and gilded panels and four uprights for a mosquito-net canopy. And I had teak chests with carved drawers, and polished rosewood chairs, and brassware and pewter. These and my books. I had nothing else – no plates or dinnerware, no glasses, no cooking pots, nothing practical.

I wanted Sophie to see my collection of Asian things. I knew she would be impressed. She would marvel at them; she would want me more. I longed to leave my small hotel room on Chelsea Embankment and spread out in Overstrand Mansions. I yearned to be with her.

She had picked out the flat, and in buying it I had never acted so quickly, so decisively. I was glad. She had made me bold. But I tried not to think that I had bought it for us, because it was too early – she was not mine yet. I hoped she knew how badly I wanted her. I could not imagine that a desire as strong as mine could be thwarted. At times it seemed simple: I would have her because I wanted her.

I thought: *If only she could see these treasures from Asia!* And I tried to imagine our life together. It was a wonderful combination of bliss and purpose, and it made my bachelor solitude seem selfish. What was the point in living alone? Secretly, I believed we were the perfect couple.

All this happened in the space of three weeks – the exchanged contracts, the arrival of my furniture, the numerous phone calls. I did not see Sophie in the third week, and it was frustrating because now it was Sunday. The German had given me the key yesterday; I was moving in tomorrow.

I moved in. She had led me here. I was grateful to her that morning as the men carried my tea chests of Asian treasures upstairs (and they called their moving van a 'pantechnicon' – I had never heard the word before and it pleased me). There was space for everything. This was the apartment I needed. She had known that, somehow, or guessed – another indication that she understood me. I was delighted because Sophie had made this her concern. But where was she?

I called her but got no answer. I tried again and managed, by speaking slowly, to leave a message with her charlady, who was exasperated at having to write it down. She read the message back to me with uncertainty and resentment.

That night I woke up and was so excited to be in a place of my own that I got out of bed and walked up and down, and through all the rooms, and finally onto the balcony. I was so pleased at this outcome, I vowed that I would send Sophie a case of champagne. I lingered on the balcony – I liked everyone out there in the dark.

My roaming in the night made me oversleep. I did not get to the Embassy until after eleven, and my desk was stacked with pink *While You Were Out* message slips. Scaduto had called and so had Horton's secretary, and there was still some paperwork to do on my apartment – insurance and some estimates for painting it. But most of the messages were from Sophie. Five slips of paper – she had been ringing at twenty-minute intervals.

My happiness was complete. It was what I wanted most, and it seemed to me as if I had everything I wanted and was in danger of being overwhelmed by it. The phone calls were the proof that she wanted me. I would send her the case of champagne, of course;

but that was a detail. She could move in with me anytime. We would do what people did these days – live together, see how we got along. It was a wonderfully tolerant world that made such arrangements possible. I would have a routine security check done on Sophie, but if Horton questioned the wisdom of our living together I could always reply that I had met her at his house and that he had had a share in creating this romance.

The phone rang. Sophie's voice was eager. 'You've moved in – that's super.'

'You've been a great help,' I said. 'When can you come over to look around?'

'My life's a bit fraught at the moment,' she said. Her voice became cautious and a bit detached. But she had rung me five times this morning! Then all the eagerness was out of her voice and with composure she said, 'I expect I'll be able to manage it one of these days. I'm not far away.'

'We could have a drink on the balcony. The way you like it. Right up.'

'Yes,' she said, with uncertainty. She had forgotten.

Then I felt awkward and overintimate. Had I said too much?

'It's a very nice flat,' I said.

'I'm so glad for you. I knew you'd like it.'

I wanted to say *Come and live with me! There's enough room for both of us! I won't crowd you – I'll make you happy in my Chinese bed!*

We worked at the London Embassy with the doors open. I could see Vic Scaduto just outside my office, talking to my secretary. He was impatient and held a file in his hand that he clearly wanted to show me. He made all the motions of wanting to interrupt me; he made his impatience look like patience. At times like this, Scaduto tap-danced.

I said, 'Sophie, I have to go.'

'There was something else,' she said.

'I'll call you back.'

'I've rung you half a dozen times this morning. Please. I've got so much else to do.'

She sounded irritated, and I could see Scaduto's feet – shuffle-tap, shuffle-tap – and the flap of the file as he juggled it.

I said to Sophie, 'What is it?'

'You've moved in – you've got the flat. So it's all settled.'

'I'm going to buy you a case of champagne,' I said. 'I'll help you drink it. I know a place –'

'That's very sweet of you,' she said. 'But two percent is the usual commission.'

I waited for her to say more. There was no more.

I said, 'Are you joking?'

'No.' She sounded more than irritated now. She was angry: I was being willfully stupid.

'Is that why you've been ringing me this morning – for your commission?'

'I found you a flat. You had an exclusive viewing. You bought it for a reasonable price –'

I said, 'Did you fix the price?'

But she was still talking.

'– and now you seem to be jibbing at paying me my commission.'

Scaduto put his head into my office and said, 'Have you got a minute?'

'Write me a letter,' I said, and still heard her voice protesting in the little arc the receiver made, the distance between my ear and the desk.

Scaduto smiled. He said, 'For a minute there you looked married.'

Because Sophie's letter was delivered by hand and arrived at the front door of the Embassy, it was treated as if it contained a bomb or a threat or an explosive device. It was X-rayed; it was passed through a metal detector; it was sniffed by a trained dog. I complained to the security guard about the delay, but in the event I wished that the letter had never come.

It could not have been more businesslike or broken my spirit more. It was one chilly paragraph telling me that I had moved in, that she had been instrumental in finding me the flat – 'following your instructions' – and that in such a situation two percent was the usual commission.

It was not a great deal of money, the equivalent of a few thousand dollars – not enough to be really useful, only enough to ruin a friendship. I could have paid her immediately, but I didn't want her to be my agent – I wanted her love.

Instead of writing what I felt, I wrote logically: I had not given her an order to find me a flat; she had not negotiated the price; she had not been present when I reached agreement with the owner;

she had played no part in the contract or any subsequent negoti-ations. Hers had been an informal, friendly function. If I had known that the fee was going to be two percent I would have taken it into account and adjusted my offer. She was, I said, presuming.

Then I contemplated tearing up the letter. I had either to destroy it or send it – I didn't want it around.

Sophie rang me two days later. She said, 'How dare you! Don't write me letters like that. What do you take me for?'

I said, 'I thought you were an actress.'

She turned abusive. She swore at me. Until that moment I had marveled at how different her English was from mine. And then, with a few blunt swears, she lost her nationality and became any loud, crude, bad-tempered bitch spitting thorns at me.

I sent her the champagne. She did not acknowledge it. And she dropped out of my life.

I learned one thing more. One day I found an earring in the kitchen. I called the German, who now lived in a smaller place in Pimlico. He came over and had a drink. He was grateful – it had belonged not to his wife but to his mother. He showed no signs of wanting to leave. My whiskey made him sentimental. He said that we were both foreigners here in London. We had a lot in common. We ought to be friends.

To get him off the subject, I asked him about Sophie.

'She brought us together, you and me,' the German said. 'She charged me two percent. But it was worth it. Here we are, drinking together as friends.' He glanced around the flat. He said, 'These English girls – especially the ones with money – can be very businesslike. And did you notice? She is very pretty. She lives with an Iranian chap. They all want Iranians these days.' The German laughed out loud. 'Even if you call them Persians they still seem boring!'

And then, to my relief, he began telling me about his ex-wife.

Children

'Vic's got this theory. Parents owe their children everything, but children don't owe their parents anything. Why should they? They didn't ask to be born. People tell their kids, "You treat this place like a hotel." My father used to tell me that! It's funny, because family homes are exactly like hotels – where you've been brought. No kid ever checked in of his own free will, did he? And Vic says if the parents keep their part of the bargain – I mean, discharge their responsibility and do everything they can for their kids – they'll never have a problem. Hey, it's amazing how irresponsible most parents are. Some of these embassy people you just would not believe –'

Marietta Scaduto's voice was dropping to a whisper: Vic was on his way back to the room with his children and some other people's children. They were all boys – even Vic, come to think of it.

'I don't know why I'm bothering to tell you this – you don't have any kids,' Marietta said.

'Or parents either,' I said. 'Does Vic have a theory about orphans? I only ask because I lost my parents in an air crash when I was five. But you do get over these things, you know. I had a happy childhood; I suppose it's a bit like being blind from an early age. I adapted. The kind of orphan I was – bright, solitary, with my trust fund from the insurance money – it was like being privileged, inheriting a title early. And I seem to have managed. I'm not looking for a mother figure. Maybe that explains why I'm not married.'

I had said too much. It was then that she gave me a look of pure murder.

This conversation came later, over coffee, after she had told me about her poems and said she was unhappy and – rolling her lower lip down sourly – 'I know your type.'

But Vic had a theory! She made him sound serious. The man's wife – when she's angry or incautious – can reveal such surprising secrets. And so can the man expose the wife. And the children most of all. But who would have thought that man sat around theorizing?

Vic Scaduto – 'Skiddoo' to the office – all gestures, all heel clicks on the corridor tiles, shooting his pink cuffs, tugging at his earlobe, pinching his face at his reflection in the elevator mirror, tap-dancing as he talked and as his bubblegum snapped, saying, 'The royal facility in Kensington has a really spacious function room,' then interrupting himself with 'I've got a stack of cables waiting' and 'I'm one of those rare people who has a nose for detail,' neighing his hideous laugh – 'It's my Italian blood,' he explained – and he was never breathless. He had teeth like piano keys, and spit flew out of his mouth when he talked.

More than anything he wanted a good post in Italy – running a binational center in Florence or Palermo, or being public affairs officer in Rome. Some of his relatives still lived in Sicily, farming an acre of thorns and procrastinating about selling the pig, so he said.

'It's not that I'm bucking for a promotion; it's just that with my cultural background I think I deserve Italy.' It was a sure sign of his Italian-ness that he mispronounced it, giving it two syllables and making it sound even more like an adverb: 'It-lee.'

He had been interviewed for the transfer, he had taken the language proficiency exam, he was waiting for his report.

'I think they were impressed.' He meant the pair of assessment officers from Washington. Scaduto had invited them to his house. 'I didn't just invite them – I threw the place open to them.'

He had arranged it so that the assessment officers could spend a whole day with his family – Marietta and the three boys.

'I wanted to show them what cultural enrichment really means.'

I said, 'Is that Italian job so important?'

'Not to me, but to my parents. If you've got immigrant parents you'll understand. They left Italy' – *It-lee* – 'with nothing and came to America. They spent Christmas on Ellis Island in nineteen twenty-two.'

'They must be proud of your success,' I said.

'That's just it – my success is the only thing that matters to them. They left home, left their house, gave up their country, and abandoned their own parents for their children, my sister and me. They ran off and got married. My parents were bad children! They put me through college, they lived poor, they're still poor. No one thinks about that, but it's funny – some people who used to be poor are still poor, living where they always lived and dying in the same place. My folks live in an old row house in Queens, with planes going overhead all day – some people in the neighborhood are on disability, the noise is so bad. My father is over seventy. He hasn't retired! He cuts fish. You should see his hands. *His* father probably had hands like that, in Caccamo. Then I get this London job. It's a terrific job. I offer to pay his fare over here so he can have a vacation, and what happens? Does he come to visit? No. "Why don't they give you Italy? Ain't you good enough?" He gives me *braciol'* until my head hurts. My mother's worse. She drives me nuts with her phone calls. I mean, both of them sit on Long Island waiting for me to take them back to Italy. Proud of me? Not on your life! I'm disloyal – this isn't the way children are supposed to treat their parents. Hey, children have obligations, don't you know that? But I'll get Italy.'

It-lee: waiting for him to say the word made me inattentive.

'They've got this image in their minds,' he was saying. 'They're on a plane. Jumbo jet, transatlantic flight. Someone in the next seat asks them where they're going. They say, "We're visiting our son. He's got this big job at the American Embassy in Roma. Hey, he's doing all right. Me, I put him through school – working nights, working weekends. My wife and I, hey, we're going home. We're from Italy –"'

It-lee again; but Scaduto had started to object.

'It's a fantasy! Listen, old people are really stubborn about their fantasies. You got no idea! Ask Marietta.'

Scaduto had not said anything about his parents to the assessment officers, and yet he had done all he could to emphasize that he was overdue for a post in Italy. Such officials often visited Foreign Service personnel at home – the crowded party, the powerful drinks, the bonhomie and 'My family's flexible' – but it was rare for them to spend an entire day at the house. Scaduto wanted to impress them with his complete honesty, his willingness to admit strangers to the privacy of his home. It was a considerable risk, but Scaduto said he was sure it would pay off. Anyway, he said, he liked having visitors – so did Marietta and the boys. Hey, wasn't that the point about being in the Foreign Service? Hey, if you didn't like people you were in the wrong job! So he said.

I was interested when he made the same offer to me, of spending the whole day with him, from just after breakfast until just after midnight. He lived far enough from the center of London for such a long visit not to seem absurd. His house was in Putney, but the western part, near Roehampton Vale and Richmond Park. It took him over an hour to get to work in the morning by car.

American couples, I discovered, lived in Notting Hill and Islington and Chelsea, and they especially favored Hampstead. But when they wanted to breed, and exchange their two-bedroom apartment for a four-bedroom house, they crossed the river. The larger the family, the farther they penetrated into the suburbs – and all the real suburbs were in the south and west. North was distant and dull – 'the country'; but all the south was London. Vic and Marietta Scaduto and their three boys lived on a leafy street off the Upper Richmond Road, on the 37 bus route.

The house was large – probably six bedrooms, something like a turret on the left, and (the rarest of features in London) a driveway. The wistaria at the front had a stem the thickness of a human leg and (it was now May) was in hanging bloom. The rooms were furnished with treasures Vic had picked up in his previous posts. You could tell where an officer had been by looking at his living room or his bookshelf. Vic had brassware and carpets from Turkey, tables with ivory inlay from Pakistan, Kamba carvings and Kikuyu shields from Kenya. He was not a specialist in anything: he went where he was sent. (So many of us can be described, accurately, as traveling salesmen!)

In a poor country, objects – such as the ones Scaduto had in his living room – often look like treasures. But the farther they get from home, the less marvelous and exotic they seem. In a middle-class London house, these looked cheap and vulgar and badly made. Bazaar merchandise does not travel well, and most of it is so hard to dust it grows fur.

There was a smell – dusty, pollenous, knife wounds on wood, hair, and feathers: curio stink – in the room where we were all now seated. I had just arrived – by bus, quite a novelty, and certainly a conversation piece, but I was a student of London's bus routes and told them how I had transferred at Clapham Junction from the 19, which ran near Overstrand Mansions, to the 37. Vic said I was in time for coffee, and Marietta showed me into the conservatory – it was her word for the glassed-in patio area. Vic made a show of arranging chairs around a small table, and then grinding the coffee noisily – the sound made my head spin – and then explaining how he made coffee the real Italian way, before bringing it in on a little rattling table on wheels, which Marietta was quick to call a trolley.

'The boys are very anxious to meet you,' Vic said. 'The older two have been studying about the Dyaks. I told them you were in Malaysia. They'll be full of questions.'

'Most Dyaks are in Sarawak, Vic,' I said. 'I never went there.'

'You were near enough,' he said. 'God, the things they learn in geography class. A far cry from my junior high. "Coffee production in Brazil," "Lumbering in Murmansk," "Eskimos on the McClintock Channel." They're not called igloos, by the way. They're *igluviga*. They wear *mukluks*. They light their *igluviga* with oil lamps called *koodlies*. Are these kids getting an education or what? English schools are awesome. Latin, French, science, Scripture. No fingerpainting, no bull sessions, no Little League. Hey, they learn the basics!'

Scaduto was not merely proud of his children – he was respectful in a way that suggested that these children had taught him new things about the world and given him fresh ideas and surprised him with his own ignorance.

'So they don't go to the American school,' I said.

'Or to the state school either,' he said. 'No, all three of them are at PL.'

I smiled inquiringly at Marietta Scaduto. My smile was a request for information – and she understood.

'Prince's Lodge,' she said.

'It's a prep school,' Vic said. 'A really fine one. Where are the kids, honey?'

'Upstairs.'

Vic said to me, 'They've got some school friends over.' He winked – it was a gesture of helpless admiration for his children: Scaduto had the Italian gift of being able to wink meaningfully, and he had as many winks as other people had smiles. 'I'll get them,' he went on. 'They're amazing. You won't understand a word they say. I mean, they're incredibly bright.'

He was infatuated. That was touching, but I saw no reason why in order to praise his children's intelligence he had to belittle mine.

He said, 'You can ask them anything!'

I said, 'Can I tell them anything?'

He frowned, and I wished I had kept my mouth shut.

While Vic was out of the room, Marietta said, 'I wrote a poem.'

I did not know what to say. I had just spoken a bit unwisely to Vic. So I hesitated, and that was my mistake. It made her defiant.

She said, 'You think it's a waste of time.'

She had black hair that hung in long lank strands, and large dark eyes. Her eyebrows were bushy, her face and arms thin, covered with hair that made her skin appear almost gray. Vic was too fat and too bald and too silly for his age, which was about forty-four; she was very thin – spiderlike and brittle. She held herself straight in the chair and, instead of moving her eyes, turned her whole head stiffly at me.

'No, that's marvelous,' I said. 'Do you write many poems, or was that the first one?'

She said nothing. Had she heard?

'I've always loved poetry,' I said, and felt ridiculous. But she had thrown me. Marietta Scaduto was one of those people who can say, 'I just wrote a poem,' and make it sound like 'I just flushed the canary down the toilet' – like the maddest, most irrational act on earth.

Her eyes did not register my stupid remark ('I've always loved poetry') or even that I had spoken. She was staring, entranced, at my forehead, as if trying to guess my age.

She said, 'I got the idea at Kennedy Airport. You know those signs above the escalator telling you about the rest rooms and the gates and the baggage and all that? "Men, Women, Telephones"? That's what gave me the idea. That's what it's called.'

'"Men, Women, Telephones,"' I said. 'It's nice – it's got drama!'

I wished then that I had stayed home. Today, this Saturday at the Scadutos', was my fortieth birthday. I had always resisted birthday celebrations – cakes, candles, presents. It is all forced and false and embarrassing, and the song 'Happy Birthday to You' – monotonous and excruciating – has driven me out of restaurants. I had not wanted anyone to know that this was my birthday; I hadn't wanted a party. This day with Vic and Marietta was the best possible alternative, I had thought. I could leave the birthday at home, be anonymous here, and, somehow, wake up forty tomorrow morning. I had considered it an event of no importance, but now I regretted that I wasn't at Rule's or Leith's or the Connaught with a woman and getting a little drunk and telling her, 'It's my birthday.' I thought that, because I had just realized that I could never mention my age or anyone's age to Marietta Scaduto.

She was still staring at me.

She said, 'You won't like this poem. It's a woman's poem. It's about women's problems.'

I tried to protest. She didn't hear.

'You could write a whole book about those signs,' she said. '"Customs," "Refreshments," "Food," "Handicapped Exit," "Ramp," "Concourse to Ground Transportation," "Way Out." Signs can be poetry. Listen, this is nineteen eighty-one! I could write a book. Men write books. Why shouldn't women?'

I said, 'But women do write books, Marietta, and some of them are awfully good.' Why was I saying these idiotic things? I suppose I was afraid of the childish resentment in her eyes. 'Why, look at George Eliot and Emily Dickinson and Edna Millay –'

'They're always putting us down,' she said.

'Who do you mean?'

'Vic,' she said.

'Vic puts you down?'

'Constantly.'

'But isn't that different from people like Edna –'

'That's why I wrote my poem,' she said.

'"Men, Women, Telephones"? That one?'

'And "Rest Rooms – Women and Handicapped,"' she said. 'And "Customs." And "Children." I think that's one of my best, "Children," based on the sign. I mean, there's more honest pain in it – I hope you don't think I'm being pretentious or that I talk about my poems all day, because I don't. In some states, the sign "Children" is a boy. You've seen it a million times – everyone has. It's like a stencil. It's from about nineteen twenty-two. He's running – his legs are all over the place, and he's smiling. He's wearing these old-fashioned knickers. "Children."'

'It sounds –' I couldn't finish. I didn't know how.

'You're smiling.'

'No!' But, protesting, I began to smile.

'You're just like Vic.'

They called him 'Skiddoo'; he tap-danced; he wanted a post in Italy; he complained about his parents; he boasted about his children; he bitched about this sad crazy woman he was married to.

I said – and didn't know why I was being so polite – 'You hardly know me.'

'I know your type,' she said.

Why hadn't I stayed home? This was my birthday!

'Judgmental. You think I'm wasting my time. You're completely absorbed by your job and do nothing but talk about the Embassy, as if the Embassy's so goddamned important and there's going to be World War Three if you're late for work or you miss a party. You're probably worse than Vic, you're probably like my father – he used to say that education was wasted on a girl –'

Being with her was like reading a letter to a stranger, chosen at random from the dead letter office. It was, at once, both meaningless and embarrassing – you were embarrassed to be holding these sentiments in your hand. Who was she talking to? I did not know her. I was not even moved, and I should at least have pitied her.

It was perhaps more like a glimpse of poor bare flesh – not the beauty of nudity but the wobble of nakedness.

She was still talking – was her father the link? – and then, 'Vic's got this theory –'

Parents owed their children everything, but children did not owe their parents anything; and then that business about how irresponsible most parents were.

Then I told her I was an orphan, and Vic entered with the six boys and said, 'I'm glad to see you two are hitting it off.'

We managed to get through lunch. Marietta did not mention her poems again, or the signs, or her father. Like Vic, she was devoted to her children and she tolerated their friends. In the role of hostess, serving lunch, she was mute and efficient and wholly unlike the mad poetess I had seen over coffee. The boys did not eat with us.

But I still wanted to leave – not stay for dinner, not have to face whatever plans Scaduto had made for the afternoon. I wanted to go back to Overstrand Mansions and turn forty alone.

The married couple believe – unreasonably – that when the single person is on his own he is lonely. I am usually happier alone than in company, and I felt trapped at this house. I can be contented in the narrowest space – but there is a kind of social claustrophobia that afflicts me, the persistence of uncongenial people, who crowd a room and make it airless and give me actual physical discomfort: I wanted to go.

But because I had no excuse for going, I gave myself a reason for staying. Scaduto had mentioned his parents, how they had married young and left their parents in Italy – 'My parents were bad children!' His grandparents had stayed in Sicily. He had told me something of himself, and Marietta had told me his theory – and she had griped about her father. Vic had then promised that I would be impressed with his boys. I forced myself to be interested in these generations of children. At last, after lunch, Vic brought the boys out to meet me properly. I was fascinated and horrified and instructed, and I would not have left that house for anything.

He had suggested a walk in Richmond Park – spending the afternoon there – and then back to the house for dinner. Each of his three boys had a friend. We set off for the park, the eight of us, like the Beaver Patrol – boys ahead, scoutmasters behind. After about half a mile, the Upper Richmond Road entered East Sheen, and we turned into the genteel streets that fringed the park, passing brick and mock-Tudor villas and the trim rose gardens and the well-washed milk bottles that are the very emblem of the Tory suburbs.

Scaduto said, 'Their school is on the next street. It's one of these completely anachronistic schools. They sing hymns loud and out of tune, they're forced to run cross-country in the rain, they do Latin and Scripture –'

'And – was it *lumbering*?' I said.

'"Lumbering in Murmansk." One of their topics, and if you don't know it backward and forward you get a hundred sentences – "I must remember to do my homework thoroughly." Their matron's a hag. They have to sit in the corner if they misbehave. They get beaten – it works! They put on old-fashioned plays and eat disgusting food. And that's not half of it.'

'It would age me twenty years,' I said.

'It's good for them,' Vic said. 'What do you know? You don't have any kids.'

We had entered the park at Sheen Gate. The boys were waiting for us and walked with us across the meadow toward the deer – thirty or forty deer, placidly cropping grass. Vic had told them earlier, when we were introduced, that I had been in Malaysia. Now he reminded them of that and said that if there was anything they wanted to ask me this was the time.

'My father was born in Malaysia,' one of the boys said. 'He still owns part of a tea estate there. My uncle owns the rest of it, but my uncle does all the work. They have thousands of workers – Indians, mostly.'

'They grow lots of tea in Malaysia,' I said.

'My father shot a tiger in the Cameron Highlands,' the boy went on. 'We've got the skin on the wall of our billiard room. My father shot him in the eye. That's why there aren't any bullet holes in the skin.'

This impressive fact – the tiger shot through the eye – silenced the rest of the boys for a while, and the boy called Jocko, who had told the story, marched ahead like a brigadier.

'My father was born in India,' another boy said. This was Nigel. He was Mario Scaduto's friend. He was tall and had a rather debauched-looking face. 'They've got more tigers in India than they know what to do with. But they've been wiped out in Malaysia. Jocko's father probably killed the last one. My parents say that most blood sports are nothing more than vandalism.'

'You've been to India, haven't you, Dad?' Scaduto's youngest son looked pleadingly at him to verify the fact, and then glanced at his school friend, a mouse-faced boy the others called Little-fair.

'Lots of times,' Scaduto said. 'We had a facility right near the border in Pakistan. I used to pop over all the time.'

'We went out there last summer for a holiday,' Jocko said.

'India?' Scaduto asked.

'Hong Kong.' Jocko, I noticed, had a mustache, though he could not have been more than eleven or twelve.

'That's nowhere near India,' Nigel said. 'Jocko's confusing Hong Kong with India.'

'The place is full of ruddy Indians,' Jocko said, facing the others and setting his brigadier's jaw at them. 'Indians own shops there. They're in competition with the Chinese. The Chinese work jolly hard, but they're sneaky. The Indians are arrogant – most of them lie worse than that little git Norris in Form Two, the one they call Ananiarse.'

'We saw some Indians in Trinidad last summer.' This was Littlefair. He was small and bent-over and watchful in a rather elderly way. He was mouse-faced even to the twitching of his pointed nose. 'They were having a Hindu festival. They made a hell of a racket.'

'That's the trouble with England,' Jocko said. 'Too many colored people.'

'Too many Scotsmen is what I say! Send them all back to their rotten old backward villages –' Nigel stopped speaking suddenly and turned to Mario Scaduto. 'Crikey, I'm sorry! I hope you're not Scottish!'

'They're Italian,' Jocko said. 'Scaduto's an Italian name.'

'Smart boy,' Vic said. And he whispered to me, 'They have this fantastic awareness about language.'

'Our maid's Italian,' Jocko said.

Littlefair said, 'We've got two, a husband and wife. They're Spanish. You can hear them arguing at night. All Spaniards argue after work.'

'We're not Italian,' Mario Scaduto was saying. 'We're American. We've got this huge house in Silver Springs, Maryland.' But Mario's accent, and its nervous urgent tweet, was English.

'We went to Trinidad on a yacht my father chartered,' the mouse-faced boy called Littlefair was explaining.

The word 'yacht' was heard by the others, who began to listen.

'We were in a hurricane. We almost sank. We had to put ashore in such a hurry the captain ran the yacht aground and completely smashed the hull. That was after we left Trinidad. Then we went to Jamaica. The colored people standing by the road, when they saw our limousine going by to take us to the hotel, they gobbed on it.'

Nigel said, 'I'm going to camp this summer.'

'I hate camp,' Jocko said. 'It's worse than school.'

'This camp's in Switzerland.'

I walked abreast of Vic, just behind the boys, whose voices were raised, as if they intended for us to hear them clearly. Vic looked at me and said, 'Aren't they unbelievable?' I agreed; I said they certainly were; it was the very word for them. But he was praising them. And the boys were still talking.

'My mother says it's not that they can't find jobs, it's that they just don't want to work. They'd rather draw their dole money.'

'Some of these people make a hell of a lot on the dole – twenty or thirty pounds a week. That's more than we pay our maid.'

'If you have masses of children you can make a ruddy fortune on the dole. That's what all these Pakistanis do.'

'Some of them work hard. They take jobs that English people

refuse. Ever see them at Heathrow? They're the ones who clean the bogs.'

'They work all night, too. Our plane came in at three o'clock in the morning and there were Pakistanis all over the place with mops and buckets.'

'There's a Pakistani round our way. His shop is open even on Sunday. He never closes!'

'That's the trouble with them – they're just interested in making money.'

Scaduto's children mingled with their friends. It was impossible to tell them from the others in this chorus of voices. All the accents were the same to my unpracticed ear, like the cries of 'My father says' and 'My mother says.' After vacations, and the Far East, and immigrants, and welfare, they discussed work – the best jobs – and schools – the best schools.

'How old are your children, Vic?'

'Eight-fifteen, nine-forty-five and twelve-thirty,' he said, as if reciting a timetable. 'Mario's twelve-thirty. He starts public school next September. If we go to Italy he can be a boarder.'

'Radley's a brilliant school,' one of the boys was saying. 'They did that television series about it.'

'My father says they put too much emphasis on books. I'm going to Ardingly. They've got sailing.'

Littlefair said, 'I'm going to Marlborough,' and when no one commented he became even more mouselike, and twitched his nose, and said, 'My grandfather gave them a library.'

'My father's an old boy of St Paul's.' This was the Scottish boy they called Jocko. 'That's why I want to go to Westminster.'

'American schools are rubbish,' another boy said. He was dark-haired. He was, I realized, one of the Scaduto boys.

'Tony,' Vic said sharply.

'Oh, you know they stink, Dad,' the boy said in a jeering way. 'The kids carry knives. They take drugs. There's no discipline. Half the teachers can't even read.'

'Flipping Norah!' Nigel said.

'They smoke marijuana in the bogs,' Tony Scaduto said. 'The teachers go to discos with their girl students and get them pregnant.'

'Gordon Bennett!' Jocko said, and in spite of myself I laughed out loud at the exclamation.

'I'm really impressed with English schools,' Vic said. 'But just because you like English schools doesn't mean you have to run down American ones. Compulsory free education is an American idea.'

The boy called Nigel said, 'American schools are brilliant at sports,' and then smiled patronizingly at the Scadutos.

'What does your father do?' the Littlefair boy was asking the youngest Scaduto, whose name was either Frankie or Franny.

'He works in the West End,' Mario said, helping his brother out.

'He has an office in Mayfair,' Tony said.

It was a highly imaginative way of describing Vic Scaduto's job as Cultural Affairs Officer at the American Embassy in Grosvenor Square. Vic heard and gave me a pained and apologetic look. Then, in an attempt to set the record straight, he cleared his throat and spoke loudly.

'I'm with the American Embassy, on the cultural side.'

'Hussein – that colored boy in Form Three they call "turhead" – his father's with the Saudi Arabian Embassy,' Jocko said. 'He has TV cameras in his driveway – for security reasons. And an armed guard. That weed Beavis went to a birthday party there. Hussein's father weighs about twenty stone! Beavis said he looks like a chucker-out.'

'Princes come to visit him, Beavis said' – this from Littlefair.

'Not real princes,' Nigel said. 'Colored ones, wrapped in blankets, with towels over their heads.'

Mario Scaduto said, 'The colored ones are just as good as the real ones.'

Nigel smiled and said, 'There are three thousand members of the royal family in Saudi Arabia. It's because they have all those wives. They have billions of children. Everyone you meet is a prince, even the people who do the washing-up. It doesn't mean a thing.'

The smallest Scaduto said, 'I don't believe you!'

'My father's company's got an office in Jeddah,' Nigel said. This seemed to settle the argument. He added, 'My father goes there by Concorde.'

'Concorde doesn't go to Jeddah,' Jocko said.

'It goes to Bahrain,' Nigel said. 'He changes planes there.'

We had walked across the park, from Sheen Gate to the woods on the hill to the south, passing the deer, which hardly noticed us, an older people with dogs on leashes, who never took their eyes off us and seemed to listen to the boys yelling and boasting.

'The last time we were here it was awful bleak,' Vic said.

The last time: he meant when the assessment officers had spent the day with him.

We were surrounded by azaleas and tall and tumbling rhododendrons that grew in the high shade of the woods.

'These are really pretty,' he said.

'We've got lots of these at home. My mother grows them. She's entering some in the Chelsea Flower Show.'

Oh, shut up, I thought, and walked on ahead. But I could still hear them.

'Richmond Park is famous. I'll bet you don't have parks like this in America.'

'They used to. They've all been ruined by vandals. That's what my father says.' Was this one of the Scadutos?

'I've been to America lots of times.' I turned. This was Nigel.

'So have we.' Littlefair.

'We never go to America,' Tony Scaduto said. 'We prefer it here.'

Jocko said, 'You're American.'

'I don't feel American,' Mario Scaduto said.

'Neither do I,' Tony said.

'But you are!' Littlefair said. 'Your parents are American, so that means –'

Vic had caught up with me, and he had abandoned the boys, given up on their conversation. They were screaming at each other now, and he looked sheepish.

He said, 'I'll get that job in Italy. Then everyone will be happy. My folks will come over and visit. They'll be proud – it's what they always wanted. I think I'll put these kids in the American school in Rome. You don't have to tell me they need it. I know. They won't like it, but they'll get used to it. A job like this can be hell on a family – you have no idea.'

My last memory of that day at the Scadutos' was the dinner itself – not Vic asking where the lemon for the fish was and Marietta saying, 'Get it yourself!' and not Vic (who quickly became drunk) defending the death penalty for child molesters, joined by his three boys, who said that they were in favor of capital punishment not only for murder but also stealing; it was the memory of Marietta leaning over and telling me at great length that in spite of what people said about parents teaching their children, the truth was that children taught their parents. Children, Marietta said, sort of raised her parents and helped them grow up and if it wasn't for her three she would probably never have taken up poetry. It wasn't the children who belittled women writers – it was the adults. And wasn't it a shame that I did not have any – especially here in London, where there were so many opportunities for kids? I remembered that – as a consolation – because Vic Scaduto ('All parents are children' – he wouldn't leave the topic!) of course never got the job in Italy.

Charlie Hogle's Earring

There is something athletic, something physical, in the way the most successful people reach decisions. The businessmen who plot take-overs, the upstarts who become board chairmen, the masterminds of conglomerates – they are often jocks who regard more thoughtful men as cookie-pushers, and who shoulder their way into offices and hug their allies and muscle in on deals. They move like swaggerers and snatchers, using their elbows when their money fails. And when they are in command they are puppet-masters.

Everett Horton, our number two, prized his football photograph (Yale '51) as much as he did his autographed portrait of the President. Here was another of him, posed with a Russian diplomat, each in white shorts, holding a tennis racket and shaking hands across a tennis net. And others: Horton golfing, Horton fishing, Horton sailing. Horton had interesting ears – slightly swollen, and gristlier than the average, and they did not match: 'Wrestling,' someone said. It seemed innocent vanity that Horton thought of himself as a man of action. I suppose he was a man of action. He worked hard. He succeeded where Ambassador Noyes often failed.

Erroll Jeeps used to say: 'Watch out for Horton's body English.'

He could have sent me a memo, or phoned me, or we might have had lunch. But he had not become minister by sending memos. He was a hugger, a hand-shaker, a back-slapper – body English – and when something important came up he tore downstairs and interrupted whatever I was doing and said, 'You're the only one around here who can straighten this out. You've been in the Far East, not in Washington, among the cookie-pushers!'

Today he hugged me. His sweet-whiskey fragrance of aftershave lotion stung my eyes. A file folder was tucked under his arm.

'Is that the problem?'

'That's his file,' Horton said.

I tried to catch a glimpse of the name, but he tossed the file onto a chair and kicked my office door shut.

'Let me tell you about it. That'll be quicker than reading this crap.' He sat on the edge of my desk and swung one heavy thigh over the other.

'Do you know Charlie Hogle from C and R?'

'I saw him once at your house – that reception you gave for me. I don't go down to the telex room.'

'You let your *pyoon* do it, eh?' It was the Malay word for office lackey, and he was mocking me with it. He said, 'You should get around more – you'd be amazed at some of the things you find.'

'In the telex room?'

'Especially there,' Horton said. 'This fellow Hogle – very gifted, they say, if you can describe a telex operator in that way. Very personable. Highly efficient, if a bit invisible. He's been here almost three years. No trouble, no scandal, nothing.' Horton stopped talking. He stared at me. 'I was down there this morning. What do I find?' Horton watched me again, giving me the same dramatic scrutiny as before. He wanted my full attention and a little pause.

I said, 'I give up – what did you find?'

'Hogle. With an earring.' Horton sighed, slid off the desktop, and threw himself into a chair. He was remarkably agile for such a big man.

I said, 'An earring?'

'Right. One of those gold . . . loops? Don't make me describe it.' Horton suddenly seemed cross. 'I don't know anything about earrings.'

'Was he wearing it?'

'What a dumb question! Of course he was.'

'I thought you were going to tell me that he stole it – that you found it on him.'

'He's got a hole in his ear for it.'

I said, 'So he's had his ear pierced.'

'Can you imagine? A special hole in his ear!'

I said, 'What exactly is wrong, coach?'

He had encouraged us to use this ridiculous word for him. I had so far refrained from it, and though I felt like a jackass using it today, it seemed to have the right effect. It calmed him. He smiled at me.

'Let's put it at its simplest. Let's be charitable. Let's not mock him,' Horton said. 'An earring is against regulations.'

'Which ones?'

'Dress regulations. The book. It's as if he's wearing a skirt.'

'But he's not wearing a skirt. It's jewelry. Is there a subsection for that?'

'Sure! In Muslim countries, Third World countries –'

'This is England, coach.'

'And he's a guy! And he's got this thing hanging off his ear!'

'You're not going to get him on a technicality,' I said. 'All you can do is ask him to remove it. "Would you mind taking off that earring, Mr Hogle?"'

Horton did not smile. He began lecturing me. He said, 'You act as if there's nothing wrong. Did you know there's no law against lesbianism in this country? Do you know why? Because Queen Victoria refused to believe that women indulged in that sort of behavior!'

'Hogle's earring is hardly in that category,' I said.

'Bull! It's precisely in that category. That's how serious a violation it is. It's unthinkable for a man to turn up at work wearing an earring, so there's no legislation, nothing in the rulebook for earrings *per se*. But there's a paragraph on Improper Dress –'

'That covers lewd or suggestive clothes.'

'What about Inappropriate Accessories?'

'Religious or racial taboos. Cowhide presents in Hindu countries, pigskin suitcases in Muslim countries, the New York Philharmonic touring Israel and playing Wagner.'

'What has Wagner got to do with Accessories?'

'You know what I mean. Earrings don't figure.'

'There's something,' Horton said. He came over to me and jerked my shoulder, giving me a hug. 'It doesn't matter.' He grinned. He was a big man. He hugged me sideways as we stood shoulder to shoulder. 'There's always something – just find it.'

'Why me?' I said. 'You could do it more easily.'

His eyes became narrow and dark as he said, 'I'll tell you why I can't.' He looked at the door suspiciously, as if he were about to bark at it. Then he made an ugly disgusted face and whispered, 'When I saw Hogle with that thing in his ear, and the hole, and the implications, I felt sick to my stomach.' He glanced darkly at the door again. 'He's a nice clean-cut guy. I'd lay into him – I'd lose my temper. I know I would, and I want to spare him that. You'll be more rational. You know about these nutty customs. You've been in the Far East.'

'Doesn't Hogle have a personnel officer?'

Horton gave me a disdainful look. His expression said I was letting him down, I was a coward, a weakling.

He said, 'You don't want to do this, do you?'

'What I want is of no importance,' I said. 'I do what I'm told.'

'Excellent!' he said. Horton stood up straight. The muddy green was gone from his eyes; he was smiling. 'Now get down there and tell Hogle to divest himself.'

I said, 'That's his file, right?'

'Ignore the file for now. When you've settled this problem, stick a memo in here and hand it back to me. I also want to know why he's wearing it – that's important. And, by the way, this is strictly confidential, this whole matter – everything I've said.'

I made a move toward the file.

'You don't really need that,' he said.

'Maybe not,' I said. 'But I think I'll take it home and blow on it.'

I had thought, *Why me?* But of course Horton was testing me as much as he was gunning for Hogle. He was trying to discover where my sympathies were: Would I give him an argument, or would I obey? Perhaps I was a latent earring-wearer? Horton's own reaction seemed to me extraordinary. He felt sick to his stomach. That may have been an exaggeration, but the fear that he would lose his temper was almost unbelievable in someone whose temper was always in check. Everett Horton – he wanted to be called 'coach'! – was a man of action. I could not understand his reticence now, unless I was right in assuming that I was the real subject of the inquiry.

I was new here – less than four months on the job. I had to play ball. And I must admit I was curious.

The file was thin. Charlie Hogle had come to us from the Army under a program we called Lateral Entry. He had been in the communications unit of the Signal Corps, running a C and R office in Frankfurt. He was twenty-nine, not married, a graduate – German major – of the University of Northern Iowa in Cedar Falls. He had been born and raised in nearby Waterloo, Iowa. His annual job evaluations from the State Department fault-finders were very good. In fact, one suggested – as a black mark – that Hogle had experienced 'no negative situations.' In other words, he was such a happy fellow he might prove to be a problem. I did not buy that naive analysis. Hogle was a well-adjusted, middle-level technician with a good record, and after looking through this worthy man's file I regretted what I had been ordered to do.

Lunch with him was out: it was both too businesslike and too friendly. Anyway, I hated lunch as unnecessary and time-wasting. Lunch is the ritual meal that makes fat people fat. And dinner was out – too formal. I kept telling myself that this was a small matter. I could send for him. I pictured poor Hogle, clutching his silly earring, cowering in my office, awkward in his chair.

There was only one possibility left – a drink after work. That made it less official, less intimidating, and if I got bored I could plead a previous engagement and go home.

I met him at a large overdecorated pub called the Audley, on the corner of Mount and Audley Streets, not far from the Embassy. Hogle, whom I spotted as American from fifty feet away, was tall even by the generous standards of the Midwest. He was good-looking, with a smooth polite face and clear blue eyes. His blond eyelashes made him look completely frank and unsecretive. His hands were nervous, but his face was innocent and still. His voice had the plain splintery cadences of an Iowa Lutheran being truthful. I took him to be a muscular Christian.

'I kind of like these English beers,' he was saying now. (Earlier we had talked about his Sunday school teaching.) 'They're a little flat, but they don't swell you up or make you drunk, like lager. Back home –'

As he spoke, I glanced at his earring. It was a small gold hoop, as Horton had said, but Horton had made it seem like junk jewelry, rather vulgar and obvious – and embarrassing to the onlooker. I was surprised to find it a lovely earring. And it was hardly noticeable – too small to be a pirate's, too simple for a transvestite. I thought it suited him. It was the sort of detail that makes some paintings remarkable; it gave his face position and focus – and an undeniable beauty. It was the size, and it had the charm, of Shakespeare's raffish earring in the painting in the National Portrait Gallery.

Charlie Hogle was still talking about beer. His favorite was the Colorado Coors brand, because it was made from –

This was ridiculous. We were getting nowhere. I said, 'Is that an earring you're wearing?'

His fingers went for it. 'Yes,' he said. 'What do you think of it?'
'Very nice,' I said. He smiled. I said, 'And unusual.'

'It cost me twenty-two pounds. That's almost fifty bucks, but it included getting my ear pierced. I figure it was worth it, don't you?'

Was he trying to draw me?

'You've just,' I said, 'got the one?'

'One earring's enough!'

I said, 'I'm not sure –'

'You think I should have *two*? Don't you think that'd be pushing it a little?'

'Actually,' I said, and hated my tone of voice and dreaded what was coming, 'I was wondering whether one earring might be pushing it, never mind two.'

'You said it was nice.' He looked at me closely, and sniffed. He was an honest fellow for whom a contradiction was a bad smell. 'What do you mean, "One earring might be pushing it"?'

'It *is* very nice,' I said. 'And so are those split skirts the secretaries have started to wear. But I wouldn't be very happy about your wearing a split skirt, Mr Hogle.'

He smiled. He was not threatened: he saw a joke where I had intended a warning. He said, 'I'm not wearing a split skirt, sir.'

'Yes,' I said. 'But you are wearing an earring.'

'Is that the same as wearing a skirt?'

'Not exactly, but it's the same *kind* of thing.'

'What – illegal?'

'Inappropriate,' I said. This was Horton's line, and its illogicality was hideously apparent to me as I parroted it. 'Like coming to work in your bathing suit, or dyeing your hair green, or –'

I couldn't go on. Hogle was, quite rightly, smiling at the stupidity of my argument. And now I saw that Horton's objection was really a form of abuse.

Hogle said, 'I know those things are silly and inappropriate. I wouldn't come to work dressed like a slob. I'm no punk. I don't have green hair.'

'Yes, I know.'

'I've got a pretty clean record, sir. I got a commendation from the Consul in Frankfurt for hanging on and keeping the telex room open during a Red Army Faction riot. I'm not bragging, sir. I'm just saying I take my job seriously.'

'Yes, it's mentioned in your file. I know about it.'

'You've been looking in my file,' he said. His face became sad, and his attention slackened. He had let go of his earring. 'I get it – my ass is in a crack.'

'Not yet.'

'Sir, I could have bought a cheaper earring – one of those silver dangly ones. Instead I saved up. I bought a nice one. You said so yourself.'

'I also said it's rather unusual.'

'There's nothing wrong with "unusual," is there?'

'Some people think so.'

He looked at me, with his lips compressed. He had now seen the purpose of this innocent drink. I had led him here on a false pretext; I had deceived him. His eyes went cold.

He said, 'Mr Horton, the minister. It's him, isn't it?'

'It's the regulations,' I said lamely.

'He was staring at me the other day, like the second louies used to stare at me when I was in the Army. Even though he was about fifty feet away I could feel his eyes pressing on my neck. You can tell when something's wrong.' Hogle shook his head in a heavy rueful way. 'I thought he used to like me. Now he's yanked my file and sent you to nail me down.'

Hogle was completely correct. But I could not admit it without putting Horton into a vulnerable position and exposing him as petty and spiteful. After all, Horton's was the only objection to the earring. But Horton was boss.

I said, 'Everyone thinks that it would be better if you dispensed with your earring.'

'I still don't understand why.'

'It's contrary to dress regulations. Isn't that obvious?'

He touched the earring, as if for luck. He said, 'Maybe they should change the regulations.'

'Do you think it's likely they will?'

He made a glum face and said no.

'Be a sport,' I said. 'I'm telling you this for your own good. Get rid of that thing and save yourself a headache.'

Hogle had been staring at his glass of beer. Without moving his head, he turned his eyes on me and said, 'I don't want to seem uncooperative, sir, but I paid good money for this earring. And I had a hole punched in my ear. And I like it, and it's not hurting anyone. So – no way am I going to get rid of it.'

'What if we take disciplinary action?'

'That's up to you, sir.'

'You could be suspended on half-pay. What do you say to that?'

'I wouldn't like it much,' Hogle said.

'Mr Hogle,' I said, 'does that earring represent anything? I mean, is it a sort of symbol?'

'Not any more than your tie clip is a symbol. You don't see many tie clips these days – and I think yours is neat. I think this earring is neat. That's the only reason. Don't you think that's a pretty good reason?'

I wished he would not ask me these questions. They were traps; they incriminated me; they tore me in two. I said, 'What I think doesn't matter. I'm an employee. So are you. What you think doesn't matter either. There is nothing personal about this; there's no question about opinion or tolerance or flexibility. It's strictly regulations.'

Hogle replied in a sort of wounded whisper. 'I'd like to see the regulations, sir,' he said. 'I'd like to see in black and white which rule I've broken.'

'It's a very general regulation concerning appropriate dress,' I said. 'And we can make it stick. We're going to give you a few days to decide which is more important to you – your earring or your job.'

I had lapsed into 'we' – it is hard to use it and not seem cold and bullying; it can be a terrifying pronoun. And yet I had hoped this meeting would be friendly. It was, from my point of view, disastrously cold. His resentment made me officious; my officiousness made him stubborn. In the end I had simply pulled rank on him, used the scowling 'we,' and given him a crude choice. Then I left him. He looked isolated and lonely at the table in the pub, and that saddened me, because he was handsome and intelligent and young and a very hard worker. His earring distinguished him and made him look like a prince.

The next day I went to Horton's office. Seeing me, he rushed out and gave me a playful shove. He then helped me into the office with a hug, all the while saying, 'Get in here and tell me what a great success you've been in the telex room.'

I hated this fooling. I said, 'I've had a talk with Hogle.'

'With what result?'

'He's thinking about it.'

'You mean, it's not settled? You let him *think* about it?'

I freed myself from his grasp. I said, 'Yes.'

'It's not a thinking matter,' Horton said. 'It's an order – didn't you tell him that?'

'I didn't want to throw my weight around. You said yourself there's no point making an issue out of it if it can be settled quietly.'

Horton gaped at this. He became theatrical, imitating shock and incredulity with his exaggerated squint, and there was something of an actressy whine in his voice when he said, 'So he's still down there, wearing that *thing* on his ear?'

I let him rant a bit more. Then I said, 'I didn't want to put pressure on him. If he hasn't got the sense to see that our displeasure matters, then he's hardly any use to us.'

'That's a point – I don't want any passengers in this Embassy, and I certainly won't put up with freaks.' Horton's phone was ringing; it had the effect of sobering him and making him snappish. 'I'll expect that file back by the end of the week – and I want a happy conclusion. Remember, if you can't get this chappie' – Horton wiggled his head on the word – 'to remove his earring, you can hardly expect me to have much faith in your powers of persuasion.'

'I'd like to drop the whole damned thing,' I said.

Horton paused, and he peered at me with interest in spite of his nagging phone. 'And why is that?'

'I don't see the importance of it,' I said.

'It is very important,' he said. 'And of course I'm interested in your technique. You see, in this Embassy one is constantly trying to point out that there is a sensible, productive way of doing things – and there is the British way. Tactful persuasion is such an asset, whether one is dealing with a misunderstood aspect of NATO or an infraction of the dress regulations by a serving officer – I mean, Hogle's earring. I hate even the word.'

'I'll do it,' I said. 'But my heart isn't in it.'

'That is precisely why I want you to do it,' Horton said. 'If nothing else, this should teach you that feelings have nothing to do with this job. Now, please, get it over with. It's starting to make me sick.'

I chose the pub carefully. It was in Earl's Court and notoriously male; but at six-thirty it was empty and could easily have been mistaken for the haunt of darts players and polite locals with wives and dogs. Hogle was late. Waiting there, I thought that he might not turn up at all, just to teach me a lesson. But he came with an excuse and an apology. He had been telexing an urgent cable. Only he had clearance to work with classified material after hours, and the duty officer – Yorty, a newcomer – had no idea how to use a telex machine. So Hogle had worked late. As an ex-Army man he understood many of the military cables, and he had security clearance, and he was willing; I knew from his file that he didn't make mistakes. His obedience had never been questioned – that is, until Horton spotted the earring. I began to see why this detail worried Horton so much: Hogle, in such a ticklish job, had to be absolutely reliable.

He said, 'I've been thinking over what you told me.'

He looked tired – paler than he had three days ago. It was not the extra work, I was sure – he was worrying, not sleeping well. Perhaps he had already decided to resign on a point of principle, for in spite of his wilted posture and ashen skin, his expression was full of tenacity. I suppose it was his eyes. They were narrow, as though wounded, and hot, and seemed to say *No surrender*.

I said, 'Don't say anything.'

He had been staring into the middle distance. Now he looked closely at me. He winced, but he kept his gaze on me.

I said, 'I've managed to prevail. I took it to the highest possible level. I think everyone understands now.'

'What do you mean, "understands"?' There was a hint of anxiety in his voice.

'Your earring,' I said.

'What's there to understand?'

'You've got nothing to worry about. We don't persecute people for their beliefs anymore. If that were the case I wouldn't be in the Foreign Service.'

'Wearing an earring,' Hogle said. 'Is that a belief?'

'It depends on how naive you are,' I said. 'But be glad it doesn't matter. Be glad you live in a free society, where you can dress any way you like, and where you can choose your friends, whether they're British or American, white or black, female or male –'

Hogle became very attentive.

I said, 'I'm grateful to you. It's people like you who break down barriers and increase our self-awareness.'

'I don't want to break down any barriers,' he said. 'I'm not even sure what self-awareness is all about.'

'It's about earrings,' I said. 'The other day I told you your earring was nice. I was being insincere. May I call you Charlie?'

'Sure.'

'Charlie, I think your earring is fantastic.'

His hand went to his ear. He looked wary. He did not let go of the earring or his earlobe. He sat fixedly with his fingers making this plucking gesture on his ear.

'It's a very handsome accessory,' I said. His fingers tightened. 'A real enhancement.' They moved again. 'An elegant statement –'

I thought he was going to yank his ear off. His hand was trembling, still covering the earring. He said, 'I'm not making a statement.'

'Take it easy,' I said, giving him the sort of blanket assurance of no danger that convinces people – and rightly – that they're in a tight spot. 'You've got absolutely nothing to worry about!' He looked very worried. 'You can relax with me.' I ordered him a drink and told him there was no point in discussing the earring.

'To be perfectly honest,' I said, 'I rather like your earring.'

'I'm certainly not making any kind of statement,' Hogle said. The word worried him. It had implications of being unerasable and hinted of hot water. 'I got the idea from one of the delivery men – an English guy. He wasn't making any statement. It looked neat, that's all.'

'It looks more than neat,' I said. 'It has a certain mystery. I think that's its real charm.'

He winced at this, and how he was pinching his earlobe. He lowered his eyes. He did not look up again.

'I feel funny,' he said.

'Be glad you work with people who say yes instead of no.'

I gave him a friendly punch on the shoulder, the sort of body English Horton would have approved. It made me feel uncomfortable and mannered and overhearty. It amazed me then to realize that Horton was always punching and hugging and digging in the ribs. Hogle was unresponsive, not to say wooden. His eyes darted sideways.

The night's clients had started to arrive in the pub – men in leather jackets, with close-cropped hair, and heavy chains around their necks, and tattooed thumbs, and sunglasses. Some were bald, some devilishly bearded; one wore crimson shoes; another had an enormous black dog on a leather strap. All of them wore earrings.

'Have another drink,' I said.

Hogle stood up. 'I have to go.'

'What's the hurry?'

He was breathing hard. A man encased in tight black leather was hovering near us and staring at Hogle. The man had silver chains with thick links looped around his boots and they clanked as he came closer.

'No hurry,' Hogle said. Now he was reassuring me in the way that I had reassured him earlier, giving me hollow guarantees as he backed away. 'Hey, I had a good time.' He stepped past the clanking man, whose leather, I swear, oinked and squeaked. 'No kidding. It's just that' – he looked around – 'I told this friend of mine, this girl I know, that I'd – I don't know, I'd give her a call.' He looked desperate. 'Hey, thanks a lot. I really appreciate everything you've done!'

Then he left, and then I removed my earring. That was easy enough to do – just a matter of unscrewing the little plunger and putting the foolish thing into my pocket. And I hurried out of the pub, hearing just behind me clanks and squeaks of reproach.

In my report for Charlie Hogle's file I recorded the earring incident as a minor infraction – Inappropriate Dress. I left it vague. What was the point in explaining? I noted the two meetings; I described Hogle as 'compliant' and 'reasonable.' There was no innuendo in my report. I spared him any indignity. It sounded no worse than if he had come to work without a necktie.

Indeed, it was no worse than if he had come to work without a necktie. I had had no objection to the earring, nor had any of Hogle's co-workers in the telex room. Horton had made it an issue; Horton was minister, so Horton was obeyed. And Hogle did not wear his earring again.

'It's for his own good,' Horton said later, and he squeezed my arm. I was the team member who had just played well; he was the coach. He was proud of me and pleased with himself. He was beaming. 'I feel a thousand times better, too! That really annoyed me – that kid's earring. I used to go down to the telex room a lot. I realized I was staying away – couldn't stand to look at it!'

'Aren't you being a little melodramatic?'

'I'm completely serious,' he said. 'That situation was making me sick. I mean sick. I got so mad the first time I saw that thing on his ear' – Horton turned away and paused – 'I got so mad I actually threw up. Puked! That's how angry I was.'

'You must have been very angry,' I said.

'Couldn't help it. We can't have that sort of thing –' He didn't finish the sentence. He shook his head from side to side and then said, 'You were too easy on him in your report. That kid had a problem. Incredible. I took him for a clean, stand-up guy!'

I said, 'He may have feelings of which he's unaware. It's not that uncommon.'

'No,' Horton said. 'I'll keep an eye on him.'

'Fine,' I said. 'Anyway, everyone's safe now, coach.'

He smiled and smacked my arm and sent me back to my office.

In the following weeks I saw scores of young men Hogle's age wearing earrings. They were English, and all sorts, and I was ashamed that I had been a success. It was not merely that I had succeeded by deceiving Hogle, but that I had made him think there was something dangerous and deviant in this trinket decorating his ear. And he never knew just how handsome that trinket made him. Hogle would be all right. But after what he had told me, I was not so sure about Horton.

The Exile

Everyone knows Ezra Pound's funny name, but no one can quote him. This was also the case with the American poet Walter Van Bellamy, who – like Pound long ago – lived in England. Nearly everyone knew what Bellamy stood for, but I had never met a person who could quote a single line he had written. I wondered sometimes whether the people who bought his books actually read them. Certainly they went to his readings and listened to him reciting his poems. He did so in a whisper, but it was an amazing one. Most people whisper in a monotone; Bellamy could whisper over an octave and a half, a characteristic he shared with the best actors.

His subjects were love, nature, humanity, and war. He also wrote frankly of how he had once lost the balance of his mind. That was the phrase he used. I liked 'lost the balance' very much, as if he had lost the little that remained and had none left. This confession of a recent bout of lunacy made him greatly sought after as a party guest, and it also conferred on him glamour and respectability. His poem 'I Am Naked' was about these very paradoxes.

Inevitably, his war poems concerned politics. His readings had the flavor of political meetings and some had the heat and unanimity of religious get-togethers. That was what the clippings said in his Embassy file, which was all I knew at the beginning. (I had met him once at an Embassy reception and had found him deaf on gin – we got nowhere.) To a large extent, Bellamy's audience could best be described as believers, and they were charmed by his music. He was famous for the sounds in his poems, what he called 'my throbs and gongs.' It was possible that people were so persuaded by him beforehand that there was little need afterward for them to remember anything. Still, it surprised me that no one could quote his poems. His presence was memorable, though: a broad chest, eyes as blue as gas flames, a stern bony Pilgrim Father's face, and enormous hairy hands. He was also very tall – my height, about six-three. He walked with a slight stoop, a cringing posture that had probably evolved out of a fear of banging his head.

His strong, distinctly radical views were well known – his position on South Africa, nuclear disarmament, NATO, and even such rarefied issues as the exploitation of nonunion labor in the wine-growing region of Northern California. He had led peace marches in the 1960s, when he had been regarded as the soul of propriety in his dark gray three-piece suit and hand-knotted bowtie and gold watch chain. You might have taken him for a Tory politician or a banker or an Episcopalian preacher. He had a copper-bottomed look of authority, of solidity and trustworthiness; he had a good old name. The ragged, angry protest movements of the sixties needed his respectability, and they were probably surprised by how vocal he was on their behalf. He had the appeal of John Kennedy – in fact, the two had been classmates at Harvard. His 'Elegy on the Death of JFK' was celebrated for its intimate and unexpected details of the two men's friendship. Within a very few years of this poem, Bellamy became a public figure, who stumped around the United States reading his poems and giving encouragement to the anti-Vietnam protesters. He was noted for his willingness to share a platform with a folksinger, a jailbird, or whoever. Most people agreed that he was the conscience of his generation. Bellamy seemed to have no fire, but that was not so surprising. A conscience does not shout – it murmurs.

What else? Yes, he looked wonderfully well fed. This alone was an amazing characteristic in a poet, but he was a most unrepresentative figure. The more I found out about him, the more bewildered I was. He had a large following, but he was not only a poet. He was like a spiritual leader, like one of those bearded domineering Indian gurus; but for Bellamy poetry was the medium of instruction. His humility was so conspicuous and challenging it was like arrogance; but his sense of certainty, and the preachiness of his poems – and his physical size – attracted many people to him. He had considerable influence, and I was very glad it was for the good. His followers were a peaceful and romantic bunch on the whole – the college crowd – who perhaps trusted and liked this well-dressed father figure more than the middle-aged men who also wrote poems and carried banners and played to the gallery, and who dressed like chicken farmers and long-distance truckers, and who could be pretty embarrassing in the cold light of day.

Bellamy had the strange privacies also of a spiritual leader. There were no rumors and stories of his excesses, but there were resonant and suggestive silences. To look like a banker and to be known for his nervous breakdown – that was what made him. And his marriages had also given him fame. He had been married three times. But he was no philanderer – he had been victimized and thrown into confusion by these messy affairs. Each of his wives had been extremely rich.

It was some measure of his fame that he was known as a writer to people who did not read him, and a great writer to those who did not read at all. He was all the more celebrated for not living in America. When Walter Van Bellamy came to England from New York in the early seventies he was called an exile. It did not seem the right word to describe a man who was often on television telling lively stories, or else doing something public and political before a crowd. I thought of exiles as gaunt silent men, with red eyes, pacing the rocky foreshores of barren islands; or else unshaven men in hot overcoats who spoke in thick accents and slept on sofas. Bellamy did not fit my stereotype. And were you still an exile if you occasionally flew home first class in a jumbo jet to attend a New York party? I did not think so. Some years he taught at Harvard. He had money. His rich wives had been sympathetic. They were more patronesses than wives. He was lucky. He had always lived well – he was in his way a socialite, a party-goer, if a somewhat reluctant one. He had a house in the depths of Kent and an apartment in Eaton Square. Perhaps the most unusual thing about him was that, as a poet, he made money. People bought his books, even if they didn't read them. The books were symbols or tokens of belief. Buying them was a political act, an affirmation that you were on his side – whatever side he was boosting at that moment.

I had been introduced to him at Everett Horton's house, when he was drunk and deaf. I was eager to meet him again, because I had read him at school. He too had been to Boston Latin, and his books in the school library and the thought that he had sat under these same windows, this whiff of literary history, fueled my own ambition to write, until I drifted into the State Department. I had wanted to talk to him. It is a natural desire to want to meet a writer and size him up. But I did not see him again until the Poetry Night of the London Arts Festival, where he was reading.

His poems that night were dense and full of his personal history, but his reading was vigorous and gave life to what seemed to be little more than spidery monologues about his domestic affairs – how he had cleaned out a sink and swept a room and ordered a pint of milk and so forth – modern poetry, as a lady behind me said out loud. There is a personal tone in some poetry that is so intimate it gives nothing away – so private it sounds anonymous. Bellamy's was a sort of general confession of practical untidiness with which any youngster might identify. I say 'youngster' because Bellamy seemed to be addressing younger people, implying that he understood them and offering them reassurance. This restrained snuggling was a popular approach. The audience clamored for more, and that was when I noticed how lonely he looked in the spotlight – how solitary and anxious to please.

As an encore that night he read a long poem, called 'Londoners,' about Americans in London, starting with Emerson and Hawthorne and ending with himself. In between, there were references to Mark Twain, Stephen Crane, and Henry James. The personal note was struck in such sentences as 'Tom Eliot told me –' and 'Cal Lowell used to drawl –' Afterward, he said the poem was about language and culture. With a characteristic flourish, he added, 'and schizo-phrenia.'

What I have written so far will not be news to anyone who has followed the career of Walter Van Bellamy. He was a public man; the facts are well known – but wait: it is the public men who have the darkest secrets. They have the deepest cellars and hottest attics, and they are consoled by blindness and locked doors. It is imposs-ible to guess at what truly animates these people whose surfaces we seem to know so well, and there is nothing in the world harder to know than the private life of a public man.

The London Embassy had tried to cultivate Bellamy. We needed him. He had a powerful eminence among the writers in London – partly for being American and partly because his present wife was a patroness. She was an irascible Englishwoman who, for tax reasons (ah, the resourceful English aristocracy!), held an American passport.

In the previous ten years Bellamy had signed petitions condemn-ing our intervention in Vietnam and our arming small Central American countries; about our decision to build a neutron bomb

– and more: public matters. Of course we needed his criticism, but it was unhelpful, not to say humiliating, to get it publicly. I had told Horton that I hoped there was a friendly way of gaining Bellamy's confidence. It occurred to me at the poetry reading that in another age a man like Bellamy might have chosen to be a diplomat. Even today the French, the Spanish, the Portuguese, chose poets as their cultural attachés and the Mexicans had recently sent one of their most distinguished writers to be Ambassador to France. Bellamy could, I thought, teach us a great deal. There were too few men at the London Embassy who were willing to criticize policy decisions – they felt their jobs were at stake. That sort of thing wouldn't bother Bellamy. He had a reputation as a humane poet-philosopher; he also had a private income. I felt that someone like Bellamy might keep us from making stupid mistakes. And it would certainly be a very good thing for our image in Britain if Bellamy chose to associate himself with us, for there was no question but that British intellectuals regarded our London Embassy as a stronghold of corrosive philistines, reactionaries, anti-Communists, and America Firsters – a nest of spies. Bellamy would be a good corrective.

True, he was a little unpredictable. He had been something of a prodigy; he had published while still very young and had attracted the notice of the really eminent – Robert Frost and Eliot and Pound. He had gained laureate status while still in his forties. Now, at sixty-three, and nearly always in the public eye – 'the most visible poet since Yeats' he had been called – he qualified as a bard. He was a complicated man – confused, vain, too many sleeping pills, too much wine – but he wrote like an angel. I was sure of it. I could never understand why no one remembered the lines of his poems – I don't know why I was unable to recall a single line. But, then, who can quote Ezra Pound?

When the reading – this Poetry Night – was over, Bellamy walked off the stage and was mobbed by people asking for autographs. I noticed that few people addressed him directly. They stood shyly, offering him his books, which were open to the flyleaf. He signed them without saying a word. The group around him was reverential. Out of politeness – but it might have been fear – they kept their distance and even averted their eyes as, not speaking, Bellamy scrawled his name in various editions of his books. When he was finished he saw me.

Our height was all the introduction we required. Tall people often find themselves talking to perfect strangers, merely because the stranger is also tall. Tallness is like a special racial attribute.

Bellamy spoke over the heads of his admirers: 'I think we've met before.'

'At an American Embassy reception,' I said. 'Months ago.'

'Yes,' he said and came over and shook my hand. 'I remember you well.'

His eyes were unsteady and his hair had the look of having been combed by someone other than himself. In his wincing, round-shouldered way he seemed wounded or drunk, but he was more likely just very tired after two solid hours on the stage.

'How is your wife?' he said.

'I think you have someone else in mind,' I said. 'I'm not married. I'm the man from Boston. Excuse me, that didn't sound right!'

Bellamy said, 'Is she still writing poems?'

He had not heard me, and he had mistaken me for Vic Scaduto, whose wife wrote poems – or at least she said she did.

'Not married,' I said, shaking my head.

'So am I,' he said. 'I was just leaving – why don't you come along?'

His tone was neutral, but this was the strangest thing about Bellamy. At a distance he was very friendly, but the closer you got to him the cooler he became. Giving a lecture or a reading, Bellamy had a very warm intimate tone; in public he was relaxed; but face to face, like this, he was deaf and almost completely indifferent. This I am sure will be news to many of his fans.

I followed him outside, not certain that I was really wanted.

He said, 'Have you eaten?'

'No.' But I was not particularly hungry. 'I don't want to intrude. We can meet some other time. You must be tired after your reading.'

'Time to eat,' he said. He waved a taxi toward us. 'You haven't eaten. You may as well come along. After you.'

It was off-hand, as plainly spoken as I have written it, not really an invitation but rather a nod to the inevitable. We rode in silence for a while.

I said, 'I don't feel right about this.'

'It's dinnertime,' Bellamy said. 'Too bad about your wife.'

The wife-business had taken hold of him, but I had no idea what he was imagining. It seemed a ludicrous trip in this taxi, for the fact was that I did not want to go with him, and he probably did not want me along either – and yet here we were on our way to a restaurant. I wasn't even hungry!

It was Wilton's in Bury Street – expensive, English, dark brown, and joyless. Emma, Bellamy's wife – the third – was waiting for him at the table inside the restaurant. With her were the Poulters, man and wife. I recognized the name instantly.

'Like the mustard?' I asked.

Poulter's English Mustard had a green and yellow label, and an unforgettable royal warrant: *By Appointment to HM Queen Elizabeth the Queen Mother*, with her gold crest. I often stared at this label and tried to imagine the Queen Mother painting Poulter's mustard on a royal sausage.

Mr Poulter said, 'I *am* the mustard.'

It was clear, from the way Poulter had stood up and shown Walter Van Bellamy his chair and called the waiter over for a fresh drinks order, that he was the host. Poulter was paying. I had no business there.

Bellamy said, 'For God's sake, sit down!'

But they were one chair short. They had not expected me.

Poulter was tactful. He urged me to take his chair. This proved embarrassing. I sat and left Mr Poulter, the host, standing. Every other diner in the restaurant was seated. I quickly stood up again and offered him my seat.

Bellamy turned his back on us. He was drinking wine and – his hand shook badly – spilling it.

Mrs Poulter's hair arrangement was bright mahogany and so shiny and stiff it looked shellacked. She became suddenly flustered and said, 'There seems to be something wrong. There are too many people. Norman, there's one too many!'

And Mr Poulter said, 'No, no. Our friend here' – he beckoned a waiter over – 'will get us another chair.'

The table in the cubbyhole was still set for four, and, worse, it was designed for four, so throughout the meal the discomfort reminded me that Bellamy had had no right to bring me there and make me an unwelcome guest.

Bellamy did not explain my presence to the Poulters. For a time he spoke to the waiter, who did nothing but listen and agree ('That needs saying, sir!'). Emma spoke to Norman Poulter about the treachery of postmen, and I spoke to Mrs Poulter about the weather in Indonesia.

The table jolted – Bellamy was shifting position. He stared at me and said, 'Learn of the green world what can be thy place.'

'I suppose that's good advice,' I said.

'Pull down thy vanity,' he said.

'Excuse me?'

'But to have done instead of not doing,' he said. 'This is not vanity.'

'No –'

'Here, error is all in the not done,' he said, 'all in the diffidence that faltered.'

The others, hearing this, had fallen silent and were watching me. Bellamy was smiling broadly.

'Ezra,' he said.

He was quoting Pound!

At eleven o'clock Bellamy stood up and took Emma by the arm and said, 'We have to go. We're in the country these days and our last train leaves in half an hour.'

I stayed uneasily with the Poulters.

Mrs Poulter said, 'Bingo's going through rather a bad patch.'

'Bingo?'

'Walter Bellamy, of course.' She had lipstick flecks on her teeth. 'Do you mean to say you're a friend of his and you don't even know his name?'

That was as far as I had got with Bellamy, which annoyed me, because I still admired him and we still needed him. A month later we had a request from our Binational Center, Amerikahaus in Berlin, asking whether Bellamy would be available to represent the United States in a seminar called 'Writing East and West.' Everett Horton, our number two, told me to take care of it.

I called his house in Kent. A housekeeper answered and said he was in London. I called the Eaton Square number. A tetchy voice said I could not speak to him.

'It's very important,' I said.

'He is very ill.' Was this Emma? 'In any case, he is not here.'

'May I ask where I can get in touch with him?'

'I am not obliged to answer your questions!'

The phone was slammed down.

There were two more cables from Berlin, demanding Bellamy. My secretary tried but failed to discover Bellamy's whereabouts. There was another cable, and then I went to Scaduto. He was the cultural affairs officer, I said; surely it was his job to deal with Bellamy, the literary man, the poet –

'A binational seminar in West Berlin, with writers from both sides of the Iron Curtain, and you call it literary?' He laughed at me.

'"Writing East and West" – that's what it's called.'

'Guys from East Germany,' he said. 'You call them writers?' He tap-danced for a moment, then said, 'Face it – it's political. That's why we need Bellamy to represent us. The Ambassador's going to be there! Bellamy's got the right profile – he's old, experienced, liberal, well known, active in political protest. Did you know he was arrested in 'sixty-five on a peace march in Washington? Do you have any idea what that buys in terms of credibility with these so-called Marxist writers? Plus, he's well connected, lovely wife, and he wears these terrific suits.'

'And he's sick,' I said.

'So you say,' Scaduto said. 'It might just be a story – famous men often have people around to protect them. "He's sick" – it might be a euphemism for "Take a hike" or "Don't bother him."'

It was then that I remembered the Poulters and that awkward dinner at Wilton's. I found 'Poulter's Mustard Ltd' in the phone book and called the main office. My telephone technique, to reassure people, was to call very early in the morning and leave the Embassy number and my name. They always called back: a call from the American Embassy always seemed important. Poulter was prompter than most. Yes, he remembered me.

I said, 'I know Bingo's very ill. I wonder whether you can tell me where he is – I have something to give him.'

'Doesn't he usually go to the Abbey?' Mr Poulter said.

'In London?'

'Yes,' he said, 'that clinic on the other side of the river.' *Other side* in London always meant south.

I said, 'I wasn't sure, but I can check.'

'I try to avoid the Abbey,' Poulter said. 'I've never liked those places. And anyway, Bingo will be out soon. He never stops long.'

By then, it was too late to ask what was wrong with Bellamy.

'Berlin is still waiting for a reply on that Bellamy request,' Horton said, just before I went home.

I said, 'I feel as if I've been looking for Bellamy my whole life.'

'Then it's about time you found him.'

Back home at my apartment in Overstrand Mansions, I looked up the Abbey in the phone book and discovered that it was not far from me. Its address was Spencer Park, on the 77 bus route in Wandsworth.

I switched off all the lights so that I could think, and sitting in the darkness I reflected on the fact that what I had told Horton was true: I had been aware of Walter Van Bellamy, and seeking him, since my schooldays. Then, to impress us, my English teacher, Mr Bagley, showed us Bellamy's first book of poems and the jacket flap that said: ... *attended Boston Latin School*. We were very proud of Bellamy and, because of him, were proud of ourselves. It seemed possible that we could do what he had done. For me, he was more than a fellow townsman – he was, in fact, like my alter ego; and here we both were in London, not exactly exiles but with certain likenesses and affinities.

I knew no more about him than what I have written here. Some people regarded him as one of the greatest living writers, but my image of him was indistinct – from hearsay and books, from the reception at Horton's, the reading, the terrible dinner at Wilton's. I could not say what he was really like. What was at the heart of my quandary was the suspicion that Walter Van Bellamy was a little like me.

The best news was that this private hospital – its name, the Abbey, said everything – was nearby. It was three miles at most, a fifteen-minute bus ride. I called and was told that Bellamy was indeed a patient, that he could receive visitors, and that visiting hours were not over until nine o'clock. It was now seven-thirty.

I resolved to visit him that night. On the bus, I was amazed at my audacity: here I was visiting one of the most famous American poets. I wondered if I could bring it off. It was like anticipating a hard interview. Would I measure up, and could I get him to agree to the Berlin request? I did not know much about him, but I knew he was human. At the time, I was naive enough to find that a consolation.

The Abbey was a Victorian house behind a wall, with a tower to one side. Its tall church windows were heavily leaded. A mock Gothic villa, its rear garden was part of a private park – the most inaccessible park in London – and its Frankenstein-movie façade faced Wandsworth Common, many chestnut trees, and a row of bent-over hawthorns. Its sign, in old script, was well lighted, but the building itself was in darkness – the curtains were drawn, and it was impossible to get a glimpse of anything going on inside. When I rang the bell and entered I saw that it was a very deep house. Ahead of me, past the reception desk, was a long corridor.

A nurse took swift squeaky rubber-soled steps toward me, but before I could identify myself I heard a sudden yakking and the rattle of what was almost certainly lunatic laughter.

'Sorry about that,' the nurse said. 'Are you here to see one of the guests?'

'Mr Bellamy,' I said; and I thought: *Guests?*

'Is he expecting you?'

My first impulse was to lie and say yes. But I shook my head and said that I had not had time to get in touch with Mr Bellamy on the phone.

The nurse said, 'He can't use the phone.'

'Is he that bad?'

'No, no. He'd be on the phone all day, talking nineteen to the dozen, if we let him. But we have instructions from the family. He's not allowed to use the phone.'

'Poor fellow.'

'They're afraid of what he'll do.' She smiled at me.

'What *will* he do?'

'I mean, say.' She smiled again. 'He never gets any visitors.'

'Is it contagious?'

'Being manic?' She nodded with real conviction and said, 'It may sound silly but I honestly think it is. Crazy families! If you promise not to excite him you can see him. But don't stay too long. Have you been here before?'

I said no and she told me to follow her. Bellamy's room was on the top floor. The nurse knocked, there was a grunt from inside the room, and she left me there to go in on my own.

Bellamy lay on the bed. He was fully clothed – over-dressed if anything – wearing a jacket and turtleneck sweater and tweed trousers and thick socks. The room was small and hot and brightly lit and smelled of cough remedies: Bellamy also had a cold. On a chair there were books – three were Bellamy's own, including his *Poems New and Selected*. He was reading a small black Bible.

He glanced up. It was a glance I recognized: his nod to the inevitable – not friendly, not hostile. But he was drugged – his lips were puffy and inexpressive, his eyes sleepy-looking.

He said, 'Read that,' and handed me the Bible, where a passage was circled in pencil. 'Read it out loud.'

'"I have digged and drunk strange waters, and with the soles of my feet have I dried up all the rivers of besieged places."' I gave the Bible back to him. Its leather cover was unpleasantly warm where he had been holding it.

'What does it mean?' he said.

I shrugged, and already I felt as if I had failed the interview.

'It's a poem,' Bellamy said. 'It's my poem.'

He tore the Bible page out and opened his mouth to smile. I thought he was going to eat the page. He crushed it into his pocket.

'How do you feel?' I asked.

'I don't sleep.'

'Can't they give you something?'

'That's not it,' he said in a drowsy voice. 'I haven't got time to sleep. Too much work to do. Look.' He picked up a book and said, 'Are you the tax man?'

On the bus I had thought: *Will I measure up? Am I bright enough?* The anticipation hurt my nerves. I imagined certain questions. But I had not expected this. I felt sorry for him.

I said, 'I'm from the Embassy. I have a message for you.'

'I've been getting messages for weeks. Taking them down. I don't want any more messages.' He showed me the book again, and again he said, 'Look.'

It was *Poems New and Selected*. He flipped the pages. I saw blue ink, a blue scrawl, poems scribbled over and smudged, balloons with words in them, and arrows, and asterisks. You see a person's bad handwriting and you get frightened or sad. It was the sort of book that students kept, full of underlinings and annotations and crossings-out. Now Bellamy was holding it open to a particular page. I could see that he had crossed out nearly all the lines in that poem and had rewritten them. I couldn't judge how good the new lines were – they were scarcely legible. The exclamation marks did not make me hopeful.

'You're rewriting your poems.'

'Improving them,' he said. 'I'm getting messages.'

'But these poems have already been printed,' I said.

'Full of mistakes.' His eyes brightened. He looked desperate, as if he had been tricked and trapped and could escape only through this great labor of rewriting. He looked at his hands. There were ink stains on them that brought his wrinkles into relief. He motioned to the other books, opened one – it was *Londoners*. It was a mass of blue ballpoint. The handwriting was wobbly and childish and actually frightening to look at. It indicated disorder and mania and big blue obsession: 'And these.'

His head lay to one side, on his shoulder, as if he were trying to read upside-down writing. But when he shut the book his head didn't move.

He said, 'The names of racehorses – they aren't names. They're numbers. Word-numbers. Meaningless.'

I said, 'I had never thought of that.'

'It's true. A Jew thought it up, the names, to confuse people. You can make a lot of money if you know how to confuse people.'

'How do you know it was a Jew?' I said.

'Because the Jews have all the money,' he said. 'What's wrong with you? Sit down.'

I was standing at the foot of his bed. I said, 'I can't stay. I just wanted to make sure you're all right.'

'I'm not all right,' Bellamy said. 'Didn't anyone tell you?'

'You should write some new poems – not rewrite the old ones,' I said, eager to change the subject.

'If your car was rusty, would you paint it or sell it?' he asked.

'I guess I'd fix it,' I said.

'A Jew would sell it,' he said. 'But I'm not selling these rusty poems. I'm fixing them.'

I wanted most of all to open a window. It was stuffy in here – and the smell of Vicks and old socks and last week's apples made it stuffier. I looked out through the window bars and saw a blackness: Spencer Park. I sat down.

Bellamy said, 'Tell them I'll have this book fixed pretty soon, and then I'll leave this place.'

'Whom shall I tell?'

'The rest of them,' he said. 'Roger, Philippa, all the Howletts.'

Now I was certain that I wanted to leave. He thought I was his publisher. It was a charade – and pathetic. He had no idea who I was. It was unfair and tormenting for him if I stayed longer.

'Here's one,' he said. He took up a piece of paper and cleared his throat. 'They were naked at last and had no pockets to pick.' He smiled. He said, 'The Jews.'

I stood up.

'They knew they had to be purified, an angel gave them the news.' He smiled as before. 'The Jews.'

I said, 'I get the point.'

'Their shoes –'

I could not stop him. He read on. It was a short poem, but it was poisonous, as clumsy as the scribble it was written in. It was demented, it was awful, it was wrong. And the next one he tried to read was an attempt at comedy. Anti-Jewish feeling nearly always tries to pass itself off as humor, because there is a kind of easy freemasonry in anti-Semitism – the nudge, the shared joke. And it is worse because it is completely fearless hatred mimicking sanity as it mocks its victims.

I was glad for the knock on the door as he started poem three: 'The Jewnighted States.' The door opened.

'Hello, Walter,' the man said. 'Have you taken your pill?'

Bellamy reached for the pill and put it into his mouth and drank his water. Doing this, he became childish again – the way he pulled a face and had a hard time swallowing, the way he gulped his water and wiped his mouth with the back of his hand, the way he drooled and sat forward, working his jaw.

'May I see you for a minute?' the man said to me, and led me into the corridor. 'I'm Doctor Chapman. Are you a friend of Walter's? Family?'

'Not really, no,' I said. 'Just an interested party.'

'Pity. He's doing marvelously well. But he'd do a great deal better if he got more visitors. I'm thinking of releasing him. He needs company.'

'He says some rather wild things. Racehorses. Jews. And he's rewriting his poems. I think he's crazy.'

The doctor smiled at me. 'That's not a word we use here.'

'You use all the others – why not that one?' I said. 'And Bellamy's in there babbling about the beauties of Auschwitz. Why don't you tell him there are certain words, certain ideas –'

The doctor was still smiling. It was a Bellamy smile, of a kind – impatient, patronizing, humorless. He said, 'A famous Jewish writer once said, "All men are Jews," meaning all men are victims.

It's not true, you know. The opposite is closer to the truth. All men are Nazis, really. I mean, if all men are anything, which of course they're not. What a depressing subject! But I'm keeping you from Walter. Sorry. I just wanted to find out if you were close to him.'

'I'm from the Embassy,' I said. 'We try to keep an eye on our citizens, even if they are determined to be exiles.'

'He's that, all right. Exile – it's a good word for his condition.'

I did not re-enter Bellamy's room. I did not stay. He had no idea who I was. I took a bus home and drafted a cable to Berlin, which I sent the next day, explaining that Walter Van Bellamy could not attend this seminar, or any other.

And of course, for months afterward, whenever I saw a book of Bellamy's or a newly published poem, I searched it for signs of madness or Jew-baiting or plain stupidity. But there was nothing, nothing, nothing. His poems were serene and unmemorable; they never touched these subjects; and afterward, when I couldn't remember them, they frightened me.

Tomb with a View

'There's another woman to see you,' my secretary said, giving me an old-fashioned look on 'another.'

It had been a bad morning – I knew she was thinking about Mr Fleamarsh's ashes. Mrs Fleamarsh had come in a few days before. Her husband had complained of chest pains on the train to Salisbury, missed the cathedral, collapsed on the bus, and died at Stonehenge. She insisted on having him cremated so that she could carry him in her handbag. Is there a more presumptuous statement than 'He would have wanted it this way'? Accompanying his coffin back to Baltimore would have meant her missing the tour of the Lake District, and Stratford was tomorrow. Mrs Fleamarsh gave me to understand that a whole unburned adult human corpse was a terribly inconvenient thing. 'He bowled a lot,' she said, as if this was all the explanation I needed. And even more obscurely, 'He always had one of those shiny blue jackets.'

I arranged for the cremation, but as Mrs Fleamarsh was in Stratford, the ashes were delivered to me at the Embassy. The urn, the size and shape of a white crock of Gentleman's Relish, stood on my desk for most of the afternoon. And it put me in the mood for what happened later that day, though I would willingly have missed it all – Mrs Fleamarsh, the ashes of her husband, and Miss Gowrie and her dark lodger.

Miss Gowrie, the other woman – she had watery eyes and a wind-reddened face – introduced herself as a friend of Sir Charles Smallwood, whom I dimly remembered having met at Horton's reception. Miss Gowrie, I guessed, was nearing seventy. She sat down and planted both her feet on the carpet to steady herself and she began squashing her handbag in her lap.

She said, 'I'm afraid I have rather a shocking story to tell you. I mentioned it to Charlie' – this was the way she referred to Sir Charles Smallwood – 'and he said I should come straight to you.'

I thought she was a bit drunk or having trouble with her dentures. In fact, she was straining to speak in a dignified way – she was fighting her cockney accent, and losing. She had a voice of astounding monotony.

I said, 'Go on.'

'Well' – *wayew* – 'it's about my lodger then, isn't it?'

She looked around the office; she peered at the walls; she spoke again. She was one of those people who seem, in the way they whisper and squint, to be addressing eavesdroppers.

'Mind you, I'm not really a landlady in the normal way. It's just that I live in Mortlake and the Council put up me rates, didn't they? Practically doubled them. I had to take in lodgers to pay the additional. That's Mr Wubb. Colored.'

'What color, Miss Gowrie?'

'There's only one color,' she said. 'Black. One of yours.'

I tried to convey, with silence and cold eyes, that I did not like this at all.

'And that's why I'm here,' she said.

'Because your lodger is black?'

'Because he's a thief.' *Feef* was what Miss Gowrie said.

'British?'

'Of course not.'

'Before you go any further, I think I should remind you that this is the American Embassy,' I said. 'Properly speaking, if you have a problem with your lodger you should go to the police.'

'He's one of yours,' she repeated. 'American. And he's driving me mental. It's not fair!'

'How do you know he's a thief?'

'He keeps the rubbish under his bed, don't he?'

'Rubbish?'

'Rubbish is what he steals – pots and pans and that. He's driving me mental.'

As she spoke, I resolved to check the man's citizenship. I didn't like Miss Gowrie's manner. She behaved as if she were holding me responsible for this thieving lodger. I hoped I could get rid of her without becoming involved in her problem. I had had enough that day, dealing with the ashes of Herbert Fleamarsh. The worst problems in any office arise at roughly four in the afternoon. It was four-ten, and I wished that I had gone home early.

'Mr Wubb has no right whatsoever to come here and steal from people. Some college student! I suppose he's studying how to steal. Why don't he stay in his own country and steal?'

'That's a good question,' I said, picking up the telephone. 'Let's see if the police have an answer to it.'

'Oh, please, sir!' she said, and her fear brought forth a terrible tone of respectfulness, almost of groveling. She looked suddenly frightened and small, and I felt genuinely sorry for her. 'Please don't tell them. It would be in all the papers. There'd be talk. It would kill me.'

'That you had a dishonest lodger?'

'That I had a flaming lodger at all,' she said. 'I don't want the rest of them to know.'

'The rest?'

'The street,' she said. 'They don't take lodgers, certainly not black ones. They're awfully decent.'

She was asking me to agree with her. I said nothing.

'He's one of yours,' she said. 'You'll know what to do.'

But he wasn't, and I didn't.

It seemed no business of ours, this light-fingered lodger who might or might not have been an American. I checked the files. There was no one named Wubb registered with the Embassy – but not every American registered, and would a thief? Miss Gowrie telephoned me the next afternoon. She was desperate, and I had a free evening: the combination often ends badly. But I liked the idea of going upriver to Mortlake, so I visited her, just to look around, and perhaps to find excuses for my curiosity.

'He's rearranged all his furniture, hasn't he?' Miss Gowrie said, letting me into the tall gloomy house. It was just off the Mortlake Road, which ran along the river, and the river could be seen – we were mounting the steps to the lodger's room – from Miss Gowrie's upper windows. On this wet black afternoon the river's dampness seemed to penetrate every brick of the house, and the trees dripped gray water from the tips of their bony branches. 'In his room,' she said. 'He's moved everything, every stick.'

She threw his door open, releasing mingled smells, sweet and sour. Miss Gowrie saw me sniffing.

'He does all his own cooking,' she said. 'That pong is all his. It hums sometimes.'

I looked around the room and then turned to Miss Gowrie and said, 'Tell me, does your lodger have a small bump or bruise – a little swelling, say – right here on his upper forehead?'

'Yes – you've *seen* him!' she cried.

'Does he often wake you up in the middle of the night, padding around?'

'All the time! Gives me a fright sometimes. How do you know about his bruise –'

'And have you noticed that he cooks at night – only at night – not during the day?'

'Yes!' she said and clawed her hair straight.

'Your lodger is a very devout Muslim,' I said.

'Musselman?' she said, saying it like 'muscle-man,' and frowning. 'I don't know about that. And as for devout –'

'Oh, yes,' I said. 'Muslim certainly, because he rearranged the furniture so that he could face Mecca – over there –'

Miss Gowrie peered in the direction of Mecca and, seeing only Barnes Common, made a face.

'– and taken down those pictures,' I said, examining a pair of framed prints stacked to face the wall: two busty ladies in black lace. 'They hate pictures of human beings.'

'Spanish,' Miss Gowrie said. 'They're the same as blacks!'

'Here's his prayer mat,' I said. 'And he must be devout because he has a prayer bump on his forehead. The bruise – you've seen it. Also, if he wakes you up at night, he must be saying his prayers five times a day. They bump their heads when they pray.'

'He might not be praying – he might be cooking.'

'Of course. Because this is the Muslim period of Ramadhan. It's like Lent, and it goes on until the end of next month. He can't eat or drink anything until sundown. That's why he eats at, ah' – I had seen a small valise under the bed, and its luggage tag – 'Abdul Wahab Bin Baz. That explains it.'

Instead of looking relieved, Miss Gowrie had become progressively worried by the information I had given her. And then she said, 'Ain't you glad you come over?'

'Miss Gowrie, he's not one of ours,' I said.

'He's black,' she said.

'Arab.' The Saudia Airlines luggage tag said everything: he was a Wahabi; he had flown from Mecca to London. A fanatical traveler?

'Don't split hairs,' she said, and flung herself at me. She grasped my arm and exhaled the smell of bread and fish paste.

'You know these people and their funny ways. You can help me.

You're the only one who can. The police don't know about prayer bumps and eating after sundown, do they?'

Instead of agreeing, I asked her where her lodger was.

'College,' she said. 'It's a sort of night school. He goes out about six and comes back at nine. That's when he starts eating.'

'And praying, presumably.'

'I wouldn't know about that,' Miss Gowrie said. 'During the day he just frowsts in here. Studies and that. He's a great reader. Mad about history. That's what he told me. That's all he told me.'

'How long has he lived with you?'

'Two weeks. I only discovered he was pinching things two days ago. He must have been at it all last week. I thought, then, out you go! But I reckoned he might be dangerous, him being a thief. That's why I called Charlie Smallwood, and he give me your name. You'd know what to do – that's what he told me. Only I wish you'd do it.'

'Let's have a look at his loot,' I said.

Miss Gowrie got slowly to her knees, saying, 'I used to have a proper charlady – I used to have staff,' and went on to say that she had discovered her lodger's thievery while she was cleaning out his room. It was under the bed, in a couple of cardboard boxes. She brought out the boxes, spitting with effort as she did so, and showed me the oddest collection of stolen goods I had ever seen.

There were two brass incense burners, properly called thuribles – they could have been a hundred years old. There was a brass lamp of Oriental design and a pair of brass candlesticks. There was a metal crucifix and, lastly, a string of about twenty bells – round ones, about the size of golf balls, with a slit in each one. I had never seen any bells like this. Everything was thick with dust and coated with a kind of sour damp rind, as if it had lain on the floor of an underground cave. 'You think it's junk,' Miss Gowrie said, 'then you look closer and you realize it might be valuable. A little Brasso and a dry rag – come up a treat. But if you get very close, it looks like junk again, and that's what it is. So why go to the police? All they're going to do is laugh and say, "Steady on, love." They won't treat it as a serious matter. But they don't have to live here, do they?'

'Maybe it's not serious,' I said.

'You're joking,' she said. 'This is diabolical. You don't get this in shops or houses. This ain't the kind of thing that fell off the back of a lorry. Go on, touch it.'

I took one of the bells and shook it. It had a dull sound and no vibration – about as musical as a pebble hitting a coffin.

'Creepy, isn't it? Like from a church. I tell you, some of this stuff gives me the collywobbles, don't it?'

I knew what she meant. They weren't the sorts of things that anyone would steal, and yet where could you buy them? So they had to be stolen, probably from a church, from a derelict altar – a Muslim fanatic might do that. But what about those little round bells?

It was too late to do anything that day. I left Miss Gowrie with a promise that I would try to get to the bottom of it, and the next morning, with the aid of a good map, made a list of all the churches near her Mortlake house. There were seven. My secretary phoned each one and asked whether anything had been stolen from them. All had been burgled, but not within the previous two weeks. We tried a dozen more nearby churches: no luck.

I was still not satisfied, and so, that same afternoon, I went to the three churches nearest Miss Gowrie's. The Anglican church and Methodist chapel were both securely locked, but the Catholic church was open. I walked through it and into the deep grass of the churchyard.

'Can I help you?' It was a man with a broom, probably the caretaker, but he was suspicious of me and held his broom with the handle forward, like a weapon.

'Hello,' I said brightly, to calm him. 'Are you missing anything from the church – anything stolen? I'm thinking of things like candlesticks or crucifixes.'

'Not that I know of,' he said, and yet he had an undecided look. He wanted to say more – he had something on his mind.

I said, 'You're very lucky then,' to give him an opening.

'Not really,' he said. 'We've lost most of our outside lights – vandals. They broke every blooming one of them.'

He showed me that all the floodlights in the churchyard had been broken, and as it was also a graveyard, the effect on this gray afternoon was somber, a sort of bleak and muffled violence.

'I'm amazed they could have broken lights that high,' I said. The spotlights were attached to the eaves of the church, thirty feet up.

'They're savages,' he said. 'They use pellets, slingshots, blow-pipes.'

'Did you see them do it?'

'No, and I'll tell you something else,' he said. 'I've worked here at St Mary Magdalene's for twenty-two years, and it's the first time this has happened. The past two weeks have been terrible. Broken glass everywhere. It's so dark at night!'

'Two weeks?' I said, and thought of Mr Wahab.

'The first week was shocking. But this week hasn't been so bad. There's no more lights to break!' He looked at me in a disgusted way and said, 'You're an American, aren't you?'

I told him I was.

'You're used to this sort of thing – vandals, queue-jumpers, lawbreakers. But this isn't New York or Chicago. This is the quietest part of London. People behave themselves here. At least, they used to.'

We stood in darkness, because of the smashed lights. But this was the early daytime dark of November; it was not yet five o'clock. I decided to stop by the Embassy before I went home.

I was at my desk, wondering whether to call Miss Gowrie to tell her I had found out nothing, when my colleague Vic Scaduto appeared. Seeing me examining one of those strange round bells that the lodger had stolen, Scaduto said, 'You've got the craziest things in your office. Last time I was here there was a funeral urn with a tourist's ashes in your pending tray. And now you're playing with a camel bell!'

'How do you know that's a camel bell?'

'Used to see them in India. Place is full of camels. My kids bought bells like that at the bazaar. They're sort of ceremonial – they loop strings of them around a camel's neck.'

I said, 'Can you think of any reason why you might find a camel bell like this in an English church?'

'I love it!' he said, and left my office, snickering.

Just before I went home, the phone rang. It was Miss Gowrie.

'Can you come over straightaway?' she breathed. 'He's just gone out.'

'Is there anything wrong?'

She said, 'There's another parcel, isn't there? He brought it back last night, then, didn't he? The dirty devil!'

'Don't open it. Don't touch it. I'll be right over.'

She was waiting for me by the door, her hands knotted in her apron. She told me to hurry, and started upstairs. Twice she called him a *dir'ee devoo* – 'And he might be back any minute.'

Mr Wahab's room was the same as before – very neat, the prayer mat facing Barnes Common and Mecca, a slight aroma of stale spice in the air, the pictures turned to the wall. After Miss Gowrie unlocked it, she stepped into the hallway to stand sentry duty while I opened the parcel under the bed. It was a pillowcase, its top twisted and held fast with a length of wire. It gave off the same dusty underground odor as the candlesticks and the crucifix and the camel bells. It seemed to contain sticks of wood and broken pottery wrapped in newspaper. I removed them and saw at once that they were bones – old, yellow, spongy, woody bones – and the cracked bowl of a skull and a jawbone and a number of loose human teeth.

'More of the same,' I said so as not to frighten her. And I wrapped them and returned them to the innocent-looking pillowcase.

'You'll help me, won't you?'

'I'll do my best,' I said.

I was relieved that she had not seen the contents of that new parcel, for I had always considered myself as being fairly unshockable, and yet when I thought of those yellow bones and teeth and incense burners and camel bells under the bed of the Arab in that wet suburb of London, I got the shudders.

It was no longer a trivial, speculative matter about a troublesome lodger. The man from Mecca was, quite simply, a grave robber. Mr Wahab was a ghoul. Why hadn't I thought of it before? Though they looked like ecclesiastical items, they could not have come from a church. But tombs, especially the larger ones, were often a kind of underground chapel, and had an altar furnished with candlesticks, and an incense burner and crucifix.

It was almost certainly a Catholic tomb – the crucifix said that. An old tomb – this stuff had lain undisturbed for a century. A large tomb, big enough to hold an altar, and one that could be entered through a door; if there had been digging, it would have been seen and reported. The tomb was probably above ground. But what sort of a tomb contained camel bells?

This part of London was full of cemeteries – we had cremated

Herbert Fleamarsh in nearby Kew. There were five important cemeteries not far from Miss Gowrie's house, and every church had a walled-in graveyard beside it. But only one of those churches interested me: it struck me that a grave robber needed darkness to hide him, and if he did not have it he might break the sort of lights I had seen smashed at St Mary Magdalene's. But no theft had been reported there.

I did not want to see the caretaker again. He would wonder why I was back; he would be suspicious; he would ask awkward questions. I had no answers. So I let a day pass, and then I waited for the five o'clock darkness, and I entered the churchyard of St Mary's wearing a black coat and black gloves and looking left and right. I crept toward the vaults, the flat-topped granite huts with iron doors or sealed with stone blocks. They were unmarked; they were sadly neglected and overgrown with high bushes. Some were hidden in grass; others had almost burst from the ground or been yanked aside by the roots of the trees. I was behind the church and fighting my way through a tangle of bushes when I saw the tent.

It was a sort of Oriental tent, perhaps Arab, with a slanting roof and high steep sides flowing from neatly scalloped eaves. I thought for a moment that I had stumbled upon a group of campers – people often pitched tents by the roadside or in parks (I could see them from the windows of my flat in Battersea) – why not in this graveyard?

But the tent was made of stone. It was white granite or marble, with carved folds, and it bore a tablet with the legend *Captain Sir Richard F. Burton.* The explorer's tomb was the strangest I had ever seen.

I went close and tried the door. The putty surrounding the door, a marble slab, had been dug away. But a padlock on a rusty hasp remained. I shook the padlock, and it came apart in my hand: it had been sawed through. So he had broken it – I was sure that this was the work of Abdul Wahab Bin Baz. A poem was chiseled into the marble just above the door. I turned my small flashlight on it.

> *Farewell, dear friend, dead hero, the great life*
> *Is ended, the great perils, the great joys;*
> *And he to whom adventures were as toys,*
> *Who seemed to bear a charm 'gainst spear or knife*
> *Or bullet, now lies silent . . .*

What was that? A sound from the churchyard gate.

Crouching, I ran around to the back of the vault. It was not easy – trees grew close to it, and I scratched my face on a branch as I squeezed through.

At the rear of the tomb, overgrown with bushes and partly hidden by the thickness of black branches, was an iron ladder. It was fixed to the stone; it rose to the top of the tentlike roof. More to hide from the caretaker than to see where the ladder went, I climbed the iron rungs, and when I could not go any farther I looked down in amazement. I was looking straight into the chamber of the tomb.

This tomb, this stone tent, had a window! It was of thick glass and I could see in the narrow beam of my flashlight that it had not been tampered with. But I knew at a glance that the tomb had been plundered. A century of sunlight through this window had faded the stone walls in places and also printed on them the shadows of the objects I had seen in the Arab's room – the lamps, the crucifix, the string of camel bells. Where a thurible had been plucked from the dust, a disk mark remained, of its oval base. Only these shadows were left of what had once been in the tomb, except for the two coffins. They lay on the floor, at either side of a row of footprints. The larger coffin had been opened. Its lid, a fraction lopsided, had a freshly yanked nail at its end and showed a seam of darkness. But if I had not already seen Burton's bones, if I had not tried the lock that seemed so secure, I doubt that I would have noticed that the coffin lid was ajar or suspected any tampering. Even under the penetrating light of my pocket flashlight the tomb was very murky, and only serious scrutiny told me that it had been broken into. It was a terrible little coffin room; it was dusty; it was cell-like. It gave me a good idea.

The Arab, Abdul Wahab Bin Baz, had to be stopped. Now I knew how.

It was no more than a short stroll, using the footbridge over the railway tracks, to a row of shops. In one of these, with a sign saying IRONMONGERS, I bought a large, flat padlock. It was very similar to the one the fanatic from Mecca had cut through in order to enter Burton's tomb.

It was now well after six. The church was shut, the gate was locked. I scaled the brick wall of the churchyard and took up my position at the top of the ladder, where I rested against the slanting window of the tomb. I was completely hidden; the graveyard was as dark as the bottom of a deep hole. In a doggedly destructive way, by breaking all the churchyard lights, the Arab had guaranteed that I would not be seen.

I thought: *What if he doesn't come back?*

And yet, Isabel Burton's coffin had not been disturbed.

Later than I expected, after seven, when my knees were about to give out, I heard the thump of feet in the churchyard – someone had come over the wall. There was a swishing sound, of legs moving in brambles and grass. If it was Abdul, and if he entered the tomb, I would see him through the window. I heard nothing for a while, and then there was a slow millstone sound – the marble door being swung open. When he entered the tomb, I ducked, and I did not move again until, some seconds later, I heard the door being eased shut.

It was not closed entirely. I climbed down the ladder and dashed to the front of the tomb and kicked the door. At that moment there was a cry from the vault, but I was quickly straightening the hasp and clapping the padlock on. There was no sound from inside. The Arab was sealed in. No one would hear him. He had asked for this – and now he was buried alive.

If you knew he was there and you listened carefully you could hear a faint mewing, which was all that was audible of his wild screams through the thick marble walls of the tomb.

'I thought it was *him*,' Miss Gowrie said, opening the door and with a look of apprehension still on her face. Fright takes a while to fade.

'He won't be back tonight,' I said. 'He may not be back at all.'

'He's out haunting houses, I expect.'

'Not exactly.'

'You come in and have a nice cup of tea,' Miss Gowrie said. 'Put your feet up. Look at the time! It's gone eight – you've had a long day.'

My day was not over. I told Miss Gowrie I had discovered where Wahab had stolen his brassware. I gathered up the objects and put them into a sack. I would return them to their rightful place, I said.

'May I sleep in Mr Wubb's room tonight?' I said.

'What if he comes back?'

'Not a chance,' I said.

'You never know with blackies,' she said.

In his stale bed, in that small room that smelled of carpet dust and prayer sweat, I thought about Abdul Wahab and it occurred to me why he had broken into Burton's tomb. It was simple revenge. Hadn't Burton, the unbeliever, trampled all over Islam? In this Muslim's eyes, hadn't the English explorer violated the sanctity of his religion by dressing up as an Arab and entering Mecca? Burton was no respecter of taboos or traditions – he had plundered the secrets of Islam in his search for adventure.

This was one Muslim's reply: the Arab dressed as an English gentleman, prowling undetected in London – as anonymous as Burton had been in holy Mecca. There was a crude justice in what the disguised Arab had done to Burton's bones in the Mortlake churchyard. This was a civilized country and a different century, but the smell in that bedroom was of dust and bones and the stink of fanatical prayer.

I had set my wrist alarm to wake me before dawn. It was still dark when I crept out of Miss Gowrie's house. I liked the thrill – carrying the brassware and camel bells and Richard Burton's bones through the damp chilly streets to the graveyard where the tomb had been opened.

There was no sound at the door of the vault. I went around back and mounted the ladder and shone my flashlight inside.

Wahab lay on the floor, sleeping on his side. He woke when I turned the light on his eyes. This was the first time I had really seen him.

His dark face had a stretched look of panic – the expression certain fish have in fishbowls: trapped and pop-eyed, with fat swollen lips. His eyes were red and puffy, and he was at the last stage of terror. He was limp, making pleading faces at me – or rather at the light – and blinking at the brightness of it. He would have confessed at that moment to being Leon Trotsky.

He clasped his hands and implored me.

I breathed on the window. The vapor condensed, and with my finger I traced a cross in it and shone my flashlight on it. It is the simplest of symbols, but to the man from Mecca it was strange and unwelcome, and I was sure that it made him more fearful than the darkness he had endured in that tomb all night. It was now safe to remove the padlock: I had announced myself as the avenging Christian.

As soon as the hasp was released he pushed the door open and gasped – gave a whinny of fright – and then disappeared at the far end of the churchyard.

It was still dark. I had plenty of time to replace the thuribles, the lamps, the crucifix, and the camel bells, as well as Burton himself in his ornate and rotting coffin. Then I shut the door of the tomb and locked it. I had left everything just where it belonged in the tomb, as anyone could see.

The Man on the Clapham Omnibus

If Sir Charles Smallwood had not sent Miss Gowrie to visit me at the Embassy, and if I had not helped rid this Mortlake landlady of her vengeful lodger, I would never have given this gentleman another thought. Miss Gowrie had called him 'Charlie.' She made me curious and she allowed me an excuse to see him.

We knew him vaguely. He was usually invited to our Embassy parties and very often to dinners. He was, somehow, on the permanent guest list. But he was seldom a guest. He invariably turned down the invitations. I had seen him once, but only long enough to shake his hand – a damp, slack, small-boned hand. The only other thing about him that I could remember was that he had been wearing evening dress of an old-fashioned kind – bib and stiff collar, white scooped-out waistcoat, starched cuffs, black trousers, and tails. He should have looked like a prince; in fact, he looked like a headwaiter, though he was not so poised. It was the functionaries, the waiters and doormen in London, who dressed correctly. The rest of us seldom did. Sir Charles wore his evening dress the way an old veteran wears a uniform for a regimental reunion. He looked uncomfortable in this stiff and slightly ill-fitting suit, and it also looked forty years out of date. I could not remember his face.

His address was in the computer, and his code number – eight digits – explained why he was repeatedly invited to Embassy functions. He was a very high grade of guest, the best English ally, a baronet from an old family.

Al Sanger, from the Legal Department, had shown me which keys to hit on the computer.

'If the British knew the kind of information we had on them in this thing, they'd deep-six every one of us,' Sanger said. 'Great-grandfather's birthplace, wife's maiden name, nanny's husband's political preference, criminal record, queerness quotient, shoe size, taste in underwear, magazine subscriptions, credit rating – do me a favor!'

Smallwood's name and code had come up, and Sanger was scrutinizing the alignments of file references, the green letters and numbers.

He said, 'I don't even know this guy!'

He seemed angry with himself, so I said, 'It's nothing to be ashamed of. I only met him once.'

Sanger said, 'But this is the kind of guy we're *supposed* to know. It's why we're here!'

'Really?' I wondered if he believed what he had just said.

'Yeah – to meet the opinion-formers.'

'How do you know he's an opinion-former?'

'If you see a guy with a long white beard, wearing a red suit and carrying a bag of toys and saying, "Ho-ho-ho," you'd be pretty stupid if you didn't call him Santa Claus,' Sanger said. 'It's all in the profile. Look at Smallwood's. Look at those ratings. That's a pedigree and a half! Where'd you get his name?'

'From a little old lady.'

'That's funny, you know? We're in the business of information-gathering, and you stand there uttering pointless jokes and tiresome evasions. Give me a break. I hate unreliable witnesses.'

'It's no joke. The little old lady's name is Miss Gowrie.'

'Let's find out her bust size,' Sanger said and leered at the computer screen. 'We know everything.' Then suddenly he shouted, 'He lives in Clapham!'

'What's so funny?'

'The man on the Clapham omnibus,' he said.

It was the first time I had ever heard this picturesque description. It brought to mind the vivid image of a thinfaced man sitting alone in an old double-decker bus – a bowler hat on his head, and brass rails on the stairwell, and posters advertising Players Weights and beef tea pasted on the freshly painted red sides; the man swaying as the bus rattled on hard rubber wheels down an avenue of brown cobblestones.

I said, 'It has a nice sound.'

'It just means "the man in the street" – it's a legal term here. In American law he's called the fair and reasonable man. Didn't you go to law school?'

'I haven't had your advantages, Al.'

'I can see that,' he said. 'Anyway, a lot of Foreign Service people have law degrees. See, they know the subtleties in the law, but how

can you expect the man on the Clapham omnibus to know them?'
And he grinned. 'See what I mean?'

'The average man,' I said.

'Right. A bloke, as they say here. Only this guy' – he was tapping
the display screen of the computer, where Sir Charles Smallwood's
paragraph was illuminated – 'this guy is no ordinary bloke. One
thing's for sure. The Clapham address is a front. Probably a *pied
à terre*. Baronets don't live in Clapham.'

He had no phone, or else it was unlisted. I wrote to him in Clapham,
at the address shown on the computer, inviting him for a meal.
He was prompt in refusing. I invited him for a drink. He replied
saying he was tied up: he was going to be in the country for a few
weeks. I liked 'in the country' – it meant out of town. I let those
weeks pass. I wrote again. Was he interested in a pair of complimentary tickets to the London première of *Up North*, a black folk-opera
performed by the Harlem Arts Collective? No, he was not. There
was a practiced politeness in his refusals – he was good, not to say
graceful, even lordly, at declining invitations. His handwriting had
a black and spattery loveliness. He was a hard man to raise.

This sharpened my desire to meet him, and in the interval I had
discovered something about the Smallwoods. They were English
Catholics – it said so on our computer. There is something faintly
exotic about Catholics in England, something spooky and tribal
and secretive. They worry people. They are like Jews in the United
States, and they are seen in the same way, as outsiders and potential
conspirators. They are feared and somewhat disliked, and they are
always suspected of not supporting the Protestant monarchy for
religious reasons. The Smallwoods traced their ancestry back to
the reign of Henry VIII, when they had been recusants – dissenters
– and it was their boast that in four hundred years not a single
day had passed without holy mass being celebrated in a secret
chapel at Smallwood Park, in Hertfordshire. They were like early
Christians: they were persecuted, they hid, they clung to their faith,
they remained steadfast – and he was one of them.

He lived within walking distance of my apartment in Battersea
– up the road and just on the other side of Lavender Hill, on Parma
Crescent. I walked past the house three times before summoning
the courage to knock. The house was one in a terrace of twenty,
two-up, two-down, with the shades drawn and two trash barrels

in the front yard – the other houses had rose bushes or hydrangeas. There was an unwashed milk bottle on the front step. Surely this was the wrong house?

Not seeing a bell or knocker, I rattled the metal flap on the letter slot and waited. After a moment there was a shadow on the glass of the door. The door opened, but only a crack, and from this a hidden face spoke to me, asking me what I wanted. It was the voice of a man muttering into a blanket.

'I'm looking for Sir Charles Smallwood.'

'No admittance on business,' the man said.

What did *that* mean?

'This isn't business,' I said. 'This is a social call.'

'And you are?'

I still could not determine whether the man I was speaking to was Sir Charles Smallwood. I had a feeling that he was some sort of manservant. He was tetchy and suspicious and overprotective, and even – like some English servants I'd seen – domineering. I told him who I was and gave him my American Embassy calling card, with the eagle embossed on it in gold. It had been specially designed by a team of psychiatrists to impress foreign nationals.

'Please wait there,' he said.

He shut the door and left me on the front doorstep, but less than a minute later I heard him shooting the bolt inside, and saw his shadow again on the glass, and the door was opened to me.

There was no hallway. I walked from his front step into his front room in one stride. And I was sorry now that I had come, because clearly this was the man's bedroom. There was a cot and a chair beside it, and it was heated by an electric fire – the orange coils on one bar. It was not enough heat. On the floor, propped against the wall, was a very good painting in a heavy gilt frame. It was black and incongruous and instead of hinting at opulence it gave the room the air of a junk shop.

I said, 'I hope I'm not intruding.'

'It is rather awkward – your coming unannounced. Will you have tea?'

'No, thank you. I can't stay.'

'As you wish.'

He wore a torn sweater and paint-splashed trousers and scuffed shoes. He might have been a deckhand, spending some time ashore in this small room. If this was Sir Charles's servant, he was being treated rather poorly. He had hair like pencil shavings, the same orangy woody color, the same crinkly texture.

He said, 'Perhaps a glass of sherry?'

'I'd love one.'

He left the room and I had a chance to look it over more carefully. It was like a monk's cell; it was not improved by the old radio, the wilted geranium, or the narrow cot. I heard footsteps upstairs, a solid tread that banged against wooden planks in the ceiling. And there was a burring noise, like steam and bells, of a television behind the wall, in the next house. It was a hell of a place for a servant to sit, in this front room. I had the impression that there were a number of other people in the house – it was not only the feet on the floorboards above my head, but voices, and the sound of water humming through different pipes in the wall.

'Sorry I was so long,' the man said when he returned. He handed me a glass of sherry. 'Couldn't find the right glass.'

It was crystal, with eight sides tapering to a heavy base, and it shimmered with a lovely marmalade glint, even in the pale dirty light of this room. A coat of arms was etched on one narrow plane. It was one of the most beautiful glasses I had ever seen. But I drank from it and nearly spewed. The sherry had a vile taste, like varnish, and its smell was like the fumes of burning plastic. Tears of disgust came to my eyes, and I tried to wink them away as I swallowed.

The man watched me. He was not drinking.

'It's awful to drop in,' I said. The man said nothing. He seemed to agree that it was awful. 'But this was the only address I had.'

'This is the only address. There is no other.'

I felt uncomfortable with him waiting there and watching. I wanted him to announce me to Sir Charles, or else to shuffle away in the direction of the noise – get those noisy fools to pipe down – so that I could empty the remainder of my poisonous sherry into the geranium pot.

Just then there was a shout above our heads. We both looked at the ceiling in time for the even sharper reply – an angry but incoherent complaint.

'They're at it again. Fight like cats.'

'Can't you do anything about it?'

'They wouldn't listen.' He was silent a moment. He tucked his hands under his sweater to warm them in the thickness of the folds. 'No, not them!'

'I don't think I could stand that.'

'You'd get used to it.' He said this in a firm schoolmasterish way, as if he were telling me something I didn't know but ought to.

I said, 'I wonder.'

'You would,' he said, 'if you had no choice.'

I was put off by his know-it-all tone and thought I had been kept waiting long enough. I had had too much bad sherry and peevish advice. I was going to say *If you don't mind* –

But before my tongue could make that thought a complete sentence, he said, 'What was it you wanted?'

'I want to speak to Sir Charles Smallwood.'

'But I'm Charlie!'

You say, *Of course, what else?* It seems predictable, even perhaps an anticlimax. But only in hindsight do events seem inevitable. At the time, sitting in that monk's cell of a room under the tramping feet and humming pipes, it was the last thing in the world that I expected.

He saw the shock on my face. He said, 'Shall I explain?'

He told me about a man from an old family with a good name who, in the middle of his life, believed he had a curse on him. The man loved his family, but he felt they were to blame for the curse. It was a kind of hereditary illness – nausea sometimes. He was disgusted when he saw common red-faced wheezing men drink beer; his gorge rose when he saw their vicious hands – some of them seemed to have paws of peeling skin. He glanced at the men in horror. They stared back at him. He could not make friends with people who frightened him and, in his way, he suffered.

The things he owned had sentimental value, but they were also quite useless. He owned a magnificent portrait of an ancestor, but it was so heavy it could not hang on the wall of his tiny house. He owned a boar's head with curved tusks that had been in the family for generations; various family histories – a shelf of books – some silver plate, a chalice, and glassware that, under the terms of the legacy, he could not sell or dispose of (who wanted that family crest, anyway?); some old documents on vellum; and odds and ends of no value – Bibles, photographs, enormous latchkeys, some splinters of saints' bones, and a linen scrap from a martyr's winding sheet.

He had had no education, apart from two years at Eton. He still owned some of his Eton clothes, and he was lucky that his tails still fitted him – he had not grown at all after being withdrawn from the school at the age of fifteen. He had worn out his cricketing flannels, but not by playing cricket. He still had some of his tweeds. What clothes he had were various school uniforms – party uniform, games uniform, weekend uniform. But no occasions arose when these uniforms were suitable – only a party now and then, but that was all, because only the grandest parties required him to wear white tie.

The family collapse had come quickly. The death of his father and then his mother – within six weeks of each other. There had been no time to make any financial arrangements at all. Tax demands were made; some were met. The death duties – awful pair of words – remained unpaid. There was no more money. The house had belonged to the family for almost five hundred years. It was sold to an Australian, who boasted that he was the great-grandson of a pickpocket who had been transported to Botany Bay.

The children were shocked. Instead of legacies being handed out, debts were apportioned. They had never lived in much style, but now each of the children – there were four – found that he was nearly destitute and owed a considerable amount of money. Everything was gone; there was nothing more to sell. The children felt as though they had been turned into debtors and would soon be hunted down.

They consulted solicitors and barristers and were given a certain amount of reckless advice. 'Leave the country at once,' a man said. His name was Horace Whybrow. 'Turn yourselves into a limited company and then declare the company bankrupt,' a Queen's Counsel said. His name was Dennis Orde-Widdowson. They remembered the names because the advice was so dire, and the bills for this advice put them further into debt.

The children found that by separating, living in different parts of London and letting matters drift, they could survive. And yet this man, who was the eldest child, who had inherited his father's title, had also inherited the greatest part of the debts – this man often felt as if there were a tide of debt and disgrace rising around him. He was up to his neck. There was no one who would help him, no one who would understand.

He moved to Mortlake and lived in an upper room of a house that at times seemed to suffocate him. He had black moods. He lived with the blinds drawn. The landlady was kind, but she was no help – she too was down on her luck.

He felt he had to kill himself. He did not want to.

Wouldn't someone else in his position understand? Not exactly in his position, but a member of the aristocracy, the withered part of it, from an old family, with a meaningless title like baronet, and an important title like doctor. He knew that if he did not explain his suffering to someone soon, he would not have to kill himself – he would be too ill to prevent himself from dying.

Then a man was found. He had a small title. He was a member of the Scottish aristocracy, and his name was the Honorable Aleister Colquhoun. He was a National Health doctor. Every person, even an aristocrat, had a right in this country to see a psychiatrist, free of charge.

The doctor was sympathetic to his new patient, who seldom ate and seldom went outdoors. The doctor encouraged him to go to parties, although there were very few parties the man could go to wearing a white tie and tails.

'I'm cursed,' the patient said. 'It's a trap.'

The doctor smiled. He had a beautiful, noble face. The patient felt he could have kissed that man without any shame – and he knew he wasn't queer. He felt safe in the doctor's presence.

Doctors are the most practical of men, and psychiatrists the most practical doctors. They deal in the obscure but make it obvious, and they treat it with common sense. They argue on behalf of the patient. They are the friends we all ought to have for nothing. They take their time; they are slower than lawyers; they have a kind of selfish patience. This Dr Colquhoun listened, saying very little at first. When he did speak he said sensible things, such as, 'There are no curses. There are no traps, except the ones we make for ourselves. Your future is up to you. Don't confuse debts with faults. Life can be messy, but you don't change it by worrying –'

Clichés of that sort had a calming effect.

'My ancestors are in the history books,' the patient said.

'My ancestors wrote those books,' the doctor replied.

'But I'm a lodger in Mortlake!'

'Barnes is right next door to Mortlake.' The doctor lived in Barnes.

The patient talked about his family, his feeling of having lived under a curse – the instincts that went with his title. He was burdened by having to be this person without being able to accomplish anything. He said that sometimes he felt that he was the only man in Britain who did not believe in a hereditary title. It was as silly as a belief in reincarnation! What was this naive trust in a family name?

But when the doctor mentioned friends, the man said, 'I have none,' and when he mentioned working-class people, the man said, 'I hate them.' He told the doctor that he could not help feeling the way he did – he had been born like this.

'As if you were born somewhat malformed?'

'No,' the man said, 'as if I were born perfect. As if everyone else were malformed.'

He could see that this shook the doctor a little.

The patient said, 'I've never said these things before to anyone.'

'I've never heard them before,' the doctor said.

'Perhaps they don't matter.'

'Of course they matter!' the doctor said. He was indignant, in a sulking, aristocratic way. Some of these Scots were frightfully grand.

'But what can I do about it?'

The doctor said, 'You must tell me everything.'

The rest was bleak. It was the man incapable of making a friend or finding a job or paying the family debts. It was the humiliation of being weak and exposed, like a dream he had of finding himself naked in a public place. He despised people for their common-looking faces and the careless way they spoke. Seeing them eat made him sick. He could not bear to watch anyone eat, he said. And there were sights just as bad – watching people blow their nose, hearing them laugh, seeing their underwear on a clothesline. And he hated seeing their old shoes.

The doctor said, 'I think I know what you mean.'

He told the doctor everything. He felt much better as a consequence. He knew now that he could not change his situation, but talking about it made him feel less burdened. It did seem at times immensely complicated; but he was not imagining the curse – there really was a curse on him. It was a curse to have to live like an average man. He felt like a fallen angel, for wasn't this poverty truly like a fall from grace?

These visits to the National Health psychiatrist became his life – the life he had been born to. This was enough society for him. The doctor was, of course, an aristocrat. He was intelligent; he was a model of refinement. The way he smoked cigarettes convinced you he was a deep thinker, and very neat and economical. In a world they knew as squalid and unequal they faced each other as equals, and often at the end of a session the doctor offered his patient a glass of good sherry.

Warmed and made optimistic by the wine, the patient could forget the curse of the family name that had hobbled him so badly. Now it did not seem so cruel that he had been born an aristocrat. He had found a way out of this trap. The doctor was his social equal! And the doctor was excellent company. This wasn't therapy or the confessional feeling of well-being. This was like meeting for drinks.

'We have a great deal in common,' the patient said, and was pleased.

'A very great deal,' the doctor said, after pausing a moment. He seemed reluctant to admit it, and said no more.

'Before I met you, I didn't know which way to turn. I used to think about killing myself!'

'How do you feel now?' the doctor asked.

'I feel I have a friend who understands.'

'None of this has ever occurred to me before,' the doctor said. He went on to explain that he had never thought much about the burden of the past, or upholding the reputation of an old name, or the snobbery-nausea, an instinct that was the worst curse of all.

'I'm glad we met,' the patient said.

The doctor did not reply. In recent weeks he had seemed somewhat inattentive. Now and then he was late for his appointments with the patient. Often he cut the session short; sometimes – though rarely – he did not show up at all.

But it did not matter to the patient that the doctor no longer offered him common sense as advice, or that he fell silent when the patient spoke and remained silent long after the patient was finished. It seemed to the patient like perfect discretion. They really were frightfully grand!

His satisfaction was that, having told the doctor everything, he felt well. It was much better than confession, because each time it had become easier – there was less to confess.

There was no cure, but the humiliation, which was painful, could be eliminated. They had met as doctor and patient on the National Health, but they recognized each other as gentlemen.

The patient's depressions ceased altogether. The following week the session was canceled. It was one of the doctor's no-shows. He was ill – that was the story.

It was a lie. The doctor was dead.

The *Times* obituary was three inches: THE HON ALEISTER COLQUHOUN, it said, PIONEER IN MENTAL HEALTH.

'He hanged himself,' Sir Charles Smallwood said. 'And that's why I'm here like this. Under the circumstances, I feel I'm doing rather well, though there are those who doubt it. And sometimes people pity me.'

'Take no notice of them,' I said.

'They don't bother me a bit,' he said. '*Honi soit qui mal y pense.*'

Sex and Its Substitutes

When people said, 'Miss Duboys has a friend,' they meant something sinister, or at least pretty nasty – that she had a dark secret at home. Because we were both unmarried and grade FSO-4 at the London Embassy, we were often paired up at dinner parties as the token singles. It became a joke between us, these frequent meetings at Embassy Residences. 'You again,' she would say, and give me a velvet feline growl. She was not pretty in any conventional way, which was probably why I found her so attractive. Her eyes were green in her thin white face; her lips were overlarge and lispy-looking; her short hair jet-black; and you could see the rise of her nipples through her raincoat.

It took me a little while to get to know her. There were so many people eager to see us married, we resisted being pushed into further intimacy. I saw a lot of her at work – and at all those dinner parties! We very quickly became good friends and indeed were so tolerant of each other and so familiar that it was hard for me to know her any better. I desired her when I was with her. Our friendship did not progress. Then I began to think that people were right: she probably *did* have a secret at home.

The facts about her were unusual. She had not been to the United States in four years – she had not taken home leave, she had not visited Europe, she had not left London. She had probably not left her apartment much, except to go to work. It made people talk. But she worked very hard. Our British counterparts treated hard workers with suspicion. They would have regarded Margaret Duboys as a possible spy, for staying late all those nights. What was she really doing? people asked. Some called her conscientious; others, obsessed.

There was another characteristic Miss Duboys had that made the London Embassy people suspicious. She bought a great amount of food at the PX in Ruislip. She made a weekly trip for enormous quantities of tax-free groceries, but always of a certain kind. All our food bills were recorded on the Embassy computer, and Miss

Duboys's bills were studied closely. Steaks! Chickens! Hamburg! She bought rabbits! One week her bill was a hundred and fourteen dollars and forty-seven cents. Single woman, tax-free food! She was a carnivore and no mistake, but she bought pounds of fish, too. We looked at the computer print-out and marveled. What an appetite!

'People eat to compensate for things,' said Everett Horton, our number two, who perhaps knew what he was talking about: he was very fat.

I said, 'Margaret doesn't strike me as a compulsive eater.'

'No,' he said, 'she's got a very sweet figure. That's a better explanation.'

'She's thin – it doesn't explain anything!'

'She's pretty,' Horton said. 'She's living with a very hungry man.'

'Let's hope not,' I said, and when Horton leered at me, I added, 'For security reasons.'

She had completely reorganized the Trade Section; she dealt with priority trade matters. It was unthinkable that someone in such a trusted position was compromising this trust with a foreigner who was perhaps only a sexual adventurer. It is the unthinkable that most preoccupies me with thought. Or was she giving all the food away? Or, worse, was she selling it to grateful English people? They paid twice what we did for half as much and, in the past, there had been cases of Embassy personnel selling merchandise they had bought at bargain prices at the American PX: they had been sent home and demoted, or else fired – 'terminated' was our word. We wondered about Miss Duboys. Her grocery bill was large and mystifying.

The day came when these PX print-outs were to be examined by some visiting budget inspectors from Washington.

Horton, who knew I was fond of Miss Duboys, took me aside that morning.

'Massage these figures, will you?' he said. 'I'm sure they're not as lumpy as they look.'

I averaged them and I made them look innocent. Yet still they startled me. All that food! For any other officer it would not have looked odd, but the fact was that Miss Duboys lived alone. She never gave dinner parties. She never gave parties. No one had ever been inside her house.

There was more speculation, all of it idle and some of it rather cruel. It was worse than 'Miss Duboys has a friend.' I thought it was baseless and malicious and, in the way that gossip can do real harm by destroying a person's reputation, very dangerous. And what were people saying about me? People regarded her as 'shady' and 'sly.' 'You can't figure her out,' they said, meaning they could if you were bold and insensitive enough to listen. And there was her 'accident' – doubting people always spoke about her in quotation marks, which they indicated with raised eyebrows. It was her hospital 'scare.' Miss Duboys, who was a 'riddle,' had been 'rushed' to the hospital 'covered with bruises.' The commonest explanation was that she 'fell,' but the general belief was that she had been beaten up by her mysterious roommate – so people thought. If she had been beaten black and blue no one had seen her. Al Sanger claimed he saw her with a bandaged hand, Erroll Jeeps said it was scratches. 'Probably a feminine complaint,' Scaduto's wife said, and when I squinted she said, 'Plumbing.'

'Could be another woman,' Horton said. 'Women scratch each other, don't they? I mean, a man wouldn't do that.'

'Probably a can of tuna fish,' Jeeps said.

Al Sanger said, 'She never buys cans of tuna fish!'

He, too, had puzzled over her grocery bills.

Miss Duboys did not help matters by refusing to explain any of it: the grocery bills, the visit to the hospital, no home leave, no cocktail parties, no dinners. But she was left alone. She was an excellent officer and the only woman in the Trade Section. It would have been hard to interrogate her and practically impossible to transfer her without being accused of bias. But there were still people who regarded her behaviour as highly suspicious.

'What is it?' Horton asked me. 'Do you think it's what they say?'

I had never heard him, or any other American Embassy official, use the word 'spy.' It was a vulgar, painful, and unlucky word, like 'cancer.'

'No, not that,' I said.

'I can't imagine what it could be.'

'It's sex,' I said. 'Or one of its substitutes.'

'One of the many,' he said.

'One of the few,' I replied.

He smiled at me and said, 'It's nice to be young.'

The harsh rumors, and the way Miss Duboys treated them with contempt, made me like her the more. I began to look forward to seeing her at the dinner parties, where we were invariably the odd guests – the unmarried ones. Perhaps it was more calculated than I realized; perhaps people, seeing me as steady, solid, with a good record in overseas posts, thought that I would succeed in finding out the truth about Miss Duboys. If so, they chose the right man. I did find out the truth. It was so simple, so obvious in its way, it took either genius or luck to discover it. I had no genius, but I was very lucky.

We were at Erroll Jeeps's apartment in Hampstead. Jeeps's wife was named Lornette, which, with a kind of misplaced hauteur, she pronounced like the French eyeglasses, '*lorgnette*.' The Jeepses were black, from Chicago. A black American jazz trumpeter was also there – he was introduced as Owlie Cooper; and the Sangers – Al and Tina; and Margaret Duboys; and myself.

The Sangers' dog had just come out of quarantine. When he heard that it had cost three hundred dollars to fly the dog from Washington to London, and close to a thousand for the dog's three months at the quarantine kennel in Surrey ('We usually visited Brucie on weekends'), Owlie Cooper kicked his feet out and screamed his laughter at the Sangers. Tina asked what was so funny. Cooper said it was all funny: he was laughing at the money, the amount of time, and even the dog's name. 'Brucie!'

The Sangers looked insulted; they went into a kind of sulk – their eyes shining with anger – but they said nothing. You knew they wanted to say something like *Okay, but what kind of a name is Owlie?* But Owlie was black and it was possible that Owlie was a special black name, maybe Swahili, or else meant something interesting, which – and this was obvious – Brucie didn't.

Unexpectedly, Margaret Duboys said to Cooper, 'Taking good care of your dog – is that funny? People go to much more trouble for children. Look at all the time and money that's wasted on these Embassy kids.'

'You're not serious,' Cooper said. 'I mean, what a freaky comparison!'

'It's a fair comparison,' Margaret said. 'I've spent whole evenings at the Scadutos' listening to stories about Tony's braces. Guess how much they cost the American taxpayer? Three thousand dollars! They sent him to an orthodontist at the American base in Frankfurt –'

'I'm thinking of going there,' Lornette Jeeps said. 'I've got this vein in my leg that's got to come out.'

'They didn't even work!' Margaret was saying. 'Skiddoo says the kids still call him Bugs Bunny. And Horton's kid, eight years old, and he's got a bodyguard who just stands there earning twenty grand a year while Horton Junior plays Space Invaders at these clip joints in Leicester Square –'

'It's an antikidnap measure,' Erroll Jeeps said. 'It'd be easy as shit for some crackhead in the IRA to turn Horton Junior into hand luggage –'

And then the two Sangers smiled at each other, and while Margaret continued talking, Al Sanger said, 'We're pretty fond of Brucie. We've had him since Caracas –'

There were, generally speaking, two categories of bores at the Embassy dinner parties: people with children, and people with animals. Life in London was too hectic and expensive for people to have both children and animals. When they did, the children were teenagers and the animals disposable – hamsters and turtles. One group had school stories and the other had quarantine stories – and they were much the same: both involved time, money, patience, and self-sacrifice.

'You certainly put up with a lot of inconvenience,' I said to one woman with a long story.

'If that's what you think, you completely missed my point,' she said.

She was proud of her child – or perhaps it was a puppy.

Margaret Duboys was still talking!

I said, 'Are we discussing brats or ankle-biters?'

'It's still Brucie,' Tina Sanger said.

'Give me cats any day,' I said, sipping my gin and trying to keep a straight face. 'They're clean, they're intelligent, and they're selfish. None of this tail-wagging, no early-morning sessions in the park, no "walkies." Dogs resent strangers, they get jealous, they get bored – they stink, they stumble, they drool. Sometimes dogs turn on you for no reason! They revert! They maul people, they eat children. But cats only scratch you by accident, or if you're being a pest. Dogs want to be loved, but cats don't give a damn. They look after themselves, and they're twice as pretty.'

'What about kids?' Al Sanger said.

'They're in between,' I said.

Erroll said, 'In between what?'

'Dogs and cats.'

Margaret Duboys howled suddenly. A dark labored groan came straight out of her lungs. I had a moment of terror before I realized that she was just laughing very hard.

I had been silly, I thought, in talking about cats that way, but it produced an amazing effect. After dinner, Miss Duboys came up to me and said in a purr of urgency, 'Could you give me a lift home? My car's being fixed.'

She had never accepted a ride from me before, and this was the first time she had ever asked for one. I found this very surprising, but I had a further surprise. When we arrived at her front door, she said, 'Would you like to come in for a minute?'

I was – if the Embassy rumors were correct – the first human being to receive such an invitation from her. I found it hard to appear calm. I had never cared much about the Embassy talk or Miss Duboys's supposed secrets; but, almost from the beginning, I had been interested in offering her a passionate friendship. I liked her company and her easy conversation. But how could I know anything about her heart until I discovered her body? I felt for her, as I had felt for all the women I wanted to know better, a mixture of caution and desire and nervous panic. A lover's emotions are the same as a firebug's.

There was a sound behind the door. It was both motion and sound, like tiny children hurrying on their hands and knees.

'Don't be shocked,' Miss Duboys said. She was smiling, she looked perfectly serene. In this light her eyes were not green but gray.

Then she opened the door.

Cats, cats, cats, cats, cats, cats –

She was stooping to embrace them, then almost as an afterthought she said, 'Come in, but be careful where you step.'

There were six of them, and they were large. I knew at once that they resented my being there. They crept away from me sideways, seeming to walk on tiptoe, in that fastidious and insolent way that cats have. Their bellies were too big and detracted from their handsomeness. Why hadn't she told anyone about her cats? It was the simplest possible answer to all the Embassy gossip and speculation. And no one had a clue. People still believed she had a friend, a lover, someone with a huge appetite, who sometimes beat her up. But it was cats. That was why she had not left Britain for the duration of nearly two tours: because of the quarantine regulations she could not take her cats, and if she could not travel with them she would not travel at all.

But she had not told anyone. I was reminded then that she had never been very friendly with anyone at the Embassy – how could she have been, if no one knew this simple fact about her that explained every quirk of her behavior? She had always been remote and respectful.

That first night I said, 'No one knows about your cats.'

'Why should they?'

'They might be interested,' I said, and I thought: *Don't you want to keep them from making wild speculations?*

'Other people's pets are a bore,' she said. She seemed cross. 'And so are other people's children. No one's really interested, and I can't stand condescension. People with children think they're superior or else pity you, and people with cats think you're a fool, because their beasts are so much better behaved. You have to live your own life – thank God for that.'

It was quite an outburst, considering that all we were talking about were cats. But she was defensive, as if she knew about her mysterious reputation and 'Miss Duboys has a friend' and all those coarse rumors.

She said, 'What I do in my own home, on my own time, is my business. I usually put in a ten-hour day at the Embassy. I think I'm entitled to a little privacy. I'm not hurting anyone, am I?'

I said, no, of course not – but it struck me that her tone was exactly that of a person defending a crank religion or an out-of-the-way sexual practice. She had overreacted to my curiosity, as if she expected to be persecuted for the heresy of cat-worship.

I said, 'Why are you letting me in on your little secret?'

'I liked what you said at Erroll's – about cats.'

'I'm a secret believer in cats,' I said. 'I like them.'

'And I like you.' She was holding a bulgy orange cat and making kissing noises at it. 'That's a compliment. I'm very fussy.'

'Thanks,' I said.

'It's time for bed,' she said.

I looked up quickly with a hot face. But she was talking to the cat and helping it into a basket.

We did nothing that night except drink. It had got to the hour – about half-past two – when to go to bed with her would have been a greater disappointment than going home alone to Battersea. I made it look like gallantry – I said I had to go; tomorrow was a working day – but I was doing us both a favor, and certainly sparing her my blind bumbling late-night performance. She seemed to appreciate my tact, and she let me know, with her lips and a flick of her tongue and her little sigh of pleasure, that someday soon, when it was convenient, I would be as welcome in her bed as any of her cats.

Cat-worship was merely a handy label I had thought of to explain her behavior. Within a few weeks it seemed an amazingly accurate description, and even blunt clichés, such as *cat-lover* and *cat-freak*, seemed to me precise and perfectly fair. Cats were not her hobby or her pastime, but her passion.

I got to know her garden apartment. It was in Notting Hill, off Kensington Park Road, in a white building that had once been (I think she said) the residence of the Spanish Ambassador. Its ball-room had been subdivided into six small apartments. But hers was on the floor below these, a ground-floor apartment opening into a large communal park, Arundel Gardens. The gardens, like the apartment and most of its furnishings, were for the cats. The rent was twelve hundred dollars a month – six hundred pounds. It was too much, almost more than Miss Duboys could afford, but the cats needed fresh air and grass and flowers, and she needed the cats.

On her walls there were cat calendars and cat photographs and, in some rooms, cat wallpaper – a repeated motif of crouching cats. She had cat paperweights and cat picturebooks, and waste-baskets and lampshades with cats on them. On a set of shelves there were small porcelain cats. There were fat cats stenciled on her towels, and kittens on her coffee mugs. She had cats printed on her sheets and embroidered on her dinner napkins. Cats are peculiarly expressionless creatures, and the experience of so many images of them was rather bewildering. The carpet in the hall was cat-shaped – a sitting one in profile. She had cat notepaper, a stack of it on her desk (two weeks later I received an affectionate message on it).

And she had real cats, six of them. Five were nervous and mal-evolent, and the sixth was simple-minded – a neutered, slightly undersized one that gaped at me with the same sleepy vacuity as those on the wall and those on the coffee mugs. The largest cat weighed fifteen or twenty pounds – it was vast and fat-bellied and evil-spirited, and named Lester. It had a hiss like a gas leak. Even Margaret was a bit fearful of this monster, and she hinted to me that it had once killed another cat. Thereafter, Lester seemed to me to have the stupid, hungry – and cruel and comic – face of a cannibal.

There was nothing offensive in the air, none of that hairy suffocation that is usual in a catty household. The prevalent smell was of food, the warm buttery vapor of homecooking. Margaret cooked all the time; her cats had wonderful meals: hamburg in brown gravy, lightly poached fish, stews that were never stretched with flour or potatoes. Lester liked liver, McCool adored fish, Miss Growse never ate anything but stews, and the others – they all had human-sounding names – had different preferences. They did not eat the same thing. Sometimes they did not eat at all – did not even taste it but only glanced and sniffed at the food steaming in the dish and then walked away and yowled for something else. It made me mad: I would have eaten some of that food! The cats were spoiled and overweight and grouchy – 'fat and magnificent,' Margaret called them. Yes, yes; but their fussy food habits kept her busy for most of the hours she was home. Now I understood her huge shopping bills. She was patient with them – more patient than I had even seen her in the Embassy. When the cats did not eat their food, she put it into another dish and left it outside for the strays – the London moggies and the Notting Hill tomcats that prowled Arundel Gardens. Why the other dishes? 'My cats are very particular about who uses their personal dishes!'

I said, 'Do you use the word "personal" with cats?'

'I sure do!'

And one day she said, 'I never give them cans.'

It was the sort of statement that caused me a moment of unnecessary discomfort. I ate canned food all the time. What was wrong with it? I wanted to tell Margaret that she was talking nonsense: Good food, fresh air, no cans! Me and my cats!

No, absolutely no cans – the cats drew the line there – but they were not particular about which chair leg they scratched, or where they puked, or where they left their matted hairs. They sharpened their claws on the sofa and on the best upholstered chairs, and went at the wall and clawed it and left shredded, scratched wallpaper, like heaps of grated cheese, on the carpet. The cats were not fierce except when they were protecting their food or were faced with the London strays; but they were very destructive – needlessly so – and it made me angry to think of Margaret paying so much money for rent and having to endure the cats' vandalism. She did not mind.

I made the mistake of mentioning this only once.

She replied, 'But children are a hundred times worse.'

I said, 'How does it feel to have six children?'

If it seemed that way, she said – that they were like children – then how did it seem from the cats' point of view? I thought she was crazy, taking this line (look at it from the cats' point of view!), but she quoted Darwin. She said that Darwin had concluded that domesticated animals which grew up with people regarded human beings as members of their own species. It was in *The Voyage of the Beagle*, where the sheepdogs treated sheep in a brotherly way in Argentina. From this, it was easy to see that cats regarded us as cats – of a rather inconvenient size, but cats all the same, which fed them, and opened doors for them, and scratched them pleasantly behind their ears, and gave them a lap to sit on, and pinched fleas from around their eyes and mouths, and wormed them.

'Darwin said that?'

'More or less.'

'That cats think we're cats?'

'He was talking about dogs and sheep, but, yes,' she said uncertainly. With conviction she added, 'Anyway, these cats think I'm one.'

'What about their natural instincts?'

'Their instincts tell them no, but their sympathies and learning experience tell them yes. These cats are sympathetic. Listen, I don't even think of them as cats!'

'That's one step further than Darwin,' I said.

By now I knew a great deal about Miss Duboys's cats, and quite a lot about Miss Duboys. We had spent the past five Sundays together. Neither of us had much to do on the weekends. It became our routine to have Sunday lunch at an Indian restaurant and, after a blistering vindaloo curry, to return to her apartment and spend the afternoon in bed. When we woke, damp and entangled, from our sudden sleep – the little death that follows sex – we went to a movie, usually a bad, undemanding one, at the Gate Cinema near

577

the Notting Hill tube station. Sunday was a long day with several sleeps – the day had about six parts and seemed at times like two or three whole days – all the exertion, and then the laziness, and all the dying and dreaming and waking.

London was a city that inspired me to treasure private delights. Its weather and its rational, well-organized people had made it a city of splendid interiors – everything that was pleasurable happened indoors: the contentment of sex, food, reading, music, and talk. Margaret would have added animals to this list. When she woke blindly from one of these feverish Sunday sleeps, she bumped me with an elbow and said, 'I'm neglecting my cats.'

She had no other friends. Apart from me (but I occupied her only one day of the week), her cats were the whole of her society, and they satisfied her. It seemed to me that she was slightly at odds with me – slightly bewildered – because I offered her the one thing a cat could not provide. The cats were a substitute for everything else. Well, that was plain enough! But it made me laugh to think that for Margaret Duboys I represented Sex. *Me!* It made life difficult for us at times, because it was hard for her to see me in any other way. She judged most people by comparing them with cats. In theory this was trivial and belittling, but it was worse in practice – no one came out well; no one measured up; no humans that she knew were half so worthwhile as any of her cats.

'I make an exception in your case,' she told me – we were in bed at the time.

'Thanks, Marge!'

She didn't laugh. She said, 'Most men are prigs.'

'Did you say *prigs?*'

'No, no' – but she dived beneath the covers.

Usually she was harder on herself than on me. She seemed to despise that part of herself which needed my companionship. We saw each other at parties just as often as before, because we concealed the fact that we had become lovers. I was not naturally a concealer of such things, but she made me secretive, and I saw that this was a part of all friendship – agreeing to be a little like the other person. Margaret thought, perhaps rightly, that in an informal way the Embassy would become curious about our friendship and ask questions – certainly the boys on the third floor would keep us under observation. So we never used the internal Embassy phones for anything except the most boring trivialities. There was plenty of time at the dinner parties for us to make plans for the following Sunday. People were still trying to bring us together! When I did phone her, out of caution I used the public phone box near my apartment, on Prince of Wales Drive. Those were the only times I used that phone box, and entering it – it was a damp, stinking, vandalized cubicle – I thought always of her, and always in a tender way.

She was catlike in the panting gasping way she made love, the way she clawed my shoulders, the way she shook, and most of all in the way she slept afterward, as though on a branch or an outcrop of rock, her legs drawn up under her and her arms wrapped around her head and her nose down.

I don't think of them as cats. A number of times she repeated this observation to me. She did not theorize about it; she didn't explain it. And yet it seemed to me the perfect reply to Darwin's version of domestic animals thinking of us as animals. The person who grew up with cats for company regarded cats as people! Of course! Yet it seemed to me that these cats were the last creatures on earth to care whether or not they resembled an overworked FSO-4 in the Trade Section of the American Embassy. And if that was how she felt about cats, it made me wonder what she thought about human beings.

We seldom talked about the other people at work or about our work. We seldom talked at all. When we met it was for one thing, and when it came to sex she was single-minded. She used cats to explain her theory of the orgasm: 'Step one, chase the cat up the tree. Step two, let it worry for a while. Step three, rescue the cat.' When she failed to have an orgasm she would whisper, 'The cat is still up the tree – get her down.'

From what she told other people at dinner parties, and from Embassy talk, I gathered that her important work was concerned with helping American companies break into the British market. It was highly abstract in the telling: she provided information about industrial software, did backup for seminars, organized a clearing-house for legal and commercial alternatives in company formation, and liaised with promotional bodies.

I hated talking to people about their work. There was, first, this obscure and silly language, and then, inevitably, they asked about my work. I was always reminded, when I told them, of how grand my job as Political Officer sounded, and how little I accomplished.

These days I lived from Sunday to Sunday, and sex seemed to provide the only meaning to life – what else on earth was so important? There was nothing to compare with two warm bodies in a bed: this was wealth, freedom, and happiness; it was the object of all human endeavor. I was falling in love with Margaret Duboys.

I also feared losing her, and I hated all the other feelings that were caused by this fear – jealousy, panic, greed. This was love! It was a greater disruption in the body than an illness. But though at certain times I actually felt sick, I wanted her so badly, at other times it seemed to me – and I noted this with satisfaction – as if I had displaced those goddamned cats.

It was now December. The days were short and clammy-cold; they started late and dark; they ended early in the same darkness, which in London was like faded ink. On one of these dark afternoons Erroll Jeeps came into my office and asked whether he could have a private word with me.

'Owlie Cooper – remember him?'

'I met him at your house,' I said.

'That's the cat,' Erroll said. 'He's in a bind. He's a jazzhead – plays trumpet around town in clubs. Thing is, his work permit hasn't been renewed.'

'Union trouble?'

'No, it's the Home Office, playing tough. He thought it would just be routine, but when he went to renew it they refused. Plus, they told him that he had already overstayed his visit. So he's here illegally.'

'What can I do?'

'Give me a string to pull,' Erroll said.

'I wish I had one – he seemed a nice guy.'

'He laughs a little too much, but he's a great musician.'

My inspiration came that evening as I walked across Chelsea Bridge to Overstrand Mansions and my apartment. I passed the public phone box on Prince of Wales Drive and thought: *Owlie Cooper was a man with a skill to sell – he made music, he was American, he was here to do business. He had a product and he was in demand, so why not treat it as a trade matter, Margaret?*

I saw her the next day and said, 'There's an American here who's trying to do business with the Brits. He's got a terrific product, but his visa's run out. Do you think you can handle it?'

'Businessman,' she said. 'What kind of businessman?'

'Music.'

'What kind?' she said. 'Publishing, record company, or what?'

'He makes music,' I said. 'Owlie Cooper, the jazzman we met at Jeeps's house.'

Margaret sighed and turned back to face her desk. She spoke to her blotter. 'He can get his visa in the usual way.'

'We could help him sell his product here,' I said.

'Product! He plays the trumpet, for Pete's sake.'

'Margaret,' I said, 'this guy's in trouble. He can't get a job if he hasn't got a work permit. Look, he's a good advertisement for American export initiative.'

'I'd call it cultural initiative. Get Scaduto. He's the cultural affairs officer. Music is his line.' Then, in a persecuted voice, she said, 'Please, I'm busy.'

'You could pull a string. Skiddoo doesn't have a string.'

'This bastard Cooper –'

'What do you mean, "bastard"? He's a lost soul,' I said. 'Why should you be constantly boosting multinational corporations while a solitary man –'

'I remember him,' Margaret said. 'He hates cats.'

'No, it was dogs. And he doesn't hate them. He was mocking Al Sanger's dog.'

'I distinctly remember,' she said stiffly. 'It was cats.'

There was a catlike hiss in her cross voice as she said so.

She said, 'People will say I don't want to help him because he's black. Actually – I mean, funnily enough – that's why I do want to help him – because he's black and probably grew up disadvantaged. But I can't.'

'You can!'

'It's not my department.'

I started to speak again, but again she hissed at me. It was not part of a word but a whole warning sound – an undifferentiated hiss of fury and rebuke, as if I were a hulking, brutish stranger. It embarrassed me to think that her secretary was listening to Margaret behaving like one of her own selfish cats.

It was the only time we had ever talked business, and it was the last time. Owlie Cooper left quietly to live in Amsterdam. He claimed he was a political exile. He wasn't, of course – he was just one of the many casualties of Anglo-American bureaucracy. But I felt that in time he would become genuinely angry and see us all as enemies; he would get lonelier and duller and lazier in Holland.

Two weeks later I was calling Margaret from a telephone booth, the sort of squalid public phone box that, when I entered it, excited me with a vivid recollection of her hair and her lips. She began telling me about someone she had found in the house quite by chance, how he had stayed the night and eaten a huge breakfast, and how she was going to fatten him up.

I had by then already lost the thread of this conversation. I had taken a dislike to her for her treatment of Owlie Cooper. I hated the stink of this phone box, the broken glass and graffiti. What was she talking about? Why was she telling me this?

I said, 'What's his name?'

'Who?'

'The person who spent the night with you.'

'The little Burmese?' she said. 'I haven't given him a name yet.'

My parting words were ineffectual and unmemorable. I just stopped seeing her, canceled our usual date, and Sunday I spent the whole day bleeding in my bedroom. She hardly seemed to notice, or else – and I think this was more likely – she was relieved that I had given up.

The Honorary Siberian

One day I returned to my apartment at Overstrand Mansions and found a case of vodka outside the door – a dozen bottles of Stolichnaya Green Label. A week later it was a basket filled with small jars of caviar. Neither of these gifts contained a note or any indication of the name of the sender. But there was no question of my keeping them. I brought them to the Embassy and put them in storage – in the same basement room in which we kept the originals of hate-letters and the left-behind umbrellas – and I had their existence entered in the duty officer's log. The next parcel was a box of chocolates, and the last one an imitation leather wallet. One thing was clear: whoever was leaving these things was running out of money.

'You have a secret admirer,' Everett Horton said. 'It's got to be a Russian. They're noted for their subtlety. Like German jokes, like Mexican food. A few years ago one of our guys on the third floor was approached by a Tass correspondent. They had lunch – our man was wired up. The Russian offered him money for information. Just like that – can you imagine? They still play the tape of the conversation upstairs for laughs.'

'What should I do, coach?'

Horton said, 'I'd put him on hold.'

The next week there was no gift at my door. There was a phone call.

'My name is Yuri Kirilov,' a man said. 'You know me.'

I did know him, in the same way that millions of people in the West know Soviet defectors. But Kirilov's defection – in the middle of a television program on the BBC – had been spectacular.

'Please to meet my wife,' Kirilov said, as I threw my lunch bag into the litter bin next to the bench. We were at the Piccadilly side of Green Park.

I was embarrassed for him, because this woman gave me a hot adoring look and took my hand. She said, 'You have beautiful eyes,' and kept staring.

Under the circumstances there was nothing I could say except 'Thank you' and 'Yuri didn't tell me he was married.'

'He is ashamed!'

I said, 'If I were married to you I'd never stop boasting about you.'

It was exaggerated and insincere, but what else could I say? She had made a little melodrama out of being introduced to me in Green Park, and I was doing my best to turn it into a farce. Spouses who flirted in front of their partners seemed to me dangerous and stupid, and Helena – that was her name – had taken me by surprise. Kirilov had not mentioned his wife. He merely said that he urgently wanted to see me – somewhere quiet. I suggested my office at the Embassy. He said, 'Not that quiet.' I suggested the Serpentine, which I often walked around at lunchtime. 'Green Park,' he said. 'Is better.' *Grin Park*: he had not been out of the Soviet Union very long.

'I must kiss him for these compliments,' Helena was saying. 'Take my photo, Yuri.'

Kirilov obediently snapped a picture as Helena sat me down beside her and threw her arms around my neck. We were, for a few seconds, the classic canoodling pair, kissing on a park bench.

'I like the taste!' Helena said. 'One more time, please.'

I tried to restrain her, but it did little good. I was sure that the photograph of this embrace probably looked much more passionate. The kiss made it seem a private moment.

'There is lipstick on your mouth,' she said. 'Your boss will be very shocked!'

I said, 'It would take more than this to shock my boss.'

'What if he knew it was Russian lipstick?' Helena said.

'He'd send me to Siberia,' I said.

'I would follow you,' Helena said.

I expected Kirilov to hit her, but all he said was, 'I was in Siberia. I write my novel in Siberia. With a little pencil. With tiny sheets of paper. More than eight hundred sheets, very tiny – very small writing, two hundred words to a sheet. I bring it here. It is *Bread and Water*. No one want to read it!'

'Siberia?' I said. 'Were you in a labor camp?'

'No,' he said impatiently. 'Writers' Union! They send me to Siberia to make books.'

Helena said, 'In Soviet Union, Yuri is famous. Have money. But here, not so famous!'

Kirilov looked rueful. 'I am honorary Siberian for my work,' he said. 'I can sell two hundred thousand copies of novel.' He made an ugly face. 'This is nothing. Others can even sell half a million. Even if I go to a shop I hear people say, 'Kirilov, Kirilov,' and pulling my sleeve. Moscow shop.'

Helena said, 'Pop star,' and smiled foolishly at him.

'In Soviet Union I have a car,' Kirilov said. 'Is better than that one.'

Now we were all sitting on the bench, and Kirilov turned and pointed to a maroon Jaguar. He then let his tongue droop and with big square thumbs snapped his camera into its leather case.

Helena said, 'He have no car in London.'

'I don't have a car either,' I said.

'But you have a job,' Kirilov said. 'You have money. You can do what you like. I have nothing.'

'You have freedom,' I said.

'Hah! I have freedom,' Kirilov said. He twisted his mouth and made it liverish and ugly. 'All I have is freedom, freedom. Too much, I can say.'

Friddom: he made it sound like persecution.

'Is better more money,' Helena said. Each time she mentioned money her face became sensual. She spoke the word hungrily, with an open mouth and staring eyes. It occurred to me that you could know a great deal about a person by asking him to say 'money.'

Kirilov turned to her and said clearly in English, 'Now we make our discussion. So you go, Leni. Be careful – people can do tricks to you.'

Before she left, Helena said to me, 'You can come and visit me.'

'Perhaps I'll visit you both,' I said.

'Yes, that's nice,' she said, and made a soft sucking noise with her pursed lips.

When she was gone, Kirilov said, 'She likes you.'

'That's nice,' I said. But I wanted to say *How do you stand this damned woman?*

'She never likes anyone before in London,' he said. 'But you – she like.'

'She's a very nice person,' I said.

Kirilov laughed. He said, 'No. She is very pretty. With big what-you-can-call. But she is not nice person. We say, she is like a doll – pretty face, grass inside.' He winked at me. 'Also, like an animal.'

'I see.'

'She love to buy clothes. English clothes. American clothes. Blue jeans. In Soviet Union, I buy clothes, clothes, clothes. I have money. I have respect. But here' – he made his ugly face again – 'nothing.'

'It takes time,' I said. 'You're luckier than some. There was a man here a few years ago who asked for political asylum like you, but before he was in the clear they drugged him – your Embassy people – and sent him back.'

'He is not so unlucky,' Kirilov said.

'They might have killed him,' I said.

'You are like children – you believe anything,' he said. 'Maybe it was a trick. Just fooling the British. He is not unlucky. But I am very unlucky. These shoes – how much you think they cost?'

'Thirty-two pounds,' I said.

I must have guessed right, judging from his expression. He said, 'In Soviet Union, not more than ten pounds. And my rent! I have a tiny small flat here. Is better for a dog. I pay sixty-seven pounds a week. In Soviet Union I pay twenty for the same square meters. Is ridiculous in London.'

'Mr Kirilov,' I said, 'I thought you had something urgent to discuss with me.'

'Yes,' he said; then pettishly, 'But why you refuse me to have lunch?'

Dinner had been his first suggestion, lunch his second – 'I pay for you,' he had said. And I knew then that he wanted a favor. I wasn't interested in eating with him, and we had compromised on Green Park. If he had been any other Russian I would have refused to meet him, but he was enough of a celebrity to be harmless.

His defection, as I said, had been spectacular. He had been on a television program with his interpreter, who was also his security man. And then, in the middle of the program (something about writing and politics), Kirilov had simply stood up and walked off camera while the security man gaped. That was his defection. The clip of Kirilov hurrying away behind the wooden walls of the set, the security man squinting stupidly, was shown on the BBC many times, always with a hilarious effect, for it was known that minutes after making a run for it, Kirilov had gone into hiding, in the depths of Kent. A week later he was granted political asylum.

Kirilov was not a political dissident. He was a defector, a well-known Soviet poet, a party man, a womanizer. He had always claimed that he was free to criticize Soviet life. He had made numerous trips to foreign countries. He was thought to be safe. He was well connected. He went to writers' conferences, not only in Eastern Europe, but also in the West – in Stockholm, Paris, and Milan. He had been to Cuba five times. His poems had been translated by the American poet Walter Van Bellamy, and it was at Bellamy's house in Kent that he had hidden on the day of his defection. Anyone who read a newspaper knew these facts about Yuri Kirilov, and it was easy to tell from Kirilov's attitude on the telephone that he expected people to know him. He had the celebrity's easy presumption. He was on good terms with the world. I must have stammered or hesitated on the phone, because he had said, 'You know me.'

But he was annoyed that I had refused his invitation to lunch, and I think he objected to our sitting on this park bench in the middle of a gray winter afternoon. He had imagined something grander, and he sat tetchily on the bench, making fastidious plucks at his trouser creases, and fussing with his cuffs and his camera, and looking left and right.

I said, 'We can have lunch some other time.'

'You Americans,' he said. 'Always in a hurry. No time for relaxing. Even the British – so famous for their good manners. They behave like pigs, I can say.'

'That's nice, coming from you. I'm sure they'd love to hear you say it.'

'It is true. They are pigs.'

'When you ran away they gave you a place to hide. They let you stay. They could have sent you back. You'd be in Siberia, with your ass in a crack.'

'Siberia is lovely place! I am honorary citizen of Siberia!'

'You're an honorary citizen of Britain, too.'

He said, 'I am propaganda value. I am worth millions. You saw the newspaper – 'Famous Soviet Writer Chooses Britain.' All of that. It is good for the British government. They would never have sent me back.'

'So you think you're valuable?'

'Millions,' he said, curling his lower lip and fattening it boastfully. 'I am not like some of these dissidents – troublemakers, cripples, Jews. Listen, I tell you they make trouble in any society – *any*. Solzhenitsyn! He is a trouble in Soviet Union. Yes, he is also a trouble in United States. You hear how he criticizes Americans – journalists, drugs, pop music. He is against!'

'Can you blame him?'

Kirilov laughed, snapping his jaws at the air. 'I can blame him! I like journalists, I like pop music, and some drugs I can say so what.'

'Then you must be very happy in London.'

'I am deeply unhappy, my friend. This is a terrible country, a corrupt country. So many people unemployed. No work. And how the people live! In small rooms, very cold rooms, eating bad food, taking the tube. Aargh! I hate.' He batted the air with his hands, pushing these images aside.

'Siberia must have been much better.'

He considered this; he nodded; he had not heard any sarcasm.

'I can say, yes, better. In Siberia I am a VIP. Here I am nothing. No one to publish Russian books, no one to read. I go to the library, I drink with Walter Bellamy, I look for money. Nothing, nothing, nothing. Better VIP in Siberia than nothing in London. There are flowers in Siberia!'

'It was your choice,' I said.

'Helena's choice,' he said. He winked at me. 'She likes you very much. You know?'

'She seems happy here.'

'Happy, yes. Because I let her do whatever she like' – he nudged me hard with a sharp elbow – 'whatever make her happy. Anything.'

'I see.'

'*Anything*,' he said. 'I am not a jealous man. She is very beautiful. Like an animal, I can say. Is cruel to make her unhappy. You think she is wild?'

'It's hard to tell,' I said, and now I was sure I wanted to walk away.

'In public park she is wild –'

'Yes, yes.'

'– but in bed, in bed she is a slave,' Kirilov said. 'A slave.' He watched my face closely, leering at me and waiting for me to react.

I was determined not to. I saw what he was offering me, but he stopped short of saying, *Take her –*

Perhaps he noticed my impatience, because his face hardened.

I said, 'What do you want?'

'Brodsky,' he sneered. 'Brodsky has been declared genius.'

'I haven't got the slightest idea what you're talking about.'

'Joseph Brodsky – Jew dissident – living in New York, good jobs teaching at three universities, nice place to live, plenty of money. He writes his poems in a tiny room in Soviet Union. Fine. Good. Everyone say, "Good work – maybe a little decadent." Then he hate Soviet. He go to New York. He get free money for write poems in New York! This scumdrill have plenty of money, but he want more to write more Brodsky poems! Then! American foundation say, "Brodsky is genius"' – he pronounced it *jaynyoos* – "'we will give him money! Forty thousand dollars, every year, for five years." Brodsky! Scumdrill!'

Kirilov was shouting. He had stood up, and his shrill voice penetrated through the roar of the traffic. The wind had risen, and it rattled the branches overhead, it pulled at Kirilov's coat, it yanked his trousers against his skinny legs and white ankles, making him look weak.

I said, 'I don't know anything about it.'

'Is in library. *New York Times*. Is your country. If you don't know about it I feel sorry for you. But I think it is an injustice.'

'This is the last time I ask you,' I said. 'What do you want?'

'You must give me visa for New York City.'

'I'm not in the consular section.'

'You know the poet Bellamy. Famous American poet. He will vouch for me. He will sponsor me.'

'Bellamy's in the hospital,' I said. 'Anyway, you've already been turned down for a visa.'

'For what reason I want to know!'

'We're not obliged to give you a reason.'

He sat down beside me again – his shouting had tired him. He was a bit hoarse. He said, 'You can help me. They will believe you. Bellamy says you are the only honest man in the Embassy – that's why I phoned you up. You have a reputation for being a fair man. That's why Helena is so attracted to you. She can't help it – she admires your honesty.'

I said, 'Do you know the word "bullshit"?'

'You are trying to insult me,' he said.

'You're wasting your time. If you had told me a half an hour ago that you wanted a visa I could have saved you a lot of trouble. It's impossible.'

He said, 'It is not I who am insulted – it is my wife. You simply toss her away like a worthless thing.'

'Be careful,' I said.

His face darkened. 'Then you will be sorry.'

'Don't threaten me,' I said. I was smiling.

He said, 'You think you can mock me!'

'No, I was just thinking that you offered me lunch. All this might have been taking place in a restaurant. I would have had indigestion! Excuse me,' I said, and stood up. 'I have to go back to my office.'

'I have pictures of you with my wife!' he said. He shook the camera at me. 'I will send them to the newspaper. Hah!'

'It will be very embarrassing for you,' I said. 'In this country, pimping is a criminal offense. I would imagine that if the authorities heard that you'd been pimping for your wife, they'd ship you both back to the Soviet Union.'

'That is a disgraceful lie,' he said. 'And you have no proof.'

'I've been recording our conversation,' I said.

He laughed. 'No, you haven't. When Leni kissed you she examined your clothes for a recorder. She found no wires, or she would have told me!'

I moved to the end of the bench and dipped my hand into the litter bin. I retrieved the soiled lunch bag I had thrown in, and took a small tape recorder out of it. It was still whirring softly. I stopped it, rewound it, then pressed the *Play* button.

'. . . *ship you both back* . . .'

'You are disgusting,' Kirilov said.

I said, 'Get a job.'

I knew then that this honorary Siberian would spend the rest of his life as a refugee – unemployed, uttering threats, and pitying himself. He had actually believed that I would help him – perhaps sleep with his wife, or be tempted to collaborate with him in his flight to America. How old-fashioned the Soviets were in their quaint belief in blackmail! But Kirilov believed in nothing, really, which is why he was so ignorant. A more passionate man, a believer, would have been far more resourceful, like the other honorary Siberians who had already become American writers.

Gone West

They appeared to be husband and wife – man standing, woman seated: the classic married pose of Authority flanked by Loyalty – but when I got closer I saw they were both men. It was just after eight in the morning, a smudgy winter dawn in London, on the Embassy stairs. The doors would not be open to the public for another hour. I mounted the stairs but couldn't get to the door without asking the man who was standing to move aside. He made a respectful noise, then spoke.

'We're going to America!'

Americans call it the States.

I said, 'You'll need visas.'

'That's why we're here,' the seated one said.

'You should be at the other door – the Consulate, visa section. It's right around the corner, on Upper Grosvenor Street.'

The news that they were waiting at the wrong door didn't upset them. They laughed, as the English often do in such situations. They said, 'Silly old us!' and 'What a wheeze!'

It seemed to be a national characteristic. The English had been getting bad news for so long, they had learned to cope. They disliked complainers, even when the complaint was justified, and regarded such people as spineless. Most of the English seemed rather proud of their capacity for suffering. It made them the world's best airline passengers, but had given them one of the world's worst airlines. Surely this 'mustn't grumble' attitude accounted for a great deal of Britain's decline? But of course it made the place nice and quiet. Our vices are so often our virtues as well.

'You must be cold,' I said.

'Absolutely freezing.' This was said, with one eyebrow raised, in the most matter-of-fact tone.

'Never mind. We'll soon be in California.'

'Fat lot of good that's doing me now,' the matter-of-fact one said.

'Oh, we're going to have a little moan, are we?'

'Listen to him – after his blameless weekend!'

'You said you were impervious to cold.'

'On your bike! I never said impervious – don't know what the flipping word means!'

This was all spoken with sharpness and speed, and the effect was comic – friendly, too – even in the misty brown dawn of a January morning. From that moment I began to wonder what would happen to them in California.

The dark-haired one, who was standing, faced the fairer one, who was still seated, and said, 'Lambie here got me up at the crack of dawn. Said we had to hurry – frightened me with stories about long queues and red tape. So off we go to stand at the wrong door! Feel me cheeks. They're solid ice! I haven't even had me tea!'

'Forgot our thermal underwear, didn't we, chicken?'

'I'm wearing me serviceable string vest.'

I said, 'How about a coffee inside?'

This made them go very silent. They seemed a bit suspicious. But I had noticed that a kindness to an English person often arouses unease or suspicion. It is a very nervous nation. In a wary voice, the dark-haired one said, 'Do you think it'd be all right?'

'What about security? Laser beams and that,' the other said. 'You must get ever so many bomb scares.'

I said, 'You don't look very dangerous to me.'

'Him – he's the dangerous one,' the dark-haired man said. 'Oh, he's a hard lad!'

They followed me in – our security man squinting at them and giving their colorful shoulder bags a close inspection for weapons – and I heard one of them say, 'Laser beams, you daft prat!'

The coffee urn was outside Al Sanger's office. This morning there was a plate of Danish pastries next to the urn. Sanger often bought them at a place off Curzon Street – deliberately there so that he could say, 'I just picked up some tarts in Shepherd Market. Want one?'

I poured three cups of coffee and urged them to take some pastry.

'Don't mind if I do!'

'I won't say no!'

'Our first American breakfast.'

So they had overcome their suspicion. I said, 'It's part of our job to encourage tourism.'

'It's lovely and warm in here.'

'Think I'll put me feet up!'

Their names, they said, were Cary and Lamb. Cary had the dark hair and broad shoulders, and he had a tiny Irish chin and a high sweet voice. Lamb at first glance was a young man with reddish hair, but looking closer I saw he was quite old – over sixty – with rather nasty blue eyes and his hair harshly colored and coarse-textured and spread across his crown to cover his baldness. He wore an earring, and Cary had a heavy chain around his neck.

Lamb said, 'You actually work here, do you?'

''Course he works here, you pillock!'

I said, 'But I can't give you much help with your visas.'

'We won't have any trouble,' Cary said. 'We've never been Communists or prostitutes, and we haven't been in the nick. That's the kind of thing they want to know, don't they? We've been good lads, haven't we, Lambie?'

'Apart from your occasional lapses of taste,' Lamb said.

'Listen to the incurable cottager!' Cary shrieked. He pulled a pack of cigarettes out of his back pocket. But his trousers were so tight the cigarettes were squashed and unsmokable. He said, 'There's another packet of fags gone west.'

'About time you gave up smoking. It'll stunt your growth.'

'Aren't you happy with me growth, Lambie?'

They both laughed at this. I couldn't see the joke, but the sight of them laughing so easily amused me.

'What are you planning to do in the States?'

'We're going to California,' Lamb said.

'I mean, after you get there.'

'We don't have any plans for after that. We're going to California a special way – an ingenious way. It's Cary's big plan, see. He does have the occasional brilliant scheme.'

'I'd like to hear it,' I said.

Cary had thrown his squashed cigarettes into the waste-basket. Now he was bent over the basket and reaching in, trying to retrieve them.

'Look at him,' Lamb said. 'Fossicking in the waste-bin!'

'I see one,' Cary said.

'He sees one,' Lamb said, rolling his eyes. 'Picking up fag ends – can't take him anywhere.'

It was a double-act. They were spirited and mocking, and they kept it up until my secretary arrived. They found her presence intimidating, and they asked whether they should go. I said they shouldn't hurry away, and I kicked the door shut.

Lamb heard her tuning the radio for the news. There was a moment of music.

'Music,' he said. 'Oh, be still my dancing feet!'

'Give over,' Cary said.

'Tell him your brilliant scheme.'

'Yes, mum,' Cary said, and grinned and gave himself dimples as he looked at me. 'We're secondhand furniture dealers, the kind of rubbish that innocent people call antiques. We find the stuff all over the place. You've seen the signs. "House Clearances Our Specialty."'

Lamb said, '"Top Prices Paid for Your Unwanted Furniture."'

Cary frowned. He said, '"That Old Chest in Your Attic Could Be Worth a Fortune."'

'Cary specializes in old chests. You have to watch him.'

'You flaming wally!' Cary said, and turning back to me, he said, 'It's absolute balls about the top prices, but we buy what we can afford, mainly tables, benches, mirrors, picture frames, and that. Windsor chairs. Welsh dressers if we're lucky.'

'There's an awful lot of lifting,' Lamb said. 'I've done me back I don't know how many times.'

'He's the original Welsh dresser, is Lambie,' Cary said. 'Aren't you, sunshine?'

'You're just saying that because you like me drawers.'

'That's what we should have called the shop, you know – "Chests and Drawers."'

'Do me a favor!' Lamb said in an actressy voice.

But I noticed that everything they said, no matter how mocking, was tinged with what sounded like real affection.

I said, 'What is your shop called?'

'"Pining for You" – isn't it horrid? We hate it,' Lamb said. 'We used to do stripping in our tank, to order. Anything you wanted stripped – within limits – we'd chuck in.'

Cary said, 'There's a boom in stripped pine in London at the moment. You get knackered, scrubbing the paint off, but you can sell anything if it's stripped. We got top whack for a coffin once. Can you imagine someone buying an old coffin? I suppose some clapped-out Dracula –'

'We've got a lot of American customers. They adore our refectory tables,' Lamb said. 'Or any sort of shelving. They're mad on shelving over there.'

'"Mad on shelving" – you make them sound a pack of flaming morons, Lambie.'

'Well, they are,' Lamb said, timing his pause after that word, 'mad on shelving.'

'Americans buy quality,' Cary said.

'Crawler!' Lamb said. 'You're shameless!'

Cary said, 'And that's what gave me the idea of the lorry. Did you know you can ship a lorry across the Atlantic and it costs the same whether it's full or empty?'

'That's Cary's brilliant scheme. We're going to take a lorry-load of country pine furniture to California.'

'And flog it,' Cary said. 'To pay our way.'

'We reckon on making a tidy fortune on it.'

'Don't tell me too much,' I said. 'If you do, I'll have to advise you about the regulations governing the import of dutiable goods.'

'Muggins put his foot in it,' Lamb said.

'Oh, belt up,' Cary said. But he was laughing.

'I won't report you,' I said. 'But you'd better go get your visas. The Consulate opens pretty soon.'

'Crikey, I feel better. I needed that coffee. You're awfully kind,' Cary said.

'You're welcome,' I said.

'That's nice, isn't it? "You're welcome." English people never say that.' He looked at Lamb and said, 'You're welcome, sunshine.'

'Send me a postcard,' I said.

'We'll do better than that,' Lamb said. 'We'll report back.'

'When English people go to California,' I said, 'they either come back the next day or stay there for the rest of their lives.'

Lamb said, 'I wonder what we'll do.'

'You could do both,' I said. 'After all, there are two of you. Each one could –'

'There's only one,' Cary said. 'I mean to say, we're sticking together.'

Lamb gave Cary an affectionate push, and Cary lowered his eyes. I noticed again the great difference between their ages. Lamb's neck was loose and the roots of his hair were gray and his hands were mottled with liver spots. But his voice and his gestures, the promptness of his wit, made him seem youthful.

'That's the idea,' I said. 'Stick together.'

'He's my wife,' Lamb said. 'Aren't you, petal?'

I never thought I would see them again. I imagined them crossing the United States in an old English truck loaded with pine furniture – Cary at the wheel, Lamb riding shotgun, going west.

Of all the get-rich-quick schemes I had ever heard – and I had heard many – this was the best. It was a truckload of furniture, but they paid only for the truck. This would transport them to California, and the sale of the furniture paid for the trip. It had everything – sunshine, freedom, a good product, a free ride, and a guaranteed profit. It had taken a little capital, but even more enterprise; and it gave me hope. Whenever London went dead on me, whenever I thought of ditching my job and clearing out, I thought of Cary and Lamb in their truck, with their pine furniture, bumping down the highway underneath a big blue sky. It made me want to get married and go.

I was sure they would wind up in San Francisco, overstay their visas, and go to ground. Many Europeans did these days – it was only Arabs who had the confidence to head home when their visas expired. I had met the two men in early January. In late February, the security man at the main entrance phoned me and said, 'A Mr Cary and friend down here, sir. Doesn't have an appointment – name's not in the book – but he says he wants to talk to you. What shall I tell him, sir?'

A *Mr Cary and friend*: they were back!

'Send them up,' I said.

But Lamb was not the friend, and I barely recognized Cary. He was thinner, he had grown a beard, and he was dressed like a man in the English Department bucking for a promotion – tweed sports jacket, leather tie, corduroy trousers, argyle socks, and shiny shoes. He was a far cry from the junk dealer in the ragged scarf and flat cap and greasy raincoat of six weeks ago. Some people look worse, much stranger, even crooked, when they dress stylishly. That was how Cary seemed to me – as if he were trying to pull a fast one on me. He was frowning, pushing out his lips, jerking his beard with his cheeks.

And the friend was a girl with a big soft face, who chewed gum with her mouth open. She wore a man's pea jacket and a woolly hat. Cary introduced her to me as 'Honey.'

There are some nicknames that are obstacles to friendship. 'Honey' is one of them. At first it seems overaffectionate, and then it seems like mockery, and finally it sounds like a word of abuse.

Cary was holding her hand. He did not let go of it, even to smoke. He shook out a cigarette, put it to his lips, and lit it, all with one busy hand. In itself his hand-holding was not strange, but he had never once touched Lamb.

I said, 'I'm glad you kept your word about giving me a report.'

Cary didn't smile. He sat stiffly in his chair with a look of vague incomprehension on his face.

'Just stopped in to say hello,' he said. 'And to introduce you to Honey.'

The girl snapped her gum at me and said, 'Cary told me how you helped him' – she was American – 'and he really appreciated it. Usually Embassy people are such assholes. I remember once when I was in Mexico.'

Cary coughed and said, 'You must be busy.' He looked as if, already, he wanted to go.

'Tell me about the trip,' I said.

'There's so much to tell.'

'The crossing,' I said. 'What was the ship like?'

'I was seasick most of the time. It was a Polish freighter, full of butch sailors. The food was dreadful – turnips, swedes, boiled cabbage, stews of rancid mince. It was a week of misery. I stayed in my bunk the whole time.'

'What about your friend?'

'Pardon?'

'Lamb,' I said.

'Oh, him. He started acting strange. He'd disappear for hours and then when I asked where he'd been he'd say, "In the bowels of the ship." He thought he was being incredibly funny.'

I smiled, remembering Lamb, imagining how he would have said that. Where was the little old comedian? Where was the old Cary, for that matter? This one was entirely new – disapproving and full of seriousness. He was grave, but what was the point?

'It wasn't funny,' Cary said. 'He was always cracking jokes. When people who aren't funny start to make jokes it sounds stupid.'

His accent was gone, too.

I said, 'New York must have been quite a surprise.'

Cary shrugged. 'Lamb met a chap in a bar and got very excited. "He's giving us a place to kip – he's got bags of room!"' It was a flash of the old Cary – he did Lamb's effeminate voice very well, and it reminded me of how his own voice had deepened. He glanced at the girl whose hand he was holding and said, 'The chap was into S and M. Well, S really. Very keen on spanking. "How do you know you don't like it if you've never tried it?"'

'How did you get out of that one?' I asked.

'A cobbler's bench and a lot of pleading. I reckon he's cobbling someone on it right this minute.' He weighed the girl's hand in his own, lifting it and considering it. 'Hungry?'

Honey squeezed her face into an expression that said, *Sorta*, and Cary said to me, 'We have to go. I promised to show Honey around the neighborhood where I grew up – Stepney Green.'

'But what about your scheme?' I asked. 'What about the trip?'

'Don't ask. The lorry broke down on the New Jersey Turnpike. Turnpike! Why is it that the most horrid places in the States have the prettiest names?'

'Like Stepney Green – the jewel of East London?'

Cary did not respond to that. He said, 'We were towed to a garage. It seemed we needed a water pump. Two hundred for the tow, another two hundred for the pump. Nice round figures. We hadn't a penny.'

'How did you pay?'

'A refectory table, lovely it was, from a boys' school in Eastbourne. It was covered with carved initials, some of them going back to the eighteenth century. Just the thing for a garage mechanic in New Jersey.'

I had the strong sense that I did not know this man at all; that we were talking about nothing; that he did not know me.

'The radiator packed up in Virginia, on something called the Skyline Drive – Lamb loved the name. The radiator cost us a beautiful Victorian chest – two drawers, brass fittings, lots of carvings.' He looked at Honey again and waggled her hand and said, 'Hi.'

'Hi,' she said.

'Bored?'

She snorted a little air.

He kissed her. I felt I was watching someone taking a bite of candy. He licked his mouth when he finished kissing her.

'Let's go,' she said.

'So you didn't make it to California?' I said.

'We did, after a fashion. By the time we got to Missouri we'd traded most of the big pieces. And over the next three weeks, the rest of it went, to buy petrol and food. We slept in the lorry. It was getting emptier and emptier. Pretty soon, all the best pieces were gone. We'd turned them into cheeseburgers.'

'Not all of them,' Honey said. She surprised me. Her voice was brighter than Cary's, and a little malicious and lively.

'Where are you from?' I asked.

'Pomona?' She made it a polite question, as some uncertain Americans do when they give information. 'I go outside one morning and who do I see in the front yard but these two English guys.'

'So you met Mr Lamb,' I said.

'And his friend,' she said.

'Not me,' Cary said in a disgusted way. 'It was a chicken he found in Arizona. A hitchhiker. "Oh, let's pick him up – he looks lost!"' Cary squinted at me, giving me a powerful look of indignation, and he said, 'Lamb was really beastly to that kid. It was a revelation to me.'

Honey said, 'They were fags.'

Cary swallowed and said, 'I think he's sick. I think he's strange. I think he lost his bottle.'

Now Honey was smirking. 'My first husband is into English antiques. They really hit it off.' She uttered a coarse laugh and dragged Cary's hand off her lap and said, 'Let's go, sailor; we're wasting this man's valuable time.'

'We're looking for a flat,' Cary said. 'I'm not going to live over the shop anymore – especially after I've seen the way they live in America.'

'We've got this grubby little room,' Honey said, 'in a dump called Kilburn!'

'We'll find something,' Cary said in a solicitous voice.

'What about Lamb?' I said.

Cary pretended not to recognize the name for a moment, and then he said, 'We were really shocked. It opened my eyes. Lamb's a corrupter. That's where he belongs – Pomona.'

'Shut up about Pomona,' Honey said. 'It's a hundred times better than this dump. Hey, are we going or aren't we?'

So they left. What had gone wrong on the ideal trip, I could not say. But what worried me was that in a half-hour of talking, in the presence of a woman he obviously loved, this very funny man had not smiled once.

A Little Flame

'I'm downstairs.' It was a dead man's voice, like my father talking from his grave. 'They say they can't let me see you without an appointment.' It had a slight stammer of fear or anger in it. 'I want to talk to you about my wife.'

'I didn't catch your name,' I said.

'Whiting.'

'Anthony?'

'James Whiting, from Hong Kong,' he said. 'Anthony's my cousin. He said he'd met you. But Mei-lan –'

'Yes! You're married to Mei-lan! Now I remember.'

He said, 'It's in that connection that I want to talk to you. It's very important.'

'I see. I wonder if we could make it tomorrow. Lunch, say – somewhere pleasant.'

'I'll be on my way back to Hong Kong tomorrow.' He spoke with a finality in which there was no emotion.

I said, 'I'm terribly tied up at the moment.'

'I can't wait.' He sounded as if, already, he had been waiting a long time for me.

'Perhaps we could meet the next time you're here?'

'I'll never be in London again.' His voice was stone.

'I might be in Hong Kong one of these days,' I said.

'You won't find me. I'm leaving the bank for good. What time do you finish work?'

'I'll be here forever, I'm afraid.' His silence demanded that I explain. 'The Vice-President's flying in next week from Washington. We're all working overtime. It might be eleven before I can get away.'

'Midnight, then,' he said, and I saw blackness.

'Impossible,' I said.

'I must see you.' The words rapped against my ear.

'Is Mei-lan with you?' I asked.

'Mei-lan is dead.'

'Oh, God, I'm sorry,' I said. 'I'll be right down.'

He was older than I had guessed he would be, but his frailty was partly grief. The strain was on his face, in his sideways glance, and his odd, bereaved smile. He was a tough man who had been stricken with sorrow. His hair, raked into gray and white strands, was as dull as metal. His face was shadowy; there was no light behind the skin. It is that light which can make a person seem old or young.

Now that I was with him I was less anxious. He was just over sixty – I knew him to be sixty-one – not elderly, but rather old to be the husband of a Chinese girl in her mid-twenties. He had the shaky gaze of a widower. I could not match him to Mei-lan. He looked a little wild.

I had greeted him. I was still talking, commiserating, and walking much too fast. He replied in a breathless way. He followed me outside and down the Embassy steps. He seemed to be chasing me. I stayed just ahead of the flap of his footsoles, one stride away from him.

He said, 'I'm at the Connaught. Shall we go there?'

That was a bad moment. I said, 'The Connaught,' and made it an idiot's echo.

'I'm sorry to have interrupted your work.'

Was this irony? Mei-lan was dead! We were heading across the square for Carlos Place.

'It's perfectly all right. I hadn't understood. I should have asked.'

'I didn't want to tell you on the phone. I find it hard to talk about. It's only been a month. The odor of her scent is still in the house. Flammette. It's very upsetting.'

He said no more until we reached the Connaught Hotel. The doorman saluted us. James Whiting raised his head and showed the man his bereaved smile, and we went inside. In the little lobby of armchairs and engravings, he said, 'Wouldn't we be more comfortable upstairs?'

He scratched the air with his hands, pointing the way.

'Right here is perfect,' I said. I sat down to show him I was satisfied and would not go farther. I hoped he would sit down.

I felt very young then, and sad and swindled, not just visited but haunted. This man had seemed to materialize in London with terrible news, and he looked terrible – the menace was a shadow on his face. I did not want to go upstairs. I did not want a white door to close behind me, in a room smelling of burning lavender, with a blue ceiling and the purifying light from tall windows.

He frowned at the chair across from mine. He blew out his cheeks in anger – but it may have been only impatience. He sat down in that chair, he sighed, he blinked at me, he tried to start.

'She stayed here, you know,' he said.

'They say it's a lovely hotel.'

'This is where she said she was happiest in London, when she came in October for her tests. That's why I'm staying here.'

'Those tests. I thought she was taking exams. She mentioned she was studying law.'

'To take her mind off it. She was trying to overcome it by means of will power. She had so many tests! She didn't believe them. The best hospitals. The findings were always the same, even the same words – "the Black Spot," she said, when she got the reports. When she was too weak to travel – bedridden – she seemed to accept it. They gave her heroin injections. "Heroin for the heroine" – that was her joke. It was wonderful stuff. It made her death almost peaceful.'

I said, 'Please don't feel you have to talk about it.'

'I think it does me good.' He wore a look of wonderment for a few seconds. It lighted his face briefly; it made him look selfish and a little wild once more. Then it was gone, and with a kind of grumpy deference he said, 'Unless you'd rather I didn't.'

'It's painful,' I said. 'I find it painful.'

'You young people.' He raised his head at me. 'When you get cancer it goes right through you. You burn up very fast. It's usually a matter of weeks, not months. Days, sometimes. You just burn.'

'Please.'

He said, 'She was very fond of you.'

'I knew her father. I was the US Consul in Ayer Hitam. What a home town for someone like Mei-lan!'

'You don't have to tell me anything. I know about you. She spoke about you a great deal. What are you looking at?'

The waiter had slipped behind Whiting to inquire whether there was anything we wanted.

'Nothing for me,' I said.

Whiting exercised his right as a guest of the hotel and ordered a whiskey – it was after three-thirty. He did not speak again until it arrived, and then he merely held the glass, sometimes lifting and inhaling its fumes, but not drinking. It seemed to allow him to hide his glance in an innocent gesture. His eyes seldom left me and they scorched me with aching heat wherever they rested. They were deceptively dangerous, like dull metal that looks the same hot or cold.

'She greatly enjoyed her time in London.'

'The old man's customers were British – always talking about London. It was home for those colonials. Sentiment can be catching. People had so little to be sentimental about in Malaysia. I mean the Chinese. He wanted Mei-lan to come to London.'

'It wasn't London – it was you.'

Whiting, a banker, did not have the heavy-faced and chair-bound look of a banker. No paunch, no watch chain, no money-moralizing, nor any apologies that were in reality sneers. He had a lawyer's alertness showing through his bony face of grief. He had watchful eyes, the pretense of repose, the pounce ('It wasn't London –'). Bankers are bullfrogs; lawyers are lizards. And his tongue was quick for a grieving man.

He said, 'We were in London together when we first got married. It seems like yesterday. It *was* yesterday. Two years ago. Funny' – he didn't smile – 'she didn't mention you then.'

'The old man liked me to keep an eye on her. He was my first friend out there. He worried about her.'

'You call him the old man,' Whiting said, and raised his glass and looked at me over its rim. 'He and I are the same age.'

I said, 'We did some business with him. We were winding up the Consulate. I needed office equipment. It would have been expensive for me to buy things outright and sell them two years later. He leased everything to me, at a fair rate. He was one of the first in that part of Malaysia to go in for leasing in a big way. He was progressive. So were his children. Very modern-thinking. They were stifled there.'

Whiting pushed at his face with his fingertips as he listened to me.

'I left my wife for Mei-lan.' He looked at me through spread fingers. 'I have grown-up children.'

'Her father was a bit upset about that. Strife in a Chinese family can be violent. Threats, fights, suicides. It's all or nothing. The old man was worried.'

'My eldest son was Mei-lan's age,' he said.

'How did he take it? Some kids never come to terms with their parents' divorce.'

'Didn't bother him.'

'He's unusual.'

'He's divorced,' Whiting said. 'Three years ago. But he loved Mei-lan. Everyone did.'

I said, 'She was the sort of woman who inspired men to make sacrifices for her. They'd do anything.'

He merely looked at his whiskey and at me. He drew his lips up in a mock smile, like a man with a bad pain hiding his distress, and after I'd said *They'd do anything*, one of his eyes widened on me.

I said, 'Her father gave her everything. It made him a little uneasy – he knew he was in danger of spoiling her. I'm proud to say he trusted me. I liked him.'

Whiting gave me his sideways look. I noticed that his gray-white hair was yellowing in places, as it does in certain aging men. It gave his head a strange heated appearance.

He said, 'Frankly, I found the old man a bit slippery.'

'He was a businessman.'

'I don't mean that. I'm a businessman myself. He seemed sly.'

'A lot of people respected him for being careful.'

'A double-entry man. Hong Kong's full of them. Twisters.'

'I found him truthful. I knew the whole family.' As I said this, Whiting raised his head, lifting his chin at me, seeming to reject what I said. I paused, then said, 'The family must have been very sad about Mei-lan.'

'Shattered. You see, Mei-lan wasn't very truthful. All along she had denied that she was seriously ill. She claimed it was hepatitis.'

'That takes courage.'

'No.' His bright eyes challenged me to deny this. 'She found it easy to lie.'

I said, 'Perhaps in unimportant matters.'

'Unimportant? I am talking about her death. But not only that.' He now sat like a man on a wagon traveling over a bumpy road. He worked his shoulders as he spoke. 'She told lies because truth bored her. She didn't know that a good liar needs a good memory. She was always contradicting herself. It could be rather touching sometimes – like my daughter, who used to swear she hadn't touched the sweets and then would show me her purple tongue. God, I loved her.'

'You're saying she was deceitful.'

'No. She was virtuous. She didn't really know what the truth was. Lying was just a bad habit with her.'

'So she was innocent,' I said. 'She looked innocent.'

'She looked like a child,' he said. 'She was tiny. She had such a simple clean face. Some Chinese women never grow old. They have skin like silk. It grows finer, more beautiful with the years. Mei-lan was like that. A person ages and dies – the aging is a kind of preparation. But if there is no decline, no aging process – if the person looks ageless and beautiful – they seem immortal.' He glanced behind me as if a new thought had come into his head. 'Then they die and it is like the end of the world.'

'Didn't you know she was ill?'

'Having cancer isn't being ill,' he said. His head was turned toward me, but his eyes were glazed with memory. 'This is going to sound horribly naive to you, but I thought she was pregnant. It took my first wife that way. In bed all the time, that sort of ravishing pallor, the tears. I thought she was below par. It made her more beautiful.'

'She seemed fine when she was here,' I said. 'It must have been London.'

'Perhaps it was your company.'

'I saw very little of her, I'm sorry to say.'

'Somehow, she was satisfied.' He drank half his whiskey in a sudden gulp and breathed hard. He said, 'She wanted to be well.'

'Mei-lan wasn't desperate,' I said.

'It's not desperation I'm talking about – it's urgency. Do you know anything about death?'

'A certain amount. My parents were killed in an air crash when I was five. I was old enough to miss them.'

He said, 'With all respect, I'm talking about a different kind of intimacy with death. I mean, a dying woman will do anything to save herself.'

'So will a dying man.'

'For a man, death is a door. Everyone dies ugly, but that ugliness makes it terrible for a woman. You can't imagine. And there are worse things. A woman will do anything to get well, but she'll also do anything if she knows she's not going to get well. What are your restraints if you know you're doomed?'

'Mei-lan was a rational person. She was studying law,' I said. 'She had sense.'

'Law was only one distraction. She became obsessed about her appearance. She had beauty treatments. Injections. She did all the hospitals, she was tested again and again. She traveled, she needed old friends, she saw you.'

Whiting still sat solidly across from me with a patient intensity. He was large, his gaze was steady, and yet it was not a stare. He glanced from my eyes to my lips when I spoke, and at my hands when I moved them. We were not alone in that little Connaught parlor. It seemed to bother him. Whenever someone entered, Whiting flicked his eyes at them and dropped his voice.

I said, 'I hadn't really expected to hear from her.'

'She liked to startle people, show up without warning, catch them off-guard.'

'That can be charming,' I said.

'It gave her the upper hand. She could get anyone to do anything. I had never met anyone like her. Do you know, I lost most of my friends when I married her. I was glad. I didn't want them. She was everything. And such greed! I wanted someone who was greedy, who wanted me in a fiery way. That is passion. To me she was a friend, an enemy, a mother, a child.'

I must have looked puzzled.

'Wife, too,' he said slowly. 'I felt like an old man before I met her. After we married, I felt younger – she gave me youth. I had never had a real childhood. Some of us don't, you know. An English childhood can seem as serious and gray as middle age – all that silence, all those exams, we're always indoors. Mei-lan set my spirit free. My only regret was that she would outlive me – she would be on her own. I knew she had to be provided for. She gambled, you know.'

'I wasn't aware of that.'

'No?' He sat straighter. He seemed glad that I didn't know. I wondered how he got such a close shave – his skin was pink, not a hint of whiskers. It made me think of razors.

'She'd bet on anything,' he was saying. 'On an ant crossing a carpet. Very Chinese, that. I didn't mind the expense. It gave me something to spend my money on. It made her happy. Past a certain figure it's impossible to know what to do with your money. I had everything when I had her. I don't mean it was all good – it was diluted, that was the best of it. She kept my feet on the ground. You look blank.'

'I'm not sure what you're talking about.'

He shrugged. He didn't smile, yet he looked pleased – confident. In the past half-hour he had grown larger but less menacing. He said, 'When she died, nothing mattered. I came close to death myself then. What was the point in carrying on? I wanted to turn to wood. I spent a week in a chair with my mouth open. I suppose that sounds a bit crazy to you.'

I denied that it did. His eyes never left me and there was watchfulness even in his two hands, poised like crabs on his knees.

'When I finally got out of the chair, I wrote my letter of resignation. Now I want to find a smaller flat. I don't want anything more if I can't have Mei-lan.'

He turned away but glanced back at me quickly, as if he expected to catch my expression changed.

He said, 'Sometimes I can't bear to think of her.'

'That's only natural.'

'You don't understand.' He flung that sudden gaze on me again. Was he sinking, was he drowning? He said, 'But I had to trust her. I came here yesterday and realized that I was looking for her. That's not good. Don't you agree?'

'You'll never find her,' I said.

I had hesitated, and now he gave me his lizard look of scrutiny.

He said, 'No, no. That's not the point. I could find her – I could know her better. But it might be very upsetting.'

He wanted me to agree with him. But I said, 'People should be allowed to have secrets.'

'People's secrets are the most interesting thing about them,' he said. 'How could you love anyone who didn't have a secret?'

I said, 'How is it possible to go on loving someone after you know the secret?'

He was watching me very closely now. He seemed to want to trap me, lowering his judge's face on me and exerting pressure with his eyes.

He said, 'I want to think of her as I knew her – like a little flame, burning, burning, slightly malicious, tempting, loving, doing harmless damage. The coquette is a tormentor in a good cause. I want to think that she would always have been mine.' His face moved closer to mine. 'What color was her dress?'

I made a memory-prodding gesture, showing my effort by masking my eyes with my hand. I experienced a slow moment of grief, and it seemed to pinch a bruise onto my soul.

In this darkness, Whiting spoke to me. 'You don't remember,' he said. 'She wouldn't have liked that. She went to a lot of trouble to buy her London clothes.'

I said, 'She was here only a few days.'

'A week,' he said.

'I only saw her one day.'

'A day has twenty-four hours in it,' he said.

'We had tea,' I said. 'One hour. I didn't see her dress. She never took her coat off.'

Whiting frowned at me in pleasure, and lapsed into a comfortable silence. He said, 'In a hurry, that was Mei-lan. Hello, good-bye. What a life. It's perfect when you think about it. She was a little flame. She –'

At first I thought he was about to cry, but then I saw the flicker of a smile on his mouth. He had not smiled at all.

He said, 'The chaps at the bank think I'm stupid. "You're wrecking your career – throwing it all away, everything you worked for." But they didn't know Mei-lan. A woman's secret is the essence of her character, isn't it? She is what she tries to hide. They didn't know her.'

His eyes changed in focus, leaving me and peering into a greater distance.

He said, 'If I thought for a minute that she had betrayed me, I wouldn't have left the bank. I'd carry on as normal. And I don't think I'd ever trust a living soul again.'

He invited my attention with a beckoning of his head, lifting it at me and saying, 'What would you do if you were in my shoes?'

'Just what you did,' I said. He was surprised into a short silence by my prompt reply.

'She was rather special,' he said. 'What?'

'Yes,' I said.

And then he smiled. He said, 'And you hardly knew her!'

Fury

One of the first Americans Mary Snowfire met in London was a girl named Gretchen, who told her she was doing graduate work on the European Economic Community, and then smiled and smoothed her chic velvet knickerbockers and said she also worked for an escort agency. 'You have to, here. It's the only way you can manage financially.' Gretchen had a Saab Turbo and a big apartment in Fulham. She talked about 'Saudis.' 'I've met some really interesting people. It's not what you think. I'm not a hooker.'

But escort agency meant hookers for hire, didn't it?

'You have dinner usually. Or you go to a play. After that it's up to you.'

Gretchen was also a tennis player. She spoke French. She had a tan. She owned a sun-bed. Some weekends she went to Paris.

'Do they pay you?'

'You wouldn't believe how much! Some of those girls could retire. They make a fantastic amount.'

'Sure,' Mary said, 'but what do they have to do for it?'

She said 'they' but she meant Gretchen.

Gretchen said, 'They do everything.'

Everything seemed frantic, pleasureless, repetitive, exhausting.

Gretchen said, 'They're really well paid.'

'Doesn't that mean it's prostitution?' Mary asked.

'Oh, no. It's much more than they're worth,' Gretchen said. 'That's why it's not prostitution.'

Gretchen offered to introduce her to the manager of the agency, but Mary laughed and said no thanks, and she did her best to hide her disgust. She was also shocked by the easy way that Gretchen confided this matter. If you had to do these things to live here, why live here?

Gretchen changed the subject. She began talking about the EEC in a dull and knowledgeable way, and wasn't it a scandal that the

French farmers were paid a subsidy to produce butter that was sold cheap to the Soviet Union in order to keep the prices high in the European butter market?

Mary listened to the pretty girl and later got a nanny job, looking after three small children. She lived at the top of the house, which was just off the Fulham Road. She could hear the buses. For this job she was paid ten pounds a week – less than twenty dollars. Her room was part of her salary. Some girls were not paid at all, the woman said: they were jolly glad to have a place to live in return for helping with the kids! And Mary thought: *No wonder girls like Gretchen meet Arabs in the Hilton and go to bed with them.* ('At midnight you say, "I've really got to go. I've got a heavy day tomorrow at the Institute," and you walk out with three hundred pounds.')

Mary had wanted to live in London more than she wanted a husband or a lover. She was from Gainesville, Florida, an English major from the university there. She had very little spare money, but the standby fare to London was a hundred and fifty dollars. After a month at the Fulham Road house she saw that a bookstore near the cinema had a card in the window saying SALES STAFF WANTED. She was interviewed by the manager, Mr Shortridge, and hired. When she resigned from her nanny job she did not tell the woman that her husband had made an improper suggestion (kept pinching her hard and saying, 'How about it?') and that this was the main reason she was leaving.

In her new job, Mary discovered what many people like Gretchen already knew – that there was a great deal of good will toward Americans in London. We had style, we worked hard, we were full of life, we understood money, we succeeded where others failed. We were associated with luck.

By planning her life and measuring what she wanted against what she could afford, Mary established herself. She had moved to a bed-sitter that was directly over an Italian grocery store. She painted her room; she sewed new curtains; Mr Shortridge gave her Penguin posters – portraits of Virginia Woolf, Doris Lessing, and William Faulkner. Each one said A PENGUIN AUTHOR. Their orange matched her orange room. She had a bike (five pounds from a junk shop – she fixed it up), a gas fire, and a plug-in radio (batteries made radios expensive). Her geraniums, her small avocado tree, her pots of ivy she had all grown herself. The bright ferny tub of marijuana that thrived in a sunny corner of the room had been left by the last tenant.

She became friendly with the owner of the grocery store and his wife. They knew how little money she had and gave her a discount, and sometimes they gave her packaged food when the date stamp had just expired. This Italian couple, who had English accents, had relatives in Newark, New Jersey! Mary knew that they looked upon her as another exile, trying to make her way in this city of cold rooms, and hallways smelling of dust and bacon fat, and wet streets and brown skies.

London was not the London of her Gainesville dreams. It was sadder, darker, stranger, narrower, newer, dirtier, more oppressive. Now she understood why Gretchen had become a prostitute in an escort agency. But Mary felt that London was teaching her how to live against the odds.

She knew she could not have a boy friend or a lover. They required too much time, they demanded favors, they crowded her and made her careless. In her first weeks in London she had gone out a half a dozen times with men she had met. She went to pubs, to the movies, and once to a disco. She insisted on paying her share – it was expensive! One drink in a pub was around two dollars! The British seemed easier about money – no one had any. But Mary could manage only by living narrowly. It was hard and comfortless and sometimes very lonely. It was a delicate balance, but friends could be unpredictable, and everything depended on close planning, because she had so little.

She had never smoked; she stopped drinking; she became a vegetarian. She began to dislike cats for being meat-eaters. She had never felt healthier or tougher. It was a satisfaction, this kind of survival. She didn't care that it made her seem a little selfish. She had started with nothing. She had discovered how to be independent, and she was glad, because she was a woman, and they weren't expected to be loners. When she thought of Gretchen or saw a woman with a rich man who was obviously keeping her, Mary Snowfire smiled and thought: *She lays eggs for gentlemen.*

Mary was twenty-four, and slim, and had long legs. She could run five miles. She told the truth. She became so angry when someone lied to her that she couldn't sleep. Occasionally, customers in the bookstore lied to her: 'That's what I said the first time,' or 'I

gave you a ten-pound note and you gave me change for a fiver.'
She wanted to hit them.

After six months she considered that she had won her freedom.
It was then that she became friendly with the fellow Brenhouse.
He worked as a delivery man for Howletts, the book publisher,
but Brenhouse also supplied books from the Blackadder Press, a
publisher of Trotskyite literature. This bookstore reflected Mr
Shortridge's political views. Mr Shortridge had been to Cuba.

Brenhouse was extremely thin, in his early twenties, and from
Whitby, in Yorkshire, where the Blackadder Press was. He had
hair to his shoulders and a drooping mustache and a long nose.
He looked like Robert Louis Stevenson. His hands were skinny
and usually dirty, and he bit his fingernails until they bled. But
Mary regarded him as sort of romantic, because he lived outdoors,
in a lean-to on Mitcham Common. It was perfectly legal there –
it was common land: men lived there like savages, squatting near
smoky fires, and boiling soup in black kettles. In cold weather they
wore socks on their hands and lined their coats with old newspapers
and stuffed them up their pants. They carried their belongings in
baby carriages twenty miles or more. Brenhouse told her these
things. Mary thought: *The poor kid sleeps in a Surrey ditch with
hoboes and homeless men and he still works every day!* He had
built his own shelter and had a sleeping bag. He said he was better
off than many people in this country. Mary admired him for saying
that.

She had once thought she was living the life most men led, until
she met Brenhouse, who slept on the ground. There was sometimes
a cloudy droplet at the tip of his nose. He offered the information
that he kept clean by using public baths. London was full of bath
houses for people who didn't have tubs at home. This was 1981!
His talk made her grateful for what she had.

Some nights, in her warm room – the warmth brought the
scorched smell of new paint off the wood – she thought of Brenhouse and shuddered, feeling faintly ashamed. Though she knew
there was no virtue in living outdoors like that, she felt it was
beyond her capabilities. Shouldn't women be able to endure such
hardships? If you had to do it, you could, Brenhouse said. But
Mary thought: *If I had to do it, I would die.*

The cold London winter was colder even than the predictions.
Snow fell in big white crumbs and made the streets simple and

small. It was not plowed, no one shoveled it, it did not melt. After a week it was still on the ground, but dirtier, and the temperature dropped. Walking down the Fulham Road was treacherous. Mary saw dead sparrows in snow holes, where they had fallen and frozen. Cats walked in the soft snow in a high-stepping tentative way, making spider legs. Strangers spoke to each other in worried reminiscing voices. This London weather was remarkable, almost unbelievable, and everyone had something different to say about it. The first week of storms was exciting, but the city was changed and the next week similar storms were cruel.

And one night, the coldest night so far, there was a rapping on Mary's door.

It was Brenhouse. Five minutes ago she had been thinking of him! He did not ask to come in. He did not speak. His skin was red and gray, his cheeks looked bruised, but after an hour in the room he became pale. His breathing was harsh. He stayed the night, sleeping on the floor. He did not take off his clothes, and though he was wrapped in two blankets he smelled of dirt and oil smoke.

'I thought I was going to die,' he said the next morning, his first words, and he was still pale.

Mary knew that he planned to stay. He was afraid of the cold for the first time. The snow lay everywhere in London, like black slop.

She said, 'Don't you have a friend somewhere?'

'No,' he said. 'Only you.'

How could this be true of a man who lived in his own country when it was not true even of Mary, who had lived in London less than a year?

Suddenly he said, 'It's only seven-thirty!'

'I have to open the bookshop,' Mary said.

'In Mitcham I never get up before nine.'

He made it sound like luxury, and he was talking about a scrapwood lean-to on a scrubby common in the dead of winter. The rigid tip of his long nose, which had been very red last night, was pale as gristle today.

Mary said, 'What about your job?'

'I'm not going in today. I'll call in sick. Want to go to the pictures?'

This was why she hated men and boy friends. They recklessly

decided to tell lies or turn their back on things. Maybe it was their strength, but it was crooked strength.

She said, 'You'll get fired.'

Brenhouse swore. Obscenity was always an ugly foreign language to her and she translated what Brenhouse said as *To hell with them*.

'I can find work back home.' He snorted, pushing at one nostril with a knuckle. 'Whitby.'

When Mary returned to her room that night, he was wrapped in a blanket and sitting cross-legged on her bed, reading a Blackadder pamphlet, something about wealth and property. He looked contented. His hair was still damp from his bath; his nose was shiny. Where had he found the towel?

The gas fire was hissing, and the room was so warm it raised his soap smell and the paint and the geraniums and some lunch odors – he had made himself a fried egg, the greasy skillet still on the hotplate. Mary began to tidy the room and, seeing her, Brenhouse tried to help.

'I'm not used to bourgeois living,' he said.

What about the bath, the meal, his leisurely reading? And he had scrubbed the dirt out of his fingernails.

Brenhouse was at the sink doing his dishes. Mary would have done them: she liked cleaning the room alone, but with Brenhouse doing it too the housework seemed like drudgery. He was talking.

'We can go up the pub.'

'I hate pubs,' she said.

'Then I'll go out and get a bottle of plonk,' he said. 'It's the least I can do.'

That was true: it *was* the least he could do. It was a characteristic of too many Englishmen, Mary thought, this doing as little as possible, and presuming; and some of them lived like pigs. He brought back a two-liter bottle of Spanish wine, and she remembered that she had given up drinking.

She bought cheese from the Italian downstairs and made canneloni and salad. They ate, sitting on cushions in front of the gas fire.

Brenhouse said, 'There's no meat in this, love.'

'I'm a vegetarian,' she said.

'I eat anything,' Brenhouse said. He had a weevil's nose. He stared at her and smiled, and when she shrugged he filled her glass to the brim with the cheap wine.

She drank it because this bottle was his gift to her. He filled the glass again and she drank that. He began wickedly again with the big bottle. Mary tried to stand up, but couldn't; nor could she sit. She lay on the floor until the side of her face grew hot. Before she sank completely, she felt his hands on her. He was lifting her clothes in a rough and hurrying way. And then for an hour or more she had little glimpses of herself being pushed and pulled by him. At the end, he shouted at her in a doomed and adoring way.

In the morning Mary woke up in her bed and saw he was gone. The room had been turned upside down. The truth was easy to see in a room so small. He had stolen her money; he had taken her keys, her watch, her earrings, her one bracelet, her Florida paperweight, her radio. His smell was on the bed. It was that, his dreadful smell, which made her cry. Then, remembering the way he had shouted in his passion, she became angry. She ran to the bookstore. It was eight-thirty.

Mr Shortridge was already inside.

'We've had a break-in,' he said. 'It must have happened in the night. The till's empty.'

He was trying not to be cross. He always said that the Tory government deserved crime and that property owners and landlords were thieves. Now his hands were in the empty cash drawer. He said no more. He chewed his tongue.

Mary said, 'It wasn't a break-in,' and explained, and began to cry again, and only her anger stopped her tears.

Then she had no time for grief, none for tears; she was falling. She had no job – Mr Shortridge sorrowfully fired her and when she mentioned the week's pay that he owed her, his lips trembled and he said, 'You should be paying me.' Her rent was due. Brenhouse had taken her checkbook – but there was no money in the account. He had taken her Parker pen! Everything shiny, everything of value, the savage had taken. He had stuck his horrible nose everywhere.

Mary had nothing in this dark brown winter-wet city.

Gretchen was glad to hear from her, though Gretchen's first mood on the phone was a mixture of sex and suspicion – her escort voice. Then her tone was girlish. 'Have you changed your mind about the agency?'

'I need some money,' Mary said. 'A loan. Would ten pounds be all right?'

'You could earn two hundred by dinnertime,' Gretchen said.

Mary said, 'I'd kill the first man that touched me.'

They met for tea that day. Gretchen handed over some money. It was fifty pounds.

Mary counted it and cried because it was so much. She was aware that she wore a starved and crazy expression, but she couldn't help it.

'I'll pay you back.'

'Nothing to pay back,' Gretchen said. 'Fifty quid isn't money.'

But to Mary's mind it was money, but a man had given it to Gretchen, but what had she done in return? But she was really generous. But it was no way to live.

Gretchen talked about her work at the Institute, and the European oilfields, and the future of Arab oil. Mary thought only of the thief Brenhouse. There was a glut, Gretchen said, and everyone thought there was a shortage. Gretchen said, 'I could show you the figures – I've made an amazing flow-chart. Oh, God, I've got to run.' She made a friendly face. 'A date.'

Mary was still holding the money, rolled into a tube. She said, 'I have to get my bike fixed and buy a few things.'

'You're funny,' Gretchen said. 'But I think you're right. You'd hate being an escort.'

Mary felt there was a yellow flame of anger in her that kept her alive. She wanted to find this man who had treated her like an ignorant animal. He was the animal – he had the snout for it! She walked to Fulham Broadway and bought a light for her bike. She set off for Mitcham Common, pedaling fast. She knew she was behaving like the animal he had made her. But he had created this rage in her.

Two old men sat on their heels in front of the fire, watching it with pink watery eyes. They didn't know Brenhouse. Had she been over to the spinney? They sent her to this wooded part of the common, not far, but she noticed they were following her like stupid hungry hounds. There was no sign of anyone else here. They were trying to confuse her or trap her! She hissed at them, and they stood aside, and her bike took her quickly away.

There were fires and camps all over this common. Scraps of snow still lay on the ground, like filthy bandages.

She surprised a pair of schoolboys smoking cigarettes. They guiltily agreed to help her. Perhaps she looked like their teacher? Their search turned up Brenhouse's ditch and the lean-to and the dead smelly fire. Brenhouse had cleared out. She did not pity him at all when she saw this rat's nest – she hated him much more.

A man with a gray face and a coat of long rags was watching her. This place was full of tramps! This one was young, about Brenhouse's age, but heavier, and his weight made him look shabbier and nastier.

'I've got news for you,' he said.

'I hate that expression,' she said. It was a man's belittling expression, *I've got news for you*. She wanted to hit him.

The young man laughed. He knew she was wasting her time.

'He's gone home!' His gray mocking face seemed to say *And there's nothing you can do about it!*

Mary said, 'Where does he live?'

'He's a Yorkshireman, isn't he?' But it was not a question. He added, 'I've got no time for Yorkshiremen' – to insult her, because she was involved with Brenhouse; the fat young man could see that.

She remembered Whitby.

'Don't go away,' she said to the schoolboys who had helped her find this campsite. The fat young man would not touch her while they were around. The boys escorted her to the road, but said nothing, and even refused the tangerine she offered them as a present.

Howletts, the publishers, confirmed that Brenhouse was in Whitby. They were very angry with him, and when she said he owed her money they understood, and in an encouraging way – she felt – they gave Mary his address.

She did not sleep that night. The room was no longer hers. Brenhouse had robbed and ruined her. Her life had depended on a delicate balance. Brenhouse had stumbled into her little room and betrayed her, all the while looking down his nose at her. She had never once asked anything of him. He was a pig; he deserved worse than death. She cried, feeling trapped in a ditch where he had thrown her and tried to smother her. Why are men thieves?

Each night after that she cried again. But she was crying because it was dark and she could not travel in the dark. Her tears were fury.

She had sold everything that she could sell and bought an Army sleeping bag, arctic model. She had then dressed herself in her warmest clothes (bleak-brown February had turned the snowfields to dampness and mud) and set off on her bike for Whitby. In this small country of four directions she had taken the longest one.

She was fighting the wind as soon as she left London. Her head was down and her body bent double and braced over her bike frame. She had rejected the train, the bus, or hitchhiking. She needed this effort so that she could use her fury. Each day on her bike her anger gave her strength. It was food, it refreshed her, it kept her warm. She did not sleep easily beside the stone walls of villages and farms, but her fury enlivened her when she was awake. And sleep that was too deep was dangerous on cold nights: you could freeze and not know it.

The roads were clear; the thaw was general and filthy. And even with the rain pelting against her, she flew. Some days in high winds she screamed curses at him. She hated the thought of his beaky face.

She had become possessed. Fury made her a demon, but it also made her efficient. She saw nothing unusual in this speeding along back roads on her bike, but her throat burned with shrieks as she beat uphill toward Yorkshire. Men stood in muddy fields or against high brambly hedges and watched her. They were curious, but after they had had a good look at her they were afraid. She went fast; the effort strengthened her; she felt she was being flung toward Whitby by black winds.

From Ely and the Fens, she skirted the Wash and made for the Lincolnshire Wolds, then across the Humber to York and the long hills of that dark county to Scarborough. She was in Whitby the next day; she knew it by the ruined abbey – her gaze continually traveled up to it.

She did not stop. She had by now memorized Brenhouse's address and the roads to it. Hunger had increased her fury: she had not eaten since morning. It was now a cold windy midafternoon, muffled by cloud.

She had imagined him alone in an empty room and defenseless. Her mind had simplified the imagining and made it helpful, and had tricked her. The truth was a tiny brick house in a bottled-up lane, with no view of either the moor or the sea. There was no answer to her knock. She drank a cup of tea at a café. She had four pounds and sixty-seven pence left, but once this was done nothing mattered.

Her dirty face and red hands frightened the woman at the tea urn.

Leaving the café, she saw him – she was sure it was Brenhouse – walking down the road. And he saw her. But he smiled and looked away, probably guessing that he had imagined her in this distant place, and smirking at his mistake. How could she have got here so fast in the winter with no money?

Furiously, she followed him. She was impatient. Now, hearing her rapid steps, he looked again. This made her eager. She held her weapon up her sleeve. No: he had not recognized her.

He had pushed through the door of a pub, but when Mary entered she could not see him. There was smoke and chatter; nearly all were men, some staring at her. She saw her own scarf around someone's neck! It was one she had bought in London. The person's head was turned, but she knew whose it was. Two strides took her to the chair and then she had his long hair in her hand and was yanking his head back so that he faced the ceiling.

Brenhouse tried to stand up. He shouted. His look of horror filled her unexpectedly with pity, and it frightened her, too. No one made a move to help him, or to restrain her in her swift movement. The cloudy light came through the painted pub window with gulls' nagging squawks. Brenhouse was clutching his face; blood streamed from his hands. Then Mary was seized from behind.

'His throat's cut,' she heard.

And 'She never cut his throat.'

She hadn't touched his throat, but she had cut him with the scissors she surrendered to the men.

All this she told me on the train south from York, after her two weeks in the hospital. She was treated for exhaustion and dehydration, and Brenhouse was there, too, in another ward – severe laceration of the face, as the newspapers said. She had scissored a little more than half an inch from the end of his nose.

But there were no charges laid against Mary Snowfire. The London Embassy was involved because she had no money – and I was sent to escort her back to London and arrange her repatriation. We flew her to Florida. She said she would repay every cent. I felt sure she would keep her word.

Neighbors

I had two neighbors at Overstrand Mansions – we shared the same landing. In America 'neighbor' has a friendly connotation; in England it is a chilly word, nearly always a stranger, a map reference more than anything else. One of my neighbors was called R. Wigley; the other had no nameplate.

It did not surprise me at all that Corner Door had no nameplate. He owned a motorcycle and kept late nights. He wore leather – I heard it squeak; and boots – they hit the stairs like hammers on an anvil. His motorcycle was a Kawasaki – Japanese of course. The British are patriotic only in the abstract, and they can be traitorously frugal – tax havens are full of Brits. They want value for money, even when they are grease monkeys, bikers with skinny faces and sideburns and teeth missing, wearing jackboots and swastikas. That was how I imagined Corner Door, the man in 4C.

I had never seen his face, though I had heard him often enough. His hours were odd; he was always rushing off at night and returning in the early morning – waking me when he left and waking me again when he came back. He was selfish and unfriendly, scatterbrained, thoughtless – no conversation but plenty of bike noise. I pictured him wearing one of those German helmets that look like kettles, and I took him to be a coward at heart, who sneaked around whining until he had his leather suit and his boots on, until he mounted his too-big Japanese motorcycle, which he kept in the entryway of Overstrand Mansions, practically blocking it. When he was suited up and mounted on his bike he was a Storm Trooper with blood in his eye.

It also struck me that this awful man might be a woman, an awful woman. But even after several months there I never saw the person from 4C face to face. I saw him – or her – riding away, his back, the chrome studs patterned on his jacket. But women didn't behave like this. It was a man.

R. Wigley was quite different – he was a civil servant: Post

Office, Welsh I think, very methodical. He wrote leaflets. The Post Office issued all sorts of leaflets – explaining pensions, television licenses, road tax, driving permits, their savings bank, and everything else, including of course stamps. The leaflets were full of directions and advice. In this complicated literate country you were expected to read your way out of difficulty.

When I told Wigley I wouldn't be in London much longer than a couple of years, he became hospitable. No risk, you see. If I had been staying for a long time he wouldn't have been friendly – wouldn't have dared. Neighbors are a worry: they stare, they presume, they borrow things, they ask you to forgive them their trespasses. In the most privacy-conscious country in the world neighbors are a problem. But I was leaving in a year or so, and I was an American diplomat – maybe I was a spy! He suggested I call him Reg.

We met at the Prince Albert for a drink. A month later, I had him over with the Scadutos, Vic and Marietta, and it was then that talk turned to our neighbors. Wigley said there was an actor on the ground floor and that several country Members of Parliament lived in Overstrand Mansions when the Commons was in session. Scaduto asked him blunt questions I would not have dared to ask, but I was glad to hear his answers. Rent? Thirty-seven pounds a week. Married? Had been – no longer. University? Bristol. And when he asked Wigley about his job, Scaduto listened with fascination and then said, 'It's funny, but I never actually imagined anyone writing those things. It doesn't seem like real writing.'

Good old Skiddoo.

Wigley said, 'I assure you, it's quite real.'

Scaduto went on interrogating him – Americans are tremendous questioners – but Wigley's discomfort made me reticent. The British confined conversation to neutral impersonal subjects, resisting any effort to be trapped into friendship. They got to know each other by allowing details to slip out, little mentions that, gathered together, became revelations. The British liked having secrets – they had lost so much else – and that was one of their secrets.

Scaduto asked, 'What are your other neighbors like?'

I looked at Wigley. I wondered what he would say. I would not have dared to put the question to him.

He said, 'Some of them are incredibly noisy and others downright frightening.'

This encouraged me. I said, 'Our Nazi friend with the motor-cycle, for one.'

Had I gone too far?

'I was thinking of that prig, Hurst,' Wigley said, 'who has the senile Labrador that drools and squitters all over the stairs.'

'I've never seen our motorcyclist,' I said. 'But I've heard him. The bike. The squeaky leather shoulders. The boots.' I caught Wigley's eye. 'It's just the three of us on this floor, I guess.'

I had lived there just over two months without seeing anyone else.

Wigley looked uncertain, but said, 'I suppose so.'

'My kids would love to have a motorcycle,' Marietta Scaduto said. 'I've got three hulking boys, Mr Wigley.'

I said, 'Don't let them bully you into buying one.'

'Don't you worry,' Marietta said. 'I think those things are a menace.'

'Some of them aren't so bad,' Wigley said. 'Very economical.' He glanced at me. 'So I've heard.'

'It's kind of an image-thing, really. Your psychologists will tell you all about it.' Skiddoo was pleased with himself: he liked analyz-ing human behavior – 'deviants' were his favorites, he said. 'It's classic textbook-case stuff. The simp plays big tough guy on his motorcycle. Walter Mitty turns into Marlon Brando. It's an aggres-sion thing. Castration complex. What do you do for laughs, Reg?'

Wigley said, 'I'm not certain what you mean by laughs.'

'Fun,' Scaduto said. 'For example, we've got one of these home computers. About six thousand bucks, including some accessories – hardware, software. Christ, we've had hours of fun with it. The kids love it.'

'I used to be pretty keen on aircraft,' Wigley said, and looked very embarrassed saying so, as if he were revealing an aberration in his boyhood.

Scaduto said, 'Keen in what way?'

'Taking snaps of them,' Wigley said.

'Snaps?' Marietta Scaduto said. She was smiling.

'Yes,' Wigley said. 'I had one of those huge Japanese cameras that can do anything. They're absolutely idiot-proof and fiendishly expensive.'

'I never thought anyone taking dinky little pictures of planes could be described as "keen."' Scaduto said the word like a brand name for ladies' underwear.

'Some of them were big pictures,' Wigley said coldly.

'Even big pictures,' Scaduto said. 'I could understand flying in the planes, though. Getting inside, being airborne, and doing the loop-the-loop.'

Wigley said, 'They were bombers.'

'Now you're talking, Reg!' Scaduto's sudden enthusiasm warmed the atmosphere a bit, and they continued to talk about airplanes.

'My father had an encyclopedia,' Wigley said. 'You looked up "aeroplane." It said, "Aeroplane: See Flying-Machine."'

Later, Marietta said, 'These guys on their motorcycles, I was just thinking. They really have a problem. Women never do stupid things like that.'

Vic Scaduto said, 'Women put on long gowns, high heels, padded bras. They pile their hair up, they pretend they're princesses. That's worse, fantasy-wise. Or they get into really tight provocative clothes, all tits and ass, swinging and bouncing, lipstick, the whole bit, cleavage hanging down. And then – I'm not exaggerating – and then they say, "Don't touch me or I'll scream."'

Good old Skiddoo.

'You've got a big problem if you think that,' Marietta said. She spoke then to Wigley. 'Sometimes the things he says are sick.'

Wigley smiled and said nothing.

'And he works for the government,' Marietta said. 'You wouldn't think so, would you?'

That was it. The Scadutos went out arguing, and Wigley left. A highly successful evening, I thought.

Thanks to Scaduto's pesterings I knew much more about Wigley. He was decent, he was reticent, and I respected him for the way he handled Good Old Skiddoo. And we were no more friendly than before. That was all right with me: I didn't want to be burdened with his friendship any more than he wanted to be lumbered with mine. I only wished that the third tenant on the floor was as gracious a neighbor as Wigley.

Would Wigley join me in making a complaint? He said he'd rather not. That was the British way – don't make a fuss, Reggie.

He said, 'To be perfectly frank, he doesn't actually bother me.'

This was the first indication I'd had that it was definitely a man, not a woman.

'He drives me up the wall sometimes. He keeps the craziest hours. I've never laid eyes on him, but I know he's weird.'

Wigley smiled at me and I immediately regretted saying *He's weird*, because, saying so, I had revealed something of myself.

I said, 'I can't make a complaint unless you back me up.'

'I know.'

I could tell that he thought I was being unfair. It created a little distance, this annoyance of mine, which looked to him like intolerance. I knew this because Wigley had a girl friend and didn't introduce me. A dozen times I heard them on the stairs. People who live alone are authorities on noises. I knew their laughs. I got to recognize the music, the bed-springs, the bath water. He did not invite me over.

And of course there was my other subject, the Storm Trooper from 4C with his thumping jackboots at the oddest hours. I decided at last that wimpy little Wigley (as I now thought of him) had become friendly with him, perhaps ratted on me and told him that I disliked him.

Wigley worked at Post Office Headquarters, at St Martin's-le-Grand, taking the train to Victoria and then the tube to St Paul's. I sometimes saw him entering or leaving Battersea Park Station while I was at the bus stop. Occasionally, we walked together to or from Overstrand Mansions, speaking of the weather.

One day, he said, 'I might be moving soon.'

I felt certain he was getting married. I did not ask.

'Are you sick of Overstrand Mansions?'

'I need a bigger place.'

He was definitely getting married.

I had the large balcony apartment in front. Wigley had a two-room apartment just behind me. The motorcyclist's place I had never seen.

'I wish it were the Storm Trooper who was leaving, and not you.'

He was familiar with my name for the motorcyclist.

'Oh, well,' he said, and walked away.

Might be moving, he had said. It sounded pretty vague. But the following Friday he was gone. I heard noise and saw the moving van in front on Prince of Wales Drive. Bumps and curses echoed on the stairs. I didn't stir – too embarrassing to put him on the spot, especially as I had knocked on his door that morning, hoping for the last time to get him to join me in a protest against the Storm Trooper. I'm sure he saw me through his spy-hole in the door – Wigley, I mean. But he didn't open. So he didn't care about the awful racket the previous night – boots, bangs, several screams. Wigley was bailing out and leaving me to deal with it.

He went without a word. Then I realized he had sneaked away. He had not said good-bye; I had never met his girl friend; he was getting married – maybe already married. British neighbors!

I wasn't angry with him, but I was furious with the Storm Trooper, who had created a misunderstanding between Wigley and me. Wigley had tolerated the noise and I had hated it and said so. The Storm Trooper had made me seem like a brute!

But I no longer needed Wigley's signature on a complaint. Now there were only two of us here. I could go in and tell him exactly what I thought of him. I could play the obnoxious American. Wigley's going gave me unexpected courage. I banged on his door and shook it, hoping that I was waking him up. There was no answer that day or any day. And there was no more noise, no Storm Trooper, no motorcycle, from the day Wigley left.

Fighting Talk

Some repeated noises seem to erupt with numbers, making the chatter of counting, a kind of syncopation that turns *bop-bop* into *one-two*. But, staring out of the window of Vic Scaduto's office at the rear of the Embassy, I was only dimly aware that I was hearing a noise at all. I seemed to be hearing the words *three-four-five*. It was only after I saw the policeman hurry out of the glass booth near our staff garage that I realized that what I had heard were gunshots.

'What is it?' Scaduto said.

He had just been telling me about meeting the father of Hussein Something-or-other, one of his kids' school friends – at least he had thought the man was a parent, an unusually friendly guy among all those snobs at the school rugby match – and he turned out to be Hussein's bodyguard and chauffeur! 'Hey, listen, Arabs are Jews on horseback –'

'It sounded like gunfire,' I said.

Blackburne's Mews was very still for several minutes, and then it was awash with scrambling policemen setting up barriers at the mews's entrance and blocking Culross Street. I heard the ear-splitting donkey *hee-haw* of a British police siren.

Scaduto had joined me at the window. His ears twitched; the hairline of his scalp gave a little jerk. He shaped his mouth as if preparing to take a bite.

'Libyans,' he said.

We had had an urgent memo about Libyans earlier that week. Teams of gunmen had been dispatched by the wild-eyed President Qaddafi. We had been sent blurred pictures of the mustached assassins.

Scaduto's phone rang. Panic invests commonplace objects with menace. He picked the receiver up with fearful fingers – would the thing explode? He listened for perhaps twenty seconds. He said, 'We've been expecting something like this,' and then he replaced the receiver gently, again behaving as if it were explosive.

'There's been a shooting,' he told me solemnly. 'Stay inside and keep away from the windows. Those are orders. It might be Arabs. That was Horton on the phone.'

'It was right down there,' I said, pointing into the mews.

'You're a witness.'

'I didn't see anything,' I said.

Scaduto said, 'I'm glad they didn't give me Rome. It's worse there.'

While he phoned his wife I tried to determine what the police were doing with their chalk marks on the surface of the mews. It looked like the beginning of a children's game.

'I'm not kidding, honey. I heard the shots,' he was saying. 'Hey, I'm glad they didn't give me that Rome job. It's an everyday thing there. Sure, it's terrorists! No, don't worry. I can take care of myself.'

He looked pleased, even smug, when he hung up. 'How about a drink?' he said. 'Someone's bound to have the poop on this downstairs.'

The bar-restaurant in the Embassy basement had no windows, and it was perhaps this and the semidarkness that suggested a hide-out or bomb shelter to me. It was full of huddled, whispering Embassy employees rather enjoying their fear.

'Reminds me of when I was in Rawalpindi,' Scaduto said, still looking pleased. He went for two beers and returned with the name of the man who had been fired upon – Dwight Yorty, a relatively new man in Regional Projects, whom I had never met.

'I shouldn't laugh,' Scaduto said.

But near-disasters, especially when an intended victim seems to have been miraculously reprieved, are often the occasions for lively gossip.

'Yorty!' Scaduto said. 'A month or so ago, he told me the most amazing story. He hit his wife over the head. She fell down, *wham*, flat on the floor. Go ahead, ask me what he hit her with.'

'What was the weapon, Vic?'

'A cucumber,' he said, pressing his teeth against his smile. 'Isn't that incredible? You'd think he'd use something sensible, like a sledgehammer. But they were having an argument about cucumbers at the time. He had it in his hand, then he hauled off and belted her with it.'

'You can't do much damage with a cucumber,' I said.

'It paralyzed her!' Scaduto was tipping forward in his chair, trying not to laugh. 'That's what she said – she couldn't move. An ambulance came to take her away on a stretcher. The stretcher wouldn't fit through the kitchen door. She had to get up and walk into the hallway and lie down on it. That's the funny part.'

I said, 'That's not the only funny part.'

'Exactly,' he said. 'Ask me what happened to the cucumber.'

'You'll tell me anyway.'

'He ate it!' Scaduto said. 'That's what they were arguing about. She didn't want him to eat the cucumber, so he whacked her over the head with it and then he ate it. He didn't count on her faking brain damage. You don't believe this, do you?'

'It sounds a little far-fetched.'

'If you were married you'd believe it,' he said. 'You'd think it was an understatement. This kind of thing happens all the time to married people.'

'But shootings don't,' I said. 'Someone just tried to kill Yorty. Maybe it was his wife.'

'No. His wife left him – she's in the States. Poor guy.' Now Scaduto looked contrite. 'I shouldn't have told you that cucumber story. But that's all I know about him.'

The next morning, Ambassador Noyes gave the senior officers a briefing.

The crueler ones among us called him 'No-Yes.' He was a tall white-faced man with thin pale hair and the stiffness and exaggerated sense of decorum that you often associate with people of low intelligence. He often said he liked gold an awful lot. He had the shoulders and the plodding gait of a golfer. He had no interest in politics and had never before held a diplomatic post. But he was a personal friend of the President, and this post of US Ambassador to Britain was regarded by many people as membership in the ultimate country club. It was expensive, but it offered real status. It also proved that money could buy practically anything.

Ambassador Noyes had another trait I had noticed in many slow-witted people: he was tremendously interested in philosophy.

'I guess you've all heard about the shooting,' he was saying. 'As far as I'm concerned, this is just about the most serious thing that's happened since I took up this post.'

Although he was nervous and rather new, he did not find his a difficult job. His number two man, Everett Horton, was a career diplomat who had been in London ten years and had wonderful sources. And of course the eight hundred of us at the London Embassy were each working toward the same end: to prop up the Ambassador and put him in the know. I could think of twenty people who were directly responsible to the Ambassador. There was Horton, Brickhouse, Kneedler and Roscoe, besides Scaduto, Sanger and Jeeps. There was Pomeroy, MacWeeney, Geach, Baskies, Pryczinski and Frezza, Schoonmaker, Kelly, Kountz and Toomajian, Shinebald and Oberlander. There was me. There were the boys on the third floor. And that was just the inner circle. We were at his service; we were his eyes and ears; we were the best, most of us overqualified for the jobs we were doing. How could he fail?

'I'm determined to get to the bottom of it,' he went on. 'I want to show these people – whoever they are – that we are not afraid of anyone, and that we are, if provoked, quite able to hit back.'

He was a reasonable man. He was also a multimillionaire. How he had made his fortune was a mystery to me, but it was no mystery to me how he had kept it. He was unprejudiced and fair; he gave everyone a hearing; he was also unsentimental. I suspected he was strong. He was certainly practical, and I knew from the way he lived that he was a simple soul. He knew how to delegate power and how to take decisions. I was sure he knew his weaknesses – if he hadn't, he would not have been so successful.

All this is necessary background – I mean, the reasonableness of his character – because his next words were very fierce indeed.

'When I find out who did this, I can promise you that it'll be the last time they try it. We're going to jump on them hard. Our flag will not be insulted.'

The mention of 'flag' put me in mind of Dwight Yorty and the cucumber, and I lowered my eyes as I listened to Ambassador Noyes's tremulous voice.

'I spoke to the President last night and he assured me that he will support us to the hilt. I don't have to tell you gentlemen that we are more than a match for anyone who takes up arms against us.'

This was fighting talk. We muttered our approval, and there was a little burst of appreciative handclapping. But I could tell that the response was mixed. The older men seemed very pleased at the prospect of kicking someone's teeth in. The younger men and all the women were clearly irked by the threats. Most of us judged the Ambassador to be uncharacteristically credulous. Perhaps he was trying to make an impression by swearing revenge. I wondered how it would sound after it was leaked to the press.

Everett Horton spoke next. At times like this he was captain of the team rather than coach. He was correct, modest, loyal, and deferential. He gave a good imitation of controlled anger – I doubted that he had been angry at all. His voice expressed intense indignation.

'The Ambassador has been forthright – and with reason. This is the sixth terrorist incident involving American Embassy personnel in the past two months. It is the first one we've had in London. Obviously, there's a movement afoot in Europe to frighten us.' He paused and said, 'I'm not frightened, but I'm kind of mad.'

Ambassador Noyes smiled in agreement at this, and some of us shuffled our feet in embarrassment.

'One American has been killed, and another wounded – both in Paris,' Horton said. 'Three incidents have been kept out of the papers, as you know. But the Ambassador has decided, and I agree, that this attempt on the life of one of our serving officers should be given maximum publicity.'

He then read us the press release, with the details of the shooting: At approximately fifteen-thirty hours ... Dwight A. Yorty fired upon ... unknown assailant ... believed to be political. He showed us a street map of the Embassy neighborhood, and as he took us through it step by step, he looked more and more like a quarterback explaining a game plan that had gone wrong.

'Any questions?'

No hands went up, perhaps because the Ambassador was in the room, standing behind Horton with his arms folded, ready for battle.

I decided to risk a question. I stood up and said, 'Everett, you called it a terrorist incident. Have we any proof of that?'

Before Horton could speak, the Ambassador stepped forward. 'A man was terrorized – shot at,' he said. 'There's only one sort of person who does that. Everett?'

'I think we're in total agreement, Mr Ambassador,' Horton said.

I was still standing. I said, 'What I meant was, has any group like the IRA or the PLO or Black September – or anyone – claimed credit for it?'

My question exasperated the Ambassador. He sighed and stepped away, seeing me as an obstruction. He said, 'I'll let you field that one, Everett.'

'No terrorist group has come forward,' Horton said. 'In one of the Paris shootings the same pattern was followed – an unknown assailant. But it wasn't robbery in either of the incidents. It's got to be political.'

Now Oberlander was on his feet. 'Excuse me,' he said, 'but isn't it somewhat premature to call this shooting political?'

'No,' Horton said, 'because we've got a good description of the man. Dark hair, dark eyes, swarthy features, a slight build, about five-foot-six. Arab. He may be the same man who was responsible for those Paris incidents. We're sure they're linked. And frankly' – Horton made a half-turn toward the Ambassador – 'I'd love to nail him.'

Al Sanger said, 'What about the guy who was picked up right after the shooting?'

This was news to me.

'He was released,' Horton said. 'He didn't fit Yorty's description.'

'I hope you won't find this question malicious,' Erroll Jeeps said, 'but how was it the guy took six or seven shots at point-blank range and missed?'

'Five shots,' I said.

Horton said, 'We haven't found any of the cartridges, so we don't know how many shots. Maybe it was one. Apparently he missed because Yorty was parking his car at the time – in the staff garage.'

'Instead of looking for cartridges,' Sanger said, 'why not look for the slugs?'

'That is up to the British police, who, so far, have done a superb job,' Horton said.

Horton repeated that we would not give in to intimidation, and the Ambassador refolded his arms in defiant emphasis. And he fixed his jaw and nodded stiffly as Horton advised us to take all necessary precautions. If any of us had reason to think we were under threat, he said, we could apply for police protection.

Erroll Jeeps said, 'These British cops don't have guns but they got some real loud whistles.'

'We'll ignore that remark, Mr Jeeps,' Horton said. 'In the meantime, remember, the best defense is a good offense. Thank you, gentlemen.'

And then, unexpectedly, I was asked to leak it to the British press. I had been very doubtful about the whole affair, but what made my nagging questions the more urgent was the Ambassador's request, relayed by Horton, for me to see a reliable journalist on the *Telegraph* or *The Times* and spell it out.

I said I would need time to think about it.

'Thinking is not necessary in this case,' Horton said. 'I just want you to give an accurate summary of our attitude. You were at the briefing.'

'The whole team was there.'

'You were taking notes,' he said. 'I saw you.'

'I was writing down questions, and wishing I had answers to them.'

'You asked questions. I gave you answers.'

'I didn't ask you the most important one, because I thought Yorty might be in the room. I didn't want him to feel he was on trial.'

'Ask me now, if it'll make you feel better.'

'Okay,' I said. 'Yorty didn't see the gunman. I re-enacted the shooting with Scaduto standing in Culross Street. If Yorty was in the garage – and he must have been, because I was right above him – there is no way that he could have seen the man who was shooting at him.'

Horton said, 'That's a statement, not a question.'

'This is my question,' I said. 'He didn't see the gunman, so how was Yorty able to supply you with a description of him?'

'Your premise is false,' Horton said. 'Therefore, the question doesn't arise. He saw the man. That's how he gave us a description.'

'Couldn't have – impossible. And that's the problem, because it leaves us with two answers to the question. And both of them put Yorty in a bad light.'

'Yorty's a married man with a spotless record,' Horton said crossly.

'His wife's in London?'

'She's on sick leave,' Horton said. 'I don't know why I'm answering these questions.'

I said, 'Listen. He gave you a description because he knew the gunman beforehand, and he didn't have to see him to describe him accurately. That's the first possibility.'

'If Dwight Yorty was the sort of man who ran around with that sort of person, I think the boys on the third floor would know about it.'

I ignored this. 'The second possibility is that because Yorty knew the gunman, he deliberately didn't describe him accurately. In which case, he doesn't want us to catch the guy.'

'You just sit there assuming that Yorty knows this killer!' Horton said. 'That's incredible!'

'He definitely knew him,' I said.

'Prove it.'

'Because he definitely didn't see him, and he definitely gave us a description of the man.'

Horton said, 'This is interesting. Thinking always is. It's fun, let's face it. But you're not paid to contradict the Ambassador. I can tell you he's really mad. He knows that I'm asking you to pass this along to the press.' Horton put his fingertips together and flexed them. 'And when he opens his paper in a few days he will expect to see an accurate version of his point of view, not a garbled mess that impugns the honesty of a serving officer –'

I wanted to say: *Yorty hit his wife over the head with a cucumber, and then he ate it, and now she's trying to sue him for brain damage.*

I said, 'I'd like to know a little more about the man who was picked up after the shooting.'

'He didn't fit Yorty's description,' Horton said. 'He was released.'

'Yorty's description doesn't really count, because he didn't see the gunman. The suspect was seen running down Park Street.'

'Jogging,' Horton said. 'He was a jogger.'

'That's useful. He's athletic. It could explain the gun. A runner might have access to a starter's pistol – one that shoots blanks.'

'Just because no cartridges were found doesn't mean that no shots were fired.'

'True,' I said, 'but no bullet holes were found either. No slugs. No marks on the garage walls.'

Horton said, 'You've been working overtime.'

'I was looking out the window when it happened. I didn't see anything. Yorty couldn't have seen anything.'

And he hit his wife with a cucumber and she called it attempted murder.

'I'm glad you've told me all of this speculation,' Horton said, 'because if any of it gets into the paper I'll know who to blame. Maybe someone else should be found to leak the story.'

'No, no,' I said. 'I want to do it – please let me. Just give me a little time. I've got to find the right paper, one that the wire services will pick up on.'

Horton smiled. 'Remember, you're doing this for the Ambassador. He didn't like your performance at the briefing – you asked too many questions. He'll be watching you.'

'Do you trust me, coach?' I hated saying the word, but with Horton it always worked.

'Of course I do.'

'I'll do exactly what I'm told,' I said. 'But I'd appreciate it if you'd ask Yorty one question on my behalf. There's no harm in asking. It might even be a good idea. After all, since we're accusing Libya of sponsoring an assassination attempt, we really ought to have most of the facts. And it's a simple question.'

'Go ahead,' Horton said.

'Just this – and it would help if you reminded him that it doesn't matter whether he swears on a stack of Bibles that he's telling the truth, because this fact is checkable. It concerns the man who was picked up right after the shooting, the one you said was innocent. Has Yorty ever seen him before?'

'What if he says yes?'

'Then that's your man, because Yorty didn't see him at the time of the shooting. He knew him – perhaps very well, perhaps so well that he wanted to hide the fact.'

Horton said, 'Then why did the guy try to kill him?'

'He didn't,' I said. 'Only ex-lovers shoot to kill.'

Two days passed, and on the morning of the third I entered my office, to find Everett Horton seated at my desk.

He said, 'Have you leaked the story yet?'

'Not yet,' I said, but in fact I'd had no intention of doing so until we had all the information, which was why I was so eager to take sole responsibility for it.

'That's a relief,' Horton said.

'He answered the question,' I said.

Horton nodded. 'Yorty is leaving us,' he said. 'He's leaving the Foreign Service, too. And his wife is leaving him – already left him, so I understand.'

'I feel sorry for him,' I said.

'Forget it,' Horton said. 'The Ambassador wants to see you. Don't bring up the incident in our backyard to him. He was impressed, I think, by your tenacity, but it's rather a sore point.'

Ambassador Noyes said, 'I was wondering whether you're free to join us for dinner on the twenty-first. We'd like to see you at Winfield House.'

'I accept with pleasure.'

He said, 'The Prime Minister will be there.'

So that was my reward.

The Winfield Wallpaper

Dinner at Winfield House, the American Ambassador's Residence in Regent's Park, was usually regarded as a treat, not a duty. But the guests of honor tonight were the Prime Minister and her husband. I had guessed that my invitation was a reward, and then I began to suspect that I was being put to work. I did not really mind – I had nothing else to do. After more than a year in London I still had no lover, no close friends, no recreations. I had plenty of society but not much pleasure: it was not an easy city. And perhaps I overreacted to Ambassador Noyes's invitation. I bought a new dinner jacket and a formal shirt. The shirt cost me forty-seven dollars.

I was heading home to change, and reflecting on the safest topics to discuss with the Prime Minister, when I saw the car. Every Friday evening since early in January I had seen this car parked on the corner of Alexandra Avenue and Prince of Wales Drive, and always two people inside. As the weeks passed I began to be on the watch for the car. The man and woman in the front seat were either talking quietly or embracing. On some evenings they sat slightly apart, sipping from paper cups. Three months later, but always on Fridays, they were still at it.

There was something touching about this weekly romance in the front seat of an old Rover. It was ritual, not routine. Sometimes the two people seemed to me as passionate and tenacious as a pair of spies – lovers clinging together and hiding for a cause – and sometimes they made me feel like a spy.

I supposed they worked in the same office, that he drove her home, and that on Fridays – using the heavy traffic as an excuse – they made this detour in Battersea to spend an hour together. It was their secret life, this love affair. The parked car seemed to say that it was kept secret from everyone. It was probably the only hour in the week that mattered to them.

Tonight they were kissing. The spring air was mild, and the trees in the park were blossomy, pink and white, palely lit by the lingering sunset and the refracted river light that reached past the embankments and cast no shadows. We had high clouds, mountains of them, all day, and every new leaf was a different shade of green. Spring was magic in London; the city seemed to rise from the dead. There was no winter freeze, as in some northern cities, but rather a brown season of decay and bad smells. April brought grass and flowers out of the mud and healed the city with leaves and made it new. This was my second spring, and it was, again, a surprise.

The couple in the car helped my mood. I set off for Winfield House, whistling a pop song I had been hearing, called 'Dancing on the Radio.' I was wearing new clothes. I had done my exercises and had had a shower and a drink. It had been a good day. In my cable I had summarized in a thousand words yesterday's by-election; a month ago I had correctly predicted the outcome. I had borrowed Al Sanger's Jaguar, and as I drove up Park Lane I turned on the radio and heard a Mozart concerto, the one for flute and harp. It gave me optimism and a sense of victory. I had solitude and warmth, and all my bills were paid, and I had a general feeling of reassurance. Everything was going to be all right. It began to rain lightly and I thought: *Perfect*.

When I came to the iron gates of Winfield House, four armed men appeared. I opened my side window and heard noises from the zoo, grunts and bird squawks. The men examined my invitation and found my name on their clipboard, and I was waved in. The security precautions reminded me once again that the Prime Minister was coming. I was by now excited at the prospect of meeting her.

I was announced by the doorman. Ambassador Noyes sprang forward when he heard my name. He seemed nervous and rather serious. Everett Horton and Margaret Duboys were there, and soon after, more guests arrived. Most of them were nice American millionaires who lived part time in London. There was also a journalist, and an American academic and his wife, and a novelist – he was fortyish and talkative, delighted to be there, and his smug square face was gleaming with gratitude. One group of guests had already been more or less herded into the green room to admire the wallpaper.

'I think it's best if we sort of gather in there,' Ambassador Noyes said. This was an order, but he said it uncertainly, which was one of the reasons he was called No-Yes.

He was the shepherd, and Horton and I were the sheepdogs, and the nondiplomatic people were the sheep. The idea was to keep them from straying without making them panic or feel penned in.

Horton whispered, 'Not a word about interest rates tonight, please.'

Then he hurried to the far end of the room and began helpfully pointing at the wall.

The wallpaper in this room was famous. It was Chinese, four centuries old – or was it five? – and had been found in Hong Kong by a recent ambassador, who had had it restored and hung. It was the color of pale jade, and there were pictures of birds and flowers on it, hummingbirds and poppies and lotuses. It was such a classic item, it had the look of a Chinese cliché, even to the predictable pagodas. It had been so carefully repainted, it looked like a copy – it was too perfect, too bright, not a crack or a peel mark anywhere – and every figure on it was primly arranged in a pattern of curves. The pattern was old and slightly irregular, but the surface design had been scoured of its subtlety with the fresh paint, and there was not an interesting shadow on it anywhere. You scrutinized it because it was famous, and then you were disappointed because you had scrutinized it. Such interesting wallpaper, people said; but if it had been less famous it might have looked more interesting. And I felt that the prettier wallpaper was, the worse the wall it hid.

It had another feature, this wallpaper – it inspired the dullest conversation: How old was it, and was it really paper, and how much had it cost?

It made me want to change the subject. I was talking with Debbie Horton, telling her the correct version of a story about me that had been going the rounds. A few months before, I had attended a fund-raising dinner and at my table I had spoken to a man whom everyone present had been referring to as 'Sonny.' Sonny was a tall rosy-cheeked man with the subdued manner of a botanist or a handyman. 'What do you do?' I had asked. He became awfully flustered. 'Nothing much,' he then said, and was silent for the rest of the meal. Afterward, a smirking, sharp-faced woman said, 'That was Sonny Marlborough – the Duke of Marlborough, to you.' It was a good story, and, as President Nixon used to tell his aides with a sweaty little grin, it had the additional merit of being true.

Debbie had heard the gossip version – that he had said, 'What do I do? I'm a duke –'

Then I forgot everything. I couldn't think. I was looking at a young woman's back, and at her yellow hair, the way it came out in little wings over her ears, and the curve of her hip, a line, from where her small hand rested on her waist, to her knee, and the way her green dress was smooth against her thigh. I went weak, as if suddenly standing up drunk, and I felt lost in admiration and anticipated failure and the kind of hopeless fear in a flash of blindness that is known only to those who feel desire. I wanted to touch her and talk to her.

Debbie Horton was saying, 'You're not even listening to me!'

'I heard every word you said.' Insincerity made my voice overserious and emphatic.

'What are you looking at?' Debbie said.

A stir in the room saved me. There was a shifting of feet, the guests looking at each other and then at the door, which the Prime Minister and her husband were just passing through with the Ambassador and his wife. We fell silent, and the Prime Minister began talking in a loud friendly way about how much she liked the wallpaper.

'It's silk, of course,' the Prime Minister said.

This silent smiling mob at my end of the room was already tremendously impressed. This was how you talked about wallpaper!

The young woman had also turned to see the Prime Minister. She was about thirty; her face was bright with intelligence and a kind of shyness. She had a little smile of anxiety on her lips, giving her mouth a pretty pair of parentheses, and there was something lovely and unglamorous about her that gave her real beauty. Her dress was a simple one, but the neck of it was edged in lace. Her eyes were green, she had small feet, her skin looked warm.

No one spoke. The Prime Minister was being introduced, and most of us were beaming horribly at her in case she should look up.

'I have a law degree myself!' she was saying to one guest. She spoke in a hearty headmistressy shout.

Two steps took me nearer the young woman with green eyes, and I whispered, 'We haven't met.'

She smiled and looked toward the Prime Minister, who was approaching us.

I said in a low voice, 'What do you think of the wallpaper?'

She laughed a little and said, 'I like its lame uncertain curves.'

'Flora Domingo-Duncan,' Ambassador Noyes said, appearing next to her. 'Doctor Duncan is currently doing research in London.'

'On Mary Shelley,' she said, with a hesitant bow to the Prime Minister.

'Frankenstein!' the Prime Minister shouted, and moved on. She had already put herself in charge of us.

I again wanted to touch Flora Domingo-Duncan. I could not think of anything to say to her. I needed time, and I knew I looked stupid and slow.

At this point, the Prime Minister's husband came forward and was introduced. This man had been made into a celebrity by an English comedian, who had portrayed him in a popular farce as a sour-faced paranoiac in a cardigan, interested in nothing but drinking and playing golf. In this unlikely way he had become as famous as his wife, but something of a joke figure. I could see at once that the comedian had gotten him wrong. He was kindly, he was funny, and he had an easy laugh – a way of throwing his head back and braying his approval. He scowled and smiled; he was skinny and nimble; he had a very funny upper-middle-class drawl.

'Is this your first time in London?' he asked Dr Duncan.

'No,' she said. 'I did graduate work at Oxford three years ago.'

'I know who you are,' he said to me. 'You're with the firm, aren't you? Yaaas' – and threw his head back and laughed – 'you see I've done my homework! I read that sheet of names they gave me – all your little biographies.'

This was surprising candor – dinner-party homework was never mentioned – but it made me like him. He saw it properly as both a joke and a duty.

I said to Dr Duncan, 'You have a lovely name. Flora Domingo-Duncan.'

'My mother is Mexican.' She was polite and patient, and I wondered whether she was bored by me.

The Prime Minister's husband said, 'Yes, some of these Mexicans actually do have blond hair.'

'My mother's hair is brown,' Dr Duncan said.

We were getting nowhere. I wanted to be alone with her. I wanted to meet her later in the week for dinner. Maybe she had a boy friend?

Horton joined our little group; he introduced a lady by the name of Bloomsack, then whispered to me, 'That was a wonderful cable you wrote today on the by-election.'

'Thanks, coach,' I said, and for some reason thought of the old Rover car parked on the corner of Alexandra Avenue and Prince of Wales Drive, and the two people in it, kissing, and I stepped nearer to Flora Domingo-Duncan.

Horton was whispering behind me, 'If the subject of interest rates comes up with the PM, I'll give you a signal. I'll need some back-up.' And he went away.

I was watching Dr Duncan's pulse at her neck, an almost imperceptible flutter between a branch of bones.

Mrs Bloomsack said, 'I was at Carrington's last night,' to the Prime Minister's husband.

'Yaaas,' he drawled warily, tipping his head back.

The woman had equivocated – 'Carrington,' she had said, not 'Lord' or 'Peter.' Lord Carrington was the Foreign Secretary.

'Wasn't he the man,' Dr Duncan said, 'who settled the Rhodesian issue?'

'Yes,' said Mrs Bloomsack.

'No, no, no,' the Prime Minister's husband said. 'I'll tell you who did that. I'll tell you who brought both sides together and did most of the preliminary work.' And he turned and with an owlish face and immense pride he said, 'It was that lady over there. That's who it was. Yaaas.'

He was smiling fondly at the Prime Minister. She saw him and smiled back. She had a hard pleasureless smile and slightly discolored teeth, and her skin was like flawed dusty marble. Her face was vain, unimpressed, and attractive, and her body square and powerful. Her eyes were heavy-lidded, and there was a sacklike heaviness in her, a willfulness and impatience that gave her an aura of strength. Even her hair looked hard. In every way she was the opposite of her husband.

Ambassador Noyes stared at me. He was with the Prime Minister and I think he wanted help. I pretended not to see him.

'I'm interested in your research on Mary Shelley,' I said to Dr Duncan. 'I reread *Frankenstein* recently. "Misery made me a fiend.

Make me happy, and I shall again be virtuous." That poor monster.'

'Frankenstein's the doctor, not the monster,' Mrs Bloomsack said, seeming pleased with herself.

'Yaaas,' the Prime Minister's husband said, lifting his sharp nose at the woman.

'Most people get it wrong,' she said.

'Do they?' the Prime Minister's husband said. 'I had no idea.' He shook his head at her and in a gentle way watched her stumble. Did he know how funny he was?

I said, 'I have a theory that this novel represents a fear of child-birth. Mary Shelley's mother died giving birth to her, there had been several miscarriages in her family – or Shelley's family – and she wrote it when she was pregnant. Can't *Frankenstein* be seen as an expression of the fear of giving birth to a monster or a corpse?'

'A lot of people have that theory,' Dr Duncan said. She tossed her loose gold hair and smiled at me. 'But she wasn't pregnant, and anyway is Doctor Frankenstein the father or the mother of the monster?'

'Does it make a difference?'

'We are being summoned to dinner,' the Prime Minister's husband said, and stood aside to let the ladies pass.

'As a feminist, I think it makes a big difference,' Dr Duncan said. 'You don't believe me.'

'No, no, it's not that,' I said. 'Feminists are usually such scolds. But you're so nice.'

'I'm not nice,' she said lightly. 'I'm selfish, I'm bossy, I'm opinion-ated, and I'm a scold, too. My students are afraid of me.' She was grinning, giving her mouth the pretty parentheses. 'And I'm impossible to live with.'

'You're full of surprises,' I said. 'When I asked you about the Chinese wallpaper you said, "I like its lame uncertain curves." That's pretty funny.'

'It's a quotation,' she said, 'from Charlotte Perkins Gilman. You don't know her story, *The Yellow Wallpaper*?' She smiled at my ignorance. 'She was another impossible woman. It was very nice to meet you.'

And I felt, furiously, that she was saying good-bye to me.

The table was set for sixteen people. Flora Domingo-Duncan

was sitting at a distant corner, between Everett Horton and Mr Sidney Bloomsack. The Prime Minister was halfway down the table, next to Ambassador Noyes, and her husband was just across from her. I saw Dr Duncan speaking to Mr Bloomsack, who had the tanned white and brown head of a yachtsman in his sixties – he radiated money and virility – and I became uneasy and thought how funny and spirited Dr Duncan was, how self-possessed and surprising. She was pretty, she was bright-eyed, she was frank. I had nothing to offer her, but again I felt the sad urgency of desire for her.

It is customary at such a dinner to speak to the person on your immediate right. This was Mrs Fentiman, wife of the New York publisher, who was in London in a take-over bid for the English firm of Howletts.

Mrs Fentiman said, 'I can't think of anything to say to the Prime Minister's husband.'

'Ask him about Zimbabwe or North Sea oil,' I said. 'Don't mention interest rates or unemployment.'

But I was watching Flora Domingo-Duncan, and my heart ached when I saw how far away she was. I was in an undertow – I was very far from shore.

The meal was served. It began with pheasant consommé and sherry, and then we were served *Navarin de homard*. The main course was *escalopine de veau Normande*, with broccoli and dauphine potatoes and a *gâteau des carottes aux fine herbes*, and the wine with it was Pinot Noir 1977. There was red salad and deep-fried Camembert, and dessert was *bombe glacée* with fresh strawberries and cream, and I had three glasses of champagne.

I ate, I listened to Mrs Fentiman, and instead of watching the Prime Minister to see how she was getting on with the Ambassador, I stared hopelessly at Dr Duncan, trying to catch her eye. She never once glanced in my direction. Several times, while watching her, I saw her laugh – she had a loud energetic laugh. I loved her laughter, and yet it made me feel rueful. Why was I sitting so far from her?

There were toasts – to the Queen, to our President – and then speeches. The Ambassador's, made with notes, was a simple affirmation of Anglo–US friendship; the Prime Minister's speech was an eloquent and graceful rejoinder that had the effect of making Ambassador Noyes seem as if he had asked an intelligent question – he looked surprised and pleased. At their best, the British can be very courtly, and the Prime Minister made us seem that night as if we were her dearest friends.

It was one of the best meals I had ever eaten; this was one of the most distinguished guest lists imaginable; Winfield House was one of the loveliest private homes in Regent's Park; the speeches were uplifting; and all that beautiful wallpaper! But I would have swapped it all for an hour of privacy with Flora Domingo-Duncan.

'And you're a pretty fussy eater,' Mrs Fentiman said. She was still talking! 'You hardly touched your meal. Are you one of these food cranks?'

'No. I just got very strange when I was in the Far East,' I said.

She did not smile. She twitched a little. I hated women who looked like men.

'The State Department has a lot to answer for,' I said.

Having successfully bewildered Mrs Fentiman, I scrambled to get near Dr Duncan, nearly knocking down Mrs Bloomsack. Dr Duncan was smiling at me, seeming to invite me over to join her! Just behind me, I heard Horton clearing his throat, and then he threw his arm around me.

'The word is that she wants to hear about interest rates. We'll have an informal session over coffee. You're going to like her. She is really an amazing human being.'

I said, 'I don't know anything about interest rates.'

'Improvise,' Horton said.

'It seems to me that's what all the economists are doing,' I said. 'Improvising.'

'That's kind of a cute opening – why don't you use it on her? She'll appreciate it.'

Flora Domingo-Duncan had joined Margaret Duboys and Debbie Horton and the distinguished Sidney Bloomsack, who, I could tell, had taken a shine to her. He was a rich, idle man – he would make everything easy for her. He looked like the sort of man who had had every dollar and every woman he had ever wanted. It was awful to think that she and I might never have a chance to talk, and she might go off with S. Bloomsack thinking he wasn't a bad guy – generous, at least. Some women in the company of vain and ridiculous men look vain and ridiculous themselves, and some look like hookers. Dr Duncan looked serene. She had the most relaxed shoulders. She was listening, giving nothing away.

'Hurry up,' Horton said, squeezing my arm. 'She hates to be kept waiting.'

I heard a loud sudden burst of laughter and recognized it as Dr Duncan's. What a wonderful laugh! What had Bloomsack said that was so funny? They were all laughing now, over there, the millionaires, the academic, the journalist, the novelist. They were having a swell time.

My whole life had been like this. Working in second-floor offices in Africa, in Malaysia, in London, I had looked out the window and seen lovers strolling on the ground, or people smiling at nothing; I had seen the casual way that people met, the way they chatted, how they held hands. And I was always doing something else. My work was my life. I had never been idle. I was always a little late for an appointment, a little overdue with bills, a little behind in my work, and there was always someone in the next room with a problem for me. I was seen by everyone as a master; but no one was a more put-upon servant, keeping regular hours and at the mercy of anyone at all who demanded to see me.

It seemed wrong to like solitude so much, but I had always lived in empty rooms, and craved privacy, because I was overworked. And now, like any servant, I saw how completely I had surrendered and how much I had wasted. I had been praised, but praise was not enough; I was well paid, but what did money matter? I had never had the time to spend it. It seemed that I had always been a bystander, watching life through a second-storey window and expected to talk about the wallpaper. Love was for after work, but I was always at work.

This woman had woken in me desire, and a realization of my own envy, cowardice, loneliness, and disappointment – I couldn't say despair. But I began to think that I did not deserve her, which is one of the gravest sins of all, self-doubt. What a lovely name, what a ringing laugh, what a pretty mouth!

Watching Flora Domingo-Duncan, and thinking about myself, I was taking a chair in front of the Prime Minister.

'The Prime Minister was wondering about interest rates,' Horton said to me.

'I was told,' she said in a hectoring, too-loud voice, 'that you could quite easily put me in the picture. Just how long are your rates going to go on rising?'

She was known for her directness. I sat down and began explaining, and again I heard the sudden laughter of Dr Duncan. She was with that other group – the ones drinking port and cognac, who would go away thinking what a wonderful time they had had at Winfield House with the Prime Minister and those powerful London Embassy people. We were drinking water. We were talking in abstractions. From my point of view the evening was a failure, because I wanted for once to be on the far side of the room. The only thing that mattered was human happiness; however distinguished or powerful we looked here in this corner beside the expensive fake-looking wallpaper – the Prime Minister, Horton, Ambassador Noyes, and myself – we were merely temporary people, actors with small speaking roles, reciting lines that were required of us: we knew what an uncertain thing power was. We were talking about the world, and pretending that we had a measure of control over it, but it was mostly bluff. Or did we really believe that this concern was more important than that laughter?

We had done with interest rates and grain sales and the Polish debt, and then a silence fell.

To fill it, I said, 'Prime Minister, the unemployment rate in Britain strikes some of us as a serious matter. Have you any –'

'No one is more concerned about it than I am,' she said, with the force of someone who believed she might soon lose her job. 'I take it very seriously indeed. But the long-term projections are encouraging, and we believe it will be substantially reduced in the next quarter.'

'I don't see how,' I said, and I looked for Flora Domingo-Duncan across the room.

I had, through inattention, been too skeptical. This aroused the Prime Minister, and she began to speak in a venomous way. 'There are a few vicious, self-serving, greedy, desperate, power-seeking –'

Flora Domingo-Duncan was leaving.

I said, 'It seems hopeless.'

'Don't you believe that for a moment,' the Prime Minister said; she had never looked plumper, and her plumpness was like armor.

What had I started? They were all staring at me! Was it unemployment? Oh, God, I thought, and I saw that the hardest thing in the world for me to do would be to leave that little group. I had to stay, to give the Prime Minister a chance to say her piece, and to satisfy the Ambassador and Horton. But there was no time, and in the swing of that silence I stood.

'Excuse me.'

And turned my back on them.

She was in the large, wood-paneled foyer, speaking to the Bloomsacks. Mrs Noyes was saying good night to the Fentimans. Chauffeurs were being summoned from the rain and darkness.

'Do you need a ride home?' I said. 'I have a car.'

'The Bloomsacks are taking me,' Dr Duncan said. 'But thanks anyway.'

I said, 'We didn't have much of a chance to talk.'

'I saw you talking to the Prime Minister,' she said. 'I mean, you were actually *talking* to her. That was –'

'No, no!' Mrs Bloomsack exploded. 'Mine is the dark blue one!' Pumping her arms, this short stout woman crossed to the cloakroom, where a blank-faced servant held the wrong coat in both of his hands.

'May I get your coat, Flora?' Mr Bloomsack said.

'It's a green cape,' she said.

And then we were alone, Flora Domingo-Duncan and I.

'I want to see you again, very much, for a meal – or anything.' I was talking fast.

'That would be nice.' She looked at me with curiosity, and her gaze lingered in a tipsy way. She had the slightly out-of-focus look in her eyes of someone who wears contact lenses.

'What's your telephone number?'

She told me. I scribbled it on my wrist in ballpoint.

'Call me,' she said.

Mr Bloomsack was returning with her cloak. His teeth were gleaming. He was pushing toward me.

'When?' I said, with such insistence that she smiled again.

'Tonight,' she whispered, and then turned so that Mr Bloomsack could help her put on her cape.

Dancing on the Radio

Flora Domingo-Duncan said, 'I used to be a mess,' and laughed, and said, 'It was my mother. So I went to graduate school in California and put three thousand miles between us. God, am I boring!'

'You're not boring,' I said.

'I don't want you to get sick of me.'

'I'll never get sick of you.'

We were naked in bed on our backs and speaking to the ceiling.

'Anyway, I was a wreck,' she said, and clawed her blond hair away from her forehead. 'I had a shrink. I wasn't embarrassed, I just didn't want to talk about it, so I told people I was seeing my dentist. Twice a week! "You must have terrible teeth," they'd say. But it was my mind that was a mess. Hey, why are we talking about my mind?'

Because during our lovemaking we had become very private and fallen silent. I thought then that no one was more solitary than during orgasm. We were resuming an interrupted conversation.

'I like your mind,' I said. 'I like your green eyes. I like your sweet et cetera.'

'Good old e.e. cummings.' She was expert at spotting quotations. We agreed on most things, on *Wuthering Heights*, *To the Lighthouse*, *Dubliners*, and *Pale Fire*; on Joyce Cary, Henry James, Chekhov, and Emily Dickinson. We shared a loathing for Ernest Hemingway. That night we had gone to the National Theatre to see *La Ronde*, by Arthur Schnitzler; and then I made omelettes; and we went to bed, and talked about *La Ronde*, and made love. But literature was as crucial as sex – we were getting serious. Liking the same books made us equals and gave us hope; we had known the same pleasure and experience. Taste mattered: Who wanted to live with a philistine or to listen to half-baked opinions? Everything mattered. And there was her Mexican side, a whole other world. It was not exactly revealed to me, but I was aware of its existence.

In all ways, with Flora, I seemed to be kneeling at her keyhole. She loved that expression.

It was spring, and the windows were open. The night-sweet fragrance of flowering trees was in the air.

'This is luxury,' she said. She pronounced it *lugzhery*, because she knew I found it funny, like her comic pronunciation of groceries, *grosheries*.

'But I have to go,' she said.

'Stay a while longer.'

'Just a little while.'

She lived off Goldhawk Road, at Stamford Brook, in two rooms. It was there that she worked on Mary Shelley, with occasional visits to the British Library. Her time was limited. She had only until July to finish her research; then back to the States and summer school teaching. She worked every morning, and so it was important to her that she left me at night.

'I have to wake up in my own bed,' she said. 'Otherwise I won't get anything done.'

I admired her enterprise and her independence, but I was also a bit threatened by them – or perhaps made uneasy, because her life seemed complete. She had a Ph.D., an Oxford D.Phil., and was an assistant professor at Bryn Mawr. She was presently on a traveling fellowship, working on a biography of Mary Shelley. She was beautiful, and I never wanted her to go. She had never spent a whole night in my bed.

I said, 'I wish you needed me more.'

'That's silly. You should be glad I'm independent,' she said. 'I can see you more clearly. Don't you know how much I like you?'

I liked her. I craved her company. I liked myself better when I was with her. The word 'like' was useless.

'But I need you.'

'There's no reason why you have to say it like that,' she said, smiling gently and kissing me. 'Anyway, you have everything.'

'I used to think that,' I said.

She said, 'It's scary, meeting someone you like. Friendship is scarier than sex. I keep thinking, "What if he goes away? What if he stops liking me? What if . . . what if . . . ?"'

'I'm not going anywhere.'

'But I am,' she said. She could be decisive. She kissed me and got out of bed and dressed quickly. And minutes later I was watch-

ing her car pull away from Overstrand Mansions and already missing her.

I had thought that once we were sexually exhausted we would
be bored with each other, and yet boredom never came, only the
further excitement at the prospect of my seeing her again. Every
succeeding time I was with her I liked her better, and discovered
more in her – new areas of kindness, intelligence, and passion. I
lusted for her.

She was not romantic. She was gentle, she was practical, and a
little cautious. She had warned me against herself – she told me
she was selfish, bossy, opinionated, and possessive. She said, 'I'm
impossible to live with.' But later she stopped talking this way. She
said I made her happy. I had known her a month, but I saw her
regularly – almost every evening.

We had made love the first night we met, after the Ambassador's
party, at two in the morning, in distant Stamford Brook. We made
love most evenings, always as if we were running out of time. It
became like a ceremony, a ritual that was altering us. Each occasion
was slightly different and separable, and fixed in my memory. So
this continued, both of us burning, both of us expecting it to end.
But we did not become bored – we were now close friends.

I had had lovers, but I had never had such a good friend, and
for this friendship I loved her. I didn't tell her – I was afraid to
use that word. The sex was part of it, but there was something
more powerful – perhaps the recognition of how similar we were
in some ways, how different in others, how necessary to each
other's happiness.

Love is both panic and relief that you are not alone anymore.
All at once, someone else matters to your happiness. I hated to be
parted from her. But she was busier than I was! She had just until
July to finish her work, and then it was back to the States and her
teaching. We lived with a feeling that this would all end soon, but
this sense of limited time did not discourage me. I found myself making plans and, in an innocent way, falling in love with
her.

It reassured me. I had never thought that I would fall in love
with anyone. Then it seemed to me that living with another person
was the only thing that mattered on earth, that this solitary life I
had been leading was selfish and barren – and turning me into a
crank – and that Flora was my rescuer. Part of love was bluff and

fumbling and drunkenness. I knew that – but it was the pleasant afterglow of moonshine. The other part of love was real emotion: it was stony and desperate; it made all lovers shameless; and it did not spare me. I was alive, I was myself, only when I was with Flora, and that was always too seldom.

I could not see her on Friday nights. She did not say why, but Friday was out. I had a colleague – Brickhouse, in the Press Section – who told me that after he got married he and his wife decided to give themselves a night off every week – it was Wednesday. Neither could count on the other's company on Wednesday, and neither was expected to reveal his or her plans. They weren't married on Wednesday night. Of course, most Wednesdays were the same – a meal, television, and to bed – in different rooms that night. That was the agreement. But some Wednesdays found Jack Brickhouse on his own and Marilyn inexplicably elsewhere; on other Wednesdays it was the other way around. This marriage, which was childless, lasted seven years. Brickhouse said, 'It was a good marriage – better than any I know. It was a good divorce, too. Listen, my ex-wife is my best friend!'

I used to wonder if for Flora it was that kind of Friday, keeping part of her life separate from me. It certainly disturbed me, because I was free most Fridays. I spent Fridays missing her, thinking of her, and wishing I were with her. Perhaps she knew this – counted on it? On the weekends when I was duty officer I did not see her at all.

I had asked her about her Fridays once. I said, 'I get it. It's the night you go to your meeting of Alcoholics Anonymous.'

I could not have been clumsier. But worry, self-pity, and probably anger, had made me very stupid.

She said, 'Do you have to know everything?' And then, 'If it is Alcoholics Anonymous I'm hardly likely to tell you, am I? A. A. is very secret, very spiritual, and no one makes idiotic jokes about it. That's why it works.'

Maybe she was an alcoholic? But a few weeks later she told me that her father had had a drinking problem, and I knew somehow that she didn't.

Still, every Friday night I seemed to hang by my thumbs. On two successive Fridays I called her at her apartment, but there was no answer. Was she in bed with someone else and saying, 'This is our day off'? I wondered whether I could live with her and allow her her free Fridays. But of course I could – I would have allowed her anything!

And from this Friday business I came to know her as someone who could keep a secret. She did what she wanted; she stuck to a routine; she would not be bullied. So, not seeing her on Fridays, I learned to respect her and to need her more, and it made our Saturdays passionate.

She never stayed the whole night with me, not even on the weekends. On the nights when I went back to her apartment she woke me up and always said, 'You're being kicked out of bed.' It was so that she could work, she said. She was determined to finish her Mary Shelley research on time.

On one of those late nights, when I was yawning, getting dressed sleepily, like a doctor or a fireman being summoned at an unearthly hour – but I was only going home to go back to bed – she said, 'By the way, I'm busy next weekend.'

'That's okay,' I said. But the news depressed me. 'What are you doing?'

Her beautiful silent smile silenced me.

That weekend passed. I missed her badly. I saw her on the Monday, and we went to the movie *Raging Bull*. She hated its violence, and I rather liked its Italian aromas – boxing and meatballs. I took her home in a taxi, but before we reached Stamford Brook she kissed me lightly, and I knew she had something on her mind.

'Please don't come in,' she said. 'I'm terribly tired.'

Well, she looked tired, so I didn't insist. I had the taxi drop me at Victoria and I walked the rest of the way home. It was pleasant, walking home late, thinking about her. And it did not seriously worry me that there was a part of her life that she kept separate from me, because when we were together we could not have been closer. I had never met anyone I liked better. It became a point of honor with me that I did not discuss her absent Fridays or that weekend. It was the only weekend she asked for – there were no others.

Enough time had passed, and we were both committed enough, for us to think of this as a love affair. Flora must love me, I thought, because she is inspiring my love. But so far, the Embassy knew nothing about it.

This was just as well. Not long after Flora's mysterious weekend, we were given a talk on the antinuclear lobby in Britain. The feeling was fiercely against our installing nuclear missiles in various British sites. Every party hated us for it – the Labour Party because it was anti-Soviet, the Liberals because it was dangerous, the Conservatives because it was an iniquitous form of national trespass. We knew it was unpopular. We had five men gathering information on it. They had the names of the leaders of the pressure groups; they had infiltrated some of these groups; they had membership lists. They filmed the marches and demonstrations and all the speeches, whether they were at Hyde Park or at distant American bases in the English countryside, where the more passionate protestors chained themselves to the gates.

One of the films concerned a group calling itself Women Opposed to Nuclear Technology. It was not an antiwar movement: they weren't pacifists; they did not advocate unilateral disarmament. Their aims struck me as admirable. They wanted Britain to be a 'nuclear-free zone': no missiles, no neutron bombs, no reactors. And they were positive in their approach, giving seminars – so the boys on the third floor said – on alternative technology.

This film showed them marching with signs, massing in Hyde Park, and demonstrating at an American base. The highlight of this weekend of protest was an all-night vigil, which won them a great deal of publicity. They didn't shout, they didn't make speeches. They simply stood with lighted candles and informative posters. It was a remarkable show of determination, and one of the women in the film was Flora Domingo-Duncan.

I sat in the darkness of the Embassy theater and listened to the deadpan narration of one of our intelligence men, and I watched him take his little baton and point in the general direction of the woman I loved.

'This sort of person is doing us an awful lot of harm,' he said.

I smiled, and loved her more.

Did she know she was on film?

'No,' she said, 'but I'm damned glad you told me. The others will be mad as anything. Why did you tell me?'

'It's every citizen's right to know,' I said. 'Freedom of information.'

She laughed. She said, 'Now you know about my Friday nights. But I thought that if I told you about it you'd have to keep it a secret.'

'It wouldn't have mattered,' I said.

'Something else to think about. You're busy enough as it is.'

It never occurred to her that I might disapprove of her agitprop because I worked for the US Embassy. It was nothing personal. She had acted out of a sense of duty.

I said, 'If I say I admire you for this – acting on your beliefs – will you think I'm being patronizing?'

'You're very sweet,' she said. She wrinkled her nose and kissed me. 'Let's not talk about atom bombs.'

The matter was at an end. Everything she did made me love her more.

We went on loving, and then something happened to London. In the late spring heat, the city streets were unusually full of people – not tourists, but hot idle youths who stared at passersby and at cars. Battersea seemed ominously crowded. They kept near the fringes of the park and they lurked – it seemed the right word – near shops and on street corners. They carried radios. There was a tune I kept hearing – I could hum it long before I learned the words. 'Dancing on the Radio,' it was called.

> *We start the fire*
> *We break the wall*
> *We sniff the smoke*
> *Which covers all the monsters*
> *Look at us go*
> *Dancing on the radio,*
> *Hey, turn up the volume and watch!*
> *Turn up the volume and watch!*

And there was a chanting chorus that went, '*Make it, shake it, break it!*' It was a violent love song.

The youths on the streets reminded me of the sort of aimless mobs I had seen in Africa and Malaysia. These south London boys looked just as sour and destructive. They lingered, they grew in numbers, and their song played loudly around them.

Flora called them lost souls. She said you had to pity people who were unprotected.

'Then pity the poor slobs whose windows are going to be broken,' I said.

'I know. It's a mess.'

I said, 'All big cities have these little underdeveloped areas in them. They're not neighborhoods, they're nations.'

Flora said, 'They scare me – all these people waiting. They're not all waiting for the same thing, but they're all angry.'

Many were across the road from Overstrand Mansions. They sat at the edge of the park; sometimes they yelled at cars passing down Prince of Wales Drive, or they walked toward the shops behind the mansion blocks and paced back and forth. There was always that harsh music with them.

'If this was the States and I saw those people I'd be really worried,' Flora said. 'I'd say there was going to be terrible trouble. But this is England.'

'There's going to be trouble,' I said.

She looked at me.

'We're getting signals,' I said.

The boys on the third floor, the ones who had filmed Flora, were now showing us films of idle mobs.

Then the trouble came. It did not begin in London. It started from small skirmishes in Liverpool and Bristol, and it grew. It was fierce fighting, sometimes between mobs – blacks and whites fighting – sometimes against the police. The sedate BBC news showed English streets on fire. It did not have one cause; that was the disturbing part. But that also made it like the African riots I had seen. There was trouble in a town and all scores were settled – racial, financial, social, even family quarrels; and some of the violence was not anger, but high spirits, like dancing on the radio.

When it hit London there were two nights of rioting in Brixton, and then, spreading to Clapham, it touched my corner of Battersea. One Sunday morning I saw every window broken for a hundred yards of shopfronts on Queenstown Road. There had been looting. Then the shop windows were boarded up and it all looked uglier and worse.

I had been at Flora's that night. We heard the news on her bedside transistor, and on the way home I had seen the police standing helplessly, and seen the running boys and the odd surge of nighttime crowds.

I was then deeply in love with Flora. I had been looking for her, I knew. She said the same, and this well-educated woman quoted a Donne poem that began, 'Twice or thrice had I loved thee, / Before I knew thy face or name . . .' But in finding her I had discovered an aspect of my personality that was new to me – a kinder, dependent, appreciative side of me that Flora inspired. If I lost her it would vanish within me and be irretrievable, and I would be the worse for it.

She was different, but that did not surprise me. All women are different, not only in personality but in a physical sense. Each woman's body is different in contour, in weight, in odor, in the way she moves and responds. It is possible, I thought, that every sexual encounter in life is different and unique, because every woman was a different shape and size, and different in every other way. But what about men?

Flora said, 'I've stopped wondering about that. "Men" is just an abstraction. I don't think about men and women. I just think about you and me.'

We were at my apartment one Saturday, sitting on my Chinese settee from Malacca. I wanted to tell her I loved her, that sex was part of it, but that there was something more powerful, something to do with a diminishing of the fear of death. It was an elemental desire to establish a society of two.

'Let's talk about love,' I said.

'*Folie à deux*,' she said. 'It's an extreme paranoid condition.'

There was an almighty crash. I ran to the balcony and saw that a gang of boys had stoned a police car and that it had hit a telephone pole. The police scrambled out of the smashed car and ran; the boys threw stones at the car and went up to it and kicked it. Then I saw other boys, busy ones, like workers in an air raid scurrying around in the darkness, bringing bottles, splashing the car. They set the car on fire.

I shouted. No one heard.

Flora said, 'It's terrible.'

'This is the way the world ends,' I said.

She hugged me, clutched me, but tenderly, like a daughter. She was afraid. The firelight on the windows of my apartment came from the burning car, but it looked more general, like the sprawling flames from a burning city. And later there were the sounds of police sirens, and shouts, and the fizz of breaking glass, and the pathetic sound of running feet slapping the pavement.

We sat in the darkness, Flora and I, and listened. It was war out there. It seemed to me then as if we had been transported into the distant past or future, where a convulsion was taking place. How could this nightmare be the here and now, with us so unprepared? But we were lucky. We were safe and had each other. And, in each others' arms, we heard the deranged sounds of riot and, much worse, the laughter.

Past midnight, Flora said, 'I'm afraid.'

'Please stay the night,' I said.

'Yes. I'm so glad we're together. Maybe we have no right to be so safe. But nothing bad can happen to us if we're together.'

Her head lay against my chest. We had not made love, but we would sleep holding each other and we would keep death away.

She relaxed and laughed softly and said, 'You didn't really think that I'd leave you tonight. I'm not brave –'

'You're brave, you're beautiful,' I said, and I told her how every night that we spent together was special and how, when it came time to part, it hurt and made me feel lopsided. I told her how happy I was, and how many places in the world I had looked for her – in Africa and Asia – and had practically given up hope of ever finding her, though I had never doubted that she existed. All this time the windows were painted in fire, and I heard Flora's heart and felt her breathe in a little listening rhythm. Tonight was different, I said, because we could spend the whole night together – it was what I had wanted from the moment of meeting her. And what was so strange about liking her first of all for her hair and her green eyes? That's how I had recognized her! She had been funny and bright and had made me better, and this nightmare world did not seem so bad now that we were together, and –

'To make a long story short,' I said.

And then she laughed.

'Isn't it a bit late for that?' she said.

Memo

When I took up my post at the London Embassy I entered into a tacit agreement to share all the information to which I became privy that directly or indirectly had a bearing on the security of the United States of America or on my own status, regardless of my personal feelings.

I feel it is my duty therefore to report on an American national new resident in Britain.

The Subject is a thirty-two-year-old female Caucasian; slight build, blond hair, green eyes, no visible marks or scars. She is single. She has no criminal record, although our files show that she was arrested once on a charge of Obstruction; the charge was later dropped. She was born in Windsor, New Jersey, of mixed Scottish-Mexican ancestry. Education: Wellesley College and Oxford University, England. She is presently on a one-year sabbatical from Bryn Mawr College, where she is a member of the Department of English, specializing in Women in Literature.

As an undergraduate at Wellesley, the Subject was a founder-member of several feminist groups, and at Bryn Mawr she has continued to support feminist organizations by acting as faculty adviser. She was arrested in 1980 at a sit-in protesting against the nonadoption of the Equal Rights Amendment; as stated above, the charge against her was dropped. More recently, she led a demonstration at a nuclear power station in central Pennsylvania.

The Subject entered the United Kingdom on a student visa in January 1981 and became caretaker-tenant of an apartment in Stamford Brook, West London. Her stated reason for being in London was to complete her research for a biography of Mary Shelley, author of *Frankenstein* (1818), and *Lodore* (1835), as well as *Valperga, or the Life and Adventures of Castruccio, Prince of Lucca* (1823). This research did not fully occupy the Subject, and soon after her arrival, together with some British nationals, the Subject founded a group calling itself Women Opposed to Nuclear Technology.

The US Embassy Fact-Finding Task Force on Security here in London has a substantial file on this (legally registered) organization, as well as tapes and films of its activities, and a membership list on which the Subject's name appears as Chairperson of the Agitprop Committee. The Subject attends the weekly Friday meeting of this committee.

What the Fact-Finding Task Force on Security is evidently not aware of is that the Subject has twice been entertained as a guest of Ambassador L. Burrell Noyes at Winfield House. Ambassador Noyes and the Subject's father are graduates of Franklin and Marshall College, Class of '43.

It was at Winfield House earlier this year that I became acquainted with the Subject, though it was some weeks before I learned of her activities in the areas of feminism and antinuclear protest. She struck me as tough-minded, independent, and somewhat combative intellectually. She is extremely personable. She is also lovely. In a short time in England she has managed to make friends with British people – most of them women, most of them opinion-formers – representing a wide spectrum of political thought.

The Home Office has refused to extend the Subject's visa, claiming that her student status is no longer applicable, as she has completed her work on Mary Shelley. Personally, I think the Home Office is somewhat antagonized by the Subject's political activities, but there has been no direct comment on this by the Home Office.

The foregoing may be necessary to you because of the sensitive nature of my job, and my involvement with the Subject. But none of it is really of much importance, and the only fact worth recording is that roughly two months ago I fell in love with the Subject. Yesterday, having consulted no one – why should we? – we met at the Chelsea Registry Office, where my part of the dialogue went as follows:

Registrar: 'Do you, Spencer Monroe Savage, promise to take Flora Christine Domingo-Duncan as your lawfully wedded wife,' etc.

And I said, 'I do.'

He just wanted a decent book to read ...

Not too much to ask, is it? It was in 1935 when Allen Lane, Managing
Director of Bodley Head Publishers, stood on a platform at Exeter railway
station looking for something good to read on his journey back to London.
His choice was limited to popular magazines and poor-quality paperbacks –
the same choice faced every day by the vast majority of readers, few of
whom could afford hardbacks. Lane's disappointment and subsequent anger
at the range of books generally available led him to found a company – and
change the world.

*'We believed in the existence in this country of a vast reading public for intelligent
books at a low price, and staked everything on it'*
Sir Allen Lane, 1902–1970, founder of Penguin Books

The quality paperback had arrived – and not just in bookshops. Lane was
adamant that his Penguins should appear in chain stores and tobacconists,
and should cost no more than a packet of cigarettes.

Reading habits (and cigarette prices) have changed since 1935, but
Penguin still believes in publishing the best books for everybody to
enjoy. We still believe that good design costs no more than bad design,
and we still believe that quality books published passionately and responsibly
make the world a better place.

So wherever you see the little bird – whether it's on a piece of
prize-winning literary fiction or a celebrity autobiography, political tour
de force or historical masterpiece, a serial-killer thriller, reference book,
world classic or a piece of pure escapism – you can bet that it represents
the very best that the genre has to offer.

Whatever you like to read – trust Penguin.